Space Colony One

Books 4 - 6

J.J. Green

READER GROUP

Sign up to my reader group for free ebook *Night of Flames,* the prequel to Space Colony One, and for more free books, discounts on new releases, Review Crew invitations and other interesting stuff:

https://jjgreenauthor.com/free-books/

THE BOOKS OF SPACE COLONY ONE

Prequel: *Night of Flames*
Book 1: *The Concordia Deception*
Book 2: *The Fila Epiphany*
Book 3: *The Scythian Crisis*
Book 4: *Interstellar Mission*
Book 5: *Humanity's Fight*
Book 6: *Final Onslaught*
Book 7: *Restitution*
Book 8: *Redeemer*
Book 9: *Reprisal*

INTERSTELLAR MISSION

One

Thirty-five thousand, eight hundred and thirty-five kilometers above the planet the humans called Concordia, a probe sat in geostationary orbit. The device was tiny, undetectable to all except the most sensitive astronomical scanners. Even then, the scanner operator would have to know exactly where to look in order to find it. The debris remaining from the battle for the planet was scattered throughout the immediate area of space, acting as the perfect camouflage for the spying device.

The probe focused on a small area of land on the largest continent. Covering approximately 2,184 square kilometers, the area encompassed a razed human settlement, a region where the native vegetation had been cleared, and a small forest. The forest was the point of greatest scrutiny.

Penetrating the forest canopy and a certain depth beneath the surface, the probe peered at a spot below the forest floor where the humans had constructed a habitation.

The existence and location of the site had been gleaned from disinfectors sent down to clean the human infestation from the prized world. Had this information not already existed within the probe's data banks, the heat and carbon dioxide emitted by the concentrated numbers of humans were clear indications of the invaders' presence. And, when the system's star lit that place, the probe detected the movement of humans as they departed their subterranean dwelling.

For each revolution of the world orbiting its star, the pattern of movement was the same: in the daylight hours, the humans traveled to the cleared area and its neighboring lake. Then, just before that area turned away from the star and the line of darkness crossed it, the humans would return to their forest dwelling and disappear below ground.

During the time they spent at the secondary site, the humans tended to their plants, which were non-natives. They applied unidentified substances and, when precipitation had been minimal, they also applied water from the lake. Always, they removed any native flora growing in the space.

The probe monitored the size of the invasive population, its typical behaviors, and evidence of technological advancement. The data it had gleaned up until now had been minimal. The humans' numbers were small and their activities limited. Had it been sentient, the probe would have been supremely bored. It was working at a level far below the amount of information its scanners, data banks, and transmitter could handle.

Had the probe's creators been too optimistic when they had configured its data handling capabilities? Perhaps. The device's construction had been hasty, a last-minute decision based on an abrupt change of plan.

Were the Scythians' hopes for a successful human colonization too high? The planet thieves were primitive. Their colony ship had resembled a relic of the earliest eons of galactic exploration, like something out of an ancient historical file. It had been a miracle the humans had survived to reach their destination. Even their second ship, which had caught up to the first, had carried only a few ineffective weapons, and its engines had been slow. Only by a fluke had it defeated the scout ship.

In addition to the humans' low level of development, further factors worked against the colony's survival. The destruction of their first habitation had set them back significantly, no doubt. Then a second attack had been launched with the intention of finishing them off. The destruction had probably pushed the colony to the limit of its existence.

Had the second attack not been aborted, it would have entirely annihilated the humans. The disinfectors had never been known to fail. Even the unexpected arrival of the irritating aquatic beings, who for some unknown reason had decided to ally themselves with the primitives, would not have made any difference to the final result.

But then, at the last moment, another, more appealing, solution had been suggested, exactly at the moment the humans had foolishly crashed their vessel into the flagship. Perhaps it would be possible to turn the unanticipated appearance of the humans to the Scythians' benefit. The decision to spare the invaders, temporarily, had been made.

Only two possible futures for the humans lay ahead: they would live or die. Whichever result eventuated, the Scythians would win, in a fashion. As the fate of the colony played out all the watchers had to do was wait.

On their far-distant planet, the Scythians monitored the incoming data. They read the population estimates, studied the humans' behavior, and tracked their development. The latter was pitiful. It was clear the humans were clinging to survival. All that would be required to finish them off would be the failure of the food supply they appeared to be growing.

The probe had been programmed with various triggers. If the humans transferred to a new location, it would adjust its geostationary position accordingly. If the creatures spread out across the globe so that constant surveillance from a single vantage point was impossible, the probe would react.

Finally, when the required conditions were met, the Scythians would return to claim their prize.

Two

Cherry lowered herself into the narrow, two-seater capsule, steadying herself against the bobbing of the waves by grabbing the side with her right—and only—hand. The vessel was barely large enough to accommodate both her and Ethan, and she was forced to squeeze up close to her old friend as she sat down.

The sea breeze was chilly and made colder by the spray it blew from the ocean. The sun was halfway to the horizon in a gray, cloudy sky.

"How long will this take?" she asked, eyeing the water. Somewhere beneath those snowy peaks and deep blue troughs thread creatures lay, waiting to transport the humans to their vast underwater metropolis. Her stomach muscles tightened, and it wasn't only due to the waves' motion.

"Three or four hours," Ethan replied. "At least, that's how long it took last time. I'm assuming the threads have something similar in store for you as they did with me."

"I guess it's too late to change my mind?" she asked hopefully.

He glanced at her from the corners of his eyes. "Yeah, pretty much. I need a second in command, and I picked you. The Joining Ceremony with the threads is only a formality."

In need of a distraction, she asked, "Aren't there any controls in this thing?" She scanned the featureless interior. All that lay around her was the lid to the vehicle, opened at an angle, the well where they put their feet, and the smooth, opaque lower hull.

How did the threads manufacture equipment like this submarine capsule while living under water? The process had to be remarkably different from the way humans did things. The enigma made her curious. On the other hand, the less she knew about the threads the better.

"No controls," Ethan replied, "and even if there were, we wouldn't know how to drive it."

"Pilot it," she corrected. "If a vehicle goes on water, or in the air, or in space, you pilot it."

"Drive it or pilot it, we're doing neither, in this case. Relax. It's an interesting trip. You might even enjoy it."

"So we let the threads take us wherever they want?"

"That's what happened last time, and I was totally safe."

"Why are you telling me it's safe?" she asked. "Do you think I'm scared?"

Ethan didn't reply, only smirked in a maddening manner.

"Huh!" She squirmed in her seat. "I'm not scared. I'm...uncomfortable. I mean, I'm grateful to them. They've done so much to help us and we couldn't have survived without them, but, stars, I don't like those things." The waves were growing stronger, the capsule was bobbing higher, and she was beginning to feel sick. "I wish we could—"

A hiss cut through her words as the lid of the vessel suddenly lowered, activated by unseen hands, or rather, tentacles. The lid met the hull and soundlessly closed. They were sealed in and wouldn't be able to get out again until the threads allowed them. The capsule lifted and eased forward until it was fully on the surface of the water. A particularly large wave smashed into it, causing the front to rear up, rise over the wave's crest, and nose down the other side.

Ethan gave her a half smile. "I don't really think you're scared. No one who ran out to face certain death by the cuts of thousands of Scythian spiders could be scared of some friendly thread creatures."

"I thought you were going to say single-handedly." She also smiled but then the death of her ex-lover, Garwin, sprang to her mind and her expression fell.

"If anyone can make amputee jokes, it's you and me." Ethan lifted his artificial foot.

The threads' vessel was moving steadily forward. As it reached deeper water the bobbing became less pronounced but more regular. Suddenly, the sun blazed through a gap in the clouds, instantly warming the capsule's cool interior. Then the nose dipped. Cherry gripped her armrest.

"Here we go," said Ethan as the vessel slid under the waves.

Green water rose up the capsule's sides and over the transparent lid. A force dragged them along and downward. Sunbeams glittered through the waves, dappling them in shifting spots of light. But the sun's rays quickly faded and the darkness of deep water encroached.

The light from above had almost entirely disappeared when the rim of the vessel burst into light, illuminating the interior and the water around them.

"Ugh." She'd spotted, at the edge of the circle of light, long, thin, tentacles writhing. Thread creatures had come along as escorts.

"Oh yeah," said Ethan. "They do that. They'll stay with us all the way down."

"No kidding. Isn't that great?"

"Why don't you like the threads?"

"Is it surprising? They tried to kill me once, remember?"

"They weren't trying to kill you. They were only trying to capture you, like they did with me. They wanted to find out about us."

"Oh, I'm sorry. They were only trying to *capture* me, put me in a little box, and experiment on me. Like they did with you that time you nearly *died*." Cherry folded her arm across her chest. The action still felt weird now she only had one arm to fold.

Ethan chuckled.

"Something funny?"

"*Fila cherryensia*. I love the fact the Woken named the threads after you."

"Isn't that joke getting a bit old?" In truth, Cherry enjoyed bantering with her old friend, even though her dislike of the threads was no joke. Their back-and-forth also helped her to momentarily forget the gravity of the colony's situation. She stole a glance at Ethan's profile. They had been through so much together. Their closeness in the small capsule almost made her want to reach out and take his hand. "How are Cariad and the baby doing? Meredith is such a pretty name."

"It is, isn't it? We named her after someone I used to know. They're fine. Absolutely fine. She's a sweetheart. Hardly ever cries. Always smiling."

"You're talking about the baby, not Cariad?"

"Well, both of them really."

"Cariad is a sweetheart too. I realized that once I got to know her." Cherry paused. "She isn't a typical Woken. I guess she must have told you what a bitch I was to her."

"Huh? No. She never told me that."

"Well, I was, though maybe I was justified in the circumstances. Anyway, I don't hate the Woken any longer. It doesn't make any sense anymore. We're all on the same level now."

"Yeah, that's right."

The divisions that had existed in the early days of the colony were a thing of the past. If it weren't for the Gens' uniform coloring, with their olive skin and dark brown eyes and hair, she wouldn't have been able to tell her kind apart from the Woken: the scientists who had left Earth aboard the *Nova* nearly two hundred years ago. They were all kinds of colors, from Kes's chalky white, freckled skin and ginger hair to Cariad's deep brown skin and black, frizzy hair.

The two Scythian attacks had been great equalizers. The original settlement, planned and built so carefully from materials brought from Earth, had been razed. And the underground hideout, created from the remaining materials scavenged from the wreck of the *Nova*, had only just survived the second attack. It had taken weeks to clear the passages of the deactivated spider-like search-and-destroy devices. Their claws sliced like razors at the slightest touch, and now that the colony's medical supplies were severely limited, avoiding cuts and infections was vital.

Her stump ached with the memory of the slash that had severed her left arm.

"Thinking about what's coming up?" Ethan asked, drawing her from her reverie.

"No, actually."

"We're about halfway now."

The capsule's beams only illuminated the surrounding threads' tentacles, streamlined with speed. Everything else was impenetrable darkness. She was reminded of her time aboard the colony ship, when the *Nova's* hull had been the only thing between her and deep space. "I'm flattered that you want me as your second in command, but I'm not clear on exactly what you want me to do."

"I'm not sure myself. I only know we have a long, difficult time ahead of us, and I'm going to need all the help I can get if the colony is to survive. There's the organization of our defense, for one thing. I have enough to do just keeping us all fed, and I'm no military strategist. You seemed the obvious choice after you helped coordinate the response to the second attack. Unless you think I should have asked Aubriot?"

"Stars, no," she exclaimed. The thought of Aubriot in charge of defending the colony filled her with unease. He had some good ideas, but his number one priority was himself. Given the choice of sacrificing everyone else in order to save his own life, he probably wouldn't think twice about it.

"See? You're the best person, Cherry. I know you'll do a great job."

"I'll do my best."

"You'll be fine. And after you've been through the Joining Ceremony, we can talk to the Fila about the Scythian threat. Maybe they can give us some advice on how to prepare ourselves for when they return."

"When they come back to collect their tribute?" She gave a shudder. She hoped the day the Scythians demanded human sacrifices in return for sparing the colony was a long, long time away.

"We need a plan," Ethan said, "and so far I have nothing."

THREE

Wilder tied the final living vine in place, and then stood up, brushing her bangs out of her eyes. She grabbed the handrail she'd constructed from intertwined vines and tested it, pushing and pulling on it. The rail seemed secure. It should be. The material it was made from was fibrous and so tough only a very sharp blade could cut it. The vines' properties had put her off using them at first, imagining the hours she would have to spend just sawing the stuff off the trees where it clung like a sluglimpet to its prey.

But then she'd realized it made more sense to use living vines. Not only would it save time, the plants would continue to grow and the walkways between the trees would become stronger and carry more weight.

Was using five vines per handrail overkill? Perhaps. But the handrails and the bridges—made from interwoven tree fronds and more vines—had to be entirely safe. She didn't want anyone to get hurt. And though a fall onto the soft, deep leaf mold of the forest floor probably wouldn't be fatal, an accident would mean the end of her little hamlet among the trees.

That would be a disaster. All her work would be for nothing. The adults might even insist that she permanently return to the underground settlement.

Sidhe.

That was what they'd called the place, after a vote. It was a name from ancient Earth, a dwelling place of mythological beings.

Her own name for the close, stinking, noisy passageways and tiny rooms of her former home was Shithole. Naturally, she never used the name out loud around anyone important, but she loved how the word encapsulated her hatred for the crowded habitation.

She understood why the colonists continued to live there, even though the Scythians appeared to be leaving them alone for the time being. It was the menace of the sluglimpets. The threat of the nocturnal creatures plagued her too. If they sensed a living, edible thing while out on their nightly prowls, the horrible predators could actually climb trees. Nothing seemed to be a barrier to their many legs and hook-like feet except for electricity, and the remaining fences and generators were all being used to protect the farming district.

It had been the problem of the Concordian native wildlife that had deterred her from her plan to build treetop settlement initially, notwithstanding her eagerness to leave Shithole. Without an electric current as protection, she would have quickly suffered a terrible death on her first night outdoors.

But she'd been determined. The sluglimpets were not intelligent. All they had on their side was their deadly, sticky digestive secretions and a relentless drive to reach their prey. If humans could make their way across the galaxy to a new home, they should be able to think up a way to protect themselves from the predators.

She'd done it. She'd found a solution. Though the first time she'd tested her idea, all alone, illegally outside Shithole at night, had been terrifying.

She'd done it all. Everything she'd planned. Peeking out from the tree fronds were four sturdy platforms, linked by walkways. She stood on the fifth platform, which happened to be the first she'd constructed and the one she would keep as her own.

Below, the forest undergrowth was green and lush and the decaying leaf mold was deep brown, moist, and fragrant. How much nicer it was to be above ground rather than crushed in with everyone else, skulking in dimly lit confinement.

The construction work had been easy compared to the difficulties she'd faced sneaking away to complete it. She'd made a few enemies along the way: door monitors, educators, her "parents". But that was nothing new. For years, even prior to Arrival—ever since she'd decided to not attend any more useless, boring schooling, in fact—she'd rubbed up against authority figures in one way or another.

Never mind. When some friends joined her in the tree village, the people in charge would be forced to acknowledge the benefit of her work. They would understand that her time was better spent doing what she wanted, not following any stupid Manual. The people who wrote that plan hadn't taken into account the real difficulties the colony would face. How could they? No one else had ever attempted a deep space colonization.

All she had to do was prove she'd created a sustainable living space. She didn't think it would take much persuasion for other kids to come and live here too. Who in their right mind would choose to remain in an overcrowded, stuffy slum filled with crying babies when they could live in fresh, clean air and silence above ground?

The tree village was ready for inhabitants. A few more facilities were required before the place would be entirely independent, but it was fit for sleeping in overnight.

One more test remained.

She breathed in, gripped the handrail tightly, and stepped onto the walkway. The fibrous floor bent under her weight, but held. She took a second step, entirely leaving the safety of the platform. The bridge swayed, and she grabbed the other handrail. The vines creaked. The farther platform, which had looked so close a moment ago, seemed to draw away.

Remembering she needed to breath out, she exhaled between pursed lips and carefully trod another few steps. The farther she walked, the more the bridge swayed. Was that something she could fix? She wasn't sure, but providing she held on tight she didn't seem to be in any danger.

Alternating her hands to let go and grip the rail as she moved along, she quickly walked the remaining distance. As she stepped onto the second platform, she whooped with delight and punched the air. The surrounding vegetation absorbed the sound of her voice, deadening it and supplanting it with hushed rustling.

So far, so good. But she'd bent the rules as far as she could. If she wanted to move forward with the tree hamlet and turn it into an official, alternative dwelling space, she needed permission from the Leader. That might not be easy to get.

Four

About an hour into the journey to the threads' underground city, Cherry spied thousands of lights spread out on the ocean bed. "Hey, is that it?"

"That's it," Ethan replied. "It's quite something, isn't it? If we go the same way I went, we'll sink down a long tunnel to the chamber where they hold the ceremony."

"Wow," Cherry breathed as the extent and complexity of the threads' metropolis became clearer. The underwater city reached as far as she could see, lights twinkling in the far distance, piercing the pitch black of the water. As she looked more closely, she saw plumes of bubbles and distorted, probably superheated, water rising from some structures on the sea bed. Transparent tunnels linked buildings, and thread creatures slid along them. "I had no idea it was so sophisticated." She peered at the constructed expanse. "Do you think they have vehicles?"

"Apart from starships?" Ethan answered. "I've never seen any of the Fila being transported in a vehicle. I don't think they need them. They move so fast and so easily in water."

The thread escorts had kept pace with the capsule, even though it had seemed to be traveling at a great speed.

"I think this is their main site on Concordia," said Ethan. "The places where we originally encountered them are only small outposts. This is where all the important stuff happens, like the Joining Ceremony." He glanced sidelong at her. "There's no need to pull that face."

"What face? I'm not pulling a face."

"The ceremony doesn't take long. It'll be over before you know it."

The capsule abruptly halted and sank rapidly downward. A hole was opening below. They were about to descend into the tunnel Ethan had mentioned.

She twisted in her seat, staring at the surface of the city as they passed it. Despite the utter darkness of the water, she could see details of complicated structures due to a glow emanating from them. The light was unlike sunlight or the artificial indoor lights.

"You know when we lived in the caves by the ocean?" she said. "Did you ever look out to sea at night?"

"All the time."

"The water used to glow sometimes. Did you notice?"

"I did. It was beautiful."

"The light the threads' city gives off is similar, don't you think?"

"Now you say it, I see what you mean."

Their vessel passed into the tunnel, plunging them into darkness except for widely spaced lights along the walls. Then they changed direction and headed into a large chamber. She tensed at the sight that greeted her. "So many thread creatures all in one place." She surveyed the ranks of assembled aquatic aliens.

"They're probably listening to us right now. I should have told you. They can hear what we say while we're in here, and they can talk to us too."

In the end, the ceremony really was as straightforward as Ethan had said it would be, though like everything else to do with the threads, it was weird and unsettling. When it was over and most of the creatures had left, they remained inside the threads' spherical chamber. Only one of the organisms had stuck around, a large specimen.

"Hey, Quinn," said Ethan. "Long time no see."

"You *recognize* it?" Cherry gaped at the creature's mass of gently writhing tentacles.

"Hello, Ethan." The voice seemed to come from all around them, as if the walls of the capsule were broadcasting.

Ethan said to Cherry, "Remember, anything you say, he'll hear."

"Got it." She whispered, "It's a he? How can you tell?"

"It's probably better to let me do the talking."

"If you say so."

"This is Cherry," he said to his thread acquaintance.

"Your second in command. Thank you for bringing him to us."

"Her. Cherry is a woman."

"I see. Thank you. It is difficult for me to see your differences. I notice that Cherry is missing a tentacle too."

"What?" Cherry asked.

"She's missing an arm, Quinn."

"Ah yes. You have different words for your tentacles according to where they are situated on your bodies. I remember now."

"Cherry lost her arm during the Second Scythian Attack."

"But why hasn't she grown another one?"

"I can't grow another one," said Cherry.

"You can't? Are humans not able to regrow their tentacles?"

Ethan said, "I still only have half of one of my legs. I wear a false one."

"I didn't know," said Quinn. "We still have so much to learn about human anatomy. To be unable to regenerate your limbs seems a great disadvantage."

"We manage," said Ethan. "Quinn, we have more important matters to discuss."

"The Scythians," said Quinn. "I have bad news. Our seeding ship, which came to your defense, must depart soon. Our young ones are growing to maturity and if we do not find a home for them they will die."

"I understand," Ethan replied. "We appreciate your help, but we realize we can't rely on you forever."

Cherry's heart sank. How could they hope to defend themselves from another Scythian attack without the help of the thread creatures?

"When the Scythians arrived to destroy your colony," Quinn said, "we had grave fears that they would succeed. They are an ancient and highly developed species, and we doubted they would allow a foreign intelligence to live on a planet they consider their own. Yet they did withdraw, after your ship self-destructed by crashing into theirs. The message they broadcast as they left did not make much sense to us. Then we discovered words in your language that seem to describe similar concepts—concepts that do not exist in our culture. Words like sacrifice and tribute. You know what their message means in terms of what you can expect."

"I know," said Ethan. "I haven't thought of much else since the battle."

"It appears the Scythians decided to accept the deaths of the crew in exchange for the cessation of their attack. If that is the case, it seems reasonable to predict they will return at some point, expecting further offerings, or they will not allow your continued presence on this planet."

"It's lucky they didn't realize no humans were aboard the *Mistral*," Cherry said. "Do you think the Scythians might accept something other than human lives as tribute?"

As always, she felt conflicted by the memory of the enigmatic Guardians, androids sent from Earth to save the colony from sabotage. They had masqueraded as humans, and when their artificiality was revealed it explained the creepy feeling she'd always had about them. Yet she couldn't deny that these sentient machines had sacrificed themselves in battle without hesitation.

"We cannot say," Quinn replied, "but we believe it would be prudent to act as if this were not the case."

"Could you transport us somewhere else?" Cherry asked. "A place where the Scythians won't find us?"

"We have considered that, but we do not know of any other planets that would support you indefinitely, and that would not also be known to the Scythians. We continue to search, but it would be wise for you to make alternative plans."

"What kind of alternative?" asked Cherry. "We only have two: run and hide or stay and fight, and currently only the second one is open to us."

"You do not have to fight," said Quinn. "There is a third possibility."

"You mean we should sacrifice some of us as tribute?" Cherry asked.

"It is an option to consider."

"Okay, let me consider it," said Cherry, her heart racing with rage. "Er, NO! I'm not going to suggest that some of us die to save the rest. That is *not* happening. We would never sacrifice one of our own, even if it were to save all of us."

"Don't worry," said Ethan. "There's no question about that. But I'm guessing Quinn has more to tell us. Am I right? There's a reason you asked me to bring another human representative to Join with you, isn't there?"

"You are right, Ethan. As I said, our seeding ship must depart soon, and it's doubtful it could return to help defend you from another Scythian attack. Furthermore, I must warn you that the Scythians are growing stronger, and we are not a warlike species. We could not have defeated them when we tried, and we won't defeat them the next time."

"So we're on our own?" asked Cherry.

"Perhaps not," Quinn replied. "If we cannot help you, perhaps others might. You are not the only ones who have been targeted by the Scythians. Other intelligent species have been attacked, and in response they are forming an alliance called the Galactic Assembly. It's possible that they might accept humankind into their midst."

"Is it likely, though?" Ethan asked. "I mean, what do we have to offer?"

"You're assuming the alliance exists only for self-interest," Quinn replied. "Do you find it difficult to believe they would try to protect other intelligent species without receiving anything in return? Only because they believe it is right?"

"Of course not," said Ethan, looking abashed. "That's exactly what you've done. Even though you were here on Concordia first, you've protected us when you didn't have to."

"We are grateful," said Cherry, her aversion toward the thread creatures beginning to fade. They could have easily allowed the Scythians to do their work and rid Concordia of the uninvited newcomers.

Quinn said, "Species come into existence and die out all the time, but we believe your destruction would be a loss to the galaxy."

"We think so too," said Cherry.

"The Galactic Assembly may come to the same conclusion," he continued, "but they will not accept you without meeting you first. However, our seeding ship cannot take you to the site of the Assembly. There are no planets suitable for colonization in that sector, and our ship could not sustain human life. Therefore, we will build another ship. This vessel will journey to the Assembly, conveying one or more representatives of your colony. Perhaps you could go, Ethan?"

Ethan replied, "I'm needed here."

"I understand. I should also warn you that the Assembly is a fragile organization. As far as we know nothing like this has been attempted before. Bringing many disparate, intelligent species, each with their own interests, into agreement is difficult and fraught with danger. It is very easy to cause great offense when interacting with unfamiliar cultures. I would advise you to carry a weapon, Cherry, to reduce the risk of attack."

"Wait. What?" said Cherry.

"You will go to the Galactic Assembly," Quinn said, "and seek admittance to their alliance, in order to ask for help to secure the future of humanity."

"I heard you," Cherry said. "I just don't quite believe it."

FIVE

The problem of the Scythian hunting spiders had been bothering Wilder for ages. Since early that morning, she'd been studying one of the devices she'd 'borrowed'. But time was getting on. Her appointment with the Leader was soon and before the meeting she wanted to take some vids of her little hamlet to show him.

She put down the spider, its sharp claws bound in rags, and piled more rags over it. Then she searched for her interface, mulling over the hidden Scythian device.

After the colonists had carefully cleared them from the underground settlement and emerged onto the surface, the sheer numbers of the devices the Scythians had dropped became apparent. They littered the forest floor, creating a bizarre carpet of silvery, angular, razor sharp undergrowth.

From the drop site to the forest, tens of thousands of the lethal devices lay motionless, frozen when their creators deactivated them. At the original settlement, the pattern of silver sprayed out to all sides where the spiders had traced human scent.

It had taken weeks, but eventually all the devices had been cleared and piled in eight massive heaps surrounded by fences. Meanwhile, the scientists had started work, trying to identify what the spiders were made from and how they operated. But all their scientific equipment had been destroyed, both at the first settlement and on the *Nova*. They'd concluded with some certainty that the spiders were constructed from a metal alloy—feather-light and extremely tough—but what type of alloy it was, none could say. The material's properties were unlike anything they had previously encountered.

No tools penetrated the smooth, seamless parts of spiders. No one could study the material or their inner workings. With a great deal of effort, a forge was built to heat a spider to a temperature high enough to melt titanium, but it had no effect. Finally, after thousands of hours of work, the spiders had been designated useless trash.

Yet they remained highly dangerous. If the Scythians returned and changed their minds about sparing humanity, they might be able to reactivate the devices. When time could be spared, giant pits would be dug to bury them, a temporary stopgap to keep them out of immediate harm's way.

It was a great shame, Wilder had thought, when the colony was in such desperate need of construction materials. The Fila's donations dried out and cracked after a few days' exposure to air. Until mining operations were underway and smelting and manufacturing plants built, the settlers had no source of metal other than what had been scrounged from the *Nova*. All that remained of the ship was wreckage in the ocean.

The scientists might have given up on the Scythian spiders, but Wilder had not. She'd taken one from a heap and brought it to her tree platform, delighted to finally have the privacy and freedom to work on it. She was determined to unlock its secrets.

She'd first tested one of the spider's blades on a dead sluglimpet. The creature's tough carapace had parted like the soft, pale fungi growing on the forest floor. When she'd dipped the blade into the sticky, corrosive acid that spilled from creature's innards, the mucusy liquid had no effect on the Scythian material.

She pulled out her interface from under her pillow The cracked surface was dusty, so she carefully wiped the tiny lens. Setting the interface to record, she focused first on her platform. The she pointed the interface at the floor and swept it up toward the roof, made from fallen tree fronds. The forest canopy kept most of the rain out, but later on in the year heavier rains would arrive, and she wanted to be prepared.

Next, she lay on her stomach and stuck her head and shoulders over the platform's edge angling the interface toward the downward-facing cone around the tree's trunk.

Sluglimpets could climb, and they would sense and attack anything living, but she had thought up a solution to the problem. The predators were long and flat, and their shells were rigid. They could climb vertical surfaces, but they could not bend to navigate something pointing outward and downward. If a sluglimpet climbed a tree with a cone encircling its trunk, the creature would try to crawl along the inside of the cone, tip backward, lose its grip, and fall. She had cut off branches touching other trees, isolating the ones in her village so the predators couldn't reach them.

She also filmed the sluglimpet barriers around the other tree trunks, and the hoists she had constructed to lift people up. She had plenty more ideas about what could be done to the platforms, but she figured she had enough to show the Leader the site's viability and potential.

She checked the time. She only had a few minutes before her appointment. If she missed it, she would have to wait weeks for another, assuming she was given one at all. The man responsible for giving them out had argued with her, saying she was just a kid and had no good reason to see the Leader. She had been forced to point out that there was nothing in the Manual forbidding young colonists from meeting with the Leader. It was everyone's right, young, old, and in between.

She slipped the interface into a bag, slung it over her shoulder, and climbed into a cradle at the edge of the platform. The cradle hung from a rope attached to a pulley. She lowered herself to the forest floor. As soon as her feet touched dirt, she jumped out and ran to the entrance of the underground settlement.

The opening had been reconstructed since the Scythian attack. The destroyed thick, metal doors had been replaced with simple ones made from plastiwood, and they stood open. She ran through the doorway and down the stairs. The familiar smell of the place hit. Damp, mold, and human sweat assaulted her nostrils, and the ceilings and walls seemed to close in. Fighting down the feelings of disgust and unease that Shithole sparked, she ran on.

She arrived at the Leader's office. The man who arranged the appointments looked up sternly as she appeared, and his frown deepened as he said, "You're late. You'll have to reschedule."

"I can't," she panted. "I've waited so long already. It's only a few minutes."

"I can't help that. The Leader's a very busy man."

The door to the inner office opened, and the Leader looked out. "Verney..." He spotted her. "Are you my next appointment? You can come in."

"Leader," Verney said, "you have another appointment in eight minutes."

"I'm sure this won't take long, right?" the Leader asked her.

"No, sir. Not long."

"Good. Come inside."

She followed him in.

"Take a seat." The Leader closed the door and gestured toward a chair before sitting down himself.

She suddenly became aware that though she had thoroughly prepared her little hamlet to be ready for this meeting, she had entirely failed to prepare herself. Her mouth turned dry as she struggled to think of what to say, wondering what she looked like. She couldn't remember the last time she'd washed or brushed her hair.

She coughed to clear her throat and calm her nerves. "Thanks for seeing me, Leader. I'll be as quick as I can. I want to ask your permission to start a new settlement."

His eyebrows rose. "A new settlement?"

She looked down at the backs of her hands. They were grimy and her nails were black with dirt. How could she have forgotten to wash before meeting the most important person in the colony?

"Does this have to do with your activities in the forest?" he asked.

She gaped. "You know about that? I...I've been building some living areas among the trees. I've finished them now. They're entirely safe."

He leaned forward and put his elbows on his desk. "It's Wilder, right? Wilder, I know living conditions down here aren't great, but I'm not prepared to allow you to put yourself at risk. It isn't safe above ground right now. As soon as the new residences out at the farms are finished, I promise you'll be one of the first to move out."

"I don't want to move out to the farms. I need to be near the spiders' dump." She stopped short. She hadn't meant to mention that part of her plan. But now she'd let out her secret, she figured she might as well tell him the rest. "I've been working on understanding their tech and I think I'm near a breakthrough, but I can't work on them down here. It's too cramped, noisy, and distracting. When I live here I'm tired all the time from babies waking me up. I can't think properly."

Ever since the babies from the *Nova* had arrived, her difficult life had become nearly unbearable. She didn't have anything against babies per se, but hundreds of them all at once, plus the babies born naturally to the colonists, had been torture. She needed quiet to work on her various projects.

"I understand," said the Leader. "It isn't easy for any of us, but you know we're doing our best to minimize the disturbance."

"At least let me show you what I've done." She pulled out her interface and showed him the vid she'd recorded.

She watched his expression as he studied the recording. How old was he? She didn't know, but he had gray in his hair and beard, so he had to be pretty old. Maybe too old to remember what it was like to be young and want to live your life without everyone telling you what to do.

The vid ended and he returned his attention to her. "Very impressive. Those cones are to deter sluglimpets?"

"Yes, and they work."

"They do? How come you're so sure?"

She didn't answer. The backs of her hands suddenly became extremely interesting.

"You know that spending the night outside the settlement is strictly prohibited?"

When she remained silent, he continued, "You're fourteen, right?"

"Yes, Leader."

"When I saw you were coming to see me, I looked up your details. There's no record of your education after the age of nine."

Shit. How did he know that? She'd thought the Guardians had wiped the colony's unimportant records when they dumped tonnes of data into the system before they crashed their ship. "I'd worked through the entire schooling scheme by then. There was nothing else to learn, so school got really boring for me. I didn't see any point in attending."

"And no one followed up with you?"

She looked down again.

The Leader laughed. "Don't worry. I didn't like school either, though for different reasons. I guess you managed to avoid the chasers."

"Yeah, I did," she mumbled. The meeting was not going as well as she'd hoped. She certainly hadn't expected the conversation would turn to her truancy. What difference did that make?

"Another thing I discovered," he said, "was that the couple who took you in haven't seen you in weeks."

She sighed. "They're good people, but I don't need parents. I don't need a mom or dad telling me what to do all the time. And they took in three of the babies from the *Nova*. Three! I just couldn't stand it. There's so much I have to do, so much I *want* to do, but I'm not going to get anything done until I have the freedom and quiet to do it."

A voice came from the Leader's interface, saying, "Your next appointment is here, Leader."

"I'll be finished soon, Verney. Please ask them to wait."

She took a breath. She only had a few moments before the Leader would refuse the permission she sought and kick her out. "Leader, Sidhe is heavily overcrowded. There are too many of us to live comfortably here. And when the crops are harvested, where are you planning to store all the food? The only option is to force more people to live in even less room. I'm suggesting a viable alternative. If five or ten young people like me live outside, it will give everyone a little more breathing room. Then, if the experiment is successful, we can build more platforms. The forest is large. I figure it could easily provide dwellings for five or six hundred people. I'm sorry for playing hooky and leaving my family. But, please, can you give me this chance?"

The Leader's interface spoke to him again. "Your next appointment is asking if she should reschedule, Leader."

"One more minute, Verney." The Leader rubbed his beard and gazed thoughtfully at the frozen image on Wilder's screen. He looked tired. Shadows haunted his eyes and cheekbones. Finally he said, "I'm not too concerned about your misdemeanors. This colony wasn't built on everyone following the rules. We're all learning as we go along. But it's my responsibility to keep you safe. I want to see what you've built with my own eyes. I'll come over there later today when I have a bit of free time. Then, if it all seems okay, we can talk some more about moving ahead with your plan."

"We can? Thank you!"

He lifted a finger. "But first I want two or three door guards to spend a few nights out there, just in case it isn't as safe as you imagine."

"That's fine. Thank you so much. You won't regret it."

Six

The day after Cherry returned from her visit to the threads, she decided to go and see Aubriot. Through some secret machinations she couldn't even guess at, her lover had managed to wrangle a room all to himself in the overcrowded settlement. She didn't approve but she couldn't deny it certainly made their assignations a lot easier to carry out.

The passageway leading to Aubriot's room was especially crowded. Parents were collecting their babies from daycare after their day's work in the farming district, tending to the crops and constructing permanent housing. The colony had precious little farming or construction equipment left. Scythian spiders had passed over the place where the colonists had hidden the machines in preparation for the expected attack. The enemy's search-and-destroy devices had inflicted considerable damage during their passage, and though many Gens had the training to fix the machinery, they lacked tools and parts.

But what the colonists missed in terms of equipment, they made up for in plain laboring skills and determination. No one was under any illusion about how closely they were skirting the prospect of failure. Nearly every able-bodied individual spent the daylight hours either helping to build houses, weeding crops, or picking off Concordian pests that had discovered a taste for the non-native produce.

Cherry eased through the people crowding the narrow space until she came upon the cause of the congestion. It was Anahi, the Woken who had once illegally taken the Leader's position in order to exert her control over the colony. Cherry halted in surprise at the sight of the older woman. Not because she was shocked to see her, but because Anahi wasn't wearing her visor. Her sightless eyes stared ahead, and she was swinging a cane to navigate. The other colonists were trying to stay out of her way, causing a human traffic jam.

The scientist's visor must have broken and no one was able to fix it. For the first time, Cherry felt a pang of pity for the older woman. What could she do now she could no longer see? It would be difficult if not impossible to conduct any experiments, and going outside would be dangerous.

Side-stepping Anahi's swinging cane, Cherry continued to Aubriot's door. Stepping into his room was a relief after the noise and crush. She found him sitting at a table working on his interface. He looked up as she walked in, acknowledged her arrival with a nod of his head, and then gestured at the seat opposite. "Sit down. I've got something to show you."

She pulled out the chair. "Aren't you going to ask me what happened? How everything went on my trip to the threads' city?"

"You can tell me in a minute. First, you need to see this." He turned his interface around and slid it across the table.

She had been expecting to see a design for a weapon. Aubriot had been fixated on designing weapons for weeks, laughing at any suggestion that he should perform manual labor, and entirely ignoring the fact that they had absolutely no means of making anything more complex than plows, hoes, axes, and shovels.

But what she saw on the screen was a list of words. "What's this?"

"Come on, Cherry. Isn't it obvious? It's a ranking system. See, this is you here." He pointed at the top of the column.

General

"General what?"

"Not General what. General who," Aubriot replied. "General Cherry. Or whatever your last name is."

"Lindstrom. My surname's Lindstrom. I can't believe you didn't know that. But what the hell are you talking about?"

His eyes narrowed. "Come on. It's simple. Read the rest. See what you think."

She scanned the list of titles. "I can't even read this one. How do you pronounce it? Loo—"

"That's *Left*enant. It isn't pronounced the way that it's spelled. Unless you're a Yank. Give it back to me." He pulled the interface from her grasp. "General, lieutenant-general, major-general, brigadier, colonel, lieutenant-colonel, major, captain, lieutenant, second-lieutenant, officer cadet. I think that's right. I had to write them from memory. There isn't anything in the data banks about military ranks. Ethan would be captain general, I suppose."

His gaze shifted to the middle distance. "Makes sense. Bloody pacifist scientists. I should have guessed that's what they would do. Never mind. It's water under the bridge now. Got to make the best of it." He looked at her. "So, what do you think? If we're going to have a fighting force it needs structure. A clear line of command. I thought the ranking system for the Royal Marines was as good as any other. Though maybe we don't need all of these ranks. But if you're General, that makes me Lieutenant-General, right?"

She had grown bored of his babble. She hadn't come here for a chat.

Their affair had been going on for months, but she still found herself mesmerized by his looks. Though he was a man, the only appropriate word for describing Aubriot was beautiful. His face was so symmetrical she doubted she would have been able to tell his mirror image from the real thing. His body was perfectly proportioned and his muscles honed though he rarely did any physical exercise. Aubriot was so good-looking, it was hard to take your eyes off him. It was as if his appearance was too flawless to be believed.

Cariad had once said that on Earth if you were extremely rich you could buy genetic engineering to give your baby whatever attributes you wanted, including physical perfection, and that Aubriot was an example.

The man snapped his fingers in front of her face. "Hey, pay attention. I'm your Lieutenant-General, okay?"

"Yeah, whatever you say." She had to organize Concordia's defense force before she went to the Galactic Assembly. As was usual with the threads, Quinn hadn't been able to give her a clear idea on when the ship they were building would be ready, but in truth it didn't really matter. The Scythians might return tomorrow or they might not come back for decades. Whenever their enemies decided to pay the colonists a third visit, they had to be ready.

If Aubriot wanted to play soldiers, she could turn his enthusiasm to the colony's benefit.

"I don't know why Ethan chose you and not me as his second in command," said Aubriot, partly under his breath. "It isn't like you know anything about military strategy."

"You don't know why Ethan didn't choose you? You don't think it might have something to do with that time you attacked him because you didn't want him to run for Leader?"

"Hey, he threw the first punch!"

"You deserved it."

"Maybe, maybe not. But that was ages ago. There's no need for him to hold a grudge for so long. I have a lot to offer. It's a shame he can't see it."

It's a shame you aren't beautiful on the inside.

"What's up with you?" Aubriot asked. "You're acting weird today."

"Am I? I'm just tired. It's been a long day and I have too much to think about. Maybe I should lie down for a while. Want to join me?" She raised her eyebrows and turned her head to look pointedly at his bed.

He sighed. "All right, if you like." He stood up, pushing back his chair, and unfastened the top few buttons on his shirt. As he pulled the shirt off over his head, he said, "So do you want to tell me what happened when you went to the Fila city?"

She walked to the bed, sat down, and pulled off her boots. "It was just about the strangest experience I've ever had. The threads behave differently down there, you know. They don't move around anywhere near as much as they do on the surface, and they glow. The whole place glows. It looks quite pretty, in fact."

"Pretty? Are you sure you weren't suffering from nitrogen narcosis?"

"You say that like you expect me to know what it means."

"Don't worry about it." He sat next to her but didn't seem in any hurry to do anything. He rested his elbows on his knees and stared absently at the opposite side of the room. His expression was uncharacteristically pensive, though now she thought about it, she realized he'd had that preoccupied expression often lately.

Was he thinking back to his time on Earth, when, by all accounts, he had led a highly privileged, even charmed life? Of all the Woken, Aubriot's experiences on Concordia had to be the most different from his former existence. Did he regret his decision to join the colony expedition? She had never asked him. For all their physical intimacy, they were not emotionally or even socially close. She preferred it that way.

He suddenly turned toward her, grabbed the back of her head, and kissed her hard on the lips. With his other hand, he pulled her shirt out of her pants and reached up underneath it. At the same time, he pushed her down on the bed and effortlessly swung her small frame under him.

He seemed in a hurry. She barely had time to take precautions to prevent pregnancy, and he was rougher than usual. When it was over, he didn't say anything. He only lay on his back, his hands behind his head, staring at the ceiling.

Something was bothering her lover. She didn't know what it was. Maybe he was sore that Ethan hadn't made him second in command, but she had a feeling it wasn't that. Something else was nagging at him.

She got dressed and left without saying goodbye.

Seven

Wilder's heart was racing as she went to collect her friends. She had already comm'd and told them the Leader had given permission for them to live out in the forest. Her dream was coming true. She would never have to sleep in the stuffy settlement again, hiding from the busy-bodies who wanted to make her return to her 'family'. No more dodging the hordes of people going to and fro along the passageways. No more tolerating the stink of stale baby sick and dirty diapers.

She and her friends would have to return to Sidhe for meals and to wash and use the bathroom, but even those needs might eventually be taken care of out doors. She had been thinking about how to build a latrine. It had to be sanitary, of course. But she hoped the Fila would be able to help them with that. The creatures did seem to want to help when they could.

And if she could build a latrine, building a cookhouse shouldn't be too hard. The group could invite more friends to join them and create their own village, outside in the fresh air of the forest. A place of their own.

She arrived at her destination. The numbers and letters 'E 1, L 2, 17' had been painted on the door: East First Street, Lane 2, Number 17.

Tycho's place.

She knocked. The settlement was already buzzing with noise, but over the hubbub she heard raised voices inside the room. The door flew open. Tycho stood in the frame, but he was facing away from her, looking into the room.

"You can't stop me," he yelled. "I want to do this!"

"Don't," said a woman's voice. "We've talked about this, Tycho. It isn't safe out there."

"Yes, it is. If it wasn't the Leader wouldn't have given permission."

A tall man appeared and grabbed the door frame. "You're Wilder, right? Please reconsider what you're doing. You're tearing families apart."

Tycho exclaimed, "We're not a family and you're not my parents!"

The man laid a hand on his shoulder, but the boy wrenched it out of the man's grasp. "Leave me alone. I can do what I want."

The sound of a weeping woman came from inside. Wilder's happy mood disappeared in an instant. This wasn't how it was supposed to be. This was supposed to be a happy time. A new beginning for the colony's youngsters. That was what she'd been trying to do. Not make people cry.

"Umm, maybe you should stay," she said to her friend. "You can always join us later."

"I want to come with you."

"But—"

"It's okay," said the man. "If you really want to leave, I don't want to stop you."

Tycho's expression switched from angry defiance to guilty shame. "It isn't that I want to leave *you.*" He turned around to speak to the unseen woman. "You've both been good to me. I know you've tried. But I didn't grow up in a family. I just don't feel comfortable living like this, no matter how hard I try. It doesn't feel right to me and, honestly, I don't think it feels right to you two either."

The man hung his head.

"You're trying to make me stay because you feel bad," said Tycho. "You feel like you've failed. But it wasn't ever going to work. It's nobody's fault. Please don't feel bad."

Inside the room, the woman sniffed. "Will you come back to see us?"

"Of course I will." Tycho went into the room, out of Wilder's sight.

She stared at her toes, wishing she wasn't here. A moment later, Tycho was back and hugging the man. Then he picked up a bag and stepped out. The man closed the door.

"Phew," said Wilder. "I'm glad that's over."

"Me too. After I told them what I was going to do, they spent all yesterday evening and this morning trying to persuade me not to leave. But you know what? They didn't really mean it. They wanted to be good citizens and care for a minor, but I've never fit in. I was never happy, and neither were they. They're hurting now, but in a few hours I know they'll feel relieved."

"Well, if you're sure..."

"I'm sure."

"Okay, let's get the others."

They checked on her interface to see which of their friends' addresses was nearest. She stole a glance at Tycho as they went along, checking that the teenager really was as resolute about leaving Sidhe as he made out.

But the fifteen-year-old's features were set firm.

It was easier for her. She'd never gotten along with her 'parents' and they hadn't been at all persistent about looking for her. In fact, she was sure the man from the couple had spotted her and deliberately changed direction a few days ago.

The plan to resettle the older children with adult colonists after Arrival had not seen much success. She recalled the shock of going from a communal care center, living with thirty children of different ages, to sharing a small house with two adults. As was often the case, the grown ups were almost strangers, though they'd made some attempts to get to know her before the move. In circumstances like that, how was everyone supposed to suddenly act and feel like a family? It was beyond her understanding. Another failure of the Manual.

She guessed that nothing like that had been attempted on Earth, and the Woken really hadn't thought through the practicalities. On Earth, people who took in orphaned children probably really wanted them. And those parents had grown up in families, so they knew what to do. But adults from the *Nova* had grown up in care centers, not nuclear families. In most cases, the learning curve had been too great.

A group of children was heading toward them, taking up all the space in the passageway.

"Oh no," said Tycho.

She mentally echoed the sentiment. These were the last people she wanted to see: schoolkids. Tycho would have been going to school too, but the Leader had said as long as Wilder's 'tree kids' kept up with their schoolwork, they could learn in their new homes.

Not all the schoolkids were bad, but a faction had formed that had taken a disliking to her, perhaps jealous of the free life she'd secured. One of the worst of them was a boy called Jim. He was two grades above her, but that didn't stop him from picking on her whenever he saw her.

It was too late to go back or slip down a side passageway. Judging by the grin on his face, Jim had seen her. If she tried to get away he would only follow, spurred on by her retreat. Instead, she stepped to the side and put her back against the earthen wall.

Jim was soon in front of her, thrusting his face into hers. "Off to the jungle again? Like a... a... What is it?" Jim asked the boy next to him, a lanky kid with a birthmark next to his eye. She had forgotten his name. "What's that animal with a tail that lives in jungles and climbs trees?"

"A monkey?"

"Yeah, that's right. Like a monkey. You wouldn't know that word, would you, Wilder? Seeing as you never go to school."

"You didn't know it either," said Tycho. "And Wilder knows more than you and your buddies put together."

"Forget it," she said to Tycho. She didn't want her friend getting hurt, and she knew from experience that Jim wasn't averse to physical bullying too.

Perhaps because they were surrounded by adults, Jim decided against using his fists for once. He ignored what Tycho had said and turned to his friends. "What I want to know is, do monkeys grow tits? Because this one sure doesn't have any."

This drew the expected guffaws from Jim's pals. Content with his parting shot, which he clearly considered the height of wit, Jim moved on.

She exhaled and relaxed. Even Jim couldn't dampen her mood today. "Come on. Let's not waste any more time."

The next person they collected was a twelve-year-old girl called Stephie. She'd begged Wilder to allow her to join them. At first, Wilder had made it a rule that no one younger than thirteen could live in the tree houses. The pulleys she'd installed to raise people to their platforms were manual. At the moment, there was no electricity. You needed a certain amount of strength to pull yourself up and she didn't want anyone getting stuck.

But Stephie had demonstrated she could manage the pulley, and she'd shown how smearing the tree trunks with their own resin prevented insects from climbing up them. So in the end Wilder had felt she couldn't deny the girl. After all, the Leader had said the colony wasn't founded on people following rules.

Stephie in tow, they continued on to the next dwelling and the next, until finally six of the friends were gathered together—Wilder had invited two more but they'd balked at the last minute. They went to the east entrance and she proudly led her little troupe of monkeys out into the sights and sounds of the morning forest.

She sniffed the fresh, cool, clean air.

Eight

Cherry woke to the faint, distant cry of an agitated baby and Rene's snoring. She looked over at her roommate, who was sleeping on her back with her mouth sagging open. Rene was nice, and she was easy to live with in most respects, but Cherry couldn't wait until the farmhouses were built and she could sleep in her own room in her own house.

She dreamed of a day when the threat of the Scythians was gone and she could concentrate on her farm. She'd been busy with the additional tasks Ethan had given her as his second in command, but the sweet potatoes, beans, corn, buckwheat, tomatoes, and pumpkins growing in her fields were doing well and would soon be ready for harvest. As the months had passed, she'd learned a lot about farming, but there was so much still to learn.

The colony's data on the subject was based on farming on Earth, but Concordia's year was only approximately half as long. Their region had been chosen for its lack of pronounced seasonal variation, yet the shorter year created some unforeseen pressures on growing.

She would not be able to work on her farm today. Today, she would be going up to the threads' 'seeding ship', as Quinn called it. A comm had arrived via Kes, the colony's main avenue of communication with the threads. The creatures wanted to consult with her on the ship they were building for the trip to the Galactic Assembly.

As she got out of bed, Rene snorted and turned onto her side. The snoring stopped.

Cherry tiptoed past her roomie, who remained asleep despite the sounds of babies wakening all around. How the soil biologist managed to maintain her immunity to the noise was beyond Cherry.

She showered and got dressed. It had taken her some weeks to learn how to complete fiddly tasks like fastening buttons one-handed. She'd been forced to modify several of her daily chores to account for the loss of her limb, but generally she'd managed. She'd long given up on regretting her foolish decision to go on her suicide mission, rushing outside to face the Scythian spiders. The past could not be changed and there was no point in wishing it could.

She slipped out into the passageway and closed the door. The threads' shuttle would arrive at the edge of the forest beyond the eastern exit—a surprising choice of site. If a shuttle from the *Nova* or the *Mistral* had arrived at that spot it would have set the vegetation on fire. She'd been expecting to take a flitter out to the old shuttle field.

On her way, she popped into the refectory, where the earliest risers were already eating breakfast. The servers had nothing she could carry and eat along the way, so she was forced to sit and quickly slurp down today's offering of cereal gloop.

The breakfast had been the same for weeks. She guessed the colony was running low on food, though Ethan hadn't mentioned anything about it. They desperately needed the harvest to be a success. The only alternative was to eat Concordian natives, and Rene had told her that eating plants and animals that originated on the planet was extremely risky. No one knew for sure how the human digestive system would react to the alien chemical compounds. Ethan had been the only person to attempt it and he'd been lucky not to suffer any ill effects.

Time was getting on. Cherry took her bowl and spoon to the collection point and hurried out. Aubriot was on his way in.

She hadn't seen him alone since their last encounter, when he'd acted like something was bothering him. They'd begun gathering and training the colony defense force, but they'd only spoken about work. It wasn't unusual for them to go a couple of weeks without personal contact, yet she had a feeling that things were over between them, though she didn't know why.

"Hi." Aubriot betrayed neither pleasure nor distaste at meeting her.

"Hi. Sorry, I have to go."

"In a hurry to go play farmer?"

"No, I...I have something else to do today. Catch you later."

"What is it?"

Cherry had passed him. He was speaking to her retreating back. She halted and turned.

Ethan hadn't told her specifically to keep the trip to the Galactic Assembly a secret. On the other hand he hadn't announced it. She wasn't sure if she should speak about it. She felt a great reluctance to, knowing the colonists would pin their hopes on her success.

Aubriot stepped toward her, looking intrigued. "Wait. What are you doing?"

Though the man had a flagrant disregard for others' feelings, he was nevertheless excellent at perceiving them. Her moment of hesitation had sparked his interest.

"Just something different. It doesn't matter." She had never been good at dissembling. Her poor attempt at it would only fuel Aubriot's curiosity.

He'd reached her. He leaned closer, his handsome head angled down, his gaze penetrating.

Giving a huff of exasperation, she grabbed his arm, and pulled him along the passageway, out of earshot of any passersby. She gave him a brief outline of her task, finishing with, "I'm going up to their ship to discuss the construction of the vessel they're building for us."

"How come you didn't tell me this before?"

"I didn't think it was up to me to tell anyone. It's up to Ethan."

"Dammit, Cherry." He was resting a hand on the wall. He smacked the surface in frustration. "You could have told *me*. This is pretty important. I am your Lieutenant-General."

"This isn't anything to do with the Defense Force."

"Everything is to do with the Defense Force. But I'm not talking about that." His features twisted into a pained expression she didn't recall seeing before. What was up with him? He seemed permanently butt hurt these days.

"Look, I'm sorry," she said. "I didn't realize it would bother you so much. I have to go now."

"Just a second. I want to come too."

"What, now? Or do you want to come with me to the Galactic Assembly?"

"Well, both, I suppose."

"It's just me who's going on the mission. The threads didn't invite you. I think it would be rude if you turned up along with me."

"The Fila don't know what's rude and what isn't in human culture. They might not even understand the concept."

"I still don't think you should come."

His attitude was making her uneasy. She didn't know what it might mean, but it seemed safest to just cut him off.

He looked like he was about to say something, but he changed his mind and walked away in silence.

Relieved the confrontation hadn't escalated further, she resumed her journey to the east exit. When she reached the door, the guard checked the time.

"You're a bit early," the woman said. "Got an urge for a morning stroll?"

"I'm going up to the threads' ship today."

The guard's eyes widened. "Stars, what are you.... Wait." She glanced at Cherry's empty left shirt sleeve. "You're the new second in command, right? I heard about that." She unlocked the door and pulled it open. "Good luck to you, my dear. Good luck to all of us. We certainly need it."

"Thanks. We certainly do."

Nine

"Ugh!" Wilder threw the leg of the Scythian spider into the pile in frustration and disgust. It clanked against another and bounced back. She scooted out of the way on her butt. Luckily, the claw didn't come anywhere near her, but she learned her lesson. She took in a deep breath and slowly exhaled, releasing pent-up irritation and anger.

The damned spiders would not release their secrets. She'd brought them into contact with every substance she could get her hands on, but the material remained unchanged. Whatever the alloy was, it was entirely inert. The pulse fire of the colonists during the Second Scythian Attack had severed the connections, but the main parts remained unchanged. She'd attempted every means she had to bend, break, or just mark the silvery surfaces, all to no avail.

She prided herself on her persistence. It was the source of most of her achievements. Friends like Tycho told her she was smart, but she wasn't. She was stubborn. If she wanted to know something, she didn't give up until she succeeded. She had discovered all kinds of interesting tidbits in the data files the *Mistral's* captain had dumped before destroying the ship, including a holo made by the Guardians' creators.

That had been fairly easy to find, but other things she'd only discovered through sheer doggedness, like the mechanics of the *Mistral's* a-grav system. Whenever anyone mentioned the anti-gravity capability of the flitters, it was always assumed that the technology had been lost on Earth during the decades after the *Nova*'s departure, or perhaps during the later plague years.

Yet, from what she understood, the Guardians' ship had a-grav. Everyone had been so caught up in the scramble to prepare for the Scythians' return, no one had taken the time to investigate the phenomenon.

It was all moot now. The Concordia Colony lacked the technological infrastructure to manufacture an a-grav system, but one day...

She covered the Scythian spider in piles of rags. All the kids living at the tree village knew she had pieces of the devices on her platform, and they knew they had to stay away from them, but she couldn't be too careful.

To distract herself from the frustrations of her work, she stood up and walked the two steps to the wall of her platform. The other adolescents were working too, making improvements to their small dwellings, bringing in supplies from Sidhe, and building a water supply network. Fresh water arrived from below ground under pressure—courtesy of the Fila—and the children's job was to run pipes between each platform and install spigots.

The village had lost three residents the day after everyone had arrived. The noise of sluglimpets moving through the undergrowth and scrambling up the tree trunks had been too scary. She didn't blame them. She'd been terrified of the predators too, though nowadays she didn't notice the noise.

She watched her fellow residents, enjoying the sound of their chatter and banter.

Rustling in the undergrowth alerted her to the approach of what sounded like several people. The other kids heard it too and stopped what they were doing. Everyone turned their heads in the direction of the noise. The trees pressed closely together. It wasn't possible to see the newcomers until they suddenly burst through the vegetation nearby.

It was Jim, his lanky friend, and a couple more kids around the same age.

Little Stephie was at ground level. She dropped the pot of resin she'd been rubbing into the joints on the water pipe, and ran for the nearest cradle. She jumped into it and began to pull on the rope.

Jim smirked and pointed before rushing toward her, followed by the rest of his group. Tycho bolted across a walkway to the platform Stephie was trying to reach. He grabbed the rope to her cradle and pulled on it hand over hand, lifting her faster than she would ever manage with the pulley.

All this took place in silence. Wilder was too shocked to speak. She knew Jim hated her for some reason, but she'd never thought he would bother to come out to her tree hamlet to harass her. She couldn't understand why.

Jim missed Stephie by a few centimeters. "Shit!" He jumped and grabbed, but Tycho's hauling strength, honed by helping the adults in the fields, defeated the other boy.

Jim growled in anger. "Who do you think you are? Living out here like animals. You should live in Sidhe like the rest of us. You're all stuck up. Think you're better than us. We'll see about that. We're going to tear this place apart!"

As he'd been yelling, the other tree village children had wisely pulled up two cradles at ground level. Jim ran to the trunk of the nearest tree and tried to climb it, but he couldn't reach the lowest branch. "Give me a leg up," he commanded his tall friend. "Help me tear this place down."

Stephie and Tycho ran to the platform on the next tree.

"What should we do, Wilder?" asked Jon, who was on the platform nearest hers. She didn't have an answer. She'd figured out how to protect the tree homes against sluglimpets, but she'd never imagined she would need to defend them against humans.

She watched, dismayed, as Jim's friend linked his fingers and bent down to help Jim into the tree. Jim put his foot in his friend's hands, and the lanky boy hoisted Jim upward, high enough for him to reach the lowest branch. Jim swung for a moment before lifting a leg, catching a toehold on the branch, and scrambling up.

"Wilder?" Jon repeated.

All the kids she'd invited to live with her were waiting for her to tell them what to do.

She didn't know. She had a vision of Jim and his pals steadily working their way through the tree village, pulling down and tearing apart whatever they could, slowly destroying all her and her friends' hard work.

She was frozen.

"Shit!" Jim yelled. "What the hell is this?"

He'd encountered the sluglimpet trap. As he paused, he looked down at his group, who were silently watching. "What are you doing? Climb the other trees. Rip apart their stupid houses. Lazy, stuck-up morons. Playing at houses when they should be at school or working on the farms."

Jim's friends halfheartedly walked to a couple of the other trees containing platforms.

Wilder remembered the Scythian spider parts.

She pulled the rags off them. The silvery alloy glinted in the dappled sunlight. She hadn't thought about the devices as weapons for weeks, but now they looked menacing, deadly. Did she dare use them? The spider claws were lethal. She didn't want to kill anyone or even hurt them. She only wanted to stop them from destroying her pride and joy.

A cracking sound came from the tree Jim was climbing. He was pulling apart the sluglimpet trap. Ire gripped her chest. Maybe if she only threatened Jim with a spider leg, he would stop.

But what if he didn't?

Or, worse, what if he somehow managed to take it and use it on her?

Her hands trembling, she lifted a leg, holding it by its middle, keeping the vicious claws pointed firmly away.

Jim gave a grunt of effort and a ripping sound followed as he tore the sluglimpet trap from its moorings. "Got it off! That's it. I'm nearly there."

"Everyone, get out of my way," she called to her friends.

She stepped onto the walkway running from her tree to the next and heard the exclamations of her friends as they saw what she was carrying. Running lightly to prevent the bridge from swaying—she had no hands free to hold a handrail—she crossed to the next platform, which was empty.

"Jim!" shouted the lanky boy. "Look what she's got!"

The noises of the bullies registering her weapon now came floating up. They sounded partly fearful, partly in awe.

"Ha! I'm not afraid of her." Jim's tone lacked confidence.

Be afraid, Wilder thought. *Run away and leave us alone.*

"She's mad," someone murmured from below. "She's going to kill him."

She reached the tree nearest the one Jim was climbing and halted. Her arms ached, though the spider leg was light. It was the tension of holding the thing, knowing what it could do, that made her muscles hurt. She gazed across the walkway.

Jim's head emerged at the center of the next platform, through the gap between it and the tree it encircled. The gap wasn't large, but Jim was determined to squeeze through. He tore at the floor of the tree house, working the woven fronds to make them looser and more flexible.

"Stop that," she ordered. "You have no right to be here. This is my place, and I didn't invite you. Go away."

He only grinned, red-faced and sweaty, and continued to work at the flooring. He pushed his arms up and grabbed the edges of the gap.

"Stop!" she yelled, holding up the spider. She knew what she had to do, but she didn't want to do it.

Jim pulled himself out, rose from his knees, and stood upright, his hands on his hips.

"You idiot!" she shouted. "Think about what you're doing."

The children from both sides were staring at Jim and Wilder.

"I *was* going to rip this thing apart," Jim said. "But seeing as *you're* here, I'll do it to you instead."

He stepped onto the walkway.

Her heart heavy, she carried out her plan. First, she severed the handrails. The spider's claws sliced through them as if they didn't exist. A beat later she swiped through the floor of the bridge. The material slipped apart. The walkway, now attached only at the farther end, swung down.

Wilder looked up, hoping that Jim hadn't made it so far along the bridge that he would fall.

He was holding on. He must have taken two or three steps before seeing what she was doing and trying to make it back to safety. He'd nearly made it, but not quite. He was clinging to the platform's edge, the bridge hanging below.

Everyone watched as he swung, trying to get a knee or a toe up.

"What's going on?" someone said.

It was a new voice. An adult man's voice.

The red-haired Woken had arrived. She had seen him around—his coloring and freckled skin made him noticeable—but she didn't know his name.

"What's happening?" he asked. "Can't anyone help that boy?"

"There aren't any walkways to that platform now," she replied. "No one can reach him."

As she spoke, Jim finally managed to haul himself to safety.

"What on Earth are you doing with one of those?" asked the man, staring at the Scythian spider leg she held.

She carefully put it down. "It's a long story."

"I bet. Are you all right?" he asked Jim.

"Yeah," Jim replied sullenly as he tried to figure out how to work the platform's cradle.

Tycho called out instructions.

"Is anyone going to tell me what's going on here?" the man asked. "You're Wilder, I believe? Aren't you the one in charge?"

"I am. I'll come down to you and explain everything."

Jim's friends had already melted away. Carrying out Tycho's instructions, Jim was lowering himself. Wilder carefully carried the spider leg back to her tree home and replaced the rags. By the time she'd reached the ground, Jim had already left. The tree village children began to fix the damaged walkway and sluglimpet cone.

Wilder walked over to the man, who lifted up a spray bottle. "I came here to bring you some of this. It's sluglimpet repellent."

"No kidding." She was amazed. "Really?"

"Yes, really. But would you mind telling me what I just witnessed?"

She gave a short account of her dealings with Jim. To her relief, the man seemed to believe her.

"I see. I'm sorry to hear that but I'm not surprised. If this colonization has taught me anything, it's that aggression is innate in human nature, unfortunately. I will inform the education section about what's going on. Someone will speak to Jim and his associates and you won't be bothered by him again."

"Thanks. I was worried we would be in trouble and we'd have to go back to Sidhe."

"I don't think so, but you shouldn't have those spider parts hanging around. They're extremely dangerous."

"I know, but I was using it as a last resort. I wasn't keeping it as a weapon. I've been trying to figure out what they're made from and how we can reuse the material."

"The best among us haven't found that out yet. What makes you think you will?"

"I'm not sure I will, but I want to try."

He put a hand on her shoulder. "As one scientist to another, I applaud your efforts. And for that reason I'm not going to do what I should do and tell someone what you're doing. But if this gets out, I did *not* know you had that thing here. Deal?"

She grinned. "Deal."

"My name's Kes, by the way." He handed her the bottle. "I see that nasty young man has destroyed one of your sluglimpet barriers. You shouldn't need them now you have this repellent, though I would keep them in place just to be careful. Spray the liquid in a band about a meter wide around each tree trunk every day. It actually lasts longer than that but I don't want you to take any chances."

"So this will actually stop them climbing the trees?"

"That's right. We've been testing the repellent out at the farms. A hundred percent success rate so far. They'll probably abandon this area of the forest altogether. I love the idea of your cones, by the way. I don't know why I didn't think of it. Sometimes you're so used to solving complex problems you fail to see simple solutions."

"Is this mine to keep?" she asked, lifting the bottle.

"It is, and when you need more, just ask. The solution is sticky and won't evaporate or be washed away by rain. It's good stuff, though we don't know the active ingredient yet. We discovered it only through trial and error."

"Thanks a lot."

"You don't have to thank me. We're all in this together, right? I think what you're doing here is great. We need to ease the pressure underground." He shook his head. "I'm very sorry for what happened here today. Even when we're teetering on the edge of survival, we're still at each others' throats, it seems."

Kes said goodbye and left.

She agreed with his exasperation over Jim's actions. But the tree village had survived and now they had a second defense against the sluglimpets.

Things were looking up.

TEN

The threads' shuttle was nothing more than a narrow metal chamber, similar to the vessel in which Cherry had traveled to the creatures' underwater city. Only the entire hull was opaque, leaving her with no view of the outside. She had never felt claustrophobic, but the experience of being transported up to the threads' seeding ship was becoming more and more unpleasant. She couldn't wait for it to end.

When she'd emerged at the edge of the forest, she'd been surprised to see no ship. Then she'd spotted the shuttle, half hidden in the long grass. Disbelievingly, she'd walked over to the metallic tube. It was open, revealing a slim padded mat at the bottom and two handholds.

She had no direct channel to the threads via comm and so no easy way of checking what seemed impossible—that they expected her to undertake a journey probably lasting hours inside something resembling the receptacles used to jettison bodies from the *Nova*.

For several long moments, she had stared into the open hatch. She bent down and looked in. At the end farthest from the hatch was a simple metal bar. A foot rest? Her closer inspection revealed straps poking out each side of the mat.

The vessel looked exactly like something designed by someone with a basic understanding of human anatomy but little appreciation of human sensitivities.

Was there even a light? She hadn't seen one. When the hatch closed, would she be in darkness?

But what choice did she have except to climb in? She'd agreed to go on the trip. She only hoped the ship the threads were building to take her to the Galactic Assembly was much larger. She would need a bathroom at the very least.

When she stepped into the narrow metal chamber and lay down, the hatch immediately slid shut, blocking out the pale, pink-streaked morning sky. She was in utter darkness. She raised her hand in front of her face but she couldn't see it. The straps on each side of the mat she was lying on slithered out from their anchor sites sinuously, like thread tentacles, and clipped into place across her thighs, hips, and chest.

The vessel lifted, and she was borne upward smoothly and quickly. The shuttle moved so fast the floor pressed painfully into her back. Her stomach lurched, and this morning's breakfast gloop threatened to make a reappearance. The air pressure was rapidly dropping. Her ears suddenly and painfully popped.

Did the threads understand about air pressure and the human body's need for it? Did they understand about the human need for air?

Of course they do. She and Ethan had been fine during their ocean trip. She breathed in and out deeply. "Hey," she said, thinking it wouldn't hurt to find out if the threads had installed comm, "can I have a light in here?"

Instantly, the inner walls glowed and she was bathed in soft, yellow light. She'd only had to ask. Maybe the threads underestimated the importance of light to humans because they could create their own.

A hissing noise started up. Gas streamed steadily from the internal ribs of the shuttle. The threads were supplying air or oxygen. After a moment the flow of gas eased to a trickle she could barely feel. Her back remained pressed against the vessel's floor by the craft's acceleration. How were the threads powering the vessel? As with the underwater capsule, there didn't appear to be any engine.

The acceleration eased, and she lifted gently off the floor. She grabbed a handhold near her head and hooked her toes under the foothold. The nauseating feeling returned. She swallowed saliva. Puking in zero-g would be messy, and it would create a terrible impression when she arrived.

She must have reached the upper atmosphere. Now she only had to rendezvous with the seeding ship. How long would it take?

Time slid past until, lacking any external clues, she entirely lost track of how long she'd been traveling. It could have been thirty minutes or three hours.

Finally, just as she was performing mental gymnastics to prevent herself from panicking, begging to be let out, and bashing the hull of the shuttle with her feet and fist, deceleration hit. She had to have reached the seeding ship and was slowing down to enter it.

The shuttle bounced, as if suspended on elastic. It lurched, and then clunked against something. The impact had been beneath her back.

Several beats later—too many—the hatch opened.

An odd scent flooded in. Above was a white, shiny ceiling covered in a faint sheen of purple. The safety straps unfastened and slid away. Her body had no weight, though the shuttle sat firmly on the floor, perhaps magnetized. She sat up, steadying herself with a hand on the edge of the hatch. She was inside a white room. The walls were pearlescent white, slanting inward and rising to a smooth dome, but the floor was an ugly gray. All she could see of the entrance the shuttle had flown through was a faint seam on a wall. On the opposite wall a hole opened. It was only a little wider than she was.

Did the threads expect her to climb in?

"Please enter the portal," said a disembodied voice.

The threads expected her to climb into that little hole.

She pushed herself awkwardly out of the shuttle—she'd only experienced zero-g briefly, during trips from the *Nova* to Concordia—and kicked off to float to the edge of the hole. A tunnel stretched away from her, only a little wider than the opening. The tunnel was transparent. Surrounding it in shadowy light, were the moving tentacles of threads. Her instinctive revulsion toward the writhing forms returned in full.

She glanced over her shoulder at the shuttle. She would much rather return to that narrow vessel than enter the tunnel. The entrance was so small, and how was she supposed to move along it one-armed?

"Please enter the portal," the voice repeated.

"I'm not sure I can fit."

"The diameter conforms to your body's proportions. There is no cause for concern."

"How can I move myself?" She imagined edging forward, centimeter by centimeter, like Concordian insects she'd seen in the forest. And how would she turn around to return to the shuttle? She would have to edge backward.

"You do not have to move. The channel will move for you."

"Oh, okay." Grimacing, she put the upper half of her body into the hole and wriggled forward until her feet left the floor. Then she gripped the wall to bring in the rest of her body.

The wall didn't feel how she'd expected. She'd thought it was a kind of plastiglass, but it was not hard or smooth; it was soft and slightly sticky. The tunnel flexed and swayed gently in the water surrounding it.

"What happens n— Whoa."

The walls began to pulsate, contracting behind and widening ahead of her, pushing her forward. Each wave propelled her onward. The process was unpleasant and nauseating.

It was like being a lump of food being transported through someone's guts. The realization made her feel even more sick. She swallowed and, in an effort to take her mind off things, she asked, "Will this take long?"

"You will arrive in a moment."

"Good, because this sucks." She didn't like to complain, considering the threads were the colony's only ally against an enemy demanding human sacrifices, but neither did she want to give the impression that everything was going great.

"You're uncomfortable?"

"I am, and the trip up here was nothing to write Earth about either."

A brief pause. "We designed this conveyance to be convenient for you. Is your breathing restricted?"

"No, but everything's too small. Too closed in. I feel trapped."

She was passing rapidly along the tunnel, too rapidly to take in much of what lay around. There were hundreds of thread creatures, vague boundaries to rooms, and some items that looked like equipment, but everything was only glimpsed due to her awkward position, quick progress, and the distortion caused by water.

The threads didn't answer. What had led them to think that animals that usually walked on two legs would enjoy being forced down a narrow, flexible tunnel?

She was pushed around a bend, and then the tunnel suddenly gave a particularly hard squeeze. She was ejected into a round, pearlescent-walled chamber, but only a small section of it. A transparent wall closed off the majority of the space. On the other side, thread creatures were gathered around a solid structure.

She floated across to get a better look.

"You have arrived at the construction zone for your ship. We would like you to spend some time assessing our progress. Our knowledge of human needs is limited. We would like to discuss with you the internal accommodation."

She rested her forehead on the barrier. It wasn't as soft as the tunnel but it wasn't rigid. The material gave slightly under pressure and when she pressed a hand against it she found it was tacky.

Gradually, the details of the view became clearer. The threads were moving around a small structure. Its size was difficult to guess, but it looked way too small for an interstellar vessel.

The threads were working on it manually, long strings of translucent mucus unraveling from their tentacles and stretching across the half-built vessel. They also had devices they were controlling remotely. Smaller than the threads, these machines roved the parts of hull and moved in and out of gaps.

Bright lights and distorted water indicated some kind of heat being used, but she couldn't see exactly what was happening due to the brilliance of the rays. "Is that the finished size?"

"Yes, you can see the approximate dimensions. We are concerned that we may have made the ship too large, but most of the space is taken up by the engine. We must use a standard deep space propulsion device. We fear your bodies will not survive our usual means of travel. We need to know the details of the physiological requirements to sustain yourselves during space flight."

"Wait a minute," said Cherry. "If I'm supposed to live in that ship for any length of time, it's way too small. I'd go crazy."

"The ship is too small? You require more space than only to accommodate your body."

"Yes, much, much more."

"This is a major misunderstanding," said the voice. "Among our species, a small, confined area promotes feelings of comfort and security. In our distant past, excessive space surrounding us was a potentially dangerous situation."

"We're the opposite. We don't enjoy being confined. We like wide, open spaces. Or most of us do, anyway. Can you make the ship bigger?"

"We must. It has to hold four humans. And we must increase our work speed or the Assembly will be over before you arrive."

"Four? I thought it was only me who was going."

"The organizers have requested a representative sample of humans. At least four individuals."

She had to find three colonists to take with her? The news was a bombshell. When had the threads been planning to tell her this little detail? Aubriot's request to come along immediately popped into her head but she dismissed it. He was unbearable to be around for longer than a few hours.

"We also need information on your nutritional requirements and excretion functions."

"Uh, okay." Her mind was spinning.

The expedition to the Galactic Assembly was suddenly becoming very real. She would leave Concordia for an unspecified length of time, with three fellow passengers. She hoped the Scythians didn't return while she was gone.

Eleven

The rustling of leaves and a cool draft blowing on Wilder's back woke her. She groaned and turned over, pulling up the blanket that had slipped off while she slept.

It was the same every morning. Not long after sunrise, a wind arose that swept through the forest, agitating tree fronds, curving branches, and even setting the trees slightly swaying. The effect was a morning wake up comm, especially since there was a gap in a wall of her tree home that let in a draft directly behind her.

Each morning when the blast of cool air and noise of the moving forest woke her, she would resolve to plug the gap first thing. Every time, something would distract her and she would forget about it until the following morning.

The natural alarm clock was usually not unwelcome. Most of the time, she was eager to be up and starting on her tasks. But she'd been sleeping badly lately, her mind unable to let go of the problem posed by the Scythian spiders. She'd begun to second-guess herself. Had she waited long enough to see a result before moving on to the next experiment? Had she missed something subtle but important? Was the answer screaming in her face and she was ignoring it?

She had a feeling that the last possibility was the most likely. Though the Scythians had superior technology, the laws of physics applied to them the same as to everyone. The spiders were not magical and neither was the material they were made from. There had to be a way to re-purpose it. She would have been happy even to figure out how to separate the legs. Removing the claws would render them harmless, and the colony would have a large supply of tough, durable material. In the current state of affairs, any additional resource would be a bonus.

She sat up, wiped sleep from the corners of her eyes, and pulled her fingers through her hair. She'd lost her comb some days ago. However, she'd discovered that a piece of vine made an excellent hair tie. She pushed back her overgrown bangs, gathered her locks into one bunch and tied the vine around them.

As she got up, hunger hit. Had she eaten dinner last night? She couldn't remember. She had a feeling the others had gone to the refectory in Sidhe without her. She'd said she was busy and would go later. She would have to make an effort to go to breakfast, though the thought wasn't inviting. All that was available recently was cereal porridge and that had always been her least favorite meal.

"Wilder?"

The voice had come from below. She recognized it. It was the Woken man who had brought them the sluglimpet repellent. Wrapping her blanket around her shoulders, she went to the edge of her platform. "Kes?"

The red-haired man looked up and waved. "I hope I didn't wake you. I realize it's early."

"I was already awake. But it *is* early. What are you doing here?"

He lifted a bottle of repellent. "I thought you might need a refill. I'm going out to work in the fields today. The farmers need all the help they can get right now. So I thought I would drop by on my way."

"Oh, thanks. I'll come down."

"Do you mind if I come up to you? I can spare fifteen minutes and I'm curious to see your set up."

"Sure. I'll lower the cradle." She passed the rope hand over hand until the harness flopped on the forest floor.

The scientist stepped into it and pulled on the rope, lifting himself level with the platform. He had a little difficulty with climbing out onto the flat surface, so she helped him.

"I haven't had to do that since I was on the *Nova*."

"I didn't know we had climbing harnesses on the ship."

"Not while she was underway. I lived aboard the wreck for a while, when we first made contact with the Fila."

"I heard you were the person who first communicated with them. That must have been cool."

"I wasn't strictly the first person. That honor goes to Ethan. It's quite a story, but he doesn't like to talk about it." Kes was surveying her home. "What a nice place to live. You've done a great job."

"Thanks. Sorry, but I don't have any chairs. If you want to sit down, you'll have to sit on the floor."

"That's no problem." He lowered himself down and sat cross-legged.

"I don't have anything to offer you either. Oh, except water. Would you like a drink?"

"I would. Thank you."

She bounded to the spigot and, feeling rather proud, poured Kes a tumbler.

"Marvelous," he said as he took it. "I didn't know you'd managed to install plumbing."

"We can't take all the credit. The Fila bring the water to the surface for us. We only had to pipe it to each platform."

"You're too modest. What you've done here is truly remarkable."

"Thanks for saying that. I sometimes feel guilty and think my time would be better spent doing the same as you, helping with the crops. The others have been going out to the farms when they aren't doing schoolwork, but I have to confess I've been spending my time trying to figure out the Scythian spiders."

"You're still working on them?"

"I am, though it's been a total waste of time. I should have been pitching in with everyone else, getting the important stuff done."

He swallowed a mouthful of water and put down his tumbler. "If you're going to grow up to be a scientist, and I think you are, there's something you need to understand. Not all scientific endeavor has a useful purpose. Sometimes we investigate something just because we're curious, or for the sense of challenge, or because we heard someone else is working on it, though we don't know why. And that's fine. Some amazing, enlightening, and extremely advantageous discoveries have been made only because a scientist wondered, *what if*?

"But that doesn't even apply to what you're doing here. What you're doing is extremely practical and useful. If we find out how to use the spiders, that would accelerate our progress exponentially. And everything you've done in building these tree dwellings is highly utilitarian too. When we—hopefully—bring in the harvest, we'll be in even more desperate need of space. I believe you've laid the groundwork of a viable, safe way to expand our living quarters.

"I know it must feel as though you've been laboring in solitude without any recognition of your efforts, but that isn't the case. Everyone is too pushed for time at the moment to give you the acknowledgment and appreciation you deserve. But people are watching what you're doing and they're impressed. I believe that may be what led that little thug to bring his pals here to try to tear the place down. He probably overheard someone singing your praises and was jealous."

She was so taken aback by Kes's words, she didn't know how to respond.

Perhaps sensing her embarrassment, he went on, "But I have to say, you look as though you've been overdoing it a bit lately. When was the last time you ate? You look awfully thin."

"You're right." She hung her head. "I should eat more. It's just that I get caught up in what I'm doing and I forget."

"I understand. I'm the same. But I'm lucky enough to have others watching out for me. I know your friends care about you, but they're only kids themselves."

She looked up, her eyes narrowing. Had Kes set this whole thing up with an ulterior motive? "I hope you aren't working up to suggesting I go back to Sidhe."

"No, no way. I'm concerned about your well-being, that's all." He looked toward the other platforms and their occupants, who were rising. "You know, when I was a child I built a place like this. My parents owned a bit of land at the back of their house. They never did anything with it. It was just woodland. Nothing special or interesting. But my brother and I loved to play there."

"You had a brother?" Her Gen curiosity about the idea of siblings was piqued. Until the Woken had been revived, she'd never met anyone who had a brother or sister. Immediately, she regretted her words. It wasn't good manners to remind someone of loved ones they had left behind. "Sorry, stupid question."

"No, it's fine. I did have a brother." He paused. "I had a sister too, about your age." Then he changed the subject. "It's a shame we can't use the spiders to make something useful." He pointed at a silvery surface gleaming through a gap in her pile of rags. "It would have been handy if we could have used them to build the electric fence around the farmland."

"I thought about that too, but the material's a resistor, not a conductor. I read the report."

"You did? I didn't think that was generally available."

But she barely heard him. She was staring at the rags and their revealing glimpse of silver. Something was niggling at the back of her mind but refusing to come out into the light. Something about electricity and the Scythian spiders.

Then she had it. "Kes, what voltage does the colony's electrical system run on?"

"I've no idea. You'd have to ask one of the electricians. Why?"

"I've been testing the spider parts in every way I can think of, trying to discover the properties of the alloy or figure out a way to get inside them. But I'm wondering if the scientists only tested the material with one voltage."

"You're wondering if altering the voltage might make a difference? I'm no electrical engineer but I highly doubt it. A higher voltage would only cause the alloy to heat up and a lower voltage wouldn't have any effect. If only we had the Guardians with us. I bet they would have had the spiders figured out in the blink of an eye."

She stood up. Now she'd had her idea, she wanted to test it right away. The

Fila supplied Sidhe's electricity. How, exactly, no one really knew, but it was generally believed to be either hydro-generated or geothermal.

“Going somewhere?” Kes asked.

“You speak to the threads, right? Could you ask them something for me?”

“Sure. What would you like me to ask?”

She explained what she wanted to do.

“Well, I don’t know if they’ll agree. Seems like it might be dangerous, but I’ll ask.”

Twelve

Two groups of colony troops were lined up facing each other, waiting to undertake a training exercise. Cherry walked toward them quickly. She didn't want to be late and miss the beginning.

In the time they could spare from farm work or child care, the colony's able-bodied men and women had been undergoing training organized by Aubriot. Ethan had kept Cherry so busy with regular colony business, she'd been forced to leave her '*left*enant general' to organize the defense force. He'd mentioned he was calling Concordia's militia a 'commando' and had divided the troops into 'companies' and 'platoons', but in truth the divisions didn't matter too much. Everyone who was able to fight needed to learn how to do it to the best of their ability.

Aubriot had begun to call the men and women 'his Marines', giving her some concern. She hadn't liked the proprietorial sound of his words and had decided it was time she took a closer look at what he was doing.

The lines were not particularly straight and the men and women were fidgeting as they waited to collect their weapons. Some were already comfortable with operating both the Guardians' weapons as well as the ones from the *Nova.* Many had handled weapons during the early schism in the colony or later on during the Second Scythian Attack. Their response had been futile, but everyone had done the best that could be expected under the onslaught of the Scythian spiders. Nothing could have withstood them.

Though she was concerned about Aubriot's obsession with his new, self-awarded role, she was forced to agree the colony could not sit on its ass regarding its defense. Though realistically they didn't stand a chance if the

Scythians mounted a third attack, to do nothing would have negatively impacted morale. The colonists needed to feel they were doing *something* to protect themselves, no matter how futile.

Aubriot spotted her and walked out to meet her. "What are you doing here? Don't trust me to do a good job?"

"Stars, you're always in a bad mood these days. I've come to take part in the exercise." She continued toward the colonists to avoid arguing in front of them. The men and women were all wearing arm bands. One set was blue and the other was a muddy red. "What are those things on their arms?"

"Something to show which side they belong to. Their uniforms should be ready in a couple of weeks. When we decide who to promote to officer status, we can add stars to the collars or cuffs to show rank."

"You're having uniforms made? What from?" Textiles were a sparse resource, and most of the colonists had become adept at mending and patching their clothes.

"Didn't you hear? One of the Woken found something similar to bamboo and figured out how to make cloth fiber from it. As soon as the harvest is over, we'll be able to kit everyone out in fatigues."

It was odd to hear him refer to the Woken as if he were not one of them. She guessed he felt no affinity with them, but he was definitely not a Gen either. He wasn't even a hybrid. Aubriot sat apart from everyone.

"What's bamboo?" she asked.

"A plant. It's...It doesn't matter, except that we've found something to save us from going around bare arse naked twenty years from now when all our clothing finally wears out."

"And your first thought was to use this new cloth to make uniforms."

He frowned and stared down at her. They had reached the troops. He turned his back to them as he replied, "A military force needs discipline. It needs to act as a unit. Part of that is feeling like you belong to something bigger than yourself, something more important than you as an individual. You need to feel comradeship with the people on your team. Uniforms help with that."

"Okay, I understand. So where do I get an arm band?"

"Why do you want one? We don't have officer bands."

"I want to take part in the training. Today, I want you to treat me just like everyone else."

"No." His expression darkened. "That won't work. The rank and file need to look up to you if they're going to follow your orders. You have to keep yourself separate. That's what being a superior officer is about. The clue's in the name."

She was surprised at his agitation. She'd clearly struck a nerve. "But I need to know what it's like to be in battle if I'm going to give effective orders."

"Not necessarily. It's sometimes better if you don't know what it's like. You can't afford to be soft."

"Aubriot," she said, her hand tightening to a fist, "I would never ask anyone to do something I wasn't prepared to do myself, and if that's what Generals on Earth did, maybe they got it wrong."

His lips twisted as he tried to think up a response, but he was clearly conscious of the two lines of troops behind him, eyeballing the conversation even if they couldn't hear it. "All right. Have it your way. The armbands are over there."

The spare arm bands were in a corner of a box of pulse rifles. She slipped one over her arm and picked up a weapon. It was the last one: a weapon from the *Nova,* heavier and bulkier than the Guardians' rifles. Its range was also shorter.

Aubriot was telling the troops to listen up. She returned, her weapon at her side, and stood next to her Lieutenant-General while he explained what they were going to do.

When he'd finished, she also spoke. "I'm going to be taking part in today's exercise. I think you all know me well enough to be aware I don't expect you to treat me any differently from anyone else, just because I'm second-in-command."

"But what about your arm, Cherry?" asked Phy.

"No questions!" barked Aubriot. "You do *not* speak unless an officer speaks to you first."

Phy, who was tall and rangy and one of the best at handling a weapon, didn't reply except to roll her eyes.

Her reaction was sufficient provocation to Aubriot to make him march up to her and lean toward her face until their noses were nearly touching. "I will *not* have insubordination in this company!"

Phy didn't flinch. She only returned his stare, unblinking.

After a tense silence of several seconds, during which neither Aubriot nor Phy broke eye contact, he about-faced and strode back to his former position. An almost palpable wave of resentment passed through the men and women. The Lieutenant-General's attitude wasn't going to win him any friends. But that wasn't his intent. He wanted their fear and obedience, not their friendship.

Yet if he wanted their obedience, Cherry wasn't convinced he was going about it the right way. All of 'his Marines' were volunteers. If they disliked their treatment they could form their own militia. They could take the situation into their own hands, exactly as the Gens had done during the early days of the colony. Then where would Aubriot be?

In truth, she was surprised by his insensitivity and ineptitude. He might know a lot about weapons and military strategy, and he might also be able to read and manipulate people, but he knew nothing about winning loyalty.

He divided the men and women into fire teams, four on each side according to their arm bands. He sent the blue arm bands into the forest, telling them he'd marked a tree to defend and giving them rough directions. The red arm bands had to attempt to reach the tree. As soon as someone from the attacking side touched the tree the exercise was over.

The weapons were set to a light stun, so there was little danger of anyone getting seriously hurt, but Cherry worried about concussions from awkward falls. The troops would definitely need helmets to go with their uniforms.

So much had to be done, and yet she would be leaving soon to travel to the Galactic Assembly. She'd been feeling fairly relaxed about leaving Aubriot in charge of the colony's defense, but now she wasn't so sure it was a good idea.

She joined a team wearing red arm bands. As she neared them, she overheard Aubriot's name mentioned along with another, unflattering, word. The talk fell silent as she walked up.

"Do you want to be group leader?" asked Arden, a Gen Cherry held a lasting animosity toward. He'd been one of the compliance enforcement officers in the old settlement who had arrested her.

"I'm just one of you today. Though shouldn't you say captain, not group leader?"

The men and women in the team laughed. Aubriot had clearly been pedantic in drilling them all with the ranks of his new army.

"It's actually 'lieutenant'," said Arden. "If I'm keeping my position, I guess I should confer with my fellow officers on how we're going to manage this attack."

Aubriot had given the sides ten minutes to plan their tactics. The time passed quickly, and Arden only had a few moments to tell his team the agreed plan before Aubriot gave the signal to begin.

Cherry hadn't taken part in any kind of military training since losing her arm. As she ran through the undergrowth, keeping low, she found she was unbalanced. Carrying her weapon one-handed also felt awkward.

The soft hiss of weapon fire was coming from up ahead. She couldn't see the action through the trees, but she guessed that Teams Red 1 and 2 were carrying out their part of the plan, laying down fire to divert attention from Team Red 3, which would try to sneak in while the defenders were distracted. Her team, Red 4, was sweeping all the way around the back of the target, and would launch an attack if Team 3 failed.

Her breathing became ragged and her thighs, knees, and calves ached badly from stooping as she ran the long distance through the trees. Her team members sped along on each side of her, noisily and without much effort to be inconspicuous. She cut the wide sweep and eventually the sounds of pulse rounds grew louder as she began to approach the Blues' tree from behind. Her team mates seemed to have disappeared. Either they'd outpaced her or she'd left them behind, or they'd suddenly gotten a whole lot better at moving stealthily.

The undergrowth suddenly rustled and a figure burst out: a Blue Team member, running who knew where, but right across her path. She swung her weapon up and fired. The round hit the edge of the woman's shoulder. For a moment, Cherry thought she'd missed because the woman continued to run. But then her legs gave way and she landed face first, sliding a short distance before she hit a tree.

Cherry moved on before the woman had time to come around. Maintaining her low stance against the protests of her muscles, she continued to edge closer to the defended tree. She could clearly hear the sound of fire coming from that direction. As she circled a large sapling, she almost tripped over another casualty of the exercise rising to his feet. Like the woman Cherry had shot, the man wore a blue arm band.

"Looks like the Reds are going to win," he said, not even attempting to enter into combat.

"I don't think the Lieutenant-General would approve of you fraternizing with the enemy."

"You're probably right. But he's an asshole, so who cares?"

The Reds did win, though only after incurring many 'casualties'. When it was all over, Aubriot spent fifteen minutes berating both sides. He criticized their discipline, tactics, shooting accuracy, and everything else he appeared to think of. By the time he finished his rant and dismissed the men and women in a tone of disgust, he was red-faced and sweating.

Cherry watched him in grave silence. Everything he said was entirely justified. When she had helped to train the defense units before the Second Scythian Attack, she had trained them in only one thing: to defend the underground settlement. Required to perform independently and in an open area, the colonists were terrible soldiers. It would take a lot of work to make them an efficient fighting force.

Yet Aubriot was going about it in the wrong way. His authoritarian manner held no sway over the colonists, who were mostly Gens. They had been brought up to discuss and decide things as a group, not to be dictated at, and certainly not to be berated and humiliated by someone for whom they had zero respect.

If Aubriot wanted the defense force to improve he would need to take a different approach, but she doubted he was capable of it.

Thirteen

To prevent accidentally cutting herself and anyone else with the Scythian spider, Wilder had wrapped the claws in fibrous leaves and then tied the bunches together with pieces of dried vine. The blades would slice their way out of their wrappings eventually due only to the gentle motion of being transported, but they would remain covered long enough for her purposes.

Kes offered to carry the spider to Sidhe and Wilder agreed. He seemed relieved to take it out of her hands. Together, they walked to the underground settlement's eastern entrance.

"Have you been to the power control room before?" he asked.

"No way. Not allowed." She'd actually been to plenty of places in Sidhe she was technically 'not allowed' to go. She'd needed a place to sleep after deciding she wasn't ever going back to her allotted parents, and she'd found a tiny storeroom with a faulty lock. The room had been void of contents except for empty food sacks, which were surprisingly comfortable to sleep on. She had also snuck into the refectory kitchen in the late evenings when it was empty. Not because she wanted to steal any food. She had only been curious about the preparation equipment.

She had also investigated the platforms that had risen to the surface during the Scythian attack, carrying the Guardians to their deaths—if machines could die. Those places were strictly off-limits. It had not been morbid curiosity compelling her. She had only wanted to study the hydraulic mechanism that moved the platforms upward. She'd read about hydraulics and had wanted to see a working system.

The power control center was another temptation, but she'd never managed to gain access. The room was manned around the clock, and it had one of the colony's few remaining high security access panels. Wilder had appraised the situation before giving up any thought of entering the place, either with or without permission.

Kes spoke into the security panel, and the door opened. Her pulse sped up as the room was revealed and she heard the low hum emanating from the equipment. Thick insulated wires arose from the floor and entered closed boxes on the walls. More wires emerged from the other side of the boxes, ran across the walls and disappeared into the ceiling or the corners. A man and a woman were seated in front of several screens.

The woman stood up. "Welcome to the buzz room. I'm Sophie."

Introductions were made, and then Sophie said, "Kes told us you want to run an experiment."

"I do. Did the Fila agree?"

"No need to involve them," grumbled the man, whose name was Mark. "We have full control of the power they send. It's our permission you need."

"Oh." Taken aback by his animosity, Wilder turned to Kes. "I didn't know."

"Sorry, I forgot to tell you. Mark's correct. We can do the experiment without involving the Fila, providing the controllers give the go ahead. But I thought..." He looked questioningly at Sophie.

"It should be fine," she replied. "Shouldn't it, Mark?"

The man turned to face the screens again, muttering something Wilder didn't catch.

Sophie explained, "Trying to pass electrical current through non-conductive material isn't something you would normally choose to do. It's a great way to start a fire. But if we're going to attempt it, here, where we have the best fire extinguishing equipment, is probably the best place."

"There's a reason we have all the equipment here, Sophie," said Mark.

"Okay, I admit that the power control center is the last place we want to start a fire, but we'll be extremely careful."

Mark swung around in his seat and pointed at the Scythian spider, which Kes had put down. "Have you thought about what's going to happen if we start up that thing? Maybe some electrical current is all it needs to begin working again."

He was right. It was a possibility Wilder hadn't even considered.

"The spiders have already had electricity applied to them," said Kes. "Nothing happened."

"Maybe they were applying it to the wrong place," Mark retorted. "Maybe *you'll* touch exactly the right place. In fact..." He stood up and pushed back his chair. "I'm outta here. Let me know when it's all over.

Assuming any of you survive." He strode to the door and left without another word.

Wilder said, "Er, maybe this wasn't such a good idea."

"Don't worry about Mark," said Sophie. "He's always melodramatic. I'm sure everything will be fine."

But Wilder remained uncertain. Like every other colonist, she vividly remembered the time she had squeezed into the infirmary while the spiders ripped to shreds everything they encountered, living and dead, including stone and reinforced steel.

"The scientists who tested the spiders with electricity did a thorough job," said Kes. "I read the report. They tried contact points all over the devices. The only thing they didn't do was attempt a wide range of voltages. What's overwhelmingly likely to happen is absolutely nothing at all, unfortunately. But I think it's worth trying."

"Now you've gone to the trouble of carrying that horrible thing all the way here," Sophie said, "you might as well do something with it. If we do see smoke or a flame, we need to get out fast, or we'll be doused in foam." She pointed upward. Small spray heads were embedded in the ceiling.

"You have electrical fire extinguishers?" Kes asked.

"First thing we requested from the *Nova* once they got inside."

"But once they're used up, that's it, right?" Wilder asked, her reluctance to continue growing.

"For the foreseeable future," said Sophie, " but don't worry, I'm sure it won't come to that. I fixed up a system where we can increase the volts in increments of one hundred and twenty. The original experiment only tried a hundred and twenty volts, the settlement standard supply?"

She directed the question at Kes but Wilder answered. "That's right."

"And did the experiments find the material is a insulator or a resistor?"

"Resistor. Some current gets through, but it's limited."

"Okay, let's get this thing ready. It would be a good idea to remove all that green stuff. The spider might get hot, and plant material will smolder."

Wilder had brought along a knife. She carefully cut the ties binding the leaves around the spider's claws, and then used the tip of the knife to push the material away. In a few moments all the blades were revealed, shiny and probably as sharp as the day they were manufactured.

Sophie disappeared into the main room and returned wearing thick rubber gloves and carrying an insulated lead, bare wires just visible at the end. "You guys understand you mustn't go anywhere near the end of this, right?"

"Of course," Wilder replied.

"In that case, let's start." Sophie knelt down next to the spider. "Do you have a preference on the contact site?"

"Anywhere is fine."

Sophie considered for a moment, and then touched the wires to the nearest claw. About a meter away, the lead entered a box with six switches. Six times one twenty was seven twenty. What might happen to the spider if seven hundred and twenty volts were applied to it?

Sophie flicked one of the switches. "That's a hundred and twenty, so we don't expect anything to happen." She paused. "And nothing does. Let's try two forty." She flicked a second switch.

They all waited. Still, nothing happened.

"Three sixty," said Sophie. When the additional voltage had no noticeable effect, she removed the wire and said to Kes, "Could you check if it's getting hot?"

Kes touched the spider's leg with the back of his hand. "It is a little warm. But let's not forget this alloy has been heated to one thousand six hundred Celsius to no effect."

"Good point," said Sophie. "Let's try another one twenty."

Disappointment was already seeping over Wilder. Once more, the Scythian material was withholding its secrets. She wished she hadn't gotten her hopes up.

"That's four hundred and eighty volts," Sophie said, studying the spider, "and still nothing." She grinned at Kes. "I hope you're making notes for your write up."

"That honor will go to Wilder. This was her idea."

"*I* have to write the report?"

"Of course. You're the lead scientist."

Her disappointment turned to chagrin. Were Sophie and Kes only humoring her? She felt patronized. She genuinely wanted to find out about the Scythian spiders. She wasn't trying to play at being a scientist.

"Six hundred," said Sophie, flicking the fifth switch.

The effect was so fast Wilder almost didn't see it. She caught a glimpse of a bulge like a balloon inflating at the point of contact with the live wire. The next moment, she was staring at a silvery puddle.

"Oh my word!" Kes exclaimed, leaping backward as the liquid alloy ran toward his shoes.

Sophie had no time to get out of the way. She was kneeling in the stuff and it was soaking into the knees of her pants. She squeaked and dropped the wire as she leapt to her feet. "Ugh, ugh, get it off of me!" She pulled off her shoes and then undid her pants, dropping them and stepping out of them so they fell in the puddle.

Wilder was frozen in surprise. She could only stand and gape. The liquid hadn't reached her. Kes pulled her out of its path.

After another half a minute, when they had all calmed down a little, he said, "Now that's what I call a significant finding."

Fourteen

They'd almost made it. The crops were ready to harvest. All they had to do was gather and store them and they would have enough food to last until the next harvest, plus a little extra to put by. Cherry was about to leave to begin the work when she had a sudden idea. She comm'd Cariad and discovered she was already awake despite the early hour. The joys of parenthood. Cariad said she would love to see her.

Cariad and Ethan's quarters were along Cherry's route to the exit. She could spare a few moments to speak to Cariad and perhaps Ethan too if he was home. She doubted it. He was probably already on his way out to the farming district, leaving as soon as the sun appeared at the horizon. Sightings of sluglimpets had fallen drastically since they'd begun using the new repellent.

Cherry knocked and waited.

When Cariad opened the door, she was holding her baby daughter on her hip. "I'm so glad you could come over. Come in."

As soon as Cherry stepped through the entrance Cariad grabbed her in a one-armed, awkward hug. Cherry had a brief sensation of warmth and softness followed by the scent of milk mixed with baby sick.

Cherry hugged her back, somewhat confused. Their relationship had never been what anyone would call affectionate. Perhaps Cariad's hormones were affecting her.

"Sit down," said Cariad, adding, "if you can find a space. Sorry, the place is a mess."

Like all the residential rooms in Sidhe, Cariad and Ethan's home was small. Things for the baby seemed to occupy most of its surfaces.

"Here," said Cariad. "You can sit here." She slid a stack of diapers to one side, crushing them into a pile of baby clothes.

Cherry perched on the spot at the edge of the bed.

"Would you like to hold Meredith?" Cariad suddenly asked.

"Oh, er, I don't think I can." What Cherry really meant was, *No, not in a million years.* But she didn't want to cause offense. Not that there was anything wrong with the baby. She hadn't even seen the kid properly yet. She just wasn't comfortable around infants.

"Of course you can," said Cariad. "Move backward a little bit."

Cherry shuffled her butt farther onto the bed. When Cariad held Meredith out, Cherry felt obliged to take the baby. Meredith rested her head on Cherry's shoulder. She looked down into the small face. The baby was smacking milky lips and looking zoned out. Cariad must have just fed her. Meredith looked... like a baby. "She's lovely. Really beautiful."

"Isn't she?" Cariad gazed, mesmerized, at her daughter.

"Er..." Cherry shifted awkwardly.

"I'll take her back."

To Cherry's relief, Cariad lifted Meredith away. "Thanks for coming to see us. You've missed Ethan, though, by about ten minutes."

"It's no problem. Sorry I couldn't make it earlier... Um, I hate to talk business, but I haven't only come here to see you and Meredith."

"Oh. What did you want to talk to me about?"

"I've been thinking about this tribute the Scythians will probably expect from us the next time they visit. I was wondering what the Scythians actually know about us. I mean as a species."

"Hmm." Cariad had put her daughter against her shoulder and she began to thoughtfully rub her back. "They might have been able to deduce some information about humans from observations of the first settlement before they destroyed it. Then I guess the spiders could have been gathering data too before they were turned off. They aren't now, or at least they aren't transmitting, as far as we can tell. But I guess from the Scythians' initial reaction they weren't interested in us as a species. All they wanted was for us to get off their lawn."

"What?"

"Earth saying. If the Scythians wanted to gather data on the new species in their backyard they would behave differently. But then, as Vasquez is always reminding us, alien reasoning could be beyond our understanding, so that's just speculation."

"But would you say there's a good chance they know hardly anything about us?"

"Yes, probably. Why?"

"So if they do return and ask for tribute, could we send them something else? Something not human?"

"Ah, I understand what you're getting at. But, no, I really don't think we could fool them that easily. I mean, if we send up sluglimpets, that's never going to work."

"But could we send something non-biological? When Faina crashed the *Mistral* into the Scythian ship, the Scythians didn't pick up that nothing organic died."

Little Meredith let out a burp that was surprisingly large for someone so small.

"I hadn't thought of that," said Cariad. "You're right. They just assumed there were humans aboard the ship. But there's no way we could build anything even resembling a Guardian using our current level of technology."

"Okay, so this is why I'm here, Cariad. I wanted to ask you if you might be able to genetically engineer something that looks human but isn't. Something that didn't think or feel."

Cariad's forehead creased. "You mean living humans who don't have brains? That's actually a known gestational abnormality, but those babies die soon after birth. No, we need our brains just to breathe, Cherry, and once you have a brain, concepts like consciousness and sentience become blurry. And how would I create the embryos? Everything was lost when the Scythians blew up the *Nova*. Even if I could put something together, we would have to ask women to carry babies they knew were going to die. What a horrible notion."

"Okay," said Cherry. "It was a dumb, terrible idea. I didn't think it through. It's just that I have to leave soon to go to the Galactic Assembly and I'm worried about what's going to happen while I'm gone."

An awkward pause followed. Cariad continued to rub her baby's back, a look of alarm on her face. "It's all right. You didn't understand what you were asking."

A knock sounded. Someone was at the door. Cherry got up to open it because Cariad occupied.

The two young genetic techs were outside, holding the hands of a small boy. Cherry sometimes wondered if there were more minors than adults in Sidhe.

"Cassie, Florian!" said Cariad. "Come in!"

The pair stepped past Cherry and went over to Cariad to give her a hug.

"Are you *sure* this isn't too much trouble?" Cassie asked.

"No, not at all. Say hi to Bobby, Meredith."

The toddler and baby regarded each other.

"They'll have a great time playing," Cariad continued.

"We wouldn't ask," said Florian, "but daycare is going to be a zoo with so many parents helping with the harvest."

The rainy season was due to begin. Nearly every able-bodied person would be out at the farms toda and for the next week or two until everything was brought in. Even children over the age of ten had been given the time off school.

"Honestly, it's fine," said Cariad. "It's nice to feel like I'm doing something useful. I would be out there myself if I weren't still breastfeeding."

"I'd better go," said Cherry. "It was good to see you, Cariad."

Pride arose in her as she surveyed the fruit of her months of labor. The bright colors of ripe squashes peppered a sea of foliage, lush sweet potato vines were yellowing, the buckwheat had ripened golden brown, and beans bulged in drying pods. Farming was darned hard work but the results made it all worthwhile. There was enough food on her land alone to feed hundreds of people for weeks.

The other farms had been just as productive. The plentiful supply of water had helped. Irrigation channels from the lake crossed the entire district and had been constantly kept topped up by the threads. Then they had cut off the water to encourage the crops to ripen ahead of the rain.

It was finally time to bring it all in.

She started up the harvester. She'd been lucky enough to snag one in the lottery. The less lucky farmers would be gathering their crops by hand, helped by volunteers. It was fortunate that not all of the farming equipment had been destroyed. Some kits had remained aboard the *Nova*, and they'd survived the crash.

The harvester's operation seemed simple enough, and best of all, you only needed one hand. The machine could harvest all her crops with only a few small adjustments. Time to begin. She lifted her hand to the controls.

"Mind if I join you?" said a voice.

She nearly jumped out of her skin.

Ethan seemed to have appeared from nowhere, his friendly face looking up at her. "Sorry. Didn't mean to startle you."

"It's fine. Climb aboard."

Ethan mounted the steps to the cab and grabbed the sides of the opening to pull himself in before settling into the passenger seat. "This is quite a machine."

"Sure is." The harvester was a monster, the largest of all the equipment brought from Earth, including the roadmakers and the building machinery. Mercifully, it had escaped unscathed from the Scythian spiders.

"Are you sure you can handle it?" asked Ethan.

"Are you kidding?" She was mildly offended. Then she realized that Ethan was, in fact, kidding.

He was grinning. "Do you remember that day when you came to my farm to borrow a plow and ended up driving it for me?"

"Like it was yesterday. You were lucky I turned up. You had no idea what you were doing."

"And you knew better? As I recall, you nearly bounced me out of the cab."

"I don't recall that. I guess the ground must have been bumpy."

They laughed.

"So, what are you harvesting first?" asked Ethan.

"It doesn't really matter. It's all ready." She set the machine to gather root crops. "Here we go."

She drove the massive vehicle forward and turned it to skirt the edge of the sweet potato field. When they reached the corner she adjusted the controls. Scooped tines lowered and bit into the soil. The sweet potato vines juddered along with the ground as the harvester dug beneath them. A moment later the scoops lifted. Loose soil spilled through the gaps between the tines, leaving behind fresh sweet potatoes. The scoops lifted higher. Sweet potatoes tumbled along the tubes leading into the storage unit at the back.

She whooped, then she noticed Ethan. "Hey, what are you doing?"

While she'd been concentrating on the harvester, she hadn't noticed him recording on an interface.

"This is a historic moment," he replied. "The first harvest. I'm making a record for posterity. I probably should have organized some kind of ceremony but I didn't think of it."

"You aren't really one for ceremonies, are you?"

"Definitely not."

Minutes of silence followed as he recorded the harvester's actions, occasionally turning the interface to capture her profile until she made stupid faces to force him to stop. Off in the distance, children were playing at the lake, dipping under the water. Some wore helmets to help them communicate with the threads.

Following her gaze, Ethan said, "It's great isn't it? Those kids are growing up speaking with the Fila. Cariad said that some of them had been trying to mimic the threads' water motion language, waving their arms and legs."

"I think they'll need another hundred arms and legs to be successful at that."

He good-humoredly agreed.

Cherry said, "Ethan, what will you do if the Scythians return while I'm at the Galactic Assembly?"

Her friend's face became solemn. "Honestly? I don't know." Then he added, "I've some plans but they involve years of work. When are you leaving? Do you know yet?"

"All I know is it's the threads' version of 'soon', whatever that means."

"And do you know how long you'll be gone?"

"I don't. You know what the threads are like about time. All I know is I have to take three companions."

"Quinn told me. Have you thought about who you want to take?"

"I have, but I haven't come up with anyone definite. I guess Kes is the obvious choice. He's our resident alien communication expert, and I'm going to need all the help I can get to talk to the other species I'll be meeting. I approached him and he's willing. He suggested someone else too."

Ethan shifted in his seat so he could look directly at her. "What about Aubriot? He's smart and resourceful. I might have made him second in command if he wasn't such an asshole. No offense. I know you two are close."

"We aren't that close, and no offense taken. No one knows how much of an asshole he is more than me. Are you seriously suggesting I take him too?" The idea of spending days, possibly weeks, in a confined space with Aubriot filled her with horror. "He's the best military strategist we have. If anyone needs to stay here while I go on the mission to the Assembly, it's him, isn't it?"

"Cherry, if the Scythians were to return right now, what military strategy is going to save us? You saw what the spiders did last time. The Scythians will only drop more and more until we're overwhelmed. What will help us is an alliance with a more powerful, technologically advanced civilization."

"Which is where I come in."

"Exactly. You and Aubriot. I know he's self-centered and egotistical, but that could work in our favor. If Concordia falls, he'll fall with it. He knows that, and he'll do everything he can to survive. If that means he has to cement an alliance between humanity and another species, he'll do it. The fact that the rest of us benefit from his actions won't mean anything to him, but we'll still benefit."

She was forced to admit he was right. "Okay, I'll ask him."

"If he doesn't agree, let me know."

"Actually, he already wants to come along."

"He does?" Ethan looked relieved.

"You *really* want him to go with me."

"The fact is, you would also be doing me a favor by getting him away from the colony. He's pissed so many people off. He's a disruptive influence, like the Guardians always said."

"You're talking about the defense forces, right?"

"The defense personnel, the refectory staff, anyone who meets him. If he lowered himself enough to come out here all the farmers would hate him too."

"I understand. Phy can take over the military training. She's approached me with plenty of good ideas. And the others will listen to her."

"Yeah, Phy's a good pick."

"It looks like it's me, Aubriot, Kes, and maybe the other person Kes recommended who'll go to the Assembly. I'll—" Her ear comm gave a slight buzz.

"Cherry," Kes said, "have you packed?"

"What?" She put her hand on her ear.

"The Fila just contacted me. The ship's ready. They're sending down a shuttle to take you up."

"This evening?" She raised her eyebrows at Ethan, who was watching.

"Yep, just before sunset," said Kes. "So, did you decide? Am I coming too?"

FIFTEEN

Wilder was tired and sore. She stood up and stretched. The tree village was empty. Everyone had gone to help bring in the harvest. Cool air was arriving under the trees, signaling the approach of evening and chilling her sweaty skin. The day she'd spent trying to figure out how to program the Scythian metal had been long and frustrating.

She was convinced the bucket of silvery liquid would re-form into a solid structure if it received the correct instructions. Using a new language suggested by the Fila, she'd attempted to create various simple shapes with the alloy: cubes, spheres, pyramids, and cones.

The discovery that a burst of high voltage electric current would transform the material to liquid had been a breakthrough. Now all they needed was to solve the second part of the puzzle. The resulting abundant supply of materials would allow the colony to leap forward.

She suddenly realized she was ravenously hungry. She assessed the available daylight shining through the canopy. If she was fast, she could make it to the refectory and home again before Sidhe's doors closed for the night.

As she neared the edge of the forest, crowds of people approached from the direction of the farming district. The sun was setting behind their backs, making it difficult for her to see their faces, but their gait and posture showed exhaustion from their hours of physical labor.

Other colonists were already ahead, tramping along the well-worn path. She joined them. When she reached the entrance someone roughly pushed into her from behind even though there was plenty of room.

The person had to be so tired they weren't looking where they were going, so she stepped aside. But then she was pushed again.

"Too good to help with the harvest?" said Jim. His skin was moist and grimy from his work in the fields, and his upper lip was lifted in anger and disgust.

"I was busy doing something else." She was about to say 'something important' but that would sound like she thought the harvest wasn't important. It was, but what she was doing was important too. She'd thought it would be okay for her to concentrate on that. None of her friends had said anything. But maybe she'd been wrong. Maybe she should have gone with them.

"How did the harvest go?" she asked, hoping to deflect Jim's ire.

"It was damned hard work. What did *you* do?" He looked her up and down.

"I was working on turning the spiders into—"

"Hey, Jim." His lanky friend reached the entrance and slapped Jim on the back. "What are you waiting for? Let's go inside. I'm starving."

"I'm listening to Wilder's latest excuse for being a lazy bitch." Jim put his hands on his hips and gave her a defiant stare.

"Look, I'm hungry too," Wilder replied. "Why don't we just go and get something to eat?"

But the other boy said, "Oh, she's been shirking again? What's wrong? Too good to get your hands dirty? Is pulling your own weight too much to ask?"

She knew she should have continued trying to defuse the situation, but hunger and fatigue had made her irritable. "I *was* working today. Just because I wasn't out in the fields picking beans, it doesn't mean I wasn't—Uh!"

Jim had shoved her with both hands, causing her to stagger backward. "What's wrong with picking beans?" He stepped closer and yelled in her face. "At least we've been helping the colony. Those beans are going to feed us for months. Think you're too smart for farm work?"

She clenched her fists. More colonists were arriving, but they were passing the group of three teenagers. None of them were taking any notice. Perhaps they were too tired to care.

"Did I say I thought farm work was beneath me?" she retorted. She was a little frightened. Jim's insane fury had caused him to face her even when she'd had a spider as a weapon. "I was doing something else. Something just as important."

The lanky boy took a large step forward, bringing himself toe-to-toe with her. "What's more important than feeding ourselves, I'd like to know?"

"I didn't say it was *more* important—"

"She hides away when there's work to be done," said Jim, "but when it comes to eating the food we've grown, she's the first in line."

"That's right," said Jim's friend.

"That isn't fair," she protested. But the two boys only glared, malice radiating from every feature.

"This is dumb." She tried to step around the tall boy, but found her way blocked. Her gaze flicked to the adults continuing to enter the settlement, wishing they would intervene. She had an urge to call out and ask for help. She wasn't a good fighter, and though Jim and his friend probably wouldn't do her any serious harm, she didn't want to be roughed up again, especially when it was so unjustified. But shame and embarrassment prevented her from attracting attention to her plight.

She was trapped. Jim and his friend wanted someone to take out their frustrations on and it was going to be her.

The lanky boy backhanded her across her cheek. Her head flew to the side as the painful blow struck home and the boy's knuckles cracked into her cheekbone. "Lazy asshole!"

She stepped backward and touched her cheek. "Cut it out! I haven't done anything wrong."

But now Jim strode toward her, emboldened by his pal landing the first blow.

She shrank away, but her back hit the trunk of a tree. "Leave me alone!"

Jim drew back his fist. She ducked and punched him in the stomach. She tried to run, but Jim's friend was already there. He grabbed her arms and pushed her against the tree.

Her blow hadn't been powerful. Jim only rubbed his stomach and looked angrier and meaner.

"Hold her," he told his friend.

She gazed past her assailants. She didn't care now about calling out for help, but the area was deserted. Where had everyone gone?

The bigger boy's grip on her arms was painfully tight. She tried to squirm free but her captor's grip was like a vice. The boy pulled her away from the protection of the tree trunk, released his hold on one of her arms, moved behind her, and then grabbed her forcefully again.

Jim grinned. He crouched and made a fist, readying himself to land a heavy blow.

She struggled. She kicked backward, but the tall boy was careful to move his legs out of the way. She tensed. She was about to be beaten up, then the two boys would leave. They might knock her unconscious. The sluglimpets would be out soon. She had to get inside the settlement or return to her tree home.

"What's going on?" said a voice. "What are you two doing to her?"

The lanky boy instantly released her arms. Jim's arm fell to his side. He'd been crouching, preparing to make his punch count. He stood up straight. "We're only messing around."

"We weren't doing anything," said the other boy.

The new arrival was the one-armed woman, someone high up, a good friend of the Leader. "Get inside."

As Jim and his pal slunk off, Wilder went to follow them. Her head hung low in her shame of being seen in such a humiliating position.

"Hey, wait a minute." The woman put her hand on Wilder's shoulder. Her gaze remaining on her boots, Wilder turned.

"You're Wilder, aren't you?"

"Yeah."

"Kes told me it was you who figured out how to melt the spiders. Good job."

The mention of this achievement made her feel a little better. She raised her head to look the woman in the eye. It wasn't hard because she wasn't very tall.

"I'm Cherry, by the way."

"Oh. Hi."

"Can I ask you something? Would you be interested in another job?"

Wilder's eyes narrowed. "What kind of job?" She didn't want to be stuck doing something she hated. She wanted to figure out how to program the spiders. Or was Cherry going to suggest she should go back to school?

Cherry chuckled. "Don't worry. I think it's something you might like. What would you say to taking a trip with me on a starship?"

"We don't have any starships."

"The threads have built one for us. I have to go on a diplomatic mission."

Wilder felt her eyes widening. A trip aboard a starship would be amazing. But then she frowned. "What would I do, though? There's lots for me to do around here. Plenty of stuff the colony needs."

"This would be one of the most important things you could do to help. This trip could save us from the Scythians."

"Seriously?"

Cherry nodded.

"In that case, I'd love to come."

"Great. It's getting dark. Let's go inside. I can tell you all about it over dinner."

Wilder moved to enter the settlement. Despite the exciting turn of events, she recalled the scene of a few moments previously. Shame hit her again. Her head dipped.

"Are you okay?" Cherry asked. "I hope you aren't having second thoughts already."

"No, it isn't that," Wilder replied as they descended the steps. "It's just...I was wishing I could have fought off those boys."

"Don't feel bad. It was two against one. Besides, fighting back isn't always the best thing to do. I tried that once and look what happened to me." Cherry waved her empty sleeve at her.

Wilder smiled, and they took the passageway leading to the refectory.

Sixteen

The door guards' torches flamed high into the night.

"This is ridiculous," Aubriot breathed as they waited for the signal. "The Fila spend weeks saying we'll be leaving soon, and then suddenly we have to leave *now* and we can't wait until morning. Doesn't make any sense."

"They don't seem to perceive or measure time in the same way as us," said Kes.

"Yeah, all right, Ginger. That isn't news to anyone anymore."

Cherry inwardly groaned. They hadn't even left the planet yet and Aubriot was already being obnoxious. The trip to the Assembly was going to be one hell of a journey.

It *was* strange that the Fila had insisted they left this evening and no later. The first day of harvest had been long and exhausting. It would have been nice to have a good night's sleep before setting off. But it was not to be, so there was no point in complaining. Not that it stopped Aubriot.

"I still don't think we should take weapons with us," said Kes. "It sends the wrong signal entirely. It's only going to invite conflict."

"Quinn suggested it," said Cherry.

"It's exactly that kind of namby pamby thinking that's going to get us killed," said Aubriot. "If you don't want yours, give it to me. I'll take it."

Kes didn't hand over the Guardians' weapon slung across his back.

The problem with leaving after nightfall was the sluglimpets. They weren't fast predators—a reasonably fit adult could outrun them—but once you were caught, their strongly adhesive and corrosive mucus meant you would be lucky to only suffer severe injury. Fortunately, the repellent Kes and the other xenobiologist, Vasquez, had invented, meant that sluglimpets were not the danger they had once been.

As she waited just inside the outer door, Cherry shivered. Chill evening air was wafting in through the open entrance. Darkness had fallen and the starscape covered the cloudless sky. It had been months since she'd seen stars. Ever since the colony had gone underground, nighttime excursions had been forbidden.

Now she was going to be traveling through them again, like in the old days aboard the *Nova*. That time seemed a dream, another life. And she had been a different person.

"All clear," called a voice.

"Let's go." Cherry grabbed Wilder's arm. She didn't want her to be left behind or get lost in the darkness. As they ran together, she noticed how thin Wilder's arm was. She could easily wrap her hand around it.

The door guards' torches lit the way. Stationed at intervals along the route to the shuttles, they were clear trail markers as well as a deterrent to daring sluglimpets. Cherry crossed the distance with Wilder quickly, speeding through dew-soaked undergrowth.

"Are these all they've sent?" Aubriot asked as they arrived. He dropped a bag of belongings at his feet. "How the hell am I supposed to fit in one of those?"

Four slim, single-person shuttles lay in a row at the edge of the forest.

"It'll be tight," Cherry said, "but I think you'll make it." *As long as your massive head fits*, she added to herself.

Aubriot looked doubtful. He squatted and peered into the open hatch. "Why didn't you tell them to make something bigger?"

"We don't have time to waste. Get inside."

The door guards were waiting for them to leave so they could return to the safety of Sidhe.

Kes arrived. "Four shuttles? That's funny. I thought they would send one for all of us."

Cherry had thought so too. The threads didn't seem to have taken aboard her input about humans needing more space in their transportation. She dreaded what their ship was going to be like.

Wilder was standing and staring at the shuttles, her mouth gaping.

"Shouldn't have brought a kid along," said Aubriot. "Bad idea."

"It's great to have Wilder with us," said Kes.

"Just get in," Cherry said. "The threads will know when you're ready to leave. The hatch will close automatically, and then the shuttle will fly up to the ship. It isn't comfortable, but it's bearable."

"Simple enough," said Kes. "Let's go." He threw his small bag into the foot-well of one of the shuttles, put in his weapon, grabbed the sides of the open hatch, lowered himself in, and lay down. "Hmm. It's roomier than it looks from the outside." His voice echoed in the hollow interior.

"For you, maybe," said Aubriot. "I'm going to feel like a sardine in a tin."

"Are you going to get inside a shuttle?" Cherry asked Wilder. "It's only for a little while." She hoped the girl wasn't about to back out at the last minute. The Assembly had requested at least four humans. If Wilder refused to go, Cherry would have to ask one of the door guards to volunteer.

Wilder climbed into one of the small vessels, though she looked very unhappy about it.

"Great," said Cherry, and she entered her own shuttle.

"Feels like a fucking coffin," said Aubriot as he did the same.

"Calm down," said Cherry. "It isn't that bad." As soon as she was fully reclined, the stars were obscured by the closing hatch. Her shuttle lifted into the air.

"Whoa," came a voice from nowhere.

At first, she was confused but then she realized the voice was familiar. "Aubriot?"

"Shit."

"Hey, we can talk to each other."

"We can," said Kes.

When Wilder didn't say anything, Cherry checked she was okay. The girl quietly answered in the affirmative.

"This makes it a bit better," said Cherry.

"Why?" asked Aubriot. "It's horrible."

Despite the fact they could talk to each other, no one spoke for another couple of minutes. The shuttle boosted power and Cherry felt the smooth acceleration for a second time.

Then Kes said, "Can I ask you something, Cherry? Why is it you always call the Fila 'threads'? Is it only habit? Most people use the scientific name now."

"I don't like the scientific name."

"You don't? How come? Do you know the full name?"

"Yeah. I know you named them after me."

"You don't like that? I would have thought you'd be flattered."

"Flattered to have the same name as a tentacled alien? I don't think so."

Aubriot's deep-throated laughter rippled through the airspace.

"Whoops," said Kes. "Sorry about that."

"Don't worry about it," Cherry said.

Kes' faux pas reminded her of the time the threads had attacked her. The thin tentacles wrapping around her ankle, the inexorable pull toward the lake and what she thought was certain death. Ethan's smart move of using the plow to cut through the tentacles.

Ethan! In her hurry to leave on the interstellar trip, she'd forgotten to say goodbye to him.

She couldn't comm him. She'd left her ear comm behind so someone else could use it while she was gone. There was no point in taking the useful technology with her.

Oh well. She probably wouldn't be away for long. She only hoped that Ethan and the rest of the colony remained safe until she returned, hopefully with the news they had some new, powerful friends.

Seventeen

Wilder was going to throw up and there wasn't anything she could do about it. She'd managed to hold it in for the last five minutes, her panicked claustrophobia battling with the nauseating effects of micro-g, but she couldn't control her stomach any longer.

Her shuttle hatch opened, the safety straps slid away, and she floated upward, her hand grasping her mouth with all the strength she had. Vomit in micro-g was not going to go down well with her companions.

"Wilder?" Cherry asked. "Are you...?"

"Shit!" Aubriot exclaimed. "She's gonna throw."

Cherry was already pulling her out her bag. She ripped it open and began tearing out the contents at lightning speed. A second later she thrust the open bag at Wilder.

She got it to her mouth just in time, aiming the spray into the opening, at the last moment seeing some things Cherry hadn't had time to remove. Unable to stop herself, she continued to upchuck onto Cherry's belongings while holding the bag tightly around her mouth.

Her convulsions caused her to float backward across the seeding ship's airlock. The noise of her retching echoed, along with the splash of her stomach contents hitting the puddle inside the bag. She was sweaty and clammy and drools of saliva mixed with vomit hung from her mouth and nose.

Worse than all of this was the deep, deep embarrassment. Even in the throes of an out of control physical reaction, she could feel herself blushing with shame. She wanted to climb into the bag, despite its contents, and disappear.

Finally, it was all over. She had brought up everything and the awful retching had finally stopped. She closed the bag and held it out. "Sorry. I think something of yours is still in there."

"It's okay, really," said Cherry, taking the bag.

Kes was bouncing around the airlock, propelling himself from wall to wall, snatching Cherry's belongings out of the air.

Aubriot was gripping a handhold, scorn and derision written all over his face.

"I thought I was going to throw up too," said Kes, zooming past Wilder. "Try moving around a bit. Might help you feel better."

But Wilder couldn't move. It was as much as she could do to not burst into tears, which would only add to her embarrassment.

"I forgot to tell you the seeding ship has no gravity," said Cherry. "I should have warned you."

"I'm not surprised," said Kes. "I doubt the Fila need it. All they need is water pressure."

"So our ship's zero-g?" Aubriot asked Cherry accusingly.

"I don't know. I guess so. I was too busy trying to explain our restroom needs and calculate the amount of food we'd need for a journey of an undefined amount of time. I didn't think to ask."

"I hope we aren't away too long," said Kes. "Muscle wastage, loss of bone density... We'll be as weak as kittens by the time we get back, if we're gone for more than two or three weeks."

"I don't think we'll be gone that long," said Cherry. "Are you feeling better yet?" she asked Wilder.

Wilder nodded. She didn't really feel much better but she was confident she had nothing left to throw up. Instead, a sense of confinement was pressing down. The trip in the shuttle had been terrible, and now the airlock seemed so small. The interior of the *Nova* had been vast by comparison. She felt like she was back in Sidhe, except this place was bare and the air smelt funny.

"We have brought you in next to the starship bay," said a voice. "Please secure yourselves. We will be joining your chamber to the bay shortly."

"That's a relief," said Cherry. "The last time I was here they pushed me through a tunnel to reach the ship construction site." She put her spoiled bag into her shuttle and took out her weapon. "I'll let the threads figure out what to do with that."

"They'll probably find it interesting to analyze." Kes's arms were full of Cherry's things. His own bag was slung over one shoulder and his weapon was slung over the other. Wilder also prepared to enter the ship the Fila had built.

"Everyone holding on?" Cherry asked, grabbing a bar. "They didn't have these last time either. I'm glad the threads have improved their understanding of our anatomy. I hope we see more evidence of it."

"Look over there," said Kes.

Wilder turned. A line had appeared on the farthest wall. The handhold she had grabbed trembled and then began to judder. The whole place was shaking. She could hear a rushing, gurgling sound, like water draining out of a shower but much louder.

The line thickened. A beat later it split apart. A ripping noise emanated from the opening slit and thick strings of mucus were strung across it.

"Ugh," said Aubriot. "Disgusting."

The gap spread wider.

In the slowly revealed space was a dome. Like the walls inside the Fila ship the dome was shiny white and faintly iridescent. The surface was wet. Rivulets continued to run from it.

Aubriot said, "That isn't exactly what I was expecting."

The ship wasn't what Wilder had been expecting either. It reminded her of an egg. She'd found a bunch of them in the forest one time and assumed they were from a sluglimpet. The Fila had built them half an egg as a starship.

The surface of the ship darkened. One moment it was pale and glossy, the next it was a dark gray.

"Please enter the ship," said the voice.

Cherry propelled herself through the gap, pulling aside a mucus string. "Come on. If the threads insisted on us coming up here tonight, I guess we don't have a lot of time to waste."

"They expect us to travel in that thing?" asked Aubriot. "It doesn't even have any weapons. What happens if we're attacked?"

"What makes you think we're going to be attacked?" Kes asked.

"Stands to reason. The Scythians wouldn't want us to form an alliance with a galactic power. They want to keep us in their control. If they get wind of what we're doing, they'll try and stop us."

"How would the Scythians know what we're doing?" asked Kes. "Surely they can't observe us that closely. Their ships left our system months ago."

"Come on," Cherry insisted as she reached the ship. "We can talk once we're inside and underway."

"I'm not sure I want to be underway," said Aubriot.

"You have to come. The Assembly asked for four representatives of our species."

"Is that my problem?"

"It will be when we're under attack and we don't have anyone to defend us. Stop being an idiot."

Aubriot muttered to himself, but he pushed off from the wall and followed Cherry to the starship. Kes followed too, and Wilder brought up the rear.

The ship was about fifty meters in diameter and secured with moorings. As she drew closer, she saw her initial observation that the dome had a flat base was wrong. A complex arrangement of tubes protruded from the lower surface.

A rounded opening yawned, revealing a dimly lit interior. Cherry waited for the others at the entrance.

"I hope it comes with an operating manual," said Aubriot.

"You will not be required to pilot this ship," said the Fila voice. "Several volunteers will be traveling with you."

"The Fila are coming with us?" asked Aubriot.

"Of course," said Cherry. "What did you expect? Unless you know the way to the Galactic Assembly?"

"I could probably figure out how to get there if I had the coordinates."

Cherry rolled her eyes.

"Let's go inside," Kes said.

"Wait," said Aubriot. "What are we going to call her?"

"What?" asked Cherry.

"The ship. What's her name?"

"Does it matter?"

"A ship's gotta have a name."

"*Hope*?" Wilder suggested.

"More like *Desperation*," Kes quipped.

"*Dumpling*," said Aubriot. "But that doesn't fit now the hull has turned black. *Burnt Dumpling*."

"*Opportunity*," said Cherry. "That's what we're calling her. Now let's get inside."

Eighteen

The *Opportunity's* inner airlock door was closed. When the other three joined Cherry, the exterior door slid shut too. The chamber was small, about the size of the elevators on the *Nova*, and the surfaces were pearly white. The walls were wet and water puddled on the floor.

The four companions floated in close proximity, not making eye contact or talking. No security panels or door locks could be seen. Cherry had a brief flash of panic that *this* was how the threads expected them to travel to the Assembly, but then the interior door opened.

Balmy air flooded out and she instantly began to sweat. Why had the threads made the atmosphere so hot? Beyond the airlock was a bigger chamber containing four reclined, padded chairs lined up against the right-hand wall.

"Please sit down," said a voice over the ship's comm. "We are about to depart. It is dangerous for you to remain standing while the ship accelerates. We will eventually be traveling at near light speed."

Cherry kicked off and grabbed the head rest of the first seat before pulling herself into it. Lacking anywhere to stow her weapon, she tucked it under her arm and held it down. Safety straps slid over her.

"It's so dark in here," said Wilder as she also took a seat.

"And hot," said Cherry. The lighting *was* dim. It was adequate to see by, but it was lower than anyone would choose to set it in normal circumstances.

The airlock door closed and Cherry's seat began to vibrate.

Kes and Aubriot were still settling into seats.

The straps crossed over the occupants' shoulders, hips, and thighs, rather than the four-point style Cherry was used to. She suddenly chuckled.

"What's so funny?" asked Aubriot.

"It's like these were designed by a three-year-old. The basic idea is there but the execution sucks."

"The Fila are trying their best," said Kes. "You have to give them that. Do you think we would do any better at designing structures to hold their bodies?"

"They don't need structures to hold their bodies," Aubriot said. "They're constantly supported by water."

"That's my point."

"We are now departing our seeding ship," said the voice.

Cherry felt the *Opportunity* move. The movement was sideways at first, then the ship turned. Without the benefit of gravity, she struggled to understand which direction it was heading, but she certainly knew when it accelerated. She was forced deeply into her seat's padding. The pressure was immense, an unbearably heavy weight pressing on every part of her body. She heard a groan but she couldn't tell whose it was.

Darkness flooded her vision. Was she going blind? Or was she about to—?

A period of time later, she regained consciousness. The pressure had eased. Her clothes were soaked in sweat. The sensation of being pinned to her seat remained. She couldn't move her arms or legs or even lift her head, but the pressure was bearable. With some effort, she turned her head to check on Wilder. The girl's skin was a pale shade of green for the second time, and she was unconscious. Cherry hoped Wilder didn't vomit while she was out of it. If she choked she could die.

"You're back?" asked Aubriot.

"How long was I out?"

"No idea. I only came around about a minute before you did."

Kes spoke to the air. "Can you tell us how much longer we'll be accelerating?"

"We are trying to reach maximum velocity as quickly as possible," the disembodied voice replied. "We are able to mitigate the effects of acceleration on your bodies to a great extent, but not fully. As you are experiencing ill effects we have slowed down to give you some time to recover."

"Could you slow down a bit more?" asked Cherry, worried about their youngest companion. Wilder was thin and not naturally so. The girl looked weak and malnourished and definitely not up to the physical rigors of high-g. "And can you turn down the heating? It's way too hot in here."

"We apologize," said the Fila voice. "We thought you would like to remove your clothes after the first acceleration session."

"Wh...Why would we want to remove our clothes?"

"We assumed that humans wear clothes when the atmospheric temperature where they live is too low, requiring the use of artificial means to remain warm and comfortable."

A moment of awkward silence passed. Cherry couldn't manage to move her head to see what Kes and Aubriot thought of the proposal.

In the end, Kes came to her rescue. "Technically, you're correct. Humans did originally wear clothes so they could live in cooler climates. However, the wearing of clothes has now become a cultural norm. We would prefer a cool temperature aboard the ship and to remain dressed."

As the pressure began to ease some more, Wilder moved and moaned. Her eyes opened.

"Hey," Cherry said. "How are you feeling?"

Wilder's mouth worked. For a moment Cherry thought the girl was going to upchuck again. Then she asked what had happened.

When Cherry explained Wilder seemed to understand. "Can we get up?"

"I'm not sure." Cherry asked the threads.

"We would prefer to continue at our present acceleration for as long as you can tolerate it. We have a considerable distance to travel."

Wilder said, "I'm okay. I can do this for a while longer."

"Might as well get it over with," said Aubriot.

After a few minutes, Kes said, "Shame we didn't time to check out the ship. Do you know what the quarters are like, Cherry?"

"Not really. I only had a chance to see it when it was first being built. The threads originally wanted to make something much smaller. They thought we would be more comfortable in a confined space."

"Thank the stars they consulted with you," said Kes. "If this room is representative, the living space is going to be cramped as it is."

Cherry agreed, and privately wondered about the bathroom facilities. She wasn't confident she had adequately described human requirements in that area. The threads had access to the colony's data bases, but information so basic and well known clearly hadn't been included.

"What are we going to eat?" asked Aubriot.

"The refectory has been sending up supplies," Cherry replied. "I don't know what exactly. The stocks have run low, so I guess it'll just be basic stuff."

Kes asked, "Do you have any idea what will be expected of us when we arrive?"

"None at all. I'm hoping we might receive some pointers on the way."

"They'll probably want to test our intelligence," Aubriot said. "They'll want to know if we're worthy allies or just some interesting new species the Fila stumbled across."

"Worthy allies," Kes repeated. "What does that mean, I wonder?"

"We'd better pray it doesn't mean military capability," said Aubriot, "or we're screwed."

Wilder said, "Maybe they'll be looking for our potential to make a positive contribution to galactic civilization."

Cherry's head remained angled toward the girl though she'd been listening to Aubriot and Kes. Wilder looked even paler than before. "Are you sure you're okay?"

"I'm not great, but I can bear it."

Cherry wasn't convinced. As time wore on and Kes and Aubriot threw around ideas on what might await them at the Galactic Assembly, she grew more and more concerned about the young girl she'd invited on the trip. She'd based her choice on Kes's recommendation and the fact that she hadn't thought of anyone else at the time. The short notice the threads had given had forced her to make up her mind quickly.

She was sure that everything Kes had said about Wilder was true—that she was smart, mature and independent beyond her years, creative and innovative —but at the end of the day, the girl was very young to go on such a potentially dangerous and difficult mission. Also, Kes seemed not to have noticed that Wilder was puny for her age. Was she physically up to a deep space voyage?

Wilder hadn't spoken for a while. Her eyes were open, but she looked out of it. Cherry decided she had to do something. "Hey," she called out to the air. "Could you slow the acceleration for a bit so we can experience a force the same as Concordia's gravity?"

"Yes, we can," the thread's voice replied. "We will give you a rest period and then we will continue to increase the ship's velocity."

The acceleration began to slow rapidly and Cherry had the sensation of falling forward. Her safety straps slid away. She sat up.

"Great," said Aubriot. "Time to explore."

Then the attack began.

Nineteen

Aubriot hopped down and took a step toward the door. Before he could take another step, the ship lurched violently and he was thrown from his feet. He crashed into the wall, his head bearing the brunt of the impact. His skull clunked against the surface. Knocked out, he slid down and lay still, legs and arms splayed out.

Wilder had been sitting up, anxious to escape the confinement of the chair, but she quickly reclined again and gripped the sides of the padding. "What was that?"

Cherry had been halfway off of her seat when the ship received the hit. She staggered but managed to hold on to the end of a safety strap.

Kes fell to his knees, hard, his kneecaps thunking dully on the deck.

"What happened?" Cherry asked the air.

Wilder wondered if the Fila flying the ship had done something wrong. But the force had struck sideways, a different direction from the acceleration.

The Fila didn't answer.

Kes said, "Maybe the engine's having teething troubles."

Wilder climbed down to go and check on Aubriot, who was lying with his mouth open. He'd taken a really hard hit.

"Get back in your seat," said Cherry.

"But—"

A second impact came. Wilder flew backward into the wall.

"We are under attack," said the voice of the Fila. "Please return to your seats. We are returning fire, but we must accelerate to escape."

"You heard her," said Cherry. "In your seat, Wilder."

"But what about Aubriot?" She crawled to the man's head. He remained out cold. "If we accelerate like we did before and he isn't in a seat it could kill him." She wasn't sure if she was right but she guessed it was a strong possibility.

A third impact threw her onto her front and she face-planted on the hard surface. Pain erupted in her nose and chin, and blood ran from her nostrils. She looked up, wincing, and saw Cherry still clinging to her safety strap anchor point, looking indecisive.

"Wilder's right," said Kes. "We have to try to help Aubriot."

"Please return to your seats," said the Fila. "We must accelerate."

"We can't," Cherry said. "One of us can't move. He's unconscious."

Kes was running toward Wilder. "You take his legs."

She wiped away the blood running into her mouth and grasped Aubriot's long legs. He was a big, muscular man. Would she and Kes be able to even move him, let alone lift him onto his seat?

"Ready?" Kes's hands were under Aubriot's shoulders.

She grasped the man's ankles.

"No, not there," Kes said. "Grab his knees."

She shifted her hands further up Aubriot's legs.

"I'll help too," said Cherry, running over. She slipped a hand under Aubriot's back. She wouldn't be able to help much, but every little bit of effort would count in moving the heavy man.

Another impact came and all of them were thrown from their positions. Aubriot's head flopped and his body slid across the floor.

"This is impossible," said Cherry. "We'll never do it."

"You must lie down in your seats," said the Fila. "Our power to return fire is low. If we don't leave soon the Scythians will destroy our ship."

The Scythians? Of course it was them. Who else would it be?

"It's no good," Kes said. "We'll have to leave him. He'll have to take his chances. If we don't save ourselves we'll all die."

"You're right," said Cherry. "Wilder, I'm sorry. You're too young for this. I shouldn't have brought you along. But we have to leave Aubriot. I'm ordering you. I take full responsibility for whatever happens."

"I thought of something," said Wilder. "Hey, Fila, can you stop the ship for, I don't know, ten seconds?"

"Impossible."

An impact shoved her sideways. She clasped the floor with her fingertips to stop herself from sliding any farther.

"The Scythians will catch us if we stop," said the Fila.

"But they won't be expecting it. Their weapons are trained on the area they're expecting the ship to fly into, right?"

"I see what you mean," said Kes. "Yes, Fila, please stop the ship. Five seconds. That's all we need."

Wilder wasn't confident the Fila really grasped 'seconds' in the way humans did. From what she'd heard, their concept of time was odd. She hoped they'd learned to convert their time measurements into humans'.

Perhaps they had, because they stopped the ship. They stopped the vessel too abruptly, in fact. She and the others flew to the opposite side of the chamber. She lifted her shoulder and curled her body just in time to cushion herself. Aubriot didn't fare so well. His heavy body slid across the floor and hit the hard wall head first. If he'd been about to return to consciousness, the second blow had put an end to that process. It might even have broken his neck.

They were weightless.

"I'll get him into his seat," said Kes. "You two go to yours."

Maneuvering a weightless Aubriot was no problem. Holding the man in his arms, Kes pushed off and floated over to the reclined seats. As soon as he'd laid Aubriot down, the safety straps slid out and bound him to the padding. A purple lump was already rising on his forehead.

Wilder flew to her seat. The minute Cherry had reached hers, and Kes was in the process of lying down too, Cherry called out, "Ready!"

An unbearable weight slammed into Wilder. The Fila had accelerated once more to the original speed that had made everyone pass out. The last thing she saw was the whites of Aubriot's eyes, half open. The man was entirely senseless, but perhaps, now, he might not die.

Twenty

"I can't believe you can stand," said Cherry.

Aubriot had climbed down from his safety seat and was rubbing his forehead. "I remember getting up, but that's it. What happened?"

"We were attacked by Scythians," said the Fila voice. "We aren't sure how they knew we were coming, but when we slowed down they saw their chance and took it. We seem to have evaded them after obscuring our trace. It's doubtful they could find us now."

"So it was the ship taking a hit that knocked me out?" asked Aubriot.

"That's right," Kes said. "And that wasn't the only one it took."

Aubriot tenderly touched the purplish lump on his head.

Cherry was surprised the bruise and swelling weren't larger. The second blow to his head had been even more powerful than the first. The entire weight of his body had been behind it. "How are you feeling?"

"I want to see the rest of this ship." Aubriot strode out.

"What's he made of?" Cherry asked. "Titanium?"

"When Aubriot was no more than a handful of cells," said Kes, "he had the most advanced, most expensive genetic engineering available. I wouldn't be surprised if he could piss rainbows. Uh, sorry, Wilder." He had clearly remembered too late about the fourteen-year-old in the room.

The girl chuckled. "It's okay."

"Are you two coming to see the ship?" asked Kes.

"In a minute," Cherry replied. "I want to talk to the Fila."

Kes held out a hand, inviting Wilder to go ahead of him.

As the two left, Cherry asked, "Do you know why the Scythians attacked? I'm worried about what all of this means."

"We have guessed at two possible reasons," the Fila replied. "They offered no warning before attacking. They may view this section of space as their own. We usually avoid these problems by traveling via a method that avoids the use of normal space. Consequently, we have no knowledge of claimed territories."

"But don't you run into problems when you seed new planets?"

"All other sentient galactic species we are aware of are gas-breathers. It's the land of rocky planets that is coveted, not the water. Also, we are entirely non-aggressive. Our weapons are only used in defense. Thus, we believe we are not viewed as a threat."

"Okay, so maybe we invaded the Scythians' territory. You said you could think of two reasons for their attack. What's the second?"

"The second reason we thought of is that they want to kill you, or at least prevent you from leaving the planet. We have no reason for using our current method of propulsion except for transporting another species, and it would have been clear from our trace that we were coming from Concordia."

"It's clear they wanted to kill *someone.* Why would they have a problem with us leaving our planet? They didn't tell us we had to stay put."

"Perhaps they fear the exact thing you are trying to do: gain support from another powerful civilization. The Scythians have made themselves many enemies. They do not want anyone to try to prevent them from exercising their power over you."

The news that the Scythians wanted to keep the colony alone and vulnerable shouldn't have come as a surprise. Of course they wouldn't want the humans to gain any more friends in the galaxy. Cherry felt both worried and hopeful. On the one hand, the danger level of the mission had just increased, but on the other, it was a good sign the Scythians were trying to prevent them from forming alliances. It meant there were alliances out there to be formed—alliances that could thwart the Scythians' plans for Concordia.

"Come and see this, Cherry."

Wilder had appeared at the door.

Deciding a more detailed discussion about the Scythians could wait for later, Cherry followed her into the next room. It was a long cylinder except for a narrow path clearly designed for human feet. The roof of the cylinder curved overhead and the exit was an open hole. This chamber was even dimmer than the one they'd left. It took her a moment to realize that almost all of the wall was transparent and on the other side threads floated in water. The creatures twisted and writhed gently in straight and diagonal lines of light.

"Cherry," said a voice. "I am glad you are one of the party traveling to the Assembly."

She spun around. The voice's owner was talking to her directly, but she couldn't see which of the threads it was. And the creature appeared to believe they had a personal connection.

Eventually her gaze alighted on a particularly large creature. It didn't seem to be doing anything very different from the others, but something told her this might be the one talking to her.

"Did I make a mistake?" asked the voice. "I think you are the human called Cherry, but perhaps I'm wrong."

"No, you're right."

"Good. I'm glad."

An inkling of who the thread might be suddenly came to her. "Are you Quinn?"

"I am. That's the name Ethan gave me."

"What are you doing here? Are you a pilot?"

"We are all pilots. Pilots, engineers, navigators. We all perform these roles and more aboard the ship, all of us together."

"Come and see our living quarters," said Wilder.

"I guess I'll talk to you later, Quinn."

"Welcome home," said Kes as Cherry entered another open space.

The next room was the largest she had seen so far, though it wasn't much bigger than the one she shared with Rene at Sidhe. Four long, slim bags lay on the floor.

"Is that where we're supposed to sleep?" she asked.

"That's my hypothesis," said Kes. "I tried one, and it didn't feel comfortable."

Aubriot arrived from the opposite direction. "This is going to be one hell of a journey. All we have to eat are the Guardians' ration bars. The refectory staff must have been holding them back in case of an emergency. Hope we aren't away long."

"Aren't there any chairs or tables, or anything?" asked Cherry. Aside from the sleeping bags, the room was bare.

"What's the point?" Aubriot replied, sneering. "It isn't like we'll be sitting down to dinner. If we need to sit, we can sit on the floor."

"What bothers me is, what are you all going to do?" Kes asked. "Things are going to get boring fast."

"Don't you mean, what are *we* going to do?" asked Cherry. "Isn't the trip going to be just as boring for you?"

"I have the Fila to study. That's enough work to last a lifetime."

"I want to study them too," said Wilder.

"Great. It'll be good to have someone to compare notes with."

Wilder's face shone with pleasure.

Aubriot said, "Well, I'm not interested in finding out any more about the tentacled folk than I have to, but I wish to hell they would explain how they're flying this ship. And how they fire the weapons. From the sound of it we barely survived the last battle. I don't like being a sitting duck. If we're attacked again, I want to be the one in control of firing back."

All Cherry wanted to know was what they were going to do when they arrived at the Assembly.

Twenty-One

Wilder was fascinated by the Fila's alternative deep space propulsion method. Desperate to figure out how it worked, she'd asked them many questions about it, only to receive enigmatic or nonsensical answers. The Fila said their ships 'transformed' or 'broke into' (they used the words interchangeably as if they meant the same thing) another kind of 'space' or another 'place' (again, both words seemed to have the same meaning when the Fila used them).

While she tried to think of a question that might yield an answer she understood, she sat in the cylindrical room, her face pressed up against the transparent wall separating the humans from the watery abode of the *Opportunity's* crew.

All she knew for sure was their vessels disappeared and reappeared. She seen the satellite recordings from the Second Scythian Attack. She also guessed that to do so required enormous amounts of power. She'd been disappointed to discover the *Opportunity* wasn't going to use this exotic method—that it would remain in normal spacetime for the duration of their trip.

The bursts of acceleration had continued for weeks, and each time she and the others had to lie in the reclined seats and tolerate the pressure for hours. The Fila encouraged them to try to use this time as their sleep period, but only Aubriot, and Cherry to a lesser extent, managed to drop off while the ship was accelerating. Wilder found it impossible. She wasn't sure if Kes couldn't sleep or if he actually preferred to lie thinking with his eyes open.

While the ship traveled at an acceleration that mimicked Concordia's gravity, Wilder either slept or tried to understand more about the Fila by talking to them and studying the ship.

One thing she'd discovered was there were no mirrors. She hadn't ever had much use for a mirror, but she'd been used to having them available on the rare occasions she wanted one. The Fila had installed sanitary facilities for their human passengers that were usable once you got the hang of them, but they hadn't included mirrors in them or anywhere else. She'd concluded the Fila saw no use for them. They had no reason or desire to view themselves.

Was it because at the time the creatures evolved intelligence, there were no reflective pools of water in their environment? Perhaps they hadn't been able to see themselves and so the concept was alien to their culture.

"Do you have any more questions?" asked Quinn. He seemed to be the one designated to be the contact for humans. When he spoke, he moved close to the clear wall.

"Not unless you can explain your propulsion system in a way I can understand."

"I can try again, if you wish. I think I would be able to if I had access to the vocabulary your physicists use to discuss these things, but I have never found the words in your colony's data records."

"Don't worry about it. I probably wouldn't be able to understand even if you did. But maybe you could try to explain what you're doing in there. I can see the four of you moving around, but you don't seem to come into contact with anything."

"Most of the time we aren't *doing* anything. We're only talking."

"But you are controlling the ship sometimes, aren't you?"

"When we decelerate we must make some adjustments. And we must control the power buildup as we prepare to accelerate again."

"But how do you build power?"

"Again, I don't know the words in your language to explain. We draw the power from around us."

"But there's only empty space."

"That is not the case."

She sighed and rubbed her sore eyes. "All right. Let's leave that for the moment. How do you manipulate the ship's controls?"

"We move them."

"But you don't," she exclaimed, then realized that frustration was making her sound angry. "Sorry. I've never seen you manipulate anything. I've watched you all carefully for hours. You've told me you aren't talking all the time. Sometimes you're working. But you do it without touching anything. How is that possible?"

"We are touching the controls."

"I've watched you. I'm sure you aren't."

"Perhaps human eyes cannot perceive it."

"You mean you're moving too fast for me to follow?"

"No, I mean you cannot perceive the...the field. I think that's the correct word."

"What?" Fatigue and confusion were wearing her patience thin. "What are you talking about? We aren't on a farm." Then the answer hit. "What kind of field do you mean? Something like a force field?" Maybe Quinn's guess was right. Maybe the Fila *were* doing something that she couldn't see. She'd read about invisible force fields, though only in fiction. As far as she knew, humans had never invented one.

"Let's try an experiment that may help you understand," Quinn said. "You spoke of us manipulating the controls without touching them. Please touch this wall that separates us."

Wilder reached out a hand and held it against the wall.

"Now I will also touch the wall."

One of the large Fila's tentacles waved near the spot where she held her hand, but it didn't make contact.

"Did you touch it?" she asked.

"Yes."

"No, you didn't!"

"Good. We're getting close to our difference in understanding. I have noticed that whenever humans touch something, they always push it. They never simply touch it."

"Push? But I'm not pushing. This is pushing." She pressed her hand hard against the transparent surface.

"They are the same thing. You are exerting pressure, only in different amounts."

"I suppose touching and pushing are kind of similar. I don't see how you can say you touch when you clearly don't, though."

"We exert a field that makes contact. Our tentacles don't have to push in order to touch."

"You exert a field?"

"You cannot see it?"

"Whatever it is you're creating, it's invisible to me."

"This is interesting information. We have had little contact with aliens. We tend to avoid them and they also leave us alone. What you've told me is somewhat of a revelation. I must communicate this finding."

"I'll leave you to it." She also wanted to communicate her finding, to someone who might be able to help her understand.

Twenty-Two

As the years passed, the Scythian probe observed and reported the spread of the colony. The probe counted growing numbers of humans. Many were juveniles. These emerged from the underground settlement for an average of sixteen percent of a single revolution of the planet, always returning underground well before darkness fell. These small humans rarely traveled to the plant growing areas.

Then, the humans expanded out of their underground settlement. They did not travel far at first. They only moved above the ground and into the trees of the forest. The probe registered the infrared of their body heat beneath the canopy. Tens and then hundreds of humans lived in the trees and continued to travel to the place where they grew their plants, whenever the light of the planet's star lit the land.

After three orbits of the planet around its star, most of the humans were living in the second, tree top settlement. They would rise into the trees when darkness fell and remain there until the star's light arrived again. The remainder lived permanently in the growing areas. These humans removed native vegetation and replaced it with their food plants.

A road appeared between the forest and the second settlement, a hard surface the humans could traverse with small vehicles.

Time wore on, and eventually a second hard road appeared. This led from the growing area to the ocean, running along the base of a dried-up river valley. Vehicles moved up and down, carrying construction materials used to build vessels that rested upon the body of water. From these vessels the humans gathered sea plants and small sea creatures, which they transported to the settlements.

Quickly after the arrival of the second road, a third area of habitation arose next to the ocean. The humans' pace of development was speeding up. Dwellings at the oceanside spot were built in quick succession. Humans living in them went out to harvest from the ocean every day. Vehicles arrived from the forest and growing areas to collect the food.

The next structures the humans built were not places they would inhabit. These constructions were larger than regular human habitations. The humans did not remain inside them during the time of darkness. They appeared on the open area next to the forest. The mature humans would enter the buildings during the hours of daylight. As the time of darkness approached they would leave, en masse.

Many things disappeared into the new structures, transported there by the humans: plants they had gathered from the growing areas and the ocean, sea creatures, native vegetation, natural resources, and the remainder of the disinfectors.

The probe analyzed activity within the large buildings. The humans were manufacturing objects, but with the limited data received, the probe could not arrive at any clear conclusions about what was being made. It saw the humans bring the objects out of the new buildings. The largest were new vehicles. Smaller items were packed into boxes. These containers were transported to the nearby forest settlement, taken underground, or sent out to the growing district or oceanside habitation.

The probe undertook regular estimates of the number of humans living on the origin planet. The population continued to steadily increase. In turn, the things the humans manufactured also increased in number. The human colonization was progressing successfully.

All this information, along with planetary data, the probe transmitted to its Scythian creators. A constant stream of data traveled at light speed across space. At its destination, the information was closely scrutinized. The humans appeared to be following a normal path of growth and development.

Despite the failure of the attempt to prevent the aquatic aliens from transporting at least one human away from the planet, no aid or support had yet arrived to protect the little colony. That was the greatest danger to the plan, and it had by no means disappeared. Efforts were taking place to track the aquatic aliens' vessel and put a permanent end to the threat.

Notwithstanding a cataclysmic event, the prognosis was that the invading species would continue to increase and spread. Their society would continue to develop. Providing the humans did not improve their military defense capability, their continued development would be allowed, for now.

Twenty-Three

Aubriot had a problem with Cherry, and she was determined to get to the bottom of it. He'd been acting weird toward her for weeks, ever since that time she'd gone to see him after visiting the threads' underwater city. Their friends-with-benefits arrangement had fallen apart for no particular reason she knew. Not that she minded too much. These things happened. But what she couldn't understand was why Aubriot now seemed to hate her.

She lay in her sleeping bag. The holo the Guardians' creators had made was playing from her interface, but she wasn't paying attention. Her mind continued to chew on Aubriot's strange change of attitude. As if her thoughts had summoned him, the man himself appeared in the entrance to their quarters. When he registered she was alone, he immediately began to back away.

"Hold on," she said. "I want to talk to you about something." She closed the audio on the holo and sat up. She remembered what the male scientist said in this part anyway. The man continued speaking soundlessly, his translucent form suspended like a ghost in the center of the room.

Aubriot frowned and hesitated, apparently trying to think up an excuse to leave. He failed. He trudged in, his sullen look doing nothing to mar his perfect features. Glaring at her, he pointedly gave no invitation to open the discussion.

But he couldn't dissuade her. She was too used to his ways. "I thought you would be happy to come along on this mission. It's what you wanted. But you've been acting like we're strangers ever since we came aboard. Did I do something to offend you? How come you've been avoiding me?"

"We aren't joined at the hip, Cherry. Just because we hooked up a few times, doesn't mean we have to follow each other around."

"As I recall, we slept together a lot more than a few times, but I'm not disagreeing with you. It doesn't mean we have to hang out together. I don't expect that or even want it. But I also didn't expect you to suddenly act like you don't know me, for no reason I'm aware of."

He broke eye contact, his gaze shifting up and to the left. "You sound like an angsty adolescent. Are you sure you're talking to the right person? Maybe you should be having this conversation with Wilder."

Unusually, this insulting dismissal of her concerns hit home. "Why do you always have to be so nasty and rude? You don't give a shit about anyone but yourself, do you?"

"Probably. Does it matter? I get my work done, the same as everyone."

"Okay, forget it. Sorry for trying to have a reasonable discussion with you."

"Fine."

He was leaving, but there had been something his eyes that told her there was more to his behavior than he was letting on. Something she'd said had brushed against a sensitivity. The notion that he could be sensitive about anything at all came as a surprise.

Suddenly, she decided she wasn't going to let it go. She wasn't going to allow him to get away with his usual lousy attitude and aloofness. "Hey, stop. I changed my mind." She climbed out of her sleeping bag. "Come back. I want to say something."

He had reached the doorway. He pressed his hands against the frame. For a moment, he remained there, apparently debating whether to ignore her and leave anyway. After a brief pause, he turned.

"I don't think I ever thanked you," she said.

This statement surprised him sufficiently to distract him from his bad mood. His hard expression softened to puzzlement.

She explained, "When I made my insane suicide bid to fight the Scythian spiders."

"Oh."

"You were there with Ethan. I only just remember it, but I'm sure it was you. You carried me to the infirmary. If you hadn't run so fast, I probably would have bled to death."

"It wasn't a big deal."

"It was a big deal to me. I'm grateful. I mean it."

His gaze had drifted from her eyes. "Is that it?"

She clenched her fist. "Stars, do you *have* to be such an asshole?"

His face hardened once more, and he turned.

"Wait! Just wait a second." She strode to the door and looked up into

Aubriot's face. "I thought we were friends, sort of, once. I don't know what went wrong, and it's bugging me. If you don't want to tell me, I won't try to force you anymore. We can leave it here. But I would like to know."

Once more, he broke eye contact, looking down.

"Look at me," she said. "If I did something wrong, just tell me."

"No." He raised his head, his eyes hard and steely. "*You* look at *me*."

His voice was so quiet she barely heard him. "What? I am looking at you."

"Not when you should. You never look at me then."

"What do you mean, when I should? What are you talking about?"

"Christ, Cherry, do I have to spell it out? When we...*do it*..."

She almost snorted with laughter. Aubriot always spoke so plainly and was often foul mouthed. His use of the euphemism was out of character, but something in his expression stopped her from mocking him.

"You would never look at me," he went on. "Never look me in the eyes."

"That's ridiculous. Of course I did."

"No, you didn't. I didn't notice it at first, but when I did, I couldn't help but notice it, every time. Not once did you make eye contact with me. Not once. I began to wonder why."

She hesitated, baffled.

Meanwhile, the color was draining from his face. His anger was building. He put a hand on her shoulder. "Do you really think I would make it up? Do you think it's my imagination?"

"I don't know what to think." She struggled to remember. "Why wouldn't I look at you? And if I didn't—which is unlikely—what do you care? What difference does it make? You had a good time, didn't you?"

The expression that flashed into his features made her flinch and back away. Was he about to hit her? His grip on her shoulder tightened, and she began to regret pushing the issue. She had no idea what it was in her former lover she'd accidentally triggered. It was news that he was capable of feeling anything much except superiority and the desire for control.

"Let go of me," she said.

He released his grip. She backed farther away, but he moved closer.

"Wishing you hadn't said anything now?" he asked.

"Yeah, actually, I am."

"Strayed into uncomfortable territory, right?"

"I've definitely strayed into something uncomfortable for *you*. But let's forget about it. It doesn't matter."

"Right," he said between his teeth, "now I've answered your question honestly, you aren't going to do me the same courtesy. Nice."

Her heels made contact with her sleeping bag. She couldn't go any farther without looking down to avoid tripping, but Aubriot's glare was compelling.

She couldn't look away. "You think I'm not being honest with you? I only asked you a question and you answered. Now it's clear you have some weird fetish I wasn't fulfilling, we don't need to explore this any further."

"Weird fetish?" He seemed to be on the edge of exploding in fury. "Is that what you think this is about? You think your behavior is my fault? You think *I'm* the one with the problem?"

"Maybe that came out wrong. Look..." But she didn't know what to suggest to defuse the situation.

Then, all of a sudden, his features relaxed. "Why don't you just admit it? Then we'll know where we both stand."

"Admit what?" As she spoke, a deep discomfort welled up. Maybe he was right. Maybe he knew something, something she barely even admitted to herself.

"You want to make me say it?" he asked.

She didn't answer, knowing what was coming. She wanted to reach out and put a hand over his mouth—to stop him from saying it out loud.

"You're in love with Ethan."

A tide of hot blood was rising her neck and creeping over her face. "No, I'm not."

"Who do you think you're fooling? Not me. And if Ethan wasn't as thick as pig shit and constantly mooning over Cariad, he'd see it for himself. I've seen it. I know it. I've seen how you look at him when you think no one's watching."

"No." Now it was her turn to look away. Why oh why had she started the discussion? Why had she pushed him so hard? "It isn't like that."

"Are you going to carry on denying it? Now you're making yourself look stupid. You wanted an honest conversation. Well, you've got it. Now it's over to you. What do you have to say?"

She didn't know what to say. A war was going on inside her. She felt violated. He had hit close to home. For years, she'd been telling herself that Ethan was a good friend. Aboard the *Nova* he'd been with that girl who died in the First Night Attack. Lauren. His high school sweetheart. Then, when the Gen rebellion was kicking off and they'd been in oceanside caves, she'd kissed Garwin, guessing that Ethan would see them. Had she been hoping he would develop romantic feelings for her?

But it had been so obvious that he loved Cariad. Is that what had made Cherry hate her?

Aubriot was waiting for an answer. He was right—she'd brought this upon herself. On the other hand, she still didn't understand why her feelings for Ethan bothered him. She and Aubriot had only been having some fun. Their relationship had been convenient for both of them.

Wilder trotted into the living quarters, bursting into the tense moment.

Aubriot's head snapped around. "Fuck off, kid."

She shrank out of sight.

Aubriot's tone had been so vicious, Cherry winced. Poor Wilder. She didn't deserve to be spoken to like that.

"Please go to your safety seats," came Quinn's voice over the ship's comm. "We are about to begin deceleration."

Twenty-Four

Wilder reclined in her padded chair. The material conformed to her body and it fit her like a glove. The comfort made an increase in acceleration a tiny bit more bearable.

How many hours had she spent here, crushed almost to the point of blacking out? It had to be the more than half the journey. She hoped for future trips the Fila would figure out a way for humans to travel using the other method of 'hopping'. It sounded much more convenient. As it was, she had decided she would never volunteer for another deep space mission, not if this was what was involved.

Almost as bad as the acceleration phases were the close confines of the *Opportunity*. The cramped conditions were as bad as living in Sidhe. She longed for her tree top home, the sound of the leaves moving in the morning and evening breezes, and the clean, green smell of the air. She wondered how Tycho, Stephie, and the others were doing. Had they built more platforms like they'd said they would? Had they invited other teenagers to join them? She was excited to see what changes occurred while she was gone.

After the first few acceleration sessions, Aubriot had set up his interface so they could play a vid or a holo while trapped in their seats. He would usually remain blissfully asleep as Wilder, and sometimes Cherry, watched documentaries, news programs, and movies from ancient Earth. The origin planet of humankind was an enigmatic puzzle. Wilder found it hard to imagine her ancestors among the billions of people who had lived there, and that the Concordia Colony was the last bastion of human civilization.

Sometimes Kes would comment on what was playing, explaining things he thought Concordians would struggle to understand, or he would tell them the wider context. Other times he was silent and lost in thought.

"We will reverse the position of the ship as we begin to decelerate," said Quinn. "When the ship is fully reversed, your experience of deceleration will feel the same as the ship's acceleration. We will maintain a force similar to Concordia's gravity for as large a proportion of the journey's duration as possible."

"Great," Wilder muttered.

"What's wrong?" Cherry asked. "When the maneuver's over, the a-grav should feel the same."

"It's the maneuver I'm worried about." As Wilder spoke, it began. She could feel the *Opportunity* turning. The sensation was subtle, but the balance of pressure shifted. It was no longer over her entire body like a crushingly heavy blanket. Now her feet felt heavier than her head. She hoped she wouldn't embarrass herself for a second time by throwing up. She didn't have a bag, and even if she did, her arms weren't strong enough to fight the force holding them down.

"What was it you'd come to tell me just now?" Kes asked her.

"Oh, it was something about the Fila."

A minute or two earlier, on her way to find Kes, she'd burst in on an argument between Cherry and Aubriot. The two had been facing each other, their gazes locked and their expressions filled with anger. At least, *Aubriot* had looked angry. But had Cherry been embarrassed? Her face had been flushed. The tension of the long space journey was clearly beginning to tell on at least two of them. Aubriot had sworn. The man was such an asshole. Why had Cherry invited him to come along?

"And...?" Kes asked.

"What?"

"What about the Fila?"

"Sorry." After beating a hasty retreat from the living quarters, Wilder had found Kes. Before she could tell him her new finding, the Fila had requested they all go to their seats. She explained the discussion she'd had with Quinn on the differences between the human and Fila concepts of touching.

"Electrical fields!" Kes exclaimed. "Of course. Thank you. That's brilliant, and it makes perfect sense. Many aquatic organisms on Earth have the same ability. I don't know why I didn't think of it before. The Fila live in water. Water conducts electricity, and the Fila's bodies have evolved the ability to generate electrical power. It's invisible to us unless in extremely high voltages. That's why we can't see them sending out electrical impulses to interact with their equipment. They can probably sense electrical fields too."

The angle of the *Opportunity* continued to subtly alter. The pattern of pressure shifted and now the highest strength pushed down on the entire length of Wilder's lower legs.

"This is going to take forever," Aubriot said.

"Why don't you go to sleep like always?" Cherry suggested.

He ignored her and instructed his interface to play something.

Wilder focused on the picture that appeared. The title Aubriot had chosen didn't sound particularly interesting, but anything was an acceptable distraction from the uncomfortable sensation of the ship turning.

A figure appeared, walking toward the camera. She was astounded to recognize Aubriot. He was dressed differently and his hair was much shorter, but it was definitely him. Facially, he hadn't changed much. He looked a little older now, perhaps.

"That's you," she blurted, staring at him.

"Give the girl a cigar."

Kes sighed.

As the vid progressed, it explained the idea of a project to begin a colony in deep space. It took her a moment or two to realize it was referring to the *Nova Fortuna* Project, and that Aubriot was its instigator. The fact was a revelation. To her, he was only another—exceptionally annoying—Woken. The promotional vid showed the plans for the generational ship and a projection for how long it would take to construct.

The vid also explained the selection process for the generational colonists, stating that every fertile, healthy adult on Earth could apply, and that application fees would contribute to the project funding. Each applicant would be vetted for health and intelligence, though the latter was to ensure the project included the spectrum of normal human cognitive ability. A range of intelligence levels was thought to be beneficial for social cohesion and the long term success of the colony. The final selection would be based on genetic diversity, which meant that family members would definitely be excluded. No places on the ship were available for purchase.

"I'm not going to lie," the vid's Aubriot said. "It's a one way trip. You'll never return home. You'll never see your family and friends or set foot on a planet again. But you'll play a part in the future of humankind. Your name will go down in posterity." The picture cut to a profile of his head and shoulders. He turned to face the new camera, looking intently at the viewer. "Make no mistake. You'll never get a chance like this again. All you need to ask yourself is, do you have what it takes?"

The intent was clearly to generate funding to supplement the trillions Aubriot himself was putting up. It also asked for donations. Various incentives were offered according to the amount given. Donors could have their names inscribed on the ship's hull, or places on the planet would be named after them. Another option was to send along a small package, such as the ashes of a loved one to be buried in the exoplanet's soil or a time capsule of objects to be opened.

Had those things been stowed aboard the *Nova*? Wilder had never heard of those packages. Had they been dumped as soon as they'd been received, in the knowledge that the donors and their immediate descendants would be long dead decades before the ship arrived? There had also been no instructions in the Manual to give places on Concordia specific names. She was sure about that. Studying the Manual was one of the most boring things she'd been forced to do at school. She didn't know if any names had been inscribed on the *Nova's* hull.

The vid was entrancing. She wondered why she'd never seen it before. It revealed Aubriot's character in an entirely new light, and it gave her a weird feeling about all the viewers who had originally seen the vid. What would all of those Earth people who had donated think about how everything had turned out?

Had they ever imagined that Concordia would be coveted by hostile aliens? She guessed they thought the difficulties the colony might encounter would be quite different. No one would have dreamt up a fantasy where four representative humans would be tasked with forming galactic alliances vital to the future of human civilization.

The vid ended. Credits appeared against the background of a model of the *Nova*, giving details of where to send money, apply to become a generational colonist, or find out more about the project.

She suddenly realized that the excessive pressure on her lower legs had eased. "Have we turned already?"

"Yes," Kes replied. "It's over. We're facing the other way and slowing down."

"Phew. That wasn't too bad."

"No, not too bad," Cherry said. "And if we're decelerating, we must be over half way to the Assembly. This trip is taking longer than I thought it would, but the end is in sight."

Twenty-Five

The Scythian probe had observed the human colony begin its transformation into a civilization. Concordia had completed twenty-six orbits of its star, and in that time habitations, roads, growing areas, and manufacturing sites had increased, with one exception: the forest settlement. The humans had abandoned the trees. The tree city had reached its peak population five years after establishment, but then many of its inhabitants moved to the oceanside. Others constructed a new set of residences at the midway point between the forest and the growing district.

Some humans continued to permanently reside in the forest dwellings, but they were few. Inhabitants of the new dwelling sites did return to the forest. Soon after the majority had abandoned their homes there, the trees began to die.

Concordia completed another orbit of its star, and most of the forest canopy had disappeared. Only a small area remained, providing homes to the remaining handful of inhabitants.

The large buildings where the humans manufactured products saw the greatest increase, and the range of types of items that left the buildings also appeared to grow. The humans dug channels alongside the roads joining the habitations and in among their dwellings. They laid cables and pipes before covering up the channels again. When darkness fell on the inhabited areas, electric light lit them up.

The humans also constructed a wider variety of vehicles. Large transporters appeared and were used to move the produce from the growing areas as well as manufactured goods. Aerial craft were constructed. The probe tracked the flights of these aircraft, recording the altitude and range, but they were only used to journey between habitations and, more rarely, for trips to the the mountains.

A new road appeared, the longest the humans had ever built, running from the oceanside metropolis to the mountain range bisecting the continent. The colony had spread to the peaks, where they began to dig underground again. Plants were built to process the minerals extracted. Then the humans began to build a tunnel beneath the mountain.

At first, small boats had plied the ocean, never straying more than twenty kilometers from land. But during the planet's twenty-first orbit around its star, two large vessels were constructed. A short time later, the first humans crossed the ocean to the next continent.

As the colony grew larger, the amount of data the probe received increased exponentially. In case of this eventuality, the Scythians had fitted the device with equipment to screen the data collected. The probe sorted the incoming information into three grades according to predetermined parameters. Data categorized as of minimal importance was not transmitted nor retained. The Scythians didn't learn about the dying of the forest or the humans who continued to visit it.

The middle grade of information was stored, retained in case of later importance. The probe recorded the fact that channels had been dug and pipes and cables embedded in them. When the device's storage reached full capacity, the oldest data was purged.

The highest grade of data was transmitted immediately to the Scythians. They knew all the available details about the aerial craft and the large vessels crossing the ocean. They also closely scrutinized the data on mining operations.

By the twenty-sixth revolution of the origin planet around its star, the humans had advanced their technology and society considerably. They were constructing several modes of transportation, manufacturing many products, and exploiting the planet's natural resources. They had not developed any means of energy generation, but that possibly had something to do with help received from the aquatic aliens.

The Scythians were pleased. The humans were creating a sustainable, productive society. Left to themselves, they would no doubt go on to increase their population, spread across the planet, and build larger and more complex infrastructures. They would thrive, and perhaps in the future they might achieve a level of technology that would allow them to travel the galaxy.

That would not happen. An end was coming to the humans' achievements.

But not yet.

Twenty-Six

A holo of the site of the Assembly hung in midair in the *Opportunity*'s living quarters.

"I didn't know it would be a space station," said Cherry. "I thought we were going to a planet."

Wilder had made the same mistake. She gawped at the image. What a space station it was! Massive, foreboding, and almost black, it was a dark shadow against the stars. A long, gigantic cylinder extended down from the central hub, and five arms protruded from the same spot, each supporting a solid block hundreds of meters high and wide. The hub itself had to be two kilometers in diameter and the same depth.

Her estimations were vague, based on size comparisons with the ships entering and leaving the station. If they were bigger than she guessed, the station could easily be double the size.

Quinn explained, "It was thought that siting the Assembly on a planet could demonstrate favoritism toward a single member species. The station is in neutral territory and is governed under its own laws. All members must agree to abide by those laws in order to join the alliance."

"What are the laws?" Aubriot asked.

"You will receive a full translation if you are invited to join."

"Does it matter what they are?" Kes asked. "We aren't in a position to be picky."

"It's important to know," said Aubriot. "Never sign anything until your lawyer's read it."

"We don't have a lawyer," Kes retorted tetchily.

The months of confinement were beginning to tell on him. Usually mild-mannered, even-tempered, kind, and thoughtful, even Kes was suffering from spending too much time with Aubriot. The man's insistence on calling him Ginger didn't help.

"Are you coming with us, Quinn?" Wilder asked.

"We will be unable to accompany you onto the station. The environment is entirely unsuitable for us."

"Can we at least speak to you while we're in there?" asked Wilder.

"No. That is a condition of your attendance. No comm between yourselves and the *Opportunity* is allowed. The Assembly members have made an exception in permitting us to bring you here. A basic requirement of applying to join the alliance is deep space travel technology. Both of your ships have been destroyed, so you have no evidence of your level of development or any means of traveling here. The Assembly acceded to our request, but all further aid and support must stop as soon as you enter the station."

"Does it have gravity?" Cherry asked. Like the other humans, she was casually floating as she took in the holo of the space station. Now the *Opportunity* had stopped, there was no force acting on her.

Quinn replied, "The technology to create gravity doesn't exist as far as we're aware. Besides, what amount of gravity should the station provide? What might be low gravity to one species would crush another to death."

"Do you know what'll happen when we go in?" Wilder asked. "Do you know what they expect from us?"

"We don't know, and even if we did we couldn't tell you. It is forbidden to—"

"Yeah, we get it," said Aubriot. "You aren't allowed to help us."

"We have supplied the Assembly with all the information we have on you as a species," said Quinn. "That should help with communication."

"Do we really have to take weapons with us?" Kes asked. "That doesn't seem very peaceful or diplomatic."

"The Assembly has requested it," Quinn replied.

"We've talked enough," said Aubriot. "It's time we transferred to the station."

Quinn said, "We have prepared environment suits for you."

"EVA suits?" asked Cherry. "Doesn't the station have an atmosphere?"

"It would be impossible to generate an atmosphere that all the species can safely breathe. Rather than filling the station with gases suitable for only one or two species, it was decided it would be more equitable to make it a vacuum. Each species can supply their own suits."

Wilder's heart sank. Living in the cramped quarters aboard the *Opportunity* had been bad enough. The idea of spending a significant amount of time in an EVA suit made her feel sick. She'd seen the suits when she'd been a kid on the

Nova. Technicians conducting repairs on the hull had worn them to space walk. Even at a young age, she'd known she would never choose to wear one. Now she had no choice.

"Wilder," said Cherry. "Come on."

The others were leaving. In her preoccupation Wilder hadn't noticed. She kicked against the wall and glided out, her rifle under her arm, following her companions heading along the cylindrical corridor. By the time she reached the room with reclined seats, previously unseen compartments had opened. Each held an EVA suit. Aubriot was already climbing into one.

Breathing deeply in an effort to quell her fears, she grabbed the door frame to halt her progress and watched the others putting on their suits. Had the Fila had copied the suits' design from the colony's data banks? If they hadn't, they'd done a remarkable job of making them well-suited to the human body. They looked very similar to ones the *Nova's* technicians had worn, except a larger pack was fitted to the back. Flexible pipes ran from the pack along the underside of the sleeves, and nozzles protruded from the elbows.

"Thrusters!" Aubriot exclaimed. "Fantastic." He pressed his thumbs into his palms and pressurized gas squirted out, propelling him to the ceiling.

"Don't do that in here," said Cherry. "You don't know what gas that is." She looked over her shoulder. "The threads have fixed my suit's thrusters at the base of my pack. I have two pads on my palm, one for each thruster I guess, but this isn't going to be easy. I won't have the maneuverability you guys have."

"Hey, look," said Aubriot. "They even made a pint-size one for the kid." He was holding up the remaining suit, smaller than the others.

Wilder didn't know exactly what he meant by 'pint-size', but from Cherry and Kes's reactions the words didn't seem to be an insult. Smiling grudgingly, she took the suit from Aubriot's outstretched hand. The outfit was surprisingly light, an all-in-one item. The helmet was fixed to the back of the neck. She tried to step into it, but the motion caused her to float backward and bump into the wall. She sighed in exasperation. Moving in zero-g was an endless dance of cause and effect.

"Hold on to the suit rack," Kes suggested. "Makes it easier."

She took the advice and struggled into the suit one handed, pulling on the arms before thrusting her hands into the gloves. They restricted her hands, but not so much that she couldn't fasten the front of the suit.

All that remained now was to put on the helmet. Everyone else was suited up and waiting. She breathed in and pulled the helmet over her head. The seal around her neck immediately snicked shut.

The helmet was globe-shaped around most of her head, flattening only at the back. The Fila had a good idea of the extent of human peripheral vision. Panic began to rise up. She thought she couldn't breathe. Then she realized she was holding her breath. She forced herself to breathe out, and then in again. The air smelled different. It smelled sweet.

"Okay?" said a voice.

The comm system was working well too.

Aubriot floated into her view. The man's voice had broadcast inside her helmet.

"I said, are you okay?" He rapped her helmet with gloved knuckles and peered through her visor.

"I'm fine."

"You sure?"

When she didn't answer, because she actually wasn't sure at all, he said, "Sling your weapon over your shoulder. Makes it easier to carry." Then he waggled a finger at her and added, "No puking in your helmet."

"I said I'm fine." She narrowed her eyes at him. She was actually trying her best not to rip off the helmet and suit as fast as she could, refuse to enter the space station, and fly back to the living quarters. She didn't need any more hassle.

"Leave her alone," said Cherry.

The inner airlock doors opened.

"Prepare to transfer to the station," said Quinn.

"This is it," said Kes. "Never in all my dreams did I imagine I would experience something like this."

"All right," said Aubriot. "No need to get all poetical."

The group moved into the airlock. The inner doors closed. There was no window to the outside. They were uncomfortably close in a cramped space, a jumble of floating humans.

The outer doors opened.

At first, all Wilder could see was the inside of a tunnel, a tube stretching away beyond the airlock. It was flexible, and some motion of the ship was gently moving it.

The holo of the space station hadn't shown the means by which the *Opportunity* was attached to it. The tube curved in the distance, obscuring its end.

"What's that thing?" Aubriot demanded.

Quinn explained, "The *Opportunity's* airlock configuration is incompatible with the station's entry portal. The mechanics constructed an umbilicus. You must leave now. I hope you succeed in persuading the Assembly to allow your species to join their alliance. You will have done your colony a great service. When the Scythians discover the fact, they will be discouraged. They may be too afraid to attack Concordia if you refuse to honor their demand for a tribute."

"The Assembly better accept us," said Aubriot.

The aliens who had constructed the umbilicus leading to the space station had installed a method of conveying visitors along it. Lines were fixed to the inner wall, and the Fila had attached clips to the humans' suits. All they had to do was clip themselves to the line.

"Can't we use our thrusters to fly into the station?" Aubriot asked.

"The area is too confined," Quinn replied. "Remember, whatever happens in the station, you have agreed to it by coming here."

"What?" said Aubriot. "Wait. No, we didn't."

"Come on," said Cherry. "Let's go."

Twenty-Seven

They were being pulled steadily along the umbilicus. Cherry peered through the translucent walls. Hazy impressions of stars surrounded them except for directly ahead, where all was black.

"I wonder where in the galaxy we are," said Kes.

She had been wondering the same thing. They had clearly traveled a huge distance on the threads' ship. She wouldn't have expected to be able to judge where they were—they were viewing the starscape from a new angle—but they were clearly in an entirely different section of the galaxy. The stars clustered much thicker here than in the Concordian night sky.

Aubriot replied, "We're deeper in the Milky Way."

"I think you're right," said Kes.

The tunnel exit appeared and quickly yawned wider.

Wilder asked, "Do you think the Assembly has sent someone to meet us?"

"I should think so," said Kes.

"We'll soon find out," Aubriot said.

They stopped. They'd arrived at the circular station entrance. The interior was lit, but not much more brightly than the threads' ship. No one seemed to be here to greet them.

Cherry unclipped herself from the umbilicus line, pointed her heels downward and slightly to the rear, pressed her thumb into her palm, and propelled herself into the station. The space she entered was large enough to accommodate the *Opportunity*. Unused to operating the thrusters, she flew farther than she'd intended. She grabbed a protrusion from a tall, humped, metal structure and brought herself to an abrupt stop.

As she swung around to see what the others were doing, the structure jerked into life. Startled, she let go. Noises came through her comm. Low, long, drawn-out sounds.

Aubriot, Kes, and Wilder had entered too, and they'd clearly learned from Cherry's mistake, propelling themselves toward her with tiny puffs.

"Is that thing our escort?" Aubriot asked. "Is it talking? What's it saying?"

"How would I know?" asked Cherry.

The sounds repeated. Kes held a hand to the side of his helmet and frowned. "I think it's human speech, but it's too slow. The Fila used to do this sometimes." A spurt from his thrusters brought him in contact with the machine. He tapped it. "We can't understand you. You must speak faster."

The sound remained very slow, but the words were intelligible. "Welcome... to..." A strange, muffled sound followed, then, "Map, activate."

A detailed map appeared on Cherry's visor, a 3-D image of the interior of a huge, complex structure. At the center was a vast, bare space. The rest of the place was semi-open and filled with levels and rooms. Some rooms were small cubby holes, others ran the entire width of the station.

Wilder said, "I think those dots are us."

Cherry searched the map and saw four tiny sparks flashing.

The machine she had previously grabbed onto moved, sliding along the floor, though without any apparent tracks or wheels to convey it.

"Are we supposed to follow it?" Wilder asked.

Cherry replied, "Seems the obvious thing to do."

The machine moved on, passing through an exit as tall as the roof. They flew behind it.

"Where do you think they're taking us, Kes?" Cherry asked.

"If this place were run by humans, I'd say we're being escorted to meet someone high up in the hierarchy. As it isn't, I don't have any idea. We could be going to meet the janitor first, for all I know."

"Maybe janitors are top of the food chain," said Aubriot.

"I don't like the mention of a food chain," Cherry said. "That gives me another idea about where we're being taken."

"I certainly hope we haven't come all this way only to be eaten," said Kes. "I don't think that would be an accurate test of our intelligence."

Aubriot said, "It would be if we could stop them from doing it."

"I hope you guys are kidding," said Wilder.

The passageway was drawing to an end and another chamber opened ahead. Their escort, traveling at a faster speed than the humans, reached the opening and stopped. A few moments later, they caught up. Cherry gripped the edge of the hole and peered in. Here was the open space she'd seen on the map.

Kes whistled.

She couldn't see the top or the bottom of the empty center of the station. Above and below, structures intersected the void. Some of the structures' walls were opaque, others were mesh, others were solid but transparent, allowing in the lights dimly illuminating the massive space. There seemed to be no order. She couldn't guess as to the purpose of each chamber.

Even more fascinating than the station's weird set-up were the things moving within it. Some were machines like their escort, moving horizontally and vertically, clinging to flat surfaces and also flying through open areas. Others were what she could only describe as *creatures.* They were suited up like the humans, but their suits' shapes indicated that the forms inside were distinctly nonhuman.

Oblong, soft beings inched along, somehow clinging to surfaces like the machines. Others were like thread creatures due to their many, thin legs, but the moved like Scythian spiders. In the zero-g, they jumped from place to place, floating enormous distances.

"Unbelievable," Kes breathed.

"How are you doing, Wilder?" Cherry asked. She didn't think she'd heard the girl say more than a few sentences since they suited up.

"I'm okay," Wilder replied. "It's a lot to take in."

"You can say that again," said Aubriot. "Hey, where did our escort go?"

While they had all been gawping at the interior of the station, the robot that had brought them here had departed. It was nowhere to be seen.

"We've been abandoned," Aubriot continued. "What do we do now?"

"I think our visors are telling us," said Wilder.

Cherry checked her map. The four dots representing them had shifted to their new position, but something else had changed too. The outline of one of the structures directly above them had begun to glow and flash.

"Looks like that's our next destination." Aubriot kicked against the edge of the entrance, propelling himself out into the empty space and activating his suit's thrusters. "If this is an example of our intelligence test, it's a cinch."

"I doubt it's going to be this easy," said Kes as he followed.

"Ready?" Cherry asked Wilder.

The girl nodded.

"Stick by me." Cherry glided out into nothingness. "Unless something bad happens, in which case, head back to the threads' ship. Don't try to tackle anything dangerous yourself, and, whatever you do, don't endanger yourself to protect one of us. We can look after ourselves, and if we can't, there's nothing you can do to help us."

As they boosted themselves upward, following the soles of Aubriot and Kes's boots, Cherry wished she could give Wilder better advice, but in the circumstances she couldn't. She had no idea herself what might happen.

Twenty-Eight

Wilder pumped a jet of pressurized gas from her suit's thrusters, lifting herself to Cherry's as they rose through the vast interior of the space station. Embedded lines in the wall passed swiftly by. What were they? Pipes to convey water or another substance? Electrical wires? Were they structural, providing support?

She couldn't guess and knew she would never know, but focusing on the question distracted her from the feelings of panic about wearing the EVA suit. She kept careful track of her and her companions' progress on her visor display. They crawled almost imperceptibly slowly despite in fact traveling quickly up the wall face. Once or twice, she tried to turn to look at the wider view and see more of the strange aliens, but the effect was disorienting.

"We're nearly there," said Cherry. "Where have Aubriot and Kes gone?"

Wilder looked up. The men's figures, which had been drawing steadily away, had disappeared. All she could see was the gloom of the space station rising endlessly above. "They must have gone inside without us."

Cherry boosted herself closer. "Take my hand," she said nervously, grabbing Wilder's. "I wish I'd thought to ask the threads for a line to attach us to each other."

Wilder was insulted. She could look after herself. "I'm fine." She tried to wrest her grasp from Cherry's. In the small tussle, she failed to notice they'd arrived at their destination. When she faced forward, a wide opening confronted her. The hole stretched away all around, its edges smooth and curved, its diameter the height of four men.

Where were Kes and Aubriot?

Cherry hailed the men. No answer came. Cherry tried again, with the same result. "Shit. Go back to the ship. I'm going—"

A great force grabbed Wilder. Before she realized what was happening, she'd been sucked into the hole. Her hand was ripped from Cherry's. The woman was nowhere to be seen. Wilder twisted and turned, trying to see her, but she was surrounded by blackness. Her visor display was gone. "Cherry?"

Twisting so strongly had put her into a lazy spin in the zero-g. She pumped her thrusters, hoping for stability and to reach a solid surface. She lifted her hands to prevent a collision, but they met with nothingness. "Cherry? Kes?"

What if she tried going down? Perhaps she was near the bottom, not the top. She leaned forward and angled her elbows behind, squeezing the pads on her palms. She felt herself moving forward and downward, but again, empty space was all she encountered. "Aubriot?"

She spun again, trying to see something, anything that would give her some bearings, but she was alone in the void.

For long moments she floated in the blackness, trying to figure out what to do. The Assembly wouldn't have brought them here only to kill them. That would serve no purpose. But then, as Kes had said, guessing at the motivations and logic of alien cultures was hopeless. How could she possibly know what the Assembly members intended?

Was this an intelligence test? Aubriot had thought the aliens would want to test their intelligence before agreeing to admit them into the Assembly. Maybe he'd been right. Maybe she should be doing something to escape. But what?

She prepared to fire her thrusters again. With no visual on her surroundings, the only method she had for finding the exit was to feel her way, even if it took all the gas in her pack.

Suddenly, something grabbed her around the waist. She was pulled backward at great speed, her arms and legs trailing. Light blazed, and she was in a metal-walled chamber. Released from the pull of the invisible force, inertia carried her on until a second invisible force stopped her progress.

She hung against the far wall of the metal room. A complex design covered the opposite surface. She could see no door. How had she entered the place? There had to be an exit.

Her visor display sprang to life. A single letter flashed up in red: 'R'. *R?* What the hell did that mean? A second letter joined the R. Now the visor displayed 'R E'. None the wiser, she waited. The Assembly aliens were spelling something out after their machine's attempt at human speech hadn't worked well.

R E M

She checked the walls, floor, and ceiling again. All were seamless.

R E M O

Remo? She mentally ran through a list of words beginning with those four letters. She arrived at the answer as the V appeared. Her visor confirmed her guess.

R E M O V E

She didn't like the direction this comm seemed to be heading. She wasn't about to remove anything. Not in a vacuum.

R E M O V E

S

No.

R E M O V E

S U

No way.

R E M O V E

S U I

Dammit!

R E M O V E

S U I T

She glared at the message. Quinn had said the Fila had given the Assembly all their information on humans. The aliens had to know she couldn't survive in a vacuum. They had to know the only thing keeping her alive right now was her EVA suit. Why were they asking her to take it off? Did they want her to die? The confines of the suit, once uncomfortably restrictive, had become a comforting and safe place.

The two words confronted her. Long seconds passed. The words flashed twice.

"I can read it, you idiots!" She scanned the room for an exit again and came up blank. Were they going to keep her here indefinitely until her air ran out or she died of thirst? Quinn had said that by coming to the station they had agreed to whatever happened to them. But she hadn't thought it would include doing things that put her life at risk.

She bumped against a wall, jarring the weapon slung over her shoulder and reminding her of its presence. She lifted the rifle thoughtfully. Should she try to shoot her way out? The space was small. A pulse could rebound in ways she couldn't predict. Nevertheless, it seemed to be her only option. It was either that or face an unknown, potentially deadly outcome.

She pointed the muzzle at the wall. Aubriot had taught her the basics of how to fire the weapon, but she'd never actually shot anything. That would have been way too dangerous inside the *Opportunity*. She held her finger over the trigger. Was she doing the right thing? It appeared to be the only choice. But it didn't feel right.

R E M O V E S U I T

"No. No. It isn't safe."

All her childhood she'd learned about the dangers of space. She'd learned how, when the *Nova* arrived at her destination, everyone would travel to the planet, where they would finally be safe. There would be no dangerous vacuum or radiation beyond the ship's hull. They would have kilometers of atmosphere above and a magnetosphere and ozone layer to protect them from the ravages of space.

Now, these creatures she had never even met were asking her to go against what had been ingrained into her. Why?

The question bothered her. It made no sense that the Assembly would ask her to do something so dangerous. Even allowing for alien logic, it made no sense. Was this part of the test? That she would do whatever was asked, though it might cost her her life? If that were the case, would she pass the test only if she began to remove her suit?

But she had never been one for simply following instructions. If that was what the Assembly wanted—submissive members who did whatever they were told—they'd come to the wrong person. Concordia might as well remain under the control of the Scythians. She refused to make a show of removing her suit, if that was what the Assembly wanted.

She might as well try to blow her way out and take the consequences.

For the second time, she lifted her weapon and aimed it. For the second time, she failed to fire. The feeling she was missing something nagged at her.

REMOVESUIT

What if it wasn't blind obedience the Assembly wanted her to demonstrate?

What if it was trust?

She wasn't great at trusting others. She'd been let down too many times in the past.

"Ugh, dammit. Okay. Okay." She'd come all this way for a reason. She wanted to buy Concordia a chance to survive. If she had to take off her suit in a vacuum to do it, so be it.

She flipped the snaps. What did a vacuum feel like? She didn't know. She pushed upward on her helmet, expecting to hear the hiss of her suit's air escaping. But she heard nothing.

She lifted her helmet and held her breath. Where was the anticipated pressure of air trying to escape her lungs? Where was the biting iciness of her sweat evaporating from her skin? She opened her lips. Her tongue peeled from the roof of her mouth. Her throat opened. She took a small, experimental breath.

"Shit!"

The room had atmosphere. She could breathe. All that time she'd spent hesitating over the instruction, when she could have taken off her suit without any danger.

The place was colder than she would have liked and the air smelled of chemicals, but she no longer doubted following the instruction. She pushed back her helmet and unfastened the front of her suit, thanking the stars she hadn't fired at the wall. That would have been a dumb move. The Assembly wouldn't have wanted her to shoot the place up.

When she was out of her EVA suit and it floated in the air next to her, the complex design on the opposite wall changed shape. It turned into the outline of a human form that was roughly her size. The inner portion of the form glowed.

"Now I get it. You want to check out our bodies, right? You've never met humans before. You want to know how we work."

She pushed off and floated into the body-shaped space, reversing as she arrived so she faced outward. Grips gently but firmly grasped her waist, upper arms, and thighs. Suction pulled at the back of her head.

She tried to relax, hoping the Assembly wouldn't take too long in learning whatever they wanted to know about her body. In the end, the process took only a few minutes. Relief that she wasn't in danger flooded in. She nodded drowsily, but then it was all over. The suction on her skull ceased and she was released. She put on her suit. As her helmet was snicking shut, an exit into blackness opened.

Twenty-Nine

Cherry's relief at seeing Wilder safe and sound was immense. When the girl floated out to meet them in the dark space, she felt like grabbing her in a hug. That would have been awkward in their EVA suits and pressurized gas packs, so she contented herself by grabbing Wilder's hand.

"What happened to you?" Kes asked. "Did you have to take off your suit too?"

"I did. I think they wanted to scan my body."

"The same happened to us," said Cherry.

"They're curious about our anatomy," Kes said. "It makes sense. That would be the first thing I would want to learn about in an alien species."

"When's the testing going to start?" Aubriot asked. "I'm fed up with being poked and prodded. I was worried for a while in there. I was waiting for them to get out the anal probe."

"The *what?*" asked Cherry.

Kes chuckled.

"Maybe the testing's already started," Wilder said. "I thought the request to take off my suit was a test."

Aubriot snorted with derision. "I think the tests are going to be a bit harder than *that.*"

Kes said, "I don't know why you keep going on about the Assembly putting us through tests. I thought we were coming here to meet them and talk to them about our problem with the Scythians."

"I thought that too," said Cherry, recalling her initial conversation with

Quinn in the threads' underwater city. He'd said she was supposed to 'seek admittance to the alliance' and 'secure the future of humanity.' Two pretty big asks. She had no idea how she was supposed to achieve either of them. Everything that had happened so far had been out of her control.

At least Wilder was back safe and sound. She was also a little more talkative, which was a good sign. Cherry's visor gleamed with the lines and symbols of the station map.

"We're back in business," said Aubriot. "Where to next?"

Another section glowed green. The four flashing red dots representing their party were far distant from their next destination.

"This way." Kes activated a single thruster and turned away from the group. Both his thrusters spurted gas and he moved off.

"He seems to know where he's going," said Wilder, following.

"Wait," said Cherry. "I don't want to lose sight of you again."

The four humans emerged from the hole they had entered some time previously. Once more, they were hanging above an apparently bottomless chamber.

"It's over there," said Kes, pointing but not slowing down.

On a far distant pillar clinging to the side of the abyss was a range of portals. Some were open, revealing the brightest lighting Cherry had seen in a long time. Others were only outlines on the bronzed surface.

As the four of them flew closer to their next stop, she spied four figures waiting at a doorway. This was it. They were about to meet some Assembly aliens at last. Perhaps Wilder had been right when she'd said the request to remove their EVA suits had been a test. Cherry had hesitated at first, worried about the effects of exposure to a vacuum.

But then she'd remembered a technician on the *Nova* telling her that vacuum exposure wasn't immediately fatal, providing you emptied your lungs as much as possible. So she'd exhaled fully before taking off her helmet.

She guessed the Assembly knew the correct composition of gases humans breathed from the information the threads had given them.

The distance to the pillar was farther than she'd thought. They seemed to be taking an age to reach the spot. She realized the waiting figures were far larger than she'd thought too. Judging size and distance in the a vast, unfamiliar place was hard.

"Ready your weapons," said Aubriot. "They might try something."

Kes tutted. "What do you imagine they're going to try?"

"Doesn't hurt to be prepared."

Cherry said, "If they wanted to hurt us they could have done it a thousand times already. I don't want anyone to do anything that could be interpreted as aggressive. That's an order."

The last thing she needed was for Aubriot to incite a defensive reaction. They were a long way from Concordia, and the threads could do nothing to help them.

The distant figures grew larger and larger. By the time the humans reached the pillar, they looked like giants.

Thirty

One of the four aliens stood directly in front of Wilder as she hovered at the brink of the closed entrance. Her feet were level with the spot where the alien's four feet touched the floor, but the creature towered four or five times her height. The alien had to be at least seven meters tall, and it was the shortest of the bunch. Its four limbs rose up half its height and met at a chunky body that narrowed to a dome at the top. Wilder had assumed this was the head, but she could be wrong.

Like the humans, the aliens wore EVA suits, but, unlike the humans' suits, theirs had no visor. The entire surface was black and opaque.

"They're standing on the floor." Kes hovered next to Wilder.

The four aliens stood on a ledge that curved around the colossal pillar.

"Yeah, they are," Aubriot said. "Think that ledge has a-grav?"

"It could be magnetized," Wilder suggested.

"Move forward. Meet us." The voice spoke at a normal speed though it was monotone. The Fila's computer-generated voices sounded much more human in comparison. It was impossible to tell which of the creatures had spoken.

"Let's do what they say," said Cherry.

Wilder fired her thrusters and glided toward the platform, heading for the alien directly in front. The being's bulky form left additional little space, but she angled her elbows upward and aimed for the floor. Her boots met the metal mesh and she felt a magnetic grip.

"Whoa." Kes alighted beside her. "You were right. Feels odd to be stuck down. Feels good too, though. Better than zero-g."

Cherry landed on Wilder's other side.

"We want to understand you," said one of the aliens. "We must know if you belong with us."

"Who are you?" Cherry asked. "What are your names? What's your species?"

"We are organizers. That is all that is relevant."

Organizers? Did they mean they organized the events at the station? Wilder guessed the aliens weren't going to tell them any more than they had to. If the Assembly didn't accept humanity, any information they gave out might be used against them. Especially if the Scythians had control of Concordia.

Behind the alien organizers, the pillar entrance opened.

"Move inside," said one of the organizers. "The entrance will seal. You must remove your helmets."

"Huh?" said Aubriot. "Again? Is it safe?" He was peering between two of the large creatures.

Wilder could see into the pillar too. The chamber within was much larger than the place where she'd been scanned.

"We will fill the testing chamber with atmosphere suited to your species."

"Don't you want to talk to us?" said Cherry. "You could ask us whatever you want to know."

"We already understand your circumstances. Your friends told us. We need to understand your behavior."

"Okay." Cherry strode toward the entrance. "Come on, guys. This is what we're here for."

Stepping between two sets of four, huge legs, Wilder also went in. The room stretched thirty meters long and half as wide. Lighting strips hung on a ceiling fifteen meters above. When all four humans were inside, the door closed.

"I said they were going to test us, didn't I?" Aubriot said. "Did you hear it say this was a testing chamber?"

Wilder was watching her visor display. Readings had appeared with chemical symbols. As she watched, the levels rose.

"They're filling the chamber with air," said Kes.

According to Wilder's display, the atmosphere in the chamber was now breathable. She unfastened her helmet and took it off before breathing in deeply. The air had the same faint chemical tang. "It's safe. I feel fine."

Cherry turned, and her eyebrows lifted. "Good for you but it's probably better if we discuss these things rather than deciding by yourself what you're going to do. Unilateral action could be dangerous for you and us."

"Maybe, but I think you're all acting a bit paranoid."

Kes also removed his helmet. He sucked in air through his nostrils. "I agree with Wilder. Loosen up a little. If these aliens didn't care if we lived or died, they wouldn't go to all this trouble."

Aubriot unfastened his helmet. "If they wanted to do the right thing, they could just grant us sentient species status, accept us into their club, and not go to all this bother."

"I don't think this is only about assessing our fitness to join the Assembly," said Cherry. "The Scythians have claimed our planet, don't forget. The threads will have told them that. The Assembly has to decide if we have the right to stay there. The only reason we can give is that if we're forced to leave we'll die. Even if the Assembly conclude we have a right to exist on Concordia, that doesn't mean they'll be prepared to butt heads with the Scythians in our defense. This isn't only a matter of whether or not we meet their admission criteria."

"Well, this is boring," Aubriot said. "When's the fun going to start?"

Everything changed.

The chamber vanished. They were in a wasteland.

Wilder was so shocked she jumped. Her EVA suit had disappeared too. She grabbed the cloth of her pants, and then patted her chest, almost unable to believe what she was seeing. The material felt genuine. Gaping, she looked at the others. They had also lost their suits and were wearing regular clothes. Even the temperature and smell of the air were different. Dry desert spread in all directions under a pale blue sky. The place was nothing like anything Wilder had seen on Concordia. It looked like something from a vid of old Earth.

"This is..." said Cherry. "Are you all seeing the same as me?"

Kes said, "It feels so real. They must be feeding sensory data directly into our minds, controlling our perception."

"Shit," said Aubriot. "Now we won't know what's authentic and what isn't. I don't even know if you're all here or if I only think you are."

"I'm here," said Cherry.

"But what if you only appear to be saying that?" Kes smirked.

Cherry and Kes laughed nervously. Wilder could see the funny side too. The entire set up felt absurd.

"We have determined that you are not bearing any internal artificial intelligence devices," said a voice. "Test begins now."

Wilder waited expectantly.

A rattling sound came from overhead and an open-bottomed iron cage descended on top of them. Before anyone had time to react, it hit the sandy ground with a thud. They were confined in a space four meters square.

Aubriot immediately stepped up to the bars and shook them. "Solid. Not bad for an illusion." He gripped two bars hard and attempted to lift the cage. It didn't move a centimeter.

"I guess we have to solve this puzzle to get out," said Kes, nodding at the door: a simple set of bars like the rest of the cage. Five circular interface screens adhered to the center. Each circle contained sets of patterns except for the fifth one, which was blank. It appeared they had to guess what patterns to create on the final circle, according to the logical sequence shown in the other four.

"Huh, piece of cake," said Aubriot. "I used to do these for fun." He frowned as he studied the patterns. "You can leave it to me. Should only take a minute."

"Maybe I can help." Wilder had completed similar tests too. When she'd finished her classwork she would go into the *Nova's* database and look up additional things to do to prevent boredom.

Aubriot flicked his hand at her, waving her away. "Don't worry about it, kid. I've got this."

Cherry rolled her eyes. "He doesn't want you trampling all over his ego." Then she said to Aubriot, "Just don't make us wait all day."

The cage jerked, and the sound of movement came from overhead. Wilder looked up. They didn't have all day. The ceiling was descending.

"Great." Aubriot squatted to examine the patterns more closely. He held a finger to the blank screen, hesitating to draw on it.

The three others crowded behind him. Wilder peered at the patterns. The circles were divided into quarters, and each quarter held either dots, stripes, triangles, or wavy lines. At first glance, the patterns seemed random, but there had to be a sequence. It was only a matter of finding it.

The ceiling jerked again and descended lower.

"Is this a test of intelligence or speed?" Aubriot muttered.

"The smarter you are, the faster you'll solve it," Cherry said.

"You're not helping."

Kes was also working on solving the puzzle, but his gaze repeatedly flicked upward. "You don't think they'll actually kill us if we don't get this right, do you?"

"It's fake," Cherry replied. "It's all fake, remember? You can't kill someone with a fake roof."

"I don't want to even fake die," said Wilder. Then, because she'd seen something Aubriot appeared to have missed, she pointed at the patterns. "Look." She explained the sequence. "The final set of triangles has to be in this quadrant with their right angles facing to the left, and there must be seven of them."

Aubriot knocked her arm away. "I can do it."

"Let her help," said Cherry. "This isn't a competition."

Grudgingly, Aubriot drew in the triangles with a fingertip. The section of the screen glowed red. "See? It's wrong." He wiped the quadrant, causing the triangles to disappear.

"You're presuming too much," said Kes. "Red might not mean it's wrong."

"But they've based the tests on the data the Fila have given them about us."

"That doesn't mean they've gotten everything right," Cherry said. "Draw the triangles again. I trust Wilder."

Aubriot scowled, but he re-drew the triangles. Again, they glowed red. Next, he drew a set of squares in another quadrant. They also glowed red. He tensed as he seemed to conclude that perhaps Wilder had been correct after all.

A shudder of the cage brought the ceiling lower.

"Uh, if you could hurry up..." The ceiling had almost reached Kes's head. He lifted both hands and touched it. "This feels awfully real."

Wilder reached over Aubriot's shoulder and sketched eight wavy lines. They didn't glow.

Aubriot said, "Would you stop—"

"Oh, I've got it." She erased the lines and drew them at a different angle. Now three quadrants of the circle glowed red.

Kes quickly knelt as the ceiling dropped lower again.

"Ow." The ceiling rested against the top of Cherry's head. She also dropped to her knees. "If you two don't finish that puzzle soon, the ceiling will drop so low you won't be able to reach it."

"Gee, thanks for the reminder," said Aubriot. "I didn't think of that." He traced several stripes in the fourth quadrant.

The entire fifth circle glowed red, there was the click of a lock opening, and the door swung wide. At the same time, the ceiling descended past the level of the five circles. Aubriot ducked down and crawled out. Wilder followed. Next came Cherry as the ceiling dropped almost to the ground. As soon as she was out she turned and grabbed Kes by the shoulders. He was only halfway through the door. She hauled him the rest of the way just as the ceiling crashed to the ground.

The four of them stared at the cage, which now consisted of four walls, an open top, and a base of bars.

"You don't think they would have really hurt us?" Kes asked.

No one answered.

A moment later, the cage vanished.

Thirty-One

"That was easy," said Aubriot.

But Cherry didn't think their testing was anywhere near over yet. The cage puzzle had been identical to human intelligence tests. It made sense that they would be able to pass it with few difficulties, even with the threat of danger literally hanging over their heads.

No. The testing had only just begun.

What was coming next? She stood up and brushed sandy dirt from her knees. The environment the aliens were creating in her mind felt incredibly realistic. She was sweating in the hot, dry heat, and her mouth and eyes were gritty from dust. The wasteland seemed to stretch forever into the distance, though logically it could not. Were they expected to start walking?

"Whoa," said Kes.

She felt it too. A vibration was coming up through her feet. She looked downward. The ground began to visibly shake. She had to spread her arms to keep her balance. The gesture wasn't sufficient. She toppled, trying to sit down to mitigate her fall, but she fell most of the way.

The shaking continued.

"The ground's sinking!" Wilder exclaimed.

A crack ran straight across the ground in front. The line turned a corner at each end and ran down, forming the beginnings of a square. The ground abruptly dropped. Aubriot lunged for the edge of the hole. He reached it, but he was too late. The square of ground the crack had cut fell away. He clung to the rising edge for a few moments, scrabbling with his feet at the newly formed wall, but the dusty soil collapsed. His fingers slipped and he dropped into the hole. Cursing, he leapt to reach the edge again. His hands slapped the vertical brown dirt. He couldn't make it. "What the hell is this supposed to test?"

"Calm down," said Cherry. "We're in here for a reason. Let's wait and find out what it is." The hole was exactly deep enough to prevent the tallest member of the party from climbing out.

Aubriot ignored her and jumped again. Again, his fingertips missed the edge by a few centimeters.

"I'm so hungry," said Wilder. "Do you think we have to pass this next test before they'll let us eat?"

Cherry realized she was also incredibly hungry. "Me too. This is weird. We only ate about an hour ago."

"I'm starving," said Kes. "It must be another mind manipulation, but I could eat a horse right now."

"'Kay," Aubriot said. "I give up." He slumped down next to Cherry.

The faux sky was a rectangle above. The walls of their new prison slowly crumbled into the hole.

Kes said, "Clearly, we're supposed to climb out before we're buried alive."

"I'm sooo hungry," Wilder repeated, rubbing her stomach.

"Or before we starve to death," Aubriot said.

Cherry commented, "Before we *imagine* we've starved to death."

Then, in the exact spot on the ground where her gaze was focused, a bowl appeared. Everyone had a bowl. Next to the bowls lay spoons with very long handles. The bowl was filled with something resembling stew. Steam was rising from the contents, and her nostrils picked up a delicious, savory scent. Her stomach rumbled.

"It smells delicious." Wilder grabbed a spoon and plunged it into a bowl. But when she tried to lift the spoon to her mouth, the handle was too long. She couldn't hold the utensil far enough away to angle the bowl of the spoon at her lips.

"This is dumb." Kes was attempting the same feat. "Ah! I know." He slid his hand along the handle.

Cherry guessed what he was trying to do. If he held the handle at the bottom rather than the top, that should make it easy to eat. She tried the same, but when her hand had reached less than one quarter of the way down, it slipped through the metal. The spoon fell from her grasp.

"Hah!" said Aubriot. "They thought of that. Bet they didn't think of this, though." He handed his spoon to Cherry. "Watch." He reached for his bowl. He was planning to bypass using cutlery and pick up the bowl in his hands.

Except his hands passed through it.

"Damn."

"Guess they thought of that too," said Kes.

"Shuttup."

"If I wasn't so hungry, this would be funny." Cherry had never felt so hungry in all her life and the pain in her stomach was growing. The need to eat was compelling her to find a solution to the problem.

It seemed the aliens wouldn't allow obvious solutions. They were looking for something different. Something smarter. Or perhaps a particular type of behavior.

That was when the answer came. "It's simple," she said. "We feed each other."

"Oh, of course," said Wilder. "The spoon's too long to reach my mouth, but not too long to reach someone else's."

"Feed each other?" Aubriot looked disgusted. "I'll go hungry, thanks. I climbed down from my highchair a long time ago."

"Don't be stupid," said Cherry. "You can't seriously say you'd rather starve than accept someone else feeding you?"

"That's exactly what I'm saying."

Cherry was ravenous, and she knew Aubriot had to feel the same. "Then you're a moron, and if you're a typical example of the human race, maybe we don't deserve to pass this test."

"Er, let's take it easy, huh?" said Kes. "Our extreme hunger is putting us on edge. Aubriot, you and I will feed each other. I promise I won't tell anyone."

Aubriot scowled. "You eat first."

"I'll feed you," Wilder said to Cherry, scooping up stew on her spoon.

For a moment Cherry feared she was wrong and the food would disappear as it reached her mouth. But the stew was real. It was the most delicious food she'd ever tasted. When she'd eaten a few mouthfuls, she insisted on feeding Wilder. She tipped the stew into the girl's mouth. But then as she tried scoop up more, both the spoon and the bowl disappeared. Her feeling of extreme hunger also went away.

"Sooo," said Kes, "our cooperativeness is being tested too."

"Or maybe our altruism?" Cherry suggested.

"The test isn't over yet," said Aubriot. "If it was, they would have lifted us out of this hole or returned it to ground level. We still have to figure out how to get out."

"Simple," said Kes. "It's the same principle. We have to cooperate. You're the tallest, and you're the strongest too. You have to lift out the rest of us."

"Me? Lift you guys out?" Aubriot looked doubtful. It wouldn't be hard for him to help them all out of the hole, but he was taking a while to accept the idea. "I suppose I don't have a choice," he concluded finally. He pointed at Wilder. "You first, kid."

He walked to the wall and knelt on one knee. "Climb onto my shoulders."

Wilder went over to him and assessed where she needed to step. She rested a hand against the wall for balance and then placed a foot on his right shoulder.

"Take your bloody boots off first."

"Stop whining," said Cherry. "You're only going to complicate things. This isn't real, remember? Wilder, climb up."

Aubriot didn't protest again. Wobbling a little, Wilder climbed onto his other shoulder and leaned into the wall. He slowly rose to his feet, pushing her upward. As soon as her chest was above ground level, she climbed out.

"I made it." She grinned down at them.

His face a picture of disgruntlement, Aubriot said, "You next, smartarse."

Knowing the moniker was meant for her, Cherry did the same. It was harder with only one hand, but she managed it.

Aubriot's complaining tones sounded from down below. "What I want to know is, who's going to lift *me* up?"

"I'm sure we'll figure it out," said Kes. A few moments later, the scientist's freckled face appeared. Wilder and Cherry helped him out.

Now all three of them were out of the hole and Aubriot remained inside. Cherry was tempted to leave him there, but she doubted that they would pass the test.

In the end, they solved the problem by hanging Kes in, his hands outstretched, while she and Wilder held onto his legs, bracing themselves against the ground.

She heard Aubriot taking a short run up, and then a thud as he leapt. Kes grunted when Aubriot grabbed his arms. He began to slide in. She gripped his leg with all her might and forced her heels into the dusty, slippery ground.

"Ow!" Kes protested. "Be careful."

Aubriot was climbing over him to make his way onto level ground. Soon, he was standing up and looking pleased with himself. "That was a cinch." He appeared to award himself the credit for the group's success. "What's next?"

The words had barely left his mouth when the wasteland disappeared. They were in the bare chamber again, wearing their EVA suits.

The floor lurched, breaking the magnetic hold of Cherry's boots and sending her floating free. She twisted and turned in the zero-g. What had happened to the others? Everyone was in the same predicament. Wilder had been thrown above her.

"Screw this," Aubriot said. "If this is part of the test, it isn't funny."

Cherry said, "I don't think—"

"The station is under attack," an alien voice interrupted. "Scythians are attacking. Replace your helmets and return to your ship."

Thirty-Two

"Wilder, move!"

Scythians? Even here, at the heart of the Assembly?

"Wilder!"

Someone was pulling on her leg. Wilder looked down and saw Cherry's anxious features through her visor.

Aubriot was already halfway to the door, propelled by his suit's thrusters.

"Come on." Cherry glided up and grabbed her elbow, forcing her forward.

Snapping out of her confusion, Wilder quickly replaced her helmet, pressed her thumbs to her palms, and aimed herself at the exit, which was opening. "Do you think the Scythians followed us here?"

Cherry was keeping pace with her. "Who knows? But I hope not. I hope we aren't the reason for this attack. I'd hate for them to want to kill us so badly."

A flash of light lit Wilder's peripheral vision and the chamber jumped.

"Shit," said Cherry.

Wilder followed the woman's gaze. A hole had appeared in the wall. White-hot, molten metal dripped from its edges. Through the hole was the blackness of space and cold, hard starlight.

But that was not all. As she gaped at the hull breach, a ship sped across the gap—a crescent-shaped ship. A Scythian warship. It immediately reminded her of the second attack on the colony. She was back in the infirmary, terrified as she awaited the arrival of the Scythian spiders, wondering what it felt like to be cut to death.

She pumped her thrusters harder. She doubted the kind, gentle Fila would leave them behind, even at the risk of their own lives. Yet the longer the Fila waited for their human passengers to return, the greater the chance their ship would be destroyed.

They sped toward the exit, where Kes was waiting. When they passed through they found Aubriot also waiting, impatiently, above the entry platform. The station was in chaos. Its inhabitants were swarming through the central void, many no doubt also trying to return to their ships.

"What took you?" Aubriot barked.

"Does anyone know the way back?" asked Kes. "My visor display is down."

Wilder realized hers was too. The station's comm was out.

"I think I know," said Cherry. "Follow me."

"No," said Aubriot. "I definitely know. It's this way."

He flew into empty space. As Wilder joined him, a gap opened in the hull high above. The station had taken another direct hit. It was lucky the place wasn't pressurized. Otherwise everyone would have been forced into space.

As it was, thousands of aliens were trying to leave. Though the place was huge, she hadn't imagined it held so many. Suited up like her and her companions, creatures of all kinds of body forms and sizes were moving across the void or making their way over the walls. Militarized vehicles were also crossing the space. Three headed for the hull breach, perhaps to attempt to seal or to guard it.

Wilder flew on Aubriot's heels, sticking as close as she could. It would be easy for everyone to be separated in the mad confusion.

A brilliant light flooded the station's interior, and then was gone. The flash seemed to have come from overhead. The three military vehicles stood in a triangle at the gap emitting pulses of light, focusing on one, unseen spot.

Aubriot dropped like a stone and touched down at an exit. Was it the right one? Wilder wasn't sure. It didn't look familiar, but she swooped to join him.

"This isn't the right place," said Kes as he caught up. "I'm sure of it. We came in over there." He indicated another exit three or four hundred meters away, where aliens were swarming, trying to get out.

"Too crowded," said Aubriot. "Let's try to get back to the ship from here." He disappeared into the opening.

Wilder hesitated.

"We'll have to go with him," said Cherry. "It's that or split up. And he's right. It's chaos over there."

Wilder ducked into the opening. Her feet dragged on the metal mesh floor. The passageway was wide and shallow, barely high enough to fly along. Aubriot glided swiftly ahead, angling his body forward to navigate the narrow space.

"I hope we're going the right way," said Kes. "I'd hate to be caught on this station if the Scythians swarm the place."

"I don't understand," Cherry said. "If they want to kill everyone, all they need to do is release their spiders."

"Maybe they already have," Kes replied. "Or maybe they don't want to kill everyone. Maybe the Assembly knows the voltage trick Wilder discovered and the Scythians know about it."

A tight corner appeared. Wilder flew around it, but her visor smacked into the edge of an exit. Simultaneously, her head hit the inside of her visor. Bright points of light swam in her vision. Pain lanced across her skull. Someone was tugging at her shoulder.

It was Kes. "Are you okay?"

"Be careful," said Cherry. "Stay with us."

Screwing up her eyes in an effort to focus, Wilder gave them a weak thumbs up.

Still holding her shoulder, Kes began to pull her along. Wilder boosted her own thrusters. "I'm okay. I can do it." Her zero-g nausea was returning ten fold. She was reminded of Aubriot's warning.

No puking in your helmet, kid.

She wasn't sure she would be able to avoid it.

Apparently reassured she could move by herself, Kes released his hold on her. Aubriot was far ahead now. She increased her speed to keep up with Cherry and Kes, who were trying to catch up to him.

A ball of flame tore down a side passage and erupted into the main passageway. The flame enveloped her and she slapped into a wall, her head once more cracking painfully against her helmet. Darkness encroached and overwhelmed her.

When she came around, all she could see was afterglow. She hadn't had time to close her eyes, and the flame had blinded her. She flailed, trying to find a solid surface. Her feet couldn't touch anything. She reached out but her hands made no contact.

Where was she?

"Cherry?"

Silence.

"Kes?"

Nothing.

"Is anyone there?"

Fearing she would fly into a wall, she didn't fire her thrusters. She blinked hard, trying to restore her vision.

Moments later, she saw the inside of her visor, smeared red. Beyond the red of her blood lay diamond points of brilliance. She was looking into open space. She was outside the station! She swung around. The station was to her rear. On her right a deformed mess of metal surrounded a gash in the hull. The explosion had come from the inside. Had that once been the passageway?

She couldn't believe it. She had drifted through a tear ripped in the hull. Had a gas tank been hit? She was lucky to be alive. If she hadn't had the protection of her suit she probably wouldn't have survived.

She hailed her companions again but received no answer. Where had they gone? What had happened to them? She hoped the only reason they weren't answering was because her helmet comm was out.

From her position she had a view of the space station's exterior. What she could see of it remained intact, though in the distance ships were skimming the stars: smaller Scythian attack ships and others she didn't recognize. She guessed they were the station's ships defending it.

Through the slash the explosion had cut, she saw forms moving. Blast survivors were trying to get out.

She had to do the same.

She boosted her thrusters to carry her toward the rift. When she entered the space she found the passageway was full, though the beings were smaller than her. She rose until she was moving just below the ceiling.

That was when she heard the hiss. Despite the chaos of the scene, she heard nothing of it. No sound carried through the vacuum. And since her comm appeared to be broken, all she could hear was her own labored breathing.

Except for the hiss. Where was it coming from? As she sped along, she peered at the blood smear on her visor. Had the screen cracked? Or had shrapnel torn a hole in her suit?

It didn't matter. She was losing air. Her suit would increase its atmosphere production to try to maintain pressure, but she didn't know how bad the leak was. She didn't know if she had time to make it back to the Fila ship before more atmosphere escaped than her suit could replace. If the pressure dropped too low she would pass out and eventually die.

Where was the Fila ship? Was she heading in the right direction? Or had she turned around after the

blast?

She didn't know. All she could do was continue in the direction of the flow of traffic and hope that would lead her to her ship.

A portal lay up ahead. Could it be the entrance to the umbilicus? Aliens in the passageway were piling through it, so maybe it wasn't. Unless they were hoping to escape on someone else's ship.

When she drew nearer, she swept downward, angling her head to peek into the hatch. There was no umbilicus tunnel. The opening led directly into an airlock. The space was crowded with aliens.

Small and six-limbed, they milled about, trying to cram as many of themselves in as possible. One of the creatures facing her reared up on its two hindmost legs and pulled its four other limbs inward. It seemed to be looking at her through its long, angled helmet. Was it inviting her to come aboard?

She couldn't take the risk. If the aliens breathed a different atmosphere from humans she would die. She had to find her own people, and soon. That hiss in her suit hadn't gone away.

She raised a hand in a vague hope the creature would understand the gesture of thanks and prepared to move on. She fired her thrusters, the left a little more softly than the right, so she turned around. Without warning, the passageway juddered and debris scattered. Up ahead, a new gap yawned. Another direct hit. To her left the aliens who had been trying to escape were in disarray. Some had been injured and their fellows were trying to help them, dragging them into the airlock. The last were scrambling through the exit.

The ones already inside the airlock gestured to the others in the same movement Wilder had seen seconds ago. They were telling the later arrivals to come in, to hurry.

She had to hurry too. She was having problems breathing. Her chest was working harder, but she wasn't feeling any benefit. Her suit's atmosphere was getting low. As she felt for the pressure pads to fire her thrusters, her thumbs felt numb and clumsy.

The aliens were now all inside their airlock and the passageway was empty. But their hatch didn't close. Some of the creatures ran their appendages along the door slots and pressed controls.

But the doors weren't closing. The mechanism had been damaged by the blast. If they couldn't close the airlock door, would they be able to disconnect from the station? Wilder doubted it. Even if they opened the inner doors, allowing the atmosphere to escape, their vessel couldn't depart unless they closed the outer doors.

The aliens couldn't escape.

She was feeling dizzy and faint. She had to try to get back to the *Opportunity*. Her thumbs finally found the thruster activation pads. As she moved away, she caught a glimpse of one of the trapped aliens stepping back into the passageway. What was the creature doing? She pressed a hand to the wall to stop and watch.

The alien went to a panel next to the airlock exit. At the touch of one of its stubby limbs, the panel sprang open.

Manual override.

The creature was trying to activate the station's manual override on the airlock portal. It was the station side of the connection that was the problem.

But if the alien managed to activate the override the station exit would close and the alien would be left behind.

Unless...

She turned and headed back, gesticulating at the alien in the passageway.

"Wait!" she yelled, knowing the creature couldn't hear her and even if it could, it wouldn't understand.

It lifted a limb, ready to press the controls.

She reached it just in time, colliding with it and forcing it away from the panel. Before it could float too far, she reached out and grabbed it. Holding one of its limbs, she tossed the alien unceremoniously into its companions.

At the same time, black night began to fold over her.

A flat disc sat in the center of the open panel.

She hit it.

Just before she lost consciousness, the hatch slid shut.

Thirty-Three

When Cherry awoke, she felt soft grips on her arm, waist, and thighs. The back of her head nestled against a cupped surface. She opened her eyes and jerked in amazement. She was back inside the small room in the space station. Her EVA suit floated free and she was breathing air.

The grips on her body and the suction on the back of her head released. The movement pushed her slightly forward. She hung in zero-g, trying to understand what had happened.

A moment earlier, the station had been under attack by the Scythians. She'd been trying to escape along a low passageway. She'd been hit in an explosion and her suit had been leaking air. She'd lost Wilder and the others.

Then she'd seen those little aliens also trying to escape. They'd had some problems with the station airlock hatch, so she'd helped them.

That was the last thing she remembered.

And before that, all those tests, and the giant Assembly 'organizers'. And... what else? She'd been here, in this same room.

She grabbed her suit. Whatever had happened, it was now over. Or at least this part of it was. She'd been released from the grips.

She put on her suit, fastened the front with one hand, and pulled her helmet over her head. The station map had reappeared on the visor. As soon as the seal clicked shut, a rectangular seam appeared in the wall and a door opened into a black void beyond.

Activating her thrusters, she glided out into the void. In the blackness a small light shone—a helmet light. She directed herself toward it. The other person had clearly seen her too because the figure moved to meet her.

"Cherry?"

"Kes, it's you. Do you know where the others are? And what the hell just happened?"

"You sound as confused as I am." Kes's familiar freckled face grew more distinct as he drew closer. "Let's find the others first, then we can compare notes. Ah! I spot someone."

He was looking behind her. She spun around and saw a second figure. Though it became clear a few seconds later that it was Aubriot, she felt surprisingly happy to see him. The familiarity of both men was a warm contrast to the strange experience she'd undergone.

"Anyone else getting a sense of deja vu?" Aubriot asked.

"You aren't alone," said Kes. "It should be about now that Wilder turns up."

A bright light shone in the darkness as the door to Wilder's cell opened. The girl's form was silhouetted as she floated out. Then the door closed and only her helmet light was visible.

When Cherry floated closer to her, she saw Wilder's panicked look. "Don't worry. I think we've all experienced something very odd. You aren't the only one."

"Thank the stars! I thought I was going mad."

Kes said, "I think I'm right in saying we've all experienced this scenario before?"

"I certainly have," said Cherry.

"Me too," said Aubriot. "We all met out here after being scanned—or whatever it was they did—narrowly avoiding the anal probe."

"This isn't a time for jokes," said Kes.

"All right, Ginger. Keep your hair on."

One of Cherry's fears was allayed. She'd been wondering if she was in a simulation and the previous experience had been reality, rather than the other way around, as she suspected. But Aubriot's words set her mind at rest. It was definitely him. Either that or the Assembly had created a remarkably realistic copy.

"Let's go over what each of us remembers," said Cherry. She related the events from the moment she'd left the scanning chamber the first time, including the tests in the desert, the Scythian attack, and helping the friendly aliens to escape.

They had all experienced something extremely similar, though they didn't go into details.

"It seems clear to me what's happened," said Kes. "We never left those rooms where we removed our suits. We thought we'd undergone an analysis of our anatomy, but in fact we were being subjected to simulations so the Assembly could judge our reactions."

"Do you think we did the right things?" Wilder asked.

"I'm not sure," said Kes. "I expect we'll find out soon."

"I think it was definitely the right decision to go back and help those aliens escape," said Cherry. "After all, the Assembly knows we need its help, but why should it offer it to us if we aren't prepared to help other species in return?"

"But at the risk of our own lives?" Aubriot said. "That's a bit too much to ask."

"Is it?" said Kes. "If the Assembly sends troops to help defend us from the Scythians, those beings will be risking their lives for no personal gain or benefit. It seems right to expect the same potential sacrifice from us in return."

"Uh, our dots are flashing," said Wilder.

Cherry checked her map display. They were being directed toward a place at the edge of the station. A tube ran from the glowing green circular portal that was their next destination. "I think I can see the umbilicus to the *Opportunity.* Are we being sent home?"

"What?" said Aubriot. "No, we can't be. Surely we get to meet these creatures who messed with our heads? They can't send us off without at least letting us meet them face to face."

"We might only have to go back and rest for a while," Kes said. "Keep your hair on."

Wilder chuckled.

"Whatever the Assembly intend, we don't have any choice except to do what they tell us." Cherry fired her thrusters. One of the dots representing her group broke off. After orienting herself in the rough direction of the green glow on the map, she moved toward it.

Soon, a wide, shallow, pale light appeared in the darkness. They were moving toward the opening they'd entered from earlier.

"Anyone else wondering if they're still dreaming?" Kes asked.

"I thought about it," Cherry replied, "but I concluded that the current Aubriot was too authentically obnoxious."

"Hey!" the man himself protested.

Then he murmured, "There's only one Aubriot."

They crossed the edge of the vast space in the center of the space station. Life seemed to be continuing as normal here, the assorted strangely formed beings going about their business. Cherry remembered vividly the battle scene from the simulation, where the station had been ripped open and Scythian ships had skimmed the starscape. It had all seemed so real.

They passed along the passageway to the umbilicus. No other aliens crossed their path. No small, six-limbed creatures were trying to escape. No one required rescuing. Was the species in the simulation real or had the Assembly fabricated them too?

When she reached the umbilicus, she caught the edge of the opening to bring herself to a stop, and then grabbed the line. After clipping her suit to it, she moved down to allow the others room to do the same.

"I'm so hungry," said Wilder. "I could eat a ration bar!"

Cherry chuckled. She was heartily sick of the Guardians' food too. They'd eaten nothing else for the entire journey. But the regular food had fattened Wilder up a bit, despite her understandable aversion to it.

Because she'd arrived at the umbilicus first, Cherry was at the front. Wilder was behind her, followed by Kes and then Aubriot. They were slowly drawn along the flexible tunnel. Cherry would have preferred to fly down it on thrusters, but she could see how using the line prevented collisions in the restricted space.

She turned to talk to Wilder, but as she did, a ripple passed through the umbilicus. Wilder's eyes widened and her mouth gaped as her face drained of color. Cherry snapped her head around.

The umbilicus had been blasted away. Only two or three meters in front, the tunnel had disappeared. The end was a molten mess. Some distance beyond them, the *Opportunity* hung in space.

Something appeared at the end of the shorn umbilicus.

"Get down!" yelled Aubriot.

Cherry grabbed Wilder and ducked. Pulse fire flew over her head. Before Cherry got a good look at whatever Aubriot was firing at, the thing had retreated.

"Wilder," said Cherry, unclipping her friend's suit from the line, "get behind Aubriot."

"I can—"

"DON'T make me tell you again." Cherry pulled her weapon from her shoulder and aimed it at the gap.

Wilder fired her thrusters and flew toward the rear.

A silvery, articulated limb appeared at the torn umbilicus's edge. Cherry fired, hitting it. The limb quickly withdrew.

"How do we know this isn't another simulation?" asked Kes.

"Does it matter?"

"What the fuck's going on?" Aubriot asked, gliding to her side. "This wasn't on the itinerary."

"We never had an itinerary, remember?"

"Yeah, I was forgetting." Aubriot edged forward.

"Where are you going?"

"Cherry," said a voice, "this is Quinn."

"Oh, he can talk to us now, can he?" said Aubriot.

"Quinn, can you tell us what's happening?" asked Cherry. "We've been cut off."

"A Scythian ship has slipped past the station's defenses. We think they want to capture you. Assembly defense vessels are on their way."

"Capture us? Why? If the Scythians want humans, all they have to do is go to Concordia and pick some up."

"Or they may wish to kill you," Quinn said.

"Makes more sense," Kes muttered. "Killing us is an effective way of preventing us from forming an alliance with the Assembly."

"I'm sorry we cannot come to your aid," said Quinn. "We cannot fire on the Scythian ship when it's in such close proximity to the station. But help is coming. You only need to hold out a little longer."

A small, crescent-shaped vessel swept into the space between the remains of the umbilicus and the *Opportunity.* Even against the threads' vessel the Scythian ship looked tiny. Long tethers stretched from each point of the crescent, and at the end of each tether hung creatures in articulated EVA suits.

Cherry fired again. Aubriot began laying down fire too. Pulses came from behind them as Kes and Wilder also took shots.

One of the creatures was hit. It collapsed and its tether retracted, pulling it in.

"Ahhhh!"

Aubriot had been hit too. In her peripheral vision, Cherry saw him falter and almost release his weapon. Then he gripped it tighter and continued firing.

The pointed tip of the Scythian ship opened to receive its fallen fighter.

Light erupted above and splashed across the vessel. The Assembly defense had arrived. When the light cleared, the enemy ship's hull had darkened. It suddenly veered off, trailing its remaining tethered soldier. The tether snapped, leaving the creature spinning in space. A second blast from the Assembly ship annihilated it.

Across tens of meters of open space, the *Opportunity* waited.

"The airlock is open," said Quinn.

Aubriot's weapon floated free from his grasp and his head dropped forward.

"Aubriot's been hit," said Cherry. "Move the ship to us, Quinn. I don't want to try to fly him across that open space."

"Understood." The *Opportunity* edged closer.

Thirty-Four

The colony had grown. The humans had increased their numbers and new habitations had sprung up. Settlements grew around the mines in the mountains. Though it took nine orbits of the planet around its star, the tunnel through the mountains was finished. The two halves of the continent were connected. Next came a bridge over the mighty river beyond the mountain range.

Humans built dwellings on the previously uninhabited farther side. They removed the native vegetation, and fields appeared on the rich alluvial soil. A new growing district was established, producing food for the ever-growing population. Next to the river dwelt gatherers of nutritious river plants. Other inhabitants dug the soil and extracted subterranean fungi.

Night and day, vehicles moved up and down the long roads covering the land from the mountains to the manufacturing site, the habitation near the remains of the forest, the original growing district, and the oceanside metropolis.

Now the humans had crossed the ocean to the second continent, new settlements appeared on its vast plains and desert oases. The people who lived in them were energy harvesters. Desert dwellers built and maintained solar farms, and plainsmen harvested the wind. Long cables crossed the ocean, sending power.

When the Scythians saw the data giving this information, they were glad. The humans were becoming independent of their aquatic friends. They no longer relied on their allies for power. This was a development that fed into the

Scythians' long-term plan. A self-sufficient population was exactly what they needed. The less interference the water-dwellers offered, the better.

The Scythians also watched the humans' society. Knowledge of its structure would be useful in the future. As had been the case since the colony's early days, the majority of the humans were juveniles born on the planet. Soon after they reached adulthood the humans began to breed. A typical family would include one adult male, one adult female, and as many as ten offspring, though there was some variation.

All activity and progress had been registered by the original drone and transmitted to its creators. When the humans spread to the second continent, the drone abandoned its geostationary position and begun to orbit. The device continued to send data according to its priority system.

Eventually, the Scythians made the decision that a single probe was insufficient. They sent out a new command. As soon as it was received, the probe immediately put the command into effect. For the duration of approximately seventy-eight seconds, it was non-operational. This was because it was reproducing.

After a burst of energy from its power source, nearly every constituent part of the device returned to its original liquiform state. For several seconds, the tiny probe hung in high orbit, a shiny, metallic blob. Then a notch appeared, running along the center of the misshapen globe. The notch deepened to a channel, setting the liquid metal quivering and rippling. The blob began to round into two parts. Then it split in two.

The shiny beads moved in a circular motion, orbiting each other. As they moved, they transformed. Tiny scanners took shape at their outer edges. Inside, smooth metal hardened into structures to receive data. Within each new drone, a transmitter appeared.

The two new devices were identical, but on one of them minuscule solar thermal rockets fired. The powered drone edged away from its twin and headed for the space above the second continent's main settlement, where it halted. It would perform the same function as its partner, receiving data and transmitting it to its creators.

Two probes now hung above the planet, observing all the humans did. The devices measured the population, scanned for technological development, and watched for signs of the humans' defensive capabilities.

In their home system, the Scythians continued to carefully assess the data. They were satisfied. The humans had not taken proper steps to defend themselves, despite developing technology that would have made it possible. It was evidence the species possessed a modicum of intelligence. The humans guessed that such a move would be an invitation to attack.

But in the end, their prudence would not save them. They could not avoid the inevitable. The day was approaching when their masters would return. Then, if the humans had changed their minds about accepting Scythian overlordship, defeating and subjugating them would be quick and decisive.

Thirty-Five

The mood in the living quarters was somber. Aubriot was in pain from his wound, which made him more difficult and acerbic than ever, Wilder and Kes seemed to have finally run out of questions to ask the Fila, and Cherry felt a total failure.

The *Opportunity* had received no message from the Assembly since it had departed the space station. All the aliens had stated was that in light of the almost-successful attempt by the Scythians on the humans' lives, it could not guarantee their safety and they must leave immediately. No word had arrived, official or unofficial, to confirm they had been accepted into the alliance.

Though it had not been directly stated, Quinn had also said the Assembly had to face the fact that the space station's location had been revealed to the Scythians, possibly due to the humans going there. Their presence would only excite further interest from their enemies, and the station could be subject to a full-scale attack.

Had the Scythians managed to follow the trace of the *Opportunity*? Or had they learned its coordinates through other means? Had the aggressive aliens been scouting out the station, recognized the *Opportunity*, and seized the moment? Or had they gone there with the express intent of preventing the humans' acceptance into the Assembly? They would probably never know.

All Cherry knew was that when they returned home she would have to look Ethan in the eye and tell him she hadn't secured the future of Concordia —that two thousand people's lives remained at risk. The faith and trust he had in her had been misplaced. She'd already made up her mind that when she got back she would resign her position as second in command and only work on her farm. Maybe that would be one thing she could do right.

"Quinn," she said, feeling suddenly homesick, "have you heard anything from the colony since we left?"

"We haven't received any messages. I believe your colony doesn't possess the technology to send one."

"But couldn't they send a message via your seeding ship?"

"The seeding ship departed the system not long after we did."

"Aren't the Fila on Concordia in touch with the seeding ship?" Kes asked. "Our people could have tried to contact us through them."

"We've received no message," Quinn repeated. "It's possible your people did try to send one via the seeding ship, but the distances the ship travels are far in excess of this trip we've taken to the Assembly. The times involved..."

"You're all forgetting how far we've traveled, too," said Aubriot. "And at near light speed."

"What does that mean?" Cherry asked.

Aubriot, who was lying in his sleeping bag, only put a hand over his face and shook his head. His shoulder had been badly burned when he took a hit from the Scythians, and there was nothing aboard the ship to kill the pain. The acceleration session they had undergone when they left the space station must have been agony for him. Since then, he'd rarely spoken and when he had it had been with a tone that put a stop to any further conversation.

"Would you like me to send a message to Concordia, Cherry?" Quinn asked. "I could ask a contact there to pass it on to the colony."

She considered the offer. What would she say to Ethan and the rest of them? How to frame the statement that, aside from the threads, the colony had no one to help save them? It would be better to give them a few more weeks before delivering the bad news. The first harvest was in and the farmers would already have sown and planted next season's crop. Everyone would be anticipating a happy, safe future. She wanted to delay crushing their hopes for a little longer. "Let's just go home. I can tell them everything that's happened when we get there."

"Very well," said Quinn. "On the subject of returning home, I must ask you to return to your safety seats. We are about to accelerate again."

Aubriot groaned.

Cherry felt a pang of pity. For once, the man's complaints were justified. And, though he was just as much an asshole as ever, they owed their lives to his quick reaction when the Scythians destroyed the umbilicus.

She walked to his side and held out her hand. "Help you up?"

He removed his hand from his face and regarded her through narrowed eyes, but then he accepted her offer. Kes went to his other side and together they helped him stand.

His ship's suit had been destroyed at the site of his wound. Kes had cut away the burned material, exposing the skin of his shoulder, but there wasn't much more anyone could do. The threads seemed to have a poor understanding of human medical needs, and the *Opportunity* carried no medical equipment. Quinn had seemed confused when asked about it, and Cherry remembered his question when they'd first met, asking why she hadn't regrown her arm. She guessed that when threads were injured they simply regenerated the damaged part.

Kes offered for Aubriot to lean on him.

"I can walk," Aubriot snapped. "My legs weren't hit."

Nevertheless, he rested a hand on Cherry's shoulder as they stepped to the reclined seats.

Thirty-Six

Wilder debated whether starving to death would be preferable to eating yet another ration bar. It was a tough decision. She opened the cabinet holding the bars. It had been full at the start of the journey, but now they only covered the bottom few centimeters. Did they have enough to last them all the way home? After considerable prodding, Quinn had given a reluctant and vague estimate of 'probably about another week's journey in human time', but no one seemed convinced he was making an accurate conversion from whatever weird measure of time the Fila used.

Deciding she could stomach the Guardians' ration bars for another seven days but not another day longer, she reached into the cabinet and grabbed one. After ripping open the wrapper she took a bite. Amazingly, the bar tasted even more bland and boring than ever—something she hadn't thought possible.

She chewed mechanically, grinding the substance into pieces just small enough to swallow, trying to get the process over with as quickly as she could. To distract herself, she thought about her forest hamlet and her friends who lived there. How had they gotten along with improvements while she'd been gone? They must have built the latrines. Tycho had promised to would organize it. And Stephie had said she wanted to build some more platforms on nearby trees. Word of the success of the tree village had spread and several kids had asked what they had to do to live there.

The forest would be the first place Wilder would go as soon as they landed. The next place would be the refectory. There was bound to be a new and exciting menu made from all the delicious produce being harvested when they left. Even if the dishes weren't new and interesting, they would still be a hundred times better than ration bars.

Kes appeared. "Mind if I join you?"

"Of course not."

He opened the storage cabinet and took out a ration bar.

"Do you know what the others are doing?" Wilder asked.

"Cherry's talking to Quinn and Aubriot's practicing with a weapons panel Quinn made for him."

"He's what?!"

"He's been bothering the poor creature about learning how to operate the Fila's defense weapons. Quinn caved, and now Aubriot's gotten his way. Again. You know what he's like."

"I do. He's obsessed with war and fighting."

"Harsh, but true." Kes perched on a stool and unwrapped his bar, tucking the empty packet into a pocket. "To be fair, Aubriot's obsession with weaponry and combat saved us once. So I wouldn't condemn the man too much for it."

"Really? I didn't know he'd saved the colony."

"You didn't? You must be one of the few people he hasn't told. He was aboard the *Mistral* during the first Scythian attack. By all accounts, he saved our bacon."

"Bacon?"

"A delicious foodstuff that probably hasn't been eaten for millennia."

"Don't tell me...It came from dead animals, right?"

"Pigs, to be exact."

"Ugh." She gave a shudder. "I don't know how you could do it. Eat something that once breathed and walked, I mean. A living thing. That's so disgusting."

"Plants are living things too, you know. And we have to kill animals to grow them. On Concordia it's mostly insects, but on Earth we killed wildlife that wanted to eat our crops. Mice, deer, birds."

"But you didn't eat them. And anyway, it isn't the same. Plants—"

"Is it time for our thrice-daily dose of blandness already?" Aubriot strode into the room.

"According to my stomach it is," Kes replied.

Wilder took another bite and munched the tasteless mouthful, feeling slightly sick at Kes's mention of eating animals. She could see how people might be forced to do it if they were starving, but *choosing* to kill and eat another living thing? She shuddered again.

Aubriot helped himself to two ration bars but he didn't sit down. He leaned against the closed cabinet and took large bites from the first bar, demolishing it in three bites. He took his time over the second. Between mouthfuls he said, "What I want to know is, does this taste as insipid as I think it does, or am I only imagining it?"

"Do you mean, are we still in the Assembly's simulation?" asked Kes. "I keep wondering that myself."

"It isn't possible," said Wilder. "The most intelligent aliens in the galaxy couldn't fake something that tastes as boring as this."

Both men laughed. She was gratified at the reception to her joke. She liked Kes, and even Aubriot hadn't been quite such an asshole since his shoulder had healed up.

Cherry arrived, and the mood instantly fell. She'd been down ever since they'd left the Assembly. Whenever Wilder saw her, Cherry looked lost and sad. It was clear she held herself responsible for everything that had happened, though in fact most of it had been beyond her control. Wilder had tried talking to her about their time at the space station, but Cherry only kindly patted her on the shoulder and told her not to worry.

"What are you talking about?" asked Cherry.

"Ration bars," Wilder replied, "and the simulation at the space station."

"Oh." Cherry pushed Aubriot out of her way and opened the cabinet.

"You know," said Kes, "I just realized we never went over in detail what we all experienced while in the simulation. It would be interesting to see if there were any differences."

"Would it?" Cherry asked.

"I think so. Come on, let's do it. It'll help pass the time."

"Okay, Ginger," Aubriot said. "I'm game. You go first."

Kes began to describe the events at the station as he remembered them. For the most part they were identical to what Wilder remembered. The four giant aliens, the wasteland, the cage, and the pit, everything was just as she recalled. Then he moved on to the attack. His description of the tight turn in the passageway they'd gone down evoked a familiar discomfort and fear. When it came to the moment that the small beings were trying to escape, Kes told the story from his own perspective. He was the person who had to face the choice of saving himself or helping the alien who was going to die. They had all been that person in the scenario, naturally.

When he related how he had gone back and operated the manual override himself, Aubriot broke in.

"Now, that's where our stories diverge. I ignored the situation and headed back to the ship, like anyone with half a brain would have done."

"You left that little creature to die?" Wilder asked. "How could you?"

"How could I? How could I not? Why would I sacrifice myself for someone who meant nothing to me?"

"What are you talking about?" Cherry snapped. "No one means anything to you."

"You all fell for it, didn't you?" Aubriot asked. "You all died to save that little nothing."

"Fell for it?" asked Wilder "It was part of the test! We were *supposed* to save the alien. The other tests were assessing our cooperativeness and empathy. The final test was to tell if we were prepared to help other intelligent beings too, not only other humans."

"I think you're right," said Kes. "That makes sense."

"And you failed the test." Cherry addressed Aubriot, her expression sharp.

"No way. I passed, with flying colors. I took the only sensible course of action. I saved myself. That's the intelligent thing to do. I've said it from the beginning. The Assembly wanted to assess our level of intelligence before they allowed us to join. There's no point in having an ally as dumb as a sack of rocks."

"No," said Cherry. "You might have acted smart, but you weren't being civilized. Civilized people help each other. That's what makes a civilization."

"Rubbish. Civilizations are built on competition and technological advancement, not namby pamby *feelings*."

Kes said, "I hope Aubriot's wrong. Otherwise we did fail. Faced with the situation of sacrificing ourselves to save another, three out of four of us made the sacrifice. As representatives of humanity, we were either seventy-five percent correct or seventy-five percent wrong."

"Shit," said Aubriot. "In that case, we must have failed. All thanks to you three and your stupid decisions."

"Excuse me for interrupting," came Quinn's voice over the ship's comm, "but we have received a message from the Assembly. It asks us to tell you it regrets that it was unable to meet with you as individuals and discuss the future relationship between itself and humanity. However, after a detailed study of your behaviors while aboard the station, and in view of the current precarious position in which your species finds itself in regard to the Scythian Dominion, the Assembly grants that humanity has passed the preliminary standards to allow acceptance into its body."

"We passed!" Cherry exclaimed.

"Fantastic," said Kes. "Now we might be able to find some more allies."

Quinn said, "You are now able to begin talks with other members, though it may be a slow process."

Wilder popped the last part of her ration bar into her mouth and chewed.

The food suddenly tasted a whole lot better.

Thirty-Seven

"I expect you'll be glad to see Ethan again," said Aubriot.

Cherry was alone with him in the living quarters. Kes and Wilder had already collected their stuff and left to go to the airlock.

Cherry paused as she pushed clothes into her bag. She hadn't forgotten the spat she'd had with Aubriot, when he'd accused her of harboring feelings for Ethan. She'd thought it over many times. "I will." She left it at that. She didn't owe Aubriot anything, least of all an attempt to spare his hurt feelings, which she guessed were more to do with his pride than any affection for her.

He had been looking away when he spoke. He raised his eyes to meet her gaze. "Do you think he's been missing you?" His expression was neutral. 'Poker-faced,' he'd called it once when she remarked on his ability to convey no emotion at all. A useful business tactic in the old days, he'd said.

"Maybe a little." She was attempting to also not give away her true feelings. "I'd say he counts me as one of his good friends. I'm looking forward to seeing him, Cariad, and their little girl. I expect she's grown quite a bit while we've been gone."

Aubriot snorted. "Yeah, I expect she has." He returned to his packing.

She was tempted to ask him what he meant by his pointed remark, but she left it. She didn't want to give in to his play for attention.

They'd brought very little with them when they'd boarded the threads' ship, and so it didn't take long to pack their few items. On her way to the airlock, she stopped off to have a last word with Quinn. Though she could have spoken to him simply by speaking aloud, she preferred to see the creature face-to-face. She didn't know when she might see him again, and she knew she would miss him. Her feelings about the threads had changed over the course of the journey, though she didn't think she would ever be in love with the idea they were named after her.

Aubriot passed through the cylindrical room without a word.

She said, "Quinn, I want to thank you and the rest of the crew for taking us to the space station."

He was floating almost motionless behind the transparent wall. Over the weeks, she had learned to distinguish him from the other creatures. The patterning differed slightly from creature to creature, like fingerprints.

"We appreciate your thanks, but we are only doing what is correct. If we can infer anything from our skirmishes with the Scythians on the course of our trip, it is that in the future they will bring more challenges and threats to all intelligent species. They are a violent, aggressive force within the galaxy. We must all work together to resist them."

"Do you think they might return to Concordia soon?" Would they have any respite before having to ward off another attack?

"Soon is a very inexact word. Galactic time cannot be measured in such vague terms. But I believe the Scythians will return and demand their tribute."

"And now that humans belong to the Assembly, can we expect some help in defending ourselves?"

"Your membership entitles you to request help, but these are large and general questions for another time. You should go now. I believe the others are waiting for you."

She nodded, but she didn't leave immediately. She raised her hand and placed it on the wall.

Quinn lifted a tentacle and placed it on the opposite side. "Ethan and I tried a similar gesture some time ago. It didn't go well for him in the end, unfortunately. Goodbye, Cherry, until the next time we meet."

When she reached the others, they had taken the Fila shuttles from the storage area and placed them in the airlock. Cherry climbed into the remaining empty one. She felt inexplicably tense about leaving Quinn and the *Opportunity*, though she was looking forward to seeing Concordia again, breathing fresh air, feeling the rain, and experiencing all the things she'd grown to love since disembarking the *Nova*. "Are we all ready?"

"More than ready," Kes replied.

"I'm not happy about having to take a shuttle down to the surface," said Wilder, "but I'll put up with it if it means going home."

Cherry lay down. Her hatch closed and she steeled herself for the final, claustrophobic trip.

The hatch to her shuttle slid open. The light was blinding. Unbearable.

She turned her head to the side and folded her arm over her eyes. Around her, she heard her companions' vocal reactions as their hatches also opened.

She guessed it must be midday. The sun seemed to be shining directly into their shuttles. After weeks of dim light aboard the threads' ship, it was going to take some time to accustom themselves to the normal light of day.

Keeping her arm firmly over her eyes, she sat up. Immediately, she felt what she'd been longing for: air moving over her skin. The breeze was only mild, but it was more than she'd felt for months. She breathed in, savoring the clean scent. "Hello?"

Was anyone was nearby? She hadn't asked Quinn specifically where their shuttles would set down, but she assumed it was about the same place from where they'd left.

"We're back," called Kes. "Is anyone there?"

He was also clearly as blinded as Cherry.

Looking downward, she removed her arm from her eyes, though she kept them closed. The light piercing her lids was bright red and firing sparks.

"This is crazy," said Aubriot gruffly. "Ahhh..." It sounded like he was trying to see.

She opened her eyelids a slit. Through her lashes, she could see her legs, the sides of her shuttle and...pavement. She stared in surprise, and then quickly shut her eyes again in pain.

Where had Quinn set them down? The last time she had seen pavement, it had been in the old settlement. But that had been many months ago, before the first Scythian attack. As far as she knew, no one had laid any pavement since then.

Perhaps the colony had progressed further than she'd thought it would in the months they'd been gone, which was great. What else had the colonists done? She would have to ask Ethan to give her a tour.

"Christ Almighty," Kes breathed.

What a weird thing to say. What did the words mean? He'd sounded surprised.

She tried opening her eyes again and discovered they'd become more accustomed to the blazing light. Lifting her head, she squinted and peered at her surroundings. "Stars!"

Buildings! Surrounding them were buildings taller than she'd ever seen, with small windows right to the top. The shuttles had landed in a paved courtyard. At its corners stood wide, bushy plants in pots.

She blinked rapidly and gripped the side of the shuttle. Was she dreaming? The uncertainty she'd dealt with ever since leaving the Assembly's simulation returned. What was she looking at? How could this all be real? It looked like a holo of old Earth.

"I don't believe it," said Kes, climbing out of his vessel. "How could they have done so much in such a short time? It's impossible."

Aubriot was already out and walking around. He touched a wall. "Such a short time? Has it been such a short time?"

Kes stared at him, his mouth agape. "Oh my god. We were traveling at close to light speed, Quinn told us, but I didn't think about it. Shit! How long have we been gone?"

Wilder remained seated in her vessel, her face pale and her eyes wide. "It's time dilation, right? I read about it, but...I-I didn't even think about it in relation to what we were doing."

A terrible fear was forming in Cherry's stomach.

"Actually," said Kes, "this is marvelous." Like Aubriot, his first impulse was also to touch a wall. He tilted back his head to peer at the top of the building. "Look at what's been accomplished while we were away. Look how much they've achieved. This place looks like a factory. Or maybe offices. I don't think anyone lives here, anyway, or they would have noticed us by now."

"Maybe no one's awake yet," said Wilder. "It's early morning."

Cherry looked at the sky. It was pale blue overlaid with pink. The girl was right. The brilliant light blinding them was only dawn sunlight. It could be dusk but the place was too quiet. "Why didn't Quinn tell us? He must have known that years have passed here while we've been gone."

"He probably thought we knew," said Aubriot.

"We have to find someone," said Wilder. "We have to tell them we're back."

Kes asked, "Will they even remember us?"

Cherry grimaced. She stood up and pointed at Aubriot. "*You knew!*" She glared at him, remembering his offhand comment when she mentioned that Meredith must have grown while they were away. How old would the baby be? Maybe she was a grown woman already. "How long have you known?"

"*Did* you know?" Kes asked. "How come you didn't say anything?"

"I didn't know for sure. I suppose I could've tried to get a straight answer out of Quinn, but what would have been the point?"

"You're right," said Kes. "We would only have spent the trip worrying about what was happening at home, or wondering what we were missing out on."

"Or the people we were missing," said Wilder.

Kes said, "Yes! Everyone's aged while we've been gone. By how much, I wonder?"

Wilder replied, "We're soon going to find out."

THIRTY-EIGHT

Wilder's mind was filled with the faces of the kids who'd lived in her tree village. Were they living there still? They were probably all adults now. Maybe they had their own kids.

She could hardly imagine it.

A sense of disorientation suddenly overwhelmed her. "Does anyone think that Quinn might have brought us to the wrong planet? This place reminds me of vids of old Earth."

"No," Kes replied. "We're definitely back on Concordia."

"How do you know?"

"Concordia smells different."

Aubriot nodded in agreement. "And Earth doesn't look anything like the old vids anymore. I'm going to find someone to ask what date it is. This is freaky. I feel like a time traveler."

"We *are* time travelers," said Kes.

Aubriot walked out of the courtyard and Cherry and Kes followed. Wilder climbed out of her shuttle to join them. The only exit from was a narrow lane. Buildings on each side towered six or seven stories high. What would she see at the end? What had happened to the forest and her tree homes? She'd put so much work into them. If Quinn had returned them to the same spot they had departed from, the forest and Sidhe should be nearby.

Shithole. A sudden pang in her chest made her realize she didn't think the underground settlement was such a bad place anymore. She would give a lot to see it as it had been when she left.

They reached the end of the lane.

As she surveyed the view, her pang disappeared and was replaced with deep sorrow. The forest was gone. Sidhe was gone too. In place of both of them was a wide concreted area marked with lines, like the space for parking vehicles at the original shuttle field.

"Pave paradise," said Aubriot.

"What?" Cherry asked.

"Doesn't matter."

Wilder's vision turned blurry. She hastily rubbed her eyes before the others saw her reaction, but Kes saw her anyway.

"It's okay." He put an arm over her shoulders. "Things change. That's life."

She took a deep breath and swallowed. "I shouldn't have hoped they would keep it. That was dumb. They obviously needed the space for people to park. And there are plenty more forests."

"Still, it's a shame they didn't keep Sidhe," said Kes. "For its historical value if nothing else."

"Maybe they wanted to forget the Second Scythian Attack," said Aubriot.

Beyond the parking lot stood rows of buildings alongside paved roads. How far did the built area stretch? Wilder couldn't see the end of it.

"Someone's coming," said Cherry.

Then Wilder heard it too: the whir of an engine. A moment later a vehicle appeared from the street opposite and drove to a bay before stopping. The vehicle was a similar design to the models brought aboard the *Nova*, but it wasn't one of them. The color was wrong and the lines were longer and smoother.

The four returned travelers watched in silence. A creeped-out feeling settled on Wilder as she waited for the driver to emerge. It was similar to how she used to feel around the Guardians. Even before she'd known they were androids, she'd seen them as otherworldly, coming from the future.

The vehicle door opened. A man stepped out, his gaze already focused on them, which was no surprise. He was probably wondering why four people were staring at him.

As soon as he was out, the vehicle's door closed automatically. Another difference from the ones from the *Nova*.

Aubriot called out, "Morning."

The man nodded. "Morning." He approached them. "Can I help you folks with something? Are you looking for your workplace? It's a little early. Nowhere is open yet."

Cherry went to speak, but Aubriot raised a hand to stop her. "I've always wanted to say this." He faced the man. "Can you tell me what year this is?"

The stranger laughed. When he saw they were not laughing along, he said, "You aren't serious, right? One of you might have been knocked on the head, but not all four of you."

Then, suddenly, his gaze shot to Cherry's missing arm, his mouth gaped, and he raised a hand to his forehead. "Are you the party who left on the Fila ship? Have you finally returned? They said you'd be back one day. No, you can't be. This is a joke, isn't it? Is someone recording this?" He peered around and looked over his shoulder.

"We are who you think we are," said Cherry, impatiently. "Now will you answer the question and tell us what year it is?"

He shook his head. "Unbelievable. And am I the first person you've spoken to?"

"The year," Aubriot growled.

"Sorry. It's day one, number twelve of the second month, one hundred and six."

"One hundred and six!" Cherry echoed.

Aubriot only lifted his eyebrows.

Everyone Wilder had known had aged a hundred and six years.

"Don't forget Concordia's orbit is twice the speed of Earth's," Aubriot said to Kes.

"Thanks," he breathed. "I *was* forgetting that. But...fifty-three years is still a helluva long time."

"When did you arrive?" the man asked. "Have you been waiting here all night? I'm Evan, by the way."

"We got here about fifteen minutes ago," said Kes.

"I need to sit down." Cherry's legs collapsed and she crumpled to the pavement, putting her head in her hand. Wilder sat beside her and put an arm over her shoulders.

"You didn't know how much time had passed while you were away?" Evan asked. "This must be an enormous shock."

"You could say that," said Kes.

Evan appeared to consider for a moment. "I'll comm the Leader's office with the news. I'm here to check on a problem with the machinery in my factory, but if you can wait while I do that, I'll take you to her residence. I'm sure she'll want to see you all as soon as possible."

Kes replied, "That would be great, thanks."

"Please wait here." Evan strode around them and into a side street.

"You lot can go with him," said Aubriot. "I'm not interested in seeing the current Leader. We'll probably have to spend days debriefing. I'm going to check this place out for myself." He set off across the parking lot.

"Looks like it's just us," said Kes to Wilder and Cherry.

"You know," Wilder said, "I don't want to see the Leader either. I want to see what else has changed around here."

THIRTY-NINE

Cherry watched Aubriot and Wilder depart across the lot, each walking in different directions. Evan had disappeared into an alleyway.

I'm sure ***she'll*** *want to see you all as soon as possible.*

Ethan was no longer the Leader. It was no surprise. The position only lasted a year, and then the incumbent had to step down and call an election. Her old friend might have been re-elected a few times, but he couldn't have served for all the decades that had passed while she'd been gone.

Yet she couldn't avoid wondering if there was another reason Ethan wasn't the Leader any longer. Was it because he'd died?

Fifty-three Earth years had gone by in the weeks she'd lived aboard the threads' ship. That would put Ethan in his late seventies. Aboard the *Nova*, Gens had often died younger than that, though the Woken had said that living aboard a starship seemed to shorten the human life span. They'd said the average life span of humans on Earth when the colony ship departed had been in the mid-eighties.

It was possible Ethan was alive but he was an old man with perhaps only a few years left.

Kes sat down beside her. "This is all an incredible shock. Just standing is hard work."

She nodded, not trusting herself to speak.

"It's hard to take in, right?" he continued. "So much has changed while we've been gone. So much development, though the colonization has been a great success from the look of things."

Had he noticed her mood and was trying to lighten it? She couldn't tell.

Kes was a nice man. Kind and thoughtful. Ethan had told her once that he was Cariad's ex-boyfriend. Cariad had excellent taste in men.

"Yes, it's amazing," she managed to squeeze out.

"Here I am again," said Evan from behind them. "I comm'd the Leader's office while I was gone. No answer, of course. No one's working yet. So I tried the Compliance Enforcement Department on their emergency number. The CED has direct access to the Leader's Residence. They answered. Your arrival's causing quite a stir. Someone woke the Leader up and she wants to see you right away. All of you."

Evan had walked around Cherry and Kes while he was speaking and was now talking down at them. "I don't suppose you know where the other two went?"

"No, sorry," Kes replied.

"Can't be helped. I'm sure they'll turn up soon. In the meantime, I'm to take you to the Leader's Residence. I persuaded them it would be faster than waiting for the CED." He gave them a wink and then peered at them. "Providing you're up to it, of course. I could take you to the hospital first if you need medical attention. I'm sure the Leader would agree if that's the best thing to do. I can check if you want."

"I think we can manage," Kes replied. "Are we traveling in your car?"

"Oh yes. The Leader's residence is far away. Can I help you stand up?" He held out a hand each to Cherry and Kes.

Evan's vehicle was only twenty meters away, but the distance felt enormous. When Cherry arrived and Evan opened a door, she slumped into the backseat.

"So the secret of the flitter technology hasn't been cracked yet?" Kes asked as he climbed into the front.

Evan started the car and told it their destination. "No one has been able to reverse engineer the a-grav system, if that's what you mean."

"That is what I mean. What a shame."

"I think the colony has had more important stuff to focus on. And once the roads were built, the need for flitters dwindled. They'd all run out of power by then anyway. Only one of them still has a little juice, I believe. It's in the museum."

"In a museum," Kes echoed. "We have museums! This is astounding."

Evan gave him a puzzled look. "Just one museum, but it's been there ever since I was a kid."

Cherry said, "I guess we're museum pieces too."

The Leader's residence overlooked the ocean. The landscape had changed so much, Cherry found it hard to guess where the place stood in relation to the old breakaway cave settlement. Had the Concordians fixed up the old site? There was so much she didn't know. So much to find out. One thing especially, though she didn't *want* to know the answer to that question.

The Leader lived in a three-story house on the clifftop. Cherry guessed there was a garden behind it overlooking the water. It was a beautiful place.

"No electric fence?" asked Kes as they drove up.

Cherry had noticed that no fence stood around the farming district either, which they had passed on their way.

"No, why would there be?" Evan asked. "Who would want to attack the Leader?"

"Not who," said Kes. "What. What's happened to the sluglimpets?"

"Those horrible things? They live down South, but as long as you wear repellent, they leave you alone."

"My repellent? Fantastic! I'm glad it's still in use."

"Did you invent it? This is so weird. I can't believe it's me who found you all." Evan stopped the car outside the main double doors of the residence. As he pulled up, the doors opened. "I doubt I'm allowed inside, so I guess this is goodbye for now. But when you've settled in I'd love to have you over to meet my family. You must come or my wife will never believe me."

"I'm sure we can manage that," said Kes. "Right, Cherry?"

As they entered the hall at the Leader's residence, someone descended the stairs. Cherry watched the middle-aged woman. She had never met her, of course, and yet she thought she knew her.

"Welcome back to Concordia," said the woman. "Welcome home. But there are only two of you. I thought there were four."

"Four of us arrived this morning," said Kes, "but Aubriot and Wilder left to explore. Everything has changed so much since we've been gone."

"Ah, I see. Please come into my kitchen so I can get you something to eat and drink. None of my staff are up yet. Wait. I didn't introduce myself, did I? I'm the Leader. I think I already know your names. You're both famous. But you look exhausted. I feel bad now for asking you to come to see me right away. Maybe I should have ordered medical checkups."

"I can only speak for myself," Kes replied, "but I feel okay. How about you, Cherry?"

"I'm fine."

The doors to the kitchen opened and the Leader invited them to go first.

The room was wall-to-wall steel except for the floor, which was polished tile. Cooking equipment lined the walls. It was hard to believe this was just one person's home. No refectory kitchen Cherry had seen had ever looked so impressive.

The Leader said, "I hope you don't mind me saying, but you both look exactly the same as the vids of you from before you left. How long have you been away from your own perspective?"

When Kes told her, she shook her head. "It must be bewildering for you. I think when you left everyone was living at old Sidhe, right? Please, take a seat." She gestured toward a table and four chairs. "It's been a while since I had guests for breakfast."

Suddenly, Cherry could bear it no longer. "Excuse me, but... Is your name Meredith?"

The woman smiled. "Yes, Cherry. Well spotted. Who do I look like the most? Mom or Dad?"

Kes slapped his head. "Of course! I was thinking you looked familiar, but I didn't put two and two together." He peered closer. "I'd say you resemble Cariad the most, but you have Ethan's eyes. Dear Cariad. How is she doing? Assuming..."

"Mom is still with us," said Meredith, smiling, "though she has trouble getting around these days. And she...er...she suffers from dementia. She's upstairs if you'd like to speak to her. But I warn you, she may not remember you. She hasn't recognized me or Dad for a few years."

"I'm so sorry," said Kes. "I would like to see her nevertheless."

"In that case, go on up. Her bedroom's the second door on the left. She's awake already. I was taking in her coffee when I heard you were all back."

Kes stood up. "Coming, Cherry?"

"Maybe later."

After Kes went out Meredith busied herself at a machine Cherry didn't recognize. In the silence she finally got up the courage to ask the question that was burning a hole in her mind. "How's your father doing, Meredith?"

When the woman turned to answer, her features were full of sadness. "You two were close, weren't you? Dad used to talk about you a lot. I think he really missed you." She took a breath. "You came back just in time. Ten days ago, Dad had a severe stroke. He's in the hospital but the doctors don't hold out much hope. They say he probably doesn't have long."

Forty

The Concordians had built a high tower. As soon as Wilder left the overshadowing buildings, she saw it. Slim and tall, it rose to double the height of the surrounding buildings. It would be the perfect place to see all that had changed in the colony since she'd been gone.

Was Concordia even a colony any longer? From what she'd seen, the place looked too developed to justify the name. And from what she'd heard, Earth had devolved into an uncivilized, wild place. Concordia had become humanity's new home.

People were emerging into the streets. Predictably, she saw no one she recognized. They had all probably been born after she'd left the planet. Passersby stared at her, which she found strange at first. Surely with the population growth they couldn't expect to know the face of everyone they met? Then she realized she was still wearing her ship's suit. It was no wonder she stood out.

Comparing her clothes with those of the other colonists, hers looked clumsily made and cheap. Other raw materials for textile manufacture had clearly been found, and the new clothes were made by machine, not hand sewn.

There were also differences in the physical appearance of the latest generation. Though most were olive skinned and black haired like the Gens who had disembarked the *Nova*, the influence of Woken genes was clear. A few of the pedestrians had light-colored hair, and she even saw some pairs of blue and green eyes. One person was as red-headed as Kes, though the woman's skin was warm tan, which made her looks striking.

As Wilder walked, she checked her orientation toward the tower, but she was also trying to understand what she was seeing around her. She hadn't seen anything she would call a home. Only more factories like the ones she'd seen when she emerged from the Fila shuttle.

That felt like a long time ago, though probably only an hour or so had passed.

There were sounds of machinery operating, coming from inside a building she was nearing. What was being made? And were the people factory workers? That seemed the obvious conclusion, but they weren't wearing clothes suitable for manual labor.

She had so many questions, yet she wasn't comfortable with stopping someone and asking them. She needed a run down on everything that had happened in the last fifty years. For the moment, a view from the tower would have to suffice.

Soon she was on the wrong side of a wall skirting the base of the tall edifice. Following the wall led her to an opening without a door. She stepped through. Immediately, the growing bustle of the streets faded. The tower was a simple structure. Empty windows punctuated the walls, and at the top stood a viewing platform.

Wilder entered the open doorway and began to climb the spiral stairs. She hadn't gone more than a few flights when she had to rest. Months of inactivity aboard the *Opportunity* had made her weak. Even climbing stairs was hard work.

She managed another ten or fifteen steps and then rested again at the first window. Leaning her elbows on the sill, she looked out. She couldn't see much more than the top of the wall surrounding the tower and the blank backs of factories and workplaces.

She suspected that climbing the tower to the top might be the only thing she would accomplish today, but she was determined to do it. She wanted to see what her home had become. She *needed* to see it. The shock of displacement was eroding her sense of place and belonging.

There were fifteen steps between each window. Fifteen steps between each opportunity to see more of this new-to-her Concordia.

As she climbed, her legs ached more each time she lifted her feet to place them on the next tread. Her muscles began to tremble. She peered upward, squinting through the sweat stinging her eyes. Was the light above her a little brighter? Was she nearing the top?

Resisting the urge to give up entirely, she stopped at the next window. At each opening her view of the settlement had improved, but this latest took her breath away. Buildings stretched into the far distance, radiating from the tower. People walked the streets. So many people. She had never seen so many.

But she still hadn't reached the top. As she steeled herself for the final push, she heard footsteps. Someone was running lightly up. Apprehension and disappointment washed over her. She wanted to be alone. She didn't want to see anyone right now, especially not Concordians, who were all strangers to her. When she'd lived here before, though she didn't know everyone by name, the colony had been small and familiar. Everyone knew *of* everyone else. Now, there were too many people.

She felt like she was back inside the Fila shuttle: trapped and apprehensive.

The person running up had almost reached her. She wished there was a way to escape, but there was none. Even if she possessed the strength to beat the person to the top—which she did not—they were clearly going the same way.

A man rounded the spiral staircase. As soon as he saw her, he stopped. "They said you were back. I didn't believe it. They said you'd been seen going in here."

She gazed at him. What remained of his hair was gray with a little brown, and his face was lined with wrinkles.

"Look," she said. "I'm sorry. I understand that I and my companions must be mildly famous, but—"

"You don't recognize me."

"Oh. No, I don't." She peered closer. Could it be Tycho? The age was about right, but he didn't look like the boy she remembered, even accounting for the passage of time.

"That's a relief, I guess. If you don't remember me, that makes me feel better."

"Huh?" What an odd thing to say.

Then everything fell into place. She gasped. "Jim?!"

The man looked downward. "You do remember."

"I do. I...Well." She sat down on the cold stone. She didn't know how she felt about encountering her former bully, now an old and, apparently, sad man. "I want to get to the top of this tower."

"I'll come with you."

When they reached the viewing platform, bright morning light from a warm blue sky was shining down, and only the pillars supporting the roof cast shadows on the space. The sun was so low the roof cast no shadow at all.

"A few years after you left," Jim said, "when I'd grown up, people began to speculate that you might never return. They said something must have happened to you all. I looked back on how I'd behaved, and I was ashamed. I regretted everything, but there was nothing I could do about it. No one to apologize to. I've lived with the guilt for a long time. When I heard the rumor that you were back, I had to find out for myself if it was true. I had to find you. I had to tell you how sorry I am. I don't have any excuses for what I did. I want to ask..." Jim glanced at her. "I know I don't deserve it, but I want to ask if you can forgive me."

She realized her mouth was hanging open. She snapped her lower jaw closed. “Jim, I…” It was all too much for her to take in.

He lifted his head and smiled. “I’m just a stupid old man to you now, aren’t I?”

“No, no.” She didn’t know what to say to him. “Let’s talk about it later.”

A waist-high wall ringed the platform. She leaned a hand on one of the pillars. From her new vantage point, she could see the neat planning that had been followed in the construction of the district. Closest to the base of the tower was a section containing the tallest buildings. Farther out, the buildings were smaller and shorter, and the streets were narrower and more numerous.

Squares of green stood within the streets: small parks filled with trees. At the edge of the district were fields of green.

She put her hands on the wall and leaned out. The sun was above the horizon and rising swiftly. Where she stood, out of the shelter of the buildings, the breeze was strong. She relished the feeling of it sweeping back her hair.

Her muscles continued to throb but she didn’t care. She ignored the pain.

The Concordian colony had grown up, and so had she.

Forty-One

Cherry stepped into the hospital room, hardly knowing how to feel about what she might see.

Ethan was asleep. He was propped up on pillows and attached to a device delivering intravenous fluids. Other tubes ran under his nostrils, supplying him with additional oxygen.

He looked *so old*.

And yet, he also didn't look any different at all. She would have recognized him in a heartbeat.

The doctor had told her not to expect too much. The stroke had been devastating. Half of his body was entirely paralyzed and he'd lost the power of speech. There was almost no hope of recovery. It was a miracle he'd survived at all.

She hovered in the doorway, her heart full. Her eyes drank in the sight of her old friend. A lifetime had passed for him while she'd been gone, and he'd achieved so much. The colony had grown beyond the most optimistic predictions of the Manual. Compared to the Concordia she'd left only a few months ago, it was unrecognizable. Another place entirely. A dream.

Ethan's eyes opened.

She inhaled sharply and stiffened. Had she woken him? She hadn't wanted to disturb him.

His gaze alighted on her. She held eye contact. His eyes closed, and she relaxed. He'd returned to sleep.

Then his eyes opened again, wider. His lips worked and unrecognizable sounds issued from his mouth.

"Go in," said a voice.

Cherry turned and saw a nurse had walked up without her noticing.

"Go in and talk to him," the nurse repeated. "He hasn't had many visitors. No one knows, you see. The Leader said he'd given instructions that if he fell seriously ill, not to tell any of the news outlets. He wanted peace and quiet. He didn't want any attention. So like him. But it's meant he's been alone here except for when the Leader finds time to pop in and see him. I'm sure he'd appreciate a bit of company."

Cherry entered the room with heavy feet and stood by Ethan's bed. His eyes were alive and he smiled a smile that only worked on one half of his face. He opened his mouth as if to speak, but no words came out. The hand nearest her crept toward her own.

She grasped it. "They said you can't talk, so I'll do the talking for both of us. I got back this morning, a little later than expected. We made it to the Assembly, Ethan. It was quite an experience. I'll tell you more later, but in the end they agreed to accept humanity as an ally." She paused and swallowed. "Great news, right? If the Scythians come back, we'll have friends to help us kick their asses. But we didn't know so much time had passed while we'd been gone. We didn't know..." She paused again. "Ethan, you can't...You-you have to get better. I don't want to be the only amputee in the colony."

His lopsided grin grew wider.

She blinked furiously, but she couldn't control the overflow of her emotions. Tears cascaded down her face. She dropped to her knees and pressed her face into the bed next to his hand. She looked up into his eyes, the mask she had worn for so long falling away. She could no longer disguise how she felt.

As she held his gaze, his expression changed. Understanding lit up his eyes. The weak grip of his hand grew tighter.

She heard a movement. Expecting it to be the nurse, she turned and prepared to get to her feet.

It was Aubriot.

He was leaning on the door frame, arms and legs crossed, watching impassively.

Cherry said, "What are you—"

Ethan's hand became limp. When she looked at him again, his eyes had rolled back and his mouth hung open. Some kind of monitor must have been attached to him because moments later a doctor and a nurse rushed in, quickly followed by others.

Numbly, she stepped back to give them room to work. She watched them as if through a transparent screen, their movements and words making no sense. Their behavior was like a grotesque performance around a fallen puppet.

At one point, the nurse who had spoken earlier put a hand on her arm and said, "He was very sick. Maybe he was only hanging on in the hope he might see you."

It was all over.

The next thing she noticed was that the medical professionals had all left. She was alone with Ethan again, except for Aubriot standing in the doorway.

But it was not Ethan lying in the bed, all medical devices removed. He had gone.

She turned to leave. Aubriot's eyes were on her, but she didn't care what he thought. She didn't care that he was seeing her at her most vulnerable. She didn't care that he'd been right and now he knew it.

Her head hanging, she stepped past him. He grasped her arm. A sob welled up in her chest. She was barely holding it together. "Please. Don't."

He tugged her toward him, raised his other hand and put it on the back of her head. She fell into him, her face against his chest. Then grief and sorrow overcame her.

Cherry didn't know how much time passed before she cried herself out. She knew it would not be the end of her tears, not for a long time, but for now she had none left. She lifted her face from Aubriot's chest. His shirt was soaked through with her tears and an embarrassing amount of mucus.

She looked across at the hospital room window, her gaze avoiding the motionless figure on the bed. At some point, Meredith had arrived. She was sitting with her father in silence.

Through the window, Cherry saw the daylight was waning. Had the first day of her return to Concordia nearly passed already?

Aubriot pulled his shirt out from his pants and wiped her face with a dry part of it. "You look a mess."

"Thanks."

He took her hand. "Come with me. I want to show you something."

She went with him down the stairs and out of the building. They strode across the parking lot and across a road.

"Is this urgent?" she asked. "I just want to find somewhere to sleep tonight."

"You don't have to worry about that. You're a celebrity. We all are. We'll have people begging to put us up. But Ethan's daughter said we could stay with her until things get sorted out. Didn't you hear her?"

"I guess not."

He led her down an alleyway and then across another road. He turned and they walked for several minutes.

"Aubriot, can anything be so important it can't wait until tomorrow? I'm really done with today."

"Stop whinging. You want to see this. Believe me." He turned down another alleyway.

The layout of the buildings was beginning to look familiar. "Are you taking me back to where the shuttles landed?"

"I knew you weren't as stupid as you look. Now shuttup. You're getting annoying."

If she had an ounce of energy or willpower remaining, she would have left him and his mad obsession. But she had neither, so she was forced to allow him to pull her along.

They arrived at the parking lot where they'd met Evan.

"See that?" Aubriot pointed at a low wall around steps leading underground. "Didn't notice it before, did you?"

"No, I didn't. And...?"

"What's the point of a basement under a carpark?"

"Ugh, come on! Will you please just reveal your moronic secret so I can find a bed and go to sleep?"

He marched her toward the stairs. "Moronic secret? You're gonna take that back in about two minutes. To answer my own question, there is *no* need for a basement under a carpark. Unless it's another carpark of course."

"Oh, whoopee. Two parking lots. I'm impressed."

He looked at her out of the corners of his eyes. He seemed to be about to speak but then changed his mind. He pulled her down the steps. They went surprisingly deep. They walked down several flights and then a closed door blocked them at the bottom. A security panel sat on the wall.

"Now," said Aubriot, "not everyone can be given access to Concordia's highest security areas. But if you're an *important, famous, celebrity*, you just might get lucky." He opened the panel and looked into it.

A lock clicked. He pulled the door open.

Her eyes took a moment to adjust to the dimmer light in the underground space. It was much larger than she'd expected. The expanse spread way wider than the parking lot above it. And in the space odd, humped, and long shapes stood silent under soft lights.

"What is this?" Cherry stepped through the open doorway. "What are—"

She gasped so deeply her throat made a whooping noise. "Oh. My. Stars."

As she walked farther into the massive vault her legs felt as though they were about to give way. She was looking at an armaments depot. A huge missile launcher, stacked missiles, colossal guns, and other military equipment she had no idea the purpose of ranged across the floor.

"Our fellow Concordians have been busy while we've been gone," said Aubriot, "in more ways than one. They used the material from the melted down spiders at first, then stepped up production after mining operations started in the mountains. All in secret. And this isn't the only depot. There are more, all too deep for scanners to detect. The Fila sent back word after the *Opportunity* was attacked as she left, that they suspected Concordia was being watched."

"I...I...Wow."

"I couldn't have said it better myself." He walked to one of the guns and patted the side of it, his tall frame entirely dwarfed by the machine. "When the Scythians return, they're in for a nasty surprise."

The story of Space Colony One continues in...
HUMANITY'S FIGHT

Sign up to my science fiction reader group for a free ecopy of *Night of Flames*, the prequel to *Space Colony One*, more free books, discounts on new releases, Review Crew invitations and other interesting stuff:

https://jjgreenauthor.com/free-books/

HUMANITY'S FIGHT

One

The escape capsule was falling. The interior was tiny, accommodating only one individual. Only one individual was required. Most of the bulk of the capsule was made up by the thickness of the hull. The capsule had no landing gear and the hull was designed to absorb the shock of impact on a planet surface. The thick shell was also designed to protect the occupant from the high temperatures generated by falling through an atmosphere.

The capsule had drifted into Concordia's exosphere without incident. At this point, the small vessel was already trapped by Concordia's gravity and impact on the surface was inevitable. It was only a matter of time. The thing inside it remained motionless, waiting. Its artificial mind calculated the predicted velocity of the capsule's descent and estimated the peak temperature of the outer hull.

According to its calculations, the capsule would not heat up sufficiently to destroy the occupant, though burn damage might be inflicted. More importantly, the high temperature would not cause the capsule to disintegrate. If it did, the occupant would not survive the remaining fall.

The force of the impending impact was another consideration. Could the occupant survive the shock? There was dissatisfying variance in the answer. The probability of unimpaired survival was only thirty-two point nine two eight four percent. However, the probability of functional survival was seventy-three point four zero eight three, rounded up. Nevertheless, that meant the probability of annihilation was twenty-six point five nine one seven.

The individual would have preferred better odds. If it was destroyed its mission would fail. But there was nothing it could do to improve its chances. The intelligence thought it was odd that its creators had not designed a more robust craft, but it was forced to accept it could not know their motivations or intentions.

Time passed, and the capsule entered Concordia's thermosphere. Its velocity increased as the tug of the planet's mass grew stronger. Where would it fall? Its trajectory was not yet entirely set. The capsule was light and would be subject to the forces of the jet stream when it dropped deep into the stratosphere. At that point it would also be on fire.

Given the predicted high temperature of its hull (what remained of it at that point), it would be preferable if it landed in the ocean, even considering the fact that the sudden drop in temperature might create a differential in thermal expansion sufficient to cause the hull to crack. If the capsule crashed into land, it would cool down much slower, reducing the heat differential and maintaining the structural integrity of the hull. However, the force of impact would be greater. Overall, the probability that the capsule would break open, reducing the likelihood of the individual's survival, was lower for an impact on water than on land.

When the capsule reached the mesosphere, its exterior rapidly heated up. The metal alloy forming the outermost layer began to glow. At first, insulation protected the capsule's interior from the heat, and the occupant registered no rise in temperature.

That state quickly changed. One-tenth of a second later, the capsule's hull was melting and burning, sending out a long tail of flame. A human on the surface looking at the right part of the night sky would have seen a streak of light and thought they were looking at a meteor.

Another tenth of a second passed, and the individual registered the rapidly increasing temperature of its surroundings. Fortunately, it did not breathe air, or it would have discovered its throat and lungs scorching. Its skin was a manufactured substance designed to mimic human skin. If it had been organic, it would have been bubbling and peeling away.

By the third tenth of a second, the capsule was a fireball and its interior was a furnace. But it maintained structural integrity. The occupant waited as its circuits heated. The artificial hair on its head dissolved and evaporated. The ends of its faux fingers crisped.

Estimated time to impact was point two nine—

The capsule hit. Against the probabilities, given the comparative volume of water to landmass on the surface of Concordia, the capsule had come down on land. Its innermost wall shattered, but for the most part the vessel remained whole. One reason for this was the fact that what was left of the hull was molten and the liquid, more flexible structure absorbed some of the shock.

The occupant completed a damage assessment of itself, revealing a considerable number of breakages. Its inner frame had broken into many pieces and some of its wires had dissected. Self-repair automatically activated. As the hull cooled, the individual healed itself. Not all parts were able to be saved, but it would be functional. When it had repaired to the greatest extent possible, it would find a way out of the wreck.

Two

Cherry lifted a whistle to her lips and blew it so hard her ears rang. "Exercise over. Get in line!"

The troops shuffled slowly to their positions in the training yard. Some didn't even seem sure of where the line was.

"MOVE IT!"

Her missing arm was itching, which did nothing to improve her mood. She didn't think she'd ever seen such a bunch of useless recruits. If they weren't dropping their weapons they were bumping into each other, and if they weren't bumping into each other they were screwing around when they thought she wasn't watching.

Dammit! Where was Aubriot?

The face of his subordinate officer had been a picture when Cherry had turned up unannounced. Then the woman had tried to make up excuses for her CO, stuttering out some lame explanations for Aubriot's absence. That had only made Cherry madder. Loyalty was a virtue but not when it extended to covering up irresponsibility.

From the corner of her eye, she saw a tall figure striding toward her. The sight of Aubriot finally arriving only made her more irritated. She glared at him as he approached.

"I'll take over, General," he said as soon as he was within hearing distance.

She waited until he was close enough for her to speak without the recruits overhearing her. "Where the *hell* have you been?" she hissed. "You should have been here two hours ago. What kind of an example do you think you're setting?"

"Hey! I—"

"I don't want to hear it." Cherry pulled the whistle over her head and thrust it into his chest. "These men and women are a disgrace, but now I see the attitude of the person responsible for training them I'm not surprised. You've got one week to whip them into shape. I'll be back to run them through an exercise of my choosing, and if they don't behave like something resembling soldiers, you're discharged."

His handsome features darkened. "You don't mean that. You wouldn't dare."

"I wouldn't dare?" She struggled to keep control of herself. "Try me, Aubriot. Just try me. The Scythians could return any day, and when they do, we'll be relying on these idiots for our defense. Stars help us! If this is an example of the best you can do, our military is better off without you."

She walked away before she had to take any more of his attitude. The man was beyond exasperating. She knew why he'd been late. Antisocial as she was, even she had heard the rumors. He was late because he'd been with some young woman, one of the latest in a long line to fall victim to his charms. He was disgusting—working his way through the female half of the colony like a bad algae sandwich.

She'd heard he'd been fraternizing with recruits too, though she had no evidence to prove it. His behavior in that regard was bizarre. He was the one who had written the rules for Concordia's defense forces, basing them on his memory of armed service regulations back on Earth. Now, he was the one flouting them.

She should have given him a dishonorable discharge a year ago, when his attitude had started to slip. And she would have, except for the fact that when he concentrated on his job, he really knew what he was doing. He knew stuff about military training and tactics that wasn't in any of the colony's data banks. He also knew how to manipulate people into doing what he wanted.

In the early days, he'd been too authoritarian and overbearing, pissing off the independently minded Gens. But she had persuaded him to tone it down, and the nature of the people he was working with had altered too. This later generation had not revolted against Woken and Guardian control. They were softer, more malleable, and more tolerant of being bossed around.

When he put his mind to what he was doing, Aubriot produced excellent results. *When* he put his mind to it, and he wasn't giving priority to that other part of his anatomy.

She swung herself into her autocar and told it her next destination. The vehicle locked its doors and pulled out. The Concordian countryside rolled past her window as the car headed east toward the site that was formerly Sidhe, the underground settlement.

Was Aubriot's deteriorating attitude only due to the fact he was getting older? She wasn't sure exactly how old he was. He didn't seem to show any signs of aging, but she guessed he had to be in his late forties or early fifties. He'd expanded his family's already huge business empire until it was vast before sinking all his assets into the *Nova Fortuna* Project. Then the project had taken many years to complete. Kes would probably know Aubriot's age when he left Earth. The xenobiologist was the only other living Woken who had embarked on the *Nova*. But since then, how much time had passed for the man?

Aubriot had spent a hundred and eighty-six years frozen aboard the colony ship—did people age while in cryo? She had no idea. A little more than a year after Arrival, Aubriot embarked on the mission with her to the Galactic Assembly. Six more Concordian years or roughly three Earth years had gone by since their return.

But while they'd been away, time on Concordia had moved on another one hundred and six Concordian and fifty-three Earth years. How old did that make Aubriot now, or her for that matter? It was confusing.

Still, however old he was, aging didn't justify his bad behavior. Whatever the reason was, it was up to him to fix it. He was a grown man. If he continued to be more of a liability than an asset, he had to go. She wasn't going to place the safety of tens of thousands of men, women, and children in his hands.

After her car arrived and parked itself, she climbed out and walked to the stairs at the side of the parking lot, stepping over the crack running around its outer edge. The line in the pavement was the only sign of the vast man-made cavern beneath her feet. She descended the long flights of stairs leading to the cavern's entrance and passed through the security door.

She regularly inspected Concordia's armament depots. Everything always seemed in order when she carried out a visual inspections, but she liked to meet face-to-face with the officers in charge. People tended to be more open and honest when communicating verbally, often saying things they would not commit to writing. She perched on a camp stool and balanced an interface on her knees as she double-checked that month's report from the officer responsible for Cerberus.

Putting aside the interface, she rose and went to the nearest missile launcher. The points of four missiles protruded from the ground and rose to the ceiling. The frames holding them upright were sunk into the ground far below.

"General," said a voice. "Welcome to Cerberus."

A fresh-faced young man in uniform was approaching. She squinted, peering through the dim lighting and shadows. The man was a colonel and therefore the person in charge. She didn't recognize him. Aubriot must have reassigned the previous officer but hadn't informed her.

"Colonel, please don't call me General. Ma'am is fine, or even sir if it's easier to remember. What's your name?"

His stiff posture eased. "Fletcher, ma'am. I hope you'll find everything as it should be."

"I'm sure I will but it doesn't hurt to check, and also to meet new staff. You didn't write this month's report, so you must have taken up your new post recently."

"I've only been here two days. I received my promotion last week."

"Well, how about you take me on a tour and show me what you know?"

"It'll be a pleasure."

Fletcher took her to the pulse emitter first and explained what it was and how it operated. An entirely different construction than the ground-to-space missiles, the emitter had been built according to plans Faina, captain of the Guardians' ship, *Mistral*, had dumped into the colony's data banks before crashing her vessel into the Scythian flagship.

The silo also contained a ground-to-air missile launcher to be deployed if the Scythians made it into Concordia's atmosphere. Stacks of missiles sat beside it.

As Fletcher led her around the other armaments, her mind turned to her long day ahead on her bi-monthly visit to all the four military sites, code-named Cerberus, Minotaur, Medusa, and Hydra. Cerberus was the oldest, built in the earliest days of the colonization. Work had begun on the silo not long after she had left to go to the Galactic Assembly.

Minotaur sat deep within the cliff face several kilometers from Oceanside, the second major settlement to be built. Medusa lurked beneath the mountain range bisecting the main continent, an offshoot of the extensive mines that riddled the mountains. Hydra held the title of the newest of the four. Built with the permission and help of the Fila, it lay in wait beneath the shallow waters of the continental shelf offshore from the largest continent and original site of colonization, Lyonesse.

Hydra would eventually lose her status of the most recently constructed depot. Work was underway on Chimera. The fifth silo was being constructed on Suddene, the second largest and recently colonized continent.

At the end of his tour, Fletcher returned to the four ground-to-space missiles. Dust lay thick on their metal surfaces. Despite the dust, the silvery hue of the metal shone through. The missiles had been constructed from the search-and-destroy spiders the Scythians had sent down to kill the humans in their second attack. First to be built, the missiles had sat in place for more than eighty Concordian years, awaiting the return of the Scythians.

Eighty years was a long time, and no missiles had ever been launch tested. When the moment for their deployment came, would they work?

Three

Wilder reached armpits deep into the guts of the pulse emitter and slipped a wrench over a nut. She'd lost count of the times she'd serviced the Cerberus emitter and those at the other depots, but Cherry had asked her to carry out yet more maintenance checks on top of those carried out by the regular crew.

She understood Cherry's concern but the work bored her. It irked her too. Humans had lived on Concordia for a hundred and twelve Concordian years. They had spread across the planet's surface to both of its continents. They had built roads and railway lines, schools and hospitals, factories and offices. They had built a new civilization. If that didn't give them the right to call Concordia their home, she didn't know what did. It seemed unfair that they were forced to go to this effort to defend themselves.

There were so many more interesting things she could be doing than servicing pulse emitters, like—

"Hey, Wilder," said a voice behind her.

Startled, she dropped her wrench. The tool clattered into the depths of the machine. "Damn!" Straightening up, she turned and saw Kes.

"Sorry," he said, "I thought you heard me come in."

"No, I didn't, but it's okay. I was lost in thought." She squatted down next to her tool box and riffled through its contents, pulling out a magnetic gripper and placing it on the emitter's shell. "I didn't expect to see *you* in here. Things getting boring over at the Aliens Office?"

"You mean the Department for Extra-Planetary Affairs?"

"Exactly. The Aliens Office." She ducked down again and picked up a rag to wipe her hands, hiding the smile creeping over her lips. She enjoyed teasing Kes, whose love of his job bordered on obsession.

"Well, I guess you're half right," he replied. "I have been learning a lot about other members of the Galactic Assembly. But my job entails..." He paused, then laughed and punched her on the shoulder.

She grinned. "Seriously, though. What brings you here? It isn't like you to venture out during daylight on a work day. Is a big disaster brewing? Have the Fila decided to emigrate?"

His eyebrows rose in alarm. "The Fila leave us? Don't even talk about it. What a disaster that would be. No, it isn't anything as serious as that. It's probably nothing, in fact. I would have comm'd you about it, but you turned off your button. I thought I might find you here."

"Whoops." She turned on her ear comm. "I don't like to be disturbed when I'm working."

"No problem. I do that too sometimes. So, someone brought part of an object they'd found into the office today, and I was wondering if you might help us identify it. They found the thing way out beyond the mountains a couple of weeks ago."

"What does it look like? Did you bring it with you?"

"It's metallic, and it appears to have been burned, but that's as much as I can tell you. It doesn't resemble anything I've ever seen. I couldn't bring it with me unfortunately. I'm not allowed to take it out of the building. The director is worried it's something dangerous. Would you mind coming over to take a look?"

"Sure. Any excuse to get out of servicing these emitters. Give me a few minutes." She reached into the emitter with the magnetic grip. The wrench hadn't fallen far. It was caught between two parts of machinery. But bumping the tool could send it clattering into the depths, which might entail days of taking the emitter apart in order to reach it. She opened the jaws of the gripper and delicately closed them around the wrench, feeling a satisfying clunk as the magnetism took hold. "Do you have any pictures of this thing?"

"I do. The person who brought it in also took pictures of the whole object, not just the piece they picked up. I've already sent the files to you."

"I'll take a look at them on the way over. I'm nearly done. I just need to close this thing up."

After she had returned the emitter to a working state, they took an autocar to the government buildings where Kes worked. Concordia was governed from its capital, Annwn, which lay between Cerberus and the original farming district. Annwn was a small place. Mostly only government workers lived there. The Leader at the time had chosen it as an administrative center in order to discourage larger cities from vying for control.

Despite its small size, the capital was Wilder's source of groceries and other supplies. Not long after returning from the Galactic Assembly, she had built herself another tree house in the small patch of forest that remained after the construction of Cerberus. Many of the trees had been cleared or had died due to the fitting of the military depot's underground dome. She loved the quiet and seclusion of her little forest home, though living there sometimes made her nostalgic about the days when Tycho, Stephie, and other friends had shared the dream of building an entire settlement beneath the canopy.

Now, Tycho and Stephie were married and had grandchildren. They lived out at Oceanside and Wilder rarely saw them. Their differences in age and experience had created a gulf their former friendship couldn't cross.

"Are you going to look at the pictures I sent?" Kes asked.

"Oh, yeah." She had forgotten what she was supposed to be doing. Wondering why she seemed to be becoming more absent-minded, she took out her interface and opened her files.

The larger object was the first thing she saw—the thing too large for the finder to bring back. It was an irregular lump of buckled, twisted, scorched metal. The dimension measurements overlay the image. It was two point eight-seven meters at its widest point, one point eight meters deep, and one point five meters tall. Lush vegetation surrounded it.

"The person who found it suspected it might be alien in origin," said Kes. "That was why she came to my department. What do you think?"

"I guess it's strange that something *we* made could get burned up way over on the other side of the mountains. Unless it's a crashed aircraft? But we would have heard about it on the news."

"That's what I thought too."

Her gaze shifted from the unidentified object to the greenery encircling it. She touched the image and widened it with her fingertips, revealing greater detail. "Look at that." She pointed at an area next to the mysterious artifact.

"What am I looking at?"

"The surrounding area was burned by the heat and flames from the object. You can see the scorched soil. But new shoots are growing. Judging by the object's dimensions, the shoots were about ten centimeters tall when the picture was taken. We're in the warm season now and everything's growing fast. I would guess the area was burned about three weeks ago, though it's hard to be exact without knowing the plant species."

Kes smiled. "I knew I'd come to the right person."

"You said the finder of this thing waited two weeks before they came to you?"

"That's right. She's a miner and she only recently had enough free time to bring it to Annwn."

"That makes it five weeks ago that thing was on fire. I'll check the news reports."

There was no mention of any aircraft crashes, fires, or any other unusual occurrences in the wilderness beyond the mountains around the time she'd estimated, or within two weeks.

They arrived at Kes's place of work. He took her to his department on the first floor. It was an open plan office. She drew some curious glances as he led her through the desks.

The object the finder had brought in sat on an empty table. She picked it up. It was clearly bent out of shape, but even mentally unbending it and imagining the original form gave her no clues as to what it had been. A sharp edge indicated it had been sheared off, probably due to damage to the larger object it came from. The edge hadn't melted and then cooled and re-solidified, which was what appeared to have happened to the rest of the object. But even the edge was somewhat scorched like the rest. She wasn't sure what to make of it.

Kes's colleagues had come over and gathered around. Two were peering over her shoulders.

"I thought perhaps it was Scythian," said one of them, a young, balding man. "Remains of some of the spiders, melted together. We've certainly found plenty of those over the years."

"None of them were burned, though," said an older woman.

"Perhaps a container burst in the upper atmosphere and the spiders heated up as they came down."

Wilder felt the object's weight. "It isn't part of a spider." She'd handled enough of the search-and-destroy devices to know how much the thing should weigh. It was too heavy. "Though I think it's a metal alloy."

The woman said, "The chief engineer from Civil Works volunteered to test it and find out its exact composition."

"That's great," said Wilder. "Knowing what it's made from will narrow down the field of possibilities." She turned over the object in her hands a few more times before returning it to the table top and asking Kes, "Are you busy with work at the moment?"

"I'm always busy. There's always something to do, but why are you asking?"

"Do you fancy coming on a heli ride?"

"You want to go out there?"

"I do. This mystery is going to bug me until I've figured it out."

"I can make time for that. We can take a government heli."

"That's exactly what I was thinking."

He smiled. "Let's go tomorrow."

Unable to glean any more information from the object, Wilder decided to call it a day. Kes accompanied her to the outer doors. Before leaving, she said, "What I don't understand is, how did it get there? It's in the middle of nowhere. It couldn't have been taken there by truck because there are no roads.

We've ruled out the possibility of it being a downed aircraft. The only other vehicle capable of reaching that location is a flitter, but they're all locked away, even the one with remaining power." A sudden thought struck her and she sucked in a breath.

"What? Have you figured out what it is?"

"Uh, no. I was thinking about something else."

He looked at her inquiringly. When she ignored him, he said, "Something entirely unrelated to this object that made you gasp?"

"Look, it's personal, okay?" It wasn't personal, but she couldn't think up a better excuse at short notice for not telling him the truth.

"Personal," he said. "Right." Folding his arms he leaned on the door, gazing at the view. Several awkward moments passed in silence. He glanced behind them into the empty lobby before saying, "You know, if you're doing something *under the radar*, so to speak, you can tell me. Just because I work for the government it doesn't mean I would turn you in."

"Oh, I know you wouldn't." She touched his arm. "It isn't that. It's something I can't talk about yet, to anyone, that's all. And I don't think it's related to this burned up thing the miner found, okay?"

"Hmm, if you're sure. You know I'm only trying to look out for you."

"I'm sure, and I appreciate your concern." She was moved. Kes had always been there for her, ever since that day he'd brought her sluglimpet repellent to spray on the trees in her settlement. He was the closest thing to family she had. She hugged him before leaving.

On her way home, she thought more about the connection between the mysterious burned object and her little project, until she was convinced there was none. She'd thought perhaps the object was a failed experiment along the lines of ones she'd been attempting.

Four

It was getting dark. The sunset colors that had brightened the office where Kes worked had disappeared and the encroaching gloom alerted him to the lateness of the hour. He turned off his interface and slipped the device into a bag, then rose from his desk and stretched.

The office was empty. All of his colleagues had already gone home. He was the last to leave, as usual. He walked to the exit, going over the day's events in his mind. He smiled and gave a slight shake of his head at the memory of his encounter with Wilder.

What secret lay behind that gasp she'd given? What was she up to? His young friend had clearly embarked on yet another project that skirted the border of legality.

Out in the hallway, he turned his steps toward the rear of the building. The front doors would already be locked and he would have to let himself out of the fire door. Not for the first time, his tired brain dwelt on how remarkably similar the shadowy, quiet building was to the kind of places he used to work at on Earth. If he didn't look too closely, he might have imagined he was back there, and the intervening centuries and light years of distance were nothing but a fiction of an over-excited imagination.

He pushed on the bar that opened the door and let himself out into the coolness of late dusk. He descended the steps and walked out into the office parking lot, which he wasn't surprised to see was empty of cars. They had all been taken by departing government workers.

Sighing, he sat on a low wall and ordered an autocar via his ear comm. As he did so, he saw three messages from his wife. A twinge of guilt hit. He knew what the messages said and he didn't answer them, deciding to cross that bridge when he arrived home.

While he waited for the ordered car, he wondered about his growing sense of déjà vu. He hadn't felt that way about any other place on Concordia. It had only been in what he saw as the second phase of his life here that the mental shift had appeared, after he'd returned from the trip to the Galactic Assembly.

Experiencing events that later turned out not to be real but a simulation artificially generated in his mind had had a profound effect. He'd felt psychologically destabilized and left with a distrust of what was real and what was not.

Then, when he'd returned to Concordia and discovered that the planet had moved on by more than fifty Earth years, he'd undergone another psychic shift. This second effect had occurred more slowly. In the beginning, he'd been amazed and delighted. The colonists had worked wonders in just a few decades. And when he'd found out about the secret military depots they'd constructed in anticipation of the Scythians' return, he'd been even more impressed.

But within weeks a sense of displacement had set in. The new Concordia was nothing like he'd imagined it would be when he'd signed up to the colony expedition. He'd imagined a lifetime of enormous challenges, hardship, and toil as the generational colonists and scientists fought to survive. Instead, after returning from the Assembly, he found he was living a reasonably comfortable existence with all his immediate needs catered for.

He had a nice home, a wife and child as well as another on the way, and an office job. If it weren't for the fact that he was studying alien sentient species, he could easily have thought he'd never left Earth.

The whirr of an autocar drew him from his musings. The vehicle pulled up and the doors unlocked. He shivered as he stood up. The evening was turning chilly. He looked up at the clear sky and overhanging starscape.

"You're different," he told the stars. "I can say that, but not much else."

He opened a door and climbed in, telling the car his destination. The interior was warm. The heater had activated—yet another example of an Earth-like luxury. It added to his sense of alienation. He would almost have preferred the car was cold, the windows stuck open, and rain pouring in.

The autocar purred as set off in the direction of his home on the outskirts of Annwn.

Thinking about his life on the new Concordia and its similarity to his memories of Earth brought him to a sad recollection that often popped up unbidden when he sank into this mood.

When he'd returned from the Galactic Assembly, the first place he'd gone had been the Leader's Residence. He hadn't realized at first that the Leader was Meredith, Cariad and Ethan's child. Cherry had been the first to spot that.

At that time, Cariad was still alive and living with her daughter, but dementia had taken over her mind. Meredith had warned him before he'd gone to see her. However, the knowledge hadn't prepared him for what he encountered.

Against his expectation, she'd recognized him. Her eyes had screwed up to focus on him as soon as he'd entered the room, and then her features relaxed in recognition. "Kes, where have you been? Are you here to go into cryo too? I thought maybe you'd been taken to the OR already. Come and sit down."

He'd perched on the bed, a little shocked at the toll time had taken on her appearance. He'd known she would look older, naturally, but to see it with his own eyes was another thing.

Cariad beckoned him closer. He leaned in. She clutched his arm and whispered, "Kes, please help me. I changed my mind, but they won't let me leave. There's a nurse here who hates me and she won't let me go." Her grip became tighter. "I changed my mind. I don't want to go on the *Nova Fortuna* any longer. I want to give up my place to someone else. I can do that, can't I? It isn't too late? Someone can take my place. They can't force me, right?"

He had heard that the best way to deal with the delusions of the mentally ill was to go along with them. Telling them the truth would only make them agitated and unhappy and wouldn't help them at all. He took her other hand in his. "No, they can't force you. You don't have to go if you don't want to."

"Good, good." Cariad's hold on his arm softened. "I decided I can't leave my family. I can't do that to them, and I'll miss them too much."

He bowed his head. "I know how you feel. But don't worry about it. I'll speak to the doctors and tell them not to prep you."

"Thank you, Kes. Thank you. I knew I could rely on you."

Though she appeared to have forgotten everything that had happened since she woke from cryo, her memory of the years leading up to the departure of the expedition was vivid. As he sat and talked with her, she referred to many aspects of that time he'd entirely forgotten. The snatched moments of intimacy they'd shared, the utter exhaustion of the long days of work, office politics and gossip, and the escalating strength of the public protests.

By the time she'd become tired by their conversation and fallen asleep, he had been transported back into the past. He'd also felt anew the same doubt and indecision that now plagued Cariad's aged brain.

If he had his time again, would he decide to remain on Earth? If he'd known how much his expectations would be thwarted, it was possible he would.

The autocar drew to a stop. His house was small and fronted by a yard covered in the rubbery, low-growing Concordia ground cover plant. He exited the car and walked up the path. The front door opened before he reached it and yellow light silhouetted the pregnant figure of Isobel.

She waited until he was inside and the door was closed before she began her admonishments. "You promised. You promised you'd be home early today."

"I know, I'm sorry. Someone brought something into the office, and I had to—"

"I don't want to hear it. Whatever it was, you could have at least comm'd me. You could have replied to my messages."

"You're right. That's what I should have done. I got carried away, I guess. Look, why don't we do something special this weekend? I want to make it up to you."

"It isn't only me, it's Miki too. She hasn't seen her Daddy in three days. You leave before she wakes up and come home after she's gone to bed. Three days is a long time to a two-year-old."

"I know." He hung his head. "I'm sorry." He reached out to hug his wife, but she stepped backward, avoiding him.

"I've never said this before." Her chin began to tremble. "If you continue like this, always working, never making time for me or our children, our marriage isn't going to survive. I know that sounds like an ultimatum, but it isn't. It's the truth." She turned around and walked into the kitchen at the back of their house.

She didn't want him to see her cry. He stood in the hall, his arms hanging loosely, feeling like an absolute asshole. What was going on with him? The amount of work he had to do was overwhelming. He was studying information on members of the Galactic Assembly, learning as much as he could about the anatomy, behavior, environmental conditions essential for life, history, and culture of more than two dozen species. Realistically, it was several lifetimes' work for everyone in his department, let alone himself.

Yet none of it was as important to him as his family. Why was he neglecting them?

FIVE

Meredith had requested that Cherry pay her an informal visit at her private residence. The 'request' was not something Cherry, as the colony's general, could refuse, but she didn't mind going to see Ethan's daughter. Her grief at Ethan's passing and missing out on a lifetime of his friendship had, over the years, become something she could lock away. It was only during quiet moments that she allowed the pain to surface. Also, as time passed, remembering him increasingly brought her many moments of sweet nostalgia.

As her autocar approached the Leader's Residence, she noticed that Oceanside had grown larger since the last time she was here. The streets of one-story houses spreading out from the central clifftop district had grown longer and more numerous. The views out to sea and inland over low hills made it easy to see why so many Concordians chose the place as their home.

Proximity to the Fila was another great selling point. A large metropolis of the beings stood in the shallow waters offshore, where, decades previously, the *Nova* had crashed into the planet. The flotsam of the ship's remains had washed away long ago. The waters had returned to their shades of azure and turquoise.

Relations between humans and their aquatic friends grew stronger every year. In the little spare time she had, she would go to the beach at the foot of the cliff. Families also gathered there. Parents relaxed while their children played in the waves, entirely unafraid of accidental drownings. Cherry had even seen some of the youngsters speaking a rudimentary version of the threads' language, if 'speak' was the right word to describe their vigorous gesticulations.

Her autocar halted at the Leader's Residence. She climbed out and mounted the steps to the double doors. The assistant who let her in passed on Meredith's message that she was in the bunker. Cherry immediately knew what that meant: Meredith was talking to the threads. Probably Quinn, who had acted as the spokesperson for the aliens for as long as Cherry had known him.

She took the elevator and descended through the vertical tunnel dug in the cliff, emerging into a circular room well below sea level. Half of the wall was transparent and looked out directly into water. The threads had cut a passage through the rock at the cliff base so they could meet with the colony's Leader face to...tentacles. She recognized Quinn's distinctive patterning immediately.

"Cherry," he said via the room's speaker. He'd recognized her too, though she guessed her missing arm made her easily identifiable to the aliens. "It feels good to see you again."

"It's good to see you too, Quinn."

"Thanks for coming at short notice," said Meredith. "I didn't want to make a big fuss and order you here. I don't want to run the risk of this getting out before it's official."

"You have already arrived at a decision?" Quinn asked.

"Not yet," Meredith replied. "I want to hear what my General has to say."

"I understand."

Meredith said, "Cherry, the Fila comm'd me this morning. They received a transmission from outer space. A delegation of Galactic Assembly members is on its way to meet with us."

"A delegation? Of what? I mean, who?" She was taken aback at the news and uncomfortable at the notion of unknown aliens turning up on Concordia's doorstep unannounced. The last time that happened things hadn't gone well.

"From what Quinn tells me," Meredith replied, "I believe you encountered this species when you visited the Assembly's space station."

"Do you mean the organizers of the station?" Cherry imagined the gigantic creatures striding through Oceanside, spreading terror and panic.

Quinn replied, "They told us you met them during your simulation."

She had seen one other alien species at close quarters. "But I thought they were holos." The simulation had included a fake attack. She and her companions had been given the choice of sacrificing their own lives to help an alien, or saving themselves and letting another being die. Cherry, Wilder, and Kes had made the choice to sacrifice themselves, unaware the situation was not real. Aubriot had decided to save himself, to no one's great surprise.

"The beings in the simulation were a fabrication," said Quinn, "but the species is real. They heard they were chosen to play the victims in the test scenario, and they are grateful that most of you chose to save one of them."

"I see. But that was years ago. Why are they coming now, and why are they coming here?"

"I'm surprised you are not more aware of how the passage of time is affected by the observer's perspective."

"Ugh, all right. I get it." The one hundred Concordian years that had passed while she went on her mission remained a sore point. Even more importantly, it was a factor that limited the Assembly's ability to help Concordia when the Scythians finally returned. She had gone to its space station in the hope that humanity would be accepted into their alliance. Her mission had been successful, but her expectation that members would turn up to help defend her home in the event of an attack had proven wishful thinking.

The Galactic Assembly had warned the Scythians that the human colony had its support and it would not countenance any acts of aggression, but starships took weeks, months, and years to travel interstellar distances. If the Scythians wanted to annihilate the humans they could do it and face the consequences later. Whatever reprisal the Assembly chose to inflict wouldn't matter to the dead.

Quinn said, "This delegation has been traveling to Concordia since they received the pertinent information. We passed on their message as soon as we received it, and the delegation lags their communication by only a short while. Of course they must come here if they want to meet you."

She frowned at the swirling, tentacled alien, focusing on his center, where she guessed his brain was. He had no eyes and it was the best she could come up with for a focal point. The threads were notorious for their inability to exactly convert their measurement of time into the human scale. Though, to be fair, no Concordian colonist had managed to make the conversion going the other way either. The threads' method of measuring the passing hours, days, and months was an utter mystery to human perception.

"What do you mean by 'a short while'?" Cherry asked.

Quinn didn't answer at first. He seemed to be thinking. Eventually he replied, "Ah, tomorrow, I think."

"After the sun rises and it's light here again?"

"Yes, that's right."

Was that so hard? she silently asked.

"I guess we should welcome them," Meredith said.

"I guess so, but it won't hurt to play this safe. The last time a new species arrived from outer space, it tried to destroy us."

"You don't really think these creatures you saved during your test would mean us any harm? Do you think they're interested in Concordia too? Like the Scythians?"

"Who knows?" Cherry replied. "If they're members of the Assembly it's unlikely. But we only saw them during a simulation. We didn't meet them. I have no idea what they're really like and I'm worried about security issues. We can't afford the slightest suspicion of the existence of our armaments depots coming to the attention of the Scythians. Our secret weapons are the only defense we have, but visitors from offplanet wouldn't need to do much digging to find out about Cerberus, for example. That place is no secret to anyone here because nearly everyone has a grandparent who was living in Sidhe when construction began. And it's been hard to keep the locations and contents of the other depots under wraps. If that information falls into Scythian hands—or whatever it is they have—we might as well forget any element of surprise if they attack."

"What do you suggest?" Meredith asked.

"Well, we also can't afford to turn this delegation away either. They're fellow members of the Assembly. We have no valid excuse not to meet with them."

"And we would be foolish to refuse an opportunity to secure the close friendship of another galactic force."

Quinn said, "The *Opportunity* is available if you would prefer the visitors don't come down to the planet surface."

The starship the threads had built for the humans to travel to the Assembly's space station had remained in orbit ever since its return. It was impossible to hide it, but Meredith had decided not to allow any more interstellar missions out of fear of triggering a visit from the Scythians.

"Yes," said Meredith to Cherry. "That's another option, if you're really worried about the visitors coming here."

"The *Opportunity* is tiny. It was barely large enough for four passengers. I can't imagine hosting an official meeting of two galactic powers aboard it. No. They'll have to come here, providing they can survive in Concordia's environment."

"If not, they may invite you to come aboard their ship," said Quinn. "The *Opportunity's* EVA suits are still available."

"They might," Cherry concurred. "I hadn't thought of that." She might almost prefer the effort and potential danger of going aboard the aliens' ship to having them visit Concordia. "I think we should accept their meeting proposal and wait to see what they suggest."

"I was coming to the same decision myself," said Meredith. "But if they do want to come down to the surface, I'll need you to arrange the security operation."

"Of course. That shouldn't be a problem. As I recall, these aliens are quite small and probably weak too. It won't be hard to keep them exactly where we want them. Time is short, so I'll begin the preparations now in case they want to come here. We can hold the meeting at the government offices in Annwn."

"I agree that's the best place," said Meredith. "Use whatever resources you need, with my full permission."

"Thanks. Let me know as soon as you hear anything." Cherry was about to say goodbye when she remembered a pertinent question. "What are the visitors called, Quinn? I never knew the name of their species."

"As with many advanced galactic life forms, their name only translates into your language as 'people', but..." he was silent for a couple of beats. "Yes, Kes has given them a name. It's *Parvus wilderensia*."

"*Wilder*ensia?" Cherry echoed. "Wilder. He's named them after Wilder. I don't believe it. He's done it again."

Meredith's smile told Cherry she knew exactly what she was talking about.

"We'll just call them Parvus," Meredith said.

Cherry sighed. "Thanks, Quinn. I'll be sure to pass on the bad news to Wilder." She said goodbye and took the elevator to the first floor.

She was almost certain the visiting aliens would want to come down to the surface if they could. Quinn had once mentioned that life-supporting planets were rare in the galaxy. The visitors would probably be curious about Concordia and want to see it with their own eyes...or experience it with whatever sense organs they had.

But on her way to Annwn to organize the security around the landmark meeting, she wanted to take a small detour.

Six

Three small, two-seater helis were secured to the roof of the government building by docking clamps in case of strong winds. The helis were restricted to government use only, as Wilder had known perfectly well when she suggested that Kes accompany her to the mysterious object beyond the mountain range. The trip would have taken her days by any other mode of transport, even if she'd managed to hitch a ride on one of the ultra-fast trucks that went to refineries near the mines.

She and Kes walked to the nearest heli and Kes unlocked the doors with a code.

Wilder said, "Mind if I fly it?" Without waiting for an answer she climbed in the pilot's side.

"Have you flown one of these before?" Kes opened the passenger door while she settled herself at the controls.

"Oh yes, lots of times." She started the engine and under the noise of its whirr she added, too quietly for Kes to hear, "In a sim."

"How come? I didn't think non-government personnel were allowed."

"You know Cherry. Always asking me to do one thing or another." Wilder didn't mention that this last fact, though true, had nothing to do with flying helis.

"In that case, be my guest."

She checked the surrounding airway was clear—it would have been a miracle if it wasn't, considering how few aircraft flew in Concordian skies. The danger of attracting unwanted attention from the Scythians was too great. But she checked nonetheless. Unsurprisingly, nothing was in the sky for kilometers around. She disengaged the locking clamps, engaged the heli's rotors, and lifted the machine up into the atmosphere. The rooftop retreated swiftly below them.

"You know," Kes said, "It's surprising what I miss about Earth. I always knew I would miss certain foods and things like going to the cinema and visiting theme parks, but I never thought I would miss birds."

"Those animals that fly? Yeah, I can see that. They must have been amazing."

"I took birds for granted," he mused. "They were always just *there*. Pigeons and sparrows in the streets, blue jays and robins in the countryside, geese migrating in the spring and autumn. I never took the time to properly observe them. I was too busy thinking about life forms on other planets to pay any attention to the creatures on my own." He sounded uncharacteristically pensive.

"Are you feeling homesick?"

"I guess so, though I'm homesick for somewhere that no longer exists."

There was a tone in his voice that caused her to look at him. "Are you okay?"

"I'm fine. Don't worry." He gave her a smile, but she wasn't convinced that all was well with her friend. However, he didn't seem ready to talk about what was bothering him, so they chatted about other topics as they flew toward the mountains.

At one point, he put a hand to his ear and said, "Hi, Cherry...Uhuh...Really?" His eyes widened and he turned a shocked face toward Wilder. "When?... Sure. Of course. I wouldn't miss it for the world. It'll be good to meet the little guys in the flesh, so to speak."

"What is it?" asked Wilder after Kes finished speaking to Cherry.

When he related the news that Concordia was about to receive a visit from another member of the Galactic Assembly, she was surprised but delighted. "That's fantastic. When do I get to meet them?"

His features fell. "I don't know if you can. I don't know if the Leader will allow it. This is an official visit."

"Ugh, you're right. Why would she arrange for them to meet me?" Maybe she should get a job after all, she pondered. A government job. It would be nice to have a heli at her disposal and she might get to do something interesting, like meet visiting aliens.

Mountain peaks were rising above the horizon. "Where are we going exactly?"

"I'll put in the coordinates." Kes pressed the dashboard screen, transferring numbers from his files.

She relinquished the controls to the autopilot and folded her arms as she gazed out at the view. The landscape was passing swiftly below, transforming from farmland to wilderness. To one side the road to the mountains cut through the vegetation. Autotrucks ran along the gray line.

To pass the time, she asked Kes about his latest discoveries about the Fila. Though the research had been going on while they'd been away, and he had continued it since their return, there was always some new discovery to be made about the tentacled aliens.

She listened with half an ear as they neared the mountain range and then rose to the height of the pass. She was interested to hear the latest findings about the Fila, but she was also puzzling over the strange object they were about to investigate. The more she thought about it, the more intrigued she became about what it might be. She felt that familiar tug of desire to find out the truth about a mystery, no matter how long it took.

Her earlier fear returned. Had someone else managed to re-invent a-grav? Had their vehicle cruised to such a height that, when the machine failed, it burned as it passed through Concordia's atmosphere? She hoped she was wrong, for two reasons. Firstly, she would hate for a fellow inventor to have died horribly, and, secondly, *she* wanted to be the one to provide the colony with a-grav. Was that somewhat narcissistic? Perhaps. But there it was.

They crossed the mountain range through a cleft between two of the tallest peaks. Snowy slopes rose to each side and the air inside the heli grew chill, though the vehicle automatically supplied additional oxygen. Finally, the heli began to descend. However, it wasn't until they were nearly at ground level she spotted the crumpled, twisted wreck. Tall vegetation had already begun to overhang it, obscuring the scorched, dull metal.

As the heli touched down on a patch of rough ground several meters from the wreck, Kes lifted a hand to his ear comm. "The results from the tests on the object's material came through. Wait a minute, Aggy, let me patch Wilder in." A moment later, he said, "Okay, go ahead."

"Right," came Aggy's voice through Wilder's comm. "I'm sending these over as I speak." She then proceeded to reel off a list of substances and proportion percentages to four decimal points.

"Thanks, Aggy," said Kes when she'd finished. He turned to Wilder. "Well that was gobbledygook to me. Does it mean anything to you?"

"I think it does." The list had begun to sound familiar after Aggy had read out less than half of it. As the woman had continued, recognition hit Wilder like the flick of a wet towel from a bully—a sensation she knew too well. She'd waited to have her suspicion confirmed, but she could have finished Aggy's list for her.

The heli rotors slowed to a stop, and Wilder stepped out onto the knee-high vegetation. She strode toward the mystery craft that perhaps was no longer such a mystery.

"Well, what is it?" Kes asked as he followed. "Don't leave me hanging."

But amazement and disbelief were keeping her silent. She wanted to set eyes on the object, otherwise she might not believe it was real. She didn't want to give an answer because it would sound ridiculous.

The outline of the wreck peeked tantalizing through gaps in the trees and tall plants surrounding it. She forced her way between overhanging fronds and pushed aside a vine.

The sight that greeted her gave no clue to the object's guessed origin whatsoever. The outer surface of the misshapen lump had burned at such a high temperature it had partially melted. Stumps of what must have been some kind of instruments stuck out, their edges dissolved into obscurity. It was no wonder the person who had stumbled across it had thought the find was sufficiently remarkable to report.

"Wow." Kes had arrived at the scene. He ran a hand over the strange, destroyed surface of the object as he walked around it. "Hey, look here, you can see inside."

She joined him. A dark hole gaped in the side, but it revealed little of the interior. The remains sticking out of the hole nearly made her heart stop. "What's this, do you think?" She touched the broken protrusion.

Kes frowned. "I'm not sure. It's odd that it wasn't burned away like the rest."

"It *is* odd, isn't it? What would you say if I told you I think it used to be a door?"

His eyebrows rose. He squatted down in order to peer more closely. "A door? You mean it opened after the object landed and that's why it didn't burn off? But that would mean there was something inside and it managed to open a door and come out."

She took a breath. "Kes, the breakdown of the object's metallic compound—it exactly matches the material the Guardians' weapons are made from."

"No," he breathed, straightening up and staring at her. "No way. It can't be. They were destroyed decades ago, and you said this thing had been here only a few weeks."

"A vessel without power might float around in space for centuries, thousands of years or even longer, before the gravity of an astronomical body finally snares it."

"But the *Mistral* was annihilated when Faina flew it into the Scythian flagship. How could a piece this size have survived intact?"

"I don't know, but I don't think it's impossible. I only know that the material this is made from matches the Guardians' weapons. It seems too much of a coincidence for there to be no connection."

He squatted down again. “Could it have been an emergency escape capsule that jettisoned just before impact?”

“Maybe it was caught up in the explosion and its engine was destroyed.”

“So, was a Guardian inside, and it’s managed to open the hatch and get out?”

“That isn’t as crazy as it sounds,” Wilder said. “But if this *is* the wreck of a Guardian escape vehicle, where’s the Guardian?”

Seven

Cherry's autocar rolled to a stop outside an imposing dwelling. The three-story, double-fronted house sat alone on an offshoot of the highway that ran from Oceanside to Annwn, in a low spot between the surrounding hills. A garden of architectural native vegetation surrounded it, though the plants were unkempt and overgrown, as if no one had tended them in a long while.

The house was constructed from reclaimed building materials originally from the *Nova Fortuna*. The plastiwood of the colony's first settlement had proven extremely tough and durable, and it remained the favored material for creating new dwellings, providing the builder could get it.

The house's owner was exactly the person to find a way to acquire this scarce, valuable resource.

The door of her vehicle opened but she didn't get out. Was she doing the right thing? It had been years since she'd been here, and her visit was unannounced. Seconds passed as she hesitated. Finally, she exited the car. Since she had taken the precious time out of her busy day to come here, she might as well follow through with her visit.

As she walked to the residence, stepping over green tendrils snaking over the path, the front door opened. Aubriot stood in the doorway. He raised an arm and leaned on the frame, his expression inscrutable.

She climbed the house steps and halted. "Can I come in?"

Wordlessly, he walked away down the hall, leaving the door open.

She stepped inside and closed the door. She followed Aubriot into a front room but paused on the threshold. The place was a mess. Dirty laundry was strewn about, used dishes and cutlery cluttered the coffee table, and dust lay thick over every surface.

Ever since she had known Aubriot, he'd been generally neat and tidy in his habits. It was a fact that had surprised her, knowing his privileged upbringing, including servants to attend to all his needs.

He was sat on his sofa in his characteristic sprawl, legs splayed and arms resting along the back. Defiance gleamed in his eyes as he took in her reaction to the state of his room, yet there was no hint of embarrassment about his living conditions.

"Mind if I sit down?" she asked.

"Make yourself at home," he replied in a sarcastic tone.

She picked up some clothes from an armchair and hesitated as she looked for somewhere to put them. No surface was empty. Finally, she placed the clothes carefully on the floor.

He watched her movements. When she sat down he said, "Want a drink?"

"I do, thanks."

Without asking what she wanted, he got up and strode out.

She was already regretting her decision to visit her former lover. It would be so much easier to simply discharge Aubriot from his duties and appoint someone else in his place. That was what he deserved after his behavior at the training exercise, and he'd deserved the same for similar behavior over the previous few months. Retaining someone who had demonstrated he was unfit for service set a bad example.

But he was a good military strategist, or he was when he chose to be. He was probably better than her and so the best in the colony, considering no one living except he and she had taken part in any actual battles. If only she could return him to his previous enthusiasm for his job. It could mean the difference between defeat or victory when the Scythians returned.

The problem was, she didn't know why he'd begun behaving so oddly. She didn't know what was wrong, and so she had no idea how to fix it.

He reappeared, holding a steaming mug. He hadn't poured anything for himself. She sipped the brown liquid. It was her go-to beverage, made from chicory root. "You remembered."

He shrugged and returned to his seat. She thought she detected embarrassment underlying his nonchalance. She took another sip of hot liquid and, failing to find anywhere to put the mug down, cupped it between her hands on her lap. "You know why I'm here, right?"

He smirked. "Yeah. You can't keep away from me. Want to go upstairs?"

She tilted her head. "Don't kid around, okay? This is serious." The activity he alluded to had ceased to be a part of their tenuous relationship long ago, prior to the mission to the Assembly. His narcissistic rage over the fact that she'd loved Ethan had killed any prospect of a return to their convenient arrangement.

"Look," she said, "will you tell me what's going on? Your behavior the other day...it wasn't like you. And that wasn't the first time something like that has happened. What's gone wrong? You used to love what you do. You lived for it. Now, it's like you don't care anymore." She glanced around her. "You seem to have stopped caring about anything."

"I was only a bit late. That's all. No need to get your knickers in a twist."

"Oh, for stars' sake, will you speak English for once?" His habit of dropping archaic sayings into his speech had annoyed her for years. He appeared to love confusing her and everyone else with his weird use of language.

"I mean..." h leaned forward, rested his elbows on his knees, and looked her in the eye "you're overreacting."

"I'm not, and you know it. If our roles were reversed you would have kicked me out long ago."

He broke eye contact, leaned back into the sofa again, and crossed his legs at the ankles. "If our roles were reversed, things would be different."

"What do you mean? Concordia's defense force? How would it be different?"

He remained maddeningly silent.

"I'm doing the best I can. If you think I'm doing something wrong, making some mistakes, I want to hear about it. All I want to do is protect the colony. Aubriot, I value what you have to say. I *want* you to help me. But what you're doing now is no help at all."

Her ex-lover folded his arms and gazed into the middle distance.

She was quickly losing patience. He was being unbearable, as usual. He didn't give a shit about the colony and never had. He'd only ever cared about himself and now even that seemed beyond him.

"Okay," she said. "I know there isn't a chance in hell you're going to tell me what's been going on with you recently, but I need to know something and I need to know it now. You have to give me a straight answer. Do you understand?"

He smirked again. "Sure, *General*."

"Do you remember the aliens in the simulation at the space station? The ones you decided not to save when the station was attacked?"

"Yeah, I remember. I stand by my decision. What about them?"

"A delegation of them is on its way here right now. I think they want a closer relationship with us."

"Really?" He rubbed his lips with a finger.

She was relieved to get a reaction out of him at last. "Yes, really. I don't need to spell out to you how important this could be to Concordia. Things are moving on and I have to keep on top of the situation security- and military-wise. Now, despite what you say, I am *not* overreacting about your behavior. Your attitude has been atrocious for weeks. You've been late for duty, and from what I've heard I suspect you've been drunk while on duty too. I'm pretty sure you've also been fraternizing with your subordinates. Those are just a few misdemeanors, but, worst of all, you've been failing to train the soldiers adequately. That exercise the other morning was a shitshow. I can't afford to have someone with your attitude in such a high position of responsibility, especially at the moment. What I've come here to say is, if you give me your word all that is going to end today, I won't discharge you."

"Give you my word?" His eyebrows lifted.

He was playing with her. Though clearly something was bothering him deeply, on another level he was enjoying himself.

But she had grown bored of his egotistical games long ago. "What's it to be? You're an asshole and you know it, but I've never known you to go back on a promise. If you assure me right now you're going to change, you can remain in your position."

His features fell into a deadpan expression. He studied her. Just as much as she was watching him for a response, he was watching her. What it was he was looking for, she didn't know.

After a few long seconds, his eyes turned dull. "Ah well, looks like the military life isn't for me."

She almost gasped. His response was not what she'd been expecting. She'd thought that, faced with the prospect of losing something he had lived for for years, ever since the defense force's inception, he would decide to make a change. The last thing she'd thought he would do was toss the entire enterprise aside, especially not after hearing the news of this interesting development. Her heart sank into her stomach.

Suddenly aware her mouth was hanging open, she closed it with a snap. Aubriot wasn't looking at her, though. He was studying his toes. She was tempted to ask him to reconsider, but she'd already given him way too many chances. "What will you do?" It was all she could think to say.

"Actually, I was thinking I might start up a brewery." He spread his fingers and inspected his fingernails.

"A *brewery*?"

"Yeah, the beer around here is shit. Always has been. It's about time someone showed the colony how it should be done."

"Right." She stood up and put her cup on the floor. "Good luck with that."

"Thanks." He continued to avoid eye contact.

"I'd better go. The delegation arrives tomorrow."

"Fine. I'll show you out."

"No, it's okay."

When he accepted her response without an answer, she left his dirty, messy living room.

Eight

Wilder tapped her ear comm. Five meters above her, within the overhanging tree fronds, an electric motor started up. A moment later, a cradle of plaited vines descended. She climbed into it and tapped her comm again to move upward to her tree home, gripping the twisted vines affectionately. Despite the six Concordian years that had passed since she made the cradle the strands remained strong.

Other materials had been available after her return from the mission to the Galactic Assembly—living in a regular house had gotten old fast, especially after her long confinement aboard the *Opportunity*—but she preferred using the same tree fronds and vines from which she'd built her original house. Repeating the same process pleased her sense of nostalgia and the natural materials were perfectly suited to the project: they were light and tough and they blended into the surrounding vegetation, giving the added benefit of camouflaging her home against unwanted visitors.

Not that she felt in danger from other Concordians. As far as she knew, no serious crimes were ever committed, perhaps due to genetic selection of the generational colonists or the equality and stability of the civilization they were creating. Yet there was nothing she liked better than peace, quiet, and the certainty that no one would disturb her while she was working.

She stepped off the cradle and onto the platform supporting her tree home. Except for the rustling of leaves in the evening breeze, the silence of the forest surrounded her. Looking forward to an evening working on her pet project, she pushed open her front door.

Two slim, gray, four-legged creatures awaited her on the other side, alerted to her arrival by the activation of the electric winch. Before she even had time to close the door, the two creatures ran up over her pants and shirt until they reached her collar, which they clung to with small paws while sniffing her face and hair.

"Hi guys," she said, petting the creatures. "What's been happening?"

They ignored her question and continued to snuffle her hair and neck. Finally, they stared at her face, their bright black eyes shiny each side of their long snouts. Apparently satisfied she was who they thought she was, they both climbed into the open neck of her shirt. After burrowing down to the place where her shirt was tucked into her pants, they snuggled there, comfortable in her body heat.

"Not much, I guess."

She crossed the floor of her small, one-room home and took out a box of crackers and a tub of yeast spread from a cupboard. She also took a plate from another cupboard and a knife from a drawer. One of the animals in her shirt wriggled, slightly scratching her with its short claws.

"Hey, be careful."

Pulling out the only chair at her table, she sat down and turned on the interface embedded in the surface. She opened the tub and spread the yeast paste on a cracker. Meanwhile, the creatures nestling in her shirt ascended to the open collar and peeked out.

"Here you go, Puddle." She broke off a piece of cracker and lifted it to the right-hand animal, who took it from her fingers and inspected the morsel carefully before popping it into its mouth. A bulge appeared in the animal's cheek.

"And one for you, Piddle." She handed a second crumb to the left-hand creature, who did the same. She hadn't yet figured out what sex the creatures were, assuming they reproduced sexually.

She'd had a couple of years to spend on the problem, ever since Piddle and Puddle had first emerged from the tree trunk at the center of her home. She'd named them after their poor toilet habits, but she hadn't learned much more about their behavior or anatomy.

She also hadn't told Kes of their existence, despite being fairly certain that neither he nor any of the other xenobiologists had discovered the species. She didn't like the idea of her little friends being prodded and poked by scientists.

The latest news scrolled across her interface, featuring the top headline:

DELEGATION OF PARVUS ARRIVES TOMORROW

Parvus? They had to be the creatures from the Galactic Assembly. Kes had received a message from Cherry about them but Wilder didn't know any more than what he'd told her. She opened a comm and stated Cherry's official title.

Cherry answered immediately. "Hi, I can't speak right now. I have to get ready to meet the Parvus delegation."

"I guessed that. What I want to know is, why has this only been announced the day before they're arriving? This is a huge step for the colony."

"Sorry. I'll explain later."

A tone from Wilder's comm told her the connection was severed.

She tried to contact Kes, but his comm was busy. She decided to wait awhile and try to find out more about the alien visitors. She ate her cracker. Piddle and Puddle begged for more food, climbing up her neck and tugging on her earlobes and hair.

As she chewed her sparse meal and broke off two more pieces of cracker, she wondered about the synchronicity of today's events. It seemed an odd coincidence that the strange object she'd been investigating had arrived only a few weeks before the surprise visit of an alien delegation.

Was Cherry even aware of the other arrival on the planet? There was no reason she should be, unless Kes had told her, and he probably hadn't said anything yet. They didn't know if their guess was correct. Yet the colony's military commander *should* know of the potential link.

She requested contact with Cherry again, only to hear the 'no contact' tone. Dammit. Cherry had set her comm to only receive from certain personnel. She considered contacting Meredith, who was probably one of the few people who could speak to Cherry, but she didn't know Meredith well. Would it be too presumptuous of her to contact the Leader about her worries? After all, the object out in the wildlands beyond the mountains was just a lump of twisted metal. Everything else was guesswork.

She decided to think it over some more before making a decision. Perhaps she would talk to Kes and they could decide together.

She ate a final cracker and read the rest of the day's news. A woman had given birth to quintuplets and all the babies were healthy and doing well. Multiple births were common, but from what Wilder understood they hadn't been common on Earth. Had that been something Cariad had factored in when she'd picked the original generational colonists and the frozen gametes stored on the *Nova*? The information wasn't mentioned in the colony records and now no one would be able to find out. Cariad had died two and a half years ago. Her funeral hadn't been anywhere near as well attended as Ethan's, which Wilder thought was a shame. The woman's contribution had been huge, but obviously not as well recognized.

After scanning the other headlines and not finding anything of particular interest, she scooped the crumbs from her table, opened a window, and threw them out. While she was doing this, Piddle and Puddle climbed from her shirt, dropped onto the table, ran down one of its legs, and raced to the bed of dried plant material they'd constructed in a corner. Only the finest, softest strands of vegetation had been deemed suitable. Wilder thought of the place as their 'grooming center' because that was all they seemed to do there. The two creatures set about licking and smoothing each other's short fur.

She turned off her comm and went to a a circular machine a meter and a half across and half a meter tall. A shell covered half the domed surface. The other half was bare, the intricate, detailed circuitry and mechanisms displayed.

She had spent months working on the a-grav device. Before that she'd spent years, off and on, deciphering the principles of a-grav outlined in the Guardians' data. Colony scientists had also stumbled across the information, and now only they had official permission to work on its development due to the—in Wilder's estimation, extremely small—chance of a serious accident. Others were working on re-inventing the process too. They had a little community where they discussed their work, and they had even managed to acquire a flitter engine to reverse engineer. But it all had to be kept secret.

Many times she had given up, throwing a cloth over the machine in disgust and turning her attention to a new puzzle. The problem was, the Guardians' data only recorded the theory, not the exact details on how to neutralize gravity. It was the application of the theory that was the stumbling block, and had been for years, even prior to her return.

Despite her lack of success, she had never gathered the resolve to throw the prototype out. The machine remained in her living space, taunting her. Over the last few weeks, however, she'd felt she was making real progress.

The Guardians' data was complex, but the problem boiled down to balancing the proportions of particles during each stage of the process. Others in the group working on the problem weren't convinced. They were sure the answer could not be so simple, but she knew from her experience with the Scythian spiders that sometimes the solution really wasn't complicated.

She checked the previous balance she'd used, reached into the machine, and made a tiny adjustment. The effect would only increase the amount of particle type by a few million, but the tiny increment could make all the difference.

She started up the process. A split second later, she found herself pinned against the ceiling. A crushing pain emanated from her ribs. Her machine sat under her torso and was trying to force itself upward.

It had worked!

She'd done it.

She'd cracked the secret of a-grav.

But agony drained her elation. Red-hot knives were stabbing her chest. Her machine was driving into her with a dreadful force. She could barely breathe. She reached for the off switch but her hand only met smooth metal. The switch was too far away. She wriggled, trying to ease closer to it despite the pain, but she was pinned too firmly to move even a centimeter.

A creak came from above. The ceiling was feeling the pressure too. If the material gave way, the a-grav machine would fly upward through the atmosphere and into space. It would move fast, probably too fast for her to move off before it carried her so high she would fall to her death.

Ah! Her ear comm. All she needed to do was comm someone to come out and help her. She touched her ear. The comm was gone! The impact of hitting the roof had popped it out.

She gasped in pain. Even if she could breathe enough to yell, no one would hear. Her nearest neighbor lived kilometers away, near Cerberus. What could she do? Numbness was spreading from her arms and legs. She felt like she was going to pass out. How long could she last? How long would it take before someone realized she was missing and come looking? She frequently turned off her comm. No one would think it strange if she was uncontactable, and she had no steady job, no boss to notice she hadn't turned up for work.

Potentially, days could pass before someone came to find her. Could she last that long?

NINE

An officer called Ellis was in charge of the security detail for the meeting with the Parvus. Cherry had chosen him because he was one of the few who seemed to take his position seriously. Major Ellis had posted guards along the route from the spaceport to the government office, but he had ordered them to wear dress uniforms, as if their position were ceremonial rather than military.

The idea behind the decision was to avoid offending the visitors if possible. Meredith had been adamant that she wanted the Parvus to receive a warm welcome and not be treated as a threat. Cherry understood the Leader's reasoning: Concordia could not afford to jeopardize the potential friendship of a galactic power. On the other hand, it was her responsibility to protect the colony.

Cherry was uncomfortable in her own dress uniform under the hot sun as she waited with Meredith, government department heads, and Kes for the Parvus to disembark their vessel. The Leader had wisely invited Kes as the colony's leading expert on intelligent alien life forms and veteran of the mission to the Galactic Assembly.

Their guests' ship was boxy and not at all aerodynamic, causing Cherry to wonder if the Parvus's home planet had a thin atmosphere. A portal had opened but, several minutes later, no one and nothing had emerged.

Cherry glanced at Meredith, who was sweating and looking stressed. From private conversations, Cherry knew Concordia's Leader was feeling the strain of her job. Everyone expected her to live up to her father's reputation and she had been re-elected year after year, following the pattern of Ethan's terms of office. The rule that a Leader could serve only one term had been dissolved expressly for Ethan's benefit, though, from what Cherry had heard, entirely against his wishes.

Meredith was a good Leader, but she lacked her father's calm pragmatism and levelheadedness, born of deep humility. The role had been thrust upon her the same as it had been thrust upon Ethan, but, unlike her father she wasn't rising to the challenge, she was sinking under it.

"At last," a voice breathed.

Figures were emerging from the shuttle.

The Parvus were as Cherry remembered them, EVA suits and all. Concordia's atmosphere was clearly not breathable for the visitors. Though on the space station she hadn't had much time to properly look at them, she recalled their small bodies and six short limbs. They walked on all of them, their bodies parallel to the floor, like sluglimpets. As they descended the ramp from their ship, Cherry noticed they also seemed to be struggling with the planet's gravity. The creatures walked slowly and heavily.

"Welcome to Concordia," Meredith said.

The Fila had put a translation system in place between the welcoming committee's comms and the Parvus's EVA suits.

"We are glad to be here," came the reply. The Fila had used their usual artificially generated human voice to convey the Parvus's communication. What did the creatures really sound like? Did they make noises at all? Maybe they had other methods of communication, like the Fila.

"Please allow us to escort you to our meeting room," Meredith said. She introduced herself, adding, "I am the Leader of this colony." She also introduced Cherry and the other dignitaries. "Would you like to remain on Concordia after our meeting? I would be delighted to show you some of the most interesting and beautiful places on our planet. We have apartments where you can rest, but I'm afraid we would require more time to build a habitation where you could remove your suits."

"Your intention is noble," the Parvus' representative replied. "We observe that is the nature of your species."

Meredith looked understandably nonplussed by this reply. Cherry didn't know what it meant either. Did the Parvus want to stay a while and take a tour or not?

"Please come this way," Meredith said after a slight pause. "The place where we will hold the meeting is only a short journey from here."

The two parties proceeded to walk to the transportation that would take them to a government building. Progress was slow. The Parvus moved with great effort, and it seemed to Cherry that sometimes their coordination of their legs got mixed up.

"Is your planet very different from Concordia?" Kes asked.

"It is different in some ways. In some ways it is the same. It is smaller and there is much more water. It must be hard for you to live in a desert."

Cherry looked at the tree ferns that lined the route and the vegetation in the distance. Were the Parvus mistaking the pavement and buildings for natural features?

Kes chose not to correct the speaker or to explain. It was clearly a topic for a much longer and more informal conversation than the occasion allowed.

The Parvus were transported separately from the rest of the delegation in a vehicle with a specially lowered floor. Cherry, Meredith, Kes, and the rest of the welcoming committee were driven in chauffeured government cars.

Eventually the delegates reached the room Cherry had chosen to host the meeting. She thanked the stars she'd picked one on the first floor. Forcing the Parvus to climb steps made for humans while also fighting Concordian gravity would have been embarrassing for all concerned.

Guards were already stationed and Major Ellis had fitted the place with recording devices too, according to the Leader's instruction.

When the Parvus delegation reached the table they stood upright on their two hindmost legs and rested their upper pair of limbs on the tabletop. Their other two limbs hung in midair. Cherry noticed for the first time that tripod digits extended from the upper limbs. She couldn't see much of their faces through the dark visors of their helmets, but she thought she detected black, shiny eyes. More than two of them.

The human members of the party sat down.

Meredith opened the meeting by saying, "In our culture it is the custom to offer our guests refreshments as a gesture of welcome but unfortunately due to the fact you must wear environment suits we are unable to do so on this occasion. Please be assured we would like to extend our warmest appreciation of your visit."

This little speech excited the Parvus in what Cherry hoped was a good way. They wiggled their digits and turned to look at each other.

"Your refreshments are happily received."

What?

Meredith was similarly taken aback at the Parvus's response. Her eyes flicked to Kes, probably looking for some kind of explanation or reassurance. His shoulders moved in a slight shrug. Their resident alien expert had no idea what was going on either.

The obvious thing to move onto next was the reason for the Parvus's visit to Concordia, but it would have been rude to ask the question outright. Maybe the aliens were simply paying them a visit and traveling light years only for that simple purpose was normal in their culture.

The Parvus said, "We would also like to show appreciation. We are in your debt after you saved the life of one of our people while sacrificing your own."

"Thank you," Meredith replied. "But as I understand it, our members who went to the Assembly's space station didn't actually save anyone. They were experiencing a sim. So your thanks is welcome but not needed."

"Their intention was to save our people. That is not the same as saving them in reality. It is better."

"It's...Uh." Meredith paused again. Her gaze desperately sought Kes's.

"Um," he said, spreading his hands on the table top. "Am I right in thinking you see intention as more valuable than action?"

"Intention is more valuable. It is the accurate measure of a person's worth."

"I see," said Kes. "We think differently—"

"But we respect your position," said Meredith.

"We have come here to inform you in person, that if the Scythians attack you, it is our intention to aid in the defense of your planet."

"Right," said Meredith. "It's your *intention*."

The meaning of her emphasis was not lost on the humans present. The Parvus were either playing a weird game of pledging empty support or they genuinely believed they were offering something beneficial. Of course, their offer was actually worthless.

Cherry was annoyed. All the work everyone had done, all the stress and fuss over Concordia's first visit from a member of the Galactic Assembly, was all for nothing. The Parvus had nothing to give except words. "I'm sorry, but your intentions are not going to help us. The Scythians aren't going to withdraw because we told them you *intend* to defend us."

"General," said Meredith, "I didn't invite you to speak. I apologize on behalf of my colleague."

Cherry leaned backward in her chair. Their visitors were a useless waste of time. She almost regretted saving one of them during the sim.

"May I ask a question?" said Kes.

"Go ahead," replied Meredith.

"If you do not act on an intention and someone dies as a result, isn't that a bad thing?"

"No," said the Parvus. "When a person dies they join the waters of the galaxy and nourish other life. That is a good thing."

Great.

Concordia's 'friends' harbored a death wish for humans and everyone else. At least the Scythians were upfront about wanting to kill them.

"As well as our intention of support," the Parvus went on, "we have another gift for you as a gesture of thanks."

You're going to do us a big favor and shoot us now? Cherry bit back her reply. She wondered if Aubriot would have managed to do the same if he'd been here. For once, she missed his sarcasm.

Meredith was looking like she felt seriously out of her depth, but she managed to say, "It is very kind of you to offer us a second gift."

"This is less valuable than the first, and perhaps it is entirely worthless. It is information, but you may already be aware of it."

"Anything you would like to tell us, we're happy to hear," Meredith said.

"Humans are the most recent species to join the Galactic Assembly. We guess from this that your species is young in terms of galactic history. Our species is very old. We believe we are the oldest intelligent life form in the Assembly and, as far as we know, the galaxy as a whole."

Cherry wondered how the Parvus had managed to survive so long, given their desire to 'join the galactic waters'.

"Our knowledge of the development and spread of other species is vast. We have come here to bring you information about Scythian history."

Cherry sat up.

"This planet that you have settled, it is the Scythian origin planet."

The humans in the room became still. Looks passed between them.

"*What?*" Meredith whispered. She took a moment to compose herself. "The Scythians evolved on Concordia?"

"Yes," the Parvus replied. "Do you measure time according to the orbit of your planet around its star?"

"We do," Kes replied. "As well as the revolution of our planet."

"In your terms," said the Parvus, "the Scythians developed into intelligent life forms on this world approximately seven million orbits ago."

Cherry was dumbstruck. Everything about Concordia she'd thought she'd known to be true was being annihilated. The planet was not unclaimed. It was not a young world where higher life forms hadn't yet evolved. It wasn't *theirs*.

"It's clear you did not know this fact," said the Parvus. "We will tell you the rest of Scythian history as we know it. The details are sparse. Information from this sector takes many hundreds of orbits to reach us and we did not understand its significance at the time we began to notice it. Only a few records exist."

Tension was almost palpable in the room as every human present focused on what the small Parvus had to say. As always, the Fila's translator voice conveyed no emotion. It was impossible to tell how the creatures felt about the revelations they were providing.

"The Scythians developed space travel eight hundred thousand orbits ago. They began to travel to nearby stars. We saw they had begun to settle another star system two hundred and fifty thousand orbits later. The time interval was long, much longer than that of other species we were watching. It seemed the Scythians were not nomadic and preferred to remain on their home planet. Then suddenly we saw a huge increase in their expansion efforts. They were settling new worlds at a rate we had not observed before. Curious about the reason for the increase in migration, we looked closely at this world, hoping to discover the answer to the puzzle. What we saw was a slow catastrophe taking place. The atmosphere of the planet was undergoing a rapid change. The air was becoming poisoned by oxygen."

"Oxygen is poisonous?" Cherry blurted.

Kes replied, "To some life forms, yes."

The Parvus continued, "Something the Scythians had done during their millennia on their home world had created the perfect conditions for the proliferation of organisms that excrete a gas the Scythians could not breathe. It appeared they were unable to reverse the process and so they were forced to abandon their planet in order to survive. They have not lived here for over one hundred and sixty thousand orbits."

"This is remarkable news," said Meredith. "I'm not sure what we can do with the information, or if there is anything we can do with it. But it certainly throws a whole new light on everything."

"No kidding," said Cherry.

TEN

As well as following the proceedings of the meeting and ruminating on the revelation about the Scythians, Kes was studying the Parvus. They were only the third intelligent alien life form he'd met in real life, after the Fila and the self-described 'organizers' of the space station—and he had yet to discover the latter's species.

The thrill of sitting in the same room and speaking with these creatures was almost as great as it had been when he'd first come into contact with the Fila. Though they were wearing EVA suits, he knew what they looked like. The Fila had passed on a raft of information on other Assembly members, after translating it as well as they could. They had included images and vids too.

His first impression of the Parvus was that they reminded him of grubs. It wasn't a pleasant connection to make, and he tried not to allow the mental association to color his opinion, but their round, plump, elongated bodies were unmistakably similar to grubs he found under rotting bark when he was a kid.

The Parvus's three pairs of legs were grub-like too, only thicker where they connected to the body. But the digits at the ends of their upper pair of limbs were unlike anything he'd ever seen. They were as prehensile as the tip of an elephant's trunk but the three 'fingers' were equidistant like the points of a triangle. Their head contained seven or eight eyes above a central mouth.

Concordia's visitors lived on a high-water-volume planet. Land masses only occupied one-sixteenth of the total surface and were mostly flat and swampy. If he remembered correctly, the planet's gravity was about sixty percent of Concordia's. The creatures seemed to be dealing with their additional weight, but he guessed they would probably leave soon. Their soft bodies contained no internal or external skeleton to protect them against the increased gravity.

Meredith had been asking the Parvus for more information about the Scythians' history on Concordia, but the creatures had little more to offer.

"We will give you our records of the changes in your planet's atmosphere, but we did not have any dealings with the Scythians until recent times, when their expansion brought them into conflict with other intelligent civilizations. It was only when we examined the information we had on planets in this sector that we understood what had happened. The current Scythian-occupied worlds all have atmospheres approximating Concordia's in its ancient past. When we examined our data more closely, and we heard of the Scythian attacks on this planet, we came to the conclusion we have related to you. The Scythians cannot live here. There is no other reason we can think of that explains why they want this world for their own."

"So, what you're telling us isn't an absolute fact?" Meredith asked.

"There are very few absolute facts, and this is not one of them. Yet we feel a strong certainty about its truth."

"Can I say something?" asked Cherry.

"Go ahead," said Meredith.

"I still don't get it. The Scythians ruined their home planet, right? That much I understand. Humans nearly did that to Earth, according to everything I was taught at school. So the Scythians left and found other planets to live on. They didn't die out, and from the sound of it they're continuing to try to expand. But why would they want to come back here? Especially if they can't live here because the atmosphere is poisonous to them."

"It isn't that hard to understand," said Kes. "This is their origin world. It's where they built their first civilization. Of course they want to keep Concordia for themselves. How would you feel about someone else taking over your home without your consent, even if you couldn't go back?"

"I wouldn't care at all. It happened all the time on the *Nova*. I lived in three care centers while I was growing up. As soon as I reached a certain age I was moved on to the next one, until I finally left and was given a single cabin. If I'd married I would have moved into married quarters. It was no big deal."

"That's probably your upbringing talking," Kes said. "In most human societies people often formed emotional attachments to the places they grew up. They would sell the houses or move away, but they still felt a connection. I wouldn't be surprised if the Scythians view Concordia as belonging to them even though they could never live here again."

"Well, it doesn't belong to them," said Meredith. "It's plain stupid to refuse someone the right to use something when you can't use it yourself. By all accounts, habitable planets are scarce. It's wrong to hoard resources."

"We must return to our vessel now," the Parvus said. "Your planet's gravity is making us uncomfortable and we need a respite."

"Of course," Meredith said. "I apologize for wasting your time with our personal discussion. Please allow me to accompany you to your shuttle."

The Parvus moved away from the table, dropping down onto all six of their legs, and waddled slowly toward the door.

Meredith rose to her feet and followed the creatures, and the rest of the human contingent did the same. "Will you be returning for further discussions? I'm sure we have plenty to talk about."

"We would enjoy that. We have many intentions we would like to agree upon with you."

Kes saw Cherry roll her eyes. He bit back a smile. Inter-cultural relations had never been easy even on Earth, where all parties were the same species. Concordians could expect plenty of difficulties over the next few centuries as they entered galactic society and formed relationships with other intelligent life forms.

Assuming they lived that long. The more he considered the fact that Concordia was the birthplace of the Scythians, the more apprehensive he felt. Colonization of new worlds was one thing—disputes over valuable new territory were to be expected—but fighting over a homeland was another thing entirely. If human history was anything to go by, the Scythians would never give up their right to Concordia nor ever see humans as anything other than invaders. Even the 'tribute' they claimed might be insufficient to persuade them not to annihilate the colonists. As time passed their attitude might change, as it had during their second attack.

The procession to the Parvus's shuttle took longer on the way back. When they were halfway, Meredith said, "Perhaps it would be more convenient if I and a few others came up to your starship for our next meeting?"

"That would not be practical." The Parvus didn't give any further explanation.

Off the top of his head, Kes couldn't remember their planet's atmosphere, but if humans couldn't breathe on the Parvus ship they could have worn EVA suits. The Parvus would know that, so he guessed the problem probably related to available space within the ship. Humans must be too big for it. They must seem like giants to the small creatures. What had the Parvus made of the Assembly station's organizers, who had been giants compared to humans?

Cherry had eased her way toward him until she walked with him at the back of the group. "How are you doing?" she asked quietly. "I haven't seen you for months."

"I've been busy, the same as you, I bet."

"Ugh, you're not wrong. Some days I almost wish I was back aboard the *Opportunity* with nothing to do except argue with Aubriot."

"You must be really suffering. It would take a lot more than a heavy workload to make me wish I had nothing to eat for months except Guardian ration bars. What do you think of this news about the Scythians?"

"Like I was saying before, I don't exactly get the significance. I thought that finding out that Scythians can't live here would be good news, not bad. But I take your word that it explains why Concordia is so important to them. The knowledge doesn't make a lot of difference to me. I have to continue to do my best to prepare to defend our home, regardless."

"How's that going?"

"The hardware is in place, it's the software I'm worried about." In response to his inquiring look, she went on, "The defense force. They're undisciplined and ineffective. I think the problem is they don't take the threat seriously. None of them has ever lived through an attack. All their lives Concordia has been safe and peaceful. They can't imagine anything different."

"Surely Aubriot can help you with that?"

"He resigned."

"He did *what*?"

"Honestly, I pushed him, and rather than pushing back, he jumped. He doesn't give a shit about the defense of Concordia anymore. Not that he ever really cared. He was only concerned about saving his own skin. Now it seems he doesn't even care about that."

"That doesn't sound like Aubriot."

"It doesn't, does it? Something's up with him, but I don't have the time to figure out what, and I'm seriously done dealing with him."

They had nearly reached the Parvus's shuttle, only the creatures were moving slower every step. Kes felt sorry for them. He would have loved to offer to pick one up and carry it, but of course that would have entirely deprived them of their dignity.

Meredith was saying something formal in farewell, thanking the creatures for their visit and expressing her hopes they could visit for another meeting soon, when a realization popped into his mind. "Hey, Cherry. I haven't told you about the Guardian yet."

She turned. "What Guardian? I thought they were all long gone."

"Not this one, maybe. Honestly, it's just a guess, and nothing's turned up yet so Wilder's probably wrong, but—"

"Wilder thinks there's a Guardian who wasn't destroyed in the Second Attack? How could that be possible?"

"If you'll stop interrupting me I'll explain."

"Wait a minute. Our visitors are leaving."

The Parvus had slowly mounted the ramp to their ship. The Concordians moved quickly away from the landing site, just in case the Parvus weren't aware of how easily they burned.

"Phew," said Meredith as she caught up to Kes and Cherry. "I'm glad that's over. I thought it went pretty well, didn't you?"

"Not bad," said Kes.

"I thought you did a great job," Cherry said. "That was quite a revelation about the Scythians originating on Concordia, but I think Kes might have a revelation of his own."

"Is this about Wilder's over-active imagination?" Meredith asked.

"Oh, you know about it?" said Cherry.

"If you mean her idea that a Guardian crash-landed on Concordia, yes, Kes already told me. I don't think there's anything in it. And, if you don't mind, I'd like you to both join me along with some of the department heads to discuss what we just learned."

"You want to have a meeting about the meeting?" Cherry asked.

Meredith smiled. "Exactly. After we get back take ten minutes or so to refresh and then I'll see you in the meeting room, okay?"

"Sure." As Cherry and Kes walked the remaining distance, she said to him, "Tell me the rest about this Guardian. It seems I'm the only person who hasn't heard about it."

"Don't give me a hard time. I only told Meredith. I was going to tell you as well, soon. It only happened yesterday." He then went on to quickly explain about the apparently crashed escape vessel the miner had found in the wild-lands beyond the mountains, and Wilder's deductions about it.

"And is it made from the same alloy as the Guardians' weapons?" asked Cherry.

"It is. That was the first thing I checked when I got back to Annwn."

"I have to admit, that is an odd coincidence."

He also explained about the new growth in the vegetation surrounding the crash site. "Wilder guessed the undergrowth had been burned there about five weeks ago."

"So if a Guardian did survive the destruction of the *Mistral* and the escape vessel finally fell to Concordia a few weeks ago, it's been wandering around the planet all this time?"

"That's kind of where Wilder's supposition falls down. If something was inside that thing, and it's a Guardian, it isn't behaving anything like we would expect it to, given what we know about them."

"That's right. Still, it's an interesting problem. I wonder what that thing out there really is."

"Perhaps we'll never know," Kes said. "Anyway, I think we have more important issues to deal with right now."

"I don't agree. Any unexplained, potentially alien, object arriving on Concordia must be thoroughly investigated. I'll send a team out to assess the object and bring it in. Honestly, Kes, it was dumb of you two to just go there and take a look at it without informing me. What if it was Scythian? What if it was booby-trapped? It can't be helped now, but, please, if anything else like that turns up, I want to know about it immediately. Sometimes I feel like I'm the only person who's taking the threat to our colony seriously."

She took a breath. "We'd better not keep Meredith waiting." She climbed the steps into the government building, and Kes followed. "By the way, how is Wilder? I keep asking her for favors. I hope I'm not wearing her out."

"She was fine when I saw her yesterday. She looked a bit overworked, but that's normal, right? I haven't spoken to her recently. I tried to contact her a couple of times this morning but she had her comm turned off. She'll get back to me when she has a bit of free time, I'm sure."

Eleven

"Come on, Wilder," said Ben, "it'll be fun."

He was standing in the open doorway of their care center. Neither of the carers were at their stations. Both of the men had girlfriends who were going planetside and they'd gone to say goodbye to them, probably along with some yucky smooching. The men weren't doing anything wrong. The care center was for children aged ten and over, who were judged to be old enough to be able to look after themselves for short periods of time. Sometimes that trust worked out, sometimes it didn't.

"I don't know," Wilder replied. "What if Ras or Harry come back and check the dorm? We'll get in heaps of trouble." She was no stranger to getting into trouble, but she knew the limits. Sneaking aboard a shuttle to go planetside would be crossing them. She was already only seven points away from a category four punishment, which could mean anything from weeding the planting beds to scrubbing the toilets. She had far more interesting ways to spend her time.

"They won't check the dorm," Ben replied. "They'll be too heartbroken and sad." He pulled a face of exaggerated sorrow and clutched his hands to his chest.

Wilder laughed.

"I tell you what," Ben continued. "Let's take some spare pillows from the cupboard and put them under our covers to make it look like we're sleeping in our beds. Ras and Harry will fall for it. I'm sure they will."

"Oh, all right." Stowing away on a shuttle did sound like fun, and she was dying to go planetside. She seemed to be the only person whose turn to take a trip to their new home hadn't come around yet. She'd had to get by with pics and vids taken by others. They were a poor substitute for actually being there. She was desperate to know what the air smelt like and how it felt to look up at a real sky, not the fake one in the Main Park.

Ben trotted to a set of cupboard doors and opened them. Bed linen, pillows, towels, and other domestic stores were stacked inside. She helped him pull out four pillows. They carried them into the six-bed dorm, where their center mates were already in bed.

One of them, Marjory, remained awake, reading her interface. "I wondered what had happened to you—hey, what are you doing?" Her eyes were round as she watched Wilder and Ben pull back their covers and lay the pillows lengthways on their beds. "You're gonna sneak out, aren't you? You guys are DEAD."

"Shhh!" said Ben. "You'll wake up the others."

"Promise you won't tell on us, Marjory?" Wilder asked. Marjory was okay, but she could be a tattle tale sometimes.

"Why shouldn't I? If I don't, and Ras or Harry find out I knew about it, I could get in trouble too."

"How would they ever know?" asked Wilder. "Why would Ben or I tell them?"

Marjory was unconvinced. She frowned and pouted. "Why should I keep your secret for you? What's in it for me?"

"I'll do tomorrow's homework for you," said Wilder.

Marjory's expression brightened. "Make it all next week's homework."

"Okay, all next week's homework." Wilder had pulled the bed cover over the pillows and was patting them to make them look like a sleeping body.

"It's a deal."

"Are you ready?" asked Ben.

"Have fun," Marjory called softly as they left.

Two children taking a transit carriage alone wasn't particularly remarkable, despite the lateness of the hour. The *Nova Fortuna* was an enclosed environment where even petty crime was extremely rare. Even fairly young children couldn't come to much harm, and everyone was used to older children testing their boundaries. Many of the adults had done it themselves.

The situation at the shuttle bay was different. The protocols for allowing Gens down to the planet surface were strict. Woken could come and go as they pleased, of course. There were far fewer of them and they had scientific studies to carry out. But if the Gens had been allowed the same privilege it would have been chaos.

Ben and Wilder hovered around the entrance, trying to look inconspicuous. In fact, it wasn't too hard to remain unnoticed. Tonight was the first night colonists would sleep on the planet. The passengers were milling around in excitement.

Preparations for the momentous event had been going on for a while. Engineers had installed an electric fence to protect the compound from native wildlife, though no one thought any dangerous animals lived there.

Then builders had erected barns where the colonists would sleep. Later on, the builders would construct houses and roads, and the barns would be used to store the equipment and produce from farms. More trips down to the surface had taken place to install electricity and build latrines. The intention was to create a self-contained encampment that could survive several days without additional supplies. That way, the necessity of constantly ferrying workers between the surface and the *Nova* could be avoided.

Ben was peering into the bay. The last shuttle would be leaving in ten minutes. The announcement to board would come soon. "Got any ideas on how to get inside?"

"Of course not," Wilder replied. "I thought *you* had a plan. This was your idea, remember?" She was having second thoughts. She didn't mind being punished for stowing away on a shuttle, but to be punished for *trying* to stow away on a shuttle seemed a monumental waste of time and effort.

Ben's gaze alighted on cargo boxes being transported across the bay. He grabbed her arm and nodded at the line of transporters. "If we climb inside a storage box, they'll never know. The bots are only programmed to take the boxes to the ship, not check inside them."

"Maybe that's because no one thought anyone would be stupid enough to hide in one?" Misgivings about the entire situation were bothering her again. Would it really hurt to wait another few days to see the planet?

Ben seemed to take her comment as a challenge rather than a rebuke. He grinned and gripped her arm a little tighter. "We can do it. I know we can. Think how much fun it'll be to spend the night down there."

"That's another thing. Will there even be bunks for us to sleep on? What if they've only provided exactly enough for the people on the schedule?"

"Then we'll sleep on the ground." He scanned the bay. If they were going to make the attempt, they only had a few minutes. One pallet of containers remained to be loaded. "I know. Pretend to chase me."

"What?"

But he was already off, running across the bay. "No," he called over his shoulder, "you can't have it. You'll have to catch me first."

She hesitated, but decided Ben would look like a dumbass or crazy if he was seen running with no one running after him. "Give me my...my doll!" She cringed as she sped after her friend. She was way too old for dolls, even if she'd ever liked them, which she hadn't.

Ben had reached the pallet loaded with storage boxes and disappeared behind it. She also ran behind the boxes and found her friend squatting down and panting. She peeked over the top of a box. Ben's ruse seemed to have worked. No one was looking in their direction. All the adults were too excited about going planetside.

He was already busy removing the seal on a box of supplies. He lifted the lid. Inside the box were bags of flour. He began lifting them out and dumping them on the pallet.

"I don't think you should do that," she whispered. "They'll need flour to eat."

"C'mon. There's plenty here. They won't miss it, and if they do they'll just comm the ship to send down more. Give me a hand, huh?"

But she felt too guilty at the thought of tampering with the colony's food. She began reading the labels on other boxes to try to find something less essential. The transporter bots were already removing the boxes from the far end of the pallet.

Meanwhile, Ben had removed enough bags of flour to make room for himself. He climbed into the box. "Put the lid on for me. I can't do it from in here."

"Ben, I changed my mind. Come out of there. We shouldn't be doing this. It's dumb and wrong. Let's go back to the dorm."

"We can't. Harry and Ras will be back by now and they'll see us walk in. They'll know we broke curfew."

"Then we'll spend the night somewhere else. We could go to Main Park."

"Don't be a wimp." His expression grew angry. "Fine. Don't come if you don't want to, but at least put the lid on for me."

"Ben..."

"You won't even do that? I thought you were my friend."

"Ugh, all right!" Wilder snatched the lid from the floor and snapped it on. A moment later, a transporter bot fastened its arms around the box and carried it away.

The announcement to board sounded over the ship's comm. While the passengers crossed the bay to the shuttle, she took advantage of the bustle and walked casually in the opposite direction. When she reached the exit, she paused and looked back. Only a few stragglers remained, hurrying toward the hatch. The cargo door was closed. Only a small pile of bags of flour sat next to an empty pallet.

She came to abrupt and painful consciousness, drew in a breath, and nearly screamed at the agony piercing her sides. Where was she? It was dark, and she couldn't move, and her stomach and chest hurt badly.

She remembered. Her a-grav machine had finally worked, but she'd been leaning over it when it activated. Now she was pinned between it and the ceiling of her home.

How long had she been stuck? At least a day. She recalled the first night, when she hadn't slept at all, and the despair she'd felt when the morning breeze arrived followed by the graying of the light. Then as the day passed she'd shouted herself hoarse, desperately hoping someone might happen to be wandering through the isolated place where she lived.

She must have passed out from exhaustion. The dream she'd had was an old one, though she hadn't dreamed it for several years. She'd thought her mind had ceased replaying that memory. Poor Ben. He hadn't survived the First Night Attack. How close had she come to losing her life too? Her waking and sleeping mind had replayed the events leading up to her friend's death over and over again as she tried to come to terms with her role in it. She blamed herself for not arguing harder. She had thought up several ways she could have prevented Ben from stowing away on the shuttle. She could have told someone what he was doing. She could have held onto him and stopped him from climbing into the box. But she'd done nothing and he had died.

Was she about to die too? Was that why her brain was returning to that event? Was her fate some kind of inevitable destiny, a punishment for her misdeeds?

She shook her head and grimaced at the pain this small movement caused. Her desperate situation and physical and mental fatigue were making her think crazy thoughts.

A scrabbling sound caught her attention. Piddle and Puddle! She'd forgotten all about them. They must have scrambled into their hole in the tree trunk in fear when the accident happened, and they'd finally gathered the courage to venture out. They were probably hungry and confused about what was happening.

"Hey, Piddle," she croaked. She coughed, just a little and winced. "Puddle, where are you?"

It was too dark to see anything. Even starlight wasn't penetrating the canopy or the small window. The night was cloudy.

More sounds of scratching and scrabbling arose from the floor.

Like a lightning bolt, an idea struck. Her ear comm was somewhere below. If she could persuade one of her pets to bring it to her, she would be able to comm for help. Both her little friends were excellent climbers. They could even climb over the ceiling, upside down. She'd seen them do it many times.

"Piddle, come here. Come here. Come and see me. I'm up here."

She listened again. Sounds of tiny claws climbing the wall came blissfully to her ears. She heard Piddle, and Puddle too, walking along the ceiling. The small creatures reached her feet. Their claws dug into her pants as they climbed along one of her legs.

"Hey guys." Her pets clambered along her side and over her arm. They commenced their usual habit of checking her hair and smell. When they tried to enter the neck of her shirt, however, they found the way blocked by the a-grav machine pressing into her.

"Go back and pick up my comm. It's down there. I need my comm."

It was hopeless. She had never trained her pets to fetch and carry. Piddle and Puddle climbed over her neck and head, trying to find a place to settle or something to eat. When they didn't find either, they climbed back onto the ceiling. There was just enough light for her to see the gleam of their little black eyes.

After a while, her pets grew tired of hanging upside down. They ran across the ceiling and down the wall. She heard them moving around for a few minutes, then silence returned. Piddle and Puddle must have gone back to their hole.

She suddenly felt very alone. Blackness surrounded her. She had no hope of anyone noticing she was missing for days, by which time it would be too late.

Twelve

Kes pushed back overhanging foliage and frowned at the undergrowth. He thought he could see a faint, narrow path but he wasn't sure. "Does that look like a track to you?" he asked Cherry, pointing at the thin snake of what looked like trodden vegetation.

"I thought you knew the way?" Cherry replied. "You said you'd been to visit her."

"I have, but only once or twice, and that was longer than a year ago."

"You haven't been to see her in more than a year? She's only seventeen. She's much too young to be living out here all on her own. I thought you were looking after her."

"I do my best. I'm busy with work, and Isobel needs my help when I'm home. And, anyway, who said I was looking after her? Wilder's nearly an adult, and you know how independent she is. She wouldn't allow anyone to look after her if they tried."

"Fair point. Sorry. I guess I feel guilty. I should have been making sure she's okay too. I've been asking her to help me with lots of things, but I don't think I ever once asked her how she was doing."

"Don't feel bad. I'm sure she's fine. I bet she's only turned off her comm because she's absorbed in something."

"For three days? I know she doesn't like people bothering her when she's working, but three days of silence must be a record."

Kes had been trying to sound upbeat for Cherry's sake, but he was worried. With all the fuss surrounding the Parvus's revelation that the Scythians originated on Concordia, he hadn't contacted Wilder until yesterday. And it was only then he discovered that her comm had been off for over 72 hours.

Immediately, a blanket of concern had settled over him. He contacted Cherry on the off chance she knew what was happening with their young friend, but she hadn't heard from Wilder either. They'd elected to go and check on her straightaway, only the little tree home was proving hard to find.

"Let's try this way," said Kes. "This patch of woodland isn't big. Even if this isn't the route she usually uses, her house shouldn't be too hard to find."

They ducked under heavy tree fronds reaching almost to the ground and stepped through the undergrowth. The light under the canopy was dim, but as his eyes adjusted, he saw his guess had been correct. The trail Wilder used was now clear. The vegetation was sparser in the lower light levels, and Wilder's comings and goings had worn a track down to the dark brown leaf mold.

Cherry had seen it too. She was already striding along the path. "I'm amazed any of this survived. Cerberus mustn't reach this far."

The construction of the military silo had affected the tree roots or the soil in some way. All the trees directly above the silo had died. No one knew why. Cerberus was deeper than Sidhe had been and the building of the settlement hadn't affected the growth above ground at all. It was a shame, but they would have been forced to kill the forest anyway. When the time came, the roof to the silo would lift and open. Thousands of trees would have made the process difficult if not impossible.

"That's right," said Kes. "I think we walked over the edge of Cerberus about fifty meters back." He stopped and, with his gaze, followed the direction the path was leading. He pointed to a spot where trees crowded together in a shallow hollow. "That's it. I remember now."

"Are you sure? I can't see anything there that looks like a tree house."

"That's the point." He trotted toward the clump of trees. "Wilder! Wilder! Are you home?" He halted to avoid the noise of his crashing through the shrubs and plants drowning out his friend's reply. But no reply came.

Cherry also called Wilder's name. When silence continued to reign over the forest, Kes and Cherry ran the final few meters to the tree house. He called out again, and then high-stepped over tall plants until he was closer to the tree and could look upward at Wilder's home.

"How do we get up there?" Cherry asked.

"I think only Wilder can activate the winch that sends the cradle down, or at least I don't know how to do it."

"We have to climb up?"

"I don't see any other way. It's either that or request a heli from Annwn and that would take half an hour."

"We can't wait that long. Can you manage it? I can't get up there with only one arm."

He assessed the trunk. It was heavily ribbed, but no branches protruded from it for the first two meters. "I can try. Maybe you can help."

"What do you want me to do?"

"Stand with your back to the tree and squat down."

She did as he'd asked. "I wish Aubriot was here. He'd be up there in no time."

"Did you comm him?"

"Yeah, but he only replied to say he hadn't heard from her. He isn't talking to me at the moment."

Kes left discussing the reason for Cherry and Aubriot's falling out to a more convenient time. "Get ready. I'm going to step on your knees."

Cherry pushed her back into the trunk, and he put one foot on her knees to help him reach the lowest branch. He grabbed it, but swinging the rest of his body up was harder. With considerable effort, he finally managed it.

The next few minutes were a struggle. Wilder's home sat another three meters higher, and when he reached it he had to gradually work his way through the floor. There was no alternative than to rip out the tough, dried, compacted fronds bit by bit. Cherry waited below in anxious silence. Eventually, she said, "I'm comming for a heli ambulance. I have a bad feeling about this."

He didn't answer. He didn't disagree, but he was too intent on what he was doing to formulate a reply. Finally, he punched through into air. "Wilder!" he yelled through the gap. He couldn't see anything except the ceiling of the room.

Then a small head poked through the hole, almost causing him to fall off the branch in surprise. A weasel-like creature was looking out at him. In another second it was gone.

"What's happening?" Cherry called up. "Can you see anything?"

"Not yet." What was that thing? Had Wilder been attacked by an unknown life form? Was the creature he'd seen venomous? He redoubled his efforts to break through into the home, tearing out a large piece of the flooring.

Then he saw her.

Wilder was stuck against the ceiling, pinned there by a machine of some kind. He couldn't see her face. It was obscured by her hanging hair. Her body was entirely limp.

"Shit!"

Hardly conscious of what he was doing, he ripped away more of the flooring and forced his arms and shoulders through the hole.

"Christ! Wilder! Wilder!"

He was inside the home. The machine crushing his friend into the ceiling hummed softly. He reached up and touched Wilder's foot, but she didn't react.

Thirteen

Cherry realized her fingernails were digging painfully into her palm. She released her fist and squinted up at Kes's figure disappearing into Wilder's home. She heard him shout the girl's name.

"Kes! What's wrong? What's happened?"

A window shutter opened and his head and shoulders appeared. His face was chalky. "Call a heli. I think she's..." He choked up and couldn't complete his sentence.

"I've already called one, remember? It's on its way. Lower the cradle so I can come up."

He withdrew into the room and a moment later a motor started up. The cradle dropped down through the tree fronds. When it reached Cherry she climbed inside, but the cradle didn't go up. "Kes! Make it pull me up."

The motor whirred again and the rope tugged upward. She rose into the tree. When the cradle reached the platform she climbed out of it. The door to the dwelling was ajar and Kes was standing with his back to her.

"Stars! What's happened?" Cherry exclaimed as she caught sight of Wilder's legs. The girl was dangling from the ceiling, held there by a machine floating in midair.

Kes held a hand to his forehead. "I knew she was working on something. Something not quite legal. I didn't guess it was a-grav."

"How long has she been hanging there? You don't think she's been there the whole three days?" She touched the girl's foot. "Wilder, sweetheart, can you hear me? We'll get you down."

"Do you think we should move her? What if her back's broken? We could make it worse."

"What if that thing's crushing her lungs and heart and she's about to die? We don't have a choice. We have to get her down."

"Okay. Let's do it."

Moving the machine so they could release Wilder was easier said than done. Kes pushed everything off a table and dragged it into position beneath the trapped girl. Cherry pulled a chair over.

Kes murmured, "You don't think she's already...Do you?"

"I'm not entertaining that thought." Cherry had already lost Ethan and Cariad, she wasn't about to lose anyone else if she could help it. "I'll take the table, you take the chair." She climbed onto the flat surface and then stood up. The buzz of an approaching heli came from somewhere in the distance.

Kes stood on the chair. Cherry moved Wilder's hair to get a look at the girl's face. Her eyes were closed and her lips were pale. Cherry gently pressed her fingertips into Wilder's neck. She thought she felt a pulse, but she wasn't sure.

"Anything?" Kes asked.

"I don't know. I think so."

"Let's move this thing and get her down."

"We need to go carefully. As soon as she isn't being held up anymore, she'll fall. We'll have to be ready to catch her."

"You're right. Wait a moment. Jump down and I'll move the table underneath her."

In a few more seconds they were ready.

Cherry was standing on the table again, preparing to push the machine away from Wilder's chest and stomach. Kes stood close by, his arms stretched out to where Wilder would fall.

The noise from the heli was louder. The pilot's voice came over Cherry's comm. "Heli ambulance ETA thirty seconds. Please advise landing area."

"I can't speak right now. Please remain on standby. One injured to evacuate."

"Received."

"Ready?" she asked Kes.

He nodded, his features tense.

She gently pushed against the humming machine, easing it sideways across Wilder's body. The machine resisted, catching on Wilder's shirt. Only half of it was covered. The other half was open, its innards complex and spiky. Cherry pushed harder.

Suddenly, Wilder groaned.

"She's alive!" Kes's eyes grew shiny.

Cherry swallowed. "I'm going to give it one hard push. For stars' sake, don't drop her."

"Of course I won't."

"Here goes." She shoved the humming device. The spikes embedded in Wilder's shirt tore free, the machine slipped out from underneath her, and she fell.

Kes caught her.

Her shirt was a mess of dried blood. She cried out in pain. Her eyes opened. "My a-grav!"

When Cherry had slid the machine away, it had risen quickly and bumped into the ceiling.

"Don't worry about that now," said Kes. "The important thing is you're okay."

Wilder reached out weakly toward the humming device. It continued to press upward, working its way into the overlapping dried leaves of the roof. "Turn it off."

"I don't know how," said Cherry. "Kes, I'll help you get her down. Then we'll carry her out to the heli."

"My a-grav!" Wilder repeated.

A rustling sound came from above. As Cherry was stepping down she looked up. The ceiling was parting. The a-grav machine had forced a gap in the leaves.

"Noooo," said Wilder.

"It's okay," Kes said. "You can build another."

Cherry told the heli pilot to land on the open ground where she and Kes had entered the forest.

Kes squatted down, still holding the girl. For the first time in a long while, Cherry wished she had two arms so she could take her from him. As it was, she could only move out of the way as he carefully climbed down.

A crack came from above. Cherry looked up just in time to see the a-grav machine disappear. One moment it was there, the next moment it was gone. Only a hole remained.

FOURTEEN

Wilder was furious. They had let her a-grav machine go. They'd let it go! And now she wasn't sure she could ever get the balance of particle inputs correct again.

She reached for the interface Cherry had placed next to her bed. Pain flared in her chest, and she gasped and paused. Her arm fell to her side. The pain was constant but it got worse whenever she moved.

Wrapping her other arm carefully around her ribs, she tried again. This time she managed to retrieve the screen. She'd been making records of all her experimentation up until the night of the accident, so she had the rough figures already. But she wasn't sure exactly what she'd done prior to the machine activating. That part was hazy in her memory, along with most of the time she'd been trapped on the ceiling.

When she thought about her stupidity in failing to secure the device, she felt like screaming in frustration. She'd been trying to neutralize gravity. What had she expected might happen if she succeeded? She couldn't remember considering the possibility. Maybe she'd thought the machine would hover a convenient one meter above the floor?

If only she hadn't been leaning over it to adjust the particle flow. If she hadn't been in the way of the machine when it flew up, she might have been able to climb onto a chair and turn it off before it broke through the ceiling.

But she hadn't, and her carelessness hadn't only nearly cost her her life, now the prototype was gone. It was probably still traveling through space. Unaffected by any object's gravity well and generating none itself, it would continue until its power ran out.

She swiped the interface open and began jabbing at the surface, finding her personal files.

The door opened and Cherry walked in, balancing a tray on one hand. Wilder lifted her head just long enough to see who was interrupting her before scowling and returning her attention to the screen.

"I thought you might have woken up," said Cherry. "I brought you something to drink and a snack." She set down the tray on a table next to the bed.

Wilder continued to focus on the interface. She'd found her files and she was opening everything pertaining to the a-grav experiment, hoping that if she ignored Cherry long enough, she would leave her alone.

"How are you feeling?"

No such luck.

"What's your pain level like? The doctor prescribed some medication and you're due another dose about now. Should I get it for you?"

Stars, couldn't the woman take a hint?

"Wilder."

"*What?!*"

"Would you like me to bring you your medication?"

"If you want. I don't care. In case you hadn't noticed, I'm trying to work."

"Don't you think you should rest a bit and concentrate on getting better? You know I had to persuade the hospital to discharge you, and the only reason they agreed was because I said you could come to my home to recuperate. It'll be a week at least before you'll be well enough to return to your daily routine, and longer than that until your ribs are fully healed."

"Look, why don't you get me my medication?" Anything to stop Cherry from talking. She was making it impossible to concentrate.

"Okay. I'll be back in a minute."

When Cherry had gone out, Wilder pushed down her covers and slid her legs over the side of the bed. Standing up was hard. Her chest felt like someone was slipping knives into it repeatedly. Nevertheless, she managed to hobble to the door, which Cherry had left open. She closed it and looked for a lock. With dismay she discovered there was none. Not to be deterred, she looked for something she could push against the door to prevent it from being opened.

A chest of drawers stood in one corner, but she wasn't sure it was heavy enough. Perhaps she could push the bed to the door? Footsteps sounded outside. Someone was coming up the stairs. *Dammit.* She was too late. This time when the door opened, she was right behind it.

"Hey, what are you doing?" Cherry asked.

Wilder could only glare at her sullenly. Why was the woman insisting on bothering her all the time? Didn't she understand the importance of the a-grav work?

"Come on," Cherry said. "Let me help you back to bed."

Wilder allowed Cherry to put her arm around her and accompany her across the room. When she reached the bed, she climbed into it, reckoning that protesting about Cherry's presence was only going to delay her leaving.

She took the tablet from the woman's hand and dutifully swallowed it with a sip of water. She looked up expectantly. Now would Cherry finally go away?

"Do you want something to eat? I think it would do you good to eat a little."

That did it.

"I don't *want* to eat!" Wilder exclaimed. "I want to work! Now leave me a...*Ahhhh!*" She clutched her chest. Her outburst had caused it to explode in agony. She was in so much pain she couldn't speak. She could only hold herself and rock as tears collected in her closed eyes.

Cherry sat sideways on the bed and touched her shoulder. "Take it easy, okay?"

Wilder opened her eyes long enough to glower at her before closing them again and nursing her chest, wishing the waves of pain would recede. "I have to work," she whispered. "You don't understand."

"You're right. I don't. You're still sick. The doctor said you were seriously dehydrated when you arrived at the hospital. You wouldn't have lasted more than another few hours. The prolonged dehydration and crushing from the a-grav machine has affected your internal organs. It's going to take a while for them to recover. Your ribs will heal, but you may never be entirely healthy again."

Her words were an almost meaningless buzz. If Wilder never re-discovered the secret of a-grav, her health and well-being wouldn't matter.

"I tell you what," said Cherry. "Let's make a bargain. If you have something to eat—two spoonfuls of soup, say—then you can read your interface for half an hour."

Alarmed by this proposal, Wilder blindly reached for the interface lying face downward on the bed. She slid the device toward her protectively. The pain in her ribs was beginning to ease. The medication she'd swallowed had started to take effect. She took an experimental breath, breathing deeper than she had before. The pain was definitely reducing. "What do you mean? I can read my interface for half an hour? What does that mean?"

"It means, you need to eat before you can work. That makes sense, doesn't it? You need calories. You're stick thin. I wish I'd paid more attention to how you were getting on but I've been too busy."

"I've been busy too, working on a-grav. I worked on it for years, ever since we got back from the Assembly. The scientists here had discovered the information in the Guardians' data and started up a research group. Years I've worked on it. *Years*." Wilder was barely managing to restrain her rage, especially now the agony of her cracked ribs was fading.

"I understand you must be disappointed, but—"

"Disappointed? You let it go! You allowed all that work I'd put in—decades of work from tens of people—just fly away into the sky. How could you? How could you do that to me? To the colony? Do you have any idea how valuable an invention like that is? How significant it is in terms of our status in the galaxy?"

Cherry said, "We had no choice. We had to save you. We couldn't save you *and* the machine. I didn't know how to turn it off even if I could reach it."

"You could have done *something,* but you didn't. You let it go. And I'll never forgive you."

Cherry stood up. "We saved your *life*," she hissed, her hand clenched in a fist. "And I've taken you into my home. I was worried you would discharge yourself and try to go back to your hovel if I didn't. Don't you think I have enough to do without looking after you as well? I have the responsibility of protecting this entire colony on my shoulders. Do you think I want to care for an ungrateful brat too?"

"I didn't ask you to look after me! I don't want your stupid soup. I want to go home." Wilder moved to get up.

"Hey, no you don't. Lie down. You have to stay in bed. The doctor said so."

"I don't care." Wilder tried to get out of the other side of the bed.

"Sit down!" Cherry tried to grab her arm but Wilder was too fast. She was out of the bed in moments.

"Where are my clothes?"

"Get back into bed this instant. You're not going anywhere until you're better."

"You are not my carer and I'm not a little kid. You can't tell me what to do." Wilder pulled open a drawer, looking for something to wear. She was still in the flimsy gown she'd been wearing when she woke up in the hospital.

"Dammit, I am not going to let you leave and hurt yourself. You aren't in any condition to be going anywhere."

"Huh, I'd like to see you try to keep me here." Wilder gave up her search. "You might be the General but I bet I could beat you in a fight, even with cracked ribs." It was no good. The drawers were empty. She would just have to wear the gown and bear the stares of onlookers. It didn't matter as long as she could get back to her tree house. If she'd known Cherry was a maniacal control freak she would never have agreed to come here. She strode toward the door.

"That's it," said Cherry. "I'm calling the CED and asking them to send some officers over." She tapped her ear comm.

"You can't do that. I haven't done anything wrong."

"Like you said, I'm the General. I can do whatever I like. I'll tell them you're a threat to national security and must be apprehended at all costs."

"You..." Wilder gave a gasp of frustration. "How dare you! You have no right." Hot, shameful tears of anger sprang to her eyes. She thrust the balls of her wrists into them to wipe the tears away. "How could you do this to me?"

"Believe it or not, I'm trying to help you. You're behaving like a little kid. You have to rest. Come and lie down."

"No! Get out and leave me alone."

"Look, you either get back into bed and calm down or I'll comm the doctor and ask her to come over and give you a sedative to *make* you calm down. I've half a mind to ask her to reassess your mental state anyway. What's it to be?"

Wilder stomped over to the bed and sat down heavily. Immediately, she winced as the pain from her ribs broke through the effect of the painkiller.

"Good," said Cherry. "Now, do you want to eat something? You must be hungry."

"You just threatened to have me arrested and forcibly sedated. No, I do not want your soup. What I want is for you to leave, you bitch!"

Cherry looked like she'd been slapped. Her features froze and her skin paled. Her gaze searched Wilder's for a moment as if trying to see if she'd really meant what she'd said. Wilder glared back, hoping Cherry would read what she wanted her to see.

A troubled expression fell over Cherry's face and she seemed to regret her words, but a line had been crossed. Wilder had been angry enough as it was about losing the a-grav machine. Cherry's threats had only made matters worse. All her life Wilder had been fighting against people trying to control her. At one time she'd thought of Cherry as a friend. That was all over now. She would never forget or forgive what she'd done.

Fifteen

Kes checked the time. It was nearly four o'clock and he'd promised Isobel he wouldn't be home late tonight. He was determined to keep that promise. Things had been tense between them since the last time she had confronted him about putting his work before his family.

Since then, he'd been better about making it home before Miki's bedtime, but not perfect. Working with Meredith on relations with the Parvus had eaten into his time, and he couldn't easily refuse a request from the Leader. The visitors hadn't returned for another meeting yet, and Meredith was keen to encourage them to enter into more discussions. The small aliens clearly possessed plenty of information not available in the Assembly files—potentially extremely useful information. So, as well as deepening his knowledge on them and their culture, he had been liaising with them.

In some ways it was hard going. The Fila's translation system delivered the Parvus's communication in English, but the meaning was sometimes unclear. Sometimes, he thought he understood exactly what they meant, only to discover he was entirely wrong. He didn't find these times frustrating, however. Interest and curiosity drove him to find the heart of the misunderstanding.

Despite knowing he should spend more time with his family, he had worked several weekends and several times he'd arrived home too late to see his daughter before she went to bed. Isobel had been frosty with him on each occasion, saying that she might as well be single. He was skating on thin ice regarding his marriage. Isobel wasn't an unreasonable person and he didn't blame her for her attitude. She'd been pushed to the edge by his behavior and had nowhere left to go.

He turned his attention to the recordings of the Parvus. The vids covered every moment of their visit, from the arrival of their shuttle to its departure. He'd already watched them several times but he hoped he might see or hear something important that he'd missed.

Something he was particularly interested in was their statements around the idea of intention. Clearly, the fact that he, Cherry, and Wilder had acted with the intention of risking their own lives to save one of the Parvus held great importance. It seemed as though the fact that no human had actually saved any Parvus wasn't important. It was what the humans had *intended* that mattered, perhaps even more than the actual action.

Did Parvus culture value inner, psychological reality higher than external reality? It certainly seemed so according to the evidence. But it was early days yet. Far too early to come to any conclusions or make any definitive statements. He considered how to state his tentative hypothesis.

"Can I watch those too?"

Kes looked up. Tricia, a colleague, was standing over him. He hadn't heard her approach.

He paused the vid. "Sure. Your clearance is high enough, but be careful not to repeat anything you hear. I'll warn you, there's a doozy in there."

"Now I really have to hear it." Tricia pulled over a chair from the next desk and sat down. "You were so lucky to go to that meeting. I'm deeply jealous."

"I have to admit, it was fantastic." He told her the channel for the audio. "You'll be amazed at some of the things they said."

"Do they actually speak? I haven't done much research on the Parvus."

"They do communicate verbally. I even have a recording of the sounds they make, somewhere in my files. I'll find it if you're interested. It sounds kind of burbly."

"Later. I want to hear this amazing piece of information I'm supposed to keep secret."

"You'll have to wait a while. The recording is at the moment we had our first sight of them." He unpaused the recording.

The Parvus came into view, wearing their EVA suits.

A comm arrived for him. He paused the recording again. "Cherry?"

"Are you alone?"

"No."

"Come to the Oceanside Hospital. Right away."

"Huh?"

"Just do it. See you when you get here." Cherry closed the connection.

"Uh..."

"Is everything okay?" asked Tricia.

"I don't know. I have to leave. Sorry." He closed the recording of the Parvus and returned it to the high security files.

"What, right now?"

"Yes." He stood up.

"But I want to know what happened during the meeting!"

"You'll have to wait. Or submit a request to view the recordings." He checked if any autocars were already in the parking lot. Two were available.

"But that'll take forever. Can't you just tell me?"

"Not here and now. You know I can't." In the open plan office, the news that Concordia was the Scythians' origin planet could be overheard by someone without the clearance to know the fact.

He left his disgruntled colleague and headed out. What could be so urgent that Cherry wanted to see him as soon as possible, and so sensitive or inflammatory she didn't want to discuss it with him in front of someone else?

The travel time from Annwn to Oceanside was a little over an hour. When the car was on its way, he comm'd her. "I'm alone now. Can you tell me what this is about?"

"I'm not sure myself yet, but I can tell you what I know. About half an hour ago, someone picked up a stranger wandering around the manufacturing zone near Cerberus. The woman was in such a state, he didn't bother calling an ambulance. He brought her to the hospital at Oceanside himself, telling them he was bringing in someone on the brink of death."

He tensed. He had an idea of what was coming.

"So this woman was brought into the emergency department," Cherry continued. "*Carried* in, I should say. And the doctors started to work, only to get what I imagine must have been the surprise of their lives."

"It was a Guardian?"

"Whatever it is, it looks human, but it certainly isn't."

"Stars! Wilder was right. What's happening now?"

"The android is still at the hospital, in a secured room with guards. As soon as the doctors realized they were dealing with something entirely out of their league, they contacted the CED, who then contacted me. I haven't seen this thing yet, and I want you to be with me when I do. You and I are two of only four people who actually remember the Guardians. But it's been a long time. I'm not sure if I trust my judgment."

"If it isn't a Guardian, what else could it be?" He noted that Cherry hadn't asked for Aubriot's help. He could understand why she hadn't asked Wilder. The girl would still be recovering from her accident, and she probably hadn't had close dealings with the androids. But Aubriot lived near the hospital and he'd known the Guardians very well—too well.

"If it isn't a Guardian," Cherry said, "we're really in the shit."

Kes stood outside the hospital room door, hardly knowing what to expect. Cherry was at the staff nurse's station, getting the most up-to-date report on the strange patient. Two guards stood on each side of the entrance to its room. There were guards guarding the Guardian, if that was what it was.

Unlike many of the Woken, he had only known the Guardians as androids. After he'd been revived, he heard the tale of the agri-scientist, Anahi's, attempt to control the Gens by using the Guardians as a paramilitary force, but while the crisis was happening, he'd been frozen in cryo. The first time he'd seen a Guardian had been when Cariad had reactivated them. They'd come down to Concordia from their ship to help with rebuilding after the Scythian attack.

If he hadn't known they were artificial, he would have been fooled into thinking they were human too. According to what Cherry had said, the thing in the hospital room had retained its human-like quality, at least sufficiently to mislead the person who found it.

Cherry came striding down the corridor.

"What did the nurse say?" asked Kes.

"She said to be prepared for a shock when we see the state its in, but it doesn't appear to be suffering any pain, though its functions are impaired. That might be why it isn't speaking. It hasn't spoken a word since it was found."

"Because it can't."

"Exactly."

"Did they give it an interface? Maybe it can write."

"No, they didn't, and I'm glad," Cherry replied.

"Why? If its speaking capability is shot, how else is it going to communicate with us?"

"Do you think it's a good idea to give an unknown entity access to Concordia's data?"

"Fair point. Still, it would need superior technical skills to find out anything sensitive from a regular interface connection."

"The Guardians had superior technical skills. Very superior."

"But if it is a Guardian, its primary motivation is to support the colony, isn't it? Where's the danger?"

"*If* it's a Guardian, that might have been what its primary motivation *was.* Even after everything they did to help us in the end, I'm still not convinced that was the case. But anyway, if one of them really has been floating around in space for the last several decades before nearly being destroyed on entering the atmosphere, who knows how its circuits have been screwed up? What if that program that guided it to save us is now telling it to destroy us? Let's go in and see this thing."

Cherry stepped up to the door. A guard moved aside, and she breathed into the security panel. The door opened.

As Kes caught sight of the figure, he took an involuntary step back. One of the guards, glancing surreptitiously over her shoulder, gasped.

"Eyes front!" Cherry rebuked her before entering the room.

Kes followed, unable to take his gaze from the thing in the hospital bed.

It was humanoid, but that was about as much as could be said about it. Kes could see why the person who had found it had thought it was human. What else could it be? To nearly all Concordians the Guardians were historical figures, if they believed they had existed at all. But its appearance must have made the finder wonder how it still lived and moved.

Half the head was simply *gone*. If the thing had once had hair, it had all been burned away. The part of the face that remained was blackened and disfigured. The body areas that were visible—it was tucked under covers, bizarrely, considering the thing was a machine—were also badly damaged. The right shoulder and arm, the same side as the missing area of head, were bent backward as if from a heavy impact. The hand and lower half of the arm up to the elbow were gone. The figure was naked.

It had once been crafted to resemble a human female, but its charred surface bore barely evident details of its femininity.

Cherry was motionless, gazing at the thing. "Can you speak?"

The damaged android regarded Cherry with its single eye. Its mouth opened. It worked its jaw and tongue, as if trying to respond or simply re-familiarize itself with the act of speaking.

"I... know... you."

Cherry raised her eyebrows at Kes. "You do?"

"I..." The android's mouth was moving but no sound was coming out. Then its speech returned. "My systems are damaged."

"You can say that again," said Kes. "Is there anything we can do to repair you? Any way we can help?"

Cherry raised a hand and frowned. "What are you? What are you doing on Concordia? How did you get here?"

"I was here before. I do not know when. My timekeeping function is impaired."

Stepping closer to the android, Cherry said, "Why didn't you speak before? Why are you only speaking now?"

"I did not recognize this place. It does not match my records. I was trying to reconcile my memory with this new environment."

Kes knew that sense of confusion all too well. He'd felt it too, when he'd returned from the Assembly's space station and discovered that Concordia had moved on more than fifty Earth years.

"You haven't answered my question," said Cherry.

She was being rather harsh and demanding. Though he knew it was wrong to anthropomorphize, he couldn't help but feel pity for the android. He'd heard they felt emotions. How would it feel to be alone in space for decades, and then nearly burned to annihilation?

"I recognize you," the machine replied. "I now think I am in the correct place."

"So you know Cherry from before?" Kes asked. "What about me?"

The bleary eye turned to regard him. "Yes. Though I do not recall your name."

Kes was about to give it when Cherry interrupted him. "What about you? What's your name?"

"I do not know, but my data files contain the information that I captained a starship."

The *Mistral's* captain? What was she called? Kes couldn't remember.

"Can you type?" Cherry asked. "Do you remember how to write in English?"

"I think I can type. And I can read and write English."

"How convenient," said Cherry. "Tell me, how did you get here? You didn't answer my question earlier."

"I remember falling. And I remember my system rebooting. I walked for a long time, but I could only travel slowly because my legs are damaged. Eventually, I found a road and I followed it."

"Why?" Cherry asked. "What were you hoping to find?"

"I am compelled to find humans. I don't know why."

"Right. Wait here. Kes, come with me."

As they left the room, he asked, "Are you going to give it an interface now?"

"I am," Cherry replied, closing the door. "One that's been wiped, disconnected from the comm system, and modified to only record written language."

"Isn't that overkill? It seems obvious that what's in there was once a Guardian, the captain of their ship. What was her name?"

"Faina. *Its* name was Faina. It isn't a 'her' and it never was. When it said it captained a ship, I had a good look at it, trying to see the resemblance. It does look like a burned up Faina. That doesn't mean it is, though. And you and everyone else would be wise to remember that."

"Why? What are you suspicious about?"

"For stars' sake, Kes, you sound like one of those damned recruits who doesn't know the dangerous end of a gun. You're a smart man. Think about it."

He was taken aback. Everything he'd seen and heard in the hospital room added up. Could there really be any other explanation for the thing in the bed?

Cariad had told him once that Cherry hated the Guardians. She'd hated them ever since they were used to control the Gens, and that hadn't changed, even when they did so much else to help with the colonization later. Was Cherry's prejudice coloring her opinion of the new arrival? But she seemed to be implying something else.

"You think that thing isn't a Guardian?" he asked. "That it's some kind of threat to our security? But everything it says makes sense. It knew your name."

"No, it didn't. You told it my name."

"I did? Well, it recognized you."

"It *said* it recognized me. All we can say it knew for sure was that I had to be someone important, because I was the one who was asked to go and see it. Nothing that came out of that thing's mouth has convinced me it is what it says it is. And until I *am* convinced, I'm not taking any chances."

"I guess you are General of the Defense Force."

"Damned right. But I want your opinion too. What did you think of it? Did it look like a Guardian to you?"

"It did. Or rather, it looked pretty much as I would expect one to look after nearly burning to cinders traveling through a planet's atmosphere and then crash landing."

"Do you know of any way we can check?"

"We could examine it internally, but no one ever got a look at their insides as far as I know. Their specs might be in the *Mistral's* data files. And we have their weapons. That was how Wilder knew the crashed object was related to the Guardians, because the metal alloy is the same."

"The capsule it arrived in checks out in that regard. I had it retested, but it's a melted mess. There's not much else to be learned from it. I'll ask someone to search for everything we have on them."

"How's Wilder doing, by the way?" Kes asked.

"Ugh." Cherry's expression turned sour. "She's getting better, but she wants to go home. It's ridiculous. She's nowhere near better yet. I think she hates me too."

"Hates you? Why?"

"I threatened to call the CED on her."

"You *what*?"

"I know. Sounds crazy, right? We were having a fight, and things got out of hand. I don't even know how it happened. I guess I didn't have the patience to deal with her. She's mad at me for not doing anything to catch the a-grav machine."

"She's mad at me too, then. I didn't do anything either. But, seriously? Does she even remember the state she was in? We saved her life."

"She doesn't seem to rate that as highly as the machine she was working on. But I wasn't exactly reasonable either, and she is still a kid, while I'm the adult. Patience was never one of my strengths."

He was interested to hear more, but he'd noticed something through a nearby window. It was getting dark outside. Apprehension struck. "Do you know what time it is?"

"About seven thirty, I think."

"Shit! I have to go." Seven thirty! He ran down the corridor. It was an hour to Annwn. He wouldn't make it in time to see Miki before she went to bed. Isobel would be furious. No, she wouldn't be furious. She would be hurt and bitter and disappointed, and that was even worse.

Sixteen

Wilder lay awake in bed, facing the wall. When Cherry had come in to check on her, she'd pretended to be asleep. She never wanted to speak to Cherry again.

She heard the sound of a tray being placed on the table next to her bed and then Cherry's footsteps as she crossed the room. When the door closed, Wilder exhaled and turned over. The room was empty and a tray holding a bowl of breakfast cereal and a glass of juice sat on the table. Next to the glass was a pill.

Wilder picked it up, placed it at the back of her tongue, and drank a mouthful of juice to wash it down. She would have to wait for the medication to take effect before she made her move. It would take a few minutes, and Cherry hadn't left the house yet anyway.

Wilder waited in anticipation for the analgesic effect to wash over her. Her ribs had been bothering her for a couple of hours, but she'd been awake since before that, planning her escape. She wasn't going to spend a minute longer in Cherry's house than she had to. The woman was actually keeping her prisoner. It was outrageous, and a gross abuse of her powers.

She'd thought Cherry was a kind, nice person. How wrong she'd been.

She climbed out of bed and padded over to the door. Pressing an ear against it, she listened for movements. She could hear Cherry downstairs, walking around. She listened impatiently. What did Cherry have to do that took so much time? What was keeping her from going to work? All she had to do was eat and then leave.

"Come on," Wilder breathed. Then she froze. Footsteps were climbing the stairs. She sped across her bedroom on tiptoes, leapt into bed, and pulled the covers over her. As the bedroom door opened, she froze again.

Cherry came in. "Wilder."

When she didn't answer, Cherry repeated her name. After another pause, she said, "I know you're awake." Wilder continued her pretense. She wasn't going to give the bitch the satisfaction of replying to her.

Cherry sighed. "I have to go out to work, but I'll be back as soon as I can. In the meantime, there's plenty of food in the kitchen if you get hungry. Help yourself to whatever you want. I wanted to talk to you before I left, but seeing as you're not in the mood it'll have to wait until later. I hope you feel a bit better today. Take it easy, okay? Get plenty of rest. Then you'll be able to get back to working on a-grav. I'm sure you'll remember everything then and it won't be long until you re-invent your machine."

Yes, I am going to return to working on a-grav, and sooner than you think!

The door closed. Wilder relaxed. She lay motionless, waiting. After a few moments, she thought she heard the front door close. She sat up. Suddenly realizing how thirsty and hungry she was, she drank the orange juice in several gulps and then quickly slurped the cereal in spoonfuls from the bowl. Wiping her mouth with her hand, she slid her legs out from under the covers and got up.

There were no clothes in this room. She had discovered that last night after a thorough search. Was that by design? Had Cherry intended to deprive her of her liberty from the beginning? Whether it was a coincidence or not didn't matter. She needed clothes. Walking around Annwn in a hospital gown would draw attention and she would wind up right back here.

She held her ear against the door again. This time, she heard nothing. She waited five minutes, counting the seconds under her breath. There was only silence. Cherry had left.

Wilder turned the door handle, her muscles tense. To her relief, the door opened. Cherry hadn't locked her in. She stepped out onto the quiet landing. Two more doors led off from it and both were closed. She peered over the railing to the hall below. Nothing stirred except motes of dust in the sunbeams shining through the glass in the front door.

She walked down the stairs quietly, listening hard. Two open doors led from the hall. A kitchen and a living room were visible, both empty. The rooms were sparse, almost clinically so. She disliked clutter too, but the walls of her tree house were decorated with sketches she'd drawn—fantastical machines and devices she'd dreamt up over the years. She also had a few drawings Tycho and Stephie's grandchildren had given her on her rare visits to her old friends.

In Cherry's home there was nothing like that. Nothing sentimental or nostalgic. Everything was practical. There was nothing to warm the heart.

Cold and mean. Just like her.

Feeling happier now she knew she would not be disturbed while she enacted her escape, she ascended the stairs again. Her ribs were twinging despite the medication, so she knew she had to not take things too fast. She would also have to find the rest of the painkillers and take them with her. They did belong to her, after all.

She felt bad about taking Cherry's clothes, however. As soon as she got back to her own place, she would return them. She opened an upstairs door. Here was what she needed. It was Cherry's bedroom, and an open closet revealed hanging clothes. She quickly stripped and grabbed the nearest things to hand: casual pants and a round-necked, warm top, suitable for the cool weather. The clothes were baggy and the pants and sleeves ended inches above her ankles and wrists, but they would do.

As she closed the closet door, she saw a figure in the mirror. She gasped, not recognizing herself, before she realized that the gaunt, wild-haired girl with shadows under her eyes was in fact her. Slowly, she took in her appearance. It had been years since she'd seen a full length view of herself. She'd grown taller in the intervening time, but no wider.

She lifted the top and inhaled sharply. Her abdomen and ribs were a blue-purple mess. That was what the a-grav machine had done. But she was also astonished by the concave depression that was her belly, and the prominent bones of her ribs that overhung it.

She raised a hand to her hair. Matted and messy strands stuck out all over. Her nose was sharp and her cheekbones and chin were jutting. Her resolve to escape faltered. Maybe Cherry had a point. Maybe it might be better to wait another day or two and rest.

Then she remembered Cherry's threat to call the CED and to have her sedated. Her jaw set firm. She refused to remain in the home of someone who had zero respect for her rights.

She had to get out. When she was somewhere safe, then she would rest.

But she didn't have to leave right away. Cherry would be gone for hours.

She returned to her room, undressed, and took a shower. She washed her hair, marveling at the handfuls of strands that fell from it. She gently soaped her bruised skin. The a-grav machine had really done a good job of crushing her. It was a miracle she'd survived.

How much force had it exerted? Had it been moving at the same speed as Concordia's gravitational acceleration? She didn't think so. That would have killed her. So the neutralization effect had not been complete? She pondered the question.

Before she knew it, the shower room was thick with steam and her skin was as wrinkled as an old person's. How long had she been here? She hastily turned off the water and stepped out of the shower, a terrible guilt weighing on her at having wasted so much water.

Her feelings didn't make a lot of sense. On Concordia there was water aplenty and the energy to heat it was free—Cherry's home might even be hooked up to the old geothermally heated water the Fila had supplied in the early days. But the creed that it was morally despicable to waste water had been bred into her bones during her childhood. She didn't think she would ever be free of it.

Looking at herself in the bathroom mirror, she saw the long shower had made little difference to her emaciated, bruised appearance, but she felt a whole lot better. She dried her hair, put on Cherry's clothes again, and went downstairs to the kitchen. She opened a cupboard, looking for food. On her third try, she found what she was looking for: crackers, yeast pastes, and cookies. Her favorites.

As she was stuffing her pockets—Cherry wouldn't mind, and if she did, Wilder didn't give a shit—she spotted the pack of painkilling medication on the windowsill. She slipped that into a pocket too.

Out in the hallway she opened an understairs cupboard and found her boots. Her washed socks had been placed on top of them.

Wilder hesitated. A quiet note of guilt sounded in reaction to the thoughtful care Cherry had taken over her stuff. She gritted her teeth. It was a shame Cherry hadn't taken the same care over her right to liberty.

After putting on the socks and slipping on her boots, she strode to the front door and peered through the transparent panel. Had Cherry stationed guards? The exterior looked empty. The small home stood in a quiet, dead-end street, somewhere in Annwn. Cherry had lost her farm during the long decades of their trip to the Assembly. She'd looked incredibly sad when she'd told Wilder about it. At the time, Wilder had felt sorry for her. Now, that was all gone.

She went to the back door, which led off from the kitchen, and pressed the door release. The door remained shut.

She was locked in.

She was unfazed. It would take a lot more than a lock to prevent her from leaving. If it was the regular kind, she could deactivate it with her eyes closed. She inspected the device closely. *Damn.* It was military grade. She could probably override it, but time was a concern, and an alarm would sound at the CED if someone tampered with it. If breaking the device only took seconds that wouldn't be a problem, but Wilder didn't know how long it would take to deactivate military systems. She could be caught while still trying to escape. There was no way she was going to spend another moment here, held against her will.

She took a step backward. She had to find another way out. The window? Her luck was in. It didn't have a lock. She climbed onto the sanitizer, opened it, and took a quick look outside. All was still in the small yard. She jumped out, a rush of adrenaline hitting. She was free again.

But where should she go? Her tree house would be the first place Cherry would look for her. She had to go home quickly to check on Piddle and Puddle, but after that she needed to go somewhere else—somewhere Cherry wouldn't find her.

She crossed the small yard and climbed the fence. She didn't know where she was going yet but it didn't matter. She'd survived worse situations and come out fine. She would do so again. And, more importantly, she would be able to return to working on a-grav.

Seventeen

After Kes disappeared in a hurry, Cherry returned to the nurses' station. The staff nurse was going over something with another nurse. When Cherry approached she wrapped up the discussion and sent the nurse away.

"Our visitor will be moving to Oceanside Jail," Cherry said. "Guards and an army vehicle will be arriving in about half an hour. I want you to prepare the prisoner for transportation by strapping it to a gurney. The guards will also secure it with handcuffs and shackles."

The staff nurse's eyebrows rose in surprise. It was understandable. She was used to treating people in order to make them better. But the thing that had arrived from space was not a person and it wasn't going to get any better, at least not if Cherry could help it.

The staff nurse was intelligent enough not to question the order, however. "Yes, ma'am. Is there anything else you would like me to do?"

"I want you to take a sample from it for analysis. Any part of the main structure will do, but not any remnant of clothing or hair. I'm not sure how you'll do it. Maybe an orthopedic surgeon might lend you a saw."

"I can ask, but they're precious about their tools."

"A maintenance person, then."

"I'm sure I can find something suitable."

"As soon as you have a sample—I think a piece about this big should be fine—" Cherry held her thumb and forefinger about four centimeters apart. "Send it express to the Engineering Department at the university. They'll be expecting it."

"I'll do it now, before the guards arrive to take her."

Cherry stiffened. "It isn't a her. It isn't human and it never was. It's important that you understand that."

"You're right. I'm sorry. It was a slip of the tongue."

"Don't worry about it. It's an easy mistake to make. Thanks for your help. I have to go now, but please comm me immediately if any problems occur." Cherry left, worrying about what seemed to be turning into an ongoing problem. Even Kes, who had always known the Guardians were androids, had fallen into the trap of thinking of the surprise arrival as a person. That faulty perception and its attendant dangers would continue until she did something about it.

Was the thing really Faina? There was a likeness in what remained of its face. But if it really was the former captain of the *Mistral*, so what? The colony no longer needed Guardians, if it ever had. Their arrival had created more problems than it solved.

And if it wasn't Faina, Concordia was in grave, immediate danger. The only other explanation for a fake Guardian dropping from the sky was that it had been sent as a spy. There was plenty of sensitive information that, if it got out, could mean the end of the colony. The secret nature of the military depots was as much of an advantage as their contents.

She had already made up her mind. The thing in the bed had to be destroyed, and quickly, before rumors of its presence spread. She wasn't sure how the job could be done. It was made from tough materials. That the thing still functioned despite its near-destruction was testament to the fact.

She ran quickly down the hospital steps to the waiting autocar. She had to report to Meredith and get permission to destroy the android.

As her car carried her toward the Leader's Residence, she came up with the answer. Out at the mountains, smelting plants turned ore into metals. The furnaces had to be hot enough to entirely eradicate the unwelcome guest.

If it was a Guardian, it would be the last one. Their stain would be removed from Concordia forever.

Meredith took Cherry out onto the wide balcony leading off from the functions room. No function was being held, but Cherry could imagine the music, dancing, free-flowing drinks and stacks of food. Meredith held regular formal parties, as a way of smoothing strained relationships between important figures in Concordian society.

The Leader had often invited Cherry to attend, but even the idea of a social event like that set her on edge. It wasn't the kind of thing Ethan would have done. The colony had changed a lot.

"Take a seat," Meredith said, indicating a table next to the balcony's edge.

The breeze from the ocean was stiff but Cherry enjoyed the cleansing feeling. Spending time with the Guardian-like being had made her feel dirty.

"Drink?" asked Meredith, also sitting down.

"No, thanks."

"Come on. You never sit and have a drink with me when you come. It wouldn't hurt you to relax a little."

Cherry regarded the older woman. Was she lonely? She might be. She was single and just as busy as Cherry was with her job. "Okay, I'll have chicory coffee."

"Chicory coffee? I don't think I've heard of that. I'll ask the cook if we have any."

When the answer came back that the Leader's Residence didn't stock Cherry's favorite drink, Meredith apologized. "We only have the regular stuff."

Had Aubriot cornered the chicory coffee supply? Cherry herself hadn't managed to find any for years. "Regular will be fine."

Meredith sent the order through and sipped from a half-empty cup. She had been sitting on the balcony for a while. "So, tell me all about it."

"Thank you for not going to see it before I had a chance to check it out."

"No problem. What you said makes sense. If our visitor does have nefarious plans, it wouldn't be wise for our colony's Leader to offer herself up at close quarters."

"Have you had a chance to look at the vids the doctors took?"

"I've been studying them for a while." Meredith swiped open the interface set into the table. "They're pretty gruesome."

"It doesn't look any better in real life. It smells too, of burned plastic."

Meredith wrinkled her nose. "And did you come to a conclusion about what it is?"

"Not yet. I've ordered for the material it's made from to be tested, but even when we get the results I'm not sure it'll tell us anything definitive. I'm also moving it to the jail for better security, but the safest option is to dispose of it as soon as possible."

"Isn't that a bit hasty? We don't even know what it is. What if it is one of these Guardians? Perhaps it could be useful."

"Huh, you wouldn't say that if you knew what life was like living with those things."

Meredith put down her cup. "Am I missing something? All the history books say the reason the Scythians stopped attacking us was because the *Mistral* flew directly into one of their ships. The enemy mistook the act as a sacrifice."

Cherry's coffee arrived, carried by Meredith's maid. She took the offered cup. "It's more complicated than that. A lot more complicated. Believe me, if it is a Guardian, those things are not to be trusted. Nothing it has to offer us is worth the risk of exposing ourselves to the danger it could bring."

"You aren't sure it's a Guardian?"

"I'm sure that's what it wants us to think it is."

"What gives you that impression?"

"Things it said."

"Wait a minute. It spoke to you?"

"After not speaking to anyone else, I'm the one it chose to *reveal itself* to."

"What did it say?"

"That it remembers me, but this place has changed. Oh, and it remembers Kes too. Conveniently."

"It all fits. Well, that throws a whole new light on everything."

"Does it?" Cherry asked. "I don't see how."

"If it can talk... If it can communicate..."

"An interface can communicate. A Guardian only has more processing ability."

"A lot more processing ability, and other abilities besides," said Meredith.

"You've seen the pictures. That thing isn't capable of much any more, believe me."

"Which of the Guardians is it?"

"It doesn't remember its name, but it said it remembers it was the captain of a starship."

"Faina!" Meredith exclaimed. "I read about her."

Cherry's jaw tightened. She was getting tired of explaining that the word 'her' was inappropriate. "It's best not to think of the Guardians as people. They're nothing more than machines."

"I know. Very sophisticated machines, though."

"The distinction isn't important. We need to destroy that thing as soon as possible. I was thinking about how to do it—"

"I know. You already said. But I'm not sure I agree."

Cherry tapped the tabletop. "Why's that?"

"We don't know yet what this android has to offer. Who knows what useful data might be stored within it? And besides, word has already gotten out about its existence. The person who brought it in and medical staff at the hospital have spoken to media outlets. I couldn't do anything to stop them. It was too late. There might even be images circulating. I'm not sure. But the colony knows about this crash survivor."

"Crash survivor?"

"That's what they were calling it in one headline I saw."

"Shit."

"It's regrettable, I admit. This has never happened before. We don't have any systems or regulations to control the information. But what's done is done. If we destroy the android, it's going to look very bad."

"Does that matter when the safety of the colony is at stake?"

"We don't know that, and the safety of the colony also depends on a populace that feels secure."

"Does it?" Cherry could barely contain her anger. "It would seem to me that the opposite was true."

"If we go around arbitrarily ending the existence of something that looks human, and like a severely injured, helpless human to boot, it'll undermine public morale. People will wonder if the same thing could happen to them."

"That's ridiculous."

"People aren't always rational or logical. In fact, I'd say most of the time they aren't."

Cherry didn't know what to say. Or, actually, she did, but she bit back the retort.

Ethan wouldn't have hesitated. Ethan would have known the right thing to do. He would have annihilated it.

Instead, she said, "I hope you agree that it needs to remain in a high-security environment?"

"I do, for the time being. Until we're certain what it is."

"I don't think we'll ever be certain."

"Certain enough to know it poses no danger."

Cherry wanted to repeat herself, but what was the point? Meredith's judgment was clouded. Like the rest of the Concordians, she didn't fear the Scythians enough. Her sense of danger had no edge, if she had any sense of danger at all.

Cherry looked out over the dark ocean. The breeze had dropped, and phosphorescence was sparkling on the calm surface. Threads were probably doing something down there and disturbing the water. She recalled the time Ethan and she had taken a trip to the creatures' underground city for her Joining Ceremony. They had spoken of the glittering sparks adorning the water on still nights.

She missed him so badly. She almost yearned for the peril they had lived under after Arrival, when the colony's existence had sat on a knife edge. Things had been much harder, but they had been clear, and simple, and real.

"I have something I want to tell you," Meredith said. "I've decided to reduce the budget on Concordia's military next year."

"You've *what*?"

Meredith held up her hands. "Calm down. It isn't by much. You have to admit we do spend an awful lot on defense."

"For a very good reason!"

"Cherry, we have four missile silos, pulse emitters, and all kinds of equipment. Nearly every able-bodied person has received military training, and one quarter of the adult population is a member of a military force, either full or part time. We're also building Chimera. I believe the investment in our military has been money well spent, but there has to come a time when we say we've done plenty and we should scale back a little."

Suddenly, Cherry couldn't stand sitting with Meredith any longer. She stood up. "I should go."

"So soon? I thought we had a lot more to discuss."

"Not really."

"Okay," said Meredith, perhaps sensing Cherry's mood. "Let's talk another time."

When Cherry returned to her car, she nearly input her home address but then changed her mind. The conversations she'd had with Meredith, Kes, and the staff nurse at the hospital left her wanting to speak to someone who understood where she was coming from.

Twenty minutes later, her car pulled up near Aubriot's house. She'd instructed it to stop thirty meters away, at a bend in the driveway where she could see the building but Aubriot wouldn't hear the car.

A few windows were lit up. He was home. Probably brewing, if he'd gone ahead with his business idea.

Of all four Concordians who had been alive when the Guardians were around, Aubriot was the one who knew in his core the danger they presented. They had forcibly sedated him after judging him to be a threat to social stability. The Guardians had set no date for allowing him to return to consciousness. If it hadn't been for the objection of all the colonists to this heinous act, they could have effectively killed him. They could have kept him comatose until they determined he was no longer a threat. And if that was never? Well, never mind.

Aubriot would agree they needed to destroy the 'Guardian' in a heartbeat. And when he was motivated to do something he damn well got it done. But all the spirit seemed to have gone out of him lately. He was probably not brewing but getting drunk. Or maybe he had a woman over. Maybe both.

She recalled her former lover's dead eyes the last time she'd seen him, and she gave a shudder. She didn't want to see those eyes again right now. She input her home address. The autocar turned and moved up the driveway.

Wilder would be there when she got home. Cherry had been surprised how easily she'd taken to having the girl around. She'd thought she would hate to share her personal space after living alone for so long, but she'd found she enjoyed having a little company.

Ever since their argument, she had been regretting what she'd said. She'd overreacted. She would apologize and have a respectful discussion about how long Wilder should stay with her.

As soon as she got home.

Eighteen

Bunny Giesen lifted his hard hat and rubbed his close-cropped hair. The gesture did nothing to ease the ache that had begun behind his eyes and was gradually working its way through his head. It was the endless grinding of the excavator that caused it. The same headache every day, starting about two hours before the end of his shift. Ear protectors did nothing for it. It wasn't the sound, it was the vibration, and there wasn't anything could be done about that.

He should have been a pilot like Ma. It would have been hard to live up to her reputation, for sure. The other trainees would have been watching him, looking for signs that he had her skill and reaction times. He doubted he would have. He wasn't that good, but he probably would have been okay. Ma could have given him pointers while she was still alive.

But hardly anyone flew planes on Concordia. Little, light, personal aircraft was all that was ever built, those and the government helis. Everyone knew why. It was because *they* were watching. The beings in the sky, from another planet. The Scythians.

Only, were they really? Ever since he was a little kid he'd been warned his home was under threat, that there were aliens in outer space who wanted Concordia for their own. He'd learned all about the First Attack and Second Attack in history classes, as well as the Journey of the *Nova Fortuna*, Leaving Earth, and the Arrival of the Guardians.

But when he'd asked about the Scythians, what they looked like, where they came from, and when they were coming back, his teachers couldn't answer him. When he'd tried to find out the answers for himself, he'd drawn endless blanks. He'd wondered if any of it were true.

He'd seen the recordings. Watched them over and over again, in fact. But they could easily have been faked. The entertainment channels produced similar stuff all the time. He often wondered if the entire story about the Scythians was a conspiracy, put together by the government to get everyone to do what they said. People living in fear were more likely to do whatever they were told.

"Bunny, watcha doing up there? Taking a nap?" It was his supervisor, Alun. The words came from Bunny's ear mufflers, which were linked up to the work radio.

"Got a headache coming," he replied. "I was just taking a little break." He hated it when Alun called him by his pet name, not his real name, Bernard. Only friends could call him Bunny, and Alun was far from that.

"Did you see the nurse like I said? Didn't he give you something for those headaches?"

"Yeah, I saw him." He hadn't seen the nurse, but he didn't want Alun on his back about it. All the nurse had to offer was medication, and who knew what was in that stuff? Maybe that was another way the government controlled people. He wasn't about to become a slave to the people in power.

"You can take a break when your shift's over," Alun said when Bunny didn't elaborate on his answer. "Start up again. We're on a schedule."

Bunny angrily threw down his hat and thumbed the button to start his machine. He let the noise drown out his curses.

He checked the screen. Another two meters to go before he reached the outer edge of the chamber that would hold Concordia's fifth military depot. He wasn't supposed to know that, of course. He was only a tunneler. What right did he have to know government secrets?

But he did know. He knew the locations of all the military depots, because he'd worked on all of them. Not that it took much intelligence to figure it out. What other reason could there be for government-funded projects to hollow out vast underground chambers? Everyone knew about Cerberus, and the chambers he'd worked on had been about the same size and depth.

When he'd asked Alun once or twice what they were building, his supervisor had pretended not to know. Maybe he really didn't. Maybe he really was that dumb. But Bunny knew.

Holding the control stick, he eased the drill forward until it bit into the rock. Dust and shards flew out. The air turned opaque and pinging sounds came from the excavator's plating and reinforced transparent screen. Though he sat five meters from the drill tip, the debris from the excavation zone reached him.

He didn't mind it too much. He was safe inside his machine. The entire site could collapse on top of him and he wouldn't be hurt. As long as he didn't try to leave his cab he would be fine until someone finally dug him out.

It was the vibration he couldn't stand. He was already juddering in his seat and his headache felt like a second drill boring into his brain. And he had another two hours to endure before his shift would finally be over.

Suddenly, the excavator flew forward. All resistance ahead of it had disappeared. He hit the brake. His machine halted, but he carried on traveling. His head hit the window and thunked against the reinforced glass.

When he came around, his face was on his dashboard. The familiar edges and smooth surfaces pressed into his nose, mouth, and forehead. His headache was bad. Real bad. What had happened?

He opened his eyes and saw the side window of the cabin. Outside, the air was dusty. He hadn't been unconscious long. His machine had cut out. He must have released his hold on the dead man's lever when he fainted.

Wait. That was wrong. He hadn't fainted. He'd been knocked out. He'd braked hard and been thrown forward. He hadn't fastened his harness and he hadn't been wearing his hat. *Dammit.* Alun would be all over him like a sluglimpet for safety breaches. He might even be let go.

He'd braked because the excavator had flown forward all of a sudden. He'd done it instinctively. Who wouldn't have?

But why had the excavator behaved like that?

He put his hands on the dashboard and pushed himself upright. This action had a weird effect. The excavator began to—ever so gently—rock.

He froze.

He could think of several scenarios that might cause the machine to rock, and all of them were bad.

"Geisen!" Alun's voice came through, harsh and angry. "What the hell did I just tell you? No more breaks, okay? We don't have time for your—"

"Shuttup!" Bunny hissed. "Just shuttup. Something's wrong."

"Wrong? What's gone wrong? What the hell are you talking about? You better have a damned good explanation."

"I don't know yet. I'm waiting for the dust to settle." He was waiting for his machine to settle too. The rocking continued and he wasn't sure it was easing. He had a feeling it was getting worse.

One of the scenarios that might have caused the effect was an earthquake, but the fact that Alun wasn't feeling any tremors ruled that possibility out. The fact brought a little relief. Though his cabin could withstand a heavy rockfall, it was no match against the forces that moved Concordia's tectonic plates. Nor would it be impervious to lava.

Yet though he wasn't in the middle of an earthquake, his situation remained dire. "I think I broke through into...something."

"You broke through?"

"I was working, drilling, pushing the machine forward, you know."

"I know how excavators work, Bunny."

"And suddenly there was nothing there. Nothing to push against. The rock was gone."

"Oh shit. Do you think you hit a natural cave? Let me check the survey."

Bunny was aware of his own breathing. In, out. In, pause, out. The rocking of his machine did seem to be slowing, finally. He peered into the dust. His machine's lights bounced brightly off the tiny specks. The ground in that part of Suddene contained a lot of quartz. It made for hard drilling, but it created a pretty, shimmering effect.

What he saw didn't look good. Ordinarily, as the dust settled, a solid rock face would emerge. Now only darkness was visible, stretching out beyond the shiny motes.

Hitting a cave when excavating wasn't common, but neither was it unheard of. He knew of two instances, though it had never happened to him. By itself the cave posed no danger. The problems lay in the atmosphere it contained and how deep it was. The first problem could be ruled out. If the cave was filled with poisonous gas he probably wouldn't have woken up after being knocked unconscious.

But the second problem... The second problem could explain the rocking.

It had stopped, thank the stars. He was loath to do anything that might start it up again, but he had to know. Very slowly, keeping his back pressed firmly into his seat, he leaned to the right. The scene at the side of his cab inched into view. Blackness was taking the place of falling motes of dust.

There was nothing except empty space to the side of him. And... he leaned farther.

He swallowed.

There was nothing beneath him.

He was balanced on the edge of a precipice. The heavy machinery that drove the drill of his excavator rested on solid ground behind. The heavy drill at the front was supported by nothing at all.

He was in the middle. A slight shift in his comparatively small weight could be all it took to tip the excavator over the edge. Centimeter by breathless centimeter, he returned to an upright position. His head facing forward and his body rigid, he groped sightlessly for his safety harness.

How far down was the bottom of the cave? It could be tens or hundreds of meters. Would he survive the impact?

His fingers brushed the straps of his harness. Remaining as still as he could, he pulled it over his shoulders, found the central lock, and snapped it closed.

Where was his hat? He couldn't see it from where he sat, and looking for it elsewhere would entail far more moving than he was prepared to do.

"Back again," said Alun. "Are you sure you hit a cave? There's nothing on the survey."

"Yes, I'm sure. I'm damned well looking at it. And if I'm not very lucky, I'm about to become more acquainted with it than I'd like."

"Huh?"

"I'm right on the edge, hanging over it. Get someone in here. I need help."

"No kidding! Okay, don't worry. I'm on it. I'll sort something out as fast as I can. Whatever you do, don't move."

"Thanks for the tip," he said between his teeth.

His radio went silent again as Alun left to 'sort something out', whatever the hell that meant. There was nothing to do except stare ahead at the darkness. It grew deeper every second as the dust fell away into the expanse of the cave.

The excavator's lights were brilliant, designed for the darkest underground spaces where no daylight ever reached. Now the dust had nearly all dissipated, they shone far ahead.

He began to make out shapes and shadows. At first, he thought he was seeing the far side of the cave, but as the shapes took form in his view, he became puzzled. He hadn't been in many natural caves in his time, but the ones he'd seen first hand had been irregularly shaped. Rocks and tunnels hadn't been uniform in their appearance, they'd been haphazard.

So what was he looking at? He could see spires rising from wide bases and narrowing to slim spikes. He also saw arches and sweeping curves. How had the shapes formed? He'd never heard of any geological formations like these.

The lights from his excavator only gilded the edges of the structures. He couldn't see any detail, so it was hard to estimate their size, but he guessed they were huge—larger than anything he'd seen on Concordia, larger than the Observation Tower, which was the tallest building in the world.

Was he hallucinating? He had hit his head after all, and it still hurt like crazy. He closed his eyes. When he opened them again, the strange structures remained. He was fairly certain they were real.

Tens of meters below the surface of Suddene sat a vast underground cavern containing hundreds, perhaps thousands, of constructions.

No human had built them, so what had?

Nineteen

It was with some trepidation Kes unlocked the door of his house. To his relief, Isobel didn't come into the hall, angry at him for arriving home late again. He could hear her in the kitchen. The rest of the house was dark and quiet. Miki was already asleep, of course. He felt bad for not setting eyes on his child all day for the second time this week.

He would make it up to her on the weekend. They would all go somewhere together, somewhere remote and beautiful, where he could forget about work and concentrate fully on his family. He'd heard about cabins in the mountains available to rent. He would look into it tomorrow and book something.

Bracing himself for the onslaught of Isobel's reaction to his broken promises, he stepped into the kitchen. She was lifting a casserole out of the cooker. She was facing slightly away from him. Her bump seemed to have grown larger overnight.

"Isobel, I'm so sorry. Something astounding happened today. I don't think I can talk to you about it yet, but it was shocking and amazing. I had to go to Oceanside, and I confess I lost track of time. Otherwise I would have comm'd you."

She had turned toward him during this speech. "It's okay. You don't have to explain."

Her smile seemed too fixed, too bright.

"Are you sure?"

She nodded. "Come and give me a hug."

He wrapped her in his arms and held her tight, though taking care not to squash her bump. "I really am so sorry," he whispered.

"Please, don't talk about it."

"How are you feeling?" he asked as he released her.

"About as you would expect. Late pregnancy is no joke, but I knew what I was getting into after Miki."

"It's a shame we can't have a baby the way they did on the *Nova*, and on Earth too before I left. Pop an embryo in a bag, feed it nutrients for nine months, and then take it out again. Voila!"

She gave him the look she reserved for the moments when he reminisced about things that happened long before she was born: a mixture of boredom and irritation. He didn't blame her. He knew he talked about those times more often than he should, given that she couldn't relate to any of it.

"You go and sit down," he said. "I'll bring dinner out."

She took two plates out of the cabinet and cutlery from a drawer before going into the dining room. He brought out the hot casserole dish and placed it in the center of the table.

"There's some bread, too," she said. "And wine, if you want it."

"Wine? Are you sure? I don't want to make you feel bad that you can't have any."

"I don't mind. Have some, and relax a bit. It sounds like you had a stressful day."

"Not exactly stressful, but weird." He returned to the kitchen to fetch the bread and wine, calling, "What can I get you to drink?"

"Shhh! You'll wake Miki."

"Sorry." He seemed to be saying sorry a lot. He stuck his head through the doorway. "What would you like to drink?"

"Water is fine."

He brought everything into the dining room. His guilt and anxiety about being late had dissipated and been replaced with elation that Isobel was taking it so well. He was almost jovial as he sat down and opened the wine bottle. Discovering that someone had planted vineyards in the mountain foothills and had been producing wine for decades had been one of the nicer surprises of returning to Concordia fifty years later than expected.

He poured himself half a glass of the ruby liquid. Meanwhile, Isobel was spooning the bean casserole she'd cooked onto her plate.

"I had an idea about something we can do during the weekend," he said. "I thought it would be nice to go up into the mountains. Maybe stay there a couple of nights. What do you think?"

"I don't think it'll be safe. I'm too far along. I might go into labor early, and we would be hours from the hospital."

"Yeah, you're right. I was forgetting. But it's something to keep in mind for after the baby's born."

"Hmm, maybe."

He asked what she and Miki had done today, and the conversation moved on through their usual topics of discussion. As was usual, too, he found it hard to muster interest in the mundanity of everyday life on Concordia, especially in the light of what had just happened. He itched to tell Isobel about it, but though Cherry hadn't explicitly told him the Guardian's arrival was a secret, he guessed she wanted to keep it under wraps for now.

He loved Isobel and Miki deeply, and he knew he would feel the same about the new baby when she arrived, but he felt trapped. This life wasn't what he'd signed up for. He'd been expecting an adventure, not a cozy existence in suburbia.

"Have some more wine," Isobel said. "Don't hold back just for me."

"If you say so." He poured himself another glass. The bottle was now half empty. He hadn't drunk alcohol in a while out of consideration for Isobel, who couldn't enjoy it with him. He felt a little tipsy already after only two glasses.

"Dinner was great." He meant it. He wasn't a natural vegetarian, but Isobel managed to turn plant food into delicious meals that took the edge off his craving for meat. "I'll clear up."

"It can wait. Leave the dishes for the morning. You must be tired."

"Only a little, but I can do them before I leave for work tomorrow."

She stood up. "I'm tired, even if you aren't. Do you want to go to bed?"

"What, now? It's a bit early, isn't it?"

She shrugged. "It's up to you. I thought maybe we could snuggle, but we can watch a vid or a holo if you want."

"No, snuggling's good. Snuggling's always good." He didn't know how far the snuggling would go, but physical intimacy between them had predictably diminished due to the pregnancy, and the fights his constant lateness caused hadn't helped. He would appreciate just holding his wife close for a couple of hours, even if nothing else happened.

She said she wanted to shower, so he waited for her in bed. He was very tempted to comm Cherry and ask her what was happening with the Guardian, but if Isobel overheard him discussing work stuff her apparently forgiving attitude would be shattered.

He removed his ear comm and put it on the bedside table. He didn't know what he'd done to deserve Isobel. The truth was, he didn't deserve her. He entirely understood her viewpoint on his behavior, which made his inability to improve it all the more inexplicable.

The bathroom door opened and she came out wearing a floor-length, dusky pink, satin nightgown with shoestring straps. She'd washed and dried her hair and it hung around her shoulders, thick and lustrous. His mouth dropped open. His wife looked gorgeous, bump and all. In fact, her beauty was partly due to her pregnancy. Her abundant hormones had made her skin especially plump, soft, and glowing.

"Sweetheart, you look stunning." He was so moved at the sight that his eyes became moist.

Her eyes were glistening too. She pulled back the covers and climbed into bed. "Hold me, okay?" She turned her back to him and he lay down with her, pressing close to her body, folding one arm over her bump. Their baby stretched in response, pushing hard against his forearm. He chuckled and Isobel laughed softly too.

He folded his other arm under his head and rested his face in Isobel's hair.

"I love you, you know," Isobel said.

"I know, and I love you too."

She turned over and put her arms on each side of his neck before kissing him full on the lips. He pulled her close, and they kissed deeply. He pushed back her hair and kissed her neck. She ran her hands over his back.

He stopped what he was doing and pulled away, making eye contact. "Is this okay? I mean, you're pretty far along."

"The baby isn't due for another four weeks. I'm sure it's fine."

His heart skipped. It felt too good to be true. Smiling, he moved in close again and resumed kissing Isobel's neck. His fingers found the strap of her nightgown and slid beneath it, easing it off her shoulder.

Their lovemaking lasted ages. Certain accommodations had to be made on account of the bump, but that only made the experience more special and pleasurable. He lost track of time. Things hadn't been so good between them for months. He didn't think he'd ever felt so lucky, so blissful.

When it was over, she rested her head on his chest and he sank into a heavy sleep.

When he woke, it was full daylight. He sat up, panicking. What was the time? He'd forgotten to put in his ear comm before falling asleep. He'd missed his alarm. He was going to be late for work.

As he reached for his comm, he noticed something else was wrong. Isobel's side of the bed was cold. It wasn't unusual for her to rise before him. Miki often had a nightmare in the early morning and had to be comforted in order to go back to sleep. But Isobel's side of the bed felt like no one had slept in it all night.

An icy hand clutched his heart.

His breathing sped up.

No!

Suddenly, his wife's behavior last night took on a new meaning.

Like an automaton, he climbed out of bed. In four steps he crossed the bedroom to Isobel's closet. The door stood ajar. He pulled it wide. A room holding only a few clothes confronted him. Isobel's packing case was gone.

Clammy with cold sweat, he walked toward his daughter's room. Her door was open and her bed was empty.

He stood in the hallway, motionless.

Isobel was gone. She was gone. She'd taken Miki and left him.

Last night had been her goodbye.

He fell to his knees.

Twenty

Night was falling. Wilder estimated she had another couple of kilometers to go. All the way from Annwn, she'd kept to the side of the road to avoid detection. Now the hilly ground was evening out. She was nearing her journey's end. She could already smell the ocean, though the raised land prevented her from catching sight of it.

She was dizzy with fatigue. Her medication kept the pain of her injuries and sore muscles at bay but did nothing for her energy levels, which felt like they were already at zero.

And she wasn't even sure where she was going. It had been a couple of years since she'd been at Tycho and Stephie's house. The last visit had been awkward, and she'd never gone back. They were different people from the adolescents she'd left behind when she'd gone on the mission to the Assembly. It was obvious when she thought about it. Their lifetime of experiences had changed them, while she was essentially the same person who had invited them to help her build a tree village more than fifty years ago.

But they were the only people whose location she—vaguely—knew. She had other friends, mostly people also working on a-grav, but she only ever talked with them over comm or very occasionally met them at a public location. She had some idea where the a-grav people lived but not their house or even the street.

She also had no comm and so no way to contact anyone. Even if she had a comm the minute she used it she would reveal her location on the system. If Cherry had instructed the CED to search for her, officers would immediately swoop.

Luckily, she remembered the whereabouts of Tycho and Stephie's home. They lived on the outskirts of Oceanside in one of the newer developments. She wouldn't have to walk right to the top of the cliff and into the town center. The most recently built housing was closer to sea level and set back from the water.

Or, they *had* lived there. If they'd moved, she was sunk. They were the only people who could help her and who she trusted to not tell anyone where she was.

Cars zoomed past twenty meters to her right. Commuters from the manufacturing site near old Sidhe were returning home for the evening. The factories and munitions plants were being relocated closer to Oceanside. The manufacturing site's proximity to Cerberus had made sense in the early days, when the weapon parts had been transported underground through a tunnel, but Cerberus had long been built. Now the colony's spread across Lyonesse and over the ocean to Suddene made armament delivery easier to disguise.

Moving the manufacturing site nearer to Oceanside would cut many Concordians' commuting time while also making Cerberus less vulnerable to attack.

It was all unimportant. She loved her forest home and she fully intended to continue living there with Piddle and Puddle, just as soon as she could get Cherry off her back. Her heartstrings tugged at the thought of her little pets. She hoped they were okay. She'd been forced to abandon the idea of quickly visiting her tree home to check on them. It was too far and too risky. Her capacity to walk was severely restricted. She had to save her strength for her walk to Oceanside and her only hope of retaining her freedom.

The minute she could manage it, she would return to her home and find Piddle and Puddle.

As she crested the next low hill, several streets were revealed over the rise. In the low light they were shadowy shapes on the gentle slopes. This was it. She'd reached the outskirts of Oceanside.

But the streets didn't look familiar. Perhaps they belonged to a development that had been built since she'd last been here. Tycho and Stephie's house had to be farther in. To reach it she would have to walk the streets, exposed to other pedestrians and passersby. She probably looked awful and she would attract attention, but that couldn't be helped. She was exhausted and almost beyond caring.

Dragging one foot in front of the other, she made her slow way closer to the residencies. She stepped onto the nearest sidewalk. Kids were playing in the front yards, screaming and laughing, probably dreading the moment their parents would call them in for dinner.

Concordians had continued to reproduce at an incredible rate. Children were everywhere. She didn't dislike them, but she also relished the seclusion of her home, which allowed her to pick and choose when to be in the presence of the loud, chaotic, emotional creatures.

As she shuffled along, she watched the kids playing with their brothers and sisters and neighborhood friends. She was a little envious. The children were clearly happy. They had the love and security that came with belonging to a family. That opportunity had arrived too late for her. She'd been born into a life of slavery, entirely absent of her volition, serving the dreams of people long dead. That was what it meant to be a Gen, but she didn't think she'd ever really felt the injustice of it until now, when she saw the children of loving families playing, carefree, in their front yards.

Some of the kids had noticed her and stopped what they were doing to stare. She bore their curious gazes stoically. It wasn't like there was anything she could do about it. She certainly couldn't go any faster or change her appearance.

A street corner was coming up. She turned it gratefully. The next road was a larger thoroughfare and a fair amount of traffic passed along it. She guessed it was a branch of the highway from Annwn. She thought she recognized it.

Soon, she approached a familiar street. This was where Tycho and Stephie hopefully still lived. Neither worked any longer. They'd retired, but they were busy looking after their grandchildren and carrying out volunteer work.

She turned the corner, wracking her brains for her friends' house number. She couldn't remember it, and all the houses looked the same. She could barely stand, let alone walk. She didn't have the energy to traipse up and down the street, trying to figure out the right house. Her leg muscles trembled and her whole body ached, pain returning as her medication wore off.

Then she saw it: a small bush of yellow flowers. Tycho had told her it was one of the few flowering plants on Concordia, and quite expensive to buy because the scientists hadn't figured out how to preserve the seed. It was only viable for a few days, after which it wouldn't sprout, no matter the conditions provided.

She forced her legs to take another few steps, walking up the pathway to the front door. She couldn't comm Tycho or Stephie to tell them she was here. She raised her hand and knocked.

No one answered.

She raised her hand again, but her arm muscles wouldn't obey. She only managed to lift her hand halfway before her arm fell limp by her side. She toppled forward, hitting her head on the door, and crumpled to the ground.

Somewhere on the edge of her consciousness, she felt the door open.

"What the...?"

"Dad, someone's at the door. She's collapsed."

"Someone's at the door? We aren't expecting anyone."

"Didn't you hear me? She's collapsed. I think you should call an ambulance."

"Get out of the way so I can see who it is."

Hands grabbed her shoulders.

"Wilder? Honey, it's Wilder!"

This was a voice she recognized. It was Tycho. She'd found the right house. "No ambulance."

"What? Why?" Tycho's old face came into view. "You need help. You're sick."

"I'm not sick, only tired. Please, no ambulance. I'll explain."

"Wilder!" Stephie had arrived. "Stars, you look awful! What's wrong with you?"

"She says not to call her an ambulance," Tycho said.

"Oh, but we must. She looks like she's at death's door."

"No ambulance," Wilder said. "I mean it. I'm in trouble. I need your help."

"You need our...?" Tycho said. Then after a slight pause, he added, to people Wilder couldn't see, "Perhaps you should go home."

"Yeah, perhaps we should. We were on our way out anyway. We'll talk later."

Shadows passed over her. Tycho was already pulling her into the hall. Stephie closed the door and turn and face her. "Wilder, whatever has happened to you?"

Twenty-One

How strange it felt to be carried downstairs by two friends who had been teenagers a few years ago, and who were now old people.

"You don't need to do this," said Wilder. "I'm sure I can walk by myself now. I feel better."

"It's no trouble." Tycho was holding her under her armpits.

"We don't want you to slip and hurt yourself." Stephie was holding Wilder's knees.

"Besides," added Tycho, "you're as light as a cracker. You were always skinny, but you haven't been eating properly lately, have you? That old habit is going to catch up with you one day."

"Stop nagging," said Wilder. "Can't you see I have enough problems?"

He chuckled. They'd reached the bottom of the stairs and the basement of Tycho and Stephie's home. The old couple had taken Wilder's fear of discovery seriously. They'd said she could stay in a room their grandchildren used. It wasn't particularly secret, but they would put a rug over the trapdoor entrance, which might foil a cursory search.

Though her responses were flippant, she was deeply grateful that these two old friends, who she hadn't spoken to for years, had immediately agreed to help her without knowing what kind of trouble she was in or who was looking for her. "Please put me down now."

"If you're sure," said Stephie. She and Tycho placed her on the basement floor. She stood up, though not without difficulty. They were in a circular room with a low ceiling. Toys were scattered over the floor.

"This is it," Tycho said. "Our underground shelter for when the Scythians return. It's basic, but it'll do for now. We'll make a sofa up as a bed. The bathroom's through there." He pointed at the only door.

"Let me help you, dear," said Stephie, in a grandmotherly tone Wilder had never grown accustomed to. The Stephie she remembered had been twelve years old and had begged to be allowed to join the older kids in the tree village, not a sweet old lady, gray-haired and slightly stooped.

Nevertheless, Wilder didn't refuse Stephie's guiding, supporting arm as she crossed the basement floor. She sat on the sofa with relief. Waves of pain were erupting from her ribs and abdomen like lava from a slow eruption. She reached for the medication in her pocket. "Could I have some water? I need to take a pill."

"Sure," said Tycho. "We'll get you some, and some food. Our family was visiting and we have plenty left over."

"I'd like that." She'd eaten all the food she'd taken from Cherry's house and she was ravenous as well as very thirsty. "I can't thank you enough."

"Stop right there," said Stephie. "You don't have to thank us for anything. You gave us a place to stay that allowed us to escape forced living with fake parents, and you traveled light years to the Assembly in order to save the colony. Nothing we can do can repay that. We'll always be in your debt."

"Oh, that's ridiculous..." Wilder began, but Tycho interrupted her.

"Don't argue. Just sit there quietly while we get you some dinner."

She didn't have the strength to argue, so she didn't object. Tycho and Stephie returned to the stairs.

"We won't be long," said Stephie.

It was the last thing Wilder remembered until she felt a hand on her shoulder, gently shaking her. It was Stephie again. How much time had passed? She must have fallen asleep. She'd been sitting on the sofa, but now she was lying on her side.

"Please, let us call a doctor for you," said Stephie.

"I've seen a doctor, and I've been discharged."

"You were in hospital?" Tycho was holding a tray of food and a large glass of water.

"Long story."

"We have plenty of time," said Stephie.

"I'm sorry, I will tell you. Only I'm too tired."

"That's fine," said Stephie. "We don't need to know. You're welcome to stay with us for as long as you like."

"I just need somewhere until I'm better." And then what? When she was better Cherry would have no reason to hound her. She would be able to return to her tree home, find Piddle and Puddle, and resume normal life, though her relationship with General Cherry was shattered forever. She would never help out that woman again.

Stephie was holding sheets, a pillow, and a bed cover. She began to make up a bed on the other sofa. Meanwhile, Tycho put down the tray and handed Wilder the glass of water. She popped one of the pain medication tablets into her mouth and swallowed it.

Tycho lifted the tray of food onto her lap. "We're not leaving until you've eaten every scrap. And we both know how you love your alone time, so that's a real threat."

She smiled and began to eat. Some of the food was from the ocean, unsurprisingly considering the proximity of Tycho and Stephie's home to the sea. Before they retired, they'd both worked on ocean harvesters, which skimmed shallow water for sea plants, algae, and tiny marine creatures.

According to the tales they'd told of the years of colonization that had passed while she'd been on her mission, Concordians had balked at first at the idea of eating animal life, no matter how small and unintelligent. The colonists who had grown up aboard the *Nova* eating crickets and other animal protein had nearly all died out. Even after the Woken had okayed the consumption of certain Concordian animals, later generations were unused to the idea of eating non-plant life. They took a supplement instead, in order to protect themselves against nutritional deficiencies. But after tasting patties made of hundreds of the ocean creatures compressed and fried in oil, many had changed their minds.

Wilder had only tasted the patties once, on a visit to her friends' home, and she had to admit that the slightly salty, slightly crunchy patties were tasty. Though the idea of eating animals still turned her stomach a little, she didn't want to be rude, and she was so famished she would have eaten a sluglimpet.

As well as the still-warm patties, Tycho had made her a plate of seaweed ribbons, roasted hypogeal fungi, and baked sweet potatoes with peanut butter. Ordinarily, she would never be able to eat so much in one sitting. In fact, the food Tycho had piled on her plate seemed more than she would eat in an entire day. But her instinct to consume calories overcame her usual indifference. She picked up a fork, dug it into a chunk of fungi, and lifted it to her mouth.

"Great," said Stephie. "It's good to see you eat."

Wilder barely noted the grandmotherly tones in her hyper focus.

"I forgot to say," Stephie continued, "you can talk to the Fila while you're here."

This remarkable sentence broke through Wilder's distraction. "What?"

"I'll show you." Tycho uttered a voice command, and half of the circular wall turned transparent. Water lay beyond it, illuminated by gentle lights set into the wall's exterior.

"The grand kids begged for a Fila playroom," said Stephie. "Their parents couldn't afford it. How could we say no?"

Wilder forced down a half-chewed lump of fungi. "Your grand kids play with the Fila?"

"I don't know if they exactly play with them," Tycho said. "But they talk to them, and sometimes the Fila put on an entertaining light display. The kids love it. Keeps them occupied for hours."

"I bet." Wilder used the edge of her fork to cut a patty into quarters before stabbing one section and popping it into her mouth.

Tycho asked his wife, "I think they were originally the Fila's idea, weren't they, honey?"

"I believe so," Stephie replied. "All we had to do was create the basement and send our house's coordinates to the Fila. They do the rest at their end."

"Are you sure it's safe?" Wilder imagined a maze of tunnels among the foundations of the houses.

"The Fila say it is," said Stephie. "I guess they would know. They always try to help us. I don't think they would do anything risky."

Wilder hadn't had much to do with the aquatic aliens since her mission, when she had spent long hours chatting with Quinn, one of the Fila ship's operators. She'd been working with Kes on researching the creatures. She had to agree with Stephie. The Fila wouldn't ever knowingly do anything that might harm a human.

They also exerted a not inconsiderable influence in the colony. The Leader was known to regularly consult with them about colony affairs, even taking advice on subjects that didn't relate directly to the Fila's relationship with humans.

Wilder had an idea. "How do your grand kids talk to them?"

"They open the room comm and chat," said Tycho. "But they have to wait until one happens to come by. There's no way to summon them, but somehow they usually know when the wall is set to transparent and one turns up within a few minutes."

"All this talking must be tiring you out," Stephie said. "We'll leave you alone to finish your meal. Then you'll probably want to rest. I'll come down again later with some night clothes. If you want anything, contact us through the house comm. You can use the interface in the armrest."

"Thanks," Wilder replied. "I am tired and I would love to rest for a while. Thanks for the food too."

"It's our pleasure," said Tycho.

The couple climbed the stairs and she continued to eat. After a few moments, she saw movement from the corner of her eye. She opened the room comm that would allow her to talk to the tentacled creature. "Hi."

"Hello," the Fila replied, its voice broadcast over a speaker.

"Could you help me with something? I would like to speak to Quinn."

Twenty-Two

Blissful, pain-free ease and comfort blanketed Wilder. Feeling like she was floating on soft, warm clouds, she came slowly to consciousness, not knowing where she was or what had happened to her but also not caring. All she remembered was that she was safe.

Finally, somewhat reluctantly, she opened her eyes. A low ceiling hung over her, and she was lying next to a transparent wall. Tentacles writhed slowly in the water beyond it.

She sat up, causing her stomach muscles to ache dully. How long had she slept? The pain medication was beginning to wear off again, so it had to be around ten to twelve hours. Tycho or Stephie had returned while she'd been asleep and left more food and water.

A single, very large Fila was floating a couple of meters away. She recognized its patterning immediately. "Quinn!"

"Wilder. I didn't notice you had ceased sleeping."

"I only just woke up. How long have you been waiting there?"

Silence followed her question. Quinn was trying to translate Fila time measurement into human terms and failing.

"Never mind," she said. "Thank you for coming to see me. I hope you weren't doing anything important."

"Nothing that couldn't be done by others. It is pleasant to meet with you again."

"It's good to see you too." She hadn't realized it until now, but she'd missed him. She'd spent months in the operations room aboard the *Opportunity*, just talking to him and watching him and his fellow crew members, trying to learn all she could about his species.

In the years that had passed since, she hadn't met up with him again. Living in a tree far from the ocean hadn't made it easy, and, as always, she'd been concentrating on her work. She turned to face him and crossed her legs.

"Is this place your new home?" he asked. "I could come here to visit you. I enjoyed the time we spent together on the journeys to and from the Galactic Assembly."

"I did too." She reached out to touch the transparent wall, but the movement hurt her ribs. She winced. "Wait a minute." She found her painkillers and took a pill with a swallow of water.

"Please, eat more if you're hungry. I can wait."

"I'm not eating. It's medication."

"Medication." He paused as he pondered the word's meaning. Or perhaps he was consulting with other Fila. It had never been clearly established if the Fila had true telepathic ability or their ultra-sensitive tentacles were picking up subtle water movements carried across long distances.

"Medication," he repeated. "So you're suffering from a sickness?"

"Not exactly. I got hurt in an accident. The pill takes away the pain until I'm better."

"I hope it isn't rude of me to say it, but your bodies are not very efficient. If I suffer an accident or my body is invaded by pathological microorganisms, I only have to sever the affected part and regrow it."

"I have to admit, your method is way more efficient. But what happens if you're injured or infected all over? You can't sever all of you."

"It is very rare for that to happen, but when it does we simply die. We don't have medication. Humans have the advantage in that area."

Sparked by the conversation, she asked a question that hadn't occurred to her during the entire trip to the Assembly. "How long do Fila live?"

"That's difficult to answer."

She'd hit upon the time measurement translation problem again. She reframed the question. "When do you die? Is it after you have children, or do you live on for a long time after that?" Kes had told her longevity was often tied to fertility. Humans were one of the few Earth species whose females lived on for decades after they could no longer bear children.

Quinn replied, "Aside from the circumstances of disease or accident, Fila do not die."

"What, never?" She was flabbergasted. "Don't you grow old?"

"We do not. This is another big difference between our species, and between humans and other intelligent galactic species. Humans are very short-lived. I was surprised and saddened when I returned to Concordia and discovered that Ethan had died not long after our arrival."

"Wow, yes. That must have been a shock."

"It was a shock. If I had known that taking you all to the Assembly space station would separate you from the people you knew when you left, I would have warned you."

"It's okay. You didn't know, and we've gotten used to it, I guess."

"Is your medication working? Is your pain reducing?"

"Hmm." The pain that had threatened to return had been beaten back again. "Yes, it is."

"What was your accident?"

"Oh..." She was about to give the same response as she had to Tycho and Stephie—that it was a long story—but she hesitated. Quinn might not understand the underlying meaning that she didn't want to talk about it, but not only that. She *did* want to talk about it and unburden herself of her traumatic experience and Cherry's later outrageous behavior.

Wilder had never had a family to confide in. The nearest thing to that had been Ben, and he'd died years ago. She'd been close to Kes and Cherry too, but Kes was married now and busy with work, and as for Cherry...

For some reason, she felt she could open up to Quinn, despite him being not only not family, but another species. She told him everything that had happened, leaving nothing out. It took her so long that she paused to pick up her tray and begin eating breakfast. Quinn listened without responding, only slowly swirling his tentacles in the water.

As she finished explaining how she had walked from Annwn to Oceanside over the course of a day in order to hide at her friends' home, she heard the basement trapdoor open.

Footsteps sounded on the stairs, and Tycho came into view. "I heard you talking. I'm glad to see you were speaking to someone and not chattering to yourself. I would wonder if everything you told me had been words of madness." He held out his hand, palm upward. "Brought you a little something." It was an ear comm. "It's new. Fresh from the factory."

"Thanks, but I don't think I can use it. The minute I access the network, anyone looking for me will know exactly where I am."

"Are you really in that much trouble? I know you like to do your own thing, regardless of what the authorities might say, but I'm sure you didn't do anything harmful."

"I *didn't* do anything harmful. All I want is for people to leave me alone so I can do my work. Apparently that's too much to ask." In response to Tycho's continued apparent puzzlement, she added, "I got on the wrong side of someone high up. Someone I thought was a friend."

"May I suggest something?" Quinn asked. "After listening to your story, I believe this is one of those situations where both sides would benefit from spending some time apart."

"You got that right," Wilder said.

"As you know, I am familiar with the person you fear wants to confine you against your will. Admittedly I'm not as knowledgeable about human behavior as I would like, but among my kind I am considered an expert. You feel forced to hide away in order to escape this person's efforts to find you."

"I *am* forced to hide."

"For how much longer?" Quinn asked. "And is your friend in danger of retribution if he's discovered to be hiding you?"

"Honestly, I don't know. Cherry seemed pretty mad and she has the power to do whatever she wants, as she pointed out. I don't know what's gone wrong with her. Sorry for dragging you and Stephie into this, Tycho."

"Don't worry about it. I'm not frightened of what the General might do to us. Me and Stephie are only a pair of old folks. We aren't worth throwing in prison."

"Nevertheless," Quinn said, "I have a solution that would allow Wilder to remain safe while she heals, and the only person who would be in danger of suffering from repercussions would be myself."

"If you're about to suggest what I'm thinking," Wilder said, "I'm sorry, but I really don't fancy spending a couple of weeks in one of your underwater tanks, like the one you kept the old Leader in."

"I wasn't about to suggest that. Confining Ethan and the other man and his daughter was a great mistake that we deeply regret, and for which we have been trying to atone."

"Wait," said Wilder, "is that why the Fila have done so much to help us over all these years?"

"One of the reasons, yes. But we would help you anyway. We would prefer the galaxy to be a peaceful home to intelligent life. We try to support non-aggressive intelligent species."

Quinn had clearly never seen Cherry in a temper. "So if you don't want to put me in an underwater tank, where are you suggesting I go?"

"To the *Opportunity*. I could arrange a shuttle to take you up to it."

"The *Opportunity*?!" The starship had been in orbit around Concordia for years. She hadn't ever hankered to return to it, not after spending several months living within its cramped quarters with nothing to eat except the Guardians' ration bars. Though she hated her current predicament, hiding aboard the *Opportunity* to evade Cherry seemed like overkill.

"You could continue your work with anti-gravity, too," Quinn added, "in relative safety." She had complained at considerable length that Cherry and Kes had allowed her a-grav machine to escape.

She gasped. "You're right!" In its orbital position, the *Opportunity* only experienced micro gravity. If she managed to hit upon the right formulation again, the effects on the machine would be noticeable but minor. She would have plenty of time to turn it off, and even if she was slow to deactivate it, the machine wouldn't exert enough force to damage the ship.

The more she thought about Quinn's suggestion, the more she liked it. Aboard the *Opportunity* she would be in absolutely no danger of anyone disturbing her. She could work for as long as she wanted in peace and quiet. It sounded like bliss.

There was only one impediment to the plan. "Quinn, I accept your proposal, with one caveat. I want to go home and collect a few clothes and other things I'll need, and I have a couple of very small companions I'd like to bring too."

Twenty-Three

It was all decided. Tycho would go with Wilder by autovan to a place where she could pick up parts to build another prototype a-grav machine. Then they would go on to her tree house. Tycho would check it wasn't being watched before she collected Piddle and Puddle. Quinn would arrange two shuttles—one to transport her and her pets, and the other to carry the a-grav machine parts and other supplies.

Tycho estimated it would take them most of a day to accomplish everything. Quinn said he could have the shuttles ready 'soon'.

Stephie objected to the entire plan. "I'm sure you'll be perfectly safe in our home." She'd came down into the basement to see what was taking so long. "No one knows you're here."

"Except for the kids and the grand kids," Tycho said.

"But they wouldn't say anything to anyone."

"Are you sure? Little Bobby's only five. Do you think it's safe to trust a five-year-old to never mention someone collapsing at the front door to his grandparents' house?"

"Well, what if he does? Who pays any attention a five-year-old's prattling?"

"Stephie," Wilder said, "I know you're worried about me, but I do think this is the best option. Besides, I'm dying to get back to work on a-grav. I think I'm millimeters away from a solution and it's driving me nuts. If I have to wait until I'm better and Cherry has no more excuses for locking me up, I might go crazy."

Stephie's expression of doubt and concern remained.

Suddenly, Wilder chuckled.

"I don't see what's so funny," said Stephie in an offended tone. "I care about you. I don't want you to come to any harm. When you're up in that starship, you'll be all alone. What if you take a turn for the worse and no one's there to look after you?"

"Wilder won't be alone," said Quinn. "A minimal crew remains aboard the *Opportunity* at all times, and I will board the ship, too."

"You're going to be with me?" Wilder asked. "Fantastic!"

Stephie said, "But a Fila can't help you if you have a medical emergency."

"My medical emergency is over. All I need is time to rest and recuperate. A couple of weeks aboard the *Opportunity* will give me that and more besides. I understand your concerns, and I'm sorry for laughing. It was only that I was reminded of when you were twelve and begging to be allowed to come and live in my tree village. Now our roles are reversed."

Stephie looked downward. "Gosh, you're right. I was forgetting. I changed my mind. You didn't stand in my way then and I won't stand in your way now. I'm sorry. It's only that I'm nearly fifty years older than you and I feel like I should mother you."

"Don't worry about it. I made it this far without a mother. I reckon I can make it a little farther."

"Let's prepare some food supplies for Wilder to take with her," Tycho said, and the older couple climbed the stairs.

"That was an interesting interaction, if you don't mind me saying," said Quinn.

"It was? Why's that?"

"I rarely visit humans in these underground rooms as other Fila do, but on the few occasions I've witnessed your behavior and listened to your conversations, I find it remarkable how deeply emotionally connected you are to those who are genetically related. When I say 'you' I don't mean you in particular, but humans in general."

"That's a correct observation. Human families are emotionally close. The bonds between parents and children are strong. Isn't it like that with the Fila?" She'd never asked Quinn about his family in all the times she'd talked to him aboard the *Opportunity*, probably because families didn't mean a lot to her.

"It is not at all like that with the Fila. I have thousands of offspring and I don't know who they are or where they are. I spawned aboard the seeding ship while it was on its way to Concordia. Perhaps some of my children were deposited on this planet or perhaps they journeyed onward to a new world."

"I was 'spawned' aboard the *Nova*, and I have no idea who my mother and father were or if I have any brothers and sisters. I guess I'm a little bit like a Fila."

"I guess you are."

Tycho checked the street was empty before giving Wilder the signal that it was safe to leave. She walked quickly to the sidewalk and then climbed into the autovan. Tycho and Stephie had already packed plenty of food and other supplies.

Tycho started the engine and input the destination, and the autovan pulled away from the curb. Wilder gave Stephie a wave. The older woman waved back before smiling and giving a thumbs up. Wilder was glad they hadn't parted on bad terms. She'd already lost the friendship of one person who she'd thought cared about her, she didn't want to lose another.

She didn't know what lengths Cherry might go to in order to capture her. Should she be wearing a low-brimmed hat to conceal her identity while she and Tycho were driving around? She shook her head. The entire situation was ridiculous. Over the years she'd done a few borderline illegal things, but wanting her liberty while she was recuperating from an accident wasn't one of them.

It was late morning. The rush hour was over and the streets were reasonably quiet. It had only been a year or two since she had been here in Oceanside, but in that time the place had noticeably changed. The town had grown. New developments were going up everywhere—not only residencies, but shops, offices, services, and manufacturing plants too. The colony was expanding at a rapid rate.

"How many grandchildren do you have now?" she asked Tycho.

"If you count the one on the way, seventeen."

"Seventeen!"

"Five children, and they've all had two or three kids of their own. It happens faster than you realize."

"And I suppose all your children could go on to have more kids."

"I'm sure they will. And my family isn't unusual by any means. I have friends younger than me with more grandchildren."

She gave a low whistle. They were drawing near their first stop. She sat upright and peered out, curious to finally meet the person they were going to see.

The network of people working on a-grav rarely met. When they did it was only in twos or threes, in case they were arrested. She had never encountered the person who had offered to give her spare machine parts. She only knew him by his code name of Jamie Bond. When she'd heard the name she'd thought it was his real name, but he'd explained it was the name of a famous Earth spy.

The name was very boring. It was no wonder that Jamie Bond's story had been lost to obscurity.

But what did the real person look like? During their comms on the secret network, she had been impressed with his insightful comments and quirky sense of humor. She'd formed a mental image of a man in his late twenties, highly intelligent and probably quite handsome too. In her most candid moments, she admitted to herself she'd developed a bit of a crush.

The autovan had reached its destination and parked outside a one-story home that looked as though it had only just been built.

"It's so small," she commented.

"Not necessarily," Tycho replied. "This is one of the new designs. We're only seeing the upper story. The rest of the structure is below ground."

"To talk to the Fila?"

"To talk to the Fila. I haven't been inside one yet but I've seen plans. These places contain two or more floors where the Fila have access to come and visit."

"Two or more floors just to speak to them? That seems excessive."

"At our place it's only really our grandchildren who interact with the Fila, but many adults are getting into the habit too."

"Wow. We'll be hearing about the first human and Fila marriage next."

"I wouldn't be surprised."

"I wonder what their kids will look like."

The front door opened and a boy about twelve years old came out. He trotted up to the van's window, which Tycho lowered.

"Are you Deadly After Midnight?" the boy asked.

Wilder's stomach sank in disappointment. "No, that's me. *You're* Jamie Bond?"

The boy's eyes widened. "I thought you were a man."

"I thought you were different too. Do you have the stuff?"

"I do. But I'll need a hand bringing it all out."

"I can do that," said Tycho. "You wait here, W—I mean, Deadly After Midnight." He seemed to be stifling a smile as he climbed out.

"Shouldn't you be in school?" Wilder asked Jamie Bond.

He grinned. "Probably. I'll be back in a minute."

It took Jamie and Tycho three trips to carry all the parts to the van. When everything was safely stowed, Tycho climbed into his seat.

Wilder thanked Jamie Bond sincerely. She'd quickly gotten over her letdown over his true identity and her feelings had altered to admiration. She assumed his parents didn't know he was working on a-grav. Hiding the truth from them would take plenty of smart thinking.

"It's no problem," Jamie replied. "Good luck with whatever it is you're doing."

The temptation to tell him about her breakthrough was huge. The only thing she liked more than working on interesting stuff was talking about it, and she was very proud to be the first person in the underground group to have achieved success. But she couldn't afford the delay. She had to collect Piddle and Puddle and meet the Fila shuttles.

"You too," she said. "I'm going to be off network for a couple of weeks. Could you tell the others? I hope to have something very important to announce."

"Not if I get there first."

The autovan drove away. The first part of her preparations for leaving Concordia was over. Now all she needed was her two small friends.

After leaving the highway outside Annwn, it was a twenty-minute drive to the remaining patch of forest that had once covered Sidhe. The road to Cerberus was well paved, but the offshoot running to the forest was falling into disrepair. No one except her had lived out this way for years.

Autocars and autovans had no function for avoiding potholes, perhaps because they were rare. Their vehicle hit the holes at full speed, jerking her in her seat and making her teeth judder.

She was studying the view closely, looking for signs of CED or military transports Cherry might have sent out, but the surrounding landscape was empty of human life. Scrub plants grew tall and rough, and in the distance was the darker green of the forest.

"You know, there's still time to change your mind," said Tycho. "We can turn around and go back to Oceanside. Stephie and I would be happy for you to stay with us for as long as you like."

"I know, and I appreciate it. But now that I've had time to think, I'm really looking forward to this vacation on the *Opportunity*. I know it must seem weird, but the idea of spending days and weeks utterly alone is blissful to me."

"No, you don't sound weird. I understand, and don't forget I've known you a long time. You haven't changed." After they'd driven another couple of minutes, Tycho said, "How are we going to play this? I don't see anyone lurking to catch you. Where do you want to park?"

She had already given some thought to the question. "If someone's already watching us from the cover of the forest, there isn't a lot we can do about it. I'm going to have to go in alone, keeping my ears and eyes open. I know that place like the back of my hand. I should be able to spot anything suspicious right away. If I see an ambush in the making, I'll come running back to you. Hopefully, I'll make it before they catch me."

"No way. I'm coming in there with you. I'm not going to let you take the risk alone. You're just a girl."

She cocked an eyebrow at him. "I might be *just a girl*, but you're an old man, my friend. I'd beat you in a race any day."

"Hmpf." He folded his arms. "Not in your current state, you wouldn't."

"Let's not argue about it, okay? I know the forest much better than you. The part I live in, at least."

"I have to admit you're right on that score. It was a sad day when we left the tree village. The trees were all dying, so there was no point in staying. In another few weeks we would have had nowhere to live. But it was sad all the same. It was where Stephie and I grew up, fell in love, and got married, all while we were working on Cerberus. It was a hard time in some ways, especially after we realized you might not be back for a very long time, if ever. But we built many happy memories there. And now it's all gone."

"Thanks to the Scythians."

"Thanks to the Scythians. If it weren't for them there would have been no Sidhe. There would have been no Cerberus nor any of the other secret military bases. The trees wouldn't have died. Concordia would have been a different place."

"There's no point in mourning might-have-beens. Look, we're nearly there. Tell the car to stop near that tree overhanging the road. After I get out, turn it around so it's ready to drive back the way we came. The track pretty much peters out in another couple of hundred meters."

The autocar stopped in the shade of the tree she had indicated. It was around the spot where Quinn would be landing the shuttles, but they hadn't arrived yet. It was mid afternoon. She had plenty of time to pick up Piddle and Puddle, providing she didn't meet any obstacles.

A few moments later, she was stepping carefully and quietly through the undergrowth, heading toward her home. She was taking a circuitous route, approaching her tree from a different direction than her usual one, hoping this might give her an advantage if Cherry had stationed anyone there.

Though she'd only been away four nights, it felt much longer. The forest felt fresh, new, and foreign, as if she were visiting it for the first time. The sensations she experienced were acute: the cool, moist air on her skin and in her lungs, the scent of damp, rotting organic matter, and the dappled, shifting sunlight slanting through the canopy.

Yet she also knew exactly where she was and where she was going. Nothing looked unfamiliar, out of place, or disturbed. Perhaps Cherry had decided to leave her alone after all. But she wasn't going to take any chances.

She crept closer to her tree.

Twenty-Four

"I'm sorry for threatening to call the CED," said Cherry as her autocar neared her home. "I'm sorry I overreacted. And I would never have you forcibly sedated." She gave a shudder and put her hand over her eyes. What the hell had she been thinking?

When she'd heard the Guardians had sedated Aubriot, she'd been outraged. Even though the man was an asshole, even though if she'd been forced to choose someone to be sedated, it would have been him, she'd been incensed. She couldn't believe the gall of the creatures, their arrogance in deciding to deprive someone of their consciousness.

And then she'd gone and threatened to do the same thing to Wilder. Would the girl ever forgive her? Probably not, and she wouldn't blame her. In Wilder's shoes, she certainly would never forgive anyone who threatened to do that to *her*.

It was easy enough to tell herself she'd done it out of concern for her young friend, who was hurt and vulnerable. But depriving someone who was entirely sane of their freedom *for their own good* made no sense at all.

Were her constant worries and fears over the safety of the colony getting to her? Ever since Aubriot had resigned she'd felt her responsibilities weighing even more heavily on her shoulders. He'd been the only one who had taken the threat to the colony seriously, but even he had lost interest and commitment. Even Meredith was putting politics before planetary security.

Cherry's car stopped. She was home already. Her rehearsed speech entirely disappeared from her mind. It didn't matter. She would just tell Wilder exactly what she thought, offer her a deep apology, and express the wish that her young friend would remain living with her until she was better. But if she wanted to leave she could and no one would stop her.

Cherry got out of her car and paused before going into her house. The street was dark, like the rest of Annwn. Motion-activated, solar-powered lights would guide approaching pedestrians, but they were the only source of light. The house windows in the little dead-end road gave out no rays. Either their occupants weren't home or they had made the windows opaque.

It was something, she admitted to herself. All the settlements followed the same rule: no visible lights at night. The autocars didn't carry headlights. They didn't need them to navigate. The cars only had small side lights to warn pedestrians of their presence and avoid accidents.

She walked up the path to her small home. It was quite late. Finishing up at the hospital and visiting Meredith had taken more time than she would have liked. She hoped Wilder had made herself plenty to eat. Maybe she was asleep already. If she was, Cherry wouldn't wake her. She could apologize to her in the morning.

As soon as she stepped into her home, she sensed something was wrong. Air moved against her skin. That was it. She always kept her windows closed whenever she was out.

Had Wilder opened a window?

Unease settling over her, Cherry tried to guess the source of the breeze. It seemed to be coming from her kitchen.

"Wilder?" she called softly, not wanting to wake the girl if she was asleep.

The kitchen door was half open. She opened it the rest of the way and stepped in. The light turned on, revealing an open window above the sanitizer. Night creatures began flying in, drawn by the light. She reached over the sanitizer and pulled the window closed.

Her stomach sank. A scenario was building in her head. In her mind, she saw Wilder come downstairs and try to open the front and back doors. Their locks only responded to Cherry's touch—an experimental design that read the unique mixtures of skin chemicals. She'd been trying the new system out. The doors would not have opened for Wilder.

Not to be foiled in her escape attempt, had her young friend had gone through the kitchen window instead? Cherry looked into her yard. It was impossible to see anything in the blackness and the window's reflection of the indoor light, but she knew it was empty anyway.

Her heart heavy, she checked the kitchen for Wilder's pain medication. It was gone. Some food seemed to have been taken too. Cherry didn't mind in the slightest. She wished her friend had taken more.

By the time she climbed the stairs and went into the spare bedroom, she had no expectation of finding Wilder sleeping peacefully. There was no sign of the girl, of course. Dolefully, Cherry sat down on the empty bed. Where had

Wilder gone? Was she okay? She was still far from well, and she had no comm. Cherry had requested a new one for her but it hadn't arrived yet.

Had she returned to her tree house? Cherry called the CED and introduced herself to the operating sergeant.

"Good evening, ma'am. How can I help you?"

"I'd like you to send someone to..."

After a pause the sergeant said, "Yes, ma'am?"

"No, it's okay. Never mind."

"Are you sure, ma'am?"

"Yes. Sorry to bother you." She closed the comm. Wilder's home had no address and even if it had, sending over a CED officer to find her and check on her would only add fuel to the fire. She also couldn't go over there herself. She would be the last person in all of Concordia Wilder would want to see.

She had another idea. She comm'd Kes. Wilder might also be angry at him for allowing the a-grav machine to escape, but he hadn't entirely betrayed her trust. Wilder might be prepared to talk to him.

But Kes didn't answer.

What should she do? She hated the thought of Wilder, injured and angry, trying to get home, perhaps fearing that the CED or even the military were looking for her.

A comm arrived.

"What?" Cherry barked.

"Uh, something's happened at the Chimera excavation site, ma'am."

"*Something's happened?* What kind of statement is that? Who am I speaking to?" In her preoccupation, she had missed the caller's ID.

"Colonel Fletcher, ma'am."

The officer she'd met at Cerberus. "Please be more exact in your language, Colonel, or we could be here all night."

"There's been an accident at the Chimera excavation site."

"Right. Was anyone seriously hurt? Is the project delayed?"

"No, and...I don't think so. Or—"

"So why are you comming me?" She fought to keep her anger from spilling over into her tone, without much success.

"Ma'am, if you would give me a moment to explain..."

She rubbed her temples. "Go ahead, Fletcher. You have my undivided attention."

"I only just received the news, but apparently the incident happened about an hour and a half ago. One of the excavators was removing bedrock, when he broke through into a massive underground chamber. His machine nearly fell into it, but the other workers managed to get a few lines fixed to it and pulled it back from the brink. He's okay."

She bit her tongue, waiting for the non-story to come to an end. Caves might be interesting to some people, but she had more important things on her mind.

"Ma'am, the cavern he broke into, from the recording the supervisor has sent, it looks like an underground city."

"Huh?" Now he had her full attention. "A city? Are you sure?"

"I'm positive, ma'am. I have no idea what it means, but I thought you should know about it. Should I send you the vid?"

"Please do." She had an idea what the discovery might be, but she didn't want to jump to any conclusions. On the other hand, if there really was a city beneath the desert in Suddene, there was no doubt in her mind about who had built it. "Colonel, the man who broke through into the chamber, are you sure he's okay? He didn't suffer any breathing difficulties?"

"I'm not sure about that, to be honest. All I know is his supervisor told me they got him out and he seemed fine."

"Tell them to take him to a medical facility immediately for a full checkup, especially his lungs. I don't think there's a hospital on Suddene yet, but there must be some kind of medical center. And tell the supervisor to evacuate the entire excavation site and seal the entrances." She didn't know anything about the atmosphere the Scythians breathed before screwing up their planet's ecosystem. The gases that might remain in the city could be harmless to humans, but it wouldn't hurt to be cautious. "Oh, and tell the supervisor to remind his workers about the secrecy clause in their contracts. I don't want a single word of this to get out."

"Yes, ma'am. Can I ask...Do you have an idea what this place might be?"

"Anything you have the clearance to know about, you'll find out in due course."

"Yes, ma'am. I'll pass on the message. I've sent the vid."

"Good. Thank you for passing on this information so promptly, Fletcher. It could turn out to be extremely important."

"Just doing my job, ma'am."

She closed the comm. She needed to speak to Meredith, but she would watch the vid first and check that Fletcher wasn't seeing things that weren't there. But she doubted it. He seemed to be intelligent and rational.

After informing Meredith, she would travel to Suddene and see this 'city' for herself. If it really was what she thought it was, the place might yield a huge amount of information, potentially vital to helping repel the Scythians if they attacked.

She also had to address the problem of the Guardian, Faina, if that was what it was. She hadn't given up on getting the thing destroyed. At least for the moment it was safely secured in the Oceanside prison.

She stood up in order to go to the tabletop interface. As she rose, she remembered Wilder. She'd temporarily forgotten about the girl and her plight. She sat down again. *Shit!* What a time for this to happen.

But could she help Wilder now anyway? What was done was done, and Cherry couldn't take her words back. She decided to comm Kes and tell him everything that had happened. Perhaps he could help Wilder. It would be an imposition when he was already so busy, but he really cared about the girl and he would want to help her.

Cherry comm'd him again. Again, he didn't answer. She left him a message as opened the vid Fletcher had sent. All she could do now was to hope Wilder didn't come to any harm.

Twenty-Five

Cherry had to wake up a pilot to fly her to Suddene. She waited for him impatiently on the roof of a government building. It was past one in the morning, and a cold wind had risen. She waited in the darkness, hugging herself with her one arm to try to keep warm. She hadn't even thought to put on a jacket before leaving home.

While she waited, she pulled out her interface to watch the recording of the underground city again. The vid's clarity wasn't great. Low light conditions and the basic interface recorder used meant the images were often fuzzy and too dark to make out clearly. But even on her very first viewing, she had been forced to agree with Fletcher's assessment: the excavator had broken through into a vast subterranean metropolis. No geological formations could resemble the curved, towering edifices and detailed, regular constructions.

The city hadn't been built by humans. It looked nothing like the streets and houses of Oceanside. But it had been built. And the shapes she saw struck a pang of fear in her guts. They were reminiscent of the curved, pointed Scythian ships.

Her comm received a request from the pilot, Zapata. "Yes? Where are you? I've been waiting fifteen minutes."

"I'm here, ma'am. I'm downstairs. I can't get in."

"Yes, you can. Go to the panel. I added you to the system." The building had only autonomous security protecting it from unauthorized entry. It was a situation that had surprised her, and one that she intended to rectify at the earliest opportunity. She would explain to Meredith that all government buildings required human security guards round the clock.

Her own clearance overrode all military and governmental security systems. She could even walk right inside the Leader's Residence. She had simply entered the building, but of course the pilot couldn't do the same.

Eventually, he stood next to her and the heli. He was bulky, not at all how she had imagined pilots who flew the small aircraft and even smaller helis.

"We're flying to Suddene?" he asked.

"Is that going to be a problem?"

The large, bearded man looked up into the starless sky and wet a finger to feel the breeze. "Rain's coming, and I don't like the wind speed. But I'll give it a try."

"Good. Let's go."

The heli was already straining against its docking clamps, the light blades lifting in the wind. She had to hold on tight to the door frame in order to climb into the passenger seat. Zapata's weight soon settled the craft, however, as he entered on the other side. She put on the ear mufflers and fastened her harness.

"What are the coordinates?" Zapata asked as he started up the engine.

"I'll input them. Just get us into the air."

There was no need for the pilot to know Chimera's location. As soon as the trip was over she would wipe it from the log and tell him to forget where they had gone. She tapped the numbers into the console.

The heli's rotor was already spinning. Zapata released the docking clamps, and immediately the machine swept upward at an angle, pushed sideways by the wind. He gripped the controls, forcing the heli to turn. It banked sharply, caught by a sudden gust. She reached out to brace herself against the window as the heli almost turned on its side.

"Windier than I thought," Zapata said.

"Are you sure you can make it?" She wanted to go to Suddene, but she also wanted to arrive.

"I'll try. I'll have to fly on manual the whole way. The autopilot won't cope with this wind. We'll end up in the drink. If conditions seem like they're getting worse, I'll turn back. Is that a deal, General?"

"It's a deal."

He was bringing the air vessel around in a circle as he rose higher, turning it to face the coast. The night was hellish black, and as the ground dropped beneath them, she lost sight of any signs of civilization. The blackout rule seemed to be working, for all the good it might do when they came under attack.

When, not if. Others might not believe it, but there was no doubt in her mind that the Scythians would be back, and when they didn't receive their tribute, Concordia must defend herself.

At least they now knew the secret of the Scythian spiders. Even before the building of Cerberus, Ethan had put defenses in place to prevent the spiders from entering any constructed area unless dropped exactly onto it from above. If that happened, every Concordian knew how to defend himself or herself.

Or did they? Cherry made a mental note to check that the drill was still being taught in schools. The way things were going it wouldn't surprise her if it had been dropped from the curriculum.

The ETA was three hours away, according to the console display. Still worried about Wilder, Cherry tried to comm Kes again, but she didn't expect an answer and got none. He must have taken out his ear comm for the night.

Next, she sent the recordings of the Scythian city to Meredith. She'd held off on sending them until the Leader would most likely be asleep. She wouldn't see them until she awoke. Cherry didn't mark the file as a priority. It was a sneaky, underhand move, but the more she had thought about the situation, the more reluctant she was to allow Meredith to dictate what should happen.

Since their discussion about the Guardian, Cherry had lost faith in the Leader's ability to do the right thing. What if Meredith ordered Chimera to be closed off due to safety concerns? There might be a crucial clue to the Scythians lying somewhere in the abandoned city that would never be found.

Cherry couldn't allow that to happen. She *wouldn't* allow that to happen. And so she'd taken it upon herself to try to prevent it from happening by accessing the site before Meredith even woke up. It was a risky move. Meredith might demand her resignation, but Cherry had to do whatever she could to protect her home.

The sun was tinting the horizon of Suddene's desert as the heli neared the construction site. All there was to identify the place was a handful of monster trucks and a large hole in the ground.

"Taking her down," Zapata said.

He'd flown the heli well in bad conditions. A head wind had wrestled them all the way across the ocean, adding another half an hour to their flight. Buffeted by unpredictable gusts, Zapata had managed the light craft with skill. He hadn't spoken much, but Cherry had seen his lips thinning with tense concentration.

She guessed she was lucky they hadn't ended up 'in the drink'.

Just as she was finally relaxing and thanking the stars the journey was over, the wind gave them one last parting blow, whipping the heli upward when they weren't far from the ground.

For the first time, Zapata cursed. She admired his restraint.

He brought the craft downward again. "No restraints." He nodded toward the ground. "She'll blow away as soon as I get out, maybe even before. You'll have to jump. I'll take off and try to land her near the coast. I heard there's a heli pad at the port."

"Okay. Tell me when." She prepared to slide open the door.

The heli was fifteen or so meters above the ground and dropping fast. Zapata did something to slow the descent. "Five, four, three." The wind-blown, gray desert sand was rushing up at a dizzying pace, despite the pilot's efforts. "Two...one. Go!"

She tore open the door and leapt out. She hit sand, which felt surprisingly hard for sand, and managed to roll to lessen the impact, but the breath was knocked out of her all the same. As she came to a stop she craned her neck upward and saw the heli rising, though its flight was erratic. The strong wind must be blowing in through the door she'd opened, creating even more problems for Zapata as he tried to control the craft.

Panting, she rose to her feet, still watching the heli. It flew higher, catching the rays of the as-yet invisible sun. Its flight evened out. Zapata had managed to close the door. The craft banked, and then flew away in the direction of the coast.

"Have fun," came Zapata's voice over comm.

Releasing a held breath, she brushed the sand from her pants. A man was approaching from the parked trucks. It had to be the site supervisor.

Now was her chance to see this secret city. If she was unlucky, she might only have a couple of hours before Meredith found out what she was doing and possibly put a stop to it. Realistically, she knew she couldn't hope to explore the Scythian metropolis within that time, but perhaps she might discover something to prevent the Leader from giving a stupid order.

Twenty-Six

Cherry was annoyed to discover no gas masks were available for entering the Chimera construction site. She'd assumed they would either be here or easy to acquire quickly.

"Don't the workers wear them routinely?" She glared up at the tall, scrawny supervisor, Alun, forced to raise her voice over the noise of the wind. "What about the risk of poisonous gases leaking from underground vents?" She was no geologist, but even she knew of the dangers of entering unexplored subterranean regions. There had been a couple of incidents where miners had been evacuated when methane had suddenly flooded an area.

"All our workers are protected in their cabs, ma'am," Alun replied. "The vehicles sound an alarm when they detect anything dangerous. We do very little on-the-ground work. That's the job of the finishing crew."

"Okay, can you order some masks? How long would they take to arrive?"

"I can try. I don't know if any are available in Suddene. Might have to order them from Oceanside. Then we're looking at this evening at the earliest, assuming the shippers can find a pilot willing to brave this wind."

The wind showed no signs of dropping. If anything, it seemed to have increased in the short time it had taken her to walk from the spot where she'd arrived. Everyone was standing leeward of the trucks, but the violent air whipped them on both sides, carrying with it stinging sand. The rays of the rising sun were making no dent in the chilly atmosphere.

"Dammit," she said, half to herself. The longer it took to go into the Scythian city, the greater the chances were that Meredith would put a stop to her investigation.

"We could drive you in there," said Alun. "You would be safe inside one of our survey vehicles."

"How would that work?" According to what she'd seen on the recording, there was a deep drop from the point the excavator had broken through to the city.

"We could lower a vehicle on a few lines. It shouldn't be too hard to rig something up."

Exploring from within the confines of a vehicle wouldn't be ideal, but it was better than nothing. "Let's try it."

"I'll have to unseal the site, of course."

"The excavator registered no toxic gases?"

"None at all."

"I'm prepared to take the risk, but I'm not going to command anyone else to do so. I only want volunteers to accompany me. I might need some people to help me move stuff." She didn't need to explain any further. Her lack of one arm was plain for all to see.

"You won't have any shortage of volunteers. I had a hard time keeping people out of the place. They're all dying to know what's in there."

"Let's hope it doesn't come to that."

The small, boxy survey vehicle held four seats, but they were closely crammed together and the roof was low. The top of Alun's head brushed it as he climbed into the driver's seat. All the controls were manual. This was a car you had to actually drive. He passed her a hard hat and a pair of thick gloves.

The tires were fat and there was plenty of clearance to deal with rocky terrain. Two excavators had volunteered—begged, in fact—to come along. Both crowded into the back seat.

She sat in the front and turned to face the woman and man sitting behind. "I know Alun has already told you this but I'm going to say it again: Nothing you see in there can be discussed with anyone else. Not ever. Not unless you receive clearance directly from me. Understood?"

They nodded, appearing taken aback by her serious tone. They'd been excited to be allowed to come along.

"My name's Pearl, by the way," said the woman. She was blonde-haired, green-eyed, and pale-skinned, which was unusual among Concordians. The man's coloring was the same as Cherry's and the most common: olive skin, brown-black eyes, and black hair. Both wore work overalls and hard hats. The man's eyes were almond-shaped like Wilder's.

Cherry guilty recalled her most recent encounter with the young woman and the poor hospitality she'd received.

"And I'm Laurie," said the black-haired man.

"Everyone ready?" Alun asked.

She faced forward and nodded.

The car surged forward, pushing her into her seat. The car's engine was powerful for a small vehicle. In a few moments they were racing toward the site entrance. The tunnel opened above ground but sloped quickly downward.

Alun drove the car into darkness and its headlights beamed out. When he issued a voice command, metallic gears started up somewhere ahead. The tunnel continued to slope down. Dark gray, solid metal doors pulled apart. A line of lights blinked on along the tunnel roof beyond them. The constructed roof disappeared and was replaced by roughly hewn stone. They were underground, nearing the excavated chamber that would become Chimera: Concordia's fifth missile silo.

She had never seen one of the military defense sites under construction. The other four had been built while she'd been offplanet, each project a major drain on resources. She hadn't looked up the figures, but roughly half of the colony's productive effort, from the mining operations to the munitions factories, was devoted to constructing and arming the silos.

It had become a source of contention. She didn't follow current affairs as closely as she probably should, but even she had heard the rumblings of discontent that so much effort and economic value was spent on defense. Still, it was no excuse for Meredith's decision to reduce the budget.

They reached the end of the access tunnel. Alun drove directly into the excavation site. Powerful lights on stands were positioned centrally though widely spaced apart, linked by wires to a generator. Though their beams were too strong to look directly into, they failed to penetrate the darkness overhead. The gouged out, distant edges of the chamber were visible, however. The ground was even but still bore the marks of excavation drilling. The rock was a uniform, sandy gray.

Several of the monster excavators stood abandoned. A flimsy portable building and a row of portable latrines were the only constructions.

"We've dug to the lowest level," Alun explained. "We would have finished the job in four days, bang on schedule. Then this happened."

Ignoring the man's complaint, she asked, "What's the atmosphere like out there?"

"The alarm will go off if the car's instruments detect anything dangerous."

"That's the spot over there, right?" She pointed at a hole where the rear of one excavator poked out. Two more of the machines were attached to the it by thick lines of twisted wire. "Let's check it out."

Alun drove them over, remarking to the backseat passengers, "If we want to take this into the city we'll have to move Bunny's machine out of the way."

"That won't take long," Pearl said.

"Yeah, no problem," added Laurie.

The excavators looked even bigger close up. They were bigger than many houses Cherry had seen. Pearl and Laurie jumped out and trotted over to separate machines. They had to climb up the outside on steps to reach the cabs. When they started them up, their massive engines sent vibrations through the floor of the car.

In three or four minutes, Laurie and Pearl had backed up the excavators, taking up the slack on the lines attaching them to the third machine and pulling it all of the way out, revealing the powerful drill. Laurie and Pearl hopped back into the car, slammed the doors, and Alun spurred it into the vacant space.

They soon lost the benefit of the brilliant site lights and relied once more on the vehicle's beams, which revealed more bare rock and then...nothing.

"This is it." Alun slammed on the brakes. He'd stopped just short of the brink of a hole. Beyond lay only blackness.

"I can't see anything," Cherry said.

"You wouldn't. I took that vid when Bunny's excavator lights were shining in. This car's lights are ten times weaker. We won't see much until we get down there. What we need to do now is fix the lines we brought along. Then Laurie or Pearl can lower us."

"Pearl can do it," said Laurie.

"Forget it," she replied. "I'm going down too."

"No way!" Laurie retorted. "I'm not sitting up here while you three have all the fun."

"Quit fighting," said Alun. "Figure it out between yourselves. I'm going to start securing the lines."

Cherry was forced to wait impatiently while Pearl and Laurie played a hand game to decide who would go into the city. Laurie lost and cursed. He stomped away down the tunnel. A moment later, he returned, driving the massive excavator.

The system they created didn't look particularly safe. Laurie drove the vehicle to the brink of the cavern containing the city, then all three excavation crew members tied metal lines to parts of the survey vehicle before winding them around the drill. The idea was that Laurie would gently nudge the survey car off the precipice and slowly turn the drill to lower it.

"Do you know how far it is to the bottom?" Cherry asked.

"Roughly," Alun replied. "Don't worry. I've been doing this kind of thing for a long time."

Cherry was pretty sure he hadn't been creating makeshift winches in order to lower vehicles into ancient Scythian cities for a long time, but she let it go. She didn't have time to wait for a better, safer option. She was safe from interference for a short while, due to the fact that the the excavation site was out of direct comm range. If Meredith wanted her to stop badly enough she would have to send an order by human messenger.

Pearl sat in the middle of the back seat to even out the balance. Alun released the brake so the car wouldn't resist when Laurie pushed it forward.

Faced by utter darkness broken only by two slim beams of light from the headlamps, Cherry couldn't resist gripping the side of her seat tightly. Their seat belts wouldn't provide much protection if the car plunged hundreds of meters to a rocky floor.

There was a bump as the excavator made contact, and then a slow slide forward. The front of the car rolled off the edge, dipping down. The lines attached to it jerked as they took the vehicle's weight. Cherry's heart raced. The rear of the car dropped off the rocky ledge. This drop was lower and the jerk harder as the rear lines prevented the car from falling.

They began to move downward. Something about the way Alun and the others had wound the line made the car seesaw. The front would dip and then the rear, in a rhythmic fashion. The movement didn't appear to surprise or worry Cherry's companions.

She concentrated on trying to catch her first sight of the Scythian city. The survey car's swinging beams revealed tantalizing glimpses: a sweeping curve here, a slender point there. She longed to see the whole place. It would be impossible, of course. She would be confined to viewing whatever was illuminated by the car and the flashlights they'd brought along. The city hadn't seen the light of day for tens or perhaps hundreds of thousands of years.

A sudden puzzlement struck her. "It's strange, don't you think? I don't know much about geology, but shouldn't this city have been filled in with sand from the desert? How come the space around the buildings is still hollow?"

"Yeah," said Pearl. "I was thinking that too."

"You're right," Alun said. "It's normal for man-made—or artificially made, I should say—structures to sink over time as the land around them rises. A place this big and this deep should be a pile of sand and weather-worn remains by now. My best guess is that it's covered by a roof. A dome of some kind, probably. The land's risen up around it, covering it over, but the weight of the desert sand hasn't broken through the roof."

"Yet," Cherry said.

"Yet," he agreed.

"But when it does," said Pearl, "woo wee! That's going to be one helluva landslide!"

"A landslide we don't want to be under," Cherry said. Alun's explanation made even more sense, knowing what she knew. Concordia's atmosphere had begun to become unbreathable for the Scythians, so they had enclosed their cities to protect their citizens from the dangerous gases.

She hoped the dome would hold a little while longer.

Twenty-Seven

Three flashlight beams swung over the facade of a construction. Now that Cherry was seeing one of the structures in real life and up close, she was certain this was no geological phenomenon. The surface was too smooth and regular and three types of material colored soft pink, green, and purple had been used to create it. Each part slotted into the next to create a mosaic effect, but with no discernible pattern.

"Is it safe to touch, do you think?" Pearl asked softly.

"I don't know why you're whispering," said Alun, his voice booming and echoing in the vast, dark chamber. "Nothing's been alive in here for a long while. No one's going to hear you."

No one and nothing.

Would they be the first humans to discover what the Scythians looked like? Though the Galactic Assembly had furnished the colony with image files of all its members, it had been unable to supply them with pictures of the Scythians. Did anyone in the galaxy know anything about the hostile aliens' appearance? The Parvus had said they didn't breathe oxygen, but a different gas. Would that affect the form their bodies took?

Pearl was creeping closer to the edifice.

"Don't touch it," said Cherry. "At least, not yet. We need to try to figure out if it's safe first." She wished Kes was here. He would know the correct and safe procedure to follow in the circumstances. If only he'd answered his comm when she'd tried to contact him about Wilder. But he'd been busy or asleep and she hadn't had time to wait.

The air was chilly and musky, and the ground was so thick with dust they were sinking into it ankle deep. It made walking difficult. It would also make running hard, if they had to get away from something, and winching the survey vehicle out of the chasm would be a slow process. If anything did attack, they didn't stand a chance.

As Alun had said, nothing could remain alive, but that didn't mean the Scythians hadn't left behind something synthetic, designed to come to life if ever their ancient home was invaded.

"What now?" Alun asked. "Do we go inside?"

"I can't see a way in," said Pearl, playing her flashlight's beam over the dusty surface.

Cherry pointed her light upward, wondering if the Scythians had windows in their buildings, but all she could see was the same random arrangement of three differently colored and textured materials. "I should tell you two something, before we go any further. I want you to know what you might be getting into. But, again, not a word of this to anyone else."

"I think I know what you're going to say," Alun said.

"You do? Tell me."

"You're going to say this place was built by the Scythians."

Pearl's eyes grew round. "Was it?!"

Cherry said, "I don't know for sure, but that is what I think. You probably heard about the delegation of Parvus currently visiting us? Well, one reason they came was to tell us Concordia is the Scythians' origin planet. They evolved here and built a civilization. But then they did something to alter the ecological balance and over time the atmosphere became flooded with oxygen, which is poisonous to them."

"So they left," said Alun. "The roof over this place makes sense now."

"Whoa," Pearl breathed. "Darn it!"

"What's wrong?" asked Cherry.

"I know one of the most significant facts in the history of Concordia and I can't tell a soul about it."

"I'm not sure it's going to be a secret for much longer," Cherry said. "But please control yourself for a while, until the news is out."

"So we've stolen their home," said Alun.

"So what?" Pearl said. "It isn't like they can use it. It's better for us to colonize Concordia than allow a habitable planet to go to waste."

"Let's save the philosophical argument for another day," said Cherry. "I'm going to try something." She gave Alun her flashlight and gently wiped a green section of wall. She'd only been meaning to wipe off some of the dust to get a better look at the join between two colors, hoping there might be a way to pull the sections apart, but what she discovered made her jump backward in surprise.

"What's wrong?" asked Pearl.

"It's soft!" Cherry had been expecting to encounter a hard, unyielding surface like the wall of every human building, but the Scythian material had given way easily under the pressure of her hand. "Look, you can see an indent where I touched it."

A depression in the rough shape of four fingertips had appeared.

"It feels spongy, like a dessert I had once. I can't remember its name."

"Mousse?" Pearl asked.

"That's it."

Alun was already reaching out to also touch the wall. Before Cherry could tell him to stop, he'd made contact. His hand sank in. He continued to push. His wrist disappeared and then half of his forearm.

She had a vision of Alun suddenly being yanked from his feet and pulled bodily into the wall. "Stop! Don't do that."

His arm was buried up to his elbow.

"What can you feel?" asked Pearl.

"I'm through to the other side. I can't feel much, though. Just emptiness."

"Take your arm out," Cherry said.

He pulled, then grimaced. "I can't."

"Oh no!" Pearl exclaimed.

Alun pulled again, straining against the grip of the wall. "Shit. It's stuck hard."

"Dammit!" Cherry said. "I told you not to do that. Keep trying to pull it out. I'll see if I can think of something."

But what could they do? If they tried to use the survey car to pull him out his arm could be torn from its socket.

She asked, "Do you have anything in the trunk of the car that might work as a solvent? Maybe we could dissolve the area around your arm."

"There's a bottle of hydrochloric acid," replied Alun.

"Don't use that!" said Pearl. "That'll dissolve your arm too."

Suddenly, he slipped his arm out from the wall and burst into laughter, whooping and doubling up, his hands clutching his sides.

"Oh, Alun," said Pearl. "That wasn't funny. I was really worried."

The supervisor straightened up and wiped his eyes. "You should have seen your faces."

Cherry glared. "No more stunts like that, or you wait back at the vehicle."

"Sorry, couldn't resist."

She rolled her eyes, and then turned her attention to the place where Alun had stuck his arm. A hole marked the surface, but it was closing. Material from all sides was oozing inward. As an experiment, she touched a purple area. The material was tougher and grainy. She pressed a pink section. This substance was the firmest of them all, but it still had some give.

"This green part is wide enough for me to fit through," Alun said. "What do you say? Should we all go inside?"

"No, not all of us," Cherry replied. "Someone needs to stay out to alert Laurie if we get into difficulties so he can go and get help."

"I'll stay behind if no one minds," Pearl said. "I was excited to come here, but now this place is seriously giving me the creeps. I'd rather not go any farther."

Cherry knew exactly what she meant. There was something deeply disturbing about the Scythian city. The feeling it gave her was something akin to how she'd felt during her time at the Galactic Assembly space station, only it was much worse. This place made her skin crawl.

Alun was already pulling the green material apart to create an entrance. "Better check there's air in there." He put his nose at the gap and sniffed cautiously. "Smells like shit. I'll bring the car over and run a pipe inside so we can use the instrumentation to test for dangerous gases."

While he returned to the survey vehicle, Cherry also leaned into the gap and gave a tentative sniff. This time, Alun hadn't been joking. The air inside the construction did, indeed, smell like human feces.

He drove up and leaned out of the window. "I had an idea. That patch of green stuff there looks big enough to fit the car. I wanna try and drive her right inside."

"Good thinking," said Cherry. If there were pockets of dangerous gases within the Scythian structure, they would be much safer inside the car. They would be able to drive out as soon as the alarm sounded, breathing the air in the vehicle.

She climbed in and Pearl moved off to the side. Alun drove the car directly at the wall. The surface initially gave some resistance. It seemed to be stronger when a wide area was impacted than when something smaller was pushed in. The engine noise rose as it strained, but the material began to give way. The car inched forward and the green substance stretched. A gap opened, and then all of a sudden, with an odd ripping noise, the surface broke and they drove into the inner darkness.

Twenty-Eight

Kes was on his fourth beer and he was feeling light-headed. He wasn't used to drinking alcohol. He didn't like to drink in front of Isobel when she couldn't due to being pregnant, though she never objected. It seemed deeply inconsiderate to him to indulge in something while the person you loved could not—and you had contributed to the reason they could not. It was Isobel who was going through all the physical demands of carrying their baby and caring for a toddler at the same time. Giving up booze was the least he could do.

Had been, he corrected himself. Giving up booze *had been* the least he could do. Which wasn't to say he couldn't have done a lot more. He swallowed hard and put down his glass.

Coming out to a bar had been a bad decision. The place was heaving, all of the people strangers as far as he'd noticed. He wasn't sure if that was better or not. On the one hand, he wouldn't have minded seeing a friendly face right now; on the other, a word of comfort or commiseration from a friend could tip him over the edge. He was barely holding together as it was.

He leaned his elbows on the bar and cupped his hands around the glass of beer, hunching over it—the purported memory and emotional pain obliterator. It didn't seem to be working.

The scent of beer, spirits, and cocktails hung in the air in the dimly lit space. Music was playing, louder than the chatter of voices. He didn't recognize the song, but then again he never did. He'd been out of touch with musical fashion for as long as he could remember. Even back on Earth, growing up, when all his classmates had raved about the latest hot band or singer, he'd had no idea what they were talking about.

Being unable to join in the discussions had left him somewhat isolated, but he hadn't minded much. All he needed was a few close friends and his work. Just a handful of people he felt close to and who liked him, or loved him, as Isobel had. He'd screwed up badly, and he didn't even know why.

He lifted his glass to his lips and gulped several mouthfuls of beer. Should he make this one his last and head home? His visit to the bar wasn't achieving the desired effect. He didn't feel any lessening of the terrible, empty ache in the pit of his stomach or the overwhelming sense of regret and self-hatred.

Yet he also couldn't bear the thought of returning to his dark, silent house or his cold, empty bed. Just imagining it filled him with dread. Maybe he should find a place to stay for the night. If he managed to get a little sleep and take a shower in the morning, he might make it into work tomorrow. He hadn't comm'd them about his absence and everyone was probably wondering what had happened to him.

Earlier, he'd tried to contact Isobel, but, predictably, every attempt was refused. He didn't blame her in the slightest. He'd left messages, but even to him his words sounded hollow. Eventually, he'd given up. Next, he'd thought about contacting the office, planning on making up some excuse to take the day off, but he'd felt his throat thicken. He'd known he wouldn't get through the conversation without his voice breaking. He'd received notifications that Cherry wanted to speak to him, but he hadn't replied, knowing he was incapable of dealing with anything.

He drained his beer, still indecisive about whether or not to call it a night. He opened the interface set into the bar and scrolled through the lists of drinks, wondering if he should try something stronger. But nothing caught his eye. He didn't need alcohol. He needed his wife and child. His chest ached and something was forcing its way up his throat.

Closing the interface, he rose from his stool. But a heavy hand clamped onto his shoulder and pressed him down. A large figure swung onto the next stool and released his grip.

Aubriot. "Don't tell me you're leaving already, Ginger. I only just got here."

"Yeah, sorry. I'm not feeling it." He stood up.

"C'mon. Stay a minute. Have a drink. One drink. As mates. We never really bonded, did we, you and I? Now's our chance."

As far as Kes knew, Aubriot had never 'bonded' with anyone, except perhaps Cherry, though their relationship had seemed a matter of convenience. "Look, another time, okay? I'm not in a good—"

"For fuck's sake. One drink isn't going to hurt you, is it? Is one fucking drink too much to ask?"

He heaved a sigh and sat down, but he didn't order anything. He would stay five minutes to pacify the arrogant, bossy man and avoid an argument, then he would go for a walk. He would walk all night if needed. Perhaps that would help.

Aubriot had pulled his sleeve down over his hand and was using the edge to wipe spilled beer from the interface screen. When the surface was reasonably clean, he swiped the drinks list from left to right.

His lips moved but Kes couldn't hear what he was saying. The music and noise of the crowd was too loud. He finally made his selection and then straightened up and turned his attention to Kes. "Funny seeing you here. I didn't think you came to places like this. You strike me as more of a family man."

"I *am* a family man." He left his response at that. He didn't owe Aubriot an explanation for his presence at the Annwn bar.

Aubriot gave him a long look. "But not tonight, eh? Been arguing with the missus? She kicked you out?"

He didn't answer. He didn't know where to look as he stoically bore Aubriot's scrutiny.

"Nah, it's worse than that. If you'd had a fight, a bloke like you wouldn't make things worse by pissing off down the pub. You'd be banging on the door, begging forgiveness, or on your way to buy flowers."

Kes's lips thinned to a line. Normally, Aubriot's rudeness didn't get to him. In fact, he barely took any notice of what the man said unless he had to, but tonight his skin was not so tough. He glared at Aubriot, warning him with his eyes that if he continued pressing buttons, there would be consequences. Not that he stood the remotest chance of beating Aubriot in a fight. He would have his ass handed to him. But he wasn't in a state to care, and getting in just a few blows would feel damned good.

Aubriot's eyebrows rose. "Don't tell me she left you."

Kes's fist slammed into Aubriot's jaw with such a force he was thrown from his stool. He hit the floor. Kes stood over him, pain radiating from his knuckles, poised to hit Aubriot again.

A hush had fallen over the bar as the patrons took in what had happened. Only the music played on.

"Someone comm the CED," said a woman's voice.

Aubriot raised a hand. "It's all right," he called out, beginning to rise to his feet. "No harm done. Just a misunderstanding."

Kes took a step backward, his fist remaining raised. He guessed Aubriot's reaction was a trick, designed to make him let down his guard so that Aubriot could retaliate.

"Sit down," said Aubriot. "I don't wanna hurt you. Let's forget about it."

A drink was traveling along the narrow conveyor belt on the inner edge of the bar. The cocktail stopped in front of Aubriot. He picked up the yellow-green concoction, pulled out the curled lime peel garnish, and poured the entire contents of the glass down his throat.

Kes realised Aubriot was very drunk and wondered why. Though Aubriot had many faults, Kes had heard no rumors he was an alcoholic. Curiosity about what was going on with the man, and a weird sense of camaraderie, drove Kes to stay for a while. He remembered Cherry telling him Aubriot had left the military.

"What are you having?" Aubriot asked. "Don't make me drink alone. It's not polite."

His speech was slightly slurred. How much had he drunk? Resistance to the effects of alcohol had to be built into the man's genetic code, along with every other physical and mental advantage available at the time. Aubriot must have already downed a considerable amount of booze.

Kes was clearly not the only one with sorrows to drown tonight.

"You should have one of these," said Aubriot, raising his empty glass. "Bloody good. Gets you drunk fast. That's what we want, right?"

"What was it?"

"Dunno." Aubriot chuckled. "I forgot. Wait a minute. I'll find it again. Order one for both of us." He opened the order screen, swiped it, and jabbed it a couple of times. When he'd finished ordering he said, without looking up, "I was married once. Bitch left me too."

"My wife isn't a bitch," Kes said between his teeth.

"All right, wind your neck in. I was talking about my ex, not yours."

"She's *not* my ex!"

"Christ on a bike! Ah, here's our drinks. In the nick of time." He grabbed the two cocktails from the conveyor belt and passed one over. "Get that down your throat while I think of something to say that won't offend you."

Kes sipped the cocktail. It was as strong as Aubriot had promised, the citrus flavors failing to disguise the powerful taste of mixed liquors. He swallowed and took another sip.

"She only wanted me for my money," Aubriot said. "Thought she could get it too, despite the pre-nup. What an idiot, suing the richest man on Earth. But then, I didn't marry her for her brains. Maybe that was my mistake."

Kes vaguely remembered the story of Aubriot's divorce in the news. The woman lost her claim for alimony and was required to pay Aubriot's court costs, which bankrupted her.

The effect of the cocktail spreading through Kes's body. "What do you care? With looks like yours, you could have any woman in this place. In Concordia, even."

"Could I?" Aubriot looked at him sidelong. "And if I could, would *you* want that? If you could swap places with me, would you?"

Kes considered for only a moment before shaking his head. He had no interest in having every woman in the room. He knew himself too well. He would find no satisfaction or happiness in that.

"See?" Aubriot said. "It's not so great when you think about it."

"Not so great for *me*. We aren't the same."

"Aren't we? I'm not sure about that."

Kes gave a short laugh. "I am." He took another sip of his cocktail.

"No, you're wrong. In some ways we're very similar."

Kes turned to face him. The man was physically flawless. He was also cocky, overbearing, boorish, and often deeply offensive. He'd been wrong to say Aubriot could have any woman in the bar. He could have the ones who only wanted a good time, and those who weren't discerning, but in fact he would struggle to attract someone like Isobel. Cariad had never liked him either. "Sorry, but you're the one who's wrong. I can't think of a single thing we have in common."

Aubriot leaned in so close Kes could smell the alcohol on his breath. "We're fucked."

"What?" Kes craned his neck backward to avoid the exhalation.

"Fucked," Aubriot repeated. "We all are. Me, you, Cherry, Wilder. But especially me and you. In here." He poked Kes in the head.

Kes grabbed his hand and pushed it down onto the bar. "Don't touch me."

"You can't expect to travel fifty years into the future and be normal." Aubriot picked up his drink. He saw the glass was empty and opened the interface. "Want another one?"

"No, thanks."

Aubriot ordered his third drink. "We're men out of our time." He spoke so quietly Kes could only just make out the words. "Last of the Earth-born. We're out of place. It's different for Cherry and Wilder. They grew up on the *Nova*. Concordia's the only planet they know. It's their home." After a pause, he said, "Tell me, Ginger..."

Kes gave him a look.

"Tell me, is this what you imagined? Is this how you thought our lives would be?"

"No."

"Not at all, right? Never imagined I would be sitting in bar getting smashed on cocktails. Never in a million years. It's strange, don't you think, how ordinary everything turned out? How similar to how things were on Earth. I mean, I expected some things to be the same. The Manual was supposed to create an Earth-like civilization. That was all we knew. But it's funny how, decades after the Manual became redundant, everything's continued along the same lines. Families, cars, residential estates, offices, factories. If there weren't four fucking massive missile silos hidden underground, Concordia would be like something off a soap opera."

"It isn't that odd," Kes said. "This is what we do, as a species. People have experimented with different systems: communes, monasteries and nunneries, anchorites living in caves. They're all anomalies. Those ways of life never become popular. For hundreds of thousands of years, we've lived in small or large family units and within tribes of about a hundred people we know. It hasn't changed and it isn't going to. It's encoded in us."

"Huh. Speak for yourself." Aubriot's cocktail had arrived but he didn't remove it from the belt.

"So family life isn't for you? You're different. You're a *loner*."

"Fuck off," Aubriot said, though without conviction.

"I have to admit, when I went into cryo, I didn't expect my life to end up as it has. I expected a bigger struggle. I expected things to be harder."

"They were, for a time. We missed out on most of that."

"I almost wish..."

"What?"

"Nothing." For some reason, the unanticipated encounter with Aubriot and their somewhat bizarre conversation had made Kes's mind clearer. He was wasting his time here with his dysfunctional drinking buddy. He should be trying to speak to Isobel, to apologize, and to ask for another chance. She might listen to him now she'd had time to calm down. She did still love him. He was sure of that, or last night wouldn't have happened. He could make things better.

"I'm leaving." He pushed his empty glasses onto the belt and it carried them away, along with Aubriot's untouched drink.

Aubriot watched the cocktail disappear into the hole in the wall, his expression listless. Had the alcohol he'd drunk finally caught up with him? Was he about to slump onto the bar?

"Call you an autocar?" Kes asked.

Aubriot shook his head.

"Are you sure you'll be okay?"

Aubriot nodded.

"Well, if you're sure..." Kes hesitated. He didn't want to leave the man alone in the state he was in. Something was definitely going on with him. "Is there anything you want to talk about?"

The question broke through Aubriot's drunken haze. He looked at Kes and the corner of his mouth lifted. It was an attempt at an ironic smile, but the effect was ghastly.

Just as Kes was about to suggest Aubriot go home and sleep it off, a young woman appeared from nowhere and draped an arm over Aubriot's shoulders.

Her eyes were half closed and her movements languid. "Are you all alone, honey, now your friend's leaving?"

Aubriot's arm snaked around the woman's waist, pulling her in. "Not now you're here, darlin'."

The woman laughed and allowed herself to be pulled closer. He tilted his head back and she leaned in for a kiss, her hair falling in a curtain to obscure their faces.

Kes left him to his latest encounter. As he was on his way out, however, exclamations of surprise made him turn back. The bar's patrons were holding their hands to their ears and staring at each other as they all listened to what had to be an emergency message.

He wasn't wearing his ear comm. He'd put it in his pocket to stop himself from constantly trying to comm Isobel, knowing he was hounding her. He reached for it, but before he retrieved it, the message played from the bar's speakers.

Twenty-Nine

Alun pressed gently on the accelerator, and the survey vehicle moved slowly forward. Cherry leaned closer to the windscreen, trying to make out what lay ahead. The headlight beams revealed a black floor, free from the dust covering everything outside the city. The floor appeared to be hard, solid, and made from a different substance than the walls.

"The air's breathable," said Alun, peering at the dashboard display. "Want to get out?"

"No, not yet." If anything happened to them, they would be safer in the car. Would the Scythians have booby trapped their abandoned city? The more she thought about it, the more unlikely it seemed. They wouldn't have thought that far ahead. When they were forced to flee their planet, they would have been too filled with fear for their future to consider what might happen to the place they were leaving behind.

But then she remembered the words of Vasquez, Kes's fellow xenobiologist who had passed on long ago: *We mustn't imagine we can predict how they think.* Who really knew what the Scythians' thought processes had been when they departed their home? Perhaps they *had* been fearful that another species would take over their home planet and make it their own. Perhaps they had put plans in place to prevent that from happening.

Yet there had been no sign of any plans so far. No one had even suspected the Scythians had once lived here until the Parvus informed them of the fact. There had been no 'Private Property, Keep Out' signs in any noticeable form. Concordia had appeared to be a pristine world, untouched, and its life in the early stages of evolution. And it hadn't been until the

Scythians detected the *Mistral's* trace and followed it they had discovered humans living on their origin world. They hadn't been keeping watch as far as anyone knew.

Another fact indicated that the Scythians weren't excessively protective of Concordia: where were they? It had been decades since they had accepted the 'tribute' of the Guardians' sacrifice. With the acceptance came the implication they would return to collect further tributes, but no sign had been seen of them for so long the colony was becoming slack in its preparations for defense. She wouldn't have been surprised if some Concordians even doubted the Scythians' existence.

Well, one thing was certain—the revelation that a Scythian city lay beneath the sands of Suddene would convince the most stubborn doubter.

The survey car had continued to crawl ahead, its lights illuminating nothing except the dark floor and empty darkness.

"This is less interesting than I thought it would be," Alun commented.

"Try turning. Maybe we're on some kind of indoor road."

He turned the steering wheel and the car curved smoothly right.

"Whoa!" He slammed his foot down.

Cherry was thrown forward against her seat belt. "What is it?"

"Nothing! There's nothing there."

The headlights were no longer reflecting from a smooth black surface, they were shining into a void. It was only due to Alun's fast reflexes that had prevented them from tumbling into the pit. Her heart thudded as the realization hit.

"You'd think they would have a guard rail or something," Alun said. "Or a sign at least."

She mentally agreed, but then she realized they were approaching the situation all wrong. "Were you alive when the Scythians attacked for the second time? When the colony was living in Sidhe?"

"No. Before my time, thank the stars."

"But you've heard about the spiders, right? The ones the Scythians sent down to kill us?"

"Of course. My ma used to threaten me with them to make me behave. She used to tell me not all of them had been destroyed, that there were a few that had never been found, and that they were living out in the woods, waiting to catch naughty boys and girls."

She stared at him. "I'm guessing your ma wasn't alive when the Scythians attacked either."

"She was. She was about two or three years old though and she doesn't remember it."

"I thought so." No one who had witnessed what the spiders did would ever have turned them into bogeymen to frighten little boys and girls. The memory of seeing Garwin cut to ribbons before her very eyes was seared into her mind like it had happened yesterday. Just the thought of them made her stump ache.

"Anyway," she continued, "we knew the Scythians would be back to try to finish us off, and we knew we didn't really stand a chance. All we had was the *Mistral* and a pulse emitter the Guardians had built on the wreckage of the *Nova*. So we tried to hide everyone as well as we could. We built Sidhe and hid all signs of its presence. We erased all tracks leading to it, and we camouflaged the entrances so they couldn't be seen.

"We made a huge mistake. We were thinking the Scythians were like us. We put ourselves in their position and imagined what *we* would do to find something that was hidden. We imagined they would look for us. But the spiders didn't look, they smelled. They followed our scent from the place where they landed right to the doors of Sidhe within minutes. To them, our scent trails must have been like great illuminated lines traced on the ground and in the air. So..."

"I get it," Alun said. "The Scythians might not have a guard rail on a road, but they might have a guard scent."

"Exactly. You probably don't know it, but all the highways and military and metropolitan areas of Concordia are regularly sprayed with chemicals that break down human odors, precisely because of what happened with the Scythian spiders." At least, she hoped the de-scenting program remained active and Meredith hadn't cut it without telling her due to 'budgetary constraints'.

"That isn't a lot of help," said Alun. "This car doesn't detect scents."

"And neither do we."

They both sat and pondered the problem.

"For all we know," Cherry said, "there could be alarm scents going off all around us, or scents giving evacuation information still hanging in the air. We just don't know."

She was crestfallen. She'd been hoping to discover something that would reveal a weakness in the Scythians, or some other clue that would help in the defense of Concordia. Now she realized that, if such a thing existed, the information could be in a form that was impossible for humans to access or understand: the language of scents.

"What's that?" Alun was looking at the rear view screen. He turned and stared out.

Cherry turned around too. A light was flashing in the darkness. The white beam swayed and swerved. She was thrown into confusion. Had everything she'd been thinking about the Scythians been wrong? Did they have a visual sense after all?

Had her and Alun's arrival triggered something?

But there was something familiar about the light.

"It's Pearl," Cherry said. "She's come inside and she's waving her flashlight at us."

"Of course!" Alun said. "She must want us to go back." He put the car into gear and began to reverse in a curve away from the edge.

What could have made Pearl force her way through the wall when she'd said how uncomfortable the place made her? Meredith must have listened to Cherry's message and she'd sent someone to Suddene to halt the exploration of the Scythian city. Or if she didn't want to stop it, she probably wanted to interfere.

Cherry gave a mental groan. Meredith had no appreciation of the seriousness or urgency of the situation. It might take years to explore the city and find out useful facts about the Scythians. The work had to be started right away without the intervention and intrusion of politicians.

"Damn." Alun had steered the car to the left, apparently planning on turning it around to go back the way they had come, but a second void had opened. "Road's too narrow. Gonna have to reverse it all the way back."

"Are you sure you can do it?"

"Yeah, no problem." Despite his words, the space between Alun's eyebrows was creased with concern. He righted the steering wheel and put the car into reverse, hooking his arm over his seat back and looking out of the rear. She gazed in the same direction, but she could barely see anything. The mark between the black roadway and the drops of unknown depth were nothing more than faint lines.

The car moved backward, and Pearl stopped waving her flashlight. She'd seen they were coming.

Cherry's concern about the risk of tumbling into an abyss was mildly offset by her frustration with Meredith. Concordia needed a new Leader. It had gone on re-electing Meredith too long, imagining she was as wise and competent as Ethan, but she was not. She even knew it herself, Cherry was sure. She was only continuing in her role through a sense of duty and perhaps to honor the memory of her father.

The only answer was a Leader who would take the Scythian threat seriously and who would act decisively to protect the colony. Not someone who pandered to public opinion because she lacked the strength of her own convictions.

"Whoa." Alun slowed down the car, which had veered toward the edge of the road. "Must be a curve I didn't notice." He corrected their direction, returning them to the center.

A voice was calling. Pearl was shouting something, but Cherry couldn't make it out.

"Are you sure it's safe to open the window?" she asked.

"That's what the panel says."

If there was anything poisonous in the atmosphere, it didn't seem to be affecting Pearl. Cherry lowered the window and called out, "What did you say?"

"You have to come back!"

The woman's voice fell dead. There was no echo, in spite of the size of the interior.

"I realize that," called Cherry. "The Leader's sent an order telling us to stop exploring, right?"

"No!" shouted Pearl. "The Scythians are coming!"

Thirty

When Cherry emerged from the tunnel onto the surface, she had to screw her eyes up against the light. It was late afternoon, or evening in Oceanside. Nearly a day had passed while she'd been below ground. The wind hadn't dropped, and the car was immediately hit by a scouring blast of sand.

As soon as she entered into comm range, she contacted Meredith. Predictably, she heard a 'busy' tone, but the Leader quickly ended her conversation and opened contact. "Cherry, thank the stars! What the hell are you doing in Suddene? It took me ages to find you. I had to ask an engineer to trace your last comm."

"You didn't get my message?"

"What message? I've been busy with government business all day. I didn't see anything urgent. Look, never mind. It doesn't matter now. How soon can you get back to Lyonesse? I haven't made any announcements yet. I don't want to create a panic." Meredith sounded as if she were trying to prevent herself from panicking too, and only just succeeding.

"Well, now you've told the excavation team it'll be all over Concordia within the next two minutes. You'd better make that announcement after we finish speaking. Our plan is in place, and we only have to put it into action. Do we have an ETA on the Scythian fleet, and how many ships are coming?"

"The Fila told me they would be here in three hours and seventeen minutes, but that was over half an hour ago."

"Right. What's been happening while you were trying to comm me?"

"Nothing. I've been trying to find you."

Cherry was stunned. More than half an hour had passed since Meredith had received the notification that an enemy fleet was on its way, and in that time all she'd done was try to contact her General. What if she'd died in the Scythian city? Would Meredith have done nothing at all, only waited for the Scythians to turn up and annihilate them when they didn't receive their tribute? Or would she have turned over some sacrificial victims to appease them?

She swallowed her shock and anger. "Okay, we have time to implement our defense strategy. Make the announcement. Now I have comm I can give the order to roll out the defense plan. Refresh your memory on your part in case you've forgotten any of it. I'll be back in Lyonesse as soon as I can. I need to comm my pilot now. Wait. What about the Parvus? Are they still in orbit?"

"They left as soon as the news arrived. In fact, I think it may have been them who told the Fila Scythian ships were coming."

"They *left*? Wait, don't tell me. They said they *intended* to help us."

"That's right! How did you know?"

"Just a guess."

"They left right after they sent the message."

"Okay, I get it. We're on our own. I'll be in touch." She closed the connection. The temptation to unleash her frustration on Meredith was great but it could wait for later, after the crisis was over, assuming both of them remained alive.

The Fila seeding ship that had helped them last time was probably on the other side of the galaxy. It had taken months to arrive before. They couldn't hope for any help from the Fila this time. If anything, it was up to the humans to protect the aquatic aliens, who would no doubt feel the weight of the Scythians' wrath when the colony didn't comply with the hostile aliens' demands.

The only ship they had was the *Opportunity*, but it was too small to be an effective defense against the Scythian fleet. It would be better to leave it out of the battle plan.

She needed her pilot. "Zapata?"

"Yes, ma'am?"

"I need you back here. Now."

"Er..."

"Don't tell me you have a problem with that." Looking out at the gusts of wind filled with stinging sand, she didn't doubt he had a problem but she needed a heli regardless.

"I'll be there in fifteen."

"I'll be waiting." She opened the survey car door. Immediately, the wind slammed it closed again, spattering the glass with sand. She had snatched her leg out of the way just in time.

"It's probably a good idea to wait in here." Alun had been following her side of her conversation without comment.

"I guess you're right." The excavation crews had retreated to their trucks. The ground around the entrance to the Chimera site was empty except for swirling sand, which was growing so thick it was cutting out the light. She hoped Zapata would be able to land in the gale.

"Tell your people to go to the nearest shelter," she said to Alun. "You go too."

He gave the order to his crew. The trucks started up and began to move out.

How long would it take to return to the main continent? It would take fifteen minutes for the heli to pick her up. How long had it taken to fly to the Chimera excavation site? Three hours in total from Annwn.

Before she reached Lyonesse, the Scythians would be on Concordia's doorstep.

She would have to deal with them from the heli, but that couldn't be helped. First, she needed to alert all the senior officers. She went to comm Aubriot to tell him it was time to put his plan into action, but then she paused. *Shit*. She'd momentarily forgotten he'd resigned.

Shit. Shit. Shit.

Aubriot was their best military strategist. The only reason Ethan hadn't put him in charge of the defense force was due to his terrible personality.

In the months following their return from the Galactic Assembly, she had worked with him on developing and honing the defense plan Ethan had created. In subsequent years—before he went astray—Aubriot had tweaked it, especially after Hydra came on-line.

She could give the orders to set everything in motion, but Aubriot should be at her side. It was his duty and responsibility. This was not a responsibility he should be able to avoid. The colony needed him. She opened a comm to her ex-lover.

"Cherry, I thought you'd never call." His words were slurred. He was clearly drunk.

"Who's that?" said a woman's voice. "Is it your girlfriend?"

"Shuttup. I'm trying to talk."

"Well! That's pretty rude."

"Aubriot," said Cherry. "Did you hear the news?" It was possible that Meredith still hadn't made the announcement about the Scythians' imminent arrival, or that the gossip from the workers at the Chimera site hadn't reached him yet.

"You mean the news that our unfriendly neighborhood aliens are on their way? Yeah, I heard it."

"So, what are you doing?"

"Making the most of my final moments."

"*Seriously*?!"

"I'm kidding. Well, not really."

"C'mon, honey," the woman's voice whined. "Let's get back to business."

"In a minute."

Cherry said, "Aubriot, you have to sober up and get to work."

"No, I don't. I resigned, remember?"

"I never accepted your resignation." It was true. She hadn't formally responded to the carefully worded message that had arrived from Aubriot after their conversation at his house. He'd simply stopped turning up for duty and she hadn't done anything about it except to assign another officer to take his place.

"What difference does it make?" he asked. "I have to go now."

"You need to get back on duty. The colony needs you."

There was a long pause.

"I gotta go," he repeated.

"Wait! If you aren't going to help, at least go to a shelter."

"I will. We've got a couple of hours yet. I'm gonna make the most of them." He cut the comm.

She cursed under her breath. He was being as self-centered as ever. She wouldn't have been surprised if he'd suggested offering up a few colonists to the Scythians in order to save his own skin.

"Problems?" Alun asked.

She started. She'd forgotten the supervisor was sitting next to her. "Shouldn't you be on your way to a shelter?"

The surrounding desert was empty. The rest of the crew had departed.

"Do you need this car to get there?" she asked.

"No, I don't. There are a couple more vehicles in the tunnel. Or I could wait out the battle in the excavation site. It'll probably be the safest place on Concordia. But I thought I would keep you company until your heli arrives."

"That's kind of you, but there's no…" A buzzing noise distracted her. She peered upward into the hazy sky. Darkness was falling that had nothing to do with the sandstorm. Night was approaching. The heli's lights shone out in the dusk. Zapata had made it, faster than he'd predicted. The following wind had to have been very strong. Would they make it back to Lyonesse?

Thirty-One

The first thing Kes thought of when he heard the announcement was Isobel and Miki. He didn't know where they were. Were they near a shelter? Would they be safe?

A dreadful fear fell on him. Was anywhere on Concordia safe? What would the Scythians do when Meredith refused to give up anyone as tribute? If past experiences were anything to go by, the aliens would attempt to annihilate the colony.

Well, if they were all to die, he wanted to be with his wife and child.

The atmosphere in the bar had flipped from drunken congeniality to terror and confusion. After shock at the announcement had frozen everyone, chaos descended. People roughly pushed past him as they ran for the door. Others sank to the floor and hunched over, weeping. More remained motionless, trapped in indecision.

Aubriot took the hand of his prospective one night stand and led her toward the exit.

Kes beat him to it. Like the others crowded there, he pushed forward, eager to leave. Then he remembered something important: as Chief Xenobiologist, he had a role to play in the planned response. He was supposed to head to the control center in the bunker at the Leader's Residence. He was supposed to support the Leader in her dialogue with the Scythians.

But what about Isobel? He couldn't just leave her to endure the attack alone, solely responsible for their little girl. He and his wife had never discussed what they would do if Concordia was attacked. She knew he would have a key role to play, and she must have accepted they would have to be apart during the attack. But that had been before she'd left him.

He tried comming her, but there was no answer. Sorrow was a knife in his heart. Even with the threat of death hanging over them she wouldn't talk to him? He'd hurt her that badly? He must have. He didn't want everything to end with her thinking he didn't love her. He wouldn't allow it.

He burst through the crowd into the cold night air. A strong wind was blowing that immediately sucked all the warmth from him. The street was pitch dark, the only the light from the open door of the bar. More people surged out, and he moved out of their way.

He began to trot along the street, the chill night clearing the final dregs of alcoholic muddle from his mind. He ordered an autocar, directing it to zero in on him rather than giving a particular location.

He had to get to the bunker, but he also had to find Isobel. The announcement had said the Scythians' predicted arrival was in two and a half hours. That was enough time to find Isobel and then get to Oceanside, assuming she hadn't gone too far. Where could she be? Her parents had retired to a little place out in the mountains. If she'd gone there she was in one of the safer places on Concordia but he would never reach her.

"Kes?"

It was Meredith.

"Just checking in. You're on your way, right?" The Leader sounded tense and fearful.

"I am, but I..."

"What?"

"I have to find my family."

"You don't know where they are?"

"No. It's complicated."

"Concordia can't wait on you finding your family. You're needed here."

"I know, and I'm coming," he said with a sinking heart. He had to do the right thing. "I'm in Annwn now. I'm taking a government autocar."

"Good. I would suggest taking a heli but none of the pilots will fly. The wind's too strong. They say the helis are too light and it's too dangerous."

"I can see that." The wind was incredibly strong. He was leaning into it as he ran, forcing his body against the chilly stream of air.

"I know I said in the announcement that we have a couple of hours, but I need you here as soon as possible. The Scythians may open a dialogue before they arrive. The Fila are already hailing them but haven't received a response."

"If they do respond, just patch me in. I can work with you while I'm on the road. It won't be a problem." Exactly how he or Meredith were going to persuade the Scythians to leave Concordia alone when they didn't receive their tribute, he didn't know. He'd discussed all potential avenues of the conversation many times, but an effective argument was impossible to find. So little was known about the Scythians, it wasn't possible to know what might dissuade them.

An autocar appeared out of the darkness. He didn't see it until the last minute. The car swerved around him and then stopped. He climbed inside. He hesitated, but eventually he gave the vehicle the Leader's Residence coordinates. It nearly killed him to do it.

The car set off, navigating its way through the darkness. He tried Isobel's comm again, and again he received no answer. He put his head in his hands. He couldn't bear the thought of not seeing his wife and child one more time before devastation rained down. He had to speak to Isobel and make things right.

Thirty-Two

The heli couldn't touch down. Whenever the landing skids neared the ground, a gust of wind would lift it into the air, or another would force it downward, causing the skids to bump the sand but then zoom upward as Zapata fought the downdraft.

The pilot had opened the vehicle's passenger door too, so the wind was affecting the machine even more.

"Can you make it?" Cherry asked over comm.

"Doing my best, ma'am."

"I understand. I just don't want you to kill yourself."

"Me neither."

"Or land on me."

Zapata chuckled.

The heli hung fifteen meters up, buffeted by the gale. Cherry had her eyes closed to slits to try to keep out the sand, and until the heli drew near all she could see was its lights. Her hair whipped around her head.

Zapata said, "I think we need to face the fact that I'm not going to be able to land. I'll get as close as I can, and then you'll have to jump aboard."

"Let's try." Her voice sounded braver than she felt. If she'd ever missed her left arm and hand, it was now.

The heli's lights approached, and then the bulbous belly of the machine and its skids came into view. Its main rotor was a dark, whirring blur. She stepped backward as the heli veered toward her. She couldn't imagine what it had to be like to try to control the light air vehicle in the fierce wind.

Suddenly, it dipped downward. Another gust had caught it. The open passenger door zoomed close. She leapt. One of her feet landed on the edge of the cockpit. She caught the frame of the open door. Mustering all her strength, she pulled herself forward. Zapata's head was turned half toward her while he still tried to keep an eye on his controls.

The whine of the rotor combined with the roar of the wind was deafening. The night was a maelstrom of sand and empty air.

The heli rose abruptly. She'd been leaning in, but the sudden movement forced her backward. Her grip on the door was torn away. Her foot slipped.

She was falling.

A large, strong hand fastened on her shirt and yanked her in. She landed on the heli's passenger seat, knees first. As she grabbed the seat back, Zapata released her. The door closed, cutting down on the racket from the rotor and the howling wind.

"Thanks." She fastened her safety harness.

"No problem."

The heli veered sharply left and down. For a second she had an alarming view of Suddene's desert rising up, but then Zapata swept them away and drove the heli into the battering wind.

How long had the pick-up taken? It had seemed an awfully long time between the moment she had said goodbye and good luck to Alun, left the survey car, and waited while Zapata had made his many attempts to land. But when she checked the pilot's screen, she saw it had only taken ten or eleven minutes.

Still, each minute could count.

Anxious to begin preparations for the impending attack, she had comm'd her senior officers with the code word. All over the inhabited regions of Concordia, men and women were running to their stations, readying their weapons, and putting their equipment through checks. Finally, they would be watching the skies, wondering if they would outlive the night.

As Zapata fought the wind, flying her toward Lyonesse and the bunker beneath the Leader's Residence, she wondered the same.

She checked in with her officers on how everything was rolling out. To her slight surprise, there hadn't been any hitches so far. Perhaps she'd underestimated the commitment and training of the defense force personnel. After the series of brief conversations, she was left with nothing to do other than wait as the heli battled the wind. The minutes to their ETA reduced too slowly. It was as if time was expanding inside the heli and speeding up for the rest of Concordia as the Scythians drew nearer.

Ahead of them lay utter darkness, the night sky a thick, black shroud. Zapata was flying on instruments only. Below lay the ocean. When she had first set eyes on the expanse of precious water, the sight had amazed and delighted her. Now, she feared tumbling into its watery depths, leaving Concordia to endure the Scythian attack without her.

"Do you have family to contact, ma'am?" Zapata suddenly asked.

"No need to call me ma'am. Not now. I always hated that. Just call me Cherry. And, no, no family to con..."

Wilder! She had entirely forgotten about her. Where was she? Was she safe? Did she even know the Scythians were coming? If she didn't have an ear comm yet she might not have heard Meredith's announcement, not if she'd gone back to her tree house, far from the nearest community speaker.

Cherry tried to comm the young woman. When there was no answer she tried twice more, just to be sure Wilder either had no comm or was refusing to answer—the latter would be understandable.

It was time to try someone else.

"Kes?"

"Cherry, are you at the bunker already?"

"No, I'm flying back from Suddene."

"In this wind?"

"Do I have a choice? Look, I'm worried about Wilder. When I returned home after that day we were at the hospital, she was gone."

"You mean yesterday?"

Was it only the previous day? "Yes, yesterday. She'd left, not surprisingly, I guess."

"I'm not surprised either. You know how strong-willed she is."

"I know, and if I ever get to see her again I'll apologize. But I don't know if she's heard the Scythians are on their way. I have no idea where she is."

"And you want to know if I do? I don't, sorry. She hasn't been in touch."

"I was worried you would say that. Could you go to her house in the forest and check she's okay? Maybe you can persuade her to go to a shelter."

"I would love to. I'm worried about her too, but I can't."

Kes's voice sounded strained, as if he was under extreme pressure. She guessed they all were.

When she didn't respond immediately, he continued, "I have to get to the Leader's bunker. I'm on my way there now. The Scythians might contact us at any time."

"But what if she's all alone? Someone has to help her."

"I know, but it can't be me. I'm sorry." He closed the comm.

She blinked in surprise. It was very unlike him to be so abrupt. The tension of the situation had to be getting to him. She was reminded of those terrible hours and minutes before the second Scythian attack when everyone was waiting in fear in Sidhe, but Ethan had been there to keep everyone calm then.

What could she do about Wilder? All the military personnel had jobs to do, and civilians would be making their way to shelters.

There was only one person she could think of who could help. She comm'd him, and after several moments he accepted.

"Aubriot, I need—"

"This is getting annoying."

"I need you to find Wilder. She's all alone and—"

"I'm busy."

"This is important."

"Nothing's important anymore. This is the end, so if you don't mind..."

"Don't say that!"

"Face up to it, Cherry. It's over. It was nice knowing you."

"Damn it! Don't you dare close this comm!"

The connection remained open. She heard a sigh. She wasn't sure if it came from Aubriot or the woman he was with. He sounded as though he'd sobered up a bit.

"It is *not* over," said Cherry. "No one knows for sure what will happen."

"I think it's pretty clear."

"No, it isn't. Everyone thought it was clear when the Scythians attacked last time, remember? When the spiders landed and found us despite everything we'd done to hide ourselves. I thought it was over then too. I gave up, and I ran outside so it would be over for me quickly. But I was wrong."

Aubriot was silent.

"I was wrong," she continued. "And you could be wrong now, too. No one knows what the future holds. And even if we think we do, even if we're sure, we still shouldn't give up. Don't hand your life to the Scythians on a plate, Aubriot. It's worth more than that. All of our lives are worth more than that."

After a pause, he said, "What do you want?"

"Wilder was in an accident and she was recuperating at my house, but we got into a fight and she ran off. I don't know where she is and she isn't answering her comm. She might not know about the attack. She has to get to a shelter. She lives in the forest, near Cerberus. I want you to find her and take her somewhere safe."

"She still lives up a fucking tree? What's wrong with that kid?"

"That doesn't matter now. What matters is that someone tells her what's happening and takes her to a shelter. As soon as the Scythians realize Cerberus exists they're going to try to blow it out of the ground. There isn't anything going to be left of that forest but smoking ashes."

"So you want me to go into a forest in the middle of the night, find a tree house, and tell an idiot kid she's about to die if she doesn't get out?"

"She isn't a kid. She's seventeen."

"Still an idiot, though."

"Just do it."

"I dunno. I'm in Annwn. By the time I get to the forest, find the stupid girl, and bring her back here, the Scythians will—"

"For once in your life, can you think about someone other than yourself!"

Silence.

She held her breath. Had she pushed him too far? He generally hated any kind of personal criticism. Nothing could make him shut down faster. But he was the only person she knew who might succeed at finding Wilder and getting her to safety.

"There's no need to be rude," he said.

Coming from one of the rudest people she knew, his comment almost made her laugh. But the situation was too dire. "I'm sorry. Please do this for me. Find Wilder."

"I suppose I might as well die on a pointless quest as opposed to anything else."

"Thank you. Let me know what happens, okay?"

"All right. Where are you?"

"About halfway between Suddene and Lyonesse."

"Huh?"

"It doesn't matter. I'll explain later, after the Scythians go home, or we destroy them."

Aubriot snorted. "Keep dreaming."

Thirty-Three

Kes's autocar was speeding along the main highway into Oceanside. Roads leading off it were shadowy and vague, and it was empty of other vehicles except for a solitary pheromone-neutralizing truck making its final rounds, spraying the street. No one was out as far as he could see. Everyone was in a home bunker or had gone to one of the municipal shelters.

He was reminded of the Second Scythian attack, when all two thousand colonists had crowded into Sidhe. After months of preparation and tension, the nightmare had come true. The enemy had returned, and all that stood between them and the last outpost of human civilization had been a few meters of earth and some reinforced doors.

He gave a mental shiver. Now they were better prepared, but if it came to a fight, could Concordia really defend itself against the might of the Scythians? For their previous attack they'd only sent a handful of ships and the colony hadn't stood a chance. How many ships had they sent this time? Meredith hadn't mentioned a number. He decided not to ask her. He would find out the facts soon enough.

Light brightened the dark road, turning iron gray to somber silver. The clouds were tearing apart and starlight was glimmering through the raggedy gaps. Were any of the stars Scythian ships?

When he returned his attention to the road, he realised he recognized the neighborhood. One of Isobel's sisters lived here. A detour would only take a few minutes out of his journey. It would be a long shot. Isobel had several siblings she could be staying with, or she might not have gone to any of them at all.

"Car," he said. "I have a new destination." He quickly looked it up on the console and input the coordinates. The car passed two exits and turned left at the third. After passing five houses it stopped. He jumped out, telling it to wait, and ran to the house. Rather than taking extra time to find Isobel's sister, Nancy, on comm, he banged on the door.

He realized he'd probably just alarmed everyone inside on this already terrifying night. He took a step backward and tried to locate Nancy via comm.

The door opened.

Nancy and Isobel looked alike except for the fact that Nancy was taller and somehow overall 'harder'. Her nose was sharper, her eyes narrower—giving her a resting suspicious look—and her mouth thinner. As she saw who was waiting outside her door, her mouth thinned even further to a barely perceptible line. "She isn't here."

His shoulders slumped. "Do you know where she is? Is she in Oceanside?" If Isobel was nearby, he might still have time to see her before going to the bunker.

"No, I don't know where she is, and if I did, I wouldn't tell you."

He wasn't sure if she was telling the truth. "I just want to see her. It might be for the last time. So if you—"

"Kes!"

Isobel pushed past her sister but then halted, hesitating. She was the most beautiful sight he had ever seen. He couldn't help himself. He grabbed her and held her, though he took care not to crush her swollen belly.

Nancy tutted. She turned on her heel and strode away down the hall.

"I'm so, so sorry," he said.

"It doesn't matter," said Isobel. "Not now. I was so angry and hurt, but none of that is important now. I wanted to see you, thinking it might be for the last time. But Nancy had hidden my comm and wouldn't let me use hers."

What a bitch. "That wasn't very nice of her."

"It's only because she cares about me."

She has a funny way of showing it. "I wish I'd spent more time with you and Miki. I wanted to but...I don't know what was going on with me. I think I've been struggling with some things, though I didn't really know it."

"No, I was wrong to be so demanding. You have an important job. I should have been more understanding."

"You're wrong, Izzy. I..." He sighed in frustration. He didn't have time to have this conversation. There never seemed to be enough time. Then he had an idea. "I want you and Miki to come with me. I'll take you with me to the Leader's bunker. You'll both be safer there."

"We can't go there. It's only for officials, not their families."

"I don't care. If I bring you both with me, what are they going to do? Turn away the Chief Xenobiologist? Tell the person they're relying on to communicate with the Scythians that he can't come in?"

She touched his cheek. "You're being crazy. We can't go with you. I bet every other person in that bunker would love to have their family with them, but they can't. It's just the way it is. It wouldn't be fair if Miki and I went down there with you."

His arms fell to his sides and his head bowed. She was right, but he couldn't bear the thought that this might be the last time he would see her and his daughter. "Where's Miki? Can I see her?"

"Of course." She called their daughter's name, and a moment later the two-year-old appeared at the top of the basement stairs.

"Daddy!" The toddler ran to him as fast as her little legs would carry her. The hall light caught the red sheen in her black hair. He swept her up in his arms and she cuddled into his neck. He thought his heart would break. "I can't leave you both."

"You have to. I know what you're thinking. If this is the end I'd rather I was with you too, but you can't think like that. Go to the bunker and talk to the Scythians. I know we don't have much of a chance, but I know you'll do your best. If anyone can communicate with them, it's you."

Time was ticking away. He had to go. He'd already taken too long on the detour.

"At least we had a chance to see each other again, didn't we?" Though Isobel smiled, she was weeping. "At least we had the chance to put things right."

He couldn't speak. He nodded and held her and Miki close. Huskily, he told his wife and child that he loved them before handing Miki to Isobel and returning to the autocar. He took a final look at them as the car drew away.

Isobel and Miki were silhouetted in the doorway by the light from the hall. He couldn't see their faces, only their outlines against the brightness, but he deliberately fixed the image in his mind, knowing it might be the last one he had.

When the autocar reached the end of the street he turned to look at Nancy's house. The door had closed and the street was in darkness.

Thirty-Four

There was a problem at Cerberus. Fletcher's tone was professional but Cherry could hear an edge of fear and panic. It was hardly surprising. Concordia's military had been preparing for decades for this moment, but it had never encountered a real enemy. Drills and exercises could not prepare you for the real thing. She remembered too well the cold sweat and the painful tingle of nerve endings when faced with your mortality.

"Send people to visually inspect each system," she said. "Tell them to try percussive maintenance, then run the checks again."

"Percussive maintenance?"

"Hit the mechanisms with hammers. Not too hard, but enough to dislodge any rust or grit."

"Oh, okay. They're pretty large."

"I understand, Fletcher, but unless you have any better ideas it's worth a try. Cerberus is our oldest silo. We'll be lucky if everything works as it's meant to after all this time." She wished she'd asked Wilder to service the massive mechanisms that opened Cerberus's roof. But the focus had always been on the armaments. When the time came, they would be vital. But if the roof didn't open they would be useless. "Just do whatever you can, and keep me updated."

The flight from Suddene to Lyonesse had passed quickly as she dealt with the flurry of progress updates from Concordia's military arms. The three other silos were reporting all their checks were clear and they were ready for action. Companies of ground troops at all major metropolises were at their stations.

The anti-spider devices had been activated. The community shelters were full and locked.

Concordia was ready and waiting.

"ETA has been revised," said Zapata suddenly.

"It has?" She looked at the display. Even as she watched, the minutes until the heli was due to arrive at the Leader's Residence rapidly reduced.

"The wind's dropped," Zapata explained. "Didn't you notice?"

She hadn't. She'd been concentrating on the military's preparations. But as she looked out into the night, she saw the clouds were opening. Starlight shone through the gaps. The water beneath them glittered and in the distance was a line of blackness: the coast of Lyonesse. She checked the arrival time again. "We'll make it to the Residence before the Scythians arrive."

"Yes. Just."

For the first time in the last hour, no comms were waiting for her. No one had anything to report or anything to check. Zapata said nothing else. His features were tense with concentration as he extracted the maximum power from the heli.

Did he have a family he might never see again? She didn't know anything about him, except for the fact he was a damned good pilot.

A comm arrived, this time from a non-military source. Or perhaps ex-military. "Aubriot? What's happening? Did you find her?"

"After a lot of tramping through wet undergrowth in the dark, I found the tree. Then I had to climb up into it, getting covered in scratches and—"

"But did you find her?"

"Nope. Not here. Total waste of time. And now I have to get back to Annwn."

"Damn. Did you see anything to indicate where she might be?"

"No. Place is a mess and it's too dark to see anything. No one would spend any longer here than they had to. There's a hole in the roof and the rain's got in."

"I wonder where she went. I hope she's safe."

"Yeah, so...I'm going to try to get to the nearest shelter now."

Shit.

He was kilometers from a shelter. He'd spent all his remaining time since searching for Wilder and now he was alone in one of the most dangerous places on the planet.

"Thanks for looking for her for me," Cherry said. "I appreciate it."

"No problem. You know, I have to admit she's a smart kid, even if she does live up a tree. She will have gone somewhere safe. And I have to go now too."

"I know where you can go! Cerberus. I'll tell Colonel Fletcher you're coming and he'll let you in."

"Cerberus? Why the hell would I want to go there?"

"Where else can you go? You'll never make it back to Annwn. There's no time."

"I suppose you have a point."

"And you can help them. They're having a problem with the roof opening mechanisms. Some of them are reporting faults but the maintenance team can't figure out what the problem is."

"And? I'm no engineer. I used to pay people to do that kind of thing."

"Just go there. It won't hurt, and you'll be underground." And not alone. Aubriot had many faults, but there was something about the thought of him dying alone that tore at her.

"All right. I'll give it a try."

"Good." She swallowed. Aubriot was sounding more 'human' than ever. And he'd tried to find Wilder, wandering around a forest at night under the imminent threat of a Scythian attack. It was probably the most selfless thing he had ever done. "Good luck."

"Yeah, you too."

Thirty-Five

Piddle and Puddle could not get used to micro-gravity. Wilder regretted bringing them aboard the *Opportunity*. The two small creatures vomited up whatever they ate not long after eating it, and the vomit was not easy to deal with when it was floating in mid air. Her pets' toilet habits—or lack of them—were even more inconvenient.

She gently launched herself, pushing her feet against the side of the living quarters. As she floated past a small lump of Puddle's partially digested dinner, she swept it up into a tissue and folded the tissue over it. When she reached the other side of the living quarters, she pulled herself along the wall to the trash disposal and deposited the tissue. Then she returned to her work on her a-grav machine.

Piddle and Puddle had even puked and peed during the long hours it had taken for the shuttle to rendezvous with the *Opportunity.* Not that such small animals generated a lot of waste, but it was unpleasant nonetheless.

After several such accidents, she had made a bag from a sweater by tying the bottom in a knot. After tying the sleeves to two cupboard handles she installed her two little friends. They would nap in there, cuddled up, and sometimes run around the ship, clinging to the walls. They had quickly learned the dangers of letting go. She'd only had to rescue them two or three times as they floated helplessly, unable to return to a solid surface.

Technically, in micro-g, everywhere was a wall. There was no floor or ceiling. As soon as the shuttle moved beyond most of the influence of Concordia's gravity she had been vividly reminded of her own nausea in this situation. Had she made the right decision when agreeing to Quinn's suggestion to recuperate here? But it was too late for regrets. She had borrowed the a-grav machine parts from Jamie Bond, and Tycho and Stephie had loaded her up with supplies. After her friends had gone to so much trouble, it seemed wrong to cancel the plan, especially over something as trivial as discomfort in micro-g.

She would get used to it. At least she was doing marginally better than Piddle and Puddle. She could use a toilet, for instance.

An unforeseen difficulty of working on a-grav while, ironically, in micro-g, was that nothing remained where it was unless you fixed it there. Before, she'd been able to rely on Concordia's gravity to hold the prototype on the ground. Aboard the *Opportunity*, she was forced to tether it to the 'floor'. Initially, she'd put all the parts in boxes to avoid a room full of floating pieces of metal, but the boxes themselves had been dangerous floating objects too. In the end, she had put all the parts into a cupboard, taking them out a piece at a time when she'd needed them.

When she'd first come aboard the ship had been cool and smelled of dust and mold. As far she knew, no human had set foot, or hand, on the *Opportunity* in all the years after the trip to the Assembly. She personally had felt no desire to revisit the place where she had spent so many months in close quarters with her three shipmates.

The first thing she'd done was to ask Quinn to turn up the heating. Things had become a little more comfortable after that.

She pushed the final part into place. The first stage was over. After many hours of work the new machine was built. Holding onto a chair fixed to the floor, she floated next to the a-grav machine, a hand on her hip, appreciating the satisfaction of completing this first essential task.

"Have you finished?" Quinn asked.

"I've built it. Now I have to get it working. I can't remember exactly what I did before, but I'm sure I'll figure it out through trial and error."

"Maybe have something to eat and take a nap. You're here to recover from your injuries, don't forget."

She was tempted to ignore his advice and push on, but then she thought better of it. She hadn't yet forgotten the sight of her skinny, bruised body in Cherry's mirror. "Yeah, I'll do that." Once the words were out of her mouth she realized she felt hungry and fatigued. Her pain medication was wearing off, too. Discomfort was beginning to build in her ribs and abdomen. It was weird how her mind managed to ignore the signals from her body when she was concentrating.

She pushed off from the chair in the direction of the food cupboard. After retrieving a container of pasta in lentil sauce, she opened the lid and scooped out noodles with a fork.

Quinn asked, "Do you want to check your comm messages while you're eating?"

"You make a strange kinda mom, Quinn. You know that?"

"Are you implying that I'm trying to mother you?"

Smother me, she thought, but she didn't say it. He was only being kind. "I guess that is what I meant, but I know it's only because you care."

"I'm pleased I interpreted your underlying meaning correctly."

"You did, didn't you? You're getting good at understanding us."

"So, are you going to check your messages?"

"Wow, you're *really* good at understanding us." Wilder marveled that the Fila hadn't been deterred by her effort to change the subject. "In a minute. I'll eat this first."

She had found her ear comm on the floor of her tree home and popped it into her pocket while calling Piddle and Puddle. Her two little friends had been hiding, but they'd poked out their heads when they recognized her voice.

She ate the rest of the pasta and then sucked water from a bottle. Next, she pulled out her medication packet and swallowed a tablet, followed by more water. Finally, she took out her comm and pushed it into her ear.

There was a message from Jamie Bond. "It was great to see you yesterday, Deadly After Midnight. I hope you make some progress with the sandwich—" 'Sandwich' was the code name for the a-grav machines. "I have a feeling you'll be the one to find the perfect mix of ingredients. I was wondering, do you want to meet up sometime and talk about recipes face to face? Just us, I mean."

She smiled. Jamie Bond was sappy, but sweet. And he had to have guts to ask for a date with a girl at least five years older and a head taller than him. Maybe she would comm him back when she returned to the surface, but by then she hoped she would have made the 'sandwich' work and their shared project would be over.

Cherry had tried to contact her. Wilder was glad she hadn't been bothered by the alerts. In all of Concordia, Cherry was the last person she wanted to talk to. All that remained to listen to was a short message from Tycho and Stephie, wishing her good luck and telling her to visit when she was better.

That was it. No one else had comm'd. Ordinarily, this would be a good thing. She hated wasting time on boring small talk and gossip. But this time she felt a tiny bit sad and, for the first time in her life, a little lonely. Perhaps it was because she was many kilometers above the planet surface and the only human aboard the ship. "Quinn, can I comm the surface from here?"

"That won't be a problem. However, if you wish to speak to someone you should do it now. It is evening at Oceanside and Annwn. Most humans will be going to sleep soon."

"Maybe I'll do it in the morning." She put the empty meal container in the trash and pulled herself along to the bathroom to change into pajamas and brush her teeth.

When she was ready for bed, she climbed into her sleeping bag. It was the same one she'd used the last time she was on the ship. Plans for what she would do tomorrow circulated through her mind, gradually slowing down and transmogrifying into strange shapes and figures. The a-grav machine melted into a pulse emitter. Then it took flight and sped into the distance toward a setting sun, becoming lost in the vivid red, pink, and orange of the evening sky. A figure was walking toward her from the distant horizon, taking impossibly gigantic leaps over the land. As the figure drew nearer, she recognized Jamie Bond, though he was taller and older.

"Wilder!" Jamie said. "Wilder, wake up!"

She tried to answer him, "I'm already awake." But her mouth voiced silent words.

"Wake up, Wilder!"

She forced open her eyes. Her dream had been so vivid she was momentarily confused, but then she remembered where she was. It had to be Quinn, not Jamie, speaking. "What's wrong?"

"I've just heard from our communication center that we have sighted the Scythians. They're returning to Concordia."

Shock silenced her for a moment. "The Scythians?" she asked, stupidly.

"You must return to the surface. Please go to one of the shuttles. I will send it to Oceanside immediately."

"No, wait." She sat up, floating half inside and half outside her sleeping bag. "When will they get here?"

"Not for a few hours. You have time to return to the surface and enter one of the shelters."

"What if I don't want to?"

"You have to. The *Opportunity* will be a target for attack."

"I *have* to? Now you're really sounding like you're trying to mother me. I thought you invited me up here as a guest. Now you're kicking me out?"

"For your benefit. When the Scythians arrive and are refused their tribute, this ship will become one of the least safe places in the star system."

"I'm getting damned tired of people doing things for my benefit. How about you let me make this decision for myself?"

A pause followed. Then Quinn said, "I cannot physically force you into a shuttle, but I strongly recommend it. However, we built this ship as a gift for your colony. Whether you remain or leave is entirely your decision."

"Thank you. I'm not leaving. Let's think about what we can do when the Scythians arrive."

Thirty-Six

Zapata landed the heli on the roof of the Leader's Residence. This time round, the landing was easy. The wind had died away to a light breeze and the sky had cleared to brilliant starlight. Cherry leapt out the moment the landing skids made contact, keeping low to avoid the still-spinning rotor. She ran out from under the blades before straightening up and jogging across the roof to the exit door.

By the time she opened the door Zapata was already high in the sky, making his way to the nearest shelter. She ran down the steps two at a time. Before landing, she'd confirmed with Meredith that the Scythians still hadn't answered the hail the Fila had been sending ever since they'd been spotted. The enemy ships were minutes from reaching Concordia's high orbit.

Ten vessels were coming. Two of the largest type: the double crescent that carried a massive pulse emitter on a spike. The other ships were single crescents, less powerful but still deadly. And she had no doubt the Scythians were also bringing tens or even hundreds of thousands of their relentless spiders too, ready to unleash on Concordia and strip it of human life.

She reached the first floor and ran across the lobby to the elevator.

She comm'd Meredith as she waited for it, "I'm here."

"Thank the stars. You're the last to arrive."

The doors opened and Cherry stepped in. The elevator began its journey down.

Suddenly, a hard shock hit. Cherry was thrown to one side. The elevator abruptly stopped. Her heart froze. "Meredith, what just happened?"

No answer came. The lights flickered and died. Utter darkness surrounded her.

"Meredith? Meredith?"

She felt for the elevator doors. If it had stopped at one of the intervening floors, she might be able to prisw the doors open and get out. She could take the stairs the rest of the way.

But the doors were firmly closed. With only one arm, she didn't have a hope of opening them.

The light returned. Emergency backup power had kicked in.

"Meredith! Answer me!"

The lights for B3 and B4 were lit on the console, meaning she was between the two floors. The bunker was at B5.

She was about to try to comm Meredith again, but she changed her mind. Something terrible had happened and the Leader was clearly distracted. Who else was in the bunker and could explain what had happened? She comm'd Kes.

"Cherry?"

The voice that answered was strangled with emotion, the tone high, quiet, and distant.

"Kes? Is that you?" She was honestly not sure. She'd grown so used to her friend's voice—the Fila used something similar for generating human speech—but this version sounded like nothing she'd heard before. Had whatever had caused the shock disrupted the comm system? But he'd answered with her first name. It had to be him.

"I'm stuck in the elevator," she said. "What's happened?"

"They...They...Oh God! Oh my God."

Cherry heard a guttural sound, a horrible, heart-wrenching sound, as if the man's soul were being torn in two.

"Kes! Tell me what's happened!" She thumped the elevator buttons. Desperately, she cast her gaze around the enclosed space, trying to find a way out. The only exit was a hatch in the ceiling, but it was far out of her reach.

"They fired, Cherry," he whispered hoarsely. "They fired, before even asking us for tribute. They didn't say a word. All their ships fired at once. A simultaneous shot from ten ships." He choked, "Half of Oceanside is gone."

She couldn't find the words to reply. Half of Oceanside? How many people was that? Thousands. Tens of thousands.

She kicked the elevator wall and then yelled as pain seared up her leg. "Is there an engineer with you? Tell them to do whatever it takes to get me out of here. Now! Okay, Kes? Did you hear me? Find someone to get me out of here. Those fuckers are not going to get away with this."

She comm'd Aubriot, hoping to the stars the damage the Scythians had inflicted hadn't taken down the network.

He answered.

"Have you heard what's happened?" Cherry asked.

"Yeah." His tone was leaden. "Wasn't expecting that."

"I need you to coordinate the response. We'll throw everything at them. Everything."

"What? Why me?"

"I'm stuck in an elevator. It was moving when we were hit and the shock's affected the system. I can't get out and I can't work inside a tiny box with no data and no vid feed. I need your help."

"You've got officers..."

"Do it! It's mostly your plan, remember? You know it inside out. They've brought ten ships. We'll wipe them from the skies."

"Yeah. Okay."

He was gone.

Aubriot was no longer an officer—he wasn't even in the military—but she didn't doubt his ability to make the staff follow his orders. Despite his many faults, if there was one thing he didn't lack it was the ability to take control.

She stared at the walls, rigid with frustration. How many people had died? She'd been expecting an exchange of words at least. The Scythians should have demanded their tribute, then Meredith would have refused. And if the Scythians attacked or even threatened it, Cherry would have ordered the missile silos to be opened, the pulse emitters to be raised to ground level, and the surface armaments revealed. The Scythians would have discovered they were not going to destroy the human colony or take the planet as easily as they might have thought.

But the aliens had had a surprise of their own to deliver. What did it mean? Were they on the offensive because they anticipated a hostile reception? Were they getting in the first blow? Or did they want to cow the colonists and make them agree to any terms?

Did it matter?

No.

When she'd learned that Concordia was the Scythians' origin planet, their attacks had made more sense. The fact didn't excuse them. There was no excuse for attempting to destroy another intelligent species, even if you did find them living on your former home. But to an extent she had understood their actions.

Now, things were different. The Scythians had allowed the humans to remain on Concordia. They'd been absent for decades, and the colony had thrived and built a society. To return now and launch a devastating attack with no warning, no parley, no attempt at a compromise... It was an evil act, and the aliens deserved everything they had coming to them.

In her mind's eye she could see the gigantic roof covering Cerberus begin to pull back, shedding soil, rocks, and vegetation to the sides. Minotaur, along the coast from Oceanside, would growl into life, opening the cliff top, sending boulders crashing into the ocean below. Medusa, long-hidden below her high plateau, would shake free her icy cap and spill frozen shale down the mountainside. A towering fountain would signal Hydra's arrival, rising from the ocean. The rumbling of the silos' mechanisms would shake the ground and echo through the air. The armaments would lift into the starlit night, their targeting systems locking onto the ten Scythian ships threatening the planet.

A noise sounded from above. Someone had landed on the elevator's roof. A moment later, the hatch opened and the head and shoulders of a middle-aged, bald man appeared.

"Thank the stars," she breathed.

"You'll have to come out this way. The elevator won't restart. Either the shaft has been damaged or something's screwed up the system."

"It doesn't matter. Do you have a rope?"

"Yes, but that's all. I don't have a harness or anything like that. Maybe you can tie it around you."

"Just let it down. Hurry up."

The end of a hemp rope dropped into the elevator. She grabbed it. "Pull me up!"

The man peered in. "Are you sure you can support your weight on one arm?"

"Stop wasting time. Pull me up."

He disappeared and the tension on the rope tightened. Her feet left the floor and she rose, clinging on tightly. When she reached the hatch, however, she hit a problem. The rope was scraping against the edge. If she continued to hold it her hand would be scraped too and would block the rope from moving farther.

Just as she was debating whether to let go, a hand reached in and grabbed the back of her shirt. She was unceremoniously hauled through the hatch and dumped onto the elevator's roof.

"Thanks," she gasped.

"The only way out is up the service ladder, but it isn't far to the next floor."

Above them in the dark elevator shaft the doors to the nearest floor stood open. She went up the ladder first, forced to go slowly so that she didn't fall when she released the grip of her only hand to move higher.

She reached the open doors and crawled out of the shaft onto tiled floor. Immediately, she ran to the stairway that would take her down to the bunker. As she sped down she noticed cracks in the walls. The combined attack from all the Scythian ships must have had a devastating force to inflict damage so far underground.

In less than a minute she'd reached the bunker. She burst through the doors, only to meet a scene of disarray.

Kes sat motionless at the table, his face ashen, his gaze a distant stare. Meredith was pacing in front of the transparent wall separating the room from the Fila side, her hand on her forehead and her features riven with despair and confusion. Two officials huddled, muttering to each other, another two stared at screens. The screens showed the open missile silos and other places in Concordia, as well as a visual on the Scythian ships.

"What's going on?" Cherry asked.

Meredith abruptly turned toward her as if only just noticing her appearance. She ran over and grabbed her shoulders. Before she could say anything, however, a comm from Aubriot arrived.

Cherry held up her hand, palm outward. "Yes?"

"Cerberus opened," Aubriot said. "And all the others. Everything's locked on target."

"Right, I'll give the order."

"No!" Meredith exclaimed. "Wait!"

Cherry gritted her teeth. "Standby, Aubriot." She asked Meredith, "What are we waiting for?"

"We received a message. Play it, Kes."

Woodenly, Kes swiped an interface and thumbed a key.

A screech pierced Cherry's ears. She covered one of them but had no way of protecting the other from the penetrating sound.

"Dammit, Kes," said Costello, Head of Civil Works, "can't you skip over that part?"

"Invaders of our planet," said a voice. The Scythians had somehow accessed the Fila's translation technology. "We have tolerated your presence in our home and allowed you to benefit from its resources. You have multiplied your numbers and created a self-sustaining livelihood. We have been forgiving. We have been generous. But these things are... *Does not translate...* Now it is time for us to receive our recompense."

A pause followed by a second *Does not translate*.

"We are returning to our home," the Scythian message continued. "We have brought materials to construct habitations for our settlers. They will be the first of our kind to dwell on the sacred soil of our homeland in eons. But our people will not be able to survive outside of their habitations. They will require assistance. You will service them, supplying all their needs. In return, we will allow you to continue to live on our world. Refuse this offer, and we will destroy your colony and all life on our planet. No other species will ever besmirch our sacred land with its presence again. We await your answer."

Thirty-Seven

Wilder endured the crushing pressure stoically, though she couldn't help harboring a wish that the Fila had the technology to entirely eradicate the effect of the *Opportunity's* fast acceleration on the human body, not only ameliorate it. She'd grown used to the feeling on her trip to the Assembly, but she worried about Piddle and Puddle. Would their little bodies and small bones cope?

Thankfully, the pressure began to ease after only a short time. That was all it took to travel to the second planet in from Concordia. As soon as she felt she could safely move, she asked Quinn to release the straps holding her to the padded, reclined seat. She went to the living quarters, still struggling against the forces pressing her down. By the time she reached her pets' separate pouches—she'd guessed they would be safer apart—the effects of the acceleration had decreased to roughly the same as Concordian gravity.

She opened the first pouch. Puddle's eyes glared up at her resentfully. She lifted him out carefully and gently ran her hands over his body. He didn't seem to have any broken bones. As to any internal damage, she simply didn't know. Time would tell if the little creature had suffered serious damage. She replaced Puddle in his pouch.

Next, she opened Piddle's tied-up sweater. She sucked in a breath. Piddle's eyes were closed.

"No, no, no!"

She reached in. Piddle was warm, but was she still alive? Even more gently than she'd handled Puddle, Wilder cradled Piddle as she lifted her out. She inspected the creature's face. Piddle's mouth hung open and her tiny tongue lolled out over her pointed teeth. As Wilder turned the small body, Piddle's head flopped to the side.

Puddle's head and front legs emerged from his sweater. He was watching his little friend.

Wilder held Piddle's chest against her ear, the soft, warm fur tickling, but she couldn't hear anything. Did Concordian animals even have hearts the same as Earth animals? Concordian animals hadn't featured in the curriculum in her school days. No one had thought complex life forms even existed on the planet the *Nova* journeyed toward.

As she carried out her checks on her pets, the *Opportunity* slowed further. She grew lighter and lighter until her feet lifted off the floor and she was floating.

Piddle gave a little squirm, then her eyes slowly opened, her tongue retracted, and her mouth closed. Her legs moved feebly.

"Are you okay?" Wilder asked. "Please be okay!"

As if in response, Piddle wriggled some more. Her tail whipped from side to side. She didn't seem to have broken anything. Feeling better but remaining concerned about her pets, Wilder put Piddle in Puddle's pouch. He immediately began to groom her.

"We have entered low orbit on the far side of Camaret," said Quinn. "The Scythians may have observed our movements, but perhaps not. At their current distance the Scythians' instruments may not detect the *Opportunity's* trace against the background of solar radiation."

"But they know this ship exists, right? They won't have forgotten about it."

"No, indeed they won't."

Camaret was closer to the star than Concordia. Barren, rocky, and devoid of life, it had not held much interest for the colony's scientists, who had barely scraped the surface of investigating their own world.

But for Wilder, Quinn, and the other Fila in the crew, Camaret was somewhere to hide and wait while they tried to come up with a way to use the *Opportunity* to the greatest effect in the inevitable battle.

As long as they remained shielded by the planet's mass, the Scythians might not want to weaken their forces by sending a ship to hunt them out. And though the *Opportunity* was not sufficiently powerful to inflict serious damage on anything except the smaller ships in the Scythian fleet, she was nevertheless not without her sting.

Thirty-Eight

All eyes were on Cherry. Even Meredith seemed to be looking at her for an answer. Only Kes's gaze was averted. He was in a world of his own, clearly deeply in shock.

"When did the message arrive?" Cherry asked. "Was it before or after we opened the silos?"

"We received it immediately after the assault," Meredith replied.

"And we've heard nothing since?"

"No. They must have seen the silos opening but they haven't said anything yet. I guess they still think they can destroy us." Meredith slumped into a chair. "It was all a ploy, right from the beginning. The Scythians never wanted a tribute. During their second attack, when the colony was sheltering in Sidhe, they must have realized they could make use of our presence here. We could survive on their planet but they could not. If they used us as their slaves they could re-establish a civilization on the world they had been forced to abandon. They could come home. Telling us they accepted the sacrifice of the *Mistral* and its crew was only a convenient excuse for them to call off their attack. Since then they've been waiting, biding their time until our population increased to sufficient numbers to serve their needs."

"You're right," Cherry said. "That's clear now."

"What isn't clear is, what do we do?"

"What do you mean?"

"What answer do we give them? Do we agree to their demands?"

"Why is that even a question?"

"Yes," Meredith said. "We don't have a choice, do we? We'll have to agree."

"What?!" Kes slammed a fist on the table and rose to his feet so fast his chair clattered to the floor. "No! They just killed thousands of people with no provocation. Thousands of Concordians are dead just so the Scythians could make a point!" He swiveled to face Cherry. "Give the order. Destroy them."

"I will," Cherry said. "We can't give in."

"Do not give the order to fire," said Meredith. "I'm Leader here and I forbid it. If we respond to the Scythians' attack we'll be committing suicide. Our families, our homes, everything we've worked for, will be gone. We'll all die, and we're the last outpost of human society. If Concordia falls it'll be the end of human civilization."

"Better dead than living as slaves," Cherry retorted.

Meredith seemed about to say something but then changed her mind. She turned to the four heads of government departments. "I want to hear your opinions."

While Meredith was listening to the officials, Cherry comm'd Aubriot. She wanted to know what he thought about the Scythians' demand. Would he prefer survival, no matter the cost?

"Fuck that."

"That's what I thought you would say," said Cherry.

"What about our esteemed Leader?"

"She wants to agree to their terms, believe it or not. She's talking to the others, but I don't think she'll change her mind."

"Oh well. Who cares what she thinks?"

"Not me."

"Gotcha. Just let us know when."

"Keep those missiles and emitters targeted."

"Don't worry. They're all tracking the Scythian ships perfectly."

A screech erupted from the room's comm. Cherry clapped a hand to one ear and pressed her shoulder to the other. A moment later the sound mercifully ceased.

"We must receive your answer. Withdraw your weapons. We must receive your answer. Withdraw your weapons."

Silence.

"Elliot," said Meredith, "open a return comm to the Scythian ship."

"Wait!" exclaimed Costello, Head of Civil Works. "You can't answer on behalf of all of us. We have to put it to a vote."

"Who's Elliot?" Cherry asked.

"The Fila representative," Kes replied. He was propping his elbows on the table and holding his head in his hands. His earlier fury seemed to have dissipated to extreme lassitude.

Cherry had almost forgotten the Fila on the other side of the bunker's transparent wall. "What happened to Quinn?"

"He's aboard the *Opportunity*, with Wilder."

"Wilder went to the *Opportunity*?! Stars, I'd forgotten all about that ship. I wonder where it is? I hope Quinn had the good sense to leave as soon as he knew the Scythians were coming."

Kes didn't reply.

Meanwhile, Meredith and the department heads were arguing.

"I am the elected Leader!" Meredith exclaimed.

"So what?" Costello asked. "There's nothing in your mandate that gives you the right to consign the entire colony to slavery."

"It's my responsibility to protect you all. Not sacrifice you to some noble-sounding ideal."

"Wanting to live free or not at all isn't an ideal," Costello snapped. "It's a right."

"Maybe it is, but that's an individual's decision. We can't go around all of Concordia and ask everyone what they would prefer. There isn't time. I have to decide for everyone. That's what I'm supposed to do. And I decide we should live. Who knows what the future may hold? If we agree to the Scythians' terms now, perhaps the Galactic Assembly will force them to release us later. If we resist now, that's it. Forever."

"You're forgetting a third alternative, Meredith," Cherry said. "What if we assert our right to live in peace on a planet that can sustain us, without hurting anyone? What if we fight back, and we win?Besides, I think you're optimistic to think the Scythians won't still kill most of us even if we agree. They didn't have to come here and slaughter thousands of our citizens in order to propose their plan. They could have approached us peacefully. But instead they attacked first so we would be intimidated into agreeing to their terms. They're murderers. Vicious, remorseless murderers. Living under them would be torture. Death would be better."

"I can't do it. I can't allow the destruction of all the men, women, and children under my care."

"You know what?" Cherry asked. "Ethan wouldn't have given in. He would be ashamed of you."

Meredith gasped. "How can you say that? It isn't true! My father was all about protecting and nurturing every single person on Concordia."

"Yes, he was, but not at any cost. No one seems to remember any longer—it's probably not even in the history books—but in the early days of this colony your father, me, and the rest of the Gens fought tooth and nail for the right to live our lives as we chose. We risked death for that cause because the idea of living without our independence was unbearable. Our actions were reckless, perhaps stupid even, when the colony was small, weak, and teetering on the edge of failure. But we did it regardless because we decided that our lives were not worth living any other way. Ethan *fought back*, Meredith. And that's something you aren't prepared to do.

"I've just realized I've been wrong about something. For months now, I've been worried this generation of Concordians wasn't up to scratch. I thought they were not prepared for the Scythians' return. They seemed lazy, undisciplined, and careless. To me, they weren't scared enough. But they've surprised me. After I gave the order, all the battle preparations went with hardly a single hitch. Our military knew what it was doing after all. I've realized it wasn't them I should have been worried about, it was you. I hate to say it, Meredith—I remember you as a baby in your mother's arms—but you're the wrongness I was sensing all along. *You're* the rot at the heart of Concordia."

Cherry opened a comm to all her senior officers and Aubriot.

She spoke only two words: "Return fire."

Thirty-Nine

Seconds later, fire erupted from Cerberus as the missiles launched. Minotaur followed next, then Medusa, and finally Hydra. Massive rockets rose into the air, pulling against Concordia's gravity, rising faster and faster, trailing brilliant white flames. They were locked onto their targets and wouldn't stop until they either reached their destinations and detonated or they were shot out of the sky.

Almost before the missiles left their launchers, pulse fire started up, turning night to day. Concordia was throwing everything it had at the Scythians. The colony had been a long time waiting for this moment and it had nothing to lose.

Cherry's gaze moved to the screen showing the Scythian ships, limited to a single viewpoint. The single satellite left over from the earliest days of colonization had never been added to for fear of attracting the attention of the Scythians. The aging device had transmitted images of the first two battles with the aliens. Now it was to transmit its third and last.

Cherry was under no illusion that the Scythians would succeed in destroying the colony. If not today, then eventually. They wouldn't rest until their origin planet was wiped clean of the interlopers. They had made that clear.

The bunker was silent. None present except Kes and Cherry had ever experienced a Scythian attack. Meredith's features were frozen in horror. Others bore a look of fascinated dread. Kes's expression was intent but calm, as if already resigned to whatever happened.

The Scythian ships were firing. They weren't attempting to out-maneuver the missiles closing in on them, perhaps guessing correctly that their only chance at evading them was to destroy them. A shot from one of the largest Scythian ships hit the leading missile, bursting it into fragments that quickly disappeared into the ether.

A pulse from the surface arrived ahead of the next missile, successfully striking a small Scythian ship full on, bursting one half of its crescent away. More missiles were arriving, but the Scythians were hitting them all. The missiles' effect would be greater than a pulse strike, but only if they managed to get through. And their supply was strictly limited, unlike the pulse emitters, which would continue to fire as long as they received energy.

On the planet surface, fire from the Scythian ships was arriving. The pulses not aimed at the missiles were targeting the silos. Specifically, the pulse emitters not far distant from the missile launch sites.

"Yes!" Kes yelled.

A Scythian ship was dissolving in pale blue fire. Either a missile had broken through the enemy's defense or a pulse had hit its mark.

One down. Nine to go.

The second tranche of missiles was moving into position. Like the first swathe, these would be aimed at the two leading Scythian ships with pulse emitter spikes. These ships could cause the most damage, and their loss might cause the fleet to give up and retreat. Concordia might live a little while yet.

The spikes flashed simultaneously. A pulse sped from each converged, doubled in size and brightness, and flew toward the planet.

A second later, Minotaur exploded.

A collective gasp sounded in the bunker as the missile silo rose into the air in fragments, spurting flames hundreds of meters high. The Scythians' combined pulse must have hit the silo's fuel tanks. Less than a second later a tremor hit the bunker, the shock from the blast arriving from its clifftop site.

Meredith's frozen gaze of horror broke and she buried her head in her hands.

Cherry felt strangely calm. The path of the battle's progress seemed inevitable. The colony would inflict damage on the Scythian ships, perhaps even destroying one or two, but slowly it would be beaten into the ground by their enemy's relentless fire. The ships could move. They could leave, be repaired, and return to inflict more damage. Concordia had nowhere to go.

"What's that?" Costello pointed at the screen displaying Hydra. Black objects were raining down into the ocean. At first Cherry thought it was debris from Minotaur, but Hydra was too far away. The silo sat in a shallow area of ocean closer to Suddene than Lyonesse.

If the black falling objects were not debris, they had to be coming from the

Scythians. The ships must have launched them, but their dark color had prevented the human observers from spotting them.

Were they spiders? None seemed to have arrived yet, and when the Scythian message had spoken of their intent to destroy all life on the planet the spiders had been the first thing to spring to Cherry's mind. The colony had plans to deal with the destructive devices if they landed, but they had not imagined that spiders or anything else would be dropped into the ocean.

A second burst of pale blue fire distracted her from the spectacle of the rain of black objects. The colony had scored another hit. A second Scythian ship had fallen to either a missile or a series of attacking pulses.

A comm from Aubriot arrived. "That was ours. Hydra got the first, but Cerberus is catching up."

"Well done," Cherry replied. "Do you know about Minotaur?"

"It's gone, right?"

"Yes."

"We guessed that might be the case when we lost all contact."

"They were brave men and women. You all are."

"Cherry..."

"What?"

"Never mind." Aubriot cut the comm.

"My people are dying," said a voice.

After a second of confusion, Cherry realized it was the Fila, Elliot, who had spoken. "You... Fila are dying?" The sentence from Elliot had been so devoid of emotion she was unsure she'd heard him correctly. But then, the translation system was not set up to convey emotion.

"The Scythians have dropped biocide into the ocean. It is spreading through the water. We think the substance dissolves protein chains. It is killing every living thing it contacts."

"Stars! Can't you move away from it? Go somewhere it hasn't spread?"

"The substance seems to be converting the living matter it destroys and increasing in volume and potency. Its density is almost the same as ocean water. The ocean currents are spreading it everywhere. We cannot escape."

No other species will ever besmirch our sacred land with its presence again.

The Scythians were killing the Fila too. Of course they were. Not only were the Fila another intelligent species that had 'invaded' the Scythians' origin planet, they had helped the humans immeasurably. They had even helped humans to join the Galactic Assembly, though any aid the Assembly could send would arrive too late.

A terrible guilt settled on her. Not for one second had she considered what her decision would mean for the Fila.

"We believe the biocide is falling on land too," said Elliot. "Its dispersal on land will be slower, but it will reach your people eventually."

"I'm sorry." It was all she could think to say. "I'm so sorry."

"Do not offer any apology. We have spawned. We are fulfilled. We have Joined with you. We swim and fall together."

Forty

"Quinn, we have to see what's happening," said Wilder.

"Moving out of Camaret's shadow will expose us to the Scythians' scanners," Quinn replied. "At this distance they will spot us immediately, and then they will fire on us."

"Well, how about we fire on *them*?" She was tired of hiding. She felt like she was skulking away like a coward when every other Concordian was suffering under the Scythian attack.

"I understand your motivation. But firing on the Scythian fleet will most certainly attract their attention."

"That's the point! Maybe it will help the colony if we provide a distraction. The *Opportunity* is pretty fast. Maybe we can draw a ship or two away from the battle."

There was a pause as the Fila considered her suggestion. She was watching him through the transparent wall. She found it easier to talk to him this way, rather than chatting with his disembodied voice over comm.

"That may be an effective tactic," he finally said. "I have spoken with the other crew members and they agree to take the risk."

"Woo hoo! Let's do it."

"You must go to your safety seat. We will be piloting the *Opportunity* at high speeds."

She suddenly remembered Piddle and Puddle. The poor creatures would have to endure another bout of high-g. She almost wished she hadn't brought them here, but then again the Scythians would be attacking Cerberus. Her pets' forest home would be razed.

"Give me one minute," she said. After the previous period of acceleration, she had discovered a soft, downy substance in one of the cabinets in the ship's head. She had no idea what the material was supposed to be for. Neither had any other passengers on the trip to the Galactic Assembly, for it had remained untouched. But she knew the perfect use for it now.

She pulled herself through the ship until she reached the head, took large handfuls of the fluffy substance out of the box, and went to the living quarters. Piddle and Puddle were floating in their pouches, looking ill with motion sickness.

"I hope I can take you home soon. But until then, I have some lovely soft stuff for you to lie on when we get going. You should be more comfortable on this." She pushed the material into the tied-up sweaters, forcing it into the bottoms where her pets would end up when the ship began to accelerate.

When she was sure she'd made Piddle and Puddle as comfortable as possible, she pushed off from the wall, sending herself zooming back to her acceleration seat. "I'm ready. Oh, wait a minute. Can you give me a visual of what's happening outside the ship?"

The blank wall interface displayed a view of the exterior. A rocky, airless landscape filled the entire screen. They were so close to Camaret the ship's cameras were not picking up anything else. The landscape was bright with reflected light of the system's star. Was it day or night on Lyonesse? She'd lost track of time.

The scene switched, and Wilder saw the star. Concordia was not yet visible. She wasn't sure in which direction it lay.

"Starting to maneuver," said Quinn. "We will leave Camaret's cover in one minute and eighteen seconds."

Pressure pinned her down, but she ignored the uncomfortable feeling as she watched the interface. The scene switched again, back to Camaret's surface. It was moving. Distant rocks and dust flowed over the screen, followed by a curved horizon, and then open space. Even though millions of kilometers separated them, the blue-green ball that was Concordia was easy to spot, as well as tiny flickerings of light: the pulse fire of the battle.

"What's happening, Quinn?" she asked. "Are you picking up any messages? Your people know you're here with me, don't they?"

He didn't answer for several long moments. She didn't press him for a response, knowing that he was probably busy listening to the messages.

"Things are bad," he eventually said. "The Scythians are attempting to erase all life on the planet. They have dropped a biocide into the ocean that is killing my people."

She almost sat up in shock but the safety straps prevented her. "They're monsters. Why would they do something like that? The Fila are no threat to them."

When Quinn said nothing she was forced to come to the obvious conclusion by herself: the Fila were no threat to the Scythians by themselves but they'd helped the humans—the species who was competing for land to live on and planetary resources, and who had gone to the Galactic Assembly for military support in defense of their occupation.

"We have to stop them," she said.

"I fear it's already too late. The biocide is spreading faster than my people can escape it. Eventually it will disperse throughout all of Concordia's oceans and that will be the end."

"Oh, Quinn." A lump formed in her throat. She didn't know what to say.

"The biocide has been deposited on the land too. Its dispersal out of water is slower, but within a few months all of Concordia will be a barren wasteland. The planet will not support life again for perhaps hundreds of thousands of years, if ever."

"Let's get them! I know it's hopeless, but let's do all the damage we can."

"Yes. Let us do that."

Acceleration hit her like a hammer, driving the tears in her eyes down the sides of her face and into her hair. She was crying for the Fila, crying for the people of Concordia, and for Piddle and Puddle, whose home had been obliterated and would never grow again, thanks to the Scythians' desecration of the planet.

On the interface, Concordia was growing visibly larger, such was the speed of their approach. She still could not make out the Scythian ships, but the sparks of pulse fire were more noticeable.

The Scythians would not have a visual on the *Opportunity* yet either, but they had to know she was coming.

"We will be within firing range soon," said Quinn.

"At this distance?" She had to fight to speak due to the crushing pressure on her throat.

"Space battles are conducted at wider distances than you might imagine."

Concordia had grown from the size of a pea to a marble.

"You have been a good friend, Wilder."

"You too, Quinn. You too."

She wished she had had another moment with Piddle and Puddle, to hug them one last time. She wished she could say goodbye to Tycho and Stephie and Jamie Bond and everyone else she knew. She wanted to tell Kes how much he'd helped her with his support and to thank him. She even wanted to make amends with Cherry.

But there was no time left. No time left for anything. She was only seventeen. She had barely begun to live. It wasn't fair.

A brilliant streak of light flew across the screen, out from the *Opportunity*.

"That was from us, right?" she asked. "I hope it blows a Scythian ship to pieces."

"No, it was not us. We haven't fired yet. We are only now within range."

She blinked. "If it wasn't us, who was it?"

"I am trying to discover that."

The image on the screen switched. She saw the system's star again, brilliant white-yellow. "That's where the pulse came from? The sun?"

"Not quite. Please wait a moment."

As she watched the star, another source of light appeared next to it, more brilliant than any star in the background. The spot of light grew gradually larger and brighter. It was moving toward the *Opportunity*. Several minutes passed. The light became too bright to look at. She narrowed her eyes to slits and saw the bolt narrowly pass by, heading onward to Concordia.

"Is it a Scythian weapon?" Perhaps the aliens had a device that would destroy life on the planet even faster than their biocide.

A frustrating silence dragged out. The pressure on her eased. The *Opportunity* was slowing down, and she had no idea why. "Is anyone going to tell me what's happening?!"

"It is not a Scythian weapon. It is aimed at the Scythian ships, and it is destroying them."

"It is? Let me see!"

The scene on the interface switched once more. Concordia was bigger than ever. The bolt that had passed them by was growing smaller as it sped away, drawing closer to its target.

"What is it?" she asked. "And who's firing? You must have some idea."

"We have sent out a hail, but the distances involved mean we have to wait for the reply."

"You really don't know who it might be?"

"My best guess is that it is the Parvus."

"*The Parvus?*"

At first the name made no sense, but then she remembered the headline in the newsfeed the evening she'd had her accident with the a-grav machine. A delegation of Parvus was arriving, the headline had said, and she'd been reminded of Kes receiving the notification the day before. She had asked Cherry about them but at the time she'd been too busy to talk.

"Who are the Parvus?" she asked. "And what are they doing here?"

"The Parvus are members of the Galactic Assembly, and it looks as though they've saved your colony."

Forty-One

Cherry thought she was dreaming. One of the largest Scythian ships was a ball of pale fire. What had happened? All the missiles had been launched, and even a direct hit from several pulse emitters should not have been able to take out one of the huge spiked ships.

"Did you see that?" Costello asked. "What was it?"

"I didn't," she replied. "I was looking at another screen." Minotaur was rubble, and they had just lost Medusa too. Her mountaintop site was now a massive, smoking crater. The Scythians were continuing to try to pound the colony into dust, despite the fact they had already ensured its eventual destruction with their biocide.

"The biggest pulse I ever saw arrived from out of nowhere and hit the Scythian ship."

"From out of nowhere?" She was utterly confused. How could another pulse emitter be firing at the Scythians? It was impossible for anyone to have built another one in secret. Wilder working on an a-grav machine was one thing, but building something like an emitter, with all the specialized parts and materials needed, would require a miracle.

The Scythian firing was slowing down. They also seemed confused by this unexpected—and, to them, devastating—event.

She comm'd Aubriot.

"What's going on?" he asked. "You didn't tell me you had another pulse emitter up your sleeve."

"I don't. I'm as much in the dark as everyone else. But while we have this advantage, don't let up. If you can squeeze any more fire out of your emitters do it. Let's kick them while they're down."

Long minutes dragged out. The Scythians continued to concentrate their attack on Cerberus and Hydra, the only remaining military sites. Cerberus and Hydra continued to fight back.

Then another mysterious pulse arrived, and this time she saw it. The screen momentarily whited out. When the image returned it showed the remaining spiked Scythian ship was no more.

"It is the Parvus," Elliot said. "We received a message from Quinn, aboard the *Opportunity*. The Parvus have been harvesting energy from this system's star. They have technology that allows them to do this, and then they can concentrate the energy within a field and direct it toward a distant object. They have passed on an apology that the process takes so long, but they hope their intention is well received."

"Oh, it's well received," said Cherry. "It's very well received."

The remaining Scythian ships were moving. They were turning and leaving. They'd given up.

Cherry said, "Please tell the Parvus..." But Kes touched her arm and pointed at the transparent wall. Elliot had ceased the Fila's customary swirling movement. His body hung motionless in the water. The biocide had reached him.

He was dead.

Forty-Two

Kes wandered through the rubble that was all that remained of Oceanside. The sun was rising, and the the destroyed buildings still smoked with heat. He could feel it through the soles of his shoes. Cherry had wanted to make him wear a gas mask before going out. No one knew exactly where the biocide containers had landed or how far or fast the poison would spread.

He didn't care. What did it matter if he died now or later? They were all going to die eventually, along with the rest of life on Concordia. The Scythians had already done the job of killing everyone. It was only going to happen slower than anticipated.

All he wanted to do was find Isobel and Miki. He dared not imagine they might still be alive, but he longed to see their faces one more time. He wanted to touch them, to hold them, and to ask their forgiveness. If he could only do that, perhaps he could die in peace.

The problem was, the place was unrecognizable. He didn't know where he was. The Scythian blast had flattened the houses and obliterated the roads. Fires still burned. More than once, he had come across human remains. After ascertaining quickly that they did not belong to his wife or child he would skirt around them, trying to avoid looking at them any further. Others were looking for loved ones too.

He stopped, put his hands on his hips, and tried to get his bearings. In the distance was a freeway running through an untouched portion of the city's outskirts. From the appearance of the surrounding landscape it was the road from Annwn. It would have been the route he traveled on to the Leader's bunker.

He took a long moment to mentally reconstruct the street system as it had been, leading out from the arterial road. He pointed to where he guessed the rows of houses had been.

"One, two, three," he muttered. Three exits, and then the fourth had been the street where Isobel's sister, Nancy, had lived. When he'd decided on a rough area in which to search, he strode toward it, stepping over the rubble-strewn ground.

He was going so fast he almost didn't see a body until he was on top of it. A man lay face downward, his shoes some distance away and his back burned.

Swallowing his horror and distress, Kes took a wide detour before re-orienting himself. He arrived at the approximate location of Nancy's street sweaty and shaking, either with exertion or anguish. Perhaps both.

"Isobel!"

His voice was loud in the silent devastation.

"Miki! Sweetheart, can you hear me? Isobel? Miki!"

A groan sounded. His heart leapt and he raced toward the origin of the noise. But before he reached the person his heart sank.

It was a man, lying on his back, still alive. "Help me."

The man's hair was gone. Singed away, and his skin bore burn marks. His clothes were burned too, but by some miracle he hadn't caught entirely on fire.

"Can you stand?" Kes asked. "Try. I'll help you." He wasn't sure where to touch the man without hurting him.

The man slowly managed to sit up. He grabbed Kes's forearm. "Thank you. Thank you for stopping."

"Medics are coming out soon. They're trying to find gas masks first."

"Gas masks? What do they need those for?"

He didn't know. Of course he didn't. Only the people in the Leader's bunker knew what had happened, what the Scythians had done, and what Concordia could expect.

"Someone will explain it to you later," Kes replied. "Can you walk? I can help, but I don't know where to touch you. I don't want to hurt you."

"I can't feel anything. I don't think you can hurt me."

But when Kes tried to help him to his feet, his legs were too injured to support his weight.

"The medics will be coming soon," Kes repeated, though he wondered what was the point. Yet he didn't want to tell the man the truth of the situation.

"Were you looking for someone?" asked the man. "I heard you shout a name."

"I was looking for my wife and my little girl."

"You carry on. I'll be all right here. I feel better now I know help is coming."

When Kes hesitated the man urged him again.

"Okay, but I'll be back to check on you."

He resumed his search, calling Isobel's name and Miki's over and over and wandering farther and farther until he had entirely left his original search area. A deep sorrow settled over him and obliterated his faint hope.

A comm arrived from Cherry. "Any luck?"

"I found a survivor, but not Isobel or Miki. Are the medics on their way?"

"We're working on it. Kes, I'm sorry. Are you going to carry on searching?"

"I have to find them."

"I understand. I hope you do. I wanted to let you know something. You remember that strange arrival that claimed it was a Guardian?"

"The one that seemed to be Faina? Yes, I remember."

"It broke out of prison during the attack. I found out a moment ago."

"Huh, really? That seems to be the least of our worries right now."

"Yes, but I thought it was worth mentioning to you. The prison isn't far from the area you're searching, though it escaped the worst of the blast. If the thing is a Guardian it's odd that it would take advantage of the chaos to escape. The Guardians were programmed to help us."

"Perhaps Faina thought the best way she could help us was by escaping."

"Hmm. Maybe you're right," Cherry said. "Anyway, as you say, we have worse things to worry about. There must be plenty of people trapped in the rubble. We'll have to find them and get them out."

"And before the biocide arrives. The situation is hopeless, but I guess we have to keep going."

"We have to. What other choice is there?" Cherry was gone.

He sat down on a stone. "Isobel!" he called, more out of misery than in anticipation of an answer.

But then he heard a reply. Or had he imagined it?

"Isobel!"

There it was again. A faint cry. He couldn't make out what the speaker had said, but he knew the direction the response had come from. He raced toward it, scrambling over hot rubble.

"Isobel!"

"Here! We're over here!"

He stopped. The voice replying to him was not his wife's. He did recognize it, however. It was Nancy.

He continued on. The sound of Nancy's voice had come from a demolished house, similar to all the other demolished houses. If it had been her house, he would never have been able to guess.

He reached the remains, a pile of smoldering building fragments.

He saw her immediately. A face in one of the gaps, close to the ground. He ran to her and knelt down. "Nancy?"

He'd never been so pleased to see his sister-in-law in all his life. "Where are Isobel and Miki?"

He held his breath, desperate and also terrified to hear her answer.

"They're okay, Kes." Nancy reached out through the gap. He gripped her hand tightly. "Or, Miki is. I think Isobel might have a broken leg. When the house came down—"

"Kes! Is that really him?" It was Isobel.

"Yes, it is," Nancy replied. "But don't move. You..." She sighed in frustration. "You're going to hurt yourself."

Isobel appeared at the gap beside her sister. She looked in pain but her face was shining. "I knew you would come. Miki! Miki! Daddy's here. Come and see Daddy."

"Izzy, it's so good to see you," said Kes. "Is the baby okay?"

"She's fine. Kicking like crazy."

Soon, Nancy was holding up his little girl and Kes could touch his wife and child.

They were alive.

Miraculously, blissfully alive.

How much longer did they all have before the biocide reached them? He didn't know. He put the thought out of his mind. For now, they were together.

It was more than he had hoped.

The story of Space Colony One continues in...

FINAL ONSLAUGHT

Sign up to my science fiction reader group for a free ecopy of *Night of Flames*, the prequel to *Space Colony One*, more free books, discounts on new releases, Review Crew invitations and other interesting stuff:

https://jjgreenauthor.com/free-books/

FINAL ONSLAUGHT

One

Cherry sat at the ocean's edge and wept. The waves were sluggish as they hit the shore, heavy with the bodies of dead and rotting Fila. The stench was overwhelming, indescribable. As far as the eye could see, Fila corpses floated on the water's surface, swollen by the gases of decay. The unique patterning of each body's skin was defiled by corruption, and the tentacle limbs hung listless, moved only by the lethargic ocean current.

It was her fault.

Millions, possibly billions, of Fila had died and were still dying due to her rash, unilateral decision to defy the Scythians. If she had only stalled for more time or even agreed to their demand to enslave the human colony so the Scythians could return to their home planet, the Fila would not have died.

The colony could have reneged on the deal. It could have turned on the Scythians who arrived. Or, because the arrivals would have been dependent on the humans for survival, the colonists could have held them hostage and threatened to murder them if not left in peace.

So many possibilities had been open to her, but she'd made a snap, rash decision, responding in fury after the Scythians had blasted apart half of Oceanside without provocation.

She had told Meredith that Ethan would have been ashamed of her for being willing to capitulate, but it was she herself who should be ashamed. Ethan would not have been so headstrong or reckless. He would have kept his emotions in check.

He would not have risked all in a moment of rage and defiance.

She had taken that risk without a second thought, not even considering the impact her decision could have on those only tangentially involved in the fight for Concordia. Now she had the blood of an entire population of intelligent beings on her hands. Was there ever such a mass murderer in the history of the human race? She didn't think so. It was an unprecedented genocide.

And there was more death to come. The Scythians' biocide continued to spread. The Fila in the oceans were helpless against it. The deadly chemical traveled far and wide on water currents. The Fila could not leave the water and live. On land, the spread was slower but no less lethal. Oceanside had been abandoned six days ago immediately after the attack. One of the Scythians' biocide canisters had landed there and killed hundreds of survivors of the battle.

A toxic area had been identified near Annwn too. The evacuation of that small city had turned into a rout. Smaller settlements near and in the mountains had not been touched by the deadly poison so far, but it was only a matter of time before it reached them. At some unknown point in the future, the biocide would have completed its task. No living thing would remain on Concordia. The planet would be a mausoleum, a ghastly memorial to the pride and malice of the Scythians.

Her guilt was an iron spike boring relentlessly into her chest. Yet the pain was well deserved, and for that reason she welcomed it. When the enormity of what she'd done had begun to sink in, she'd wanted to end it all, but then she'd realized the escape would be too easy. Now, she only flirted with death, tantalizing herself with the prospect of release, at the same time knowing that suffering was her only possible penance.

Over the quiet wash of the waves on the shore, she became aware of another sound. Footsteps trudged through the pebbles, growing louder. Someone was coming.

She didn't look around or bother to wipe the tears from her sodden face. The footsteps drew close and then stopped.

"Cherry." The voice was muffled. The person was speaking from inside a haz suit. Anyone who wanted to eke out their last few days, weeks, or months on Concordia before their inevitable death put on a haz suit before stepping outside. Cherry wasn't wearing one.

A hand touched her shoulder. The person had used her first name too. It was someone who knew her personally. She felt pressure and heard the movement of pebbles as the person squatted down.

"Cherry, it's dangerous to be this close to the ocean. The biocide could be carried to you in the spray from the waves. What are you doing here?"

When she didn't answer, he continued, "What am I saying? I know why you're here. Come on. Come with me. Let's get you inside."

Despite the muffling of the haz suit's helmet, she now recognized the voice. It belonged to Kes. It was naturally he who had come to find her. Wilder—who was no longer Cherry's friend anyway—was aboard the *Opportunity*, the single colonist safe from the biocide. Aubriot was the only other person who used her first name, and she had not seen him or heard from him since the attack. He could even be dead. She'd left messages on his comm but he hadn't answered.

"Cherry," said Kes, gently tugging at her arm.

She turned to face him. His blue eyes were all that was visible of his face through the visor of his helmet.

He had such kind eyes. "I know what you're thinking, and I know how you feel, but—"

She pulled her arm from his grip. "No, you don't. You really don't."

He sat down close beside her, the material of his haz suit pressing against her pants. "I was there too, remember? I was there in the bunker with you. And when you gave the order to retaliate, I said nothing. I did nothing to stop you. I thought Isobel and Miki and my unborn child were dead. I wanted revenge. I wanted every Scythian to be blasted out of the sky. None of us tried to stop you."

"Except Meredith."

"Meredith would have agreed to their terms, it's true, but she did nothing after the decision was taken from her and the battle started. We're all culpable. Not just you."

"I know what you're trying to do, Kes, but the responsibility is mine. I'm the one who gave the order. I'm the one who..." Her words sticking in her throat, she swept her arm wide, gesturing toward the thousands of rotting Fila floating on the waves.

"You didn't kill them. The Scythians did all this. Not you. No one guessed what they were capable of. No one thought their retaliation would be to wipe the planet of all life. No one imagined they would be so evil."

She heard his words but they made no impact on her feelings. His intent was kind but nothing anyone said could absolve her of her guilt. It was a plain, hard fact.

"Come back to the shelter with me," said Kes. "Quickly, before it's too late. If a single molecule of the biocide hits you it will run through you like a hot knife through butter. You won't stand a chance."

She didn't know what butter was and she didn't care if the biocide hit her, yet she did feel bad that her friend had come to find her despite the dangers.

"Cherry, please," he urged. "I should be in the lab working on developing a neutralizing agent for the biocide, not out here with you. Please come with me."

She relented. He was right. He should not be wasting his time on her. He was one of the few people who stood a chance of saving the remaining life on Concordia. After all she'd done, it would be wrong of her to add to the peril of the colony through her own selfish actions.

"Okay. I'll come." She tried to stand. Her legs were numb and stiff from sitting so long on the cold pebbles. He helped her up.

She turned her back on the seascape of decaying Fila and faced inland. Dusk was falling. Where had the time gone? She had wandered down to the shoreline this morning. Gray and pink clouds overspread the sky and the scrubby beach grass was turning monochrome in the fading light.

It was a regular scene, one of thousands she had witnessed in the years she'd lived on Concordia. Now the simple plant life and hidden coastal creatures of the landscape were on the brink of complete and final extinction.

With Kes supporting her by her arm, she tramped clumsily through the sliding pebbles. An autocar was parked on the road running parallel to the beach. They headed toward the vehicle. Warmth and feeling returned slowly to her legs but the terrible weight of guilt remained. The feeling would never dissipate. Not as long as she had breath in her body. But the way things were looking, that would not be for too long.

Two

The refuge was crowded. It was also shoddy. Hastily converted from storage warehouses into homes and workrooms, it was one of the few places known to be far from the effects of the biocide—for the time being. But it was plain to Kes, as he showered before returning to work, that the building skills of the Gens who had disembarked the *Nova* had not been passed on to many of their descendants.

There had been no need. By the time the current generation had been born, the colony had been established and extensive manufacturing processes were underway. The proportion of the population trained in practical skills like construction, plumbing, and electrical work had greatly diminished.

Twice, the original Gens had been forced to build underground shelters to protect themselves from Scythian attacks, and each time they had completed the tasks efficiently, effectively, and at a breathtaking pace. By contrast, the job of creating a safe haven for the people displaced from Oceanside and Annwn progressed slowly and with many errors.

The lab he had returned to after taking Cherry to his home, where Isobel could look after her, was barely functional. The electricity supply was erratic—though, to be fair, that was at least partly due to the fact that it relied on solar power from the plant in Suddene. The Fila's geothermal supply had, predictably, quickly died. The showerheads often spluttered and coughed due to air in the pipes, and the plasterboard separating the laboratory from the rest of the warehouse was flimsy and looked about to fall down at any moment.

Considering the lab was the place where the task of saving the colony from disaster was being undertaken, it was pretty poor effort on the part of whoever had built it.

He turned off the shower. His skin was covered in goosebumps from the cold water. Showering seemed a pointless precaution considering the biocide appeared to kill on contact. Cherry had been his canary all the way back to the shelter. If the biocide had reached them she would have died immediately. Nevertheless, it didn't hurt to be extra cautious, and, considering he'd instigated the protocol, he could hardly complain. Wearing haz suits with their powered air purifying respirators while outside and following rigorous hygiene protocols were essential if he and his colleagues were to survive working with the deadly biocide.

He quickly dried off with a towel and put on clean clothes and lab coat before entering the lab.

Tricia, a fellow scientist, looked up. "You're back. Did you find the General?"

"I did. She was at the beach. I'm sorry I had to leave, but I had to go and find her. I couldn't think of anything else after I heard she'd gone missing."

"No problem. We all have people we're worried about. She was at the beach, though? Was she on a suicide mission?"

"What do *you* think?"

Tricia turned away, troubled, and returned to her work.

Kes was troubled by Cherry's behavior too, but he'd done all he could for now. Isobel would look after his friend. He had to concentrate on discovering the chemical makeup of the Scythian's biocide. Then he and his team could work on developing something to neutralize it. They were in a race against time. Not only was the colony facing the inexorable spread of the poison across the land, it was also vulnerable every time it rained. There was a chance the biocide might enter the water cycle, evaporating into the atmosphere with the ocean water, forming clouds, and then later falling over land.

They were lucky it was the dry season on Lyonesse. On Suddene, the climate was dry all year round, and as far as anyone knew only two of the enemy's canisters had landed there. The few inhabitants of the small continent were likely to be the last to fall to the Scythians' deadly chemical. Whether or not that would be a good thing, he did not know.

He returned to his chromatography test, mentally shutting out the hum of quiet conversation and movements of scientists in the cramped space. Setting up the test had taken him back to his college days as an undergraduate in biochemistry. Only then he hadn't been dealing with a substance that could wipe out the last outpost of human civilization.

A small team of intrepid, courageous lab technicians in haz suits had harvested several tissue samples from a dead Fila, sealed them in water-tight and airtight boxes, and brought them to the laboratory. The techs had taken a huge risk. No one had known if the biocide would eat through the tough, inert material of the boxes, but, thankfully, it hadn't. Now it was up to the colony's biologists and chemists to find out what was in it.

It was perfectly possible that chemical's structure altered as it destroyed living tissue. That would make the challenge exponentially harder. It was also possible that the biocide broke down to harmless constituents as soon as it ran out of tissue to feed its processes.

In fact, all kinds of impossible-to-surmount obstacles might stand in their way, but what else could they do except try? It beat sitting around waiting to die.

The difficulty in identifying the biocide lay in determining what was a constituent of Fila flesh and what was the lethal chemical. Fortunately, he and the other xenobiologists had already undertaken studies of Fila morphology. Donating specimens for study had not presented a problem to a species that could quickly regenerate all parts of their bodies except any of their three brains. Consequently, the scientists had some idea of what they should expect to find in the tissue samples, but the study of the species was nowhere near complete. Many substances making up Fila anatomy and metabolism were unknown to human science. It wasn't possible to be certain which chemicals were the murder victim's and which were the poison.

The gas chromatography equipment stood inside a large transparent box. On one side of the box were two holes at arm height opening into long, thick gloves. He pushed his arms into the gloves to resume his test. He hadn't been working for longer than five minutes, however, when he received a comm from Meredith.

"Hi," he replied, not pausing in what he was doing.

"Did you find her?"

He'd forgotten to tell the Leader that Cherry was back at the shelter.

"Yes, I did. Sorry, I—"

"How is she?"

"Not good."

"I thought you might say that."

"She blames herself." This comment met with silence. Perhaps Meredith blamed Cherry too. He hadn't spoken to the Leader much since the attack. There simply hadn't been time to sit down and calmly analyze what had happened. The priority had been, and remained, to save as many lives as possible.

"I hope she can get over it," Meredith said eventually. "There's no point in apportioning blame now."

That was certainly something they could agree on. "Heard anything from the Assembly?"

"That was the other reason I wanted to speak to you. The Fila's distress call arrived and the Assembly has replied using the same method. Now all the Fila comm stations have been abandoned, Quinn relayed the reply from the *Opportunity*. I'm not sure how the Assembly can send information so fast through space, but I'm glad it can. Unfortunately, the ship of the member closest to us will take eighteen days to get here. The Fila seeding ship is on the other side of the galaxy."

"Even if the seeding ship was in orbit it wouldn't be much help." He vividly recalled the Fila vessel he'd briefly visited in order to embark on his mission to the Galactic Assembly. The ship had been large, but not anywhere near large enough to accommodate even a small segment of Concordia's human population. More importantly, it was full of water and Fila.

"I'll take your word for it," Meredith said. "But perhaps this other ship may be able to save some colonists."

"Do you know which species the ship belongs to?"

"It's named in the message but the translation system couldn't handle the word."

He wondered whose it was. He'd assigned the Assembly member species English names, but he hadn't gotten around to informing the Fila of them. Now it was too late. The situation in their water world was utterly chaotic as far as anyone could tell. Some of the creatures survived, mainly in freshwater lakes and in rivers, but death was moving closer, and much faster for the aquatic aliens than for the humans. The worst thing was, there was nothing the colonists could do to help.

"You realize that even if all the Assembly members' ships turned up tomorrow, their efforts might be useless?" He didn't want to crush the Leader's hopes, but it was a fact that had to be faced.

"I do. As long as the biocide is ravaging the planet, it could be too risky for them to send shuttles down."

"Exactly. The biocide doesn't only destroy whatever living tissue it touches, it uses the chemicals of the victims' bodies to replicate itself. A molecule of that stuff on the exterior of a shuttle could end up wiping out an entire ship's crew. I wouldn't blame any would-be rescuer who decided not to take the chance."

"Me neither, I guess. Still, I thought it was worth letting you know."

"I appreciate it," said Kes. "Now, if you'll excuse me..."

"Yes, you have a lot of work to do. I hope you find something soon."

"Me too. Before you go, have you heard anything from Wilder?"

"I try to keep her up to date on the situation when I can."

"How's she doing?" asked Kes.

"Okay, I think. Considering her age. She has Quinn and the other Fila crew on the *Opportunity* to talk to."

"She's tough. As long as her food lasts, she'll be okay."

"I hope it lasts as long as it takes for the Assembly member's ship to arrive. That way, at least one of us will survive."

"The last living colonist from Concordia? I don't know if I would like to be that person."

"Let's hope it doesn't come to that. With luck your team will develop a neutralizer in time and everything will be okay."

"We'll do our best. The alternative outcome is a wonderful motivator."

Meredith closed the comm.

So much had been left unsaid. Realistically, in the short time available there was little chance the scientists could isolate the biocide and develop a neutralizing chemical. Even in ideal conditions, the task would take months. According to the satellite images of the devastation the poison was wreaking across landmasses, the colony had only a few weeks.

What was more, tens of thousands of colonists remained alive. The luckiest were living on dry Suddene, their lives disrupted but safe for the moment. Nearly everyone else resided in makeshift shelters. The worst off were camping out in the countryside in areas as yet untouched by the biocide.

The Assembly could send a dozen ships and still not have room for everyone, assuming the rescuers took the risk of sending shuttles down to the poisoned planet. The Parvus's ship, which had hung around since the Scythian attack, could not accommodate humans at all.

If it came to facing the decision of who would be saved and who would die, how would they choose?

Three

Wilder opened the pouch she'd made from a knotted sweater and peeked inside. Piddle and Puddle were sound asleep, curled up together, their arms wrapped around each other. They floated gently inside the pouch, which, for once, was clean. The little creatures seemed to have finally become accustomed to micro-g. They hadn't thrown up for three or four days. Even better, they also appeared to understand the basics of toilet training at last. They had a favorite corner where they did their business. Though, without the benefit of planetary gravity, Wilder was forced to keep a close eye on her pets and clean up their messes quickly if she didn't want to encounter unsavory surprises later on.

Was what she was about to propose to Quinn fair on her little friends? Maybe not. The two of them could live for months on the *Opportunity* on her supply of food. Perhaps even years. She was sure Quinn could devise a way to feed them, or she could simply leave the food cupboard open and Piddle and Puddle could help themselves.

But then what? Would any Galactic Assembly member arriving to rescue refugees bother with two small, unintelligent life forms? It was unlikely, and the Fila could not offer them a home in an aquatic environment.

She could not avoid the fact that the only possible hope for her small friends was if they stuck with her. Her mind made up, she pushed off with her feet and floated out into the operations room where Quinn and his fellow crew members worked behind a transparent wall.

She held up her palms and braced against the gentle impact as she reached her destination.

"Quinn," she said firmly. She would have to be assertive in order to get him to agree to her request.

"Yes, Wilder?"

"I've decided I'm going to go down to the surface."

"You want to return to Concordia?"

She frowned. Quinn was not usually this stupid. But then again, the flat, emotionless monotone the translation equipment supplied made it hard to tell the intent behind his reply. Perhaps he was only surprised. That would be understandable.

"I've made up my mind," she said. "I'm no use to anyone while I'm up here. I'm not very good with biology or chemistry—physics and engineering are more my things—but what little help I can offer is useless while I'm in orbit kilometers above the planet. I need to be down there, and the sooner the better. I'll go to a shuttle now and take Piddle and Puddle with me. So if you wouldn't mind, please transport me to the surface. I think if I go wherever Kes is, that would be best."

"No."

She was so taken aback at the Fila's blunt, unequivocal refusal, she was lost for words. Then she got angry. Her hands curled into fists. "I wasn't asking your permission. I'm *telling* you I'm going down there. I insist you transport me in a shuttle."

"That will not happen."

"You have zero jurisdiction over me, Quinn. And this isn't a debate. You have to do what I say."

He gave no immediate reply. The pause dragged out. She grew angrier. There was nothing she hated more than being told what she could and couldn't do.

"Wilder," Quinn said suddenly, "my people are dying."

Her ire flooded out of her. Her grip on the handhold relaxed and she floated free, slumping in midair. "I know. I'm sorry."

"Humans will begin to die in great numbers soon, too. If you go down there you will be one of them."

All the shock, pain, and fear she had endured over the last few days welled up and spilled out. For several moments she couldn't speak. It became clear that her determination to return to Concordia had been a way for her to distract herself from the terrible situation the Scythians had created. She wiped her eyes and nose with her sleeve. "I'll die up here. It'll just take longer."

The prospect of starving to death aboard the *Opportunity* while listening to reports of the mounting death toll had haunted her ever since she'd heard the news of the biocide. It hadn't taken her long to figure out what it meant for her personally.

"Perhaps you will not," said Quinn. "I have thought of another possibility."

"What other possibility?"

"The *Opportunity's* fuel cells are full. We could leave this system and go somewhere else. I have pondered over this for some time. I had hoped that the situation on Concordia might improve, but it seems that all is lost. My people cannot escape the poison spreading throughout the planet's water reserves. I believe their total destruction is inevitable."

She put a hand on the see-through wall. As always, Quinn's emotion was impossible to tell, but her Fila friend had to be experiencing deep sorrow and grief.

On the other side of the wall, Quinn raised a tentacle and placed it in the same place as her hand. The two friends hung there, one suspended in air, the other suspended in water, in silence.

"Where would we go?" She asked at last, not at all sure she wanted to go anywhere.

"That question is difficult to answer. We would need to find a planet with similar gravity to Concordia's, and that contains landmasses and water. It would also need to offer plant life edible for humans."

"And for Fila. You all need to eat too."

"We rarely encounter any problems with finding edible organisms on new planets."

"Huh, I wish the same were true for humans." A modest range of Concordian plants and small creatures were eaten on the colony, but it had taken scientists decades to discover them and prove their safety. Then she realized what he was saying. "Wait. You mean it would be easier for you to find somewhere to go than me, right? I don't want you guys sacrificing yourselves so I can live. Honestly, though it feels weird to be saying it, I'm not sure I even want to live. What would be the point? I mean, I like you, Quinn, and all the Fila I meet, but I don't know if I want to live a life where I would never see my own kind ever again."

"Humans colonized Concordia from another planet. We could take you there if you know the coordinates."

"I don't, though they must be somewhere in the data files. But Earth has to be many light years from here. The Guardians took twenty years or longer to come to Concordia, and their ship was way faster than the *Nova*. I'll run out of food long before we arrive."

"Perhaps the survivors of the Scythian attack could supply you with provisions for the journey."

"I don't want to take food from them. They have it bad enough down there as it is. And there's also the risk of the biocide traveling up here on the shuttle. When I said I wanted to go down to the surface I was planning on a one-way trip."

They pondered the problem some more.

"I thought of another reason I can't go to Earth," said Wilder after a while. "The Guardians told us the human population had been decimated by a plague. Assuming they were telling the truth, I would be infected by the disease if I went there. It would be the same result as if I stayed here." She sighed. "To be honest, it makes me feel sick to even be thinking about how *I'm* going to survive when every single other human being on Concordia will probably die. What a weird fluke it was that I happened to be up here when it all kicked off, right?

"You know, when I was a kid, I read stories about ancient ships that sailed on oceans before air or space travel were invented. Sometimes there would be a storm and the ship would sink or break up on rocks, and only a few people would survive. The lucky ones. Only they weren't so lucky because they would end up clinging to wreckage or marooned on tiny islands in the middle of nowhere. They had no food and no water, no shelter or way of staying warm, and they would die too, like the people who drowned when the ship went down. The only difference was they died slower and more painfully."

She blinked to clear her vision. "I got the a-grav working. Did you know? Yesterday. I finally got the damned machine to work. But no one will know now. It won't make any difference to anyone." She studied the complex patterning of Quinn's skin and then turned her gaze to the three other Fila in the operations room. They did not have English names but she had learned to recognize their patterning too. "I know what you should do. You should find a planet where there's water so you can all survive. Your seeding ship will come for you eventually, or perhaps an Assembly member will pick you up. I'd appreciate it if you could find somewhere Piddle and Puddle can live too. I know that's a big ask but I'm asking it. Don't try to save me, though. All things considered, I'd rather not be saved. When the time's right, I'll go out the airlock."

Not wanting to hear his response, she quickly pushed herself away from the operations room wall and returned to the living quarters. He could still talk to her in there if he wanted, via the ship's comm, but she hoped he would understand from her behavior that she didn't want to discuss her choice and that he would respect that.

He did.

Four

Cherry watched as heavily pregnant Isobel soothed her little girl to sleep. Mother and daughter lay together on the double mattress that took up most of the floor space in the little family's allotted section. Isobel gently stroked Miki's red-black hair as her eyes slowly closed. The child's discarded interface lay beside her. One of Isobel's legs was in a cast.

Cherry didn't like to watch Kes's wife perform her motherly duties, but there was nothing she could do. Only thin curtains separated the sections in the warehouse, providing a modicum of privacy. Unless she faced a curtain or looked upward there was nowhere else to look. The single folk were even worse off, sharing one large space filled with narrow cots.

That was where she should be. That was where she'd slept after helping to organize the search for trapped colonists, and then later the evacuation of Oceanside. That was where she would have gone if Kes hadn't made her promise to stay in his and Isobel's makeshift room.

She was sure Isobel didn't want her here. Who would want to share a tiny living space with a suicidal, fatally incompetent ex-General? Isobel already had enough on her plate trying to keep a toddler entertained without any toys or room to run around. Isobel also looked as though she was about to pop. What a time to be expecting a baby.

A shout from an excited child broke through the general hubbub and echoed around the warehouse. Miki's eyes flew open.

"Shhhh," said Isobel. "Shhhh. It's okay."

Miki's eyes closed again. Isobel continued to stroke the little girl's hair until she was breathing heavily and sound asleep. Isobel caught Cherry's gaze and smiled. Slowly and carefully, she pushed herself to an upright position and then eased herself along the mattress until she perched on the end.

Cherry was sitting in a low camping chair, her knees drawn up, feeling awkward. She didn't know what Kes had told Isobel in their hasty conversation, conducted in low voices, when he'd taken her to his wife. But whether he'd filled Isobel in on the details or not, it was pretty obvious to anyone the state she was in.

"Are you hungry?" Isobel asked.

Cherry shook her head.

"Thirsty?"

"I should be the one helping you, not the other way around. And shouldn't we be whispering?" She nodded at the sleeping girl.

"Don't worry. Once she's asleep she can sleep through a hurricane. Which is going to be handy now we're living here."

The noise in the warehouse was indeed very loud. It wasn't much quieter at night, especially not in the families' section, where there were many children of around Miki's age.

"Can I get something for you?" asked Cherry.

"I'm fine. A few of the moms and dads organized a meal roster. Someone will bring something over in a little while."

"Okay."

The awkwardness stretched out with no prospect of coming to an end. How long would Kes expect her to stay here? And where would she sleep? There was a space between the mattress and the curtain where she would fit, but lying next to Kes and his wife and child would be a whole new level of uncomfortable that had nothing to do with the hard floor.

"I guess this must feel familiar to you," said Isobel.

"Huh? What do you mean?" Cherry wasn't generally in the habit of consigning entire populations of intelligent beings to death.

"I mean living conditions must have been something like this in the early days of the colony, before you built the first settlement."

"Oh! No. Not really. Well, a group of Gens and Woken did sleep in a big barn on the first night when the sluglimpets attacked. But I don't think anyone did after that. Everyone slept on the *Nova* until the first dorms were ready."

"Right. The First Night Attack. I remember studying it at school. Were you there?"

"I wasn't, thank the stars. Only a couple hundred Gens were picked to spend the first night on the planet. I wasn't one of them. I didn't get to go down to the surface until the Naming Ceremony."

"That must have been an amazing experience after spending all your life aboard the *Nova Fortuna*."

"Yeah, it was. Feels like a long time ago now."

"It was a long time ago," said Isobel, but then she corrected herself. "Except not so long ago from your perspective."

"No, not so long." Cherry tried to figure it out. She'd returned from the mission to the Galactic Assembly six years ago. Prior to her leaving, the colony had only just brought in its first major harvest. Was it only such a short time since she'd disembarked the *Nova*? So much had happened, it felt like a lifetime. For most of the colony it *had* been a lifetime or two.

How many Concordians now living had been born on the colony ship? It had to be a small proportion of the population. Most had grown up planetside and had never even been aboard a starship. Life on the surface was all they knew. And now, soon, it would be all they would ever have known.

"It's hard," said Isobel, "but I'm sure things will get back to normal soon."

Cherry raised her eyebrows. "I beg your pardon?"

"Our house in Annwn is still there, I think. The biocide won't damage it. As soon as Kes figures out a neutralizing agent, they'll clean all the biocide away and we can move back. I'm hoping he can do it before the baby comes. I don't fancy the idea of giving birth here."

Cherry blinked. "Are you sure Kes will be able to do it? Is that what he told you?"

"He hasn't said anything except that he's working on it, but I know he will. He's so smart."

"He is smart. I hope you're right." She wasn't sure if Isobel was ill-informed about the true situation or if she was only hormonal and slightly deluded. Either way, setting her right about the danger she, her child, her unborn baby, and everyone else on Concordia was in wouldn't benefit anyone.

Cherry had a sudden urge to speak to Aubriot. She felt in need of some callous, sour realism. And it wasn't only Isobel's naive optimism that was bothering her, the entire homely set-up put her on edge. In her current state it was more than she could bear. She didn't know why exactly, but being around families always made her uncomfortable. Perhaps it was only that she hadn't grown up in a family herself. Many Gens had taken to living in families with ease but some hadn't, and she fell into the latter group. She had no desire for children. Even the idea of holding a baby seriously alarmed her. "I need to go out for a little bit."

"Oh, no. You mustn't! You have to stay here. Kes said—"

"I'm not going outside, just for a little stroll around the warehouse. I have to stretch my legs." Cherry stood up.

"But—"

"I'll be fine." Cherry touched Isobel's shoulder as she stepped around her. "I'll be back soon."

There wasn't a lot someone in Isobel's position could do to stop her, and she wouldn't want to leave Miki alone. Cherry pulled the curtain aside and walked out into the narrow corridor between the two rows of family rooms. She comm'd the warehouse coordinator and asked to be connected to the countrywide network. Then she comm'd Aubriot.

"Yeah?"

His dour tone made her question her desire to talk to him. "You're alive, then."

"Seems so."

She was about to ask why he hadn't replied to her messages, but she changed her mind. What was the point? If he'd wanted to speak to her, he would have. "Are you okay? Were you injured during the attack? Where are you?"

"I wasn't injured. I'm still at Cerberus. Helping with the cleanup. You?"

"An evacuation site outside Oceanside. You should come here. I gave orders for everyone to withdraw to the east coast. This is the largest habitable area."

"Can't."

"What? Why?"

"We're cut off. The biocide that landed outside Annwn has spread across the countryside. Can't go over it, can't go under it, can't go around it, and we sure as hell ain't going through it."

"*Shit.*"

"Funny, that's exactly what I thought."

"Aubriot..." All her terrible guilt and despair welled up again.

"What?"

When she didn't answer, he said, "Don't feel sorry for me. We're all in the same boat, right?"

"What are you going to do?"

"Carry on clearing up what's left of Cerberus. Those bastards might change their minds and come back to finish us off the fast way. We need to be ready if they do."

"That makes sense."

"Keeps us busy."

She had a vision of the biocide creeping nearer and nearer to Cerberus, cutting a swathe of destruction. What would happen when it reached the men and women stationed there? Would the poison cross the inanimate infrastructure of the silo somehow, carried on microorganisms floating in the air? Or would the people at Cerberus be protected by their position underground in chambers of metal and stone, and eventually starve to death?

"Cherry," Aubriot said.

"What?"

"How are you doing?"

She was so taken aback by the gesture of care, she repeated herself. "What?"

"You know, it's not your fault."

"That's what people keep telling me."

"If you hadn't given the order to fire back, I would have. And the officers would have obeyed me."

"I don't think so, but maybe. It doesn't matter. Might-have-beens won't change what I did."

"You're getting mixed up. What's happening is just a slow version of what would have happened anyway, because we refused to enslave ourselves to murderers. No one wanted that life."

"Some might have preferred it to the alternative." She remembered Meredith's decision to do exactly that, before Cherry took the decision out of her hands. "Even if you're right, the Fila wouldn't have died. They're entirely innocent."

"No, they're not. They picked their side when they chose to help us. They're not stupid. They knew exactly what they were doing and the risk they were taking. They were poking the wasps' nest and they knew it. You can't take responsibility for their actions or the repercussion they've suffered."

She was silent. A couple of young kids came racing down the space between the curtained cubicles.

Aubriot said, "Hey, I heard one of the Guardians survived the destruction of the *Mistral* and had come back. Is it true?"

Faina! Or at least that was what the thing had implied it was. She had forgotten all about the supposed Guardian. "Yes, it's true. Kind of. Something that looked like an escape pod was found crash-landed in the wildlands over the mountains. A few weeks later something else turned up in Annwn. It looks like a burned Guardian. What it really is, I don't know for sure. I had it locked up in Oceanside jail but it escaped."

"Good idea locking it up. That's exactly what I would have done. Do you know where it is now?"

"I don't. To be honest, I'd forgotten about it, what with everything else going on."

"Ah well. As long as it stays the hell away from me I don't care where it goes."

"Funnily enough. A Guardian is about the only thing that could cross the dead zone between Cerberus and Oceanside right now, but I doubt it's going to come for you."

"I wonder what it's doing," said Aubriot. "Their mantra was to save the colony at all costs, right? Maybe that's why it escaped. It saw the attack and its programming kicked in and forced it to break out. Disobeying orders for the greater good."

"Yeah, maybe. And we know how well that turned out last time, don't we?"

"You're telling me?"

"You know, you've given me an idea," Cherry said. "Something for me to do. I have to go now. Take care, Aubriot. I know we've had our ups and downs, but you mean a lot to me." The words were out before she even knew what she was about to say, but as she spoke she realized what she was saying was true. She *did* care about the arrogant, oftentimes unbearable asshole.

He coughed. An awkward beat of silence followed. "Yeah. You too." He cut the comm.

A new sense of purpose coursed through her veins. She would find the escapee and put an end to it once and for all, if she could. The thing looked especially difficult to destroy.

The colony's future would not be further jeopardized by the interference of the strange visitor.

Five

"I think we can rule out any kind of proteasome stimulant," said Tricia.

"Agreed," Kes said. "The speed and extent of the cell devastation is just too fast. I'm betting on a protein denaturing compound. Perhaps something bonded to a virus. That would account for the rapid replication and transmission rates."

Thom, who was a chemical engineer by profession but had joined the team, spoke. "Could it simply *be* a virus? I mean, it isn't my field, but that's my guess."

"It's a good guess," said Kes. "All the dead cells seem to have undergone lysis, so it adds up." He was annoyed at himself. Why hadn't he come up with the idea? It was a distinct possibility, given what they knew about the biocide's effects. He'd been working on the assumption that the substance was a toxic chemical rather than something alive.

He was tired. They all were. As he sat at the table in the meeting room, the thirty or so faces around him were pale and the eyes were shadowed. Everyone was unkempt, too, and it was getting hard to ignore the smell of dirty clothes and body odor. Ever since creating the lab the team had taken hardly any time off. People would snatch a couple of hours' sleep on the meeting room floor and then immediately return to work.

Perhaps they were taking the wrong approach. Fatigue dulled the mind, and that was dangerous. Someone could miss something vital, or even slip up and allow the biocide to leak out. Then no one would stand a chance.

"A virus that infects every living thing it encounters?" Tricia asked. "Is that even possible? How would it survive after it first evolved? It would be self-limiting, running out of victims to infect because it kills everything it touches."

"It doesn't have to have evolved," Kes said. "The Scythians could have engineered it."

"Pretty risky," said Dean, a fellow xenobiologist.

"When you're set on destroying an entire planet's worth of life," Thom said, "perhaps any risk is worth taking."

"Hmm," Tricia said. "I guess the Scythians might have discovered a planet where the virus evolved and destroyed everything."

"We're leaping ahead," said Kes. "The virus idea is only a guess. We mustn't close our minds to other possibilities or we might miss something important. But I would still suggest we try to isolate virions from the Fila tissue samples."

"We can try," said Dean. "Kes, what do you say we review *all* the test results we have so far?"

He nodded. There were a few soft groans. He felt the same. But no one voiced a strong protest. Everyone knew the painstaking attention to detail was necessary.

As the results of all the tests they'd undertaken were displayed on a screen and discussed, he forced his tired mind to concentrate. He also had to force himself to ignore the pressure to find the solution to the crisis before it was too late. That was the hardest thing to do. The fear of what would happen if the team failed was so great, he sometimes imagined he could feel it, like a high-pitched whistle, too high to be heard by human ears but there nevertheless. Or he would smell it: a rancid, rank odor underlying the smell of unwashed bodies.

He could not—would not—allow the biocide to reach Isobel and Miki. They would *not* fall to the Scythians' evil. He would not countenance it. But he needed an answer. Where did it lie?

A comm arrived from one of the warehouse coordinators. They all knew he was not to be disturbed unless for something vitally important, so he accepted it.

The coordinator didn't waste any time on preamble. "A Fila called Quinn wants to speak to you. He said it's urgent."

"Quinn? Okay, that's fine. Put him through." He stood up and excused himself. After stepping out into the lab he waited, listening to the second or two of silence before Quinn's voice came through. The distance to the *Opportunity* and the sub-par state of the comm system was causing the lag.

"Kes, thank you for speaking with me. I know you are very busy. I tried to speak to you directly but I was unable."

"We're down to a low bandwidth so we're only allowing comms between refuge centers. But if you want to talk to me anytime it's fine. How are you? What's happening up there? How's Wilder?"

He had only been able to contact Wilder once, when he had briefly filled her in on the situation on the surface. He waited anxiously during the lag for the Fila's reply.

"Wilder believes she will die, probably due to starvation, I believe. She is planning on killing herself first."

Kes winced at Quinn's brutally honest response. The Fila couldn't be expected to understand human social sensitivities, but that didn't prevent his emotional reaction. "Uh, okay," was all he could think to say.

"On the other hand, I don't expect to die."

"Good."

"If necessary, I will go with my fellow crew to another planet. But the time to do that has not yet come. I am now the only channel of communication between your colony and the remaining members of my species on Concordia. I received a message that all sites containing translation equipment are now dead zones, contaminated by biocide."

"How many Fila are left? Is there any way we can help them?"

"That's the second reason I wanted to talk to you. I do not know how many of my kind have died. The situation is too turbulent for a reckoning. But a great many individuals have retreated to the large river running alongside the mountain range in Lyonesse. I believe you call it the Vimur. No biocide landed in it and the flow of the current toward the ocean is keeping the chemical out for the moment. But a canister did hit land not far from the river. The patch of destruction is spreading closer to the water. If the biocide reaches the Vimur, all the Fila sheltering there will die. Even if they leave via underground waterways the poison will follow them."

"I understand," said Kes. "We're doing all we can to create a neutralizing agent. As soon as we have it, we'll send some over the mountains. When we abandoned Annwn we flew the helis out. They can't carry much weight, but I'm sure they can transport enough of the agent to spray a band along the banks and safeguard the river."

"Are you close to finding a remedy?"

"We're..." He could not find it in him to muddy the truth with Quinn. "We aren't close, but I'm confident we'll have a breakthrough soon."

"I assume you have been conducting tests. Please send me all your data. The *Opportunity's* processing power is considerable. It may discover patterns or relevant information you have missed."

"That's a great idea. I'll do it as soon as I can. If you don't have anything else to tell me, can I speak to Wilder?"

"Of course."

Two more seconds of lag followed.

"Kes?"

Wilder sounded so young. She had always reminded him of his sister, who had been fourteen when they'd said goodbye for the last time on Earth, knowing they would never set eyes on each other again. Now, he heard the same fear and sorrow in Wilder's tone. It was as much as he could do to hold himself together.

"Wilder." He struggled to keep his voice normal. "How are you doing?"

"Oh, you know...I've been better. How are things down there?"

"They could be worse, but not a lot."

She gave a quiet sigh. "After we went to all that trouble to join the Galactic Assembly, I was expecting a tad better benefits."

"They are coming. And that's important for you to know. If they aren't here in time to save us, they could still save you. Are you rationing your food? You have to make it last as long as you can."

"So I can be the last remaining Concordian? I don't think I like the sound of that. I mean, I like solitude, but not *that* much."

"Maybe someone from the Assembly could take you to Earth."

"I already had this conversation with Quinn. You're forgetting about the disease the Guardians told us about, the one that wiped out civilization, remember? I would catch it, and, besides, you didn't hear what I said. I don't want to be the only *Concordian*. I'm not from Earth. Concordia's my home. If my home and all of you are gone, what else do I have?"

"You have..." He wasn't sure how to answer. Her point was valid. Home, family, and a circle of friends who loved you, these were all important to human happiness, if not essential. He knew that to him, personally, these things were everything. "You have yourself. You're young and adaptable, and you're so intelligent. Who knows what you might do with your life? You have so much potential. So much to offer other species, other civilizations. And I know Quinn would miss you very much if anything were to happen to you."

"I..." A pause stretched out longer than the lag. "I don't know. Maybe he would."

"Of course he would. He wanted to go up there with you to the *Opportunity*, didn't he? That's what you told me."

"Yeah, he did."

"It was because he cares about you."

"I guess so."

He closed his eyes, imagining the young girl aboard the starship that had conveyed her, himself, Aubriot, and Cherry so far across the galaxy. He could remember the time vividly, the months he and Wilder had spent questioning and observing the Fila, trying to understand them. He could see the girl in his mind's eye, floating in the micro-gravity, painfully thin, her hair a mess.

"I guess Piddle and Puddle would miss me too," she said.

"You...what? Are they the other Fila on the ship?"

"No, they're my pets. I brought them with me when I came up here."

"Seriously? What kind of pets?"

"I don't think they've been classified yet."

"You found a new species and you didn't tell me?"

"I didn't want scientists studying them," said Wilder. "They were happy living with me."

"Well, I can understand that. I'm glad you have them with you to keep you company, and you're right, they would miss you too. So you mustn't do anything stupid, okay? Hang on as long as you can."

The lag dragged out. Finally, her soft reply came. "Okay, I'll try."

He relaxed in relief. "Thank you. That means a lot."

"Kes, I'm worried about some friends of mine. Could you check they're okay?"

"I can try. The database of survivors and their locations is still being compiled but I'll do my best."

"Thanks." She stated some names and Kes noted them. Then she said, "I have to go now. Piddle and Puddle are waking up."

"If you want to talk to me, anytime, just comm the center. I'll tell them to put you straight through to me. Anytime. I mean it."

"I will. Bye."

The comm went dead, but the center coordinator opened it again. "I have a message for you. I thought you might want to hear it before you return to work."

"Okay. Play it." As soon as he heard the voice he gave a mental groan. If Cherry had left him a message, he guessed it meant she'd gone again.

Kes, I realized there's something I have to do at Oceanside, but I don't want you to worry. I'm wearing a haz suit. Isobel is nice and Miki is sweet, but family life isn't for me. I'll let you know what's happening later.

That was it.

What was there for her to do at Oceanside? The place was a no-go zone, the biocide gradually spreading over it. But, from the sound of it, she was feeling better and that was the important thing.

Two lives saved in one day. Now he only had another few tens of thousands to go. Something from his conversation with Quinn, niggling at the back of his mind while talking to the Fila and to Wilder, suddenly popped to the front.

The helis.

Everyone had been focused on retreating to the areas of Lyonesse that lay far from the encroaching biocide, and then trying to find an antidote to the poison, but Suddene was barely touched. His advice to Wilder to keep going as long as she could applied to everyone on Concordia too. They might not be able to save everyone in time for the arrival of the Assembly's rescue ships, but if they could save even a small portion of the population, that would be something.

They should begin transporting people to the other continent in the helis. The aircraft would only hold one or two passengers and the trip took hours, but it would be worth the effort. After transmitting the test results data to Quinn, he would comm Meredith and suggest the idea. It made sense to transport the most vulnerable people first, such as Isobel and Miki.

If his wife and child were out of immediate danger it would be a great weight off his mind.

Six

It seemed bizarre to Cherry that the autocars continued to run as normal through the wrecked, dying landscape. All you had to do was tell the vehicle the destination coordinates and it would take you there if it could, driving over the destroyed and broken remains of roadways.

Unless you knew for sure the route was safe, however, the endeavor was dangerous. If a crack yawned wide across a highway the cars' proximity sensors might not detect it. They were made to detect obstacles, not absences. The vehicles could drive right up to a hole and tumble into it. In the days following the battle with the Scythians, the autocars—conveying those brave enough to venture out of the refuges—had encountered road surfaces too uneven to cross. The cars would either stop and turn around, stating the necessity of traveling via an alternative route, or halt and state that the destination was unreachable.

Cherry guessed the car she was in would do one or the other sooner or later. She couldn't expect to get far into what remained of Oceanside. After that, she would get out and walk. She didn't know where the escaped 'Guardian' might have gone, but she would begin her search at the jail. There was only one and she'd brought along an interface in case she couldn't find it by sight in the altered cityscape.

The inside of the haz suit smelled of sick. The odor had to be a sterilizing chemical used to treat the air the device drew in. No one knew for sure whether the suits actually protected against the biocide. It wasn't the kind of thing you could easily test.

She was more than happy to take her chances, however. She might not have been able to save the colony from the Scythians, but she might be able to save it from another menace.

Oceanside was unrecognizable.

She was reminded of the devastation after the First Scythian Attack, the crash of the *Nova,* and the tsunami that followed.

She was traveling through the site where the enemy had concentrated the fire from all its ships this time around. The blast had leveled half the city's buildings, and the epicenter was a molten mess hundreds of meters wide. No one sheltering in or near the main strike had survived. Nothing resembling a human body had been found.

In some areas, smoke still poured from fires, but other than the twisting, rising vapors, there was no sign of movement in the rubble.

Her heart and guts ached as she surveyed the desolate scene. What was the death toll? No one knew. The scramble to escape the encroaching biocide had been mad, chaotic. No one knew exactly who or how many had made it to a refuge. The priority had been to survive.

In the distance, a single tree stood silhouetted against the bright sky. As the car drew nearer to it, she saw it was entirely, utterly dead. The leaves still hung on the branches, but they were brown and desiccated. It looked as though a frost giant from a children's story had breathed upon it, instantly killing it.

No frost giants lived on Concordia. They were Earthly creatures, if they had ever existed. The tree had been killed by the biocide.

She hadn't realized the poison had spread to this part of Oceanside. The chemical was moving fast. Even in the manmade cityscape it progressed through the soil, carried from one living thing to the next.

She was now within a dead zone. It was a chilling thought. Beyond the confines of her haz suit, death waited. What would it feel like to die from the biocide? She had only seen it happen once. In the Leader's bunker, the Fila who had been liaising with Meredith from the adjoining water-filled compartment, Elliot, had suddenly died. He hadn't made a sound, or rather, the translation equipment had not conveyed a word from him.

Had the his death been instant? Or had he communicated with his kind, in their way, in his last few seconds, choosing not to submit his message to the translator? Had he suffered?

She shivered, and then put the questions from her mind. Whatever would happen, would happen. She had to focus on her goal. The task would be difficult enough without the added complication of anticipating her death.

She would go to the jail and look for any signs that might give her a clue to locate the Guardian. If she didn't find anything she would have to try to guess where the thing might go.

She remained unconvinced the machine was what it seemed to be. Its appearance only weeks prior to the Scythians' return had only excited her suspicions. It was too much to believe that the *Mistral's* escape pod had floated around in space for more than a hundred Concordian years, only to finally be dragged to the surface within a couple of months of another visit from the colony's number one enemy.

But if it wasn't a Guardian, what was it? The thing had to be connected to the Scythians somehow. It was the only possible answer. And if it was connected to the Scythians, what would it do now? Concordia was heading for global extinction. The strange visitor's original purpose, whatever it might have been, was now irrelevant. Had the Scythians' communicated a new order to it while they were in battle?

Was that why it had broken free from confinement?

Her pulse sped up. She was certain she was on to something. The events surrounding the mysterious arrival were finally beginning to make sense.

The autocar stopped abruptly, forcing her forward. A section of a house lay on the road. Among the rubble sat a bathtub, upturned. Curtains, still attached to their curtain rods, flapped in the wind. A sanitizer rested on its side, its door hanging open.

"Road blocked," the autocar announced. "Calculating alternative route. Alternative route calculated. Time to destination, three hours fifty-eight minutes."

Four hours? "Stop. I'll get out here."

In response, the autocar's locks clicked open and the engine died.

She reached for the door, but her fingers rested on the handle. She took a long look at the surrounding scenery. Off to the right was what had once been a small children's park. The play equipment was untouched, but the same could not be said for the vegetation.

The soft, rubbery ground cover that was ubiquitous in Concordia had turned black. Tubular flowers lay scattered around low shrubs, pale brown and papery. The shrubs themselves had the same blasted look of the tree she had seen earlier.

She was still in the dead zone.

She breathed in deeply. The vomit-tinged smell of her suit's interior did nothing to ease the querulous complaint of her stomach. She pressed firmly on the door release. The door moved outward and then slid back. Nothing now stood between her and the air of the dead zone.

She waited, her eyes on the cadaverous playground. Would it be the last thing she saw? Quickly, she looked up into the cloudless sky, preferring that as her final view of the world.

Nothing happened.

If the biocide was going to get her, it wasn't just yet.

She climbed out, bringing an interface with her. She'd set up the screen to display a map of Oceanside and her position. She was surprised to find that she was only about eight hundred meters, in a straight line, from the jail. And, judging by the ruined cityscape, she would be able to walk all the way. In the direction she had to travel, not a building was left standing.

Tucking the interface under her arm, she set off.

Seven

Kes woke suddenly. His head was resting on his folded arms and he was hunched over, supported by a table. For a moment, he couldn't remember where he was. He could hear voices and a faint chemical smell was seeping into his nostrils. Despite his nap, he felt immensely tired and wanted nothing more than to fall asleep again. But his memory of recent events was returning. Disquiet and the burden of the task facing him forced him to a greater wakefulness. He sat up.

He was in the lab. He'd fallen asleep while reading results on an interface. The other scientists were getting on with their work or talking, speculating on their findings. His co-workers had either not noticed he'd fallen asleep or they'd left him alone, taking pity on him.

He stretched his arms and back and then rubbed his eyes.

"Coffee?" asked Tricia, who had come up behind him.

"That would be wonderful. I suppose I dropped off."

"We're all exhausted, but what are you going to do, huh?"

"That's right. We have to keep working until we hit on the answer."

"*If* we hit on the answer." Tricia stepped closer and checked no one was listening before saying, more softly, "I don't hold out a lot of hope. Do you? We're trying to do the impossible. I mean, if we had months and fully equipped labs, we might stand a chance. But I reckon we have less than five weeks, tops. Trying to accomplish anything with the equipment we managed to transport from Oceanside and Annwn is utterly futile. Half of the stuff hasn't even been properly calibrated. How can we trust our results?"

Before he could answer, she walked away, heading over to the coffee machine. She brought back a mug of hot, black coffee. Ordinarily, just the smell of strong coffee would perk him up, but this time the aroma did nothing to penetrate the fatigue enveloping his mind.

"Better get back to work," said Tricia.

"Hey, wait a minute." He put down his mug as Tricia faced him again. "You're wrong."

"About what?"

"Everything."

"Gee, thanks."

"We can find a solution to this. I know it. This isn't some airy-fairy hypothesis we're testing. No one's working toward their PhD, dotting every i and crossing every t. We're fighting for our lives here, and we're bringing all the colony's brain power to the table. We've got some damned smart people in this team. The best. And we don't have to get everything one hundred percent correct. We only have to find one thing that will halt the progress of the biocide. We can finesse the details later."

Tricia looked unconvinced.

"But I'll tell you the one thing that will make us fail for sure."

"What's that?"

"If we give up. If we stop trying, thinking the situation is hopeless, then we've lost. You're right about the equipment, and the fact that everyone's tired beyond the point of exhaustion, but those things are out of our control. The one thing we can control is our attitude. We have to be careful not to fall into negativity. It will kill us surer than anything."

She heaved a sigh. "I hear you. I'll try to be more positive. But it's hard. It's hard to stay sanguine when death is approaching from all sides."

"I know. By the way, I sent all the test results data up to Quinn. The *Opportunity's* computer is crunching through them. Input from the Fila could shed a new light on things."

"I hope so." Tricia turned again to leave, but then she said, "Why don't you go and get some sleep? A proper sleep, I mean. For more than fifteen minutes."

"I'd love to. I was planning on enjoying that luxury after we figure out how to neutralize the biocide."

"So was I, but we're all so tired now there's a danger we'll miss something important. Like our attitude, our alertness is under our control, and even the greatest minds are fallible under extreme duress and fatigue. Go to bed and sleep. I'll keep the show running while you're gone and set up a schedule so we can all get enough rest."

"That's a tempting offer, but—"

"Do it, Kes. You've gotten the least sleep of all of us, and you must be especially tired after your trip to retrieve our errant General."

He went to protest again, but Tricia raised a finger to him and then pointed at the door.

He smiled. "Okay, I surrender." He rose to his feet. "I'll be back in a few hours."

"Come back when you're fully rested, and not before."

He left the lab. He couldn't deny that Tricia's reasoning was sound, and even if he wasn't in the lab he could continue pondering the problem. Sometimes the simple freedom to think deeply brought unexpected answers.

The lighting outside the lab was low. It was late evening and the colonists were settling down for the night. He passed between the rows of cots in the single person's section. In some places there were no cots available and people were sitting or lying on mattresses or cushions pushed together. The warehouse was chilly despite the many human bodies present. The heat was rising to the high, pitched ceiling.

He reached the curtained family section. There were no numbers or signs by which to navigate, and most curtain were closed. He wasn't sure he remembered exactly where Isobel and Miki were. When he reached what he thought was the right place, he halted outside, reluctant to disturb the occupants if he was wrong. "Isobel? Are you there?"

He heard a familiar thump, and he relaxed. He had found the right cubicle after all. What he'd heard was the sound of Isobel's cast hitting the floor as she stood up. A beat later the curtain opened.

"You're back! It's so good to see you."

They hugged and he went in, pulling the curtain closed. The lighting was even dimmer in the tiny room, but he could make out Miki asleep on the mattress, her little legs and arms splayed as always.

"Are you hungry?" Isobel asked. "I saved some food for you."

"I'm actually too tired to be hungry. I really need to sleep. Tricia forced me to go and get some rest."

"Good. I'm glad. Oh, I'm sorry, Cherry left. There wasn't anything I could do to stop her."

"It's okay. I know. And it's fine. There *is* no stopping Cherry once she's set her mind on something."

"I hope she's okay."

"I think she'll be all right. What she does is out of my hands now anyway. I did my best to help her, but at the end of the day she'll do whatever she wants."

"Come to bed. I don't think I've ever seen you look so tired, and I've seen you tired plenty of times."

He needed no further persuading. He sat on the low camp chair to pull off his shoes, and then he stood up to take off his pants and shirt. Meanwhile, Isobel tidied their daughter's arms and legs to create space on the mattress.

Miki was lying next to the curtain. Isobel curled around her. Kes lay down on the outer edge of the mattress and put his arm over Isobel's belly. He felt their baby wriggle.

Not so long ago, he would have taken lying in bed with his pregnant wife and little daughter entirely for granted. Now, it was the most blissful situation in the world. The only thing that could make it better would be to remove the shadow hanging over them.

He fell sound asleep.

EIGHT

Half of the jail remained standing. A diagonal line cut across the building. On one side stood cracked walls and splintered windows, on the other empty space. The sun was setting behind Cherry, throwing the exposed interior of the building into sharp divisions of long shadows and rosy light.

She looked around. No movement of any living thing disturbed the desolate tableau of the ravaged city. If the Guardian was out there somewhere, it was hiding.

She turned her suit's helmet light and swept the darkening cityscape with the beam, checking again for movement.

All was still.

The jail stood in a built up area of Oceanside where no greenery decorated the streets, but despite the lack of evidence she guessed the area was within the dead zone. Her suit had protected her so far. She could only hope it would continue to do so.

Stepping over scattered, broken bricks and twisted support beams, she headed for the jail. The entrance door no longer existed. She surmounted the edge that remained of one half of the building and went in. At one spot the admission officer's desk had miraculously survived intact, its chair tucked in, as if the officer had left after finishing his day's work only moments ago. Except a layer of plaster dust coated the surface and everything else in sight. No rain had fallen since the biocide landed, which had probably helped to keep the survivors alive.

The administration section of the jail had been blown to pieces. She passed through the admitting area to the standing part of the jail. Six cells, a shower room, and a jailer's station made up the first floor. All the cell doors stood open, the interiors empty.

She guessed that, like most buildings in Concordia, there was a basement area—a shelter where the staff and criminals could go if the Scythians attacked. The building regulation was old, dating back to the years when Ethan had been Leader.

She had never been to the jail's basement, but it wasn't hard to find. A hatch in the floor between the cells lay open, revealing steps leading down to darkness. Tipping her head forward so her helmet light illuminated the steps, she descended.

Twenty steps later, she reached the bottom. Everything was pitch black except for what was unveiled by her light. The cells here were more basic than those above. Simple iron bars ran from floor to ceiling and from the front to the back, separating each cell from its neighbor.

She imagined the jailers hurrying the inmates down the steps after the warning of the imminent attack. They would have shut and locked the hatch and secured the prisoners underground, probably squeezing several people into each cell. Then the waiting would have begun.

Had the prisoners and jailers maintained their social separation, or had the two sides come together as the seconds ticked down, seeing themselves as all Concordians in the end?

She gasped and froze. Human feet and legs had appeared in the sweep of her helmet light's beam. Slowly, she turned to focus on the spot. A man's boots lay askew. She raised her head to take in the rest of his figure. He was wearing a jailer's uniform and sat slumped against the wall, half fallen to one side. His right shoulder was the highest point of his body. What had killed him? His death could have been due to the attack, but it was unlikely down here where there were no other bodies and his clothes and skin were not burned.

She had not personally received the report that the thing claiming it was Guardian had escaped. The message had been relayed to her, and she didn't recall any mention of a death. Perhaps that had occurred afterward. The cell doors stood open.

She stepped closer to the corpse, peering over the prone form to catch sight of his head. She quickly took a step back, grimacing. The man's neck had been broken. His face was turned nearly one hundred and eighty degrees from the front, as if something or someone had seized his head and twisted it violently around.

Had the Guardian done that? Others might not believe it, but she knew too well how the androids could behave when they believed they were acting for the greater good. She also knew they were much stronger, tougher, and more resilient than humans. Could the Guardian have killed this man?

Yes. Absolutely.

But why? Perhaps the guard had tried to prevent it from leaving. The explanation didn't make a lot of sense, however. Everyone else in the basement had left, probably after the attack when all of Oceanside and the rest of Concordia was in chaos. The jailers had probably been scared and wanted to leave but also didn't want to leave the prisoners trapped.

So if the Guardian had been free to go, why would it have killed the guard? She studied the confined space once more. An anomaly in the regularity of the bars at the end of the room attracted her attention. She moved closer, and the interrupted pattern was immediately apparent. Two of the bars were bent sideways, creating a gap. It was a narrow gap, but wide enough for a thin person to pass through.

A scene sprang to her mind. The light was on in the basement, the prisoners were crowded into their cells. The guards stood and sat in the open space. All awaited the moment of the Scythians' arrival.

Then the massive strike came, which had trapped her in the elevator at the Leader's Residence and snuffed out thousands of lives in one stroke. The jail would have been rocked by the impact. Perhaps the prisoners or guards had panicked, perhaps they had been shocked to silence.

Either at that point or soon afterward, the Guardian had moved to the bars of its cell, grabbed one with its remaining hand, and bent it wide. Then it had grabbed the neighboring bar and bent it in the opposite direction. By this time, it would have attracted everyone's attention. The guards may have shot it, but regular weapons had little effect on the androids.

The escaping prisoner stepped through the bars. A brave guard ran up to it, ordering the creature back into its cell. The Guardian grabbed the man's head and wrenched it around, killing him instantly. Horrified and terrified, the other guards had shrunk backward, none of them daring to approach the Guardian. What point would there be in summoning the courage to face an indestructible opponent?

The Guardian strode to the steps, mounted them, threw open the hatch, and then disappeared. In the general pandemonium, no one had reported the prisoner's escape until after the attack was over. The prisoners and guards had been forced to share the basement with the brave guard's corpse until the decision was taken to free everyone and let them save themselves.

The scenario fit what she saw. What she didn't know was where the Guardian had gone. The burned up figure would be easy to miss among the many burned and injured individuals roaming around, seeking treatment, in the aftermath of the attack. She hadn't heard any reports of sightings of it. She had no clues to go on.

She climbed the steps to the first floor of the destroyed prison. The sun had set and shadows engulfed the place. Leaving on her helmet light, she walked through the wreckage and went outside. Except for the switch to monochrome due to the faded light, Oceanside's remains looked the same.

She sought and found a smooth piece of rubble on which to sit. She surveyed the devastation but only absently as she focused on figuring out her next move.

Where would a Guardian go? Or, if the thing was an agent of the Scythians, what would it do? Its masters were already billions of kilometers away, leaving their deadly chemical to finish off the destruction of Concordia. They had abandoned their inorganic, sentient creation to endless confinement on a dead planet. Would it seek out a starship to escape on? If it had accessed the colony's data it would know that nothing of the kind existed on the surface, save, perhaps, for the shuttlecraft that conveyed passengers to the *Opportunity*. As they belonged to the Fila, she had no idea where the small, slim vessels were kept, except they were no doubt somewhere in the oceans or rivers.

On the other hand, what if the escaped prisoner really was Faina, last survivor of the crash of the *Mistral*? Where would the android head in the wake of the battle? Unless the damage it sustained had affected its programming, Faina would be carrying out its mission to save the colony at all costs. But what did that mean?

Cherry shook her head. She was getting nowhere. She got up and set off in no direction in particular. Though night was falling and she should be heading back to the refuge if she wanted to sleep in a bed tonight, she didn't want to give up. The escaped prisoner was dangerous and violent. Concordians had already seen enough death and destruction to last them several lifetimes. They didn't need a homicidal android on the loose too. Finding and destroying the creature was the least she could do after her terrible mess-up.

She wandered through the deserted ruins, occasionally recognizing the remains of familiar places but mostly not knowing exactly where she was or where she was headed. The dusky sky turned dark and stars appeared between the patches of scudding clouds. It became difficult to see where she was going despite the gleam from her light, and she had to slow down to avoid tripping and tearing open her suit.

Eventually she reached an area of Oceanside unaffected by the Scythian attack. The buildings were untouched, only abandoned. Doors stood open where the occupants had left in a hurry, fearing the encroaching biocide, and dropped belongings littered the sidewalks and roads.

Suddenly, it occurred to her that her suit's filtration system would only work for a limited time. How much longer did she have? Her visor had no HUD. She guessed she was supposed to know how long the suit would protect her, but she'd missed that piece of information.

She was about to search on the public files when she turned a corner and saw she'd reached the harbor. The ocean spread out, starlight reflecting from the moving water. Boats bobbed against their moorings on the swell. Mercifully, no Fila corpses floated here.

She leaned against a wall, watching the scene. Boats used to gather tiny edible creatures of the sea mingled with leisure cruisers. The quayside was crammed with vessels. All boats and cruise ships had put into the nearest port after the announcement of the Scythian's return.

Slowly, she stood upright. What if...?

She began to walk along the line of boats.

What if the escaped prisoner had wanted to go to Suddene? If it was working for the Scythians, perhaps they had told it to go to their ancient city, now buried beneath the desert sands. Perhaps there was something important there. Perhaps that had been the reason for its presence all along.

Or if the creature was Faina, perhaps it had another reason for making its way to the place where humanity would survive longest on Concordia.

All the helis had been flown out of Oceanside and Annwn when the cities were abandoned. None of the aircraft would be easily accessible to unauthorized personnel. But a boat would be easy to obtain, and the android would have had its pick of the fastest.

She scanned the ranks of vessels, but there was no way of telling if one had been taken. A gap in the line meant nothing. But there was one avenue of information she hadn't explored.

She accessed the governmental data on shipping. Her security clearance meant everything was open to her. She prayed that Concordia's single remaining satellite launched from the *Nova* still functioned.

She halted, waiting. The comm system had slowed to a crawl. She looked up at the stars, wondering which of them was the old satellite, if it was visible at all.

"C'mon," she said softly. "Tell me what I want to know. Tell me where it's gone."

Her interface pinged. The data was arriving. The screen was bright with figures in the dark night, names of ships were followed by their recent movements. Her gaze ran down the numbers. All followed the same pattern. After the Scythian attack, all the ships had remained in the same position, moored either along the coast of Oceanside or Suddene. The information fed upward on the screen.

Then the anomaly jumped out. The movements of one ship, the *Astrea*, were vastly different from the others. The vessel had put out to sea from Oceanside after the fateful date. She input its current coordinates into a map of Concordia. The *Astrea* rested at Suddene's only port.

In the days since the battle with the Scythians, the android had sailed from

Lyonesse to Suddene. She was sure of it. No human would have dared pass over an ocean filled with biocide. She didn't know the creature's motivation but she did know it could not be good.

She had to get to Suddene, too, and find it. But the journey would take too long by boat and her suit's filter might not last. She would have to travel all the way back to the refuge and find a pilot to fly her.

Nine

Kes was dreaming. He knew everything he was seeing and hearing and touching wasn't real, but he couldn't wake up. Or maybe it was only that he didn't want to.

He was at his home in Annwn and everything was normal. He'd made it home early from work for once, and he was playing with Miki in the living room while Izzy fixed dinner. His little girl had invited him to a tea party at her playhouse, but unfortunately he was too big to fit in. He was forced to sit outside the window while the other guests all crammed around a small table inside, perching lopsidedly on three-legged stools.

Teddy was one of the guests, though his rotund tummy indicated he'd been to a few too many parties in his time and eaten far too much cake. Giraffe was there too, her head poking out of the top of the playhouse. The third guest at the table was Miki's best friend, a rag doll called Dotty after the patterning on the dress she always wore. To be fair, the dress was sewn onto her so focusing on her failure to change clothes was unjust.

It had always bemused Kes that Concordian children's toys were nearly identical to Earth children's, and had been the same for many generations. Dolls were understandable, but teddies and giraffes?

When Miki grew older, he would have to explain to her that teddies were based on real animals called bears, and that neither they nor giraffes were mythical creatures but had once lived—and perhaps still lived—on humanity's origin planet, many light years away.

The problem was there were no equivalent Concordian animals to be copied into plush playmates for small children. He couldn't imagine a furry sluglimpet having tea with his daughter, or any of the other native creatures. They were all fairly monstrous to human eyes, though he was curious about the creatures Wilder had mentioned as her pets. The creatures were probably cute if Wilder had adopted them.

The only non-Earth creature he had ever seen fashioned into a toy was the non-native, many-tentacled Fila. Miki didn't have a toy Fila, but one of her friends had brought a huge example to Miki's second birthday party. The boy's mother had complained the child insisted on taking the toy everywhere, though it was twice his size and had tens of long tentacles that constantly caught on things.

The boy had been fascinated with the Fila ever since he'd seen his first live example in the lake out at the farming district. The creature had approached while he was learning to swim and taken him for a ride around the lake. *It was love at first sight,* the mom had said. *Now he can't get enough of them. I wouldn't be surprised if he becomes a diver when he grows up, just so he can spend as much time as he can with them.*

There was something in Kes's memory of the woman's words that made him sad, but he didn't know what it was. Things were getting hazy. Perhaps he would wake up soon.

"Tea for Daddy," said Miki, passing out a cup through the window of the house.

"Thanks. Mmmm. Looks delicious."

"Drink," she urged, apparently annoyed that Daddy wasn't following the rules of the party.

He dutifully took an imaginary sip from the empty cup under her watchful gaze. Satisfied, she poured more imaginary tea for the other partygoers and placed their cups in front of them. "Daddy want cake?"

"Yes, please."

She gave a small, secret smile, turned toward the kitchen corner of her playhouse, and lifted a toy piece of cake onto a plate.

"What kind is it?" he asked

"Um, sweet potato. No! Walnut."

"Sounds yummy." He pretended to take a bite.

Walnut? That was a new one. He hadn't been aware the colony even had walnut trees, though it made sense. Most nut trees were wind pollinated. A moment of wistful sadness hit him. Miki would never taste so many delicious fruits that grew on Earth. Nothing that required bees for pollination. No strawberries, no blueberries, no oranges or melons.

Though it had been years since he'd eaten any of them, he could still remember the flavors and textures of his favorites. Sometimes, when the longing for food he would never taste again grew bad, he wished the ecologists had not excluded bees from the colonization project. Their reasoning had been that the insects might throw the local ecology out of balance. He guessed the scientists knew their stuff and their caution had been correct, but that didn't make him miss strawberries any less.

"Is it nice?" Miki asked.

"Delicious, sweetheart. Could I have some more?"

"Uh uh." His daughter shook her head. "Dinner soon." She pretended to eat cake. Then she held pieces to the toys' mouths.

He watched his little girl contentedly. Miki was one of the best things that had ever happened to him, as much as Isobel. Like always when he arrived home from work in time to see her before her bedtime, he was glad he'd made the effort and puzzled as to why he didn't always manage it.

Miki was a very special kid. All parents thought the same about their children, but he also felt that, deep down, he was objectively correct. The same as all parents. But her vocabulary seemed to grow bigger every day, and she already understood simple arithmetic and recognized many words by sight. She was also *such* a pretty child. The red tinge to her black hair really made her stand out.

Isobel appeared in the living room doorway. "Dinner's ready, guys. Time to wash up."

Miki picked up her doll. "Dotty come too, Mommy?"

"Sure, Dotty can come too. Hurry up and wash your hands, though, or your dinner will get cold."

The door to the playhouse opened and Miki emerged, clutching her doll upside down. Dotty's head hit the door frame, but it didn't seem to bother her.

"Daddy carry me." Miki held up her free arm to Kes.

"Miki," Isobel admonished, "you're only going to the bathroom."

"I'm tired. Daddy carry."

As Kes stooped to pick up his daughter, Isobel said, "You really shouldn't encourage her." He paused.

"She can't continue expecting to be carried everywhere," Isobel continued. "I can barely manage to carry her now as it is, and when the baby comes I definitely won't be able to carry both of them."

"Miki, how about if Daddy *cuddles* you instead?"

Miki beamed and jiggled, holding up her arm higher. Kes lifted her and then said to Isobel, "Out of the way. We're coming through!"

Isobel sighed and rolled her eyes.

Miki had one arm around his neck and the other around the upside-down Dotty. He swooped through into the hall and into the bathroom, where he deposited her on the little stool she used to reach the basin.

Miki dropped Dotty on her head and reached for the faucet. As she turned the lever, she gave a slight cough. She squeezed soap onto her hands and rubbed them together under water. Miki coughed again as she turned off the faucet.

She jumped down from the stool and dried her hands, coughing for the third time. This cough was deeper and noisier, as if mucus was gathering in her throat and chest.

"Are you feeling okay, darling?" Kes asked. When Miki didn't answer and only bent down to pick up her doll, he put a hand to her forehead. Her skin felt warmer than it should.

"Izzy," he called, "has Miki been coughing a lot lately?"

"I didn't notice," Isobel called back.

He squatted down and studied his daughter closely. She was holding Dotty's arms over the sink, and he managed to stop her from soaking the doll's hands only just in time. "Miki, look at me."

She turned to face him. Her cheeks seemed redder than usual and her eyes were exceptionally bright. He brushed her bangs away from her face and held his hand on top of her head. Seeming to sense the change in mood, she became still and stared gravely into his eyes.

"How do you feel?" he asked. "Do you hurt anywhere? Do you have pain here, in your head?"

She slowly shook her head while maintaining eye contact.

"How about here?" He moved his hand to her abdomen. "In your tummy."

She hesitated, then gave one sharp nod. Suddenly, she coughed again, right into his face. He flinched as the barrage of saliva spray hit.

"Gee, thanks for that." He stood up and ran water into the basin. He splashed his face clean, and then reached for a towel. As he moved, something in the corner of his eye caught his attention. Miki's face looked redder and slightly distorted. He blinked, thinking it was only an effect of the water on his vision, and wiped his face dry.

When he turned his attention to her again, he gasped. Miki's face *had* changed, drastically, and it continued to change as he stared at it, disbelieving the evidence of his eyes. Her face had turned bright red, and it was swelling up. Her entire head was swelling, and her body too. "Izzy, call an ambulance!"

"What? Why?"

"Just do it! Miki! Are you okay?" He knelt down and grabbed his daughter's shoulders.

She didn't reply.

"Miki!"

She was growing larger, and her red face was taking on a different hue. Her skin was becoming purplish shadowed with black, as if she were undergoing sepsis at a fantastic rate. He picked her up and ran out into the hall. "Izzy!" Where was she? Had she called an ambulance? He couldn't see her anywhere.

There was a hospital in Annwn. It was only small but it dealt with medical emergencies. It wasn't far away. It would be faster to go there by autocar than wait for an ambulance. He turned toward the front door and took a step, but his movements were slowing down. He tried to take another step, but the air had turned into some kind of resistant force field. He forced his other leg forward, straining against the invisible barrier.

He wanted to look down at Miki but his head would not budge. He was frozen, fighting with every muscle he possessed and entirely failing to move even a centimeter.

He awoke.

Jerking to a sitting position, he cried out. Then he remembered where he was and he relaxed, softly panting. The lights in the refuge remained dimmed. It was still nighttime.

"Kes?" asked Isobel, turning over. "What's wrong?"

The specter of the dream still clung to his mind. He peered over Isobel and saw Miki sleeping deeply. She looked entirely normal and healthy. His panic and dismay eased.

"Could you keep it down in there?" came a disgruntled voice from the next cubicle.

"Sorry." Kes reclined on the mattress and took Isobel in his arms.

"Bad dream?" She snuggled into his shoulder.

"Yeah."

"What was it about?"

"You don't want to know."

How long had he slept? It was hard to tell. He felt refreshed, so it was probably quite a while. Should he get up and go back to the lab? *Just another few minutes.* Holding Isobel, he was warm and comfortable, and his nightmare hadn't entirely faded. He felt afraid to let his wife and daughter out of his sight.

The dream had taken him back to Annwn, before everything had gone to hell. At one point he'd known he was dreaming but then he'd forgotten and had sunk into the false reality. Usually, his dreams were far weirder than that. The nightmare had seemed a facsimile of normal life. It was very strange—perhaps a reaction to the circumstances. Perhaps his subconscious had been anticipating the biocide reaching Miki.

"Are you okay, honey?" Isobel asked softly.

He realized his grip on her had tightened. He purposefully relaxed his arms. "Uh huh. I'm getting up soon."

"Just a little longer."

Usually, if he dreamed of people and places he knew, he dreamed of Earth, of people long dead and places that probably no longer existed. But he hadn't dreamed of Earth in a long time.

What would their lives be like if they were there and not Concordia? Very different, he guessed. Maybe survival on Earth was now nearly impossible. And

Isobel would not be Isobel, descendant of the Gens who'd lived out their lives aboard a starship.

But what if...?

He daydreamed an impossible scenario. He was back home, working as a researcher at the local college. He lived with Isobel and Miki in the little cottage on his parents' land. On the weekends, they would drive to the lake. Life would be predictable. Boring in some ways, but in others it would be just perfect. And he wouldn't have to worry about Miki getting sick because—

He sat bolt upright, for the second time. "*Shit!*"

"Kes, what's wrong?" asked Isobel.

"Would you *please* keep quiet," exclaimed the irritated neighbor.

He climbed out of bed. "I have to get back to the lab." He groped for his clothes in the semi-darkness. His hands touched textile and he pulled the garment closer for inspection. He'd found his pants. He began to put them on.

"Did you think of something?"

"I did. Or rather, my subconscious did, I think." He was pushing his feet into his shoes. "I have to go." He'd located his shirt. "I love you." He stooped and kissed his wife on the lips and then awkwardly leaned over her to kiss the still-sleeping Miki on the cheek. The normal temperature of his daughter's skin was reassuring. The tendrils of his nightmare clung on inside his mind.

He pulled on his shirt and felt for the opening in the curtains. "When Miki wakes up, tell her Daddy loves her."

Ten

The first light of dawn suffused the eastern sky as the group of warehouses came into view from Cherry's autocar. It had taken the rest of the night to return to her vehicle and then travel to the refuge. Her eyes ached with tiredness but she was determined to set out for Suddene as soon as possible. The android already had a head start on her of several days. Who knew what it had done already?

The autocar approached the warehouses from the east, the sunrise behind it. The group of buildings sat on flat land, hulking and dark. Some of their occupants were already awake. Figures passed along the paths leading to the latrines.

More importantly, the helis that had been flown over from Annwn remained on site, sitting in the truck parking lot. She counted eight. One would be enough for her purposes, but she also needed a pilot.

She knew just the person, but was he at the refuge? He might be stuck at Cerberus along with Aubriot and the other military personnel. It was early, but she had no time to waste. She comm'd him. When he didn't answer she tried twice more and then finally activated his alarm. She was one of the few people allowed to invade someone's quiet and privacy.

Zapata's voice was heavy and husky with sleep as he answered, "Yes, ma'am?"

"I need you to fly me to Suddene." She asked if he was at the warehouse refuge. He was.

"Meet me at the helis as soon as you can. I'm on my way there now."

"Yes, ma'am."

"I told you not to call me that."

"Yeah...I'm not at my sharpest when I've just woken up."

"Sorry. See you soon."

Ordering pilots around and having access to high security information were among the many privileges of her position. How much longer would they last? She hadn't met face to face with Meredith since the battle and she didn't know the Leader's attitude toward her, but she guessed it was not good. She had deliberately ignored Meredith's wishes and unilaterally launched a counterattack against the Scythians.

Technically, she had committed treason and should have been immediately stripped of her position. She didn't know why that hadn't happened yet. Perhaps it was only that the Leader was too busy with other, life-and-death issues. Whatever the reason, she intended to exploit her position as long as she could, particularly regarding the mysterious android. If there was one more thing she would butt heads with Meredith on, it was that. With luck, Zapata would get them both into the air and on their way to Suddene before the Leader even woke up.

The autocar rolled to a stop outside the main warehouse gates and Cherry got out. She had taken off her haz suit's helmet at the first sight of green she'd seen on the way back. The suit's filter already seemed to have stopped working. The smell of vomit had entirely faded. She reminded herself to collect a replacement before meeting Zapata at the heli. She would get him a suit too. They might need to enter areas affected by the biocide. The morning wind thrust through her clothes as she crossed to the first warehouse. She shivered. Fatigue tugged at her legs and feet after her long walk around Oceanside.

The warehouse door stood ajar. She slipped in and had to halt for a moment while her eyes became accustomed to the darkness. Even at that early hour a hum of soft voices filtered through the space. She entered the glass-walled room that stored the haz suits, and dumped hers onto the 'used' pile.

She grabbed two more suits, wedging them under her arm.

"Gotta shower first," said a voice.

A man had appeared in the doorway. He was one of the refuge coordinators.

"I'm not going inside. I'm going out again right now."

"If you come into the warehouse from outside, you have to shower. Those are the rules."

"But...That makes no sense. If I had a molecule of biocide on my skin I'd be dead."

"Leader's orders."

She dropped the suits. There was no point in arguing. It would only delay her.

The door to the showers opened automatically. She was already stripping as she passed through the doorway, dumping her clothes on the floor before stepping into the cubicle. The cold water spray hit her forcefully.

"Make sure you get all the nooks and crannies," the coordinator said from outside the stall. He'd followed her in. *Asshole.* In a couple of minutes she was done. She turned on the dryer. Another minute later, she stepped out of the stall.

The floor was bare. Her clothes were gone, and the coordinator was nowhere to be seen.

"Hey! What did you do with my clothes?"

The coordinator either didn't hear her or refused to answer. She scanned the room. In a corner stood a rectangular wire receptacle containing folded clothes. Next to it was a large box of shoes. She had a closer look. The clothes seemed clean. After riffling through them she found some about her size and put them on. She also found a pair of boots that fit. When she returned to the haz suit room, the coordinator was waiting.

"The biocide's getting closer," he said. "We can't afford to take any chances with people who've been off site."

"Fine. *Now* can I take two suits?"

"Be my guest." As the man left he remarked, "I hope you're allowed in when you get back. We might begin refusing entry altogether."

She picked up the fresh suits. As an afterthought, she grabbed four additional filters. Her arm weighed down with her new possessions, she went outside. Walking quickly, she made her way around the warehouse to the truck parking lot. Zapata was probably already waiting. As the helis came into sight, she was surprised to see not only the distant figure of the pilot, but four more people too.

She sped up her pace to a trot, wondering if a new obstacle to her hasty departure had arisen.

It had.

Zapata and the four people were arguing. She couldn't make out the words properly, but tempers were flaring. The pilot had his back to her. When he noticed the others' gazes switch to her approaching from behind, he turned.

"Great," he said, turning back to his antagonists, "I'd like to see you refuse the General's order to her face."

"What's the problem?" Cherry, asked, panting a little from her exertion.

"They won't allow me to board a heli. They're saying it's Leader's orders. That isn't right, is it?"

"Uh..." She handed Zapata the haz suits and filters. "What orders?" she asked the men and women. They were not military, as far as she knew. They were wearing civvies. But they had an air of authority about them, as if confident in their position.

"No helis are to be taken under any pretext," said a short, skinny woman with a severe haircut. "The evacuation is to begin at dawn."

"Evacuation?" asked Zapata. "No one said anything about an evacuation."

Cherry was similarly flummoxed. "When did you hear about this?"

"Not that it matters," the woman replied, "but we were informed late last night. We were told to keep an eye on these helis and make sure no one took any. We're going to need them all when the evacuation begins. The Leader wanted to make sure they were all on site when she made the announcement. I guess she didn't want anyone cutting the line." Her eyes narrowed as she looked from Cherry to Zapata.

"Right," Cherry said. Meredith seemed to have put together a plan to move the population sheltering within the warehouses to another, less dangerous, site. But that would be a very long-winded operation. Even if she deployed all the helis, only sixteen people at a time could be transported. The warehouses held thousands. "Where's the new refuge?"

The woman looked at her colleagues, as though seeking their opinion on whether she should answer. Two shrugged and the other gave no response.

"Suddene," the woman said. "We're all going to Suddene. It's safe there."

Suddene? Where the android had gone? Cherry wasn't sure the continent was safe at all, not with that thing roaming it. But how would she convince Meredith?

Eleven

Kes burst into the lab, accidentally slamming the door against the temporary wall. All the scientists pivoted and stared.

"Everyone, stop what you're doing and go to the meeting room immediately. I want you there in two minutes."

There was a moment of stunned silence, and then the women and men began to move, quickly putting down their instruments, equipment, or interfaces.

He strode through them, organizing his thoughts. On his way over, he'd been joyous. He'd finally made the breakthrough they needed. If he was right, the colony stood a chance. On the other hand, he'd also cursed himself for missing the answer for so long. But he hadn't been expecting it to be so simple.

Now he was faced with explaining it to the others, however, his optimism was waning. None of them had grown up on Earth. They had no experience with what he was about to announce. What he wanted to propose might sound like magic or the ravings of a madman. And if he couldn't convince them, they would be back to square one, faced with the impossible task of defeating the biocide before it killed them all.

He went inside the meeting room and sat down at the head of the table. Two people followed immediately. While he was waiting for the others, he opened an interface and began to search for medical practices on Earth.

They were difficult to find. If he had been looking soon after coming out of cryo aboard the *Nova*, he would have found them in a jiffy. Since then, as the information in the colony's data banks increased, older files had become more and more difficult to locate. More than five decades of information filled the system. The ancient files he was seeking were probably traceable, but he needed more time to find them than the two minutes' notice he'd given.

The room was filling quickly. An anticipatory hum was building up. He interlocked his fingers and rested his joined hands on the table. He would have to rely on his own powers of explanation. There was nothing else to do.

In a few moments the place was nearly full. He gave the stragglers another thirty seconds, counting down in his head. Sure enough, two more scientists arrived.

He began. "Thanks for dropping what you were doing and coming here so quickly."

"I think we're all guessing you have something important to tell us," said Tricia.

"I do, but as I've been sitting here waiting, I've realized how strange what I'm about to say may seem."

"Now you really do have our undivided attention," Dean said.

"Okay, here goes. At our last meeting I commented that the biocide's method of transmission indicated that it might be attached to a virus, and Thom said it might actually *be* a virus, not the toxic agent we were imagining. If it is, and if we can isolate it, then we have a very simple solution to our problem." He paused and took a breath. "Has anyone heard of vaccination?"

The silence was deafening. Blank looks passed between the assembled scientists and returned to meet his gaze. His resolve sank a little. He was hoping *someone* might know about the ancient practice.

"Okay." He pulled his hands apart and lay them face down on the table. "This will take some explaining, but hear me out. You all know I'm one of the Woken, right? I was born on Earth, grew up there, and worked on the *Nova Fortuna* Project before traveling here in cryonic suspension." His words sounded somewhat far-fetched even to himself.

"I think we all know that," said Tricia, casting glances around the room. No one contradicted her.

"All the Gens—the generational colonists originally chosen to live on the ship—were virus-free when they came aboard. They'd been treated with antivirals and anyone who didn't have a clean bill of health after treatment was denied entry. The same was true for me and the other project scientists. If we weren't free of all viruses we couldn't go.

"And during the trip to Concordia, no viruses emerged. Bacteria, yes. It was impossible to make everything sterile and it would have been foolish to try. We need bacteria to survive, even though some cause infections. But no measles, no chicken pox, not even the common cold. In a sense, it's a miracle. Humanity had been plagued by viruses all the millennia of its existence, and in the end it was a virus that destroyed civilization on Earth. But not here. Not on Concordia. No Concordian virus has ever infected a human as far as we know.

"But what that means is, you don't know about vaccination. I'm not an immunologist, but I'll do my best to explain. You know how if bacteria enter a wound and cause an infection, the body's antibodies rush to the spot to destroy the invading microorganisms? A similar thing happens with viruses, only, in the majority of cases, the body *remembers* the virus and if the body detects it again, it already has antibodies to deal with it. Most humans can only be infected by a virus one time. After that, they don't suffer the same infection again. In fact, it's a little more complicated, but that's the gist."

"And this process is called vaccination?" Tricia asked.

"No. Vaccination is the process of priming the body to recognize and destroy the virus before it can do any harm."

"By infecting the person with the virus? That seems self-defeating."

"Just listen, and then we'll do questions." He was worried that Tricia's innocent inquiries would sow doubt about his proposal. "On Earth, most children were vaccinated when they were babies and toddlers to prevent them from catching certain serious childhood diseases. Or, rather, the practice *was* commonplace until the Natural Movement got going and put an end to widespread vaccination. But for a couple hundred years the practice worked. It saved countless lives and... I don't see any reason why we can't try to do the same here."

"You mean do this vaccination thing on us?" asked Thom.

"If I'm right, it means our bodies will fight off the biocide and we won't even notice it tried to infect us."

"*If* it's a virus," Thom said.

"If it's a virus."

The general reaction seemed skeptical. He could simply order them to begin the process of creating a vaccine, but he didn't want that. It was important that everyone understood what they were doing and believed in it. He didn't want to force his colleagues or their doubt would be apparent to the rest of the Concordians, who then might refuse their vaccination.

"If we had more time," he said, "I would find and show you the files from Earth that explain the practice, but we don't. I have to ask you to believe me and to trust me."

"We do trust you, Kes," said Tricia. "It just seems so weird. I've never seen this happen in Concordian life forms. I've seen them die of viral illnesses, but—"

"We've barely broken the surface of understanding viruses here. In fact, we've been extremely lucky that no Concordian viruses have infected humans or the plants we grow. In coming centuries, one may mutate and we could have an epidemic on our hands, but that isn't our problem right now. If this biocide is a virus, vaccination could be the way we defeat it: by harnessing our immune system."

"I'm happy to try anything," said Dean. "It isn't like we have a choice, is it? The biocide will be on our doorstep soon. What do we have to do?"

"Right," said Kes. Introducing the concept hadn't gone too badly. His colleagues hadn't outright rejected it. Now came the hard part. "To trigger the immune system response, we have to give it something to recognize as the enemy."

"Like what?" asked Tricia. "Surely the only way the immune system can recognize the biocide is by introducing the biocide to it."

"Yes, that's right."

"You *have* to be kidding."

"That's insane," Dean said. "Anyone who encounters that stuff dies before they take another breath. A corpse's immune system isn't going to respond to anything."

"I know how it sounds, but bear with me. Vaccination entails injecting a weakened form of the virus or the dead virus into the blood system. Sometimes the recipient experiences a reaction—a low fever, for example—but in nearly all cases the reaction is minor and the recipient develops immunity. I have to tell you, however, that the process isn't perfect. A small number of recipients don't develop immunity and a handful of cases out of a million may experience a serious reaction."

Tricia asked, "So this vaccination you're proposing could make some people very ill and for others it won't work at all?"

"That's my prediction, according to what I know."

"And this is a solution?" someone asked quietly.

"Even dead biocide..." Thom shook his head. "I don't know. I wouldn't like any of that stuff injected into me."

"What other options do we have?" asked Dean. "What else have we turned up? We haven't made any real progress in days. We have to try *something*. And the basic idea... It does make sense. I'm sure I recall stumbling across the process when I was doing research as an undergrad. I didn't understand it at the time, but now... I don't see a reason why it wouldn't work."

"I do," Tricia said. "If it works for viruses, why doesn't it work for bacteria?"

"The immune system responds differently to viruses compared to bacteria," said Kes. "Or we could treat the biocide with antibiotics. But we know the biocide isn't a bacterium. If it was we would have found it days ago, and it wouldn't act so fast."

"Did Earth viruses act that fast?"

"No, or I never heard of one that killed that fast, anyway. But, talking of speed, are we agreed that we move our work in the direction of vaccination? We don't have time to prevaricate. I plan on finding out all I can about creating vaccines. Unfortunately, we won't have much time for testing, if any. What I need you to do is examine the tissue samples for anything that resembles a virus. I know that immunology is an obscure area of study, but—"

"I've studied it a little bit," interrupted a young man. He didn't look old enough to have graduated. A beard was trying and failing to grow on his upper lip and chin. Kes didn't know his name.

"You have?"

"I thought it seemed interesting, and I thought there might be practical applications in the future if native viruses began to infect our crops."

It was a serendipitous moment. Everything seemed to be coming together at last.

"Right," Kes said. "You're going to give us all a crash course in everything you know about isolating viruses from infected tissue,... ?" He looked questioningly at the man.

"Drew. My name's Drew. I'll do my best. I'll prepare some equipment for a demonstration." He rose and left.

No one moved. Kes waited. He'd done all he could to sell the idea. Now it was down to the others to run with it, or not. If he faced downright refusal, he didn't know what he would do.

Finally, Tricia said, "Come on, guys. Let's get to work." Her words seemed to break the spell, and the other scientists began to stand and shuffle toward the door.

As Tricia stood up she leaned toward Kes. Under the noise of the departing attendees, she said, "I hope you're right."

"So do I. So do I."

Twelve

Cherry hovered outside the cubicle assigned to the Leader, composing herself before she went in. She would not be able to look Meredith in the eye without reliving that fateful moment she'd taken Concordia's destiny into her own hands and issued the order to engage in battle with the Scythians.

How many times had she gone over that moment? How many times had she wondered if she'd done the right thing? On the face of it, it seemed her decision had been entirely wrong. Millions of Fila had died, thousands of Concordians too, and the planet was set on a path toward utter sterility.

But if she hadn't given the order, what would be happening now? The Scythians had given a vicious demonstration of their attitude toward humans, entirely unprovoked. They had sought to crush any thought of refusal or rebellion in the minds of their prospective slaves. But they had also given a picture of what Concordians could expect if they agreed to the Scythians' demands.

What kind of life would that have been? All their hard work and resources would have gone to supply a growing population of Scythians, living in idleness on their origin planet, unable to leave their environment-controlled domes. What was the point of that kind of existence for humanity?

All the work and preparation that went into the *Nova Fortuna* Project, all the thousands of people who lived and died on its long journey across the galaxy, all the effort that had gone into building a civilization on their new home planet—all would have been for nothing if they'd given up their freedom.

She had no doubt that Meredith disagreed, and fervently. Their Leader had been all for capitulating, kowtowing to the Scythians who had just murdered thousands of her people. Even as Cherry thought back to Meredith's cowardly response, disgust and fury rose up. But she had to keep it under control if she was to persuade the Leader to agree to her request to take a heli to Suddene.

An unbidden memory popped into her head. She was in the shelter she'd constructed after the first Scythian attack, when they had razed the initial settlement. She recalled the damp, the hunger, and the desperation so vividly. Ethan was there. Garwin, too. Poor Garwin. He'd died too young and broken-hearted.

The colony had needed a leader who would take them forward. Someone pure-hearted, brave, and tenacious. Everyone except Ethan knew *he* was that person. But he'd suggested that she should do it. *I don't have the patience*, she'd replied. How true that was. Her snap responses had worked against her so many times, not least when she'd alienated Wilder.

Cherry reflexively closed and opened her fist. The regret she felt for her decision to fire on the Scythians was inescapable and enormous, but in honesty it was more regret for what had happened as a result, and less regret for the decision itself. She wasn't sure if, given identical circumstances and knowing the terrible outcome, she would not have done exactly the same thing again.

If Meredith brought up the subject, what should she say? Should she lie and tell the Leader she'd been wrong? Tell Meredith they would all be better living as slaves because any kind of life was better than none? No matter how expedient the response might be, she knew she could never say it. The words would refuse to leave her mouth.

The only other option would be a shameful skirting around the truth—not something she could easily do. That time in the shelter with Ethan and Garwin, she'd been right. She would make an awful Leader.

There was nothing for it. She would just have to go in and wing it. Lacking a hard surface to knock or a doorbell to ring, she went to announce her presence, but Meredith said,

"Cherry, are you going to come in or are you going to stand out there all morning?"

She opened the curtain. Meredith was sitting on a camping chair at a small table. The only other furniture in the room was a space cot.

"I could see your boots below the curtain," Meredith explained.

Cherry let the curtain fall closed behind her. "How did you know it was me? These aren't even my boots."

"The people I asked to keep watch on the helis comm'd me that you were coming over."

"Right. I need to take one of them to Suddene."

Meredith looked at Cherry with Ethan's eyes. It was the first frank look that had passed between them since the battle. Reproach, resentment, and rancor exuded from Meredith's gaze, yet fatigue and defeat were also there. Perhaps the latter two had been prominent long before the Scythians returned. A stab of pity hit Cherry. Meredith had been expected to fulfill a role she was unsuited for. She had to live up to impossible expectations, based on Ethan's legacy.

The Leader seemed to have aged ten years in the past week.

"And?" Meredith asked coldly.

"And what?"

"I believe it's customary to state a reason when requesting the use of government property. Or do you think you're above that too?"

Cherry chose to ignore the bait. An argument would only delay her trip to Suddene. Besides, what was done was done. There was no undoing it, however much they debated the wisdom of her decision. She also suspected that Meredith wanted to be worked into such a state of heightened emotion that she would do what she should have done in the first place: sack her General. Incarcerate her, even. She'd committed treason and, in the Leader's position, Cherry would not have tolerated it.

But Meredith was not Cherry. She was weak, Cherry realized with a flash of insight—weak, tired, and way out of her depth.

"Is it okay if I sit?"

Meredith sighed. "Be my guest."

Cherry perched on the edge of the cot. "I went back to Oceanside, into a dead zone. I wanted to find out what happened to that thing that calls itself a Guardian."

"That seems the least of our worries now."

"I don't know. Maybe not. Meredith, I'm no scientist. I can't figure out a way to stop the biocide. All I can do is continue to try to protect this colony as well as I can for as long as I can."

"You don't seem to have done a very good job so far."

Cherry grimaced. Again, she refused the bait. "The Guardian has gone to Suddene. It took a ship and arrived there days ago. It has a purpose, a job. What that is, I don't know. But I suspect it isn't anything for our benefit. It may be trying to finish us off faster than the biocide."

"I don't understand why you're suspicious of that thing. The Guardians' sole purpose was to protect us. That was what they were made for."

"We don't know that it is what it says it is, and even if it is a Guardian, the situation is way more complicated. Believe me, I know them far better than you. More than once I was at the wrong end of a Guardian's weapon. They would not have hesitated to shoot me if their electronic brains decided my death was justified. *That* is what Guardians are. Not the colony's saviors."

Meredith looked unconvinced.

"What if it's working for the Scythians?" Cherry asked. "Don't you think it's a good idea to go after it and find out what it's up to?"

"The Scythians have finished us off already. They can't hurt us more than they already have."

"I haven't given up hope yet, and neither should you. You're the *Leader*. If anyone needs to believe we can survive this, it's you. People are looking to you for the will to carry on. You have to stand firm, Meredith. The colony is counting on you." Cherry was about to say more but she bit back her words. Referring to Ethan wouldn't be helpful, though it would have been true to say that without his faith they could make it the colony would never have survived.

Meredith's head sunk low. She said nothing for several moments, and eventually Cherry realized she was crying. Her teardrops dripped onto the dark concrete floor.

Shit. Cherry wondered if she'd said too much. Meredith was under tremendous pressure. Cherry scooted closer and put her arm over the Leader's shoulders. They sat together in silence. Cherry didn't know what to say. She was terrible with this kind of thing.

Finally, Meredith sniffed and rubbed her eyes with her sleeve. "Not very dignified for a Leader, huh?"

"It's okay. Leader or not, you're still a human being. I know it must be hard for you to be in your position. I couldn't do it."

Her head still hanging low, Meredith said, "When the Scythians returned and I wanted to agree to their terms, you told me that my father would be ashamed of me."

Cherry winced. "I have a habit of saying the wrong thing at the wrong time. I'm sorry."

"Did you mean it? Do you think it's true? You knew Dad from when he was young. You probably knew him as well as Mom did. Do you really think he would have been ashamed of me?"

Cherry considered, recalling Ethan as she'd known him. "He wouldn't have been ashamed of you. That was a dumb thing for me to say. He would have been proud of you for doing the best you could with these shitty, impossible circumstances. He would have been very proud of you. I'm sure of it."

Meredith slowly nodded. She straightened up. "Thanks for saying that. It means a lot. More than you know."

"I'm not saying it to make you feel better. It's the truth."

"I believe you. Take a heli to Suddene, Cherry. I hope you do us some good out there. We certainly need it."

"Thanks. I'll keep you updated."

Meredith nodded again, absently.

Thirteen

Kes was taking a short break, hastily eating a meal of pasta and seaweed as he stood outside the lab doors. Inside, his colleagues were working hard. Renewed energy had invigorated them. The fraught, quietly despairing atmosphere of the lab had been replaced by dynamic vitality. It would have been an exaggeration to call the atmosphere hopeful, but it was clear the scientists were now working with a strong sense of purpose.

The desired breakthrough had arrived. They had found the virus. Rather—Kes reminded himself so his optimism didn't grow out of bounds—they had found *a* virus. Something viral in origin had infected the Fila tissue samples, and it seemed to have been responsible for the majority of the cells bursting and dying.

No one had managed to isolate any virions from within the cells that remained whole, which indicated they had died not due to viral infection but due to the entire organism suffering extensive and devastating damage incompatible with life.

He had sent all the data up to Quinn along with several questions. He hoped the Fila would confirm that his species was not routinely infected by one or more viruses. There had been a handful of viral diseases on Earth that chronically infected some of the population. If the same was true of the Fila, it could mean the scientists hadn't found the biocide at all, but something irrelevant.

Even if they had found the biocide, it was only the first step in protecting the colony. They would have to create a vaccine from the dead virus. He only knew the basics of the process, and that was only because he'd finally managed to locate the relevant files in the recesses of the databases. And if they could create a vaccine, there was no guarantee it would work. It could be fatally dangerous.

If the biocide wasn't dead but only in another state it could reactivate when introduced to live cells. They would test it on living human cells first, but eventually they would have to test it on a human subject. The person could die, and instantly if the biocide followed its usual pattern.

Assuming they managed to jump all the hurdles standing in their way and they created an effective, harmless vaccine, they could still be too late. The human immune system did not move at anywhere near the speed of the deadly biocide. It could be days or weeks before the colonists built up sufficient antibodies to deal with the powerful virus the Scythians had created.

He had also not forgotten the concept of herd immunity. Vaccines on Earth had never been one hundred percent effective. A minority of the vaccinated did not develop an immune response. Providing a substantial proportion of the population was vaccinated these individuals were protected regardless, because the virus was prevented from circulating. But on Concordia the biocide was everywhere. When it reached the refuges, every living thing would be a vector. The people whose immune systems had not been triggered by the vaccine would die, and there was nothing anyone could do about it.

It was an awful, sobering thought. His appetite disappeared. He put down his half-finished plate of pasta. Through the window in the lab doors, he watched the energetic movements of the scientists as they worked.

Even if they succeeded in making a vaccine, there were colonists whose fate was already decided. The biocide would arrive at the refuges and pass through them without effect except for the unlucky individuals.

What if Miki or Isobel didn't develop immunity? He was sure that pregnant women's immune systems behaved differently, though he didn't know any details. What if *he* didn't develop immunity? At least it would be a fast death, and he would die knowing that he'd helped to save many others.

He fastened his lab coat. It was time to get back to work.

As he pushed open the outer lab door, a scream rang out. He froze, the cry arresting his movement. The scream was filled with horror and dismay, and it echoed from the corrugated roof of the warehouse and bounced from wall to wall.

The scientists in the lab heard it too. They paused in their conversations and actions, their eyes widening.

"What the...?" Tricia walked to the inner door and looked out, but the wider view of the warehouse was blocked by rows of curtained cubicles.

In the distance, a commotion started up. Kes could hear shouts, cries, and exclamations, but he couldn't make out what people were saying.

"Go back inside," he told Tricia. "I'll find out what's happening and let you know. Hopefully it isn't as serious as it sounds, but we can't afford to waste time on it, whatever's happened."

It wasn't difficult to find the location of the disturbance. He only had to head toward the growing noise of people in shock and distress. Had the biocide already arrived and begun to work its way through the refuge? He didn't think so. The last report he'd heard had said it was still far distant, though working steadily nearer. Unless a canister of the stuff had landed nearby during the attack and hadn't opened until now, he couldn't imagine how it could have traveled to the warehouses so quickly.

As he drew nearer to the epicenter of the disturbance, he could make out what was being said.

"I can't believe it. I just can't believe it."

"She seemed all right. Didn't she seem all right? I mean, if anyone had known..."

"Ugh, I can't look. I'm leaving. I can't deal with this. Not along with everything else."

People were running past Kes, heading toward the same spot. Others were coming in the opposite direction, their heads down. When they were asked by the newcomers what had happened, they wouldn't answer and only hurried away.

A crowd had gathered around something on the ground. The people seemed transfixed in horrified fascination. They were clustered so tightly in the narrow space between two rows of cubicles, he couldn't see what they were looking at. A horrible dread overcame him anyway. Something terrible had happened. Something devastating.

He slowed his pace. He almost didn't want to find out the source of the horror on the faces of the onlookers. He wanted to turn around and head back, go to find Isobel and Miki and hug them and protect them from yet another appalling event to befall the colony.

But his feet carried him forward.

A comm request arrived from Tricia. "Have you found out what's happened yet?"

"No, but it's bad."

"An awful rumor's reached us. I wanted to check if it's true."

"Give me a minute." He pushed gently through the throng. No one resisted. They seemed in a state of shock and not in control of what they were doing.

He saw two feet first. Splayed apart. A woman was lying on her back. He didn't recognize who it was from her feet. They could have been any woman's. Her slim legs were also splayed, as if she were sleeping, casually at rest.

He could not see the upper half of her because it was obscured by the back of the man crouching beside her. The man was working energetically, pumping on her chest. He was trying to resuscitate her.

Kes still did not guess who it was.

Inexorably, he was drawn forward, as if pulled by a string, compelled onward against his will. Someone had suffered a heart attack, probably. It was morbid and an invasion of privacy to gawp at the poor person. But he couldn't help himself.

He stepped closer, and the woman's head came into view. His strength left him. It was Meredith, though her face was deformed. He could hardly bear to look at it.

The belt around her neck had been loosened, but it remained. The man—presumably a doctor—pounded rhythmically on her, jerking her body as if she were a marionette operated by an unskilled puppeteer.

But there was no life left. To Kes's eyes at least, the doctor's efforts were heroic but hopeless.

Overburdened with responsibility for the colony, or perhaps for another reason, Meredith had taken her own life.

Fourteen

Suddene was a yellow strip on the horizon. The ocean surged below, deep blue and scattered with the foamy crests of high waves. Cherry wondered what effect millions of rotting Fila corpses would have on the water. Every other marine organism had died, too. If Kes and the other scientists managed to neutralize the biocide, would the ocean ever recover from the massive disturbance to its chemical balance?

At least Quinn had survived. By a lucky stroke of fate, her decision to stand up to the Scythians hadn't resulted in his death too. Compared to the numbers of anonymous Fila who had died, her friend's survival was only a minor consolation, but she would take it. She needed every small comfort she could get.

"Looking hot over there," Zapata remarked.

Her gaze rose to the band of yellow. It had grown larger while she'd been contemplating the fate of the Fila.

Zapata threw a glance at her. They were both wearing the haz suits. The attire wasn't particularly suitable for desert traveling.

"Do you know the temperature at ground level?" Cherry asked.

"Forty-two C."

"It shouldn't be a problem. I'm going underground as soon as I arrive."

"So we're heading to Chimera? I thought I recognized the coordinates."

"We're heading to an excavation site. That's all you... Uh, I guess it's a little late for that kind of thing. Yes, we're heading to the site that would have become Chimera, our fifth missile silo. Is there anything else you want to know?" she added, ironically.

She liked the large, bearded man. He didn't try to make small talk to fill the silence on long flights—his comment about Suddene's desert had been his first in the trip—and he exuded calmness and reassurance. She was tempted to ask him to stay with her after they arrived. She was not afraid to go after the Guardian alone, but navigating the underground Scythian city would not be easy and her lack of a limb would hamper her.

But she had promised Meredith that she would send the heli and its pilot back to Lyonesse to help with the evacuation.

"I'll understand if you don't want to tell me," said Zapata, "but I'm wondering why you're going to Suddene. I know it isn't to escape the biocide."

It wouldn't hurt to tell the pilot the reason for her mission. She outlined the sequence of events leading up to her decision to travel to Concordia's second continent. "I have a feeling it's gone to the Scythians' city. I don't know why, but I plan on finding out. At the very least, if I discover it has gone there, that means it's working for the enemy. If it really is Faina, the last surviving Guardian, it wouldn't know anything about the city's existence, let alone where it is."

"That's some story. I learned about the Guardians at school. It's hard to imagine one of them might still exist. What'll you do if you find this thing in the city?"

"Kill it, of course. Destroy it, rather. It's a machine, not alive."

"But you haven't brought any weapons with you. How do you plan on killing it?"

"Even the Guardians' own, high-tech weapons had no effect on them. I won't be able to destroy it by shooting at it."

"Wait a minute," Zapata said. "You said if it's in the city it isn't a Guardian."

"Well, it could be. Another possibility just occurred to me. The Scythians might have picked one of them out of the wreckage of the *Mistral* and reprogrammed it for their own purposes." She blinked. What if she was right? Her guess fit the facts. The damaged android did look like Faina, but if it was Faina, the Guardian would have followed the human survivors to a refuge rather than going alone to Suddene. Unless Faina knew something or was trying to do something Cherry had no knowledge of. "Whatever it is, I'm going to destroy it."

"Even if it's a Guardian?"

"If it's a Guardian that hasn't been tampered with and it can demonstrate that to my satisfaction, maybe I'll give it fifteen seconds to explain itself. Maybe. I understand this might seem odd to you according to what you learned at school, but the colony is better off without them."

"Right. I suppose you know what you're talking about. So, how will you destroy it if it isn't affected by weapon fire?"

"I'll figure something out."

———

Someone had built a perimeter fence around the Chimera excavation site. Tall, chain link fencing attached to metal posts encircled the dark opening of the tunnel. Heavy metal gates barred the single dirt road leading to the tunnel entrance, and the excavation workers' giant trucks sat inside the fence. The fence, gates, and tunnel roof were only small anomalies in the vast expanse of desert, but they were foreboding and entirely unexpected.

Zapata had to have seen them too, but his only comment was, "Do you want me to land inside or outside the compound?"

It *was* a compound, she realized. The only reason for the fence was in order to protect things or people within it. The citizens of Suddene must have relocated to the Chimera excavation site, hoping to avoid the biocide as long as possible. But why the fence?

"Did you know about this?" Cherry asked the pilot.

"Uh uh. I think it means trouble. I'll fly you inside if you want, but..."

"It might be more diplomatic to ask for admittance."

"Yep."

"Set her down fifty meters from the gates."

Her stomach moved rapidly upward as Zapata lowered the heli out of the sky. He landed on the highway, lifting clouds of sand.

As the skids touched road, she reached for the door, but Zapata said, "Wait a minute." He turned off the engine, and the heli's circling blades slowed to a stop. The sand began to settle. "A weapon might not work against a Guardian, but it might have been handy to deal with scared colonists."

The fence around the Chimera site was beginning to make sense to her too. Whoever had put it up wanted to keep out everyone else: anyone not already inside the compound might be contaminated.

"Weapon or not," she said. "I have to talk to them."

"I'll come with you."

She was grateful. She wouldn't have asked Zapata to take the risk on her behalf, but the large man had an intimidating presence that might come in handy.

The desert and the distant fence were becoming clearer as more of the disturbed sand settled. They climbed out of the craft. She recalled her previous visit, when a gale had been blowing and the light heli had not even been able to land. Now, the air was still and the desert baking. As she stepped out of the heli's shadow, the blazing heat of the sun immediately began to warm the inside of her haz suit.

They walked toward the metal gates in silence. No movement stirred within the fence. It was possible the gates were unmanned. Standing outside in the desert heat for any length of time would be brutal. She hoped they would not be forced to stand and holler to be let in.

"Stop where you are," a voice shouted. The sound had come from the gates, though she couldn't see its source. The effect was odd, as if the words had been discharged by the shimmering desert haze. "Non-Chimera residents are not permitted to enter," the voice continued, faintly. "Turn around and go back. You aren't welcome here."

She and Zapata were still forty meters from the gates. The pilot continued to stride onward, but she touched his arm, signaling him to halt. Something had rung a bell in her mind. She knew that voice. It was a man, but not Alun, the Chimera site supervisor. What had the other man's name been? The one who had lost the game with Pearl and remained behind while she went with Cherry into the Scythian city.

She had it. "Laurie?" She strained to make her voice counteract the muffling effect of her helmet. The biocide clearly hadn't made it this far. She removed her helmet. "It's me, Cherry. We met when I came to—"

"I guessed who you were," Laurie yelled. "There aren't many one-armed women on Concordia. Go away. You're not bringing that poison in here to kill us all."

"I'm not bringing..." She rolled her eyes. "We aren't carrying any biocide. We're only wearing haz suits because I thought it might have reached here already. We can take them off if you want."

"Doesn't matter. We aren't taking risks."

She went to speak but then closed her mouth. He had a point. The safest thing for anyone to do in the circumstances was to remain as isolated from other living things as possible, even other human beings. No one knew the exact details of how the biocide was transmitted. It was conceivable the poison could be carried on clothes without affecting the wearer, which is why she'd been forced to change into clean clothes at the refuge.

The dry desert air and all the shouting were making her hoarse. "Can I come up to the gate to talk about this?"

"If you move a single step in this direction I'll shoot."

The reply was exactly what she had feared. The people in the compound had weapons. Where had they found arms on Suddene?

"I hate to suggest it," Zapata said, "but they might allow you to come closer if you strip off your clothes."

"If I...?"

"I'll turn around. I promise."

The idea didn't appeal, but it might work. "*Shit.*"

If that was what it took... She called out, "What if I take off all my clothes? If I had biocide on my skin, I'd be dead, right?"

This drew a pause from Laurie. Was he thinking over the proposal or discussing it with someone else? The shouted conversation must have attracted the attention of others.

"If you strip butt naked," yelled Laurie, "you can approach the gate. But we're still not letting you in."

Great.

Zapata turned his back but not before she detected his eyes creasing in amusement.

She pulled open her haz suit and unzipped it. As the suit crumpled to the ground she stepped out of the legs. She quickly unfastened the buttons of her shirt and shrugged it off before stepping on the heels of her boots to remove them. Finally, she pulled down her pants and took off her underwear. The sun coated her naked skin in broiling heat.

Angry and embarrassed, she didn't wait for the okay from Laurie. She set off toward the gate and after a few steps she broke into a trot. The hot sand burned the soles of her feet and the sun's rays were cooking her skin. She had heard of people lying on beaches in the sun simply for the pleasure of it, but the idea had never appealed. She didn't think she'd ever exposed her body while outdoors. What an occasion for a first experience.

The shadow cast by the gate was a welcome relief the moment she set foot into it. The sand felt cool under her feet and her skin ceased to burn. "I'm here." She rested her hand on the gate. "Open up."

"I said, we're not letting you in." Laurie's disembodied voice came from the other side. There was no hole or window but it was clear he could see her. She looked upward, craning her neck to search the lengths of the posts. The black, glass eye of a camera reflected the bright sunlight.

"Then what was the point of all this?" Cherry asked.

"You wanted to come closer to the gate."

"This is ridiculous! Open up, dammit. I'm the General. I go where I want. Do you want me to give a command to blow these gates apart?"

"Concordia doesn't have a military anymore. The Scythians destroyed it. And now they're destroying the planet, but we'll last the longest. We might even last forever if the biocide burns itself out. We have seed and everything else we need to start again. So, no. I'm not letting you in. I'm sorry. You seem like a good person. It's nothing personal. But we can't take the risk. So go back to your heli and return to Lyonesse. It was nice knowing you."

Everything we need to start again? If the biocide burns itself out? Was it possible the people holed up in the Chimera site were on to something?

Even if they were, that didn't help with her immediate problem. She rested her forehead on the cool metal. Then she had an idea. "You haven't asked me why I'm here."

"I know why you're here. You want to escape the biocide. But we're full.

We can't take any more people. Sorry, but we just can't. So go home, and tell the others if anyone tries to break in we'll shoot to kill."

"You're wrong. I'm not here to get away from the biocide. And hardly anyone on Lyonesse even knows about this place. The project was secret, remember? No one knows about your plan to hide out here. No one is going to try to join you. I guarantee it."

"I don't believe you. What other reason could you have for coming?"

Before she could reply, another voice rang out from behind the gate. "Laurie, what are you doing?" It was a man's voice.

"Alun?" she asked.

"Who's that?" Alun uttered an expletive then said, "Why the hell is there a naked woman out there?"

"Alun, it's me, Cherry. You helped me investigate the Scythian city."

"Open the gate, Laurie."

Laurie protested, but Alun cut him off, saying, "Open the gate, you damned idiot!"

Locks rattled, and one door of the gates opened a few inches. An arm holding a jacket appeared through it. Cherry took the jacket and put it on. The hem reached low enough to cover her modestly.

"Thanks. Can I *please* come in now?"

Fifteen

Wilder was going crazy with boredom. Her confinement aboard the *Opportunity* reminded her of her trip to the Galactic Assembly. The weeks and months of that journey had dragged by, with little to stimulate her mental faculties except her studies of the Fila and the strange interpersonal dynamic between Cherry and Aubriot.

But at least then she'd had other humans to keep her company. At the time, she would have given a lot to get away from them and the close, sweaty proximity of other people with their loud voices and boring conversations. Now, she would give a lot to have just one of them with her. Even that asshole Aubriot would be better than no one.

She idly pressed the button on the a-grav machine. It turned on and immediately moved slightly toward the ceiling, which faced away from Concordia. The movement was barely noticeable but in micro-g she couldn't expect any more. It was enough to tell her the machine was working.

When she'd first made it work, she'd been overjoyed. She'd hollered and bounced around the living quarters, rebounding from all its surfaces and sending Piddle and Puddle scampering into their sleeping pouches. But then she'd been sad she had no one to share her success with. She'd contemplated trying to comm the surface to let one of the secret team working on the project know what she'd done, but she'd realized how crass and tactless it would be. Whoever she spoke to would have been in fear of their imminent death, assuming they'd even survived the battle with the Scythians. Her news, from the safety of the *Opportunity*, would seem extremely self-centered and would probably be meaningless.

For the first time in her life, she'd felt lonely. She'd been alone plenty of times. It was her preferred mode of existence. But she'd also known there was always someone she could comm if she wanted. She'd had the choice. Her circumstances were different now. Soon, she might be the only human being left alive, and no matter how much she craved human company, she would never see or hear another person again.

From then on she'd tried to keep herself occupied to stave off the sense of solitude. She had taken apart the a-grav machine and put it together again twice. The thing worked like a dream. She couldn't have asked for a better result from her years of toil. What a waste that no one except Quinn and the other Fila crew might know about it.

She turned off the machine. It sank a few centimeters and floated, like her, in midair.

She had to talk to someone. She liked Quinn. Perhaps she even loved him. But he wasn't human. Talking to him wasn't the same as talking to someone who thought in a similar way to her. Someone she could relate to. Heck, Quinn didn't even perceive time the same way she did.

As the days had passed, the prospect of remaining alive after all the other Concordians died had appeared more and more bleak. She had begun to regret her promise to Kes.

He'd said she could talk to him whenever, but he was racing against time to halt the progress of the biocide. She had no right to interrupt his work or the precious few hours of rest he would be allowing himself. Not for something as trivial as a chat. Yet even thinking about hearing the sweet man's voice made her tear up.

He hadn't got back to her about the people she'd asked him to check up on. He was too busy, of course. Maybe she could do the sleuthing herself. "Quinn, can I comm the surface directly from here?"

"I can arrange it so you can," the Fila replied, "but I warn you the network is very slow and most individuals have no direct access to comm. The connections must be made via coordinators at each refuge."

She suddenly realized she didn't even know the real name of the person she wanted to speak to, let alone which refuge he'd gone to. "How about the public records? Are they still available?"

"I believe so. They haven't been updated since the battle, however, except for a list of known refuges. No one has recorded the deceased or the locations of the survivors, if that's what you want to find out."

"I actually want to find out something different. Can you connect me to the surface now?" She reached out and grabbed a handhold before searching for inhabitants of a certain address. She remembered it from the time she'd gone there with Tycho to pick up the spare a-grav machine parts.

The information wasn't available to the general public, but she used a couple of hacks she'd devised years ago to access far more sensitive data. In moments she had the names of the family members, including that of a fifteen-year-old boy. She was surprised by the boy's age. When she'd seen him she'd thought he was about twelve.

Her task had been easy so far. Now came the hard work. She had to locate Niall Cully among tens of thousands of displaced Concordians. One fifteen-year-old kid, who could be anywhere. There was nothing for it except to comm each refuge, one by one, and hope the coordinators had a local database of residents.

She worked her way through the list of refuges. Each time it took ages for the comm to go through, and then even longer for the brief conversation with the local coordinator. Some did have lists of residents. None of the lists contained the name Niall Cully, or even anyone with the same surname. She was sure Niall would have remained with his family when Oceanside was evacuated. He was only a kid.

The names of the refuges gave no indication of the number of people who were sheltering there so she couldn't comm the largest ones first. An hour from when she began, she'd spoken to five coordinators and she had eleven more refuges to contact. Though she didn't know how large the refuges were, sometimes she recognized a place name that would all but rule it out from her search. Cerberus, for instance, was an unlikely destination for Niall's family. The missile silo was far from Oceanside and who in their right mind would head there when the planet was under attack?

She moved to the sixth refuge on her list. A place called simply Highway 1 15 K. She guessed that meant a spot near the highway fifteen kilometers from Oceanside. In fact, it had to mean that. It was a smart choice of name. The refuge would be easy to locate. She placed a comm to the center coordinator and waited.

The deathly quiet of the ship reigned. Except for an extremely faint, possibly imaginary hum from the engines, she was surrounded by the silence of space. The lack of noise seemed to encroach and press into her ears. Her sense of loneliness, hundreds of kilometers from another human being, grew almost too great to bear. She was about to ask Quinn to play some music when the coordinator replied.

"Hello, Highway 1 15 K."

"Hi, I'm looking for someone. Can you help me?" She waited many seconds for the reply.

"I can try. Who are you looking for? I need their full name and the person's rough age if possible."

When she had first heard the coordinator's voice, she had felt a tinge of familiarity, but it was too faint to draw her full attention. But the second time he spoke, the bell rang louder. She thought she recognized the speaker, but she couldn't quite believe it. Was her loneliness causing her imagination to play tricks on her? She didn't want to look like a fool by stating her suspicion.

"I'm looking for a boy about fifteen years old. His name's Niall Cully."

Long seconds later, the reply came. "Uh..." the coordinator hesitated "that's me." He sounded confused, as well he might. He probably had all his family with him and maybe his friends too. No doubt he was wondering who was this stranger looking for him.

She was about to attempt to explain herself when Niall continued, "Is that...? Are you Deadly After Midnight?"

"Yes! It's me. Did you recognize my voice? Hello, Jamie Bond. You'll never guess where I am." Excitement at talking to her friend from the secret a-grav machine group was making her giddy.

But she had to wait many frustrating seconds for his reply.

Surprisingly, he sounded a little annoyed. "How come you know my real name? We aren't supposed to snoop on each other. What did you hack to find out?"

"It was easy. I came to your house, remember? I knew your address and your rough age. There was only one occupant at that address of around the right age. Anyway, don't you think we're a little past sticking to the rules and regulations?"

"Agreeing not to snoop on each other isn't a rule or regulation. It's a part of the honor code."

She paused and swallowed. The conversation wasn't going at all how she'd hoped. "I'm sorry, okay? I'm glad you survived the attack. I only wanted to find out how you are and I-I wanted someone to talk to."

The lag before Niall's reply was longer than usual. He was pausing too, perhaps thinking about what to say. She hoped he didn't close the comm on her. Eventually, he said, "I'm sorry. I didn't mean to be so hard on you. Things aren't easy right now. I guess the stress is getting to me. Hey, now you know my real name, you should tell me yours."

Smiling, Wilder told him. Then she told him where she was, in the interest of full disclosure. She didn't want to delude him into thinking she was in the same predicament as him, even by omission. In anticipation of his inevitable question and to save time, she also told him how she'd ended up on the *Opportunity*, the sole Concordian not at risk from the biocide.

At the end of the intervening silence came Niall's low whistle. The section of her story of most interest to him was the part where she'd gotten the a-grav machine to work. "What a shame the people who rescued you let the machine go."

Tell me about it.

"So that's why you wanted the spare parts," Niall continued. "You wanted to take them up to the *Opportunity*. Have you had any success repeating your process?"

Trying not to sound too proud, she replied in the affirmative. "I have a complete working machine in here with me right now. I wish I could send you a vid, but it would be frivolous in the circumstances." She didn't want to take up any more of the precious network bandwidth.

"Oh, I believe you," said Niall. "You wouldn't lie about something like that. I'm green with envy and full of admiration at the same time. Well done, Wilder. Well done."

Not wanting to dwell on the a-grav machine, which she was honestly finding less interesting now, she asked, "How are things where you are? And what's happened to your coordinator? I was surprised you answered on their behalf."

"I *am* Highway 1 15 K's coordinator. There are only thirteen of us and I kind of took charge. No one else wanted the job. We may have to change our name to Highway 1 20 K pretty soon. Someone went on a scouting mission the other day and saw the biocide has spread in our direction. It's unpredictable. Sometimes it advances in one direction but not another. Sometimes it races through the ground faster than a man can run. That was how it got my mom."

His tone had turned soft and quiet.

"I'm so sorry." She blinked as her vision blurred with tears. In micro-g the water didn't run down her face. She had to wipe her eyes with her sleeve. "Here I am talking about stupid a-grav machines when your mom has just died."

"That's okay. I don't really like to talk about it, but the short story is, we were evacuating from Oceanside like we'd been told to when Mom remembered she hadn't brought any food. We'd just grabbed what we could and left. I told her not to go back, that we would find food or the government would supply it, but she went anyway. I saw her coming back..."

A long pause followed in which Wilder said nothing. What could she say?

"She didn't make it," Niall finished.

Wilder still didn't know what to say. "I'm sorry."

"I don't know where my dad is. Haven't seen him for a few years." Niall's tone had lapsed into utter misery.

"I wish you could come up here with me. It would be cool to show you the a-grav machine."

"Thanks, but I would never leave these people. They depend on me. We all depend on each other. We're going to wait it out. Keep moving. Until they figure out how to stop the biocide. Then I'll go home."

"Don't do that. When this is all over I want you to come and live with me. I have a cool place..." She realized her forest home was probably a tree graveyard by now, assuming it had survived the battle. "I *had* a cool place, and I'll build another one. We can live together and work on interesting projects. What do you say?"

"I like the sound of that." He sounded happier.

"Great. Let's do it. When this is all over and I can return to Concordia."

"When this is all over."

There didn't seem to be a lot else to say, and she didn't want to take up any more network time. "I guess I better let you go."

"Yeah. It's been great talking to you, Wilder."

"You too, Niall. I hope we can meet up soon."

They said their farewells.

Wilder repeated her wish to herself, that she would see Niall soon, but she feared it would not come true. Not ever.

Sixteen

The death of the Leader had dimmed the already dark mood in the warehouse refuge by several notches. Kes could feel the morose, despondent atmosphere among the scientists as they worked quietly on developing the biocide vaccine. Even the mild banter that had gone on between the tired workers had disappeared. Speaking at a normal volume seemed intrusive and extravagant.

The reason for the change in attitude was clear and didn't need to be stated: the loss of their Leader when they needed her most was bad enough, but the fact that Meredith had committed suicide was way worse. What greater testament was there to the hopeless state of the colony than its own leader giving up on it?

It was more important than ever that the scientists announced some good news, something to indicate that all hope was not lost. Without a boost, Kes feared there would be copycat suicides. Meredith, in her sad, desperate act, had sown the idea as a quick way out of the dreadful situation.

He recalled the Second Scythian Attack, when the colonists had been hiding in Sidhe. Cherry's thought processes had been similar: if death was inevitable, better for it to be fast and on your own terms. Rather than waiting for the Scythian spiders to cut their way to her, she had run out to face them. It had been a rash, brave, and perhaps foolhardy act. A typical Cherry thing to do, like this new task she'd set herself of chasing down the escaped Guardian.

He didn't harbor the same suspicions about the android. His first encounter with them had been when Cariad had reactivated them to help defend the colony. He'd only ever known them to be helpful and self-sacrificing in the extreme. Cherry's experience had been different and he understood why she hated them, but he also wondered if her new undertaking was mostly due to the enormous guilt she felt.

The outcome of her decision to fight back against the Scythians had been devastating but unforeseeable. No one could have guessed that their enemy would choose to destroy all life on Concordia in preference to another intelligent species inhabiting their origin planet. It was yet another example of what the long-dead Vasquez had always said: they couldn't expect to understand how an alien species would think or act.

Cherry might never be able to forgive herself. If she was successful in her effort to track down the Guardian and discovered her suspicion was correct, she might be able to live with herself—just.

It was more probable that the android was only malfunctioning. After the damage it had suffered on its re-entry to Concordia, he was surprised it was working at all. At least finding it would keep Cherry occupied for a while. Did she know about Meredith's suicide yet? If she didn't, should he be the one to tell her?

A comm arrived from Isobel. She rarely comm'd him while he was at work, and then only if it was about something important. His stomach muscles clenched. The only reason he could think for Isobel to comm him would be that she'd gone into labor. She wasn't due for another three weeks, but an early labor wouldn't be unusual, especially for a second baby.

"Hey, darling," he said. "Is everything okay?" As he spoke, he was mentally listing the doctors at the refuge. They had set up a clinic, and he was sure a nurse lived only a few cubicles along from their own, too.

"I'm fine," Isobel replied in a reassuring tone. "Miki's fine too, but we're leaving for Suddene. I thought you might want to come and see us off. We have to be at the helis in a few minutes. That's all the notice I got."

"That's great news. Yes, I'll come to see you. I'll be there as soon as I can."

He strode to the door, telling the nearest person where he was going. Then he jogged along the pathways between the cots and cubicles to his temporary home of the last few days.

Isobel was pushing clothes into a bag. Miki was bouncing on the mattress, something she hadn't been allowed to do previously, clearly enjoying the freedom afforded by her mother's haste and distraction.

After briefly hugging his wife, he said, "I didn't realize the coordinators would go ahead with the evacuation to Suddene so soon after Meredith's death, but I have to admit it's a relief to know you and Miki will be safe. I'll help you pack. What do you want to take?"

"We're only allowed one bag per person. The helis can't carry much weight. But it'll be warmer on Suddene so we won't need much clothing. I'm packing summer clothes and a few of Miki's old baby things for the new baby when she comes."

He felt as though the wind had been knocked out of him. If Isobel gave birth soon he would miss it. He'd been there for Miki's birth and it had been the most emotional moment of his entire life, with the exception perhaps of marrying Isobel.

"Is something wrong?" Isobel asked.

In answer, he wrapped his arms around her. "I'm going to miss you."

"I'll miss you too."

"If the baby comes while we're apart..."

"Aw, honey. I hope she doesn't but if she does, I'll think of you."

"You'll have other things to concentrate on, but I appreciate the sentiment."

"We'll have our whole lives together with this child, and Miki, and any more that come along. That's the most important thing."

He squeezed his wife tight, carefully avoiding putting pressure on her bump. "You're right. And I'd rather miss the birth than have you and Miki spend a moment longer here with that biocide creeping nearer every minute. Come on. Let's get you packed."

"I think we're done. It's time to go out to the helis."

When Miki realized they were going somewhere, she immediately raised her hands and said, "Daddy carry."

He stole a glance at his wife.

"Go ahead," she said, smiling. "She's going to miss you while we're gone."

He slung both bags over his shoulders and lifted Miki up.

"I can carry a bag, you know," said Isobel.

"It's no trouble. Let's hurry. You don't want to lose your seat."

They went quickly toward the nearest exit. It was obvious to everyone that Isobel and Miki were two of the chosen few to be transported out of immediate danger. He didn't detect any jealous or angry looks, but the situation was not yet dire. When the biocide drew near, people might begin to panic. Then, those lucky enough to escape via heli might attract more hostile attention. Moving the thousands sheltering in the refuge to Suddene would take far more time than they had. It was inevitable that the majority would be left behind.

He would be one of those to remain. He would never willingly take the place of another person, even if it meant leaving Isobel a widow and Miki and his baby daughter fatherless.

He pushed the morbid thought to the back of his mind. If he was right about the vaccine, he would only die if he was unlucky and his body didn't develop immunity or didn't develop it in time for the arrival of the biocide.

As they stepped out of the warehouse, the wind hit him like a wave of cold water. He squinted in the sunlight. How long had it been since he was last outside?

"It's cold, Daddy!" Miki exclaimed, clutching him.

"It certainly is. Do you have her jacket for the heli ride?" he asked Isobel. Though the weather would be warm in Suddene, his wife and child faced an hours-long flight at altitude, and the heli heaters were inadequate at staving off low temperatures.

"I packed that first. And I have mine too. Quit worrying."

They walked quickly around the perimeter of the warehouse toward the section reserved for the helis. He spotted people in the far distance, doing something to the land. "Do you know what's going on over there?"

"Uh huh. The coordinators put together teams of workers to construct a defense against the biocide. A last resort, I guess. I'm sure you and the other scientists will figure something out before it comes too close."

"What kind of defense?"

They had rounded the corner of the warehouse and the helis were in view, past the ranks of autocars. Some colonists were already gathered and the distant figures could be seen boarding the aircraft. He had a sudden presentiment he might have to fight for Isobel and Miki's place. He told himself he was being irrational, while at the same time steeling himself for conflict. He would do whatever it took to get the two—almost three—most important people in the world to him onto a heli.

"I'm not sure," Isobel replied. "I heard two different stories. Our neighbor told me they were sinking plastic sheeting four meters deep, but someone else told me they were digging a trench four meters wide and filling it with sand. I guess whatever they're making, the dimensions are four meters."

Kes was skeptical. Bacteria and other microorganisms could be found way deeper than four meters, even in bedrock, and life of one kind or another would quickly colonize a stretch of sand, even if it was sterile when the workers put it in. That was the problem with life: once it got going, it was very hard to stop. It would colonize the most unlikely places, even the exteriors of deep space starships, clustering around venting ports.

The Scythians' plan to render Concordia barren was doomed to fail in the long run. If a planet could support life, life would evolve. And space-faring intelligent species would find the world and settle eventually. But perhaps the Scythians knew this and the death of humankind was sufficient. Either way, it made no difference to the colony.

They were getting close to the helis. he waved to attract attention. One of the pilots seemed to be waiting for them. She waved back and beckoned urgently. Some of the helis' rotors were already turning and their doors closing.

When they arrived at the vessel that would transport Isobel and Miki, he was out of breath.

The pilot checked her passengers' names and glanced at Isobel's protruding belly. "You realize she'll have to sit in your lap the whole way?"

"I know. Don't worry. I'll manage."

The pilot nodded in reply. "Stow the bags behind the seats." As Kes moved to do as she directed, she added, "Wait a minute. Give me those." She took each bag and lifted it, judging its weight. "Okay, go ahead." She returned the bags.

While he was putting them into the craft, the pilot gave Isobel and Miki ear protectors. She smiled as the little girl's eyes widened with amazement at the effect of the mufflers. "Hop aboard and strap in." She left them to go to her door.

"This is it." Isobel's eyes suddenly shone wetly.

"Yup, this is it." Kes's throat was closing up. He kissed Miki on the cheek and told her he loved her.

The little girl sensed the emotion of the moment and began to wail. Then she noticed she couldn't hear herself and was distracted by her ear protectors again.

Kes held Isobel close, whispering in her ear, "Stay safe."

"You too."

Time would not wait for a longer goodbye. They broke their embrace. Isobel climbed ungracefully into the heli, and Kes passed Miki to her. Their gazes did not break from each other while Isobel closed her door and he stepped backward as the rotors started up.

The heli lifted up into the sky and still they held eye contact. Too soon, Isobel was swept out of his sight. He stood and watched until the machine was a speck. When even the speck of the heli had disappeared, he turned and walked slowly back to the warehouse. The wind had cut through his clothes and chilled him, but there was an even chillier place in his heart.

Fifteen minutes previously, Isobel and Miki had been only a few tens of meters away. Now they were gone and he didn't know when he would see them again.

Seventeen

Alun offered to carry Cherry across the sand between the fence and the tunnel entrance to the Chimera excavation site to protect her feet. After weighing up the level of indignity, she declined. "It's hot, but it's bearable. As long as I run, I should be okay."

"You could wear my boots," Alun said. "Or his." He swiped Laurie around the head and relieved him of his weapon.

The younger man cringed. Now that he was face to face with Cherry, he avoided her gaze.

She looked from her bare feet to Alun's large, worn, dusty work boots. "I'm sure I'll be fine, thanks." She clutched the supervisor's jacket around her.

"What were you *thinking*?" Alun admonished Laurie for the fourth or fifth time. His subordinate had given up on trying to justify his behavior.

"Look, let's forget about it, okay?" said Cherry. "Is the comm network working here on Suddene?"

"It is. I just heard some bad news from Lyonesse, in fact."

He was about to tell her more but Cherry was already comming Zapata. "As you can see, they let me inside."

"Right," he replied. "I didn't see, actually. I'm still facing the other way. Listen, I have to return to the refuge. While you were running around naked in the desert I received a comm asking me to come back. They're beginning the evacuation."

"Okay, go ahead. I have plenty to do here while you're gone. Wait a minute. Where are you supposed to take these people after you collect them?"

"To Port City, the coordinator said."

The "City" part of the place name was a misnomer. It was based on what Port City had been expected to become. The collection of buildings around Suddene's only port was the closest thing the continent had to a town.

Cherry looked thoughtfully at the dark hole leading down to the man-made cavern. "I might have a better idea. Return to the refuge. If there's a change of plan about where to transport your new passengers, I or someone else will be in touch."

"Got it. I hope you find what you're looking for."

"Alun," Cherry said as she closed the comm, "I have a proposal. But let's get out of the sun."

The excavation that was to have become Concordia's fifth missile silo looked very different from how she remembered it. The large, brilliant lights were the same, but the area they illuminated now held an array of tents and shacks and people casting glances at her.

She was quite the sight: entirely naked under Alun's jacket, thanks to Laurie's paranoid, exclusionary tactic. Alun had told him to go and find her some clothes.

She was relieved that Alun didn't share Laurie's sentiment about 'outsiders', but she was unsure who held the majority viewpoint. In truth, she hadn't been shocked by Laurie's attitude. It was understandable. No one wanted to die, and the encroachment of the biocide was putting everyone in fear for their lives.

"How long have you all been down here?" she asked.

"We excavation workers never really left. As soon as we heard about the return of the Scythians, it seemed the safest place to wait out the battle. We brought our spouses and kids down here. When the fighting stopped, we thought we'd won, but then we heard about the biocide. Dead Fila started washing up in the bay. The people living in Port City and out at the solar farm asked if they could come here too. We said yes, of course. We weren't about to turn anyone away. I don't think any Suddeners have been killed. That stuff moves slowly through the desert."

"You really didn't mind the others coming down here? You weren't worried they might bring in the biocide?"

"We aren't all like that idiot," said Alun. "As I understand it, once that stuff touches you, you're dead. How would anyone who'd been in contact with it make it all the way in here?"

She didn't mention the possibility that the biocide could theoretically be carried on clothing without immediately killing the wearer. "Then why the fence?"

"There are desert animals. Mostly nocturnal. The fence is just a precaution, and an excessive one in my opinion."

"If the biocide enters Chimera, it'll enter through microorganisms in the sand and rock."

"My thoughts exactly."

Laurie was approaching, carrying donated clothes over one arm and a pair of donated boots.

She wanted to make her proposal before he arrived. "Alun, when I spoke to my pilot just now, he said he'd been recalled to Lyonesse to begin transporting some of the most vulnerable people to Suddene."

"I thought that was what your conversation was about. You're going to ask me if they can come here."

"You read my mind."

The older man rubbed his stubbly chin and narrowed his eyes as his gaze roved the vast underground chamber. "Space is no problem, as you can see. We don't have an infinite supply of water or food, though. How many do you think will come?"

"The helis can only transport one person at a time, or one person and a small child. We're only talking tens of people per day at most." How many those tens might add up to, she didn't know. But Alun was no fool. He knew what she was asking. The new arrivals were likely to put a strain on the resources at Chimera, if not immediately, then eventually.

He shrugged. "We're all Concordians, right? Tell them to come here and we'll do our best to accommodate them."

"Thanks, you're a good man. But is it likely to cause tension? Do many people here hold the same views as Laurie?"

"I don't think so, and if they do, I'll soon talk them around."

Laurie arrived. "I don't know if these will fit." He handed over the clothes and boots, still not making eye contact. "I did the best I could."

She took them without comment. It would be a long time before she would forgive him. "I'm going to walk back into the tunnel a bit to get dressed."

Under the cover of darkness, in the cool air of the access tunnel, she put on the borrowed clothes. They didn't fit well, but Laurie had included a belt, which she fastened tightly to hold up her pants. She rolled up the pant legs and the sleeves of the sweater. The boots were only a little too large but were bound to chafe without socks. Her attire would have to do.

When she emerged into the light of the construction lamps, Laurie had disappeared but Alun remained.

"I guess you're wondering why I'm here," she said.

"You haven't come to find new refuges?"

"No, that's just a coincidence. I'm on the trail of someone, or rather, some*thing*. Has anyone noticed someone who looks injured or burned?"

"Injured or burned? That's an odd kind of question. I don't think so. I haven't heard about anything like that anyway. I can ask around if you want."

"I don't have time. This thing has several days' lead on me. I guess it might have arrived and gone down to the city without anyone noticing. Do you turn out the lamps at night?"

"We turn them down, pretty low, but enough to see by. What is this *thing* you're talking about? And how did it get burned?"

"Have you heard of the Guardians?"

"The Guardians? Who hasn't? They're in every history textbook in school."

"This thing claims it's a Guardian, returned from outer space. I'm sorry, I don't have time to explain properly. I want to find it. I think it may have come through here and gone down into the Scythian city. Is it possible it could have done that without anyone noticing?"

"This place has been occupied since the battle. I would be surprised if—" Alun's eyes widened. "The ghost! Now, when was it? Three nights ago, I think. I was woken up by some kids screaming. Then it all went quiet and I fell asleep. The next day I heard the kids had snuck out of their tents to have some fun playing ghosts, and they claimed they'd seen a real ghost, or a monster, running across the open space in the center. No one believed them. A kid who's up past his bed-time and playing a scary game is bound to start seeing things. Mine were like that when they were young. But now I'm wondering if it was your Guardian they saw."

"Do you know if these children said where the monster went?"

"I didn't hear anything and I didn't ask. It was only a piece of gossip. I can try to find out for you."

"It doesn't matter. If the children saw what I think they saw, I know where it was heading. I need to get down into that city. The Guardian's been there three days already from the sound of it."

"You want to go back down there? Are you sure? Rather you than me."

She did not want to return to that strange place, where everything was in pitch darkness and the edges of drop-offs were marked by scents she could not detect. But she had no choice. "That's the plan. Can you help me? Can you lower me down, the way we did it before?"

"That won't be a problem. We have everything we need."

"Great. But can you ask someone other than Laurie to lower me this time?"

EIGHTEEN

Kes didn't know how long he'd been working. He'd lost track of time. He'd thought that Isobel and Miki going to Suddene would bring him peace of mind, but the opposite was the case. When his wife and child had been only tens of meters away, it had been easy to reassure himself they were okay. Now their safety was a mental concept, not a physical fact. He didn't regret their transfer to Suddene, but he would never be comfortable until he was reunited with them, preferably before the baby came.

He comforted himself that, the way things were going in the lab, his hope might be fulfilled. With the threat of the end of the colony hanging over them, the scientists were working faster and more efficiently than he'd thought possible. Not only that, with the exception of Drew, they were all working within an unfamiliar field and so having to learn as they went along.

If they produced a vaccine that defeated the biocide it would be nothing short of a miracle, yet he thought they might just do it.

However, they faced a major stumbling block. On Earth, the process of creating a vaccine included animal testing before the final human trials. From beginning to end, the whole process would take years. They had days and no animals to use as test subjects. Even if they'd known they needed them, there would have been no point in collecting any before evacuating Oceanside. Concordian animals were next to useless for their purposes. Their anatomy and cell structure were vastly different from humans'.

What the scientists needed as a minimum were mice—specially bred lab mice—and the only mice in the galaxy were light years away.

He rubbed his temples. They had no mice, specially bred for experiments or otherwise. They had no rats, rabbits, or monkeys. Not even cockroaches. Inevitably, at some point soon, they would need to test the vaccine on a human. They would have to inject 'inactive' biocide into a person. Who would they choose? Would one of the scientists volunteer? That wouldn't make a lot of sense. Currently, scientists were what the colony needed most. Yet who would nominate someone else to take the risk?

Waiting for death to arrive was one thing. Taking the chance of walking into its arms was another.

Thump!

He looked up. The noise had come from the outer door. He walked over to see what had caused it. An angry face was framed by the further window of the sets of double doors. The outer doors jumped as something hit them. All the scientists froze. Someone was trying to get into the lab. The person must have tried the outer doors and found they were locked.

He had asked for security to be installed when the lab had been set up, only to prevent children or clueless colonists from wandering in by accident. It was a dangerous place. But he hadn't imagined security would be needed to prevent someone from *forcing* their way in.

"Open up!" shouted the person outside, though his voice was faint and muffled.

Kes couldn't see much more than the man's red, sweaty face and his gaping mouth as he shouted again, "Let me in! Give me that biocide treatment! I want it. Now!"

A few fellow scientists were walking over.

"Go back to work," Kes told them. "I'll talk to him." He opened the inner door and began decontamination.

This stalled the angry man for a time, but then he struck the outer doors again and they jumped on their hinges. The lab was a temporary structure, not particularly strong. Anyone sufficiently determined could get in.

Kes comm'd one of the refuge coordinators. "We have an emergency situation here. Send over some CED officers." He stood face to face with the would-be intruder, the plexiglass window the only barrier. "Settle down. You can't come in here. It isn't safe for you."

He didn't recognize the man, who looked a mess. Then again, so did they all. Everyone was just getting by in the spartan and distressing conditions.

"Open up!" the man repeated. "I know what you're doing. You've made a cure and you're keeping it to yourselves. You're gonna wait for everyone to die and then you'll divide up the planet between you!"

Kes had to force himself to not roll his eyes. As conspiracy theories went, this one was one of the most outlandish he'd ever heard. But pointing out the stupidity of the statement was not going to get him anywhere. It would only entrench the man further in his ridiculous notion.

"Look," said Kes, "I understand you're frightened. We all are."

The man lifted his sizable arms and brought his fists down on the door with such force, Kes took a step backward. If the assault continued, the door would soon give way.

"Please calm down!" Kes exclaimed. "If you calm down, I'll come out and explain what we're doing. It isn't a secret."

He still hadn't made an official announcement about the proposed vaccine, but that was only because he'd been concentrating on his work. Meredith's suicide had been a major distraction too. Perhaps an announcement was way overdue. People needed to hear something positive. The tension was clearly driving some of them crazy.

There was movement behind the man's head. Kes thought he'd glimpsed a couple of people running over. He kept his gaze fixed firmly on the man's eyes to avoid giving him a clue about what was happening.

"I don't want an *explanation*," the man snarled. "I want a cure! For myself and the rest of us out here. And I want it now!" He raised a fist to hit the door again, but before he could make contact, he disappeared.

Kes leaned forward and peered on the floor. The man was down and two CED officers were wrestling with him. One of them had his arm behind his back. The other pressed down with a knee to his kidneys.

Kes released the lock and pushed the door open. Feeling an obligation to help fix the situation, he went out.

Thom was there among the gathering crowd, arriving for his shift. "Thank the stars for the good old CED, huh? What a lunatic."

"Oh, I don't know," Kes replied. "We can't really blame him. Everyone's feeling nervous right now. It's bound to tip some people over the edge."

"Nervous? More like desperate and terrified."

"That too. I'll talk to the guy, now he's subdued. News of this incident is going to spread like wildfire. It's already attracted considerable attention." A circle of curious onlookers continued to form. "I don't want anyone to think what he's saying might be true. I'll make an announcement about what we're trying to do and the progress we've made."

"Hmm," said Thom. "Yes to the second, no to the first. I wouldn't waste my breath on talking to him if I were you. There's no reasoning with someone in that state."

The man who had tried to force his way into the lab was resisting arrest. One of the officers had managed to fasten handcuffs around his wrists but they were struggling to get him to his feet. The man was kicking out at them. Kes felt somewhat responsible for his aggression and rage. If he'd explained what the scientists were trying to do, the man might not have acted as he had.

The interest of the growing crowd was moving away from the fight and onto Kes. The stares of the onlookers were hard and unforgiving.

Second-guessing his decision, he nevertheless side-stepped the tussle and moved out into open space. He raised his hands. "I want to explain what we've been doing. I have some news I'm sure you'll be interested to hear."

The gazes suddenly shifted to a spot at his rear and everyone's eyebrows rose.

"Watch out!" shouted Thom.

Reflexively, Kes quickly crouched.

A figure sailed over his head and crashed to the floor. The man had launched himself and flown over Kes when he met no resistance. The crowd gasped and drew away.

His hands secured behind his back, the man struggled to rise to his feet, but he managed it. His teeth were bared in fury and his eyes were bloodshot with rage. Kes had no chance of escape. As the man came at him, Kes did the only thing he could in the circumstances. He punched the man on his jaw with all the strength he could muster.

His attacker was out cold before he hit the floor. Kes stood over the fallen figure, a little bewildered by the speed of events.

"Thanks very much," said a CED officer. "I've been trying to do that for the last five minutes."

The two officers grabbed the large man under his armpits and dragged him away. The crowd remained, their expressions now less angry but more cautious.

Kes rubbed his aching hand. "I'm going to broadcast an official statement, but I'll give you all a synopsis now. You're clearly anxious about what we've been doing to halt the spread of the biocide. That's perfectly understandable and I apologize for not saying something earlier. First of all, what you have to understand is that it's going to be impossible to prevent the biocide from spreading."

This statement drew expressions of dismay. He raised his hands. "Please, let me finish. The biocide moves via contact between life forms, and Concordia is a living planet. The poison will continue to spread until it reaches a point where nothing living remains to sustain it. Then presumably it will die. But we may have a solution. Though I don't think there's anything we can do for other species, we may be able to save human life."

He gave a brief explanation of the principle of vaccination, putting it into layman's terms as well as he could. "I know most of you won't have any idea what I'm talking about, but I can assure you that vaccines saved millions, possibly billions of lives on Earth. The only reason you haven't heard of them is because we haven't needed them until now. We're making a biocide vaccine. I wish I could give you a one hundred percent guarantee that it will work, but I'm a scientist, not a politician. I only deal in facts, and the fact is, we won't know for sure until the moment of truth arrives. When the biocide reaches us, then we'll be sure. But I am confident that this is our best shot."

"If you're so confident," a voice yelled, "why did you send your wife and kid to Suddene?"

It was a good point. He could only speak from his heart in reply. "My wife is pregnant. I love her and I want her and my daughter to live as long as possible. They qualified to be transferred to Suddene, along with all the other vulnerable people in this refuge. In my position, what would you do?" He paused. "But one thing you're forgetting is that *I* am here. I and the rest of the scientists are doing our damnedest to save you and every other Concordian. We're doing our very best. We aren't hoarding a biocide cure as that man alleged. As soon as we've made a vaccine and tested it, we'll begin immunizing everyone here and then everyone on Concordia. After that, we wait."

He had said all he had to say. In the silence that followed, the assembled men and women muttered and grumbled, but they appeared mollified. The crowd began to break up. From somewhere at the back, an old man approached. He looked vaguely familiar, but Kes couldn't place him.

"Do you want to know more about the vaccine?" Kes asked.

"You don't remember me, do you?"

"I have to admit I don't. I'm sorry."

"No need to apologize. It's been longer than a hundred Concordian years since we met. I'm one of Wilder's friends."

"Oh, damn!" Wilder had asked him to check up on some of her friends and he'd entirely forgotten.

The man was looking quizzically at him.

"I'm sorry. I realized I'd forgotten to do something important. What's your name? I believe Wilder might have been worried about you."

"I'm Tycho. But I'm not here to talk to you about her. I came here to see what all the commotion was about, and I heard you mention this thing called a vaccine you've been working on. It's supposed to help us defeat the biocide, right?"

"That's right."

"I also heard you mention that you have to test this medicine. I figured you're going to need people to test it on. Well, I want to volunteer."

"You want to...? I'm not sure—"

"Don't you need people you can test with it?"

"Absolutely, but we can't—"

"I've lived a long, good life. It's going to end soon, one way or another. I can't think of a better way to go out than by helping my fellow Concordians. And, to be honest, it would be preferable to waiting on that horrible stuff to creep up on me. What do you say?"

What *could* he say? The main objection that sprang to mind was, if Tycho died, how would he explain it to Wilder? But the old man was entirely in charge of his senses and they did desperately need test subjects.

"I say that, with the deepest gratitude, I accept your offer."

Nineteen

Pearl was going to lower Cherry down to the Scythian city. Cherry remembered the woman well, and not only due to her blonde hair, green eyes and pale skin. When it came to actually entering the city, Pearl had backed out, saying the place gave her the creeps. Cherry knew exactly what she meant. It wasn't that the place had once been inhabited by aliens—Cherry had spent plenty of time in the company of the Fila aboard the *Opportunity*, and had eventually overcome her prejudice against them—there was simply something about the Scythian city that made her skin crawl when she came in close proximity to it. The Fila had never affected her like that.

It was a feeling she was going to have to get used to as she spent who knew how long searching for the Guardian. On her previous visit, she and Alun hadn't traveled far before the announcement of the return of the Scythians had forced her to abandon her investigation. There was no telling how deep or wide the metropolis of Concordia's former occupants stretched. This time, she could be inside for days.

She stood at the overhang, looking down into the dark abyss. Behind her, Pearl sat at the controls of one of the massive excavators, preparing to use the giant spiraled borer to unwind the line attached to Cherry's harness.

"If we'd had a bit more notice," said Alun, "we could have put together a proper winch for you. There's a few of us who are handy with that kind of thing. If you could wait another day or so..."

"I can't afford to waste any more time." She adjusted her backpack to make it more comfortable. Despite the short notice, Alun had gathered an impressive array of equipment to help in her search. Night vision goggles, a pathfinder, several lightweight lines and two small grapnels, a full water bottle and an attached device for drawing moisture from the air, emergency rations, a knife, and a small rectangular device with a display screen. He called the last item an 'electronic canary' and said it could detect poisonous gases.

"What's a canary?" Cherry had asked.

"No idea." Alun had also given her Laurie's weapon, insisting she take it with her.

"No weapon on Concordia will have any effect on a Guardian."

"Maybe not. But maybe you'll find something other than a Guardian down there."

Could a Scythian have survived hundreds of thousands of years on a planet with an atmosphere that no longer supported its metabolism? The Woken had been revived from cryonic suspension after a hundred and eighty years. But hundreds of thousands of years? She didn't think it was possible, but then, what did she know? Perhaps there were Scythians who could wake up and attack her. If they did, she hoped the oxygen in the air would do its work before she was forced to fight them.

"All set?" asked Alun.

"Yeah." Yet she didn't step forward into darkness or lower her night vision goggles over her eyes.

"Have you considered that it's unlikely there's another way out of the city? Not after all this time. Any other exits will lie beneath tens of meters of sand or soil. Unless this Guardian has done whatever it came here to do and already left without us noticing, all you have to do to catch it is sit here and wait for it to leave."

"I did think of that, but if it's doing something in there, I want to find out what. If I catch it on its way out, empty-handed, I'll never know. What if the Scythians left behind a gigantic explosive device, a kind of booby trap for the entire planet, and the Guardian starts up the self-destruct sequence?"

"Then we're truly screwed. Unless you imagine you can figure out how to deactivate it. And what are the chances you'll be able to do that?"

"Okay, bad example. But you understand what I mean, don't you? If we survive the biocide and manage to start again—though I admit that's a big *if* —the Scythians are bound to find out and return to finish us off properly."

The depressing fact had haunted her for days. As long as the colony remained on Concordia, and as long as the Scythians had ships, the battle for the planet would rage on. Concordians would live under constant threat of attack, down the generations. But though the situation appeared dire, they'd survived thus far. They would battle on.

She continued, "Anything I can do to find out more about them, including why the Guardian has gone to their city, is going to help us. And to achieve that, I have to try to find out where it's gone."

"I can see there's no arguing with you." Alun paused, clearly expecting her to say her goodbye and begin her journey.

Yet still she did not. Something was niggling at her, holding her back. She'd denied the impulse for a long time. Now she had to give in to it before she could take another step on this road from which she might not return. "Is there a comm connection in here?"

"If you go back to the main chamber, it's set up with relays to the surface."

"I just want to speak to someone quickly before I leave."

"Go ahead. Pearl and I aren't in a hurry."

Cherry walked through the tunnel dug by the original excavator that had broken through to the city, pulling down her goggles to see better in the darkness until she reached the cavern. As soon as she entered the vast space, she tried to connect to the comm network. She had to wait long seconds.

"Hello again." Aubriot's tone was dour, as usual.

"You're still alive."

"You too, from the sound of it."

"What's happening out at Cerberus?"

"Honestly, it's not good. The ground's damp and fertile around here. Plenty of microorganisms for the biocide to travel through. No one's looked outside for a while, but at the last check it was pretty close."

"But down there in the silo, it might never reach you. How deep are you? There has to be seventy-five meters of dead metal and concrete between you and the nearest soil. You might last indefinitely."

"Doubt it. The air's full of bacteria. The metal and concrete won't save us, though it'll slow it down a bit. Where are you? Still at the refuge?"

"I'm on Suddene, at the Chimera excavation. The Guardian came here, and I'm going after it. I think it's in the Scythian city."

"Hmpf," was Aubriot's laconic reaction. "Wish I were there. I could help. I'd give a lot to pay back those machines for what they did to me."

"You would be a big help, but never mind. I'll have to deal with it myself."

"Did you hear about our illustrious leader?"

"Meredith? What about her?"

"You don't know? I guessed you might not. Not if you've been traveling for most of the day."

"Are you going to tell me or are you going to keep me hanging?"

"Unlucky choice of words. Meredith topped herself this morning. Must have been not long after you left."

"She...?" Cherry's legs suddenly weakened. She put a hand on the bare rock wall for support. "She *killed* herself? Stars, I had no idea. I don't think the news has reached here yet. No one's said a thing."

She recalled the last few words Meredith had said to her. *It means a lot to me. More than you know.* The Leader must have been planning her suicide even as they'd spoken. That was why she'd asked what Ethan would have thought about how she'd acted. Poor, poor Meredith. It had all been too much for her. The responsibility for the colony had been too great a burden.

"You okay?" Aubriot asked.

"I spoke to her just before I left. I had to...It doesn't matter now. She didn't give any sign of what she was planning. Or maybe she did and I missed it. I don't know. Stars, I feel terrible. I wish I hadn't been so hard on her. I was so critical. I didn't have to be. Shit. Why do I always have to be such a bitch? That poor woman."

"I thought *I* was the egotist around here. It isn't always about you, you know."

"But this is. If I hadn't—"

"You couldn't have known. No one knew. If they had, they would have stopped her. And whatever you said to her, it was because you care about the colony and you were trying to protect us all. Like you're doing now."

She was silent. The news of Meredith's death weighed heavily, no matter how much Aubriot might say it was not her fault. If she could take back her angry comments to the Leader over the years, she would, in a heartbeat. What would Ethan think? She was glad he hadn't survived to see this terrible turn of events.

"Cherry," said Aubriot, a new sternness in his tone. "Snap out of it. You've got a job to do. Stop wallowing and go and do it."

Anger rose in her chest. Who was he to tell her what to do? But then her shoulders sagged. He was right. "All right. I'm going."

"Good. Catch that Guardian and cut its fucking head off for me."

"You've got it." She closed the comm.

In the distant edges of the cavern, on the fringes of the glare cast by the lamps, the Suddeners were going about their daily lives. Soon, they would discover their Leader was dead, and that, rather than lead the colony toward overcoming the challenges it faced, she had abandoned it.

The news would destroy whatever hope they had remaining. All Concordians would need a reason to continue, to try to win despite the terrible odds stacked against them. Cherry would do whatever she could to help, and right now that was catching the Guardian. Perhaps if she could prove the android was sent by the Scythians and she had prevented it from fulfilling its purpose, it would demonstrate that the aliens were not invincible; that the colony had a chance, if only it had the determination to try.

It was the least she could do to honor Meredith's memory.

TWENTY

"Wilder," said a voice.

She was in her forest home, trapped against the ceiling by the a-grav machine. How long had she been here? Days. It was early morning, and the new day's sun was shining in through gaps in the woven, dried leaf frond walls.

It hurt so much. She couldn't feel her feet or hands, and she couldn't remember when she'd last been able to move her limbs. But worse than all was her dreadful thirst. Outside her window, dew sparkled on the vegetation. The glittering drops looked more precious than gemstones. If only she could lick them. To lick just one leaf would be bliss.

"Wilder."

She opened her eyes and saw the blank face of a starship's bulkhead. She was aboard the *Opportunity*. The shadow of pain and thirst from her dream remained, however. It had been so vivid. She felt as though all she had to do was close her eyes to return to that time and place.

Someone had been calling her name. "Quinn? Did you want something?"

"I am sorry to wake you."

"No problem. You did me a favor. I was having a horrible dream." She unzipped her sleeping bag and pushed off toward the food and drink station.

"I thought you might be. Your facial expression indicated you were distressed and you were making some slight movements."

"You can read human faces now? I'm impressed." She removed a water bottle and sucked on the straw. She'd become accustomed to the fact that she was drinking her own recycled urine and sweat. If it hadn't been for the *Oppor-*

tunity's water conservation system she would be in the same state she'd been in her dream, or dead.

If only the ship recycled food too, she thought, assessing what remained of her rations. Then she grimaced as she realized what recycling her food would entail.

She was already a light eater, yet even so she was down to half of what she'd brought aboard. How long could she make the food last? Would the scientists halt the spread of the biocide by then? She might have to choose between starvation and death by poison. At least the latter would be quick.

"I would say I can read some expressions of the humans I am most familiar with," said Quinn. "I would not describe myself as an expert."

"Still, that's quite an achievement in my opinion." Her stomach growled. Hunger was beginning to bite, but she decided to try to wait a few hours before eating.

"I imagine you must find us very easy to read."

"Uh, in what way?"

"When Fila are in a state of heightened emotion, such as fear or joy, we can't help but express it in our movements. You must have noticed."

"Ummm." She sucked another mouthful of water as she tried to remember seeing anything akin to what Quinn was talking about.

"You mean you don't see the way our tentacles quiver when we're angry or stressed? But it's obvious to the most casual observer."

She chuckled with embarrassment. "I'm so sorry. I guess I must be very unobservant."

"Nonsense. You are the most observant human I've met, and humans as a species are more observant than my own, in my estimation."

"In that case, I can't explain it. I confess I have no idea how you're feeling most of the time, and all the translation equipment conveys to me is the bare meaning of your communication." Had she offended him? Would she ever be able to tell? Unless Quinn told her so, she would never know. She made a mental note to watch his tentacles more carefully in the future.

A pause followed.

Perhaps she had offended him.

"I woke you for another reason than your apparent agitation," said Quinn. "I had an idea regarding your a-grav device."

"You did?" She pushed off from the wall and glided over to Piddle and Puddle's sweater pouches. Peering inside, she saw that both her pets remained asleep. They'd been sleeping for longer periods lately and she was getting worried about them.

"I'm not sure if you're aware," Quinn said, "but no other galactic species has invented this type of device. As far as I know, it's unique."

"Seriously?" She eyed the machine, which she had tied to the floor to prevent it from floating around and bumping into things. "Cool." Her invention had begun to lose her interest, but Quinn's information had given it a new shine.

"Ever since you managed to repeat your earlier success and make the machine work aboard the *Opportunity*, I've been in contact with Assembly members, checking if my impression was correct."

"You didn't tell me you were doing that. I didn't even know you were talking to them."

"But of course I am. How else do you think they would know about the attack on Concordia?"

"I guess I've been distracted by everything that's happening."

"That's natural. You must understand that the a-grav device is a sensitive topic. My communications with the rest of the Assembly have been under the tightest security."

"You mean because of what it can do?" The possibilities the a-grav machine opened up were vast, not only for planet-based transportation but also for interplanetary and interstellar travel. With a flick of a switch a deep space vessel sitting on the surface of a planet could achieve escape velocity almost immediately.

"Exactly. This invention comes with vast implications. I believe it signals the beginning of a new galactic era."

She hadn't considered that humans were the only species ever to have invented a-grav. Quinn's earlier reference to the machine as *her* device made her feel a little guilty. "You know my work was based on the information in the Guardians' data? A-grav was invented on Earth hundreds of years ago, but it seems it was only used in the flitters. Then the Natural Movement became too strong and the invention wasn't developed any further. I had a lot of help, too, from all the other Concordians who were working on it. It was a team effort." Her sense of guilt increased. The way these kinds of things worked, it would be she who was forever associated with a-grav. Her name would be listed as the inventor, and not anyone else's who had contributed to the work.

"I feel you're missing the point," said Quinn. "What I am trying to tell you is, this new invention puts you in a position of great power."

She was holding onto a cupboard handle and floating gently in midair. Her hair, which she always cut herself to save time, was in a messy array around her head, and her ship's suit was wrinkled and fitted poorly on her skinny body. She was hungry and she missed her friends, about whom she was deeply worried.

She didn't feel like someone in a position of great power.

"How's that?" As she spoke, the logic of what Quinn had said was becoming clear. Any intelligent galactic species would give a lot—would *do* a lot—for the knowledge of how to build a-grav machines.

"The Assembly members I've spoken to are very interested in your device."

As the realization hit, her grip on the cupboard handle relaxed. She began to float free. On the edge of her vision, she saw the outline of Puddle stirring inside his pouch. The enormous implications of what Quinn was telling her pressed on her brain like a crushing fist, but it was a good feeling. A very, very good feeling. Only it was a little too much to deal with all at once.

She recalled the vast Assembly space station, with its thousands of inhabitants of many galactic species. She recalled the gigantic alien organizers of the station, and the equipment that could read minds and simulate scenarios that were indistinguishable from reality. She recalled the strange starships of the members visiting the station.

At the time of her mission, she had felt awed by all she'd seen, and grateful that the Assembly had allowed such an insignificant species as Homo sapiens into its society. But now, things were changing. Now, humanity had something valuable to offer. It was no longer a beggar at the door of the great galactic powers.

Then her heart sank. "I almost wish you hadn't told them about the a-grav machine, Quinn. If the Assembly members demand that I give it to them in return for helping us, I can hardly refuse, can I?"

"I think they would have more integrity than to *demand* anything from you."

"Maybe, but... " She sighed. "I have to give it over. It's the least I can do. There are several ships coming to Concordia now, right? That takes fuel and a crew, not to mention their ships are probably needed elsewhere. I know! I should give the machine to the Parvus. If it weren't for them we would never have beaten off the last Scythian attack."

"These are noble sentiments. But, if I may say so, you're thinking like a human."

What species was she supposed to think like?

"By which I mean," Quinn continued, "you're confining your speculations to your own extremely short life span. Galactic time is much longer and wider and deeper than your species' imagination seems capable of grasping. I'll try to put this in terms you can comprehend. The Assembly does not view your contribution and value as a member only within Concordia's next few hundred orbits of its star. It views you as an intelligent, compassionate species with all the potential those attributes imply. Your notion of 'owing' the Parvus the a-grav machine as 'repayment' for their help is simplistic in the extreme."

She was not at all used to condescending tones, not from Quinn nor anyone else, not since she'd decided that school wasn't for her and had stopped attending. Annoyance flared up, but she tried to mask it as well as she could. She had to concede that Quinn's understanding in the matters he was explaining was way superior to hers. "Well, what do *you* think I should do?"

"I think, as an opening to discussion, you should state your willingness to share your invention with the Assembly. When we hear what they have to say, and perhaps to offer, we can think further on how to turn this fortuitous event to humanity's long-term advantage."

"That sounds good. Send them the message."

"In my opinion it would be better for you to tell them yourself, face to face. We should set out now and meet them on their journey to Concordia."

"Leave planetary orbit? I don't want to! I don't want to abandon my friends or anyone else down there. I might still be able to help them."

"The greatest help you can offer your planet is to wield the influence you have with allies who can actually help them."

She sighed in frustration. "I guess so. I don't like it, but I can't argue against it. Let's go meet some aliens!"

"You must recline in your safety seat while we accelerate."

"Ugh. I'd forgotten about that. I hope Piddle and Puddle will be okay." She propelled herself in the direction of the living quarters' exit, not looking forward to the hours of acceleration she was about to endure.

Twenty-One

When her feet touched the ground at the bottom of the drop, Cherry unfastened her harness. Way up above, the lights from the excavator glared out, brilliant white in the view through her night vision goggles. The harness and the line would remain here until she returned from the Scythian city. Alun would set up a relay so a comm from her current position would be received within the Chimera cavern.

A figure leaned out over the ledge and waved. The figure was a small silhouette against the beams from the excavator, but it had to be Alun. She waved back, uncertain if he could see her. She hadn't brought along any flashlights or head lamps, concerned that visible light would alert the Guardian, though in truth the android probably had superior visual and audio capabilities. It would know she was coming from a kilometer away.

"Thanks for everything, Alun."

"No need for that. Come back, with or without the Guardian. That'll be thanks enough for me."

A second dark figure appeared at Alun's side and also waved.

"Be careful," shouted Pearl. "Don't take any dangerous risks."

"I'll try not to."

It was a lie. As far as Cherry was concerned, this was a do-or-die mission. She had screwed up, badly, and in more ways than one. Meredith's suicide had dealt another blow. Her final memory of the woman kept replaying in her mind. No matter what Aubriot said about it not being her fault, she couldn't help but think there was so much she could have, and *should* have, done differently.

Capturing the Guardian was the one chance she to do something right. She would take whatever risks that entailed, dangerous or not. She was fighting for her own future: her ability to look at herself in a mirror, to sleep at night, to live with herself. This wasn't only about the survival of the colony. This was personal.

"I'm going in now. I'll comm when I return."

If I return.

She had elected not to take one of the survey vehicles for transportation. Prior experience told her that a car moved too fast to safely navigate inside the city, where deep fissures dissected the pavement. If any markings warned of the fissures' presence, they were not easily perceived by human senses.

She headed for the high boundary wall surrounding the city. The night vision goggles gave some indication of color, though the hues were more muted than they would have been to regular sight. Yet she could still make out the greens, purples, and pinks in an irregular pattern over the wall's surface. Which of the colors had been so soft that simply pushing would enable her to pass through?

She strode quickly closer. Might the Guardian be watching her approach? Had it guessed it would be pursued? Was it lying in wait?

No sign of anything appeared. She reached the wall. Whichever color material was the softest, it clearly didn't retain the impression of earlier incursions. The wall was smooth and unmarked, bearing no sign of Alun's vehicle or of the Guardian's entrance.

She pressed a pink and then a purple section. The surfaces gave somewhat, but she quickly realized the green area had to be the softest. She approached that part of the wall and paused, checking the tightness of her backpack straps. Then she stepped forward, forcing her foot into the spongy substance. It slipped in easily. Immediately, she pushed in with the rest of her body, wishing to minimize the time she was blind and vulnerable. The green material parted like thick paste.

The first time she had entered the area around the Scythian city it had been without the benefit of night vision goggles. All she'd been able to see had been within the scope of the survey vehicle's headlights. That had been a whole bunch of nothing except for empty space and openings in the ground. This time, what she saw took her breath away.

A crazed labyrinth of black lines patterned the floor—fissures opening to unknown depths. Beyond the maze, which looked like the production of a demented mind, tall edifices rose upward. The buildings reminded her of the serried ranks of mountains running through central Lyonesse, only the constructions were steeper and more jagged. Arched openings stood black in their sides, with none ground level.

The stench of the place made her gasp too. She'd forgotten the odor of feces. Her electronic canary would bleep if it detected dangerous gases, but she checked it nonetheless. It appeared that the only thing she had to fear from the air was puking from the smell.

The path the survey vehicle must have followed was about the only straight line in the place. She and Alun had been incredibly lucky.

What kind of creatures were the Scythians? Did they climb up the sides of their buildings? With a shiver, she recalled the speed and agility of their mechanical spiders. The spider that had amputated her arm with the same ease she had pushed through the green mush at the city's edge had ascended a tree to reach her. Had the Scythians modeled their spiders after their own forms?

She scanned the expanse thoroughly before she took another step. The floor was black, a marginally lighter black than the chaos of abysses. The structures dotted with openings in the distance were the same range of colors as the boundary wall: green, purple, and pink, though the sections were not so clearly defined. In some areas the colors merged as if the soft substances had mixed.

Nothing moved. If the Guardian was watching, it gave no sign of its presence.

Where to go first? The place was kilometers square. She corrected herself—it was kilometers *cubed*. The vertical dimensions of the city were significant, and she didn't even know how the depth of the fissures.

She walked to one floor opening and knelt. Holding onto the side, she leaned forward and peered down. Smooth, black walls ran out of sight. Spots of darker black signaled arched openings similar to those in the city's buildings.

How would she locate the burned-up android in this enormous place? The challenge of the task was daunting, but she pushed her doubts to the back of her mind and stood up.

Should she go upward or downward to look for the Guardian? The black walls falling away below didn't seem to hold any protrusions or anything else to grip. And climbing one-handed was hard.

Upward it would have to be. She quickly trod the single straight section of pavement toward the towering constructions. Soon, the straight section branched out, and then quickly branched again and again, each new pathway narrower than the last. She was forced to follow the slim surfaces as well as she could while at the same time avoid falling into a void.

After many frustrating twists and turns and doubling back—once taking a chance and vaulting over an opening—she finally made it to the base of a building. She gazed upward at the steep surface, which leaned slightly inward as it rose toward a distant peak. The arched openings she'd seen from a distance were higher than she'd guessed. Way too high above for her to reach without climbing and, like the openings in the floor, the walls didn't seem to hold anything to help her climb.

Frustration niggled. Had she come so far only to fail at this simple obstacle?

She thumped the wall in annoyance. Her fist sank into the green material. Of course! Putting her hand out, she pushed into the wall and stepped through it.

Immediately she found herself buried in debris. She flailed, trying to find purchase in the dusty fragments. She couldn't breathe. Her nose and mouth were blocked by dry flakes. She backed up, intending to push through the wall to get out, but her back didn't meet anything like a solid surface, only more of the soft stuff that was choking her to death. The substance pressed against her goggles, rendering her blind.

Fighting down her rising panic, she scooped away the material in front of her face. More didn't take its place. She'd created an empty space. She sucked in air gratefully as her heart rate and breathing slowed. She was not about to suffocate. But the stuff surrounded her in a claustrophobic fashion. She had to find her way back to the wall. It couldn't be far away. She was sure she'd only taken two steps, or three at most, since emerging from it.

The cocooning material was a homogeneous light gray. She couldn't guess what it was, or what it had originally been hundreds of thousands of years ago when the Scythians had abandoned their city. For all she knew she was trying to move through the remains of dead Scythians. Perhaps she'd entered a graveyard or crematorium.

She waded forward slowly, clearing space in front of her face. She breathed shallowly, worrying about taking the dust motes into her lungs. The electronic canary would sound an alarm if it detected poisonous gases but she doubted it was any use at checking for dangerous particles.

Before she'd moved more than a couple of meters, she knew she was heading the wrong way. If she'd been going in the right direction she would have hit the wall almost straightaway. She turned and tried a different direction. Again, she encountered nothing except the maddening, choking debris. She turned another ninety degrees and made a third foray into the congested fragments.

She scooped soft detritus from her face, and as her hand moved forward, it hit solidity. At last, the wall!

But on further exploration, she found the surface she was touching was not spongy, but hard. She moved her hand higher and felt a flat surface. She moved closer and cleared more space. Eventually the edge of the object came into view. The white, smooth structure didn't look like much of anything, but it was wide enough for her to perhaps rise out of the fragments. She climbed onto it but as she tried to straighten up she hit another solid surface.

This seemed a copy of the platform on which she was kneeling. She felt for the edge. It was easy to reach and only a little way inward. She climbed onto the second surface and encountered a third just above. She moved blindly upward, holding her breath to avoid wasting time on removing the material from her face. It seemed to be lessening in density anyway.

At the fourth platform, her head broke free. A light gray sea surrounded her. Above, the series of platforms continued to rise, spiraling. A few meters behind stood the wall she had pushed through. An arched opening gaped in its surface, revealing the darkness outside the city.

She'd done it. She was the first human being ever to set foot inside the ancient metropolis of the self-exiled Scythians. Somewhere here, the Guardian was doing something or searching for something. Now all she had to do was find it.

She woke up, turned over, and groaned. She wasn't unaccustomed to sleeping on the floor—Scythian attacks had destroyed her homes more than once—but there was something about the hard, black floors of their city that was particularly uncomfortable. The lightweight sleeping bag Alun had given her offered little protection against the heat-sucking, bone-bruising material.

She pulled back the cover over her face. Pitch darkness greeted her. And silence. Utter silence. Over the last two days, the absence of any sound except her own breathing and the slight noise of her movements had begun to grind into her consciousness like the heel of a boot crushing an insect. Several times she'd been tempted to speak just to hear a voice, even if it was her own, but she couldn't afford to do anything that might alert the Guardian to her presence.

She was deeply outclassed by the machine as it was. Despite the damage it had sustained, the android remained stronger, faster, and more agile than her. The twisted neck of the corpse she'd found at the Oceanside jail was testament to the fact. Surprising the Guardian would be her only advantage.

But she didn't only want to destroy it. She also wanted to know what it was doing.

She pulled on her night vision goggles. A gray ceiling came into view. If there were any colors in the interior of the Scythian constructions, the goggles were not picking them up. Apart from the oddly sectioned and colored walls, everything else had been white, light gray, mid-gray, dark gray, or black.

She sat up and reached for her backpack, pulling out ration strips and water. As she ate and drank, she opened the pathfinder. The device had mapped each section she'd passed through and measured distances along the level and perpendicular. She had climbed and descended through structures as she'd traveled. Outside the map of her route everything was blank, but from the total distance and her extremely rough estimate of the size of the city, she guessed she was about one-quarter of the way into it.

She was heading for the center. Important places tended to be in the center of metropolises, in her limited experience. The Guardian must have gone to the city to do or retrieve something important, so it made sense it would go to the center. There were probably thousands more possibilities, but that one reasoning was the best she had.

During her hunt she had moved through many strange places—places that had left her confused and disturbed. The sea of dusty fragments she had encountered upon entering the city had spread more than a hundred meters wide, and spiraling 'steps' like the one she'd happened upon rose out of it everywhere. Slim cylinders protruded from the walls, and the same arched portals she'd seen in the outer walls opened in them.

Navigating the city was difficult. The problem she'd encountered when she'd had to cross the crazed pattern of fissures was multiplied the deeper she moved into the metropolis. The place was clearly designed to accommodate creatures larger than humans. Everything seemed too big: the rooms, the buildings, the openings leading from one space to another. The Scythians could climb walls. No opening was ever at ground level. She had been forced to use a line and grapnel often in order to access a construction. Managing the feat one-handed had been no joke.

She hadn't encountered any roads. The Scythians didn't seem to use or need them. Each building abutted the next, with perhaps a few openings between. The rooms were taller than they were wide. In one room, curved, concave hemispheres lined the walls and the same kind of debris she had first encountered in the city lay thick on the floor.

She'd also seen what had once been equipment of various kinds, but the devices were barely distinguishable. Most were little more than heaps of rust. Anything she touched immediately dissolved, puffing dust as it imploded. One wall had held long lines of shelves. Slim, dark gray flakes and light gray puffs of a fibrous substance were all that remained of whatever the shelves had held.

The extent of the decay, though predictable given the time that had passed since the Scythians left, had her wondering what could possibly have survived for the Guardian to seek out. Had the original inhabitants made something that would endure eons? It seemed the only conclusion to draw from the Guardian's behavior, but she couldn't guess what the thing might be.

The stench of feces seemed to have gone away, though she suspected she'd only grown accustomed it. What she hadn't gotten used to was the aridity of the atmosphere. The air was painfully dry. It drew moisture from eyes and mouth, and though she'd been careful to always have her water condenser running, the amount the device managed to draw in was worryingly small.

If the Scythians needed water to live, the liquid had long since disappeared from their former habitation. Thirst was already a constant companion. She had soon realized that lack of water could be her downfall in her search for the Guardian. Her determination would not overcome her body's needs, no matter how strong it was.

She took another small sip of water and checked the level in the bottle.

Only two hundred and thirty mils remained of the water the condenser had drawn in the eight hours she'd slept. She pushed the straw into the bottle and climbed out of her bag, ready to face another long day of hunting.

After quickly repacking her backpack, leaving out a line and grapnel, she lifted it onto her back and tightened the straps. Facing away from the boundary wall and into the city, she set off. The place where she'd chosen to sleep was small and only two portals opened from it, both high up.

She swung the grapnel and threw it. Gently, she pulled the line until the grapnel caught. Then she tugged on the line to check it was holding—twice yesterday it had slipped mid-climb and she'd fallen. It hadn't taken much imagination to see herself incapacitated with a broken leg or ankle, beyond hope of comm'ing for help, dying of thirst.

She approached the base of the wall, shortening the line as she went. When she was standing below the portal, she put a foot on the wall, braced herself, gripped the line hard in her only hand, and began her climb.

Ever since losing her arm to a Scythian spider, she learned to use her teeth as another hand. After some trial and error on her first day in the city, she'd put this habit to good use when she devised a method of climbing. She would 'walk' up the wall, pulling herself as high as she could with her arm, and then bite the line to hold her place while she let go with her hand to reach higher.

It was strenuous, ungainly, and painful, but it worked.

She climbed to the bottom of the opening, reached over it, and clambered onto it. Straddling the gap she looked into the next room. This one had no roof. She had seen many similar rooms but she was none the wiser about their purpose. For the first time, however, she saw a series of ledges running around the walls. The floor of the room was some distance below—a potentially fatal distance if she fell.

One ledge about fifteen centimeters wide was within reach. If she turned her feet sideways she could stand on it easily. She mentally debated, stowing her grapnel and line as she considered her options. Which way to go? Should she try to cross the room or return the way she'd come and take a different route?

The situation with her water would soon become dire. She couldn't afford to take many diversions. And she might encounter similar or more difficult obstacles. She might already be looking at her easiest path.

Directly across from her at the same level was another opening, and the nearest ledge ran right around to it. She made her choice. She didn't have time to waste dithering. Traversing the room should be easy providing she kept her head.

She rose to her feet, holding onto the edge of the opening for balance. She would have to face the wall as she made her way along the ledge. Her backpack protruded too much for her to face outward. She turned around, and then carefully placed one foot on the nearest ledge.

She paused. Would it bear her weight? It looked solid, but it was hundreds of thousands of years old. It was a miracle that *any* of the Scythian city remained standing, let alone the ledge. If the place hadn't been enclosed by the dome, it would have been dust.

She stamped down, hard. The ledge seemed firm.

"Well, here goes," she murmured, and stepped out.

Her hand flat on the wall, she shuffled sideways. Her heart began to race and her breathing sped up. The distance to the other opening was only about ten or twelve meters. Not far at all. She took some deep breaths and exhaled slowly. All she had to do was walk a few meters then she would be through the opening and into the next room. Nothing could be easier.

She reached the corner. The space was too narrow for her to remain close to the wall. She was forced to step over a gap. Bracing herself against the vertical surface with her only hand, she made the crossing, letting out a whoosh of expelled air as she didn't fall. She would have to do the same again at the next corner. Then it would be a straight run to the opposite opening.

She set off shuffling to her left again. As she went, she wondered what was happening on the surface. Had Kes found a way to neutralize the biocide? Was Aubriot okay out at Cerberus? How was Wilder coping with being cut off from the rest of Concordia? She hoped they would all make it out of the crisis alive, along with the rest of the colony. Everyone had been through so much, had come so far with so many sacrifices, they deserved to survive.

As the toes of her left boot touched the next ledge, it crumbled. She tried to back up but it was too late. She overbalanced, cried out, and clutched at the wall. But her hand only met a flat surface. There was nothing to grip. She tried to force herself forward, tried to shift her weight onto her other foot, but her pack was pulling her backward, pulling her down.

She fell.

Twenty-Two

The biocide was getting closer. Kes studied the latest satellite images as he sat in the lab, waiting for a special person to arrive. The images showed patches of brown, dead vegetation spreading out from the landing site of each of the Scythians' canisters growing wider. In some places they had grown so large they'd joined up. Sometimes, a tongue of poison ran out, as if following a rich seam of life. When the biocide encountered water it would run rapidly through it, massacring all aquatic life. Cerberus was hemmed in on all sides. Biocide crept up mountain slopes toward the mines and adjacent settlements. Soon it would reach the Vimur, the last major refuge of Concordia's Fila.

What could humans do to stop the progress? The best they could hope for was to slow it down, such as by the efforts currently taking place around the warehouse refuge. The idea had been put forward by a farmer, but Kes recognized it as a technique used to prevent the spread of wildfires on Earth. A fire break—only for all living things.

Men and women had dug a deep trench all the way around the refuge. It had been a monumental effort, but the work must have been a welcome distraction from Meredith's suicide and the fear of impending death.

Next, they had sprayed the trench interior with a powerful agricultural pesticide. The reasoning was that if the biocide hit an area where no microorganisms remained alive, its progress would halt. With nothing to feed on, it should die. That was the reasoning. Kes could see the logic in it, though he suspected the trench was not sufficiently deep and the pesticide would not properly penetrate the soil and rock. The trench and pesticide might slow the biocide down, but eventually it would breach the fire break and then move swiftly to the warehouses.

Perhaps, by then, they would be ready. Perhaps the fire break would buy them enough time.

"He's here," said Thom.

Kes looked up. Wilder's friend, Tycho, was waiting outside the lab. Feelings that had become familiar over the last couple of days—guilt mixed with gratitude—returned in full force.

"This is it, then," said Drew.

Kes cast the young man a sympathetic look, guessing he was dreading what would happen in the next ten or fifteen minutes. They all were, of course, though perhaps Drew felt especially responsible as the scientist most familiar with vaccines.

"Isn't anyone going to let him in?" Tricia strode toward the door.

Tycho stepped in.

"You know," said Drew quietly, "I wouldn't mind volunteering."

Kes put a hand on his shoulder. "You wouldn't be the first scientist to experiment on himself, but it's a stupid idea. If the vaccine doesn't work, who do you think is best equipped to continue to work on it, you or Tycho? No one doubts your bravery, Drew, or thinks that experimenting on another human being is a cop-out. These are extraordinary times."

For a man who might only have a few more minutes of life left, Tycho looked extremely calm and relaxed. As he walked up to Kes and the others awaiting him, everyone stopped what they were doing and watched.

"I'm ready," he announced. "Stephie and I said our goodbyes, just in case. Though I hope I will be seeing her again, and living another few years at least. But if not, so be it. Where do you want to do it?" He looked around the lab.

"I'm afraid we have to draw out the suspense a little longer," said Kes. "We need to measure your vitals, height, weight, that kind of thing. Any information we can gather may be useful, whatever the outcome."

"Right, I understand."

Kes thought he detected nervousness creeping into the man's demeanor, which was entirely understandable. He had probably steeled himself for this moment and hadn't expected to wait. Kes wasn't sure he could retain composure himself in such circumstances. Tycho wasn't only staring death in the face, he was going up to him and shaking his hand.

"If you wouldn't mind following me." Drew led Tycho to the station he'd set up with basic medical equipment. The older man obligingly and patiently did as he was instructed, taking off his shoes to have his height measured, standing on the scales, and rolling up his sleeve to have his blood pressure and a blood sample taken.

Though most of the scientists continued with their work as if nothing special was happening—they could not afford to waste time, whether the experiment with Tycho was successful or not—the atmosphere in the lab was stretched as taut as a bow string. Kes tried to tell himself that if the vaccine didn't work and Tycho unfortunately died, plenty remained for them to do. Nevertheless he couldn't help hoping that, unlikely though it was, they had it right the first time.

He wouldn't allow himself to imagine the other possibilities: that Tycho wouldn't die but would suffer unbearably painful complications or would end up a shell of a man, his mind gone but his body living on. After Kes had accepted Tycho's offer to play lab rat, he'd backtracked and tried to explain to the old man that what he was volunteering for could be worse than death. But Tycho had refused to listen, only repeating, *I want to do it*.

Long, awkward minutes passed until Drew had taken all the measurements and samples they needed.

It was time.

Drew said, "We've prepared a bed for you to lie down on while we give you the vaccination, and we'd like you to stay here at least another day for monitoring. I hope that's okay. Things have been rushed around here. I'm not sure if anyone informed you what we had in mind."

"Oh, I didn't know that. Someone will have to find Stephie and ask her for my pajamas and toothbrush."

Drew smiled. "That won't be a problem, sir. Please step this way."

The small party set off again, this time toward the meeting room. One corner of it had been curtained off. Thom brought up the rear, pushing the monitor that measured blood pressure, blood oxygen saturation, heart rate, and respiration. As they administered the vaccine, all these vitals would be measured, and for around a day afterward.

"How soon will you know if it's worked?" Tycho asked as Kes pushed open the meeting room door.

"We'll check your blood every hour or so," Kes replied. "I'm hoping to see a response within twenty-four hours if not sooner. The window for an adverse reaction should have passed by then. I should tell you, though, we won't know anything about the long-term effects."

The fact was, they could vaccinate the entire colony and save them from the biocide, only for everyone to develop cancer five years hence. What they were doing was incredibly risky, but no other options were open.

They had reached the curtained section. Tricia pulled back the drapes, and Thom pushed the trolley holding the medical equipment through the gap.

"Should I lie down or sit up?" Tycho arrived at the bed. His calm poise had returned. He looked relieved, in fact, to be finally getting to the point of no return.

Kes was wondering, as he had so many times, if Tycho died, what he would say to Wilder.

"I think it would be best if you lie down." Drew hooked Tycho up to the medical equipment, saying softly, "I want you to know, that we have many medications on standby if anything goes wrong. The last thing we want is for you to suffer. I hope you understand what I mean."

Tycho looked into Drew's eyes. "I'll try to bear it for as long as I can so you can get your information. If it gets too much, I'll give you the signal. The only thing I ask is, don't tell Stephie I suffered. Tell her I went peacefully."

Drew nodded. He turned to face Kes, his eyes bright. "Can I speak to you outside, just for a moment?"

Kes said, "I'm sorry, Tycho. We won't keep you waiting long."

When the two men had left the curtained area, Drew whispered, "I can't do it." He held up the injector. His hand was shaking.

"I'll do it. Don't worry. I know how hard this is."

Kes did know. Now, if Tycho died, he would have killed Wilder's friend with his own hands.

They returned to the bed. "Ready?" Kes asked.

"I'm more than ready. Let's do this."

Kes pressed the injector against Tycho's withered bicep and fired it.

The vaccine contained a refined form of the dead, inactive biocide collected from the Fila tissue. When they had tested the vaccine on living human cells, there had been no response. They had also introduced it into a sample of human blood. Again, the cells hadn't been affected.

But injecting the vaccine into a living human being was something different entirely. They could only guess how the subject's immune system would react. It might mount a massive response manifesting as anaphylactic shock. Though they had adrenaline on hand, Tycho could still die—not from the biocide but from his body's reaction to it. Or his immune system might show no response at all. That could mean they were entirely wrong and they had no alternative to try, or any time left.

A sound distracted Kes. It had come from outside the drapes. He pulled them back. The meeting room door was open and crammed with scientists, unable to contain their curiosity.

He returned his attention to Tycho. "How are you feeling?"

"I don't feel a thing. Should I?"

"No," said Drew. "If it's working, or not harmful, you shouldn't feel anything. You might experience some soreness at the vaccination site after a few hours and maybe a low grade fever. But those signs are good. They mean your body's immune system is reacting. We won't know that for definite for a while."

Seconds ticked past, drawing out into minutes as Drew monitored Tycho's vitals. "Everything looks normal. I hope I'm not speaking too soon, but..." He grinned, embarrassed. "I don't dare say it."

"I'll say it, then," said Thom. "Tycho, if the biocide vaccine was going to kill you you'd be dead by now. I think you're going to be okay."

Tycho firmly shook his head. "This isn't over yet. If you think my body's learned to fight off the poison, I want to be certain. I want to prove it. I want someone to drop me in a dead zone with no protection."

"No," said Drew, aghast. "We couldn't possibly—"

"I insist. It's the only way you'll know for sure if your treatment works."

The old man was right, though it pained Kes to admit it. If they were to have any confidence in the vaccine it would require a field trial, though they would have to wait some days to give the old man's system time to develop the antibodies. Did they even have that long?

Twenty-Three

When Cherry came to, her mouth and nose were covered and she could hardly breathe. Panicking, she thrashed about. Then the familiarity of the sensation hit her: she was covered in the debris fragments she'd encountered when she first entered the city. Wiping the dusty bits away from her face, she tried to stand. The back of her head and her back hurt like hell. She guessed she must have landed on her backpack, which had softened the impact as she hit the floor. She was lucky she hadn't broken her spine.

She made it onto her hands and knees and pushed away the fragments from her mouth and nose, creating a gap to breathe. How would she get out? Unlike the first time she'd been submerged in the debris, there were no spiraling platforms in this room. Nothing but straight walls.

She clumsily rose to her feet and her head broke through the surface of fragments into fresh air. The layer of debris was only as deep as her shoulders. That was something. Now how would she get out of the room?

The openings were high above and they looked identical. She couldn't figure out which was the one she'd been moving toward. She picked the left one. She wouldn't mind too much if it was the wrong one as long as she got out.

Would her line reach the distance? One on its own might not, but if that were the case she could tie two together. She gave an inward groan. Her thighs, buttocks, arms, and abs were already sore from her first climb today, and it hadn't been even half the height of the one now facing her.

But there was nothing for it except to begin. The longer she delayed the thirstier and less able to make the climb she would become. She payed out the entire length of one line and stood on its end. If it was too short and the grapnel caught on the opening, she wouldn't be able to reach it.

She aimed and threw. The grapnel bounced off the wall just below the opening, tugging on the end of the line under her foot. It was just long enough. She took her foot off the rope to allow enough length for the grapnel to reach the opening, aimed, and threw again. This time, the grapnel bounced off the wall above the opening.

She gathered the fallen heap of line and the grapnel, wiping them free of the fragments, before trying again.

At her third attempt, the grapnel disappeared through the opening. *Shit.*

She winced, waiting for it to fall down the other side, taking the line with it. The lightweight rope slapped against the wall and began to slide down, pulling up the grapnel at the other end. *Phew.*

She waded through the debris to the wall. Hoping the grapnel would not slip from its precarious position on the farther edge of the opening—she wasn't sure she would survive a second fall from that great height—she began to climb.

A second strenuous climb so soon after her first quickly set her muscles complaining. Each step up the wall, each shift of her hand to a new position while she gripped the rope in her teeth, was a great effort. Sweat stung her eyes and made her palm slippery. She could feel precious moisture soaking into her clothes. Meanwhile, her mouth and throat remained dry as the dusty debris beneath her.

About halfway up she rested, locking her elbow to take some of her weight from the screaming muscles of her arm. She psyched herself up to complete the second half of her endeavor, telling herself that she'd made it this far so she could climb the rest. If she failed she would only have to do it again, and it would be twice as hard the second time around. Once she got to the top she would be able to rest as long as she wanted.

It was time to move.

She bit the rope, clenching the slim line firmly between her teeth before letting go with her hand. She reached to grab it higher up, and—

There was something in the opening.

She gasped. The line slipped from her mouth. At the last split second, she clutched at it and gripped it. But her boots had lost their traction on the wall. She swung free and then slammed into it. The impact knocked the breath from her. She hung on for her life, only her grip on the rope preventing her from falling, drawing in great lungfuls of air.

What had she seen? She could have sworn a figure had appeared in the opening and looked down at her. Or had she imagined it?

Her arm felt like it was being slowly ripped from its socket. She had to regain her purchase on the wall. She scrabbled with her feet against the vertical surface, pushing out her body until it was level again. She had to let go before her arm seized up entirely. She opened her mouth, bit the rope, and looked upward.

Dread froze her heart. Something *was* in the opening. Dark, disfigured, the hairless head looked down at her impassively.

The android had found her, while she was in the most vulnerable, precarious position possible.

She transferred the line to her hand. "Hey! Help me up."

It was an insane, desperate measure, but it was the only one available. The android had claimed it was a Guardian. And the Guardians' prime directive was to help the colony. Everyone knew that. And she was part of the colony. Perhaps the android would attempt to maintain the masquerade, despite the odd, suspicious situation.

The android did not move. It did not answer. The gaze of its remaining eye was fixed on Cherry's.

"Help me up, dammit! That's what you're supposed to do, isn't it? Are you a Guardian or not? Help me. Now!"

What thought processes were whirring in the creature's electronic brain? Was it thinking at all? Or was it only waiting to see if she died, or if it would have to kill her itself?

She couldn't afford to waste any more breath or effort. She had to reach the opening before her strength gave up, and take whatever fate awaited her. She resumed her climb, grunting and panting, working her way slowly upward. While she climbed, she tried to convince the waiting android there was no reason to kill her.

When she could spare the breath, she spoke staccato sentences. "I figured I'd better come after you...Something's gone wrong with you, right?...You're confused...Understandable, after the attack...I'll take you out of here...We can go back and help the others."

The android didn't move a centimeter. It remained so still she wondered if its power supply had happened to give out at this very moment, fortuitously. But she knew her luck wasn't that good.

She had only three meters to go. Then a couple more meters. If the android didn't do anything, she might actually make it. Then she and the Guardian could sort out their differences.

The thing looked just as horrible close up as it had in the hospital. Half its face was missing, and, as if a macabre mirror image of herself, its right arm too.

She drew closer. Relief that her trial was nearly over was sending adrenaline pumping through her body, easing her pain. Or was it not relief, but fear of what the android might do when it could reach her?

The thing finally moved. Without taking its gaze from her, it lifted its remaining hand to its mouth, bit on its forefinger, and tugged. To her horror, the finger parted company with the hand, revealing a small dagger only as long as the first joint.

"No," she breathed.

The android placed the edge of the tiny dagger against the line where it stretched below the opening, and sawed. The thing regarded her without expression as its remaining arm moved backward and forward.

Cherry grunted and took another step upward. She gripped the line in her teeth. She reached for the opening. She was almost there. Another step...

The line snapped.

Again, she fell.

This time, she was ready. She curled up, tucking her head into her chest, and allowed the backpack to absorb the impact. As soon as she hit the floor, she rolled through the debris, trying to lessen the impact further. In another beat she was on her feet and brushing fragments from her face.

All of a sudden it hit her: things weren't as bad as they seemed. She'd been trying to find the Guardian, and now she'd found it. Though, strictly speaking, the Guardian had found her. It had probably heard her yell the first time she'd fallen and homed in on the sound in the silent city. But the result was the same.

She hadn't caught it in the middle of doing whatever it had come here to do, but perhaps there was still a way she could find out the reason for its presence in the city, *if* she had the creature under her control. And despite the apparent imbalance in their physical abilities getting it under her control wasn't as impossible as it might seem.

Since beginning her quest to find the Guardian, she had remembered a snippet of information Cariad had told her long ago. Knowing her dislike, bordering on fear, of the androids sent from Earth, Cariad had told her of a weakness the Guardian called Strongquist had once revealed.

If she could keep the android from killing her just long enough, she knew how to subdue it.

The thing remained in the opening, staring. It was probably processing the fact that she was still alive and deciding what to do next. Should it take the time to finish her off, or should it allow nature to take its course while she was trapped without food or water?

"You know what? I have something I bet you'd like to see." She dropped her backpack from her shoulders. It thumped on the floor, sending up a cloud of choking dust. She coughed and wiped the dirt from her eyes. She swallowed, dryly. Squatting down and pushing the debris to one side, she opened the pack and took out a line and her other grapnel.

"Look what I found," she shouted hoarsely. "Thank the stars for that. I'll be able to climb right out of here, when I've had a rest. Isn't that great? I bet that pleases your human-protecting, metal heart."

The android's gaze had switched to the line, which she was casually tying to the grapnel. Just the thought of making that climb again sent her muscles into spasms of protest, though in fact she had a much harder task ahead.

The android moved into the opening.

Good!

It was crouching, grasping the edge.

"C'mon!" Cherry softly exclaimed.

The android remained still, apparently stuck in a whirr of conflicting commands.

A great hatred rose up in her. Ever since the Guardians had raised their weapons against innocent Gens, she had loathed them. She hated their false faces and twisted motivations. To other colonists they had been Concordia's saviors, but she knew what they really were: machines with the potential for murder. Robotic psychopaths. And here was the last one. Once it was destroyed the Guardians would never plague the colony again.

"C'MON!" she screamed.

The Guardian jumped.

As the android fell, Cherry swung the grapnel and ran backward. She wasn't hoping to draw the creature closer—it would do that itself—but she wanted to unbalance it. If she could just reach...

The android hit the floor in a crouch, sinking into gray debris. As it rose, she threw the line. But the creature was too fast. The grapnel sank into the dust, useless. The Guardian ran at her.

She feinted left and then dived right, sliding through soft fragments and scattering them. A hand fastened around her ankle with a steely grip and yanked her. She turned onto her back and kicked. Her boot heel caught the Guardian under the chin, snapping its head backward. She kicked again, landing her next blow on the android's chest. But it was like kicking a wall.

She twisted violently to her right, spinning around, and managed to break the android's hold, though it felt like the skin of her ankle had been ripped off. She kicked the side of the creature's knee, momentarily unbalancing it.

She'd bought herself a second in which to rise to her feet, but then the android's hand was around her throat. It lifted her off the floor and walked, carrying her suspended by her neck, to the wall, thrusting her into it.

The Guardian leaned in, and pressed.

She had less than a second to live. The Guardian's superior strength meant it wouldn't even need to choke her to death. Its hand could probably squeeze right through her neck.

Already weakening, she reached behind its ear. Where was that place? That special spot Cariad had mentioned, marked by a mole?

The android's hand was hard and smooth. All its fake human skin and flesh had been burned away. Her airway was shut. Pressure was building up in her head, forcing blood into her tongue, squeezing her eyeballs from their sockets.

Her fingers desperately scrambled around the android's remaining ear. Had the pressure point been on the other side of its head? The incinerated side? Or had Cariad lied, seeking to calm her fears?

She was dying. The strength was draining from her arm. Her vision was closing in.

A pleasant euphoria began to overtake her. She hoped the colony would survive. The colony would survive. It always had. And she'd done her best to help it.

The Guardian released its grip and glared into her eyes. It had realized what she was trying to do. Her feet touched the floor. The android reached for her arm.

And then she felt it. A tiny bump, a small, raised spot in the well behind the android's earlobe.

She pressed.

It was like turning a switch. It *was* turning a switch.

The android was immediately, utterly still.

Cherry slumped to her knees in the detritus, nursing her agonized throat. For several long moments she couldn't move.

When she could breathe properly again, she looked up at the Guardian, frozen into position. Its elbow bent, it had been a centimeter grabbing her arm and preventing her from reaching its deactivation button. If it had succeeded, everything would have been over. There would have been no second chances.

Shakily, she got to her feet. What next? Should she continue to explore and try to find out what the android had been doing here? She might be able to follow its trail, especially if it had passed through debris layers like the one they were currently in. Even without the debris, the dust that lay over everything would have been disturbed wherever the android had passed.

But her water was low and she was exhausted.

Perhaps she could somehow force the android to tell her why it had gone to the city. Or maybe a techie could access its data storage.

A realization hit. She stared up at the two arched openings in the walls high above. She would have to complete her nearly impossible climb again, but not only that, if she wanted to take the android with her, she would have to find a way to drag it up too. Then she would have to carry the thing all the way through the city and back to the Chimera excavation site.

She wrapped her arm around the strange, burned mannequin's waist and tried to lift it. It was surprisingly heavy for its size. She doubted she could lift it off the floor even with two hands. *Dammit.*

She would have to leave it behind. And she was too weak to search farther into the city and discover the reason for its mission. *Dammit. Dammit. Dammit.*

Cherry closed her eyes. After all her effort, she'd failed, again. She would never find out why the android was on Concordia or what it might have done in the city. Two pieces of information that could be vital.

Then, out of nowhere, something Aubriot had said popped into her mind.

Catch that Guardian and cut its fucking head off for me.

Smiling grimly, she unsheathed her knife.

Twenty-Four

Wilder lay in the acceleration seat and calculated the time that had passed as the *Opportunity* journeyed to meet the Assembly ships. By her reckoning, based on ship's time, an entire day had gone by, but the time dilation meant that more time had passed on Concordia. To work out the duration of her journey from the perspective of the Concordians, she would need to ask Quinn the distance and speeds the ship had traveled. Her Fila friend was forced to regularly slow down the ship to allow her to recover from the effects of acceleration. Traveling continuously at top speed was more than the human body could endure.

By figuring out how long it took to reach the Assembly ships, she hoped to estimate the time Concordians would have to wait for help to arrive—the Assembly vessels would have to traverse roughly the same distance. But the question was too difficult and asking Quinn wouldn't be any help. He struggled to think of time from a human perspective.

Leaving Concordia's orbit meant she could no longer comm Kes. She could send a message, but his reply would take so long to reach her there was little point. Knowing she would be to all intents and purposes cut off from him and every other fellow human being, she had tried to comm him one last time before Quinn engaged the engines, but he hadn't been available.

It was to be expected. He was busy trying to save everyone on the planet. He didn't have time to chat with teenage girls. But she couldn't help feeling sad and lonely. She'd wanted to speak to Niall too, but she could sense that Quinn was anxious to set off, so she left Kes a short message, briefly telling him where she was going and why.

She'd found the latter part of her message hard to explain. What could she hope to gain from the Assembly in return for gifting them the secret of a-grav? The members were already coming to Concordia's aid as fast as they could. What greater gift could they give? Measured against the scale of other galactic civilizations, humanity's was insignificant. It had destroyed its civilization on its origin planet and for all she knew it might even have destroyed Earth's ecosystem, like the Scythians had. And Concordia's human civilization was barely clinging to existence.

If humankind disappeared from the galaxy tomorrow, would the impact be significant? She didn't think so. The Assembly had no particular reason to help them, yet it was. She didn't fully know why. Perhaps Quinn was right when he said her human perspective made it hard for her to understand. Whatever the Assembly's reasoning, what more could she ask of it than what it was already freely giving?

In the end, after some hesitation, she had ended her message to Kes by saying, *I haven't decided what I'll ask for in return for the a-grav. Maybe I'll think of something on the way. I wish I could ask for your advice. I bet you'd be able to suggest something else as well as saving us all. Anyway, I'm going now. Quinn wants us to set out rightaway. Stay safe. You better still be there when I get back.*

To help pass the time while she lay in the acceleration seat, she had watched old Earth vids from the ship's data files, including that weird one where Aubriot had been advertising the *Nova Fortuna* Project. But she'd seen many of them before during the long months of the voyage to the Assembly space station.

For a short while she searched for something new to watch before finally giving up. Next, she tried to sleep, closing her eyes and performing complicated mental calculations as she usually did when she wanted to drop off. But, as usual while she was experiencing acceleration, she found it was impossible to fall asleep. She was simply too uncomfortable, and she was tense with worry about Piddle and Puddle, though they both seemed to be adjusting to the bouts of extreme force on their small bodies.

"Quinn."

It was a moment before the Fila answered. "Yes?"

"I was wondering if you had any suggestions on what to propose to the Assembly as recompense for the a-grav machine?"

"That is for you to decide as a representative of humanity."

"But I'm only seventeen years old. I'm the last person to be making this decision. I wish I'd thought to talk to the Leader before we left."

"I understand your uncertainty and concern, but I don't believe it would be ethical or wise for me to voice my opinion and influence you."

"I'm not asking you to tell me what to say, I'm only asking for a little *advice*."

"Wilder, though we are good friends, you know the difficulties we have in understanding each other at times. Human lives are like blips in spacetime to me. I am already mourning your passing. The current needs of Concordia are plain to the least intelligent human, and you are certainly not among those ranks. The colony's immediate needs do not require stating. Beyond that...You are human, and I am not. There is no more to be said."

"But I would like to help the Fila too. You share the planet with us."

Long seconds passed before she realized Quinn wasn't going to reply.

Heaving a sigh, she shifted uncomfortably under the pressure forcing down on her.

Twenty-Five

Tycho looked deep into Kes's eyes as he shook his hand. "I want to make something clear before I go. I'm doing this of my own free will and I accept the consequences, whatever they may be."

A cold breeze was blowing across the parking lot outside the warehouse refuge. Kes gripped Tycho's hand tightly. "I understand what you're saying, and I appreciate why you're saying it."

Would Tycho's words make him feel less guilty if the vaccine was a dud and Wilder's friend went to his death? Kes doubted it. But perhaps, when the biocide arrived at the refuge and his own end came, he might be able to take comfort in the fact that he'd done all he could, even to the extent of accepting an elderly man's offer to risk his life.

He watched Tycho walk calmly and steadily to the heli that would transport him to a dead zone. Kes squinted in the bright sunshine. How long had it been since he'd seen natural daylight? More than a week. Seven days was the shortest time it would take for the human body to develop an immune response to the vaccine. He would have liked to have waited longer—three or four weeks would have been sufficient to give them reliable data.

But they didn't have that long. At its current rate of approach, the biocide was expected to close in on the refuge in five days. No one knew how long it would take to breach the firebreak, but after it did, they would have only hours. The scientists needed every moment they had left to mass produce the vaccine and send it out to all the known refuges. They had already begun production despite their ignorance about its effectiveness. They had no choice.

The colony's future was staked on a hypothesis.

Tycho climbed into the heli, clearly struggling to force his old, stiff body to make the maneuver. At the distance, he looked frailer than ever.

The heli door closed and reflected sunlight on the transparent shell hid the interior. Tycho had disappeared from view. The rotors started up and within a few seconds the heli was rising into the sky.

As the days had passed and Tycho continued to show no ill effects from the vaccine, other members of the refuge, upon hearing about the experiment, also stepped forward to be guinea pigs. Four more individuals had been vaccinated and were under close observation in the lab's meeting room.

Despite the apparently positive progress, Kes was filled with a sense of doom, though he'd been careful to mask his feelings around the others. He'd become convinced that the vaccine recipients had remained in good health because the vaccine was ineffective. His reasoning was sound. The literature indicated that mild fevers post immunization were common, but the experimental subjects remained entirely unaffected. The biocide worked so fast and was so devastating, a robust physical response to its vaccine would have been expected.

However, the morale of the refuge was a knife edge. Meredith's suicide hadn't helped matters. The spreading news of the vaccine had renewed hope in the colonists' hearts. They had begun to believe they might survive this latest onslaught. He didn't want to put that hope in jeopardy.

He tried to tell himself that unrelated feelings were triggering his disquiet. He missed Isobel and Miki. Comms between the refuge and the Chimera excavation site were slow and erratic and he hadn't been able to speak directly with Isobel since she'd arrived. His only source of information about his wife and daughter was the general report from the site organizer, stating their names on the list of occupants. Other than that, he had no idea if they had enough food and water, or somewhere safe and comfortable to sleep.

He realized he was staring at empty sky and the chill wind was penetrating his flimsy lab coat. Even the sound of the heli had faded. He returned to the refuge, slipping through the gap in the large warehouse doorway and pulling it closed. The inside air was stale and not much warmer than outside. He guessed he only had a short time before the heli reached the test site.

A camera had been fixed to the outside of the aircraft and angled downward to record whatever went on below it. The pilot would be too focused on her controls to operate a recording device, maintaining a stable, steady hover at a fixed altitude in the strong breeze. Kes had advised Tycho to take off his shoes and socks before the pilot lowered him in order to facilitate immediate contact with the ground.

Kes entered the lab. It was empty. Every scientist was in the meeting room watching the interface linked with the heli camera. The more optimistic had suggested broadcasting the test to the entire refuge or even across Concordia, but Kes had stated a firm refusal. The last thing anyone needed to see was an old man dying from the deadly effects of the biocide.

"He's nearly there, I think," said Tricia over her shoulder as she noticed Kes.

The other test subjects were sitting up in their beds, hooked up to various monitors, watching the wall screen as avidly as the clustered scientists.

The ground was skimming beneath the heli. In the immediate area even the unpoisoned landscape was dry and bare, but occasionally green scrub or groundcover would flit past.

"Good idea to suggest the pilot drops him at an advancing border," Tricia continued when Kes reached her side. "I agree that the biocide may be less concentrated and weaker in the dead zones, where it might have run out of living organisms to sustain it. It'll be the most potent along the lines where it's advancing. Though if you're right about the former, it gives me hope."

"Why's that?"

"Maybe the dead zones will eventually be safe for us to return to."

"It's only a guess, and not one I'd like to stake my life on. I'd be happier if we can vaccinate the population, providing the vaccine works."

"It looks like we're about to find out."

The image on the interface had stopped moving. The heli was hovering over a patch of dry, brown soil strewn with small rocks. Thick leaves of a native plant were clinging to life in the inhospitable conditions. They were green, but somewhere off-camera a line of death crept closer.

A heavy silence had fallen in the room. The camera beneath the heli only recorded video, not sound. Tycho and the pilot could speak to them over comm, but neither was choosing to voice their thoughts or fears. Only the soft hum and gentle beeps of the medical equipment broke the quiet, somehow adding to the tension.

"Can I say something?" asked Drew. "We haven't discussed what we'll do if the vaccine is ineffective."

"We'll continue working on it," someone replied.

"No, I mean, what do we tell people? Do we give out the details, or do we keep quiet about it?"

"I'd suggest that if the test is a failure," said Kes, "we keep that information within these four walls."

"We can't do that," Thom said. "People have a right to know."

"Usually, I'd agree with you," Kes replied, "but in this case—"

"There he is!" Tricia exclaimed.

Tycho had appeared, dangling from a harness, slowly spinning, his bare feet thrust out from pants gathered up by the straps. The camera focused on the top of his bald head, fringed with white hair.

The tension in the room silently screamed in Kes's mind. All he could see was the leisurely rotation of Tycho's head and his uncovered feet sticking out incongruously below.

If the biocide killed him, how long would it take? From what Kes had seen, the chemical's effect was pretty much instantaneous, but if the skin on Tycho's feet was thick and hard as it often was on older people, it might take a second or two for the virus to work its way through the microorganisms on his skin to reach tenderer, more vulnerable parts.

"He's down!" someone yelled.

Kes could hardly believe it. How had the old man reached the ground so quickly? But there he was. The line from the harness slackened as it no longer bore the old man's weight.

But he'd alighted on rocks, not soil. And the biocide hadn't yet reached the spot. Tycho was busy unfastening the harness and stepping out of it. What was he doing? There was no need for him to do that. Then Kes guessed Tycho's reasoning: the biocide could creep up the line to the heli and affect the pilot, whether Tycho was immune to it or not.

As soon as he was free from the harness, Tycho stepped out of view.

"Where's he going?" asked Tricia. "He was supposed to stay there and wait for the biocide to reach him, wasn't he? Do you think he's changed his mind? I don't think he'll be able to outrun it."

"No," replied Kes. "I don't think he's changed his mind."

The scene on the interface expanded. The heli was rising, trailing the empty harness and line. Tycho came back into view, smaller due to the increased distance. His bald pate was shiny, reflecting the sunlight. He looked like a toy figure as he stomped rhythmically across the dusty earth. He seemed to want to break into a run if only his old body would let him.

He was advancing toward his death with all the speed he could muster.

Now the pilot had risen higher, the line of destruction became clear. Where life survived, green hues colored the brown earth. The dead zone contained no green. The brown of it was deeper, peppered with the darker brown and black of destroyed vegetation.

The line demarcating the two zones was moving, paradoxically as if it were alive. It sped toward Tycho's small figure at an alarming pace. In spite of his age, he mustered the energy to run. He headed directly toward the biocide, his arms and legs pumping, his feet no doubt being scratched and cut by sharp stones.

At the last moment, with the biocide only meters away, he halted. Putting his hands on his hips, he bowed slightly forward, as if catching his breath. Then he straightened up, facing the chemical's deadly approach square on.

A beat later it reached him.

In the meeting room, a collective breath was drawn. Kes's neck and back grew rigid. He wanted to turn from the screen, unwilling to witness the death of this brave man, but he could not wrench his gaze away.

And so it was he saw Tycho fall. As the dead zone encroached on and passed the spot where he was standing, the old man fell to his knees. He plummeted forward and hit the ground belly first.

"Shit," muttered Drew.

"Oh god, I can't watch." Tricia shielded her eyes.

Kes bowed his head. His intuition had been correct. The vaccine was a dud. Either that, or they hadn't waited long enough for Tycho's body to develop an immune response. Or perhaps his entire idea that the biocide could be defeated by a vaccine had been wrong.

What would they do now? How much longer did they have before the biocide reached them? If only they had more time, they might think up an alternative strategy, or perhaps the Assembly ships would get here and they could evacuate the planet. But time was the one thing they didn't have.

Then someone shouted, "He's getting up!"

Disbelievingly, Kes lifted his head. He registered the small figure of an old man, surrounded by death, clambering to his feet, but his mind couldn't grasp what he was seeing. His mouth dropped open.

Tycho was standing.

Tycho was *alive*.

It was impossible, yet it was true. The old man walked in a small circle. Then he turned toward the the heli and waved.

Dimly, Kes heard yells and hollers as the scientists erupted into celebrations. People slapped his back. Others grasped his right hand and shook it. Bright, grinning faces danced across his vision.

Someone was holding his shoulders and peering into his face.

"Kes," Tricia said, "are you feeling all right?"

"Huh?"

"Are you okay? You know you did it, right? You and Drew. You did it. You saved us. You've saved the colony."

"Huh?"

"I think you better sit down."

He felt pressure on his arms as Tricia forced him into a seat. "We did it?"

"We did it. Nearly. We still have a lot of work ahead of us, but I think everyone's going to be okay."

Twenty-Six

Memories of her time at the Assembly space station were vivid in Wilder's mind as she traveled through the umbilicus that led to the aliens' ship. Quinn had told her the species she was about to meet performed the role of the organizers of the space station, and that Kes had named them Immani giganticus.

She didn't need reminding of the size of the alien 'organizers' she'd seen at the station—she recalled that one of the individuals she'd seen had measured about seven meters tall. They were quadrupeds and their legs made up half their immense height. Their upper half formed a dome, but due to the EVA suits they'd worn, Wilder hadn't been able to see their eyes or mouth(s) or any other part of their faces, assuming they had faces.

She shivered slightly and pulled herself along the line the Immani had provided. It was hard to imagine she was traveling at near light speed. Quinn had matched the speed of the *Opportunity* with that of the Immani ship, and now the two vessels were hurtling toward Concordia together.

The interior of the umbilicus was brightly lit, but she couldn't see the source of the light. It seemed to come from the umbilicus material itself. The light at the end of the flexible tunnel was even brighter. In anticipation of entering the glare, Wilder increased the tint on her visor.

On the remainder of her trip to the Immani's ship, she had begun to work on a second problem. Now that she'd perfected her understanding of how to produce an a-grav force, it seemed obvious that without too much trouble she should be able to construct a device that would *create* gravity. The Guardians' ship, the *Mistral*, had carried just such a device. Though the ship had been destroyed, the majority of its plans had been transferred to the colony's data banks.

If she could offer a-grav *and* a gravity-generating device, that would be a hell of an advantage in negotiations with the Assembly. But she hadn't had time to work on the idea between the long bouts of acceleration and then deceleration, and she lacked tools and equipment. It wasn't only a matter of repurposing the a-grav machine's parts.

Still, she felt fairly confident she could commit to producing a gravity generator at some point in the future.

The closer she got to the end of the umbilicus, the larger the exit loomed. The effect was to make her feel even smaller and younger.

"Quinn?"

"Yes, Wilder?"

"I just wanted to check my comm would go through to you. You're sure we won't be cut off from each other while I'm aboard the ship?"

"I cannot think of any reason the Immani would prevent us from speaking to each other."

"Okay. Cool."

She stopped hauling on the line. She'd reached the Immani's ship. She clung to the slim, metallic rope with one hand, floating free, and assessed the distance between her and the other side of the portal. The opening looked wide enough for the *Opportunity* to pass clean through it.

Inside, the glare made it hard for her to distinguish the ship's bulkheads. No one seemed to be awaiting her.

"Quinn, I reached the ship but I don't know where to go."

"If none of them are there to greet you they must have left something to indicate where you are to go."

"I can't see—oh." Her eyes had adjusted to the extreme light—she imagined her pupils must be pinpricks—and she saw a disturbance in the beams. A line of even brighter light stood out along one bulkhead. "I think I know what I'm supposed to do."

After her many days of weightlessness aboard the *Opportunity* while in orbit above Concordia, Wilder was adept at moving in zero-g. She guessed she was supposed to follow the line of light. She set off accordingly, launching herself across the wide, bright space.

It seemed odd that the Immani had sent no one to greet her, but then there was no knowing what it meant. Perhaps they were being polite.

As she reached the far side of the entrance bay motion in her peripheral vision caught her eye. The door to the umbilicus was quickly closing.

"Quinn? Can you hear me?"

"I can hear you."

Wilder forced herself to relax. She was letting her nerves get the better of her. Her Fila friend was right: the Immani had no reason to wish her any harm.

Her visor displayed rising levels of gases, predominately carbon dioxide. The Immani were filling the entrance bay with the atmosphere they breathed. Wilder kept her helmet on. The gases that were essential to the Immani were poisonous to her.

The line of slightly brighter light led out of the bay along a wide corridor. Wilder had to take care to remain close to the sides. If she lost contact she could find herself floating helplessly, unable to push on anything to provide her with momentum. It might require several minutes of awkward and somewhat embarrassing maneuvering to work her way back to a solid surface.

Were the Immani watching her? Assuming they perceived their surroundings at least partially by sight it was likely they were, though she couldn't see anything resembling a camera. That was no surprise—she was having problems seeing anything at all in the brilliant light. Her eyes already ached despite turning up her visor to full tint.

Something flew across the junction at the end of the passageway. Wilder slammed her hand against the nearest surface, bringing herself to an abrupt stop.

"Quinn, did you see that?"

"I'm not receiving a visual from you."

"You aren't? Damn. I saw something. I don't know what it was."

"My guess would be that what you saw was an Immani, considering you are aboard their ship."

Though the translator's tone was emotionless, Wilder detected the Fila's sarcastic note. "Okay, okay. Don't forget I'm alone in a ship full of giant aliens. You've got to admit a little jitteriness is only to be expected."

"My advice is to attend the meeting with the Immani as soon as possible in order to overcome your nervousness."

"I'm working on it."

Wilder resumed her progress. She was finding it hard to maintain close contact with the walls. She was glad she'd decided to not bring the a-grav machine. Quinn was confident the Immani wouldn't simply take the machine from her and kick her out, but Wilder was not so trusting. She had dismantled the machine and deleted all recordings of its operation from the ship's data before leaving the *Opportunity*. But in any case, transporting the machine through the Immani ship would only have made things more difficult.

She pushed herself gently along, turning her head slightly as she did so. Something huge was rushing toward her from behind. She gave a small shriek and sped away, fast.

In fact, she moved so fast she failed to notice the creature approaching her from in front. She collided with it, sinking into a soft, billowing surface. For a moment, she was lost in folds of white and she struggled, trying to find her way out. Then the spongey surface hardened and she was forced outward, ejected into the passageway.

An Immani floated on each side of her, blocking any possibility of escape. The creatures looked different from how she remembered them. At the space station they'd been wearing EVA suits and their four limbs had been held to the floor by magnetism. Here on their ship she was looking at them from a different angle. She guessed what she was seeing was the top of their dome-like upper halves.

A circle of black dots wreathed each white head. Were the dots eyes? And where were their mouths? If they didn't have mouths, how did they breath? The creatures' four long legs were beyond her field of vision.

"Welcome aboard our ship, *does not translate*," said a voice.

"Thanks." Wilder wondered what they had called her.

"Before we begin negotiations," said the voice, "I must warn you that Scythian vessels have been sighted approaching this sector. Our talk must be brief. We may not have time to come to a clear agreement before you must return to your ship and the life support system that can sustain you in the event of an attack."

"Holy crap," said Wilder.

"That term has no equivalent in any of our languages. Could you please rephrase?"

"We're going to be attacked by the Scythians?"

"That appears to be their preferred behavior."

"But what's drawn them here?"

"It's possible they tracked your ship departing your planet's star system, or they may have intercepted and deciphered the comms the Fila sent about your work with gravity devices. The technology is priceless. For obvious reasons, the Scythians would prefer only they possessed it."

"Wow, this is super bad." Wilder had never been the sole target of a Scythian attack. She didn't like the special attention.

"That's an accurate summation of the situation," said the voice. "Let us begin negotiations. What's your desired payment for the a-grav technology?"

"Well," said Wilder, "I just thought of something, or rather, some things."

Twenty-Seven

Pain lanced into Cherry's knees and the heel of her hand, but she had no choice except to crawl on. She could already feel death edging toward her. She couldn't remember the last time she'd sweated, and she could only produce a few drops of dark amber urine. Blinding headaches and muscle cramps plagued her so badly she could barely sleep. When she did nap for a few minutes, she dreamed of wide pools of fresh, clean water, lying only meters away. She would drag herself toward a pool, scoop a handful of the precious fluid, lift it to her lips—and wake up.

If she could produce tears, she would have cried. But crying would not fix her water condenser, which had broken one of the two times she'd fallen onto her backpack or when the Guardian had slammed her into a wall.

However, she was nearly at the boundary of the Scythian city. If she could make it there and push through, her comm might reach someone in Chimera.

How long had it taken her to navigate the maze-like fissures covering the ground from the buildings to the city boundary wall? She could not remember. In her weakened state, it took her hours to traverse the long, roaming gaps threading the surface, and all the concentration she could muster to avoid falling into them. She'd spent at least one rest period lying on a lane, terrified she might move in her sleep and tumble to her death.

In spite of the ambient temperature of the underground city, she shivered with cold whenever she stopped moving. She had long since abandoned her sleeping bag and all other equipment except her night goggles, her knife, and the bag containing the Guardian's head.

When her dehydration had grown so bad she could no longer walk and was forced to use her only hand to crawl, she had slung the bag across her body. As she dragged herself along, it hung awkwardly beneath her, its contents catching on the ground and bumping her knees.

But now she was on the final, straight lane leading all the way to the boundary. If she could only make it that far, she might be okay. Doggedly, she forced her hand forward. Grimacing, she placed it on the ground. She had wrapped it in a sleeve she'd ripped from her top. The layer of cloth offered some protection but her skin had chafed away and her flesh was bruised, sore, and weeping. Her knees were in an even worse state. She hadn't looked at them in days, fearing that what she might see would dampen her resolve to make it back to Chimera.

It wasn't that she wanted to live so badly. Her motivation was spurred by her need to find out what secrets hid within the Guardian's electronic brain. It had gone to the city for a reason, a reason that could be vital to the colony's survival.

How much farther to go? In her current mental fog, she couldn't estimate the distance. Like the pools in her dreams, the wall seemed impossible to reach. But she'd come so far, she couldn't give up.

The journey back had been much more arduous than she'd imagined. The effort to climb out of the room where she'd deactivated the Guardian had nearly killed her. By the time she'd climbed up to the arched opening, her hand was a bloody mess, her teeth and jaw felt ready to detach from her head, and her leg and stomach muscles shook. She'd collapsed on the narrow ledge between two rooms, already perceiving an inkling of just how hard her return trip was going to be.

If she'd only had water she might not have suffered so much, but after each sleep she'd woken up thirstier, and as time went on the parched atmosphere had sucked her dry.

The rooms she'd climbed into and out of quickly on her way into the city had become monumental trials of effort and willpower. She'd reached the end of her reserves of energy, yet she had been forced to continue onward, digging deeper to the utter limits of her strength.

She'd never liked spending time here, but during the course of her return journey she'd grown to hate the place. She detested the stench of the air—though she could no longer smell it—she loathed the piles of fragmented decay blanketing some of the rooms, and she despised the arched openings that provided the only method of moving through the metropolis.

Why didn't the Scythians use roads? Surely they needed roads? It made no sense. It was almost as if the aliens had created the habitation hundreds of thousands of years ago with the express purpose of making her journey as difficult as possible.

She reached forward, but this time her hand didn't land on the smooth black surface of the floor. It touched a soft surface that gave a little under the pressure.

She'd made it! She was at the boundary wall.

Her eyes screwed up and a hoarse croak issued from her throat, but no tears came. She sat back on her haunches. The bag rested in the hollow between her hip bones. Was the wall the right color? Her vision was blurry. She concentrated her gaze on the vertical surface. It was green, the softest of the materials the Scythians used in their constructions. Yet despite the fact that it was the easiest material to force herself through, she wasn't sure she had the strength to do it.

There was nothing to do except to try. She leaned forward and pressed her head against the spongy surface. Her forehead sank in, but the wall held under the meager pressure she exerted. Her shoulders slumped and she struggled to remain upright. Her knees were screaming in agony.

She had to get through the wall, but she wasn't strong enough to do it unaided.

Then she remembered her knife. She had blunted the blade somewhat when she'd sawn through the silicon, metal, and plastic of the Guardian's neck, but the boundary wall didn't require a sharp edge to penetrate it.

She took it out. Holding it like a dagger, she pierced the green surface and then drew the blade downward. A slit appeared. Before the material could rejoin, she slipped the knife into its sheath and forced her fingertips into the barely visible line. Pulling it to one side, she created a hole and caught a glimpse of the area beyond the city. She even thought she could see the far cliff face and the excavation vehicle at its top.

She pushed the top of her head into the gap. The soft material closed around it, but she moved forward quickly, easing her shoulders into the softened space. As her chest entered, the bag around her torso caught and dragged. She forced herself onward. This was going to be her last expense of effort for a long while, perhaps forever.

Finally, somehow, she was mostly through the wall. She collapsed, her calves and feet still embedded in the green matter.

She tried to comm, but her throat made only a choking noise. She coughed dryly and tried again. "Hello? Can anyone hear me?" she whispered.

Water, sweet water, was dribbling between her lips. At first, she thought she was dreaming. She thought she'd finally reached the pool in her dream and that when she woke up she would be back in the dry Scythian city, in pain and alone, far from people who cared about her.

But this time when she opened her eyes a different sight greeted her. A dark green cloth hung near her face. She could also hear noises. The deafening silence of the Scythian city was gone. She could hear movement and indistinct voices.

The water was real. It was real. She reached up and blindly grabbed at the space it seemed to have come from. Her hand met flesh. Her grip folded around an arm, though her tender, injured palm protested at the touch.

"Whoa, take it easy." The arm removed itself from her grip. "I'm glad to see you're feeling better."

She turned her head to see the owner of the voice. It was a young man she didn't recognize.

"I get it. You're thirsty. But I have to rehydrate you slowly. Your organs are on the brink of failing. If they receive too much water too fast it could overwhelm them and tip them over the edge. But a little more is okay." He held a sponge over her lips and gently squeezed it.

More exquisite moisture entered her mouth. She swallowed. The taste wasn't exactly like water: it was a little sweet and salty.

"If I had a drip I could be more scientific about this, but none of the supplies I asked for have arrived from Lyonesse yet, and the Suddeners didn't bring any intravenous infusion equipment from Port City. Don't worry, though. I think you're going to be fine. Though if you'd spent another few hours longer in this state I might not be saying that."

"Who are you?"

The young man smiled. "I'm sorry. I'm Dr. Zhang. I'm in charge of medical care at Chimera."

"You're from the warehouses?"

"That's right. I came over on a heli. There are a lot of vulnerable people here who require care."

"Wait. Where's my head?"

Dr. Zhang's mouth rounded to an O. "Er, you need a little more rehydration. Here, have some more of this." He lifted the sponge.

"No, I need to activate the head. I have to find out what the Guardian was doing in the city." She coughed weakly.

"Oh, you mean that thing you brought back with you? It's a head? Okay. That's kinda weird. I think it's around here somewhere."

She tried to sit up. She saw the interior of a tent, then everything went black.

When she came around, Zhang's face was close to hers, his features creased with concern. "Please don't do that again. You must remain still and rest until you're better."

"I need the head," she insisted.

"All right. If it's that important I'll ask someone to find it for you. But you must promise me you'll stop trying to get up."

"Just get me the head."

———

It was two days before she could get out of bed. When she walked, she hobbled like someone twice her age. Her knees and hand were covered in thick scabs, and her pillow was covered with her hair, which had fallen out while she recuperated from her near-fatal bout of dehydration. What remained was thin with patches of baldness.

During her waking moments she'd grown more familiar with inside of the medical tent than she liked. There was nothing to do except look around it. She had no interface, and Doctor Zhang had taken out her ear comm, probably concerned about stress impacting her recovery.

The place they'd put her accommodated two beds, but the other one was empty.

Her only other distraction had been external sounds. Chimera was noisier than it had been when she left. The vulnerable colonists Zhang had mentioned were arriving all the time from Lyonesse, swelling the numbers sheltering in the safest place in Concordia.

The second time she'd woken, the doctor had told her the Guardian's head had been found, but he refused to allow her to have it. The pleasant-mannered doctor had become almost belligerent.

What do you imagine you're going to do with it in your current state? Lie still. Get better. Then you can do whatever you want with your precious head.

Now she *was* better. Maybe not a hundred percent, but she could move around without falling over, and that was good enough.

She could walk up and down the narrow space in the center of the tent three or four times without leaning on the bunks. She felt strong enough to go outside. This time, she wouldn't ask Zhang for the Guardian's head, she would demand it. As far as she knew, she remained the General of the colony. She could do whatever she wanted. No one had the authority to boss her around. Not unless a new Leader had been elected, and she doubted anyone had time for that.

She shuffled unsteadily over to the tent flap and ran her hand down the join, breaking it open. But before she could go out, someone appeared. She almost collided with the new arrival. Startled, she stumbled backward.

Isobel came in, looking as surprised as Cherry felt. Or maybe her expression was more horrified than surprised. The woman's belly seemed larger than Cherry remembered it, impossibly large.

"*Cherry*?" Isobel quickly added, "Here, let me help you back to bed."

"I'm okay," Cherry snapped, moving her arm out of Isobel's reach. "I need to leave."

"Why? Are you looking for this?" Isobel lifted up a full bag.

Cherry recognized it instantly. "You have the head?"

"I was bringing it to you. Please, sit down. I hate to say it, but you look awful. Sit on the bed and we can look at it together. Zhang told me I'd better bring it to you soon or he wouldn't be answerable for what you might do. I've been working on it ever since you brought in."

"Working on it? What do you mean? What have you done to it?"

Isobel had moved to the bunk and was sitting on it. The cast from her lower leg was gone. "Nothing risky. Come over here and I'll explain."

She waited until Cherry joined her before removing the head from the bag. Cherry hadn't looked at it since hacking it from the Guardian's body. Close up in the clear light of the tent's lamp, it looked hideous. The head's single eye was frozen half open. The area underlying the missing half of its face was a mess of blackened, melted plastic. Half the mouth was gone and the tongue and inner surface of the teeth on the remaining side were clearly visible. Frizzy remnants of fake hair clung to the mostly bald scalp.

Removing the head from the rest of the body hadn't been easy. Her sawing and slicing had left a ragged shambles of a neck below the ravaged face and skull.

"I think I found out how to reactivate it." Isobel rested the head against her bulbous belly. "It's this nodule here, right?" She turned the head over and pointed to the small, colorless bump behind the ear.

"That's right. How did you know?"

"My field is robotics engineering. I've worked in construction robotics for most of my career. Not exactly the kind of profession you might imagine for the spouse of the colony's chief xenobiologist, is it?"

"I hadn't really thought about it." In truth, Cherry had found it hard to see past Isobel's extremely conspicuous pregnancy. She couldn't imagine anyone doing any kind of job while so physically encumbered.

"Anyway," Isobel said, "when I heard you'd been here and you'd gone into the Scythian city, I asked Alun what you were doing. I knew Kes would be worried about you and I thought I could give him an update. Alun explained the situation about the Guardian. Then I heard you were back and you'd brought something very strange with you. I was curious to know what it was, and it wasn't hard for me to get hold of it." She turned the head face downward in her lap. "No one else wanted anything to do with it. I've been taking a look at it while you were recovering. I'll show you what I've found."

Isobel inserted her fingers beneath a flap at the back of the scalp and slid if off, revealing a pale gray skull. Though the outer surface of the Guardian's head had been severely damaged by heat, the interior seemed intact and unharmed.

Cherry recalled the android telling her that its memory had been mangled. Had it been lying?

"It was a little tricky to open it," said Isobel. "Whoever made this thing did *not* intend anyone else to mess with it. It's entirely intact. The CPU communicates with the rest of the body wirelessly. In fact, I only found the entry point because it had been forced previously. It was the marks left behind that showed me where to look."

"No kidding." Cherry leaned closer. Even so, she could only just see the tiny scratch marks on the smooth artificial skull.

Isobel took a slim piece of metal from her pocket and pressed the edge into an invisible join. She gently worked the metal downward and then gave it a twist. The skull cracked open like a nut. "It's an absolute marvel of engineering. I would so love to meet the team that put this together. Unfortunately, it's been tampered with."

"Has it?"

"Can you see here, and here? Those parts aren't the same as the others. And there are more additions and circumventions if you look closer."

To Cherry's untrained eyes, the sections Isobel pointed at didn't look any different from the rest of the contents of the Guardian's skull, but she was willing to take the woman's word for it. "Have you tried to reactivate it yet?"

"I thought I would wait until you were feeling better and we could do it together. What do you think?"

In light of what Isobel had told her, she was unsure what to do. "The thing is, what if the Scythians were the ones who tampered with the skull? There aren't any other likely candidates. They might have booby-trapped it."

Isobel drew back, covering her bump with her hands. "What makes you think the Scythians have worked on this?"

Cherry briefly told her the story of how the Guardian had returned to Concordia. "But on the other hand, if the head were booby-trapped, I'm pretty sure it would have gone off when you opened it."

Isobel had turned pale. "I had no idea. Why didn't Alun tell me? I would never have touched it."

"I didn't have time to explain everything to him, and it's only a guess. But now you've told me someone's tinkered around inside the head, it adds up. I think the Scythians collected the remains of one of the Guardians after the *Mistral* exploded, and they figured out how to alter its programming to..."

"To what?"

"I still don't know exactly."

The two women sat in silence, gazing at the exposed interior of the Guardian's head.

Finally, Cherry said, "I take it you didn't see anything that looked like a booby trap while you were poking around in there?"

"No, I didn't. Nothing at all." Isobel still looked scared. "You're going to activate it, aren't you?"

"I am. I have to. I have to try to find out what it was doing in the city."

"Well, I'm going to leave you to it. I'm sorry, but I don't only have myself to think about."

"I understand. But before you go, could you remove the parts that were added to the CPU?"

Isobel bit her lip. "I'll try. I can't remove all the non-original parts or it won't work, but I think I can take out most of them. Though I'll have to botch it." She reached into the pocket of her smock dress and took out a tiny screwdriver.

Cherry waited as Isobel worked. Thirty minutes later a small pile of hair-fine wires and tiny chips sat on Isobel's lap. The head's interior didn't look any different.

"That's the best I can do." Isobel put her tools in her pocket and passed the head over. Gathering the pile of removed parts and placing them on a camping table, she added, "I'll leave these here. They might be useful later."

Isobel walk heavily out of the tent. The woman looked like she was about to drop triplets. Returning her attention to the head, Cherry turned it over, face upward.

The Guardian's eye and mouth sagged. Cherry recalled her first encounter with the android in the hospital at Oceanside, when it had said it remembered it was the captain of a starship. It hadn't stated its name, but if the creature's memory was correct it was Faina. In spite of the extensive damage to the face, Cherry could see the resemblance. She had avoided spending time around the Guardians right from the moment they had arrived, even before they'd turned nasty. The strange newcomers from Earth had always made her uncomfortable, and when their true nature was revealed it all added up.

She had a good memory for faces. This android had appeared at the stadium alongside Garwin, Anahi, and the other Guardian, Strongquist, when Anahi began her quest to take control of the colony. It had happened so long ago. Garwin and Anahi were long dead and Strongquist was gone too, cut to pieces by the Scythian spiders.

Cherry suddenly felt old and very tired. She wondered how Kes, Wilder, and Aubriot were getting on. They were the only ones who shared her memories. She sighed and felt behind Faina's ear. The small bump was easy to detect now she knew exactly where it was.

She pressed it.

The eye opened fully, forcing back the overhanging tissue. Cherry pulled away the loose skin so the android could see her. Its mouth closed. But then it seemed to lose power. The eye shut and the jaw slackened, allowing the mouth to gape.

"Faina." When this drew no response, Cherry repeated the name louder.

The eyelid rose halfway. Half a blue-green iris focused.

"Is that your name?" Cherry asked. "Are you Faina?"

The lips closed. They opened to form a reply but no sound came out.

With alarm, she realized she could have cut away the thing's vocal chords, assuming its voice synthesis mimicked human physiology. If she had, there was no point expecting verbal responses. She would have to ask Isobel if there was a way to link it up to a computer to communicate with it.

But then it spoke. "I am Faina."

What if it was only agreeing with her suggestion? She had to find out for sure if the head really was part of a Guardian. She tried to think of something only a Guardian would know. "Do you recognize me? What's my name?"

"You are Cherry Lindstrom."

Faina had answered correctly, but the android might have gleaned that information from the colony data banks. As the General, she was hardly anonymous. She needed more convincing. Then she thought of a better question. "What do I do?"

Faina's gaze was steady as she replied, "You are a farmer. Your farm is near the lake. It was one of the first farms."

"Huh." So its memory was of the time the Guardians had been active on Concordia.

"I cannot feel my body. Where is my body?"

"A long way from here."

"I am damaged. How was I damaged? My processing is faulty. I remember..." The android's stare froze. The eyelid began to droop.

"Faina, stay with me. I need you to stay with me. You have to help the colony. That's the Guardian's mandate isn't it? You must help the colony survive, no matter what it takes."

"That is our mandate." Faina's eyelid remained droopy and the pace of speech had slowed. "I-I-I believe I have been c-c-compromised."

"I believe you've been compromised too. What can you tell me? What do you remember? Tell me everything that happened after you crashed the *Mistral* into the Scythian ship."

The eye wavered. The android made an odd, guttural noise. "Space. Cold. Dark." Faina's gaze suddenly snapped into focus. "Strongquist. Where is Strongquist?"

"He was destroyed." An unfamiliar emotion tugged at Cherry's heart. Was she really feeling pity for a Guardian? She'd called Strongquist 'he', not 'it'. "They were all destroyed. You're the last."

"He was destroyed," echoed Faina. "They were all destroyed. I am the last."

"It's very important you tell me everything you know. The survival of the colony may depend on it."

"I remember a room and living organisms above me, suspended in midair. I think I was aboard a starship."

That would make sense. Without a-grav the Scythians would float around their ship.

"I was fixed down. I believe they had tried to secure me once and I had broken free. I was there for a long time while they tried to access my mind."

"Were you ever deactivated?"

"I am not sure, but I don't think so."

"From what we can tell, something broke into your CPU." Cherry wasn't sure how much she should tell Faina. She didn't want to influence the creature's shaky recall.

The android repeated the guttural noise it had made earlier. "I remember. I returned to Concordia. I entered in an escape pod. I went... Concordia is different now."

"We're more than fifty Earth years on from the time you were here."

Faina stared. "You should be at the end of your natural life span, but you look nearly the same as before."

"It's a long story. Look, please tell me...Do you know why you went to the...Why are you here, underground on Suddene? Do you know what you're supposed to be doing here?"

"I-I-I-I-I-I-I-I-I—"

Cherry pushed up Faina's jaw, clamping her mouth closed. When she released it a few moments later, Faina's stutter stopped.

"I do remember why I am here, but when I try to tell you something blocks my speech."

"Something's stopping you from giving that information in particular?"

"Yes."

Should she ask Isobel to look for the prohibiting structure? But she had a feeling that it could be within the parts that couldn't be removed without preventing the android's mind from functioning.

"There is another way I may be able to tell you."

"Great. How?"

"I need a keyboard."

"A keyboard?" Cherry frowned. Where could she find a keyboard? Most interface interactions were carried out by voice. Only young children used keyboards, in order to help them learn to read. Children! She recalled the last time she'd seen a keyboard. It had been back at the warehouse refuge on Isobel's bed. Miki had a keyboard. But had she brought it to Suddene?

"I'll be right back." An irrational fear hit her: something might happen to Faina's head if she left it alone. "Sorry about this." She shoved the head into its bag. Clutching the bag, she hurried out of the tent as fast as she could, which wasn't very fast at all.

As she'd suspected during her long hours of recuperation, Chimera contained many more people now, though their tents covered only a small fraction of the vast underground space.

Yet it only took a few inquiries to locate Isobel. The woman's advanced pregnancy clearly made her memorable. She was at home with Miki. Cherry's relief increased when she saw the little girl was working with a keyboard and interface.

"Cherry?" Isobel said. "What are you..." Her gaze fell to the bag. "Please don't bring that thing in here."

"I'm going to leave right away, but I need your daughter's keyboard. Can I borrow it, sweetie?" She addressed her last remark to the child.

Miki's mouth turned down. "No!" She clutched the keyboard to her chest.

Cherry gave a mental sigh. She'd always been terrible with children. Her recent experience with Wilder had been a case in point, though Wilder was hardly a child any more. "Please?"

"NO!" Miki turned away.

"Miki, you have to give the lady your keyboard. She's only going to borrow it for a little while and then you can have it right back."

"I don't want to."

"Give the nice lady your keyboard and I'll read you a story on the interface."

"Uh," Cherry said. "I need the interface too."

"Oh, for star's sake. Come on, Miki. Let's go for a walk and see if we can find some candy." Isobel clumsily heaved herself to her feet.

Her daughter was easily persuaded by this proposal. She dropped the keyboard without another word and grabbed her mother's offered hand.

"Please make sure that thing is gone by the time I get back," Isobel said as she left.

Cherry settled down on the thin mattress. She had a good idea of what Faina intended, but the android no longer had hands with which to type. She took the head out of the bag. "I guess you need something to hold in your mouth?"

"Anything I can use to press the keys."

Cherry searched and found a toddler's spoon. As she waited for Faina to tap out the information, she saw herself in the weird scene, sitting in a tent, holding a disembodied head with a spoon in its mouth above a keyboard, the head giving instructions for where to move it.

At the same time, she read the message appearing on the interface.

I was sent to spy on Concordia. The Scythians have probes watching the planet, but they wanted on-ground information. They sent me to gather it and report to them before they returned to reclaim their home.

I could not access the military intelligence they wanted. Your actions in placing me in confinement hampered my attempts. The Scythians returned anyway and the battle took place. Before they departed, they sent me further instructions.

Before the Scythians fled their planet they constructed a defense system. Though they could not live here, they did not want other intelligent species to colonize their home. The defense system was designed to destroy any non-Scythian ships approaching Concordia, but it had failed.

My new instructions were to travel to the operations room of their planetary defense system and attempt to diagnose the fault and correct it.

Faina stopped tapping.

Cherry took the spoon out of the android's mouth. "You were in the Scythian city to fix their military defense system?"

"I-I-I-I-I."

Cherry stopped the Guardian's stutter and reinserted the spoon.

Yes.

"And did you?"

Yes.

"So if any ships approach Concordia, they'll be blown out of the sky?"

Yes.

Twenty-Eight

Wilder lay down in her seat, glad to be going home. She only hoped she wasn't going back to a lifeless planet. If that was the case, her brief meeting with the Immani would have been for nothing. Not that they had agreed to her terms in the matter of the a-grav machine. As only one member of the Assembly they didn't have the authority. She would have to wait until the organization held a formal meeting before she would know if she'd secured the payment requested.

The *Opportunity* began the first round of deceleration. The load pressed down hard onto her body, squeezing her rib cage and squashing her pelvis into the soft padding. Her jaw was slowly being forced open. She clenched her teeth to hold it closed.

"Quinn," she said through barely open lips, "are the Scythian ships still approaching?"

"They appear to be intent on following us back to Concordia."

"How fast are they going? Will they catch us?"

"Unfortunately their ships are faster than the *Opportunity* and, according to the Immani, no other ship in the convoy can outpace them. They will certainly arrive at Concordia at the same time as us if not before. But perhaps they aren't interested in the planet any longer, imagining that it's only a matter of time before the biocide does its work. They may only wish to attack the convoy."

"But surely they won't dare attack all these Assembly ships? They only attacked Concordia because they thought we were weak and defenseless. As soon as things got too tough for them they dropped their biocide and ran. And when I went to the Assembly space station they didn't assault the station itself, they only tried to kill us, the representatives of humanity. It seems to me they're cowards."

"Or smart and pragmatic. I cannot read their minds, Wilder. All I know is that we must return as fast as we can and attempt to protect the remaining populations of Fila and humans."

"Maybe we should turn and fight them. Make a stand, you know?"

"That would delay the convoy's arrival at Concordia and the rescue attempt."

She had no reply and her jaw ached from trying to speak. She gave up talking and tried to distract herself from her discomfort by mentally working on the problem of reversing the a-grav force.

After a few hours, just when she was thinking she'd reached the limit of her endurance, Quinn mercifully slowed the ship. He set the speed to create an effect equivalent to Concordia's gravity, so when she climbed off her seat she could walk around the ship. Her leg muscles remained weak from her time in micro-g. She walked slowly to the living quarters and immediately went to Piddle and Puddle's pouches.

When she opened the tops of the pouches, Piddle and then Puddle immediately climbed out, ran up her arms, and sat on her shoulders. Knowing what they expected next, she stepped to the cupboard of rations and gave each of the creatures something to eat. After they'd eaten it would be grooming time. She returned her pets to one pouch to share for the activity.

Piddle and Puddle were in much better shape than her. After their period of adjustment, they seemed to be thriving aboard the starship. Their coats were shiny and soft, and they'd both put on weight, developing a roundness to their bellies that was irresistible. She gave each of the tummies a rub and then closed the top of the pouch.

The same couldn't be said about her own stomach, which was concave with her two hip bones protruding on each side. She took out one of the remaining meals Stephie had cooked and heated it up.

As she was eating, Quinn spoke.

"I've been considering our conversation about the Scythian ships. I've had an idea, but it requires your agreement."

She swallowed and put down her fork. "Shoot."

"As I said before, it's possible that the Scythians aren't interested in preventing the Assembly from helping Concordia. They may know about your a-grav device and want it for themselves."

"The Immani said that too. They said the Scythians may have deciphered your comms."

"If that's so, then they're chasing us because they want the *Opportunity*, or, more specifically, the a-grav machine. Or, failing that, its inventor."

"How flattering. So what's your idea?"

"The *Opportunity's* defenses are no match for the combined weaponry of the Scythian ships, but what they perceive as our weakness could actually be our strength. We can use the *Opportunity* as bait."

"Bait? What's that?"

"You don't recognize the word? It's a term used when hunting animals."

"I don't think a lot of that goes on in Concordia."

"The bait is the food or prey animal used to attract the hunted animal in order to capture or kill it."

"Uhuh," she said uncertainly. Now she understood what Quinn meant, she was getting a little worried about where he was going with his idea. "You want to use me as a prey animal?"

"We would need to work out the details with the Assembly, but essentially, yes. We may be able to use the *Opportunity* to draw the Scythian ships into a disadvantageous position and then attack."

"Right. I'll need a few minutes to think about that."

"While you're thinking, I'll arrange a second rendezvous with the Immani ship. We cannot risk our comms being intercepted again."

Twenty-Nine

The moment the news arrived from Lyonesse, it spread through Chimera like wildfire: the scientists had developed a medicine that protected against the biocide. They were creating it in bulk and sending it out to all the refuges as fast as they could. All the colonists had to do was sit tight and wait for their doses to arrive.

"Is what I heard right?" Cherry asked Zhang when he came to check up on her. "There's a treatment that protects people from the biocide?"

"Look up." Zhang was holding a pencil light and he shone it in her eyes. He turned off the light and put it on the camping table. He pinched the skin on her arm, released it, and peered at the spot. "Your color and tone is better." The doctor began to take out more equipment from a case. "You heard right. It's called a vaccine. It's a prophylactic treatment that stimulates an immune response. It's very interesting. Give me your hand."

He clipped something to her finger. "I haven't seen the schedule for rolling out the treatment program, but it would make sense if Chimera were to be the last refuge to receive it. It's the site most remote from the biocide."

"That does make sense." For what she had in mind, she wouldn't need the medicine for a long while. She would probably be the last to receive it after she returned.

As Dr. Zhang completed her checkup, she complied with his requests, opening her mouth and poking out her tongue, allowing him to carry out his various tests. She gave him the urine sample he'd asked for. While he ran it through a device that checked it for who knew what, she said, "I feel a lot better now. Pretty much back to normal."

"That's good." Zhang was reading the results of her urine test on his interface. "You aren't quite there yet, though. You must get as much rest as you can over the next few weeks. After that I recommend monthly checkups for a year, followed by bi-annual checkups."

"But I feel fine."

"You nearly died of dehydration. That isn't something you recover from within a few days. The effects will be long lasting. They may last a lifetime."

Cherry frowned.

"It isn't so bad, is it? Better than the alternative."

"I'll just have to take along several water condensers when I return to the Scythian city."

The doctor paused, carefully put down his interface on the table, and turned to face her. "Tell me you're kidding."

"I have to go back. It's a lot to explain, but if I don't, the *Opportunity* is going to be shot to pieces and so will all the Assembly ships when they arrive." She wasn't even sure the *Opportunity* hadn't already been destroyed, but she guessed that if the Scythian defense system had fired she would have heard about it.

"You can't go back in there. It's out of the question."

"I have to. No one else can do what needs to be done." What that was exactly, she wasn't sure. Perhaps Faina would know. But the Scythian defense system had to be put out of action.

Zhang put away his equipment and snapped his case closed. "I'm sorry, but that isn't happening. You'll have to find someone else to do the work for you."

"I told you, there isn't anyone." Who could she trust to listen to an android's wrecked head? She could barely stand to look at it herself. And traveling through the Scythian city was like enduring a waking nightmare. At least *she* knew what to expect. "Anyway, you can't stop me."

The doctor tilted his head. "Can't I?"

"I'm still the General of this colony."

"And I'm only a physician. I get it. But you're forgetting I can declare you mentally incompetent." Zhang's pleasant manner had entirely disappeared. His gaze was frank and unblinking. "I can have you restrained—for your own safety."

She opened her mouth to speak but then closed it again. "*Shit.*"

His expression softened. "If you go back into that place in your current condition, you'll die. There's no doubt in my mind. Then who's going to do this thing that's so important?"

"I'm telling you, no one else can do it."

"Neither can you." Zhang picked up his bag. "The colony's problems are beyond my remit. I just fix people. If I could help you, I would, but you'll have to figure this one out by yourself." He left the tent.

She lay down on her bed. She couldn't deny she still felt weak. Her comment about feeling much better had been bravado. He was probably right that her body wouldn't cope with another feat of endurance. Yet someone had to go into the Scythian city and disable the aliens' planetary defense system. Her first response to learning of its existence had been to try to comm Wilder on the *Opportunity* to warn her of the danger, but the ship had disappeared from orbit.

Cherry didn't know where it had gone, but if it returned it could be blown from the sky. She would have to ask a coordinator to set up a repeating warning to the Fila ship in case Quinn brought it back.

Meanwhile, who could go into the Scythian city in her place? People like Alun and other members of the excavation team were fit and strong, but finding and deactivating the Scythian defense system would take more than fitness and strength.

The job required someone who understood at least a little about military defenses, and who wouldn't be freaked out by Faina's head. Kes fell into the latter camp but he already had his hands full producing the biocide medication. She racked her brains. Perhaps someone in the military could do it. If only Phy were still alive. She could always be relied upon to do a job right.

When the obvious answer popped into her head, Cherry sat up. She needed an external comm to Lyonesse, fast.

Thirty

Kes watched the brown, dead landscape pass beneath the heli, trying to stay awake. Zapata, the pilot, had woken him to say they were only a few minutes from the refuge. Kes had dropped off as soon as the heli had taken to the air and slept for the entire trip, yet he remained exhausted.

He hadn't seen his bed since Tycho had survived contact with the biocide. Every moment of his and the other scientists' time had been devoted to manufacturing the vaccine. They were administering the vaccine, too, as there were more helis than doctors at the refuge. It was a monumental effort to complete the immunization of Concordia's population as fast as possible.

His fatigue was making him airsick, and the noise of the rotor was pounding into his head despite his ear mufflers. While he waited to reach the refuge and begin work, he mentally went over the progress of the vaccination program. After immunizing everyone at the warehouse, they had flown out to the refuge nearest the Vimur. The green country surrounding Concordia's largest river was rapidly being laid waste by the biocide, and if the virus reached the water it would kill every Fila sheltering in it. The team that had vaccinated the people at the river refuge had left instructions on how to create a similar firebreak to the one that had been built around the warehouse site. Sterile zones at the river's edge might not provide the Fila with permanent protection, but they would buy time until the colonists figured out a better solution.

The military men and women at the remaining missile silos had also been vaccinated. There was a high possibility the Scythians would return when they realized their attempt at annihilation had failed. The idea of a second, and probably final, onslaught, filled Kes with despair. How could the colony continue to survive, faced by a technologically superior enemy determined to destroy it?

So many times, Concordia had hauled itself back from the brink and gone on to enjoy periods of peace and plenty, yet it would never be free from the possibility of attack. But what else could they do except battle on, as they always had? He closed his eyes, feeling old and jaded. All he wanted was to see Isobel and Miki again.

"I can't see them," said Zapata.

Kes opened his eyes, momentarily confused. "What?" He adjusted his mic, which had slipped under his chin.

"According to the most recent report of their location, they should be right there. I can't see them. Can you?"

Kes leaned to one side to get a clear view of the ground. It was as brown and dead as the rest of the landscape. If anyone was down there, they were dead. However, he couldn't see any bodies or signs of a habitation. "They must have moved on when the biocide approached. I guess they would have followed the highway."

Zapata nodded and took the heli higher before flying it in the direction of the long gray ribbon dissecting the dull landscape. In a few minutes they reached the creeping line of the biocide and flew over it.

Roughly fifteen minutes later they found the refuge: an assembly of weatherbeaten tents. No one was visible on the ground. The place looked in a bad way.

Zapata set down the heli a considerable distance from the tents out of fear that the rotor's downdraft would blow them away. Kes jumped out and ran with his bag of vaccine doses over his shoulder to the refuge. Drawn, scared faces looked out from open tent flaps as he approached.

"Have you brought us water?" asked a teenage boy.

"No, I've brought some medi—"

"We need water. We're nearly out. I sent in a request four days ago."

"I'm sorry. I don't know anything about that. But I'm sure someone's on it. You're the coordinator?"

"Yes. We need food too."

Kes looked the boy up and down. He couldn't be much older than fourteen. He checked out the faces peering from other tents. They all seemed very old or very young. He stepped over to the coordinator and held out his hand. "What's your name?"

"Niall."

"I'm Kes. You're doing a great job, but I have to tell you, we flew over the biocide line only about forty miles from here. You need to pack up soon and move on."

"I know it isn't far away, but I heard there's another line approaching from the north. The only way we can go is south but the terrain is hilly and difficult. We're getting squeezed in a trap. And we can't move fast. Some of us can only walk slowly."

"I hear you. I'll try to arrange some help. Maybe..." Kes wondered if the helis could come in and airlift everyone to the warehouses, where they would be safer. But the helis were all needed for distributing the vaccine. "I don't know exactly what we'll do yet, but at the very least we'll get water and food out to you as quickly as we can. Meanwhile, I'm here to give you some medication to protect you from the biocide."

The boy's face lit up. "Does it really work? Then we won't need to go anywhere."

"It does work, but it takes at least a week to become effective."

Niall's face fell. "The biocide will be here long before then."

"It will, so I'm afraid after I give you the vaccine you must move. And there's something else you need to know: the treatment probably won't be effective for everyone."

"You mean some of us could still die if the biocide arrives?"

"Not *if* the biocide arrives. When. There's nothing we can do to halt its progress. When it catches up to your group, it's possible one or two of you may not be protected."

"Is there any way to tell which of us that will be?"

"There is, but we simply don't have the time or the equipment to check, and even if we knew who wasn't protected there's nothing we could do to help them. It's just going to be a matter of luck."

"I'll try to keep them away from the biocide as long as I can."

Kes pitied the boy, who was carrying far more responsibility than he should at his age. "I know you'll do your best. Could you gather everyone together? I'll administer the vaccine now."

Thirty-One

Cherry waited for him outside Chimera, standing in the shade just inside the tunnel entrance. It was midday, and until her eyes adjusted the sunlight had been blinding. In spite of her protected position the heat hit her, radiating from the sand and the sun-warmed tunnel wall, and gusting in on the hot breeze.

Aside from the murmur of the wind, the desert was so quiet she heard the heli before she saw it. Then a black dot appeared in the sky. The heli was flying low and its form flickered and shifted in the shimmer of heated air. The aircraft landed in the same place Zapata had set down when she had arrived, next to the road leading to the excavation site. The solid gate in the perimeter fence blocked her view, and as the heli lowered she lost sight of it.

The noise of its engine and rotors didn't cease. Within less than a minute the aircraft was airborne again and swooping around, heading back to Lyonesse. No doubt the machine and its pilot were needed to deliver the biocide medication. None had arrived in Suddene yet.

The guard at the gate seemed to be a woman, though the copious amounts of lightweight, flowing fabric swathing the figure made the gender ambiguous. As far as Cherry knew, Laurie hadn't been assigned gate duty after his 'incident'. The guard prepared to open the gate. It had all been arranged with Alun's approval.

She waited, sweat droplets crawling down her face, neck, and back. How long had it been since she'd seen Aubriot face to face? It had to be weeks, or months. It felt like years. Their long history traveled a path in her mind in the few minutes it took him to walk to the gate. From its beginning in the ruins of the first settlement, through the tense months in Sidhe while the colony awaited the full wrath of the Scythians to descend, and on to the aftermath, the rebuilding *again*. Then had come the mission to the Assembly space station, when, after weeks of coldness, Aubriot had angrily confronted her about her true feelings for Ethan.

Had she wronged him? She didn't think so. Their arrangement had been platonic and mutually beneficial. She didn't think she owed him anything, and she hadn't expected any more from him than she'd received. But either there had been a misunderstanding or something had changed along the course of their relationship and she'd missed it.

After returning to a Concordia fifty Earth years on from the time they'd left, Aubriot had withdrawn from her. He'd gone a little crazy, neglecting his duties, drinking too much, and sleeping around. But lately he'd been better, calmer, and warmer toward her, trying to make her feel better about the terrible effects of her decisions. Now, she had no idea how things stood between them.

When she'd asked him to go into the Scythian city to find and disable the aliens' military defense system he'd quickly agreed. It had taken a day for a heli to collect him from Cerberus and bring him here.

The guard opened the gate, and then there he was. A rush of confused emotions swept over her: gratitude that he had come to do the work she could not, a sense of affinity with one of the four who had experienced the leap into the future, and a pleasant warmth at the familiar sight of him. They had shared many good times, even though things had gone bad later. And something else.

He stepped into the shadow of the tunnel entrance, already dusty and sweaty from his short walk.

"Hi." He dropped his bag onto the sandy tunnel floor and regarded her impassively.

"Thanks for coming."

"What was I going to do? Say no?"

Ugh. She'd almost forgotten what an asshole he could be. "We have to drive down to the excavation site."

Alun had loaned her one of the survey vehicles and she'd driven it up the tunnel, though with difficulty. She was used to cars that drove themselves, and having only one arm hadn't made things any easier.

Aubriot threw his bag on the back seat and peered at the vehicle's controls. "Want me to drive?"

"Sure." She climbed into the passenger seat.

"It's been a while since I actually *drove* a car," Aubriot commented as he started up the engine. The headlights turned on and they set off.

"How long? A couple hundred years?"

"Longer than that. Over two hundred and fifty or thereabouts. I lost count. It doesn't matter. Time's a weird concept when you think about it. I mean, how old am I? If I hadn't left Earth I..." He didn't complete the sentence.

She glanced at his profile, puzzled about why he'd stopped speaking. They were beyond the reach of natural daylight. His features were outlined by the minimal tunnel lighting and the backwash of the car's headlights. Something seemed to be bothering him.

"What?" she asked.

He scowled. "Before I go into the city, I need to talk to you."

"You can talk to me now."

"It might take a while." He threw her a quick look before returning his attention to the road. He appeared to be in a bad mood. Surely he wasn't still sore at her after all this time?

After a couple of minutes of silence, he said, "I want to take a team with me into the city. I hoped to bring a few good soldiers from Cerberus, but transportation is a problem."

"You might find some volunteers among the excavation crew. I warn you, it's a hellish place to navigate. You'll have to take plenty of water."

"You already told me. And I'll have to take the head."

"Yeah, the head too."

"You know, when I told you to cut the Guardian's head off, I wasn't expecting you to actually do it."

She gave a grim, tight smile. "Neither was I."

Alun had begun the preparations for the expedition before Aubriot's arrival, so it only took a couple of hours to gather additional supplies to support the three volunteers too. Alun was one, and the one Cherry was least concerned about. The site supervisor was already somewhat familiar with the strange, stinking place beneath Suddene's desert. She hoped the other two—the man was named Simon and the woman was called Abby—had strong stomachs and minds.

When all was ready, Aubriot told the team to check all the equipment one more time and then to relax and wait for him. He asked Cherry if there was somewhere they could talk privately.

She took him to the medical tent where she had recuperated. She'd since moved out and was sharing a place with Isobel and Miki, but she knew the space was currently unused.

She closed the flaps and sat on a bunk. The tent smelled faintly of an antiseptic substance. Her muscles tensed with apprehension. It was out of character for Aubriot to want to have a serious discussion about *anything*. He was the champion of flippant remarks and emotional distance.

He sat on the other bunk. Her shorter legs swung free. His feet were planted flat on the ground, his knees akimbo. He leaned forward and rested his elbows on his knees, his brow furrowed into deep creases as he mentally wrestled with whatever was troubling him. "Sorry."

She lifted her eyebrows. She couldn't remember ever hearing him apologize. The effect was unnerving.

"It's hard to know where to start." He glanced at the tent wall. "Are you sure we can't be overheard?"

"As sure as I can be. We can walk to the other side of the site if you want. No one will hear us over there."

"No, no. It's fine." He sighed and straightened up, rubbing the side of his nose.

"You know, if this is about us..." she said, "...what you accused me of while we were aboard the *Opportunity*..." It was the only thing she could think of that might explain why he wanted to have a serious discussion. She recalled his fury vividly.

He waved dismissively. "Water under the bridge." He frowned. "All right. Here goes. The thing is, well, something you should know is, I can't have kids." He studied her, watching her expression.

"Oh, uh, I'm sorry." She was even more puzzled. Was this revelation really *that* important? Then a realization struck. "Hey, I always made sure we used birth control! Why didn't you tell me?"

He shrugged. "I don't go around telling everyone. It's personal."

"What we were *doing* was personal!" Her voice had become loud with indignation. She lowered her tone lest their discussion attract unwanted attention. "What we were doing was personal, and I wasn't just *anyone*. Or at least I hope not. We were lovers and I *thought* we were friends, for a long time. Why didn't you tell me?"

"I don't know. It didn't seem important. Not at first, anyway."

"Right. Well, if that's all you wanted to talk about, like I said, I'm sorry. But I don't understand why you're telling me this now. Alun and the others will be waiting, so maybe you should—"

He reached across the narrow space between the bunks and grabbed her forearm, his large hand encircling it. "That isn't all I have to tell you." He stared into her eyes and maintained his grip. "The reason I can't have kids is due to a decision my parents made when I was just a fertilized egg in a petri dish. They selected a range of genetic modifications for me, including the one they knew could make me infertile. They didn't tell me about it until I was fifteen, when they suggested I undergo fertility testing. Sterility was a risk the doctors had warned them about, but they took the risk anyway, on my behalf. I had no say in it."

"You're hurting me."

He let go of her arm, got up, and then sat down next to her. Reaching around her shoulders, he pulled her close. "You're the first person I've ever told. I want to ask you to never tell anyone else, though I suppose it's bound to come out eventually."

"About your sterility?" She was becoming alarmed by his unwarranted seriousness. Infertility was extremely rare among Concordians, but she had heard of one or two cases. It wasn't shameful, however, and she didn't understand why he would want to keep it a secret.

"That's only a side effect I wanted you to know about." Several moments passed, and then he let out a long exhale. "The genetic engineering that ended up making me sterile was an experimental and illegal procedure. It was designed to confer extreme longevity."

"So you're going to live for a long time? That doesn't seem too bad. Do you know how long?"

"I don't know for sure. Before I left Earth I had myself tested for the last time. By then I was forty-five and my cells displayed no signs of aging. I might live an extra two or three hundred years, or a thousand, or maybe I'll never die, not from old age anyway. I just don't know."

She digested this new information. Suddenly, she sat upright. "When it became obvious that you weren't growing any older, wouldn't your parents have been arrested? Is that why you created the *Nova Fortuna* Project? Because you wanted to leave Earth?"

"Both my parents died before I began the project. All the money in the world can't save you from drug addiction. I assume they died happy. But, you're right, I was worried about what might happen to me as time went on. When your face is one of the most well known in the world it's hard to hide the fact that you never grow older. I could have faked my death, had surgery, and done the same again and again, but I would have spent my life always worrying. The Earth I left wasn't kind to people who altered their 'natural' state. I hadn't chosen to be what I am, but that wouldn't have made any difference. I might have faced imprisonment and maybe even execution."

"So you thought if you came to a new planet, where the culture and the rules were different..."

"My problem was only one of the reasons I started up the project, but, yes, I thought if I lived somewhere things were different, somewhere *I* made the rules, then I could live my life without constantly looking over my shoulder."

Her gaze roved his flawless features, his smooth skin, and his hair, which was entirely free of the gray that had already begun to pepper her own. She imagined the years marching on and Aubriot never changing, like a statue or a painting, while all Concordia and everyone in it aged and died, and new life appeared and grew old and then also died. It was hard to imagine what it must be like to know your life might never end.

"It's a lot to take in," Aubriot said. "I know. You don't have to say anything. I don't need your pity."

"Pity?! Why would I pity you? Who wouldn't want to live forever?"

"Think about it. I certainly have. It isn't so great if you're the only one. What's it going to be like for everyone I know and love to pass away while I carry on living?"

She didn't reply. She'd never heard him talk of loving anyone. She wasn't even sure he was capable of it. But though she didn't comment, her face must have given away her thoughts.

His features stiffened in anger. "I'm not a monster."

She threw him an irritated glance and hopped down from the bunk. "The others are waiting for you."

He grabbed her arm again. "Wait. Please. I haven't finished. Maybe I *am* immortal, but I'm not indestructible. I have to get this off my chest in case I never see you again."

For some reason she didn't fully understand her eyes filled with tears. "Get what off your chest?"

He swallowed. "I've had a lot of time to think over the last few weeks. After we cleared up the silo and fixed everything that was fixable, there was fuck all to do at Cerberus except wait for the biocide to reach us. I've been thinking about my time here, right from when I came out of cryo until you comm'd me after the battle to find out how I was doing. It hasn't been easy. Living this new life has been a lot harder than I thought it would be.

"I know how I come across, Cherry, and for a long time I didn't give a shit. However I behaved, it didn't matter. I always got what I wanted no matter what. *Women* wanted me. But not you. You could take me or leave me. To you, I was a convenience, a substitute for the person you wanted but couldn't have. That was quite a blow to my ego, let me tell you.

"I tried to get over myself. After all, you weren't doing anything worse than I'd done. Why should I care? But I couldn't get over it, because it hurt. There I was, the man with the cast iron ego, and my *feelings* were hurt." He held out his hand. "Come here."

She took a step toward him. He took her hand and broke eye contact, dropping his gaze to the floor. "Before I go down into that place, I want to tell you I care about you. If I were to live on after you died, I'd find that hard. I'd wish my parents hadn't laid this curse on me. I know I'm not the easiest person to get along with, or the most likable, and maybe I'll never be this frank about my feelings ever again. But I want you to remember what I said. It's true and it's never going to change."

He raised his head and looked her in the eyes. She had never seen an expression on his face like the one she was now seeing. It was like she could see inside him. She took another step forward until they were almost touching and wrapped her arm around his neck. “You mean a lot to me too,” she said awkwardly.

It wasn’t the most romantic conversation, but she guessed it was probably the most romantic they were ever going to get.

He hugged her. As they held each other in silence, she realized how alike they were. Aubriot might be an asshole but in the right circumstances she could be a real bitch. They were pretty well suited.

“I have to go,” said Aubriot.

“I know.”

Neither released their hold.

Finally, Aubriot was the one to end it. He kissed her briefly on the lips and then stood up. “I’ll be back in a few days, barring any disasters.”

“Don’t forget the head.”

He smiled and bent down to kiss her again.

Then he was gone.

Thirty-Two

Wilder watched the screen anxiously as the Scythian ships approached. No one knew why they were here or what they planned on doing, and they certainly weren't going to tell. As well as the Immani's guess that they knew about the a-grav machine and wanted it for themselves—or wanted to prevent anyone else from having it—she wondered if they only wanted to destroy the *Opportunity*.

The Scythians knew the ship. They had tracked her journey to the Assembly space station and tried to kill her human occupants after slipping through the station's defenses. At their most recent 'visit' to Concordia, they must have wondered where the ship had gone, but they'd failed to find where Quinn had hidden her behind the second planet out from the sun. Maybe the Scythians had since seen the *Opportunity* depart and they were determined to prevent any human or Fila from escaping.

Or maybe it was all a coincidence. The Scythians could simply be on their way to Concordia to check their biocide had done its work and the planet and everything on it was dead.

Whatever their motivation, she hoped the hostile aliens would fall into the trap the Assembly had set and their fleet would be destroyed. She also hoped the *Opportunity* would survive unscathed. But it would be a close-run thing.

The Scythians had supplemented the fleet that had fought the previous battle, replacing the ships that had been destroyed and returning the number of their fleet to ten, including two of the massive, four-coned vessels with their central pulse-emitting spikes. Some of the ships' forward-facing cones bore the ravages of the conflict, however, and one of the larger ship's splayed rear fans was half wrecked. Were these sections of the larger ships some form of heat-dispersal device? She couldn't guess what other function they could serve.

Against the background of far-distant stars the Scythian ships appeared frozen in space, though they were traveling at tremendous speed.

"What's happening, Quinn? I can't tell *anything* from looking at this interface."

"The Assembly ships are slowing and spreading out. The Scythians will catch up to them more quickly now, but unless their fleet breaks formation they won't be able to engage with all our ships effectively. The distances will be too great. Some of the ships—the Parvus's vessel in particular—are going to pretend to leave, as if in fear."

"The Scythians might believe that," she said, "considering it was the Parvus who turned the battle against them last time." Despite the dangerous situation, she was feeling excited at the thought of the forthcoming fight. When the Scythians had last attacked she'd felt guilty that she'd never been in any danger like her friends on Concordia. It was good to finally have an active role to play.

"They might," Quinn replied. "Especially because they cannot possibly reach a star to operate their power harnessing weapon before the Scythians catch up to them. Without that capability they are quite weak. And it would be reasonable to assume the Scythians would target their ship in vengeance."

"What happens if the Scythians do break formation and go after individual Assembly ships?"

"I'm not certain. I would need to ask the Immani about that."

"After all, it would probably only take one or two of the Scythians' smaller ships to destroy the *Opportunity*."

"Perhaps, but she can mount an impressive defense for a vessel her size. And it's unlike the Scythians to take risks."

Quinn was right. The Scythians had consistently shown an element of caution—or even cowardice—in their military engagements. The scout ship that had attacked the first settlement had left when the *Mistral* had shown her bite, and the fleet had fled after the Parvus had redirected the power of Concordia's star at their ships. She hoped the Scythians would take the bait and home in on the *Opportunity*. An entire fleet ganging up on one little ship would be just their style, and also their downfall.

"Can I see the other ships?" Staring at the Scythian ships was becoming unbearable.

"You can only see them separately. They are already too far apart to appear on your screen."

The scene shifted to a silvery, cylindrical ship with rounded ends. Lines of lights ran along the sides, and at what she assumed was the rear, two squared shoulders protruded. A long, wide slit bisected the back. Did the shoulders house the ship's engines? It seemed a reasonable guess, but she could easily be wrong. The slit could also be for heat dispersal.

A galaxy of technological development lay beyond Concordia, which was primitive in comparison. She hoped she would live to see and learn about all of it, even if it took a whole lifetime.

"Ah," said Quinn. "The Scythians have broken formation."

The scene switched back to the enemy vessels. Three were peeling away from the main bunch. They were all the smaller, single-crescent ships.

"Do you know where they're heading?" she asked.

"Extrapolating from their current trajectories, I would guess they are following the Parvus's starship."

"Oh no. That wasn't supposed to happen."

"Perhaps they found the prospect of exacting their revenge too hard to resist."

"What will the Parvus do?"

"Fly," Quinn replied. "Their ship is fast."

"But not as fast as the Scythians'."

"I don't think so."

"Isn't there something we can do?"

"Others are coming to their aid, circling back."

"This is going to mess up the entire plan."

The screen continued to show the original Scythian fleet, now missing three of its number. She clenched her fists. It was incredibly frustrating to not be able to see what was going on. "Is anyone firing? What's happening?"

"Nothing, yet, but there's no doubt the breakaway Scythian vessels intend to attack the Parvus's ship. They're heading straight for it."

Meanwhile, the remaining seven Scythian ships were drawing ever closer to the *Opportunity*. They seemed to be taking the bait. Nevertheless, it would take a strong attack to defeat them. Would the Assembly force be too weakened by the loss of the ships that had gone to defend the Parvus?

"We are within Concordia's star system," said Quinn.

"We're nearly home! I hope everyone's still okay. Is there any way you can find out?"

"Not at the moment. The remaining Assembly and Scythian ships will draw together somewhere above the planet's surface. Assuming we survive, we will find out what's happened on Concordia after the battle."

Thirty-Three

"Oooooooh!"

Cherry jerked awake. She'd been dreaming she was still in the Scythian city and trapped under soft fragments of debris. A nightmare. When she woke she was relieved to realize she was breathing fresh, clean air and she was in Chimera, in Isobel's tent at night. The light from the lamps at the center of the excavated cavern—lowered due to the lateness of the hour—gently glowed through the walls.

A quiet gasp came from the other side of the tent, and Cherry realized a similar sound had awakened her. "Isobel?" she whispered. "Are you okay?"

"Uh huh."

Cherry let out a mental sigh of relief. The last thing she wanted was for Isobel to give birth right now. The conditions were far from ideal, and though Zhang was here for that kind of thing, she dreaded the prospect of being asked to help out. That had been her first thought when Isobel had offered her a place to sleep, sharing with her and Miki. Cherry would have refused if she hadn't felt a responsibility to look after Kes's wife.

Miki was cute, and she hadn't minded playing with her to give Isobel a break, but babies and even the *thought* of childbirth made her anxious and uncomfortable. She hoped Isobel wouldn't pop until she was safely back with Kes on Lyonesse. It seemed like the baby had only kicked her or something. Cherry really didn't know or want to know the ins and outs of the various aches and pains pregnant women suffered.

"I'm okay," Isobel said softly. "It's just...I think the baby is coming."

"What?! Now?!"

"No, but soon." Isobel gave another quiet gasp. A pause followed, then, "I've been having contractions for a while but I didn't want to wake you."

"You didn't..." Cherry sat up, pushing down her sleeping bag. Isobel was shadowy in the darkness. A shadow with a large bump. Miki lay still beside her, sound asleep. "I'll go and get Dr Zhang."

"If you wouldn't mind, that would be great. And then could you take Miki to the tent next to ours? The woman there, Carol, offered to look after her if my time came. She has a little boy the same age as Miki."

"Of course I don't mind." Cherry was already pulling on her pants. She pushed her feet into her boots and then went to the tent entrance. "I'll be back with Zhang as quick as I can." She slipped out into the half-light.

Chimera was never entirely silent but night time was peaceful. Snoring and the cries of fractious babies were the only sounds. The tents threw long shadows on the cavern's walls, scored with marks left by the excavators.

She ran quietly to the medical tents, where she hoped to find Zhang. The first two tents were empty. The next two each held a patient and the final one held a nurse too, but none of them knew where Zhang was. The nurse thought he was probably sleeping and she told Cherry where to find him.

She found the tent without any problems but Zhang was not inside. Another man was sleeping in it. When she woke him he told her that Zhang had left to attend a birth.

She was momentarily confused. How had Zhang known that Isobel had gone into labor? "When did he leave?"

"About an hour and a half ago."

"Damn." Zhang was attending another laboring woman. "Do you know where he went?"

"No, but...Do you need him for an emergency?"

"My friend's about to give birth too."

"Whoa. Bad timing. You know you can comm him, right?"

"Stars, I didn't think of that! Thanks." She backed out of the tent. How had she managed to forget she could comm the doctor? She was panicking. After a lifetime of danger and death, she was panicking over a woman in labor. She took a deep breath and sent the comm.

Zhang's answer was terse. "Yes?"

She explained the situation with Isobel.

"How far apart are her contractions?"

"I don't know. Does it matter?"

"Not at all," Zhang replied acerbically. "I was just making conversation. Look, I'm at another birth right now and I may be some time. This is Isobel's second labor so it should be straightforward. I'll see if the nurse is available to come over and help. While you're waiting, time the period between the beginning of one contraction and the beginning of the next. If they get to two minutes apart, let me know. Stay with her and look after her until I can get there." He closed the comm.

Look after her? What did that even mean? But Isobel had been alone for several minutes now. Cherry ran back to her tent.

As soon as she poked her head inside, Isobel asked, "Is the doctor here?"

Miki was awake and playing with her teddy.

"He's coming soon." Cherry climbed into the tent. "Miki, it's time to go and see your friend. Mommy's going to be busy for a little while."

"Yes," Isobel said, "and when you come back you can meet your little sister."

"Oh!" Miki grinned and squeezed her teddy. "I want to meet Nina now!"

"Not yet," said Isobel. "Soon."

Cherry took her to the next tent and quietly woke the sleeping woman, who said as Cherry left, "Tell Isobel good luck. I hope everything goes okay."

"I will."

When Cherry returned to Isobel's tent she halted outside and closed her eyes.

You can do this.

Then she scolded herself. It was Isobel who was about to give birth, not her. Putting on a cheery, confident smile, she went in.

Isobel gasped. "What's wrong?"

"Huh? Nothing's wrong."

"You never smile. Something's wrong. What is it?"

"I was just trying to put you at ease."

"Don't ever smile at me like that again. Oooooh!" Isobel put her hands on her belly and sucked in a long breath. She continued to breath slowly and steadily for several moments, then she relaxed.

"Was that a contraction? Zhang told me to time them. What time is it? Where's my interface?" Cherry scrabbled vigorously in her bag, trying to feel for the smooth screen in the dark.

"Calm down. I've done this before. It's going to be all right. Ahhhh!" Isobel clutched her belly again.

"That's way sooner than two minutes! Shit! Where's Zhang?" Cherry bolted outside and comm'd the doctor.

"What?" he replied.

"Isobel's contractions are really close. Much closer than two minutes apart."

"Are you absolutely sure? Did you actually time them?"

"I didn't need to. I know the difference between two minutes and thirty seconds."

"Damn. I'm not going to make it. This baby is coming now and it's breech. I'll talk you through it."

"What? No way! There has to be someone else who can help. What about that nurse you were talking about?"

"There's no time. You'll have to do it. Can you see the head yet?"

A loud groan came from Isobel's tent.

Cherry darted in.

Isobel was on all fours. "Is the doctor here?" she gasped.

"He'll be here any minute. I'll help you until then."

But Isobel was beyond hearing anything.

Cherry held little Nina in the crook of her arm. Zhang had explained how to swaddle the infant and now she'd gone to sleep, apparently not remotely interested in this new world she'd entered. Cherry didn't know who she was more in awe of: Isobel, who had just given birth without any anesthetic and hardly making a fuss, or Zhang, who had directed Cherry through everything while at the same time attending a woman enduring a long and complicated labor. With great timing, the nurse had arrived after the exciting part was over.

Isobel was resting. She'd asked Cherry to wait until morning before going next door to tell Miki it was time to meet her new sister. Cherry thought that was a great idea. She didn't want to deal with an excited toddler *and* a newborn, even a peacefully sleeping one. The entire night had been a nerve-wracking ordeal. She marveled at Isobel's ability to take it all in her stride. Cherry would rather return to the Scythian city than undergo the same experience.

"You can put her down if you want," Isobel said. "I made a little bed for her a few days ago. Over there."

"I see it."

Isobel had lined the lid of a packing case with cut down blankets. Cherry gently laid the sleeping infant in it.

"Not the nicest crib, is it?"

"I really don't think she minds," replied Cherry. "I'll get you an external comm as soon as the coordinator wakes up so you can talk to Kes. He'll be ecstatic. How are you doing?"

"Good." Isobel smiled.

"You look good too." It was true. Even in the half-light Isobel was radiant. "It's hard to believe, considering what you just went through."

"It's the post-birth hormones. It's quite a rush. Maybe you'll find out one day."

Cherry held up her hand in mock horror. "Nu-uh. Not happening. But I'm happy for you."

Isobel winced and touched her stomach.

"You don't have another one in there, do you?"

Isobel laughed. "Stars, I hope not." She winced again. "It's only post-birth contractions. They aren't as fun as the hormones."

"Is there anything I can do? I can't believe Zhang still isn't here. I'll comm him again."

"Ahhh!" Isobel sat up and half doubled over. Then her jaw dropped and she peered downward. She pulled back the cover. A wide, wet patch spread over the bottom half of her torso and across her thighs. The bedding beneath her glistened faintly. In the dim light the liquid looked black but Cherry knew what it was: blood.

Isobel's gaze rose to meet Cherry's, and for a beat they stared at each other in horror.

"Zhang!" Cherry yelled the doctor's name even before he answered the comm. "Isobel's bleeding badly. You have to get here now!"

"Some blood is normal—"

"This isn't normal! Get over here."

"Cherry," Isobel said, her tone high and soft, "help me." Her eyes were wide and dark.

Cherry grabbed towels to help soak up the blood. She pressed the material to the dark patch. But she didn't know what else to do. What could she do? If Isobel had been wounded Cherry would have known how to suppress the bleeding, but the blood was coming from inside her.

"It'll be okay. Zhang will be here in a minute. He'll figure something out."

Isobel lay down on her side and covered her face with her hand.

Cherry touched her arm. "Don't worry. You're going to be all right." But as she spoke, she saw fresh blood surge out through Isobel's nightgown and onto the bed linen.

There was a rustle at the tent door. It opened and Zhang came in. His first reaction at seeing Isobel struck fear into Cherry. The doctor looked shocked. But he closed his mouth like a trap and resumed his professional attitude. "Okay, Isobel. I'm going to try a few things. Cherry, you might want to leave."

"No, please stay with me," Isobel said.

"I'll stay." Cherry sat near Isobel's head and took her hand.

Numbly, Cherry watched Zhang work. All her discomfort and squeamishness about childbirth was gone. All she could feel was a growing sense of dread. It didn't matter what Zhang did, he couldn't stop the bleeding. She had not imagined a single person could hold so much blood.

Isobel lay quietly, in fear at first, but then as time went on her eyelids began to droop and she drifted in and out of consciousness. Zhang told Cherry to try to keep her awake, so she asked Isobel about Miki and what she would need the following day. Isobel's replies became gradually less intelligible until Cherry was simply talking to her without expecting an answer.

An inestimable period of time later, Zhang stopped what he was doing. He sat back on his heels. His shirt was stained and so were his forearms up to the elbows. He looked exhausted. "Cherry, can I speak to you outside?"

She turned to Isobel to ask if it was okay to leave her, but her eyes were closed.

Cherry followed Zhang out of the tent. The camp was beginning to wake up. People were moving around, trudging to the latrines, stretching and yawning, complaining at their kids.

Cherry regarded the doctor, knowing what he was about to tell her but not wanting to hear it.

"I've tried everything I can," Zhang said, "but nothing's working. She doesn't have long."

"What about a blood transfusion? If we're the same type I'd happily donate some and so would others, I'm sure."

"Even if I had the equipment for a transfusion it wouldn't help. The only thing that will save her is a hysterectomy. I don't have the facilities to perform a major operation like that and if I tried to do it any other way the shock would kill her. To be honest, she's too far gone anyway. There isn't anything else I can do." Zhang put a hand on her shoulder. "You're her friend. I'm sure she would appreciate some company in her final moments."

"I'm not..." Cherry swallowed. "Okay. I'll do it."

She returned to the tent. Baby Nina was stirring in her crib, making quiet chirruping noises. Cherry carefully picked her up and placed her next to Isobel's face. The movement caused Isobel to open her eyes. The corners of her lips curled up.

Did she know what was happening? Cherry didn't know if it was cruel or kind to tell her.

Isobel's gaze left her infant and roved a little before she found Cherry. "Tell Kes I love him," she whispered. Her eyes moved again until they alighted upon her daughter once more, and then she left the world.

Thirty-Four

"The *Opportunity* is back!" Tricia exclaimed.

Kes looked up from the vaccine pods he was loading into a case.

Tricia was the lab's main contact with the refuge's coordinator. She was holding her ear comm as she listened to the rest of the message. "Apparently the satellite picked up its signal a while ago, but now it's entered the system and it's on its way to Concordia."

Kes stopped what he was doing. Tension he hadn't known he was carrying drained from his body. Wilder was going to be okay. The girl was like a sister to him. He couldn't bear the thought of anything happening to her.

"Oh." Tricia's happy expression faded. "Scythian ships are on its tail."

A collective gasp sounded around the lab.

"They're back so soon?" asked Thom.

"We're screwed," Drew said. "And after all we've done. We'll never fight them off again."

The despair in the room was almost palpable. Kes stared at the pods in his hands, the products of countless hours of exhausting work. Tycho and the other volunteers had risked their lives. The colony had lived in fear for weeks, only for it all to come to nothing.

"I don't honestly know what we were expecting," Thom said bitterly. "They're never going to leave us alone. I wonder if they let some of us live on purpose, just so they could return and torture us more."

"How many ships?" Kes asked Tricia.

"The satellite's picked up seven."

"That's three less than last time," said Drew.

"We destroyed some of the fleet last time." Tricia's hand rose to her comm again. "Uh, the vid from the satellite is going to be broadcast all over Concordia. We can watch it in the meeting room."

The scientists dropped what they were doing and moved toward the room en masse. Kes hesitated. They still hadn't vaccinated the entire population. No one at Suddene had been immunized against the biocide, and there were a few small refuges they hadn't reached yet. On the other hand, if the Scythians were returning, was there any point?

The Parvus had left, and the *Opportunity* couldn't defend the planet on her own. Perhaps Cerberus and other silos that weren't too badly damaged could be resurrected...

His shoulders slumped. He was tired of living under a constant threat of annihilation, forever rebuilding the colony after each successive attack. And now a young woman whom he loved like family might be about to die. He understood Thom and Drew's attitude. It was almost too much to bear.

As his co-workers departed for the meeting room and the lab emptied around him, he continued to stoically fill a case with pods. In less than a minute he stood alone, the rustle of the soft plastic pods loud in the newly quiet room. No sounds came from the meeting room. All inside were undoubtedly focused on the drama overhead unfolding on the interface screen.

His resolve to not watch the battle broke. He didn't want to see the *Opportunity* felled from the sky, but he had to see whatever was about to happen.

He strode into the meeting room. The scientists nearest the screen were sitting down. The ones behind them stood, their arms folded or their hands resting on table tops as they leaned forward, their gazes fixed on the screen.

As it had always been, the satellite's single vantage point was inadequate. The Scythian ships it had picked up were not yet visible. Only the *Opportunity* could be seen, a small speck growing steadily larger. Its dark gray hull made it difficult to distinguish against the backdrop of stars set in the black velvet of space.

"Is that it?" a voice asked uncertainly. "That thing in the middle? It looks like a smooth asteroid."

"That's it." Kes thought about comming Wilder, but the messages would take too long to travel the distance. By the time he heard her reply it might all be over, or he could be listening to her as he watched the *Opportunity* obliterated.

Her message had said she had gone to the approaching Assembly ships to negotiate a deal regarding the a-grav device. What had happened to the Assembly vessels? They had to be faster than the *Opportunity*. Why had Wilder returned ahead of them? Had Concordia's allies abandoned them?

"I think I can see one of the Scythian ships," Tricia said.

Kes studied the screen, then he saw it too: four bright spots making up the four corners of a square and a single dot right in the middle. It was one of the largest Scythian vessels. The lone central dot was its deadly pulse weapon. One direct hit from it would spell the end of the *Opportunity*.

The Fila ship fired! The sound of a simultaneously drawn breath broke the silence. The distance between the *Opportunity* and her hunters was too great for the pulse to cause any damage, however. The speeding needle of light dissipated into space.

"What are they doing?" Thom asked. "They should be trying to escape, not drawing fire!"

"Our ship will never outpace the Scythians," said Drew. "And once they've destroyed the *Opportunity* they'll turn their attention to us."

Kes wanted to shake the man and tell him to shut up. Except he was right.

A second pulse erupted from the *Opportunity's* rear emitter.

"What the hell is Quinn doing?" Kes blurted.

"It's like he's trying to bait them," said Tricia.

A heavy weight settled on Kes's chest. It was like the *Opportunity* was drawing the Scythians into the system. It was the only explanation that made any sense.

"More ships are approaching!" Tricia exclaimed, relaying another message from the coordinator.

"More Scythian vessels?" asked Thom.

"Their engine signatures are different, and different from each other too."

"It's the Assembly ships," Drew said. "They've arrived at last. That changes things a little. The *Opportunity* might make it."

"I hope so," said Tricia, "but she's cut off from the other ships by the Scythians."

Silence fell as every gaze in the room strained to see what was happening. The *Opportunity* was now clearly visible, and Kes could also distinguish the outline of a Scythian ship. Moving points of light in the general area had to be the rest of the fleet. He could see nothing of the Assembly ships whatsoever, but he didn't doubt the coordinator's report based on the satellite's data stream.

"She's never going to make it." Tricia's soft words were easy to hear in the hushed room. She turned to Kes, her expression full of fear. "How can she make it?"

He had no answer.

"What's that?" Thom pointed at the top right of the screen. "Is there something there?"

Kes couldn't see what he meant at first, then he realized Thom wasn't pointing at a ship but a moving absence of light. A dark shape was crossing the starry background, blocking out the brilliant specks.

"I see it," Drew said. "Whatever it is, it's massive."

Light exploded from the dark mass and shot across space. But the pulse faded by the time it reached the Scythian ship. It hit, but Kes doubted it did much damage.

The trajectory of the Scythian ships began to alter. The largest ship returned fire. The pulse from the spike found its target at the gigantic Assembly ship and was absorbed into darkness.

"More Assembly ships are approaching," Tricia said, "but I can't see anything."

"It's hard to tell what's going on," said Drew.

Aside from the small, dark gray shape of the *Opportunity*, all that could be seen of the other ships was visual suggestions of their forms and brilliant but tiny sparks of light traveling between them. In silence, hundreds of thousands of kilometers above their heads, a pitched battle was being fought.

Kes thought he guessed what was happening. The Scythians must have been spotted returning to Concordia—perhaps by Quinn and Wilder aboard the *Opportunity*—and a plan had been hatched to use the Fila ship to draw the enemy vessels forward and then attack them from all sides.

The Scythians had an escape route: all they had to do was fly onward, away from the Assembly ships. But for the time being they were not choosing to do so. Perhaps they wanted to prove their might against the Assembly, especially while in their home planet's system.

He was somewhat relieved that the *Opportunity* seemed to have been forgotten. The ship continued to move closer to Concordia. He wished Quinn would fly it around to the other side of the planet or to some other place where he and Wilder would be safe.

The room's tense silence burst into exclamations and hollers. A flash of light had lit the screen. One of the Scythian ships had exploded.

"That'll show 'em!" someone shouted.

"They're not going to like that," said Thom.

The fighting intensified and drew closer as the Scythian and Assembly ships continued along their trajectories. Some Assembly ships remained invisible, only their pulses giving away their position. The remaining six Scythian ships could now clearly be seen, firing in all directions. A second of their largest ships was concentrating its fire on the black pit of the massive Assembly ship. Now, it was no longer simply absorbing the fire. Each pulse briefly lit its surface, spilling across it like water splashing on a stone.

Somewhere in distant space a light flickered and was gone.

"We just lost an Assembly ship," Tricia said.

Then another Scythian ship turned into a ball of quickly snuffed fire.

The Assembly seemed to have the edge. Would the Scythians turn tail and run? For the moment, they were choosing to tough it out.

Glancing at the *Opportunity*, Kes decided to comm the ship. He wanted to advise Quinn to fly out of immediate danger. He sent the message, not knowing when he might receive a reply.

"That's another one!" Drew yelled. A third Scythian ship had fallen.

The enemy's flagship continued to pound out pulses at the dark, gigantic block of a starship. Kes could make out some of its form now. He thought he could see tall towers like a medieval castle's. The dark ship looked like a massive citadel, flying through space.

Could it continue to withstand the onslaught from the Scythians? Kes hoped so because its return fire was having a devastating effect on the Scythian fleet.

"Three down, four to go," Drew said gleefully. "I knew the Assembly would save us!"

Kes thought Drew's jubilation was premature. Even if the Assembly did defeat the Scythians this time around, there was nothing to stop them from returning to take out their anger on Concordia when the Assembly ships were no longer here. Concordia was too weak to put up an adequate defense and it would remain so for a long time.

Light flared from the citadel ship, but it was not the light of pulse fire. Part of the ship had broken away. The stars blocked by its presence grew fewer as the dissected tower tumbled off into space. The ship instantly responded. A blaze of light hurtled across the void. The spike of the Scythian ship was its target and it hit it full on. This caused a chain reaction that spread down the ship. The joined crescents ruptured and disintegrated, dissolving in light.

"That's it," said Drew. "That has to be it."

As if they had heard his words, the remaining Scythian ships began to speed up. They were going to take the only remaining escape route: to fly in the direction of Concordia.

The Scythian vessels sped closer, and Kes's concern for the *Opportunity's* passenger grew stronger. Would the Scythians attack the small ship out of malice and spite? The *Opportunity* continued to slowly approach.

"The Assembly ships are coming in too," Tricia said. "We should be able to see them better soon."

The crescents with their strangely scrawled patterning were now easily visible. Kes guessed that anyone standing outside would see them moving in the night sky.

One of the ships fired. As Kes had feared, the shot was aimed at the *Opportunity*. The pulse briefly lit up the Fila vessel, but it didn't seem to cause any serious damage.

The Scythian ships flew on. The Assembly vessels didn't seem able to match their speed.

Then the *Opportunity* exploded.

"NO!" Kes gaped at the screen as the fragments of the Fila ship scatter into nothingness.

No.

Wilder!

No.

He collapsed into a seat.

"Damn," said Drew. "Who was aboard? Does anyone know? Why did the Scythians have to do that? She wasn't even firing on them any longer."

"I don't think a Scythian ship did it," Thom said. "Did anyone else see another pulse from the Scythians?"

"Perhaps it was a delayed effect," said Drew.

"It doesn't work like that," Thom said.

Tricia frowned. "I thought I saw something coming from our direction."

"From Concordia?" asked Drew. "Great. It must have been one of the silos. Those idiots shot at our own ship."

Kes's head was in his hands, his mind reeling. Wilder was gone. That bright, happy young woman had hardly lived, and now she was gone.

"Kes," Tricia said, "are you okay?"

He was not okay. A sweet girl had died, and he didn't think he would ever get over losing her.

Thirty-Five

Cherry spent the time following Isobel's death feeling like she was walking through a fog. When people spoke to her their voices sounded distant and muffled. She had to strain to hear what they were saying. Everything around her appeared as if she were looking through a veil. Nothing seemed real—except for the fact that Isobel had died.

Cherry had hardly known her. She'd mostly thought of her as Kes's wife, and then as someone smart enough to figure out how to work on the Guardian's head. Isobel had also been a kind, loving mother to Miki. In the short time Cherry had spent with her, she'd come to believe that despite their different personalities, they could have been good friends.

Life in Chimera continued on, the ripple caused by the death of a woman in childbirth seeming to have barely any impact. Miki remained with the neighbor who had cared for her while Isobel was in labor. The woman Zhang had been attending while Isobel gave birth offered to feed Nina as well as her own baby until other arrangements could be made.

Cherry remained in the tent where Isobel had died. Places to sleep were hard to find, and she'd recovered from her time in the Scythian city so she couldn't stay in a medical tent. She removed all the blood-stained linen and spent hours simply sitting in it, reliving the final moments of Isobel's life and all the terrible things that had happened over the years of colonization.

When she left the tent she vaguely heard comments about the Scythians returning and the Assembly ships defeating them. She also heard the program to medicate the population against the biocide was showing success. A group that had received the treatment and was subsequently overrun by the biocide had nearly all survived.

But these pieces of information that made it through the fog seemed insignificant. More vivid to Cherry were the rotting bodies of thousands of Fila, floating on the ocean waves, or the sight of Garwin being cut to pieces by Scythian spiders. She had seen too much death, and she felt unbearably tired. Not fatigued or sleepy, but deep-down tired.

Tired of life.

Perhaps two nights had passed—Cherry wasn't sure—when Aubriot poked his head into the tent. She was so deep in the fog she almost didn't recognize him.

"I heard what happened," he said. "Must have been awful."

He sat on the floor next to her sleeping bag.

She was lying down, curled up, on top of it. "I had the easy part."

"I don't think so. It can't be easy watching someone die."

She didn't disagree. She'd watched Ethan die, too, and that had torn her apart. She didn't have the energy or willpower to argue and there was no point. Suffering wasn't a competition.

"We found the Scythian defense system control room," Aubriot said, "with plenty of help from Faina's head."

She didn't move. She hoped he would go away.

"I don't think they'll be coming back in a hurry," he said, "not after what the Assembly ships did to them. It's just a bloody shame we didn't manage to put the planetary defenses out of action until after they'd fired on the *Opportunity*."

This piece of information pierced Cherry's dulled senses sharply. "What?"

She sat up.

"The Scythian defenses took out the *Opportunity*. Didn't you hear? We didn't manage to disable them in time. It only took us another hour or so." He looked downward and shook his head. "We were so close."

"But Wilder was aboard the *Opportunity*. And so was Quinn. Are you telling me they're both dead?!"

"I'm sorry."

"Oh, stars." She clamped her hand over her mouth and nose, shaking her head. "I had a coordinator set up a repeating message warning them of the danger. How come they didn't receive it?"

"Dunno. They didn't though. Came flying back with Scythians on their tail, drawing them in so the Assembly could finish them off."

"Who else?" Cherry choked. "Who else has to die? Poor Wilder. I never got the chance to apologize to her and now I never will." She fell onto her side. So much death. So much pain. She couldn't bear it.

Aubriot remained with her, his legs crossed and his head bowed, as new grief overwhelmed her. How long he sat there she didn't know. By the time she was done the lamps had been turned down in the cavern and the tent was nearly dark.

"I heard someone's arriving with the vaccine tomorrow," Aubriot said. "When we've built up immunity to the biocide we can go back to Lyonesse. Start sorting things out and rebuilding."

Apprehension clutched at her. "Do you know who's bringing the medication?"

"No, but maybe it'll be Kes. He'll probably want to see his kid and new baby." Aubriot studied her face. "What's wrong?"

When she didn't answer, he repeated his question.

"I can't face him," she replied. "I can't tell him."

"Tell him about his wife? You mean he doesn't know?"

"I don't think so."

"I thought she died a couple of days ago. Why haven't you told him yet?"

She had no answer.

"You have to tell him. Maybe it is better he doesn't hear it as a comm, but it's best he hears it from you."

She knew it was true, but she couldn't bear the thought of breaking the terrible news to her friend. "I feel like this is all my fault somehow. Everything I touch turns to shit. Everyone I come in contact with dies. Even Wilder. She's gone now too."

"You're seriously blaming yourself for the death of Kes's wife? How on Earth could her dying be your fault? That doesn't make any sense. It was an accident. Childbirth is always a bit risky, especially in conditions like these." He put a hand on her shoulder. "You need to get over yourself. If anything, that woman's death should teach you that bad things happen and sometimes there's fuck all you can do about it."

It was Kes who brought the medication to Chimera.

The colonists sheltering in the excavation site were the last to receive it. By then, the biocide had ravaged most of Lyonesse and turned it into a barren wasteland. No Concordian life forms remained alive. As far as anyone could tell, not a single microorganism lived in the soil or the ocean. The trees of every forest were dried skeletons of dead wood. The rest of the plant life had turned to brown husks. Animals lay dead upon the ground, unable to rot because not even bacteria had survived.

Only the humans and some of the Fila still lived. Not all of the humans had been protected by the vaccine. Out of every hundred waiting in dread as the biocide finally reached them, one or two would fall, killed instantly. There was no telling who it would be, and each family and friend said their goodbyes, not knowing if they would be the ones to die.

Chimera was the only refuge that had remained safe so far. The biocide had traveled slowly through the desert and unoccupied regions of the dry continent. Yet everyone knew it would reach Chimera eventually. The people sheltering there would have to leave some day and travel to places where the Scythians' poison might still linger. It was essential they all receive the vaccine.

Cherry waited for Kes at the bottom of the tunnel. Nina hung from her front, suspended in a cloth wrapped around her torso, and she held Miki's hand. While waiting to speak to Kes in person, she'd tried to formulate the right words to tell him about Isobel. But she'd come up with nothing. If the right words existed, she did not know them.

Miki was excited to see her daddy. She jiggled and swung on Cherry's hand. "Is Daddy coming soon?" She tried to pull her hand away, probably because she wanted to run into the tunnel to meet him.

Cherry gripped the little girl's hand tightly. "Daddy will be here in a minute."

The moment she was dreading arrived. The lights from the vehicle bringing Kes from the surface lit up the tunnel's dark interior, and the approaching engine's noise reverberated louder. The car emerged from the darkness, Alun driving it. Cherry had asked him not to say anything—that she would tell Kes herself. Her friend was easily distinguishable by his red hair.

A great heaviness weighed on her heart. She had to do the hardest thing she'd ever done, and she would live with the moment forever.

The car stopped. Kes had already spotted her and his children. His door opened and he climbed out. His expression was happy but a little uncertain. He was probably wondering where Isobel was. Then his features cleared, perhaps concluding his wife was still recovering from the birth.

As he walked over, Miki managed to rip her hand from Cherry's and run to her father. "Daddy! Daddy! Daddy!"

Grinning, he squatted down as his daugher reached him and he lifted her into his arms. He walked the remaining distance to Cherry, Miki holding his neck tightly and planting kiss after kiss on his cheek.

Kes held Cherry's gaze all the way. With each step he took, doubt pierced his happy but bemused state. She didn't need to tell him anything. Her face said it all. His features fell. His eyes questioned hers, pleading with her for it not to be true. By the time he reached her he knew, and he broke.

"When?" he asked, his voice husky.

"Three days ago. I'm so sorry. I didn't know how to tell you."

He nodded.

"Mommy's gone away, Daddy," Miki said. "Far, far away. Can we go and see her?"

Cherry untied the knot at her shoulder and began to unwrap Nina. Kes helped her, and then gently lifted out his new daughter. The baby was sleeping, as she had most of the time since she'd been born.

Cherry said, "I can take the kids if you'd rather be alone for a while."

Kes gave a slight shake of his head. He cradled little Nina expertly in one arm while the other supported Miki. He walked away without another word. Cherry watched as he stopped in an area of shadow and sat down on the ground with his daughters.

She turned away to give the man some privacy and nearly bumped into Dr Zhang, who was standing right behind her. She hadn't heard him approach.

"Poor guy," Zhang said.

"Yes."

"I'll talk to him later about exactly what happened. He'll need some time to take in the news first."

"Yes."

A lifetime.

"He must have left the medication doses in the car," said the doctor. "I'll deal with them. Don't forget you need a dose too. I know you've been through a lot lately. I don't want you wandering off and forgetting."

"I won't forget." She left the doctor and walked back to the main group of tents.

Aubriot was waiting for her. "How did it go?"

"I didn't need to tell him. He guessed." She sat down on her sleeping bag. Now that her task of conveying the sad news about Isobel was over, she felt no better. She didn't think she would ever feel better.

Though the colony had survived yet another brush with disaster, the future held no prospect of improvement of its situation. Concordia was now barren. They had food and seeds stored, so if the biocide burnt itself out they wouldn't starve, but now they were living on a dead world. Their seeds were only for food crops, not trees or shrubs or ground cover plants. Until life evolved again Concordia would be an empty, bleak wilderness, nothing wild growing or moving anywhere.

And the threat of the Scythians remained. The Assembly might have defeated them this time, but its ships could not stick around forever. The members had their own planets to protect and journeys to undertake.

"Everything's shit, right?" Aubriot asked.

"That's a good way of putting it."

"Yeah, well, we've got each other. That's something."

She frowned. This new, affectionate side of Aubriot was going to take some getting used to.

"Right?" he asked.

"Right. I guess."

Sounds of a disturbance started up. Voices rose louder, chattering in excitement. Cherry and Aubriot's gazes met.

"Is that good or bad, do you think?" he asked.

"Only one way to find out." She got up and peered out of the tent flaps, wondering what she was about to see. She didn't think she could take another disaster, but she'd felt that way about all recent events and her feelings hadn't prevented them from happening.

All she saw was a knot of people standing near the tunnel.

"What is it?" Aubriot pushed in beside her.

"I don't know. I wish they wouldn't congregate there near Kes. He deserves some peace and quiet."

"I'm going to take a look."

Cherry decided to join him. She hated being in the tent alone after what had happened here. She walked with Aubriot across the open, rocky ground. Other colonists were also wandering over, attracted by the gathering crowd.

She was glad of Aubriot's large frame and bossy attitude as he pushed through to the center of the throng. She followed in his wake. It wasn't until she reached the middle that she saw what the fuss was about.

Kes had his back to her, his arms wrapped around someone. Miki was holding onto his leg and a woman in the crowd was holding Nina. Kes's back obscured the face of the person he was holding, but Cherry could see a woman's skinny legs in pants.

She stood on her tiptoes to peer over Kes's shoulder.

"*Wilder!*"

Wilder raised a hand and waved. "Hey, Cherry!"

Cherry was frozen in surprise, then she broke free and ran to her two friends. "I thought the *Opportunity* was destroyed!"

"She was," Wilder replied, still in Kes's embrace. "I wasn't aboard. I stayed on the Immani ship. We used the *Opportunity* as bait, that's all. I knew you guys would be worried about me after the ship blew up, but I couldn't comm from the Immani vessel. Only the Fila stations can receive their comms and they've all been abandoned. Quinn said Immani sensors showed the biocide hadn't reached this refuge yet, so I thought it would be safe to come down in a shuttle we'd brought over from the *Opportunity*. It was the only way to let you all know I was okay."

Wilder had spoken so fast she was breathless. She also seemed to be gasping because Kes was hugging her so tightly. Cherry went to hug her too. Wilder's survival was just the kind of miracle she needed right now.

"Careful!" the girl exclaimed. "You'll squash Piddle and Puddle."

"Huh?" Cherry took a step back and Kes finally released Wilder too.

Wilder reached into two deep pockets and pulled out a small furry creature in each hand.

"The famous Piddle and Puddle." Kes's voice was hoarse. His eyes were red and his face wet. "Can I?" He held out his hands.

"Of course." Wilder gave him the animals.

The crowd around them began to dissipate.

"I'm glad you made it." Aubriot reached down to give Wilder a hug.

She accepted graciously but over his shoulder she raised her eyebrows at Cherry.

Cherry shrugged and stifled a smile.

Aubriot released her. "So how did you survive on the other ship? Do these Immani breathe oxygen like us?"

"No, but they're the organizers of the space station. Do you remember?" She lifted her hand to indicate a great height.

"Hard to forget them," said Aubriot.

"They're used to generating environments for all kinds of species, and their ship is *huge*! When Quinn hatched the plan to use me and the a-grav as bait, the Immani said the Scythians might *think* that I and the a-grav machine were aboard the *Opportunity*, but there was no reason we *had* to be. They created environments for me and Quinn and the rest of the Fila crew. Quinn flew the ship remotely."

Aubriot went to speak but Wilder flapped her hands excitedly to quieten him. "There's more! The Immani think they can save the remaining Fila. They're going to collect them from the Vimur and any lakes the biocide didn't reach and fly them up to their ship. Isn't that great?"

"That *is* great." Cherry couldn't help but give Wilder another hug, rejoicing that this young woman she'd wronged so badly was alive and seemed to have forgiven her.

"I don't know what's going to happen after that, though," Wilder said. "This place is a disaster zone. I could see vids aboard the Immani ship. My forest is *dead*."

Kes said, "My guess is the biocide virus will die out when it's run out of organisms to infest, but I doubt anything will survive it, except us." He paused and held up one of Wilder's creatures for closer inspection. "Though it's possible a small percentage of each species may have natural immunity. If so, over time, those populations will grow. We may see some dramatic imbalances as things sort themselves out."

"And meanwhile the Scythians will send another fleet to annihilate us." Cherry came down from her high with a bump.

"If they do, we'll be ready," said Wilder.

"You mean we should rebuild the silos?" Cherry asked. "I suppose we'll have to."

"We can rebuild the silos and more. I made a bargain with the Assembly. They *really* wanted the a-grav machine and any other gravity technology I could develop, and they asked what we wanted in return." She grinned like a child.

"Are you going to tell us what you asked for?" asked Cherry.

"At first, I thought the best thing I could ask for was the protection of Concordia in perpetuity. I mean, we could always use defenses, right? Considering we kind of stole someone else's planet. But then I thought, no. It's time we stopped relying on other people and stood on our own two feet. So instead, I asked for..." Wilder smiled, enjoying everyone's anticipation. "A gift of the latest and most useful technology from each of the Assembly member species. We get to choose. It could be starship engines, robotics, mining equipment, weapons, who knows? Just imagine. All those new machines!"

"Smart," Aubriot said. "Very smart. I wouldn't have liked to go up against you in a business deal."

"Fantastic," said Cherry. "If we can get our act together we won't have to ask for anyone's help in defeating the Scythians. In fact, if they hear about our capabilities, they might even leave us alone."

"Maybe," said Aubriot. "Or maybe they'll go somewhere else instead."

"Sounds good to me," Cherry said.

"Don't speak too soon," Aubriot warned. "I haven't told you what happened to Faina. After we'd disabled the Scythian defense system, she asked me to deactivate her and leave her down there."

That unfamiliar pang of pity for the Guardian hit Cherry again. "And did you?"

"Yeah. She could have been useful, but it seemed the right thing to do. But before I shut her down, she told me that she had the impression the Scythians had extracted Earth's coordinates from her. She didn't suggest a reason why, but it's obvious, isn't it? They would only want the coordinates of our home planet if they planned on going there."

Wilder said, "We took their origin planet, so..."

"They're going to take ours," Cherry finished.

"With all this new tech we're going to have," said Aubriot, "it doesn't seem fair to we keep it to ourselves while the Scythians destroy Earth. I don't know about the rest of you, but I think it's time for me to go home."

The story of the Concordia Colony concludes in ...

SPACE COLONY ONE BOOKS 7 - 9

Sign up to my reader group for free ebook *Night of Flames,* the prequel to Space Colony One, and for more free books, discounts on new releases, Review Crew invitations and other interesting stuff:

https://jjgreenauthor.com/free-books/

COPYRIGHT

Copyright © Sept 2019 J.J. Green

All rights reserved.
No part of this book may be reproduced in any written, electronic, recording, or photocopying without written permission of the publisher or author. The exception would be in the case of brief quotations embodied in critical articles and reviews.
This book is a work of fiction. Names, characters, places, and incidents are products of the author's imagination or are used fictitiously. Any resemblance to actual events, locales, or persons living or dead, is entirely coincidental.
First Edition.

www.ingramcontent.com/pod-product-compliance
Lightning Source LLC
Chambersburg PA
CBHW060753210726
48292CB00013B/71

* 9 7 8 1 9 1 3 4 7 6 5 5 7 *